UNDER THE FIFTH SUN

UNDER THE

FIFTH SUN

A NOVEL OF PANCHO VILLA

BY EARL SHORRIS

DELACORTE PRESS/NEW YORK

Published by
DELACORTE PRESS
1 Dag Hammarskjold Plaza
New York, N.Y. 10017

Manufactured in the United States of America

First printing

Designed by MaryJane DiMassi

LIBRARY OF CONGRESS CATALOGING IN PUBLICATION DATA

Shorris, Earl, 1936–
Under the fifth sun.

1. Villa, Francisco, 1878–1923—Fiction. I. Title.
PZ4.S5593Un [PS3569.H584] 813′.54 80-15714

ISBN: 0-440-09388-0

For Tony, as if lies could be lessons

To the Mexican there are only two possibilities in life: either he inflicts the actions implied by *chingar* on others, or else he suffers them himself at the hands of others. This conception of social life as combat fatally divides society into the strong and the weak. The strong—the hard unscrupulous *chingones*—surround themselves with eager followers. This servility toward the strong, especially among the *politicos* (that is, the professionals of public business), is one of the more deplorable consequences of the situation. Another, no less degrading, is the devotion to personalities rather than to principles.

The *macho* is the *gran chingón*. One word sums up the aggressiveness, insensitivity, invulnerability and other attributes of the *macho*: power, the will without reins and without a set course.

Unpredictability adds another element to the character of the *macho*. He is a humorist. His jokes are huge and individual, and they always end in absurdity. The anecdote about the man who "cured" the headache of a drinking companion by emptying his pistol into his head is well known.

OCTAVIO PAZ
The Labyrinth of Solitude

Machize is derived from the passive form of *mati,* "to know," which is *macho,* "to be known."

MIGUEL LEON-PORTILLA
Aztec Thought and Culture

BOOK ONE

1

She sat in the corner of my garden room, close to the roses, as if flowers could hide the smell of blood. Her legs trembled with weariness from the long climb into the saddle of the mountain. There were streaks of gray on her calves where she had rubbed them with peyote to give herself strength. The child lay sleeping in her rebozo; it was still one day before the milk.

I gave her soaproot and water to make herself clean while I prepared the black mirror and gathered the smoke into my fingers. Before we began the calculations, she said, "Tlamatini Popoca, I was not a good wife." I cleansed her with an egg and gave the egg to her to bury in a distant place. There was no need to ask her about the infidelities, which is the style of the coño priests; I knew. I am smoke and flowers, night and wind, keeper of the tonalpohualli, reader of the tonalámatl, and thinker of inquiries. Even then I was the last of my kind, the only defiance that remained.

Few people sought me out anymore, although I sat in the plaza of San Juan del Río on Saturday nights and asked the difficult questions to intrigue them. The Spanish coños, the French, and the Basques had corrupted the people with ludicrous certainties; everyone in the municipality wore spurs. She would not have sought my knowledge, either, if the birth had not been attended by so many omens: although they had rubbed her belly with oils and put a knife under the mat, the birth had come slowly and painfully, the crowning at the hour of Itzli, the God of the Obsidian Knife; and the child was the size of a monster, more than five kilos, with redcurling hair and the eyes of an owl.

Perhaps it was the glance of her husband, Agustín, that sent her up the mountain. He was thin and lacking wind, a man who stumbled in the grass; he had reason to be suspicious. Nevertheless, it was not Agustín that his wife feared, only his thoughts. She said that she wanted a peaceful house for her child and her husband and that she went with the Presidente Municipal only because he made certain adjustments in the accounts she kept in his store. Without the adjustments, she said, they could not survive; the weakness of her husband could be seen in the size of the crop he brought in each year. She swore that the land owned by a man made of weak corn produces lean fruit, kernels that cannot grow beyond infancy. Perhaps. I learned long ago not to expect truth in this world. I trust only in metaphor.

After she had washed, I put copal in the fire to mix with the scent of the roses and I brought her close to me to look into the mirror. She saw her face in the obsidian darkness, colors without the light of the earlier sun. The lines of her cheeks had grown long and deep, and there was no light around her eyes. I mixed yellow colors and painted a square over each of her eyes to make her beautiful again. Then I warmed the mirror near the fire and injected it with the smoke of my fingers to make the clouds in which the calculations of the child could be seen. She touched her face as the image disappeared. I told her not to be afraid, for we are here only to dream.

There are rules of divination, intersections of the round of days and the round of nights, a beginning from which all calculations must be made. I could not deceive her; the child had been born at a bad time: the intersection of ceremonial robbery and drowning children. If he was also named that day, he would be an outlaw who would die too soon and by the hand of another man.

With her permission, I pierced the child's penis with a maguey thorn and let the blood fall on the surface of the mirror. She was fearful, but the child did not cry out, and she understood then that the act of supplication would be accepted and the new day and time of his life, the naming, would affect his calculations. In thirty days, I told her, he should be named. Then he would be of the feast of rulers and new corn, but also of the sacrifice of women. I chose an hour in keeping with the intersection, Piltzintecuhtli, the Lord of Princes, the sungod. The gift of blood assured the child of power, perhaps of riches. Only the women of his life, even his mother, were in danger. She promised to give him a name that would spare the women. I did not tell her that the name itself is meaningless, everything is determined by the time. Tezcatlipoca, the Smoking Mirror himself, teaches the value of illusion.

She gave me six reales and I gave her an ointment of mandrake root to ward off the afterpains. On July 6, 1878, by their calendar, she named the child Doroteo; and on the following day she registered his birth in the office of the municipality. I began my watch over the child; his life was to be influenced by my calculations, and I wanted to know what face he would make, if he took a face at all, for nothing is certain in this world but that the Place of Mystery awaits us. I do not know that we live. Only the Lord of Duality made himself by his own thoughts; the rest of us are in the grasp of our dreams.

Canatlán is a dead, dry land in winter; but in early summer the clouds lift themselves over the mountains and the rains come: corn grows, and beans, onions, chiles, squash, cotton, carrots, fruit trees, and yellow roses; the cactus blooms and turns to fruit; the milk of the maguey is the honey of the high desert; foals learn to run and the new pigs are ready for the spit. There is always one day of too much rain when the people save what they can from the sudden rivers; then the clouds stop crossing the mountains and the sun begins to burn: the people and the animals covet the waterholes and streams until the clouds come again in the next summer. Time is a circle turned by an old woman who lives in the secret shade of a cool white house in Canatlán. All the people know her; they are her children and they do not dispute her rounds.

Micaela Arango delivered four more live children and one that was strangled in the womb. She was a response to the little fever of her husband, fattening as he lost his flesh, preening her eyes and the heavy fruit of her lips as his eyes sank into darkness and his lips fell away from his teeth. He died in the field, his feet in the furrows, full of sand and his constant sweat. The blood ran out of his mouth until his heart stopped.

Doroteo, seven years old, came with her to take the body back to the house. They could not lift him, even thought the years of fever had wasted all but the bones and the soft sack of skin. They dragged him; the heels of his sandals were like little plows. The woman and her son washed the body, pulling clots of blood from the nostrils and the mouth, dressed it in clean clothes, and laid it on the table for a bier. Then they lit candles; and while Hipólito, the third oldest, went to get a priest and some neighbors for the deathwatch, the mother and her first son washed and put on clean clothes. In the arranged room, they smelled the shit of death through the scented candles, and they wept.

The priest said his Latin words over the body; but he told them it was too late, the man had not confessed before he died: the unforgiven soul had departed with no hope of Heaven; it would be the long death, the eternal desert. In the night, after the others had gone and only Micaela and Doroteo sat with the body, I brought butterflies and the ashes of a small snake to put inside the burial clothes. Micaela told me the details of his death; and I reminded her that in the way of our race, which is not like that of the catzopines, the man could be said to have died by drowning: having choked on his own blood, he had gone to the Heaven of warriors, women who die in childbirth, and those who drown. She gave me a peso. I told her that flowers and song are the only truth on this earth. They buried him in the morning in the Catholic way, but with aguamiel and gordas at his side and the butterflies and ashes still in his clothes.

They were clumsy farmers, without the strength to work fourteen hectares of dry land edging into hills. No one helped them; the cousins were too far and the uncles were too old. They hired a man, but he only watched

Micaela and ate. After a week, he stole two pigs and went away. The circle turned to rain before a fourth of the corn was planted. The boy continued to walk the rows, pushing seeds into the mud, but the wet seed rotted. A wandering cowboy in a raincape made of palm leaves stopped in the field one afternoon and explained to the boy that it was too late for planting. He advised him to save the seed for winter. Cut grass when it is dry, he said, and in the winter you'll be able to eat the corn yourself; otherwise, you'll starve to save the animals.

The corn came up in rows near the house and some grew wildly near the hills. Doroteo, his mother, and his brothers, Antonio and Hipólito, chopped weeds with a hoe and pulled out the deep roots with their hands. They hunted for chiles on the mountain. After every rain, they milked the maguey. They cut nopal and pickled it in earthen crocks. Their hands were sore and sick with the deceptive thorns; their clothes went without mending and they ate only in the morning and before sleep. On some nights Micaela went into San Juan del Río and came back the next morning with meat, cloth, and salt. They found a dead steer in the hills between their farm and the mountain; but when they saw that neither the buzzards nor the coyotes touched the dead animal, they were afraid to eat it. They peeled the skin from the bubbling corpse and staked it out to dry. For a week, the boy scraped the drying skin with the blade of a machete. Micaela cut the stiff hide into winter vests and boiled them in a suds of ashes until they were soft.

There was no thread, the needles broke, when the traces snapped they did not know how to mend them, the plow was lost to a stone, the blade of the hoe chipped and dulled, they were without shoes or buttons. Micaela dreamed of carrion eaters entering her house. She held the babies on her lap and cried over them. She thanked the chickens for every egg. Doroteo forgot to plant tomatoes. She cooked tortilla soup and beans. Doroteo killed a rabbit with a stone, and they buried the head out of gratitude. They ate the meat of snakes and squirrels. Antonio found a crow with a broken wing, and they had soup one day, meat the next, and tacos the day after that. Doroteo buried cow manure and pig shit beside the young corn.

Before the corn ripened they killed a chicken. They rested: Micaela cooked and sewed, Antonio and Hipólito brought clean dirt for the floor of the house, and Doroteo dug a new cesspool for the outhouse. For two days they stayed away from the fields except to inspect the progress of the corn. They talked and sang, and the children remembered how to tease each other.

Micaela separated strings from the seams of their clothes to make thread. She sharpened the broken edge of the needle on a stone. After the death of Agustín, the owners of the three stores in San Juan had come to the farm to gauge the crop. They fingered the new corn, paced off the length of the furrows, clucked, whispered, asked the help of God for the widow and her orphans, and refused to give her credit. She argued that the death of Agustín meant one less person to feed; she would be able to sell more of the crop. They offered to buy the cows and half the chickens for cash. She said she would rather eat the chickens than sell them. The owner of the grocery shrugged: such talk was further evidence of the widow's inability to manage her affairs.

The following morning she gave Doroteo the machete and told him they would eat chicken and rest until the corn was ready. On the second night, she gathered the children about her, robing herself in the last of her expectations, and spoke to them of their father, telling of the great crops he had brought in, of the chicken and even the beef they would have been eating if he had lived. They sat together in a hill of mourning, weeping for themselves, praising the memory of great onions, squashes no child could lift, corn that could be chewed raw like cane for its sweetness. They wept for tomatoes, chiles dipped in cornmeal and fried in lard, marrow bones, crisp pieces of pork, and chocolate sauce; all but the oldest son, who moved away from them to sit against the wall and look the lie at his mother.

Micaela curled the babies to her, as if to ward off the glare of his more naïve history. She waited, solemn and dreaming. The house was darkening, cool; a breeze touched the curtain at the door. The chickens had immersed themselves in their feathers, the tethered cows had begun their night of kneeling, the sow rested on her fat, the cooking fire was quiet and red. The boy did not look away. "I don't like it when you make those cinnamon eyes," she told him. "They're ugly." Doroteo took the machete down from its peg and left the house.

He walked across the corn rows carefully, not wanting to break the stalks. There was a taste of pollen in his mouth. He saw the color of marigolds in the flowering moon. It seemed to him that he was crossing his own footsteps in the furrows, making a religious sign with every step, assuring his progress. The machete that hung in his rope belt was his fang and his claw; when the puma came for him in the night he would meet it with the machete in his hand; after the battle he would eat the heart of the puma or the puma would eat the heart of him. If he won, no one would ever know; but there would be a legend in Canatlán of a boy with the heart of a puma. The grocers would hear his snarl in their dreams, and sometimes in the place where his mother lived there would be a freshly killed steer at the door in the morning, its throat torn away as if by some invincible animal.

He walked toward the moon. The world was a shadow, the slopes had no substance. Darkness lifted him. The tears of his mother erupted on his arms and his scalp, then froze away in tiny streams of salted ice. Trees,

[7]

curved like the tails of scorpions, grew up beside him. He counted the white segments, feeling the imagined spread of the twilight leaves like red sunbursts on the surface of his eyes. Serpents carrying rain in their jaws wriggled past him. He wrapped himself in a husk of corn and rolled up the side of the mountain to the saddle.

He came upon a horse tied to a cactus plant, a small fire, a man in a soft felt hat kneeling over the carcass of a steer, separating the quarters with a knife as thick and heavy as an axe. Everything glowed red in the low light of the fire—shadowless, as in dreams. To test the reality of the moment he sniffed the wind, finding blood, manure, smoke, and the sourness of the man. Doroteo announced himself by stepping into the firelight; but the man paid no attention to his presence, as if one of them were a ghost. The knife sliced through the bloody bulk of the meat, finding joints, isolating them, raising up to chop the sinew. The man's hands and forearms shone bloody. Lines and tears of blood decorated his face.

The man finished his work, wiped the blood off his hands and arms on the hide of the butchered steer, and sat against a tree to smoke a corn-husk cigarette. After he smoked and rested, he cut some strips from the beef, impaled them on a stick, and put them in the fire. The fat burst out of the fire in little stars. The meat cooked in shivers. When the strips were charred on both sides, the man invited Doroteo to come and eat with him. The boy went and sat beside the man. They put tortillas in the ashes to warm, then used the softened tortillas to pull the strips of meat off the stick, wrapping each piece of meat. "You can live without meat," the man said, "but not without corn. For that reason and for no other, it is not easy to live in the mountains."

After they had eaten, they drank cold water from a canteen and leaned against smooth rocks to watch the fire and the stars. The man spoke slowly and with the formality of the people of the northern mountains who live and speak at great distances from each other. His voice was low and dry:

"Tomorrow, perhaps the next day, the rurales will come to this municipality. They will ask everyone if the bandit Manuel Reyes was seen here. The captain of the troop, who was himself a bandit until two years ago, will say that Manuel Reyes killed three men in Durango on this past Saturday. It is true. But he will not tell how the men were killed or why. In answer, some of the people will say they saw me, and some will say I am not a man but a story. They will say that I am their anger, their whisper. You will say nothing, because I am your friend: I gave you meat and tortillas and fresh water; like an animal, you came upon me silently in the night, and I did not kill you."

The boy made no answer. He was thinking of a song he had heard, a ballad of Manolo Reyes. The man pushed his hat down over his eyes and let his head fall forward onto his chest, as if in sleep. But he did not sleep, or perhaps he was awake in a dream, for during the darkness he spoke and was silent in irregular intervals. His voice was so soft that it was often lost in the fire or the wind, and he spoke sometimes in Spanish and sometimes in the language of the kings of Aztlán. He spoke of forgotten caves and limitless seas, the god who lived in the navel of the universe, war and violation, the twos and the fours of existence. He gave the boy advice on the lessons of animals and the use of weapons. He spoke of the honor of a man and the anger of the hungry; he called for rage, he demanded rage.

Doroteo was awake and asleep, hearing but unable to answer. He felt questions but he could not speak them. The night seemed to be running, the silences of the man grew into fires in the boy, who wished against the dawn. But the adumbration of the birds came, followed by the light. The man raised his hat and looked in the direction of the light. Doroteo saw that he was a young man with an old face—his eyes lay like heavy secrets in his face. They ate again and drank more cold water. The man chewed a root that seemed to boil in his mouth, then he saddled the horse and tied some of the meat across the saddle. The rest, he said, was for Doroteo. He told him to lay the part he could not carry on a stone and cover it with ashes to keep the animals away.

When the man mounted his horse, the boy cried and begged to be allowed to go with him, but the man shook his head and looked away with his secret eyes, saying that he was going to a canyon where the devil lived. Doroteo said he knew of the place and of other men who had gone there to bargain for courage; he swore that he was not afraid. The man told the boy that his time would come, but later, when he was able to bargain with more than his dreams.

The boy said, "I have no father."

"From our mothers," the man said, "we learn the names of our fathers. That is our history."

Micaela brought five kilos of beef in a sack to pay for the consultation. It was too little for the cure she desired, but my interest in the boy and the difficulty of her situation made it a fair price. I took him into the inner room of my house, where the walls are thick and the door fits so perfectly that neither smoke nor sound can enter or escape the room. I made him run without moving until he was damp with sweat, then I listened to him breathe, covering first his nose, then his mouth, to determine whether it was ribwort or mullein that was needed. The problem was in the passage between the nose and the mouth; he breathed like a tired man even after the sweat had dried. I gave him wine aged in a smooth orange gourd and the pollen from the yellowest mullein flowers to mix with it. The nose and mouth worked together for a while; but when he ran again, the problem reappeared. With the help of his mother, I poured the mixture into his nose and made him spit it out through his mouth. Then I purified him with smoke and sent them home. It is not a certain cure, I told them. Such problems are determined by the hour of conception; and like crossed eyes, extra toes, and constant fits, they are the product of an intersection that cannot be undone: the sufferer must live in the midst of the struggle for dominance between the nose and the mouth. He should learn never to be far from fresh water and to eat fruit with every meal. She thanked me, but I could see by the sharpness of her shadow that she was not pleased. Those who wish to change nature before they understand the meaning of intersections are best comforted by the lies of the coño priests.

They gathered the corn and planted wheat, but it was not enough: the winter was too dry for the wheat, the corn was too soon eaten, a festering sore in its belly killed one of the cows. Micaela went into San Juan del Río and came back with food and credit, but there was not enough; the failure was inevitable. She talked about it to her children on the dead winter afternoons, naming the demands and the lacks of their lives, cursing the relentlessness of the appetites of children and chickens. They ate cactus, rabbits, roots, eggs, a crippled fawn born too late to climb to the tree line in the sierras. They ate birds, a dog, pine nuts, hot water, a nest of sleeping ants. Then they ate the seed they had saved for the next season, and there was no more reason to pray for the winter to pass. There was nothing, there would be nothing. Micaela told her children of the terrors of forever. The babies cried in the night. When they ceased to cry, she became frightened and sold the land, and they went to the Hacienda Gogojito to work shares. On the day they arrived at the new house she tied up her hair and let her eyes fall into narrowness. There were no more nights in San Juan del Río; she was an old woman, leaning on her hips. She scolded chickens.

The boy worked, sharing whatever he harvested with the owner, dividing his half among the six people who lived in the small house. He stood in the fields and waited for dawn, which was the beginning of his day, and he walked home in moonlight. The sun burned him and browned him and baked him, sealing his skin against the sand and manure in which he walked through his days. He dreamed, he ceased to dream, he dreamed again, living the round of seasons, of days, learning horses, birds, snakes, clouds, roots, the intricacies of corn and squash, the deviousness and tenacity of insects. His shoulders grew, his hands thickened, he took on the color and the smell of the earth of Santa Isabel de Berros. He was the father of the fields and the child of the house; he could not imagine oceans or cities; he examined the elegance of the owner as if it were a disease.

Winter was his freedom: he slept and wandered, a student of canyons and ravines, the son of every traveling cowboy and muledriver. He went to the house of his cousins the Francos, who had arranged for his family to sharecrop on the López Negrete land. They taught him to use a rifle and a pistol; his mother's sister worried about his labored breathing, bemoaning the death of his father, the weak lungs of the Arango family, the failure of God to provide for orphans. They praised him for growing taller, giving him gifts of chocolate and worn-out clothing. He sat in their house and listened to his aunt and his cousins, buying their concern with lowered eyes and dust in his hair. They gave him stewed chicken and expressions of sympathy to carry home to his mother, Micaela Arambula Widow of Arango, who dressed in shabby mourning clothes and walked on her knees up the aisles of churches to cast her prayers toward Heaven. His uncle said that he was more beast than boy, that there had been people who spoke a strange language, Basques, in the Arango family, and that their blood had affected Doroteo's brain as well as his body: his chest was too thick, his legs were too short, his hair was pure chino, he had a memory for everything but his catechism, his taste for red meat was subhuman, he could not sing, and his disdain of sleep was unnatural. Doroteo was grateful to them, following the advice of his mother, who said that they all lived by the grace of God and the generosity of the Francos.

At the end of the first year, the foreman of the hacienda came to count the corn. He said there was not enough. Micaela apologized for the laziness of her son. She and the foreman complained to each other of the hard life, the failures of children, the Indian blood that showed up in the sluggish movements of a boy and his lack of concern for the needs of decent people. The foreman touched the widow's hand, patted her shoulder, offered to whip the boy for her. They moved around the room of the house, touching and sliding, as if in dance. She slipped from under his hands; she was still graceful, although she dressed in black and the frankness was gone from her eyes. The foreman asked to come again to be her comforter, her partner in conversation, her protector, a disciplinarian for her children. She smiled; she weaved her words, her eyes; she told him no. When he had gone, she said to the children that there would be trouble.

"Then I'll kill him," Doroteo said.

Micaela went outside and gathered two handfuls of pebbles and spread them on the floor in the corner farthest from the door. Then she told Doroteo to kneel there on the pebbles and repent his sinful thoughts. He went quietly, not even complaining with his eyes. Once during the evening

[*11*]

and the night of kneeling, she thought she saw him smiling, but she dismissed it as a trick of the dying firelight. In the morning, his trousers were stained with blood, and she and Hipólito had to help him to his feet. She put a wet cloth over his swollen eyes and Marianita brought him a bowl of tortilla soup. When his eyes were calmed, Micaela asked him if he was truly repentant. "Mama," he said, "I love you."

She and Hipólito and Antonio dragged him from the chair to the corner and lowered him again onto the pebbles; he had stayed the night, now he would stay the day. "It's a sin to kill," she said. Then she took her other children and left the house. In the empty room, attended by chickens and the comings and goings of the sow and her children, the boy wept and dreamed. His father came to kneel beside him, healthier than Doroteo remembered, with a red mustache and thick forearms. They leaned against each other for strength, though neither of them could control the muscles of his legs. The man smelled good and sweaty, his voice was strong, and he gave no sign that the pebbles pained him.

They knelt together through the morning in the empty house. In the afternoon Micaela returned, accompanied by the foreman. The boy and his father could not see her or the man who followed her into the house, for their heads were turned to the wall; but they heard, they knew the voices. When Micaela screamed, they tried to stand up, but their legs were paralyzed from the hours of kneeling. While they struggled, lifting each other with their arms, the adobe wall became a mirror, and they saw. Every detail was presented to them in a series of tableaux painted on the mirror: they saw her widened eyes, a shred of mourning dress, a lacerated thigh, the exposure of her breast, the wound itself. They saw, too, when he left her lying on the woven straw, with her collapsed hands and her knees turned out in despair. Then they wept together, mother, father, and son, but they could not move; they were made of corn, they grew in their places.

For two weeks afterward Doroteo could not walk at all. His knees swelled with pus and the joints locked together like an old man's fingers. Micaela painted them with melted wax to draw out the pus and loosen the bones. The Francos came to visit, bringing chicken and garlic to give him strength. His aunt prayed over him while his cousins played outside the house. Through the sound of his aunt's prayers he heard the laughter when Antonio told how he found his brother kneeling in a pool of urine.

He came to me on a Saturday night in winter when I sat in the plaza wrapped in my blanket, listening to the violinists and waiting for someone to ask the true name of the day or how to cure the breathlessness that came with the cold. He told me everything, even the words of the coño priest who said to Micaela that she had the perseverance of a saint. I touched his knees with the feather of a blue hummingbird and told him to dance.

[*12*]

2

Motecuhzoma Xocoyotzin is dead, Cuauhtémoc could not save us, the weeping woman of the streets of Mexico is not an illusion. We are poor people now. We work like ants in a place surrounded by endless seas. Perhaps this is the last world, the final sun. I am merely the smoke that sits in the plaza of San Juan del Río or Canatlán on Saturday nights. I know nothing but the names of the directions, the thirteen heavens, the nine hells and the One-who-made-himself-of-his-own-thoughts. There is a Place of Mystery called Death, which is the only name that has no face. These are the truths I tell to the children on Saturday nights when they come to the plaza to listen to the music and learn the glances of courtship. These are the things I tell them in the vulnerable moment when they dream that they are not ants.

I am an old man with no teeth to eat meat and I wear a blanket in summer. The children suspect that I am the father of the pingos who come in the form of dogs with serpents' tails to bring them strange luck. They fear me; but knowing no greater misfortune can come to them than the lives that have already been calculated, they gather around my bench and tell me their dreams. There is no one who will listen to them but me, for I am more than the interpreter of dreams, I am the comforter of their bloody knees and the first preacher of revolt, the student of Cuauhtémoc and the teacher of Morelos and Juárez. I am the spirit of the Tezcatlipocas, the smoke that cannot be dispelled from the houses of the catzopines. The center of the world is not yet lost; I am the possessor of names that no white man can speak.

His days are like a parade: first there is the horse, then the plow, then the boy. The horse sweats. The point of the plow is made of wood hardened in fire. The boy walks on brown feet. His skin is tough and horny. He does not feel the edges of stones or the splinters of last year's stalks. He walks slowly, the horse walks slowly, the plow twists in the hard places. They are harnessed together: the horse, the plow, and the boy. Their days are like a parade under the sun, in the wind under the sun. They walk, opening the earth, following the path of the sun. It is their light and their guide, the mother and the father of the young corn.

The point of the plow breaks. The boy sweats. He cannot match the speed of his days. The seed waits. The parade will continue by moonlight, by starlight; it will begin with the awakening sun. They are harnessed together: the sun, the seed, and the boy. They will march until the first rain. The boy is the midwife of corn, an acolyte to the fields. He counts the rows and weighs the seed; he fears the rain and prays for rain. His only hope is in the agreement of the days and the fields. The counting goes on; the highest number is known.

He was twelve years old when he came to me in the plaza of Cantalán to kiss my hand and say goodbye. The fields had made him as broad and as red as a man, and he had already begun to smell of his own steam. We sat together on a bench and listened to the violinists and the trumpeters. Old men came selling roasted corn and sweets, the women came in their mourning clothes to spy on the glances of their daughters, the young men shone like leather in the long red summer evening. The rurales in their gray skin lolled among us, touching their rough fingers to the dreaming eyes of the children. The boys and girls walked in opposite circles, passing and passing. There was light in the church, pulque in the cantina, and the sheriff sat in the cool anteroom of the jail, wearing his fat pistols, waiting for the first mistakes of the night.

A blind man sat on the next bench, holding a gutstring harp between his legs, waiting for the musicians on the bandstand to go into the cantina. His eyes were without centers, orange reflections of the late sun. Doroteo asked how a man who could not see had learned to play the harp. I explained to him that everyone and everything has a position in space and time; the blind man had come to know the time and place of himself and his strings, which is the secret of music. The boy nodded. "And it's the same for dancing?"

"Yes, dancing is the music of the body."

The oil lamps were lit, the blind man had his chance to play his soft music and sing in his woman's voice, there was dancing, the women in black cloth and dust feared for their daughters, the pulque drinkers began to fall asleep on the grass. Doroteo sat beside me, holding his blanket roll on his knees. "I'm running away," he said.

"It's too soon."

"I hate the corn."

He kissed my hand. I touched his heart with a stone that had come from the holy city of Teotihuacan, but I knew that even the protection of the loving god would not be enough; he was too young, it was too soon, and he had blasphemed—we are made of corn.

He walked north, following the Río de Ramos to the lake, then up the

[*14*]

Río Oro to where it meets the Río San Juan south of Hidalgo del Parral, avoiding the roads and the gray wood of the mines, trading meat for corn, speaking his watery Spanish in answer to the more certain sounds of the mountain people. He caught fish with a pointed stick and played naked in the cold streams like a young frog splashing. He sang. He caught a wild horse one day and lost it on the next day. I am rich, he said to a woodcutter, who came down from the high mountains, leading his doddering burros with shrugs and whimperings. The woodcutter reached for his pistol.

A young Tarahumara boy traded him a straw face for a cut of dried meat, then raced him up a hill, disappearing over the top, white wrappings, thick wool, flying black hair, gone; and Doroteo far behind, panting, the dust of the mountains sticking to his tongue. When he went back to his camp, the rest of the meat was gone and the straw face was laughing. There was more meat to be found; he could also laugh; he was rich.

There was gold in the mountains, there was silver; he saw it in the streams, and he left it there, having no use for anything that could not be eaten. He stayed in the sun of the mountains, which was different from the sun of the fields, dry as an old woman's hands on his child's face. An itinerant Tarascan fiddler walked with him for three days, teaching him the roots that could be eaten, playing thankful songs to the generous earth. They could not speak to each other; but when on the fourth morning the fiddler turned off to a mining camp, he gave Doroteo a piece of the ribbon from his hat and played him a farewell song on the narrow throat of his tiny fiddle.

On the forty-third day of his rich life, he awakened to the sound of three men in gray skins discussing whether to shoot him or take him back to the hacienda from which he had run away. Doroteo said he was only twelve years old. They laughed, he was too big to be only twelve years old. The muzzle of a rifle touched his foot. He pulled himself away, sliding on his blanket. Three rifles pointed at his head. He raised his hands above his head. They laughed. The muzzles poked in his ribs, under his arms, felt across his waist. They questioned him, they said his answers were lies; he was a thief, a cattle rustler, perhaps a murderer. The sun whitened, his mouth was dry, he gasped and sobbed.

"Don't kill me, my father is dead; don't kill me, my father is dead; don't kill me."

"A boy should be with his father."

He saw that one of the silver buttons was missing on the gray legging of the man closest to him, and he stopped crying, believing that they would not kill him; they were men whose buttons fall off, not angels of death. Then he thought of the Tarahumara boy disappearing over the hill, and he wept again, knowing that they were mere men and that men can kill. He lost his

[*15*]

sight for an instant. He could not hear their voices for the ringing that rose through their words. He called for his mother, he named his sisters and brothers and cousins and aunts and uncles.

"It's two hundred kilometers to Canatlán. Shoot him."

"I'm only twelve years old; my father is dead."

"Shoot him. What's your name? We always have to tell the name of the people we shoot."

"Doroteo."

"Son of a bitch! It's a girl. How can we shoot a girl?"

"I'm not a girl."

"You piss sitting down or standing up?"

"Standing up."

"Then how come you have a girl's name?"

"I have the name my mother gave me."

They hobbled him and bound his wrists. Two of the rurales rode north and the third one headed south with Doroteo walking behind him, tied to the horn of his saddle by a long rope that ended in a noose. "Mister," the boy said, "the horse could be scared by a rabbit or a snake." The man shrugged. "If I'm a good rider, you don't have to worry. If you think I don't know how to ride a horse, I could shoot you now. I could say I found out you weren't telling the truth. You know, you didn't even tell us about the piece of ribbon the fiddler gave you."

For eight days they walked south, following roads rather than rivers, passing villages and work camps, a common sight, no less the life than corn or cotton, straw drying in cakes of mud; noted, but not with the interest caused by rain or the most subtle change in the flavor of water.

At night, the man tied Doroteo into a ball, knotting the hobbles around his ankles to his hands. After the long day of walking, Doroteo's legs cramped in the new position. The first time he felt the cramps he asked for the knots to be loosened. The man, who lay on the other side of the campsite, smoking, resting his head on his saddle, did not even look up at the boy's complaint. When the pain became unbearable and the boy cried out, the man gave a long sigh of cigarette smoke, picked up his rifle and walked around the campfire to where Doroteo lay. He stood over the boy, watching the squirming of his cramped legs. When the boy cried out again, the man smacked the butt of the rifle against his head.

Twice each day the man cooked a meal of dried beef, chiles, beans, and thick tortillas. When he had eaten his fill, he gave Doroteo whatever was left, more in the morning, less at night. There were no conversations. Doroteo made requests for food or water or permission to relieve himself. The man answered with a nod or the butt of his rifle. He refused to untie Doroteo even to enable him to get his hands between his hobbled legs to clean himself after he shat. By the fourth day, his rectum was filthy and bleeding. He begged to be allowed to clean himself, but the man would do no more than permit him to walk a few feet downstream and sit in the water while the man filled his canteens and the horse drank.

The night before they reached Canatlán, the man rode into the hills and made camp in a small box canyon away from the road. He tied the horse to a mesquite bush instead of hobbling it and letting it forage, and he did not build a cooking fire as he had on the other nights. Nor did he sleep or even rest his head on his saddle, smoking and looking up at the stars. He sat with his back against the wall of the canyon, his rifle across his lap and his pistol beside him on his saddle blanket. He studied the rim of the canyon and the narrow entrance, watching for new shadows, sudden reflections. Several times the man raised his rifle and pointed it at the wind or the flight of a bird.

Late into the night, long after midnight, when the moon was falling, the Tarascan fiddler entered the canyon. His white shirt and trousers were ghostly bright. He glided across the sandy rubble to where the rural sat. They spoke softly in Spanish; the fiddler accepted a coin from the man in gray, then he backed away across the canyon, bowed over his fiddle and his ribboned hat. Magically, Doroteo rose up out of his bonds, picked up his machete, and followed the fiddler out of the canyon. When they were out of the rural's sight and hearing, Doroteo called out to the fiddler. The man turned around slowly, removing his hat, bending as he turned. "Look," Doroteo told him. "Look up at me." He waited until he saw the surprise of recognition in the fiddler's eyes, then he killed him.

They tied him to a post, the foreman beat him with a knotted rope; it is the punishment of living children. He was not brave, because he was not dead. He heard laughter, the weeping of his mother, the startled inhalations of his sisters, the singing of the rope, the foreman's sweaty breath. He asked for his father, he cried out for the help of his mother.

The people had come in from the fields by the light of the red sun of optimism. They stood in rows and knots. Women sat in the dust with babies at their breasts. There was gossip and the eating of fruit while the rope battered his breath and his toes lost their hold in the rutted sand. He begged, he screamed for the satisfaction of the foreman, the rope burned red on the sunbrowned skin of his back. There were fifty-one blows, revenge according to the days of his freedom. Near the end he felt only the eyes of the observers. His father choked, coughing up blood onto his son's back, dying, lacking the depth in his chest to survive the demands of corn. He bellowed to God and then he slept, among the gossipers and the laughers and the weeping widow of San Juan, who was not an illusion.

[*17*]

*　*　*

The corn grew. He was the owner of every second kernel and all of the husks. His portion was divided among the widow and the children of Agustín Arango, who had died, in his thirty-second year, of breathing his own blood. Since the fall of Quetzalcóatl we have all suffered; the loving god has abandoned us, he sailed away in a paper boat, he vanished at the eastern edge of the endless sea. Without him, we are halves, dust without blood, blood without dust, fixed in contemplation of the empty space, students of the mirror.

In the rainless winter, when the corn dried, he smelled of woodsmoke and sweetgrass, his eyes opened to the softer sun, and he laughed. With his brother Antonio, Doroteo went to the house of Retana the tailor to build a new room to house Retana's overflow of children. There were eleven girls and eight boys living with Retana and his wife in the one room behind the small shop. The tailor, who was losing his eyesight from working by the light of pitchpine torches, complained to everyone in Canatlán that he could no longer cope with his family. At night, after he and his wife were asleep, the small children wandered out of the crowded room into the tailor shop and slept on top of the clothes. There were the inevitable accidents, said Retana, costly ones for a man who tried to support twenty-one people by the efforts of his fast fingers and failing eyes.

All summer the old man and all of his children had made bricks; but when it came time to stack the adobe bricks into walls, the old man could not overcome the flaws of his eyes: he saw two plumb lines and sometimes three. The first wall rose with the smoothness of a staircase until it reached the height of his other rooms and collapsed. He built a second wall, which was smoother but also leaned, like one face of a pyramid. It collapsed upon the rubble of the first wall. Neighbors said he must be blind. Retana complained that the children had not mixed the straw and mud properly when they made the bricks, for he did not want his customers to know that their tailor could not see straight. The seams, he confessed to Micaela Arambula Widow of Arango, who will ever trust the seams of a man who can't see straight? She sent her sons to build the walls of the tailor's new room.

They worked for two weeks, slowed by the need to make use of the broken bricks, which they chopped and rubbed into squares to make the top rows of the walls. Even so, the walls of the new room were barely five feet high when they ran out of bricks. They studied Retana's family; the oldest of the boys was not yet nine years old, obviously the room had been fated to house the boys, so they named it Shortie's Place and put a roof on it. In gratitude for their work, the tailor did not complain when the Arango brothers spied on his daughters. He also sewed them each a pair of underpants, though he made the error in his blurred world of sewing openings into the front

[18]

and back of one pair and no openings at all in the other. Doroteo, being the older brother, took the pair with two openings and gave the undamaged pair to his brother.

Thereafter, the tailor shared his ends of cloth and the mistakes caused by his failing eyesight with the Widow of Arango. From such things as a coat with three sleeves, a piece of red cotton the size of a handkerchief, a strip of silk, a shirt without a neck, and a ball of knotted thread—the debris of Retana's sight and the leftovers of the desires of merchants and hacendados—Micaela clothed her children. There was a boon of erroneously made garments as Retana sank into blindness, and then the dearth that came as he was unable to attract many customers to his groping work.

Cousin Romualdo Franco went away that winter to work in a mine in Chihuahua. He left happily, clothed in expectations. His blanket roll was filled with tortillas and dried beef for the journey. Doroteo gave him his underwear for protection against the cold in the high mountains where the silver mines were being dug. Micaela made him a pair of mittens in three colors. He had shoes from León, a knife from Spain, and a jorongo so long and thick that he wobbled under the weight of it. He returned in three weeks, a shivering child with one arm tied to his chest. The jorongo, the shoes, the knife, and the mittens were gone; something for the doctor, something for the railroad ticket, the rest for food. On the second day, his arm had been crushed between two mule-drawn carts loaded with ore. A doctor from Parral had set his arm and sent him out into the streets of the mining town, weak and frightened, watching the blood ooze from the places where the bone had come through his skin. An old woman made soup for him from the food that was left in his blanket roll. He slept in the open, dreaming of scorpions and coyotes, waiting for the day when he could go back to the mine; there was a horse to buy and a saddle to inspect, the life of a man with a Stetson and long boots. He waited until he thought he was dying, then he went home.

The young men of Canatlán came to the Franco house to hear Romualdo speak of life in the mines; dreaming as they listened to his evolving memories, feeling the weight of real money as he spoke of pay wagons and cockfights and whores. He told of the darkness of the lives of miners, their dead skin and the surprise of their eyes, their scarred and unfitting limbs, a fingerless man who worked beside him on the carts, a crew of crippled diggers, the brother of a timber fitter who lay in a tent at the edge of the camp alone and without feeling or strength in his legs. He laughed for having worked with brave men. He prided himself on the motionless anarchy of the fingers of his right hand, saying that when he was strong again he was going back to the mine; to live on scrip, begging credit at the tienda de raya, was not a fit life for a brave man. He sobbed in his sleep and kissed his mother's hands when she brought him wine in the night and stroked his steaming forehead until he became cool in the next round of sleep.

It was also the year of the killing of the Presidente Municipal of Canatlán. On the day after the creditors took the Parra farm, the oldest of the sons, Ignacio, rode into Canatlán on his mare. He sat in the saddle as cowboys do, half sleeping, his hat low over his eyes and his shoulders rolled forward over his hips. At the beginning of the cobblestones, he halted the animal and waited. It was just before noon on a day in the end of winter. The clouds had not yet come, the sun was cold but bright on the white walls of the houses that lined the street. In the market, a man from the east had set up a marimba. Men slept on the benches in the plaza undisturbed by the soft sound of the musician's work. Pablo Valenzuela arranged the display of needles and metal pots in his store. A barefoot woman fished in her straw bag to buy five centavos worth of iodine in the musty darkness of the apothecary's shop. The cantina was empty, the barber slept in his chair. The Presidente stepped out of his office, crossed the waiting room, put on his hat, and walked out into the sun, heading up the street toward his lunch and siesta. Ignacio Parra slipped his rifle out of the scabbard, raised it to his shoulder, and shot the Presidente through the head. While the sound of the shot still echoed between the white walls, he turned his mare and rode west toward the Mountain of the Wise Turks. The Presidente fell backward onto the cobblestones. His collar cracked and broke open. The sun looked into his eyes.

The soldiers came in the early evening of the next day. The major set up his office in the anteroom of the deceased Presidente's office. One by one the soldiers brought the townspeople before him. He threatened to beat each of them with the flat of his sword and each of them told him the same name: Ignacio Parra, a twenty-two-year-old man riding a four-year-old chestnut mare. They were not afraid for Parra; he was beyond the reach of the telegraph at Papasquiaro, climbing the sierras toward the source of the Río de Ramos.

For the purpose of the funeral, the barber, who was also the undertaker, filled the hole in the front of the Presidente's head with a plug of wax and covered it with face powder. The priest spoke at length of the good works of the deceased. Those whose land he had taken and those whose sons he had sent to the army crossed themselves and followed the instructions of the little bell. The clouds had begun to cross the mountains by then, but there was still no rain. The ragged widows comforted the widow of the Presidente. The burial was in dry ground.

The rurales imitated their leader, offering the people five fingers or five bullets. The people gave their hands and hid their eyes; they carried roses and cactus flowers to lay upon the grave of the Presidente. No one spoke above a whisper, the bells of the church were muffled, the hooves of the horses and the iron-rimmed wheels of the hearse rang on the cobblestones; there was no green, there was no yellow in Canatlán on that afternoon; the wind was from the north. An old woman with a face of arid earth told the mother of Ignacio Parra that the Lord of Death and His Lady were the judges of lives.

"The Presidente?"

"He was a thief."

"And my son?"

"He is standing in the bank of Santa Catarina de Tepehuanes."

"Then my son is also a thief."

"Why do we walk carefully now?"

"Because the snakes are blind."

"They know."

A week after the funeral there was still no rain. Holes appeared in the fields where the mice found the seed. New seed was planted. The mice were joined by the crows. The people walked in the fields, shouting and waving sticks to protect the seed. At night, they carried pitchpine torches. The hacendados, who do not understand that rain is loosed by the tears of children, announced a charreada to distract the people and prevent them from weeping. Wild horses were brought down from the mountains, calves were brought in from the range, and four bulls were led in from a ranch near Guadalupe Victoria. There was a prize of five pesos in each of the contests.

They came to sit and stand around the adobe circle; everyone, all of Canatlán came, farmers, merchants, cowboys, even the priests, even López Negrete himself with his silk and splinters wife and his pale sons. Mule skinners came in their leather pants and stood with their great arms around the waists of fat whores. Thieves and gamblers moved through the crowd, their eyes like birds' eyes in their stuttering heads. Campesinos walked down from the mountains to stand in silence and sell the woven and painted complications of their dreams. There was pulque, aguamiel, and sotol to drink, and the sheriff, walking with his hand on his pistol, to watch the drinkers. The old women carried their trays of sugary cakes or sat before their clay griddles, patting and folding, pinching tortillas out of the hot grease. It was last year's corn, last year's sugar, last year's cotton, old wood; there was no rain, the fires complained. The rich ate and laughed, the poor looked away and laughed louder.

López Negrete made gifts of sugar cakes and thin coins. He touched the faces of babies and patted the heads of the older children. He strode through the crowd, followed by two cowboys carrying Winchesters. A belly on stilts, dressed in black and silver, with a macaw's nose and soft brown hair, he evaluated the doffing of hats and the downcasting of eyes. He was the leader of the laughter, the instructor of the band, the timekeeper and the judge, the lord of Canatlán.

The Widow of Arango brought her children, four of them to watch, and Doroteo, who promised to win a prize. They carried their own food and stood in their own place, speaking first to the priests and then to the acquaintances who passed by them in the slowly wheeling crowd. They listened to the band, they smiled and saluted away the vendors, they brushed the dust from their clothes. The girls stood with their hands tight by their sides, smiling and nodding, speaking after their mother spoke, careful of the softness of their voices and the brevity of their laughter. Their hair shone, their skin was cool in the hot and white day; they wore their dresses made of Retana's mistakes as if they were the tiny gowns of López Negrete's daughters.

Doroteo stood behind his sisters, the protector of their arrogance, dressed in huaraches and a broken hat. He waited his turn, he dreamed his prize; five pesos in all their forms: a pair of shoes, the beginning of a rifle, thirty cartridges, a sword, a felt hat, candles for his father, a shawl for his mother, a silver belt buckle, candies, meat, a kerosene lamp, a cooking pot, needles, thread, cloth, buttons, a shell comb, a soft brush, a scissors, a pair of spurs, a chair, a wooden bed, a window of glass, a colored shirt, a pair of narrow pants, shoes for Marianita, Martina, Hipólito, and Antonio, wool, cured leather, an axe, an awl, the weight of the five pieces of silver in his hand assuming his warmth. He had one centavo in his pocket to pay for using the latrine before he went to the chutes to begin his ride.

"My friend," he said to the old man who sat at the men's entrance of the public baths, "will you permit me to use the services?"

"One centavo, kid."

"Old man, I'm going to ride a bull."

"One centavo."

"And if I don't have a centavo?"

"Dogs piss in the street."

"You would do that to me?"

"One centavo."

"You're a thief; you get my piss and my money too."

"And for this lesson in business I make no charge."

Doroteo gave the old man his centavo and went inside. The baths were dark and steaming with vapors of excrement. He went to the nearest trough and began to urinate. Further down the trough a cowboy leaned forward, balancing himself with one hand against the wall, directing his urine with the other. The cowboy's head was bent so that the crown of his hat nearly touched the wall. Doroteo saw a tremor go through the cowboy's body, flinging his head back and forward again, throwing off his hat. An enormous gout of blood flew out of his mouth and into the trough. The man leaned forward, resting the top of his head against the wall. Doroteo closed his pants and ran down the length of the trough to where the man stood, beginning to crumple, sliding down the wall toward the trough. He put his shoulder into the man's armpit and propped him up.

"What's going on?"

"Nothing. The broncos."

"I saw the blood."

"It's nothing. My fault."

"I'll help you."

"Just hold me up a few minutes. It passes."

"I got to go. I'll call the old man. I got to go; my turn is coming."

The cowboy raised his head and turned to look at Doroteo. There were spatters of blood on his face; one eye was swollen shut; he appeared to have two different faces joined at the center, one long and bony and the other fat and blackening. His breath stank of half-digested blood. He said: "Hide your face, kid. Make yourself into a ball. Remember. If you don't, it will be your own fault."

"The bulls don't kick."

"Idiot!"

On his way out Doroteo told the old man at the entrance that there was a cowboy inside vomiting blood. The old man shrugged: "He wanted a prize. He won."

"The bulls don't kick."

"As you like," the old man said. "But remember—" he wagged a finger —"no centavo, no entrance."

"I salute your mother, old man."

"I'm waiting for you."

Antonio stayed with the women and Hipólito went with Doroteo to the chutes. They stopped to look at the four bulls standing in a pen; three browns and a black eating hay, their ears down even in the midst of the noise of the charreada, their hindquarters greened with manure, all of them with heavy forequarters, bulls built for goring and butting, not for bucking. They were still studying the animals when the call came for the riders to draw for their turns. Hipólito went to the little knot of men near the entrance to the ring to draw for his brother. He came back with the number three.

"I'm sorry," he told Doroteo; "they say it's better to get them on the second time after they're tired out."

[*23*]

"I heard it was better to get them the first time when they're not so mean."

"You're not afraid?"

"If I get thrown, I'll just make myself into a ball and wait for someone to help me. There's no way to get hurt if you do that; the ground is soft."

"I heard it's better to get up right away and try to run."

"We'll see."

Doroteo climbed the fence to wait for his bull to come into the chute. He gave his broken hat and huaraches to Hipólito, who stood beside him, watching Doroteo's bull as it was prodded into the narrow chute. It was one of the browns, a stubborn animal, but seemingly calm, not tossing its head, stopping, then walking a step or two after it was prodded, stopping and walking, stopping again. Hipólito reached up and patted his brother's leg, whispering: "It's an ox, Doro, an ox."

When the animal was below him and the gate was closed behind it, Doroteo climbed over the top rail and lowered himself onto the bull's back. Two cowboys passed a rope under the bull's belly and knotted it. The animal felt the steel burrs tied to the part of the rope under its belly and it shivered; the burrs would not cut until Doroteo cinched the rope around his hand and turned it tight.

One of the cowboys touched Doroteo's leg. "Now," he said. Doroteo slipped his right hand under the rope. He took a deep breath and let it out slowly to mask the sound of his heart. Then he turned the rope around his hand once, grasped the twist with his fingers and turned it again. The animal raised up off the ground. "Now!"

The bull bucked, kicked, spun, bucked, jumped, bucked and bucked again. There was no rhythm, no way to prepare for the next move. Doroteo held on. The horizon staggered, flickered. He held on. The bull wheeled to the right. The rope slipped to the left. The bull wheeled harder, spinning. Doroteo held on, counting the pesos, slipping off to his left, reaching up with his left hand, grasping, trying to climb up the side of the bull. The sky and the ground were lost; he saw only the brown flank and the rising dust. He heard the people screaming, but he could not make out what they were saying: the roaring breath of the bull, the thudding of the hooves, his own wordless shouts, obscured everything else. The bull smashed him against the adobe wall.

A cowboy grabbed the animal's tail and it pulled away, mooing and turning after him with its horns. Two other cowboys dragged Doroteo through a narrow opening in the wall and laid him on the ground, arranging him neatly, with his feet together, his arms folded across his chest, and his eyes closed but aimed heavenward. Blood trickled slowly out of his nose and both ears. Small bubbles of blood formed and broke on his lips.

[24]

Micaela fell on him, crying that he was dead, calling for a priest. Two mountain women knelt beside her and lifted her up to a kneeling position. They pointed to the small bubbles made by Doroteo's breath, and they took her hand and put it on his neck so that she could feel the life. Their men came and laid out blankets on the ground beside the boy, then they lifted him over onto the blankets. The Francos came and the Retanas and the Mojicos and Lalo Clavialco who could speak the language of the Tepehuanes. Together they guided the woman and carried her son to the Arango house.

One of the mountain women crushed a pepper seed and rubbed it under Doroteo's nose to awaken him. They mixed a powder of the pink-flowered rue anemone in egg white and gave it to him to stop the bleeding. Micaela brought a bowl of water and a cloth to clean the dust and blood from his face. Marianita brought a cornhusk pillow to put under his head.

When the bleeding had stopped, one of the mountain women examined him. He was all right, she said, but for his left leg, which had been torn or broken at the knee. Clavialco translated their diagnosis and their willingness to repair the damaged leg. Beatriz Franco said that it would be better to get the doctor from Papasquiaro, but Micaela remembered how he had set Romualdo's broken arm so that it healed stiff and crooked. She told the mountain woman to go ahead with her cure, which was begun by sending two of her men running out the door waving their machetes.

Speaking through Clavialco, the woman asked for a cup of cooking grease, which Micaela brought from a shelf in the darkest corner of the house. The woman raised Doroteo's pants leg well above his knee, smiling up at him, reassuring him all the while she worked; then she covered the knee with grease and began to rub it into his skin, warming the wounded place with the lightness and quickness of her hands.

She rubbed steadily with the same lightness for more than two hours. There are quicker ways to relieve such pains using an ointment made of the crushed seed or even the leaves of jimsonweed, but after an hour Doroteo said the pain had passed and he felt able to walk on the leg. Clavialco translated for the woman, who smiled more broadly and advised Doroteo not to move until her men returned.

Except for those few words and Doroteo's apology for having failed to win a prize, the room was quiet, intent upon the woman, who further focused attention upon the boy's knee, drawing their gaze with her hands, taking their strength for him. She began to sing softly, still watching the boy's face, smiling at him. It was a cooing song, without words, light and warming, like her hands. She sang to Doroteo until he slept, and she continued to sing as the sleep took him more deeply and his body softened.

After another hour her men returned carrying the ribs of a giant cactus.

[25]

Doroteo was as limp and lost as the dead. She directed the men to cut the springy wood into two-foot lengths, which she placed around the injured knee, completely encircling it. Then she asked for some cloth, which she tore into strips and tied loosely around the wood, holding it in place. One of the men knelt at Doroteo's head and held him under the arms, the other went to his feet and took a good grasp on the ankle of his injured leg. The woman gave a nod and both men pulled. She felt the knee through the splints, nodding at the men to pull harder. When she was satisfied, she quickly tightened the cloth strips to hold the splints in place.

Doroteo lay unmoving, as if he were absent from his body. The woman awakened him only when she was ready, and then she had but to touch the corner of his eye with her forefinger and he was immediately awake. Micaela thanked her, speaking through Clavialco, but addressing her with maternal eyes. "We are poor people," she said, "but I would like to make some gift to you. Anything in my house is yours."

The mountain woman walked once around the room of the house, a barefoot assessor with lines of white in her hair and the remains of yellow and red paint on her face. "Our rooster died," she said. "Give us one fertilized egg."

Clavialco translated.

Micaela asked, "How can you be certain it will be a rooster?"

The woman stuck out her tongue and grinned.

There was no rain. The hacendados went to Mexico and Paris, the animals and people of Canatlán lived by the streams, by the sweetwater wells; but there was not enough to share with the fields: the corn had no strength, the cotton was naked, we ate nopal and bought wheat flour in the company stores, which are the promises of hunger, of years of halves of halves of the halves we farmed. I begged for rain; I wept. But there was no rain, neither was there sun; the sky was made of ashes, the earth turned to dust. We burned butterflies and incense.

Near the end of summer the rains came, alternating with the sun; time and space moved back into their proper conjunction. We went back to the fields, we picked the first beans, we ate the young corn, making ourselves strong again, hoeing and browning in the sun. We took what there was and survived; we are like the cactus on which the eagle chose to stand; we are like Tezcatlipoca the sorcerer, formed to fit the moment, wolves or sheep, cactus or mountain pine; that is what it means to be human.

I told these thoughts to Doroteo, who came to my house in the saddle of the mountain to find out if it was time to remove the splints. I gave him water to drink and water to wash himself, and while he drank a bowl of corn meal and cocoa to refresh himself, I made the mirror ready. The splints were beginning to harden and crack, which is the sign that they may be removed, for their strength has been assumed by the limb. I cut away the bindings, removed the splints and greased and warmed his leg. The woman had healed him well; the foot was turned inward, but not so much that it would keep him from walking. I passed an egg over his body to cleanse him, then we sat beside the fire to look into the mirror and talk of what the smoke said.

In the mirror he saw his face, then the smoke came and he saw his heart and a face of smoke, an unformed, changing face.

No, I told him, not the wizard; he is the smoke, he speaks, he is change itself, that is his power. Face and heart is what you saw, signs of a man. The obsidian mirror comes from the south, from the old way that was before the catzopines came; it was the beginning of the Fifth Sun.

Face and heart. They are two words and they are one word, they are the duality of a man, and they are his measure. In the old way, in the time of the grandfather of the grandfather of my grandfather, in the old city that stood in the navel of the world, and before that in the land of the cranes, and before that in the seven caves, and before that on the hill that is the throne of the Lady of Birth and Death, the Mother of Movement, since humans were born of ashes and the blood of the son of the God of Duality, it has been the work of a man to have a heart of powerful movement and a face as solid as stone.

Face and heart, cara y corazón, ixtli in yóllotl.

There are many faces: a face of glory belongs to one who can do nothing, a face of wood belongs to one whose secret crimes are known to everyone. We are born with a heart, but a man must assume a face or he remains in the earth, in dreams. Without a well-formed face, a man is nothing more than transitions. His heart may teach him to love flowers, to love song, but without a face he cannot love flowers and song. Dreams cannot dream; a man must learn to have a face like stone. I am the last of the tlamatinime; it is my name and my work to teach you to have a face.

In our history there are the faces of Tlacaélel, which is the face of wisdom, and the face of Ahuitzotl, who gave the blood of forty thousand captives to keep the sun moving in the sky, and the face of the Swooping Eagle, who was the last defender of Tenochtitlán. To have a face you must be serious, you may not be dissolute or lazy. Neither be a dragging talker nor a swallow-mouth. Be clean and quick. Know your own nose. Do not eat the young corn. Then you will be greatly esteemed, and when one man speaks of the solidity of your face, another will answer, How is one seen?

Face and heart; you have seen it in the black mirror, you know what the smoke said, you can dream.

[27]

3

The clerk in the company store had brought the problem of his nervousness to five doctors and nine healers, and neither the doctors nor the healers had been able to help his stammering or relieve his itching or slow the sweat that poured out of his skin. Each transaction took twice as long as it should because he had such difficulty in stammering out the prices; and his thanks and farewells were as long as operas. He dripped on his ledgers, causing the ink to run, and he often paused in cutting cheese or measuring out flour to scratch his testicles or the damp crevice of his buttocks. Now and then he lost a sale to those who remembered the more fastidious ways of the old times. More often he made his customers laugh. He was the fastest man in the entire state of Durango: hopping, chopping, stammering, sweating, and scratching at the same time.

The doctors and the healers explained their failure by the situation of the clerk's life: he earned ten times as much as a peón, two pesos a day, but he pretended to the life of the rich; six of his children attended the church school in Canatlán, he wore shoes and brown trousers and a storebought shirt, and his wife went by train twice each year to visit her relatives in Coahuila. On Sundays he wore a suit and smoked cigars. He was a city man, hired by the López Negretes to run their store and keep their books; country life did not suit him. People said he was used to the bite of a different kind of flea.

His customers often stood at the counter in the rectangular adobe building, pretending to be staring at the shelves behind the counter, deciding which beans or chiles to buy, when they were really only being entertained by the clerk's nervousness. Antonio Paloduro, who had been to the jungles to milk the rubber trees, said that the clerk moved exactly like a monkey he had seen in Yucatán. So the clerk came to be known as The Monkey, and the children from Canatlán and even San Juan del Río and Papasquiaro came to see him.

The people who enjoyed The Monkey most, however, were three crippled cowboys who came every morning at dawn and sat on the wooden bench that faced the counter. They sat all day until the clerk closed his store. At noon every day they bought a bottle of aguardiente and drank it off in nine even gulps, passing the bottle back and forth until it had been fairly shared. They never laughed and they never spoke. They sat in their sombreros and tattered cowboy boots, straight and serious, following him with their eyes. The clerk did not complain about them to the foreman because each of the crippled cowboys carried a pistol, which he thought was good protection against bandits.

He was a fat man, full of laughter along with his scratchings and stammerings; he always laughed at the children who laughed at him. He even laughed when the people insulted him over the price of corn or rice in the store. Prices were going up, he told them with a shrug; if a kilo of rice and a kilo of beans cost a full day's pay, there was nothing he could do about it. Did he not also eat? Then they laughed with him while he added to the debt that would be inherited by their children and their children's children. That's life, he said. That's life, they said.

Then he caught a fever and nearly died. For fifty days he lay in his house. His educated children and his traveling wife attended him carefully for the first weeks of his fever, then they abandoned him to die, doing only the little that was necessary for the weak, shrinking man who lay under the blanket. But he surprised them; the fever passed, he regained his strength, and in less than three weeks he was back behind the counter of the company store.

The three crippled cowboys did not hear of his return until he had been back for three days. Then they came and took their places on the bench to resume their watching. It was a different man behind the counter, however; The Monkey was thin and calm, he neither scratched nor sweated. They watched him all morning and did not see him hop even once. At noon, they drank their bottle of aguardiente in nine gulps, took out their pistols, and shot him.

Doroteo was returning a horse to the stables when he heard that The Monkey had been shot. He ran the length of the main compound to the store to see what had happened. The rurales were already there when he arrived. The captain was beating the crippled cowboys with the flat of his sword, demanding that they confess to their crime, though they admitted with each blow of the sword that they had killed The Monkey.

They were being driven away from the main house, stumbling and shouting their guilt as they went. The flat of the sword tore their shirts and opened long shallow cuts in their skin. Their arms were gashed and bloody, trailing strips of skin and cotton. A crowd gathered and followed them, waiting to see whether the rurales would shoot them or hang them. Dogs licked at the blood that pooled wherever one of the cowboys fell.

One of the dogs went into the company store, where The Monkey still lay. Doroteo followed the dog into the store, intending to chase it out. He saw the dog frantically running up and back along the length of the counter, trying to get to the body that lay on the other side. It was a thin yellow dog with a white belly and an almost hairless tail that curled down and between its legs. He kicked the dog and shouted at it to get out, but it turned on him, laying its ears back and growling. He kicked it again, and the dog ran out.

The back wall of the store was dotted with blood and hair. A sack of wheat flour that had been torn by a bullet poured a white stream onto the floor. The room smelled of blood and vinegar and shit and gunpowder. He leaned across the counter to look at The Monkey. The clerk's head and part of his face had been torn away by the fusillade; Doroteo would not have recognized the parts that were left. The identifying sign was the fat ledger that lay open beside the body, half covered by a dead arm. Doroteo climbed over the counter and slid the ledger out from under the clerk's arm. He looked through it, turning the pages, trying to identify the one that listed the debts of the Arango family. All the pages seemed to be the same, so he put the ledger under his shirt, taking it with him out of the store to a secret place at the foot of the Mountain of Asphodels, there to study the dried, yellowing pages, to learn how everyone came to be in debt, to understand why López Negrete was rich and everyone else was poor. It was all in the book, Micaela had said; the power of the book had made the clerk into The Monkey, the hopping, stammering victim of evil.

He held the ledger in his lap and slowly turned the pages, seeking some order in it, some clue to its power. The pages spoke of his family, the family of Romualdo, the Clavialcos, the Parras, the Navarros, the Ibarras, the old woman Muñoz, the Hueniles, the Morenos, everyone. They were all there on the pages, made into marks cast in curled lines as the future is cast in the book of horoscopes. But which and where? How did one family begin and another end? How were children made into lines with a pen? What was wheat? What was corn? It was the tale of Canatlán, the book of generations, a chain, permission for the foreman to beat a runaway orphan, the candle-light and laughter of the great house of the owner, and the woodsmoke and weeping of the huts.

It was a book of tears, the burden of continuity, the division of the world into those with shoes and those whose feet took on the color of dust, whose skin took on the consistency of baked mud. And it was without reason, colorless, thin, without a face, without the music of words. His mother was right: the priest had the book of God and this was the book of the Devil. He tore out a page and burned it. He tore out another and another. The smoke rose and became nothing, the ashes were taken by the wind and lost in the mountains; the book was more like a dream than like a stone. It had no words, nothing to remember; it died, leaving neither its name nor the

[*30*]

color of its eyes nor the shape of its nose. The ledger was nothing compared to a man. He laughed; the air was clear.

There were three of them in the fields where once Doroteo had worked alone, and there was not enough for three; they started late, they finished early, and the Arango debt in the company store increased, for every year they needed more and every year the land gave less. They permitted no weeds, they defeated the birds, they drove out the mice, they removed the weak leaves and shored up the leaning stalks, they picked the corn and mowed the hay at the best moment, they took each bean as it ripened, and still there was less; the land was losing its life, like a sun dying. They carried wood and leaves down from the hills to burn over the land, mixing those ashes with the ashes of cornstalks and dried cotton plants, but the old ways would not do; the wind and the rain scraped away the land, and the corn ate before it was eaten. The Widow of Arango dwindled to an old woman's width; her skin and her skirts fell in folds; she looked often at her hands, watching the knuckles grow. The girls bloomed like morning flowers, lacking sinew, racing toward the moment when they would begin to collapse under the weight of their own petals. Marianita's eyes became her stately negotiators. Hipólito dreamed aloud, Antonio labored, Doroteo learned to laugh. They felt an ending on its way, they waited to be dispersed.

Doroteo left home in the quiet months after the corn had been harvested. He took with him his blanket roll, a pair of boots and spurs he had won at a rodeo in Guadalupe Victoria, a tiny deerskin pouch containing Quetzal feathers and two splinters of jade from the ruins of the City of God, salt, a little ball of copal, ten matches, a fourth of a box of .30–.30 cartridges, a coil of old and soft rope, a poncho that had been dipped in rubber sap, a snake's tooth, five fat tortillas, a piece of stone from La Coyotada, and much advice from Micaela.

She had sat on the wooden chair near the fire, chilled even in the first days of winter, wrapped in the long black shawl, huddled, her quick and trembling hands passing over the brown beads. "O my little son, where are you going?"

"With the mule trains."

"They're drunkards and marijuanos."

"There are bad people everywhere, Mama."

"You're so young."

"I'm fifteen years old."

"There are bandits, there will be snow in the mountains—what will you eat? Where will you find food? You can't live on meat alone, like a savage. What will you say to the women in the towns? You'll go to the cantinas, won't you? You'll go with those men, the drunkards. Haven't you seen them in Canatlán, in San Juan, in Papasquiaro, in Guadalupe? They lie in the streets like animals, like pigs with the souls of wolves. The devil marks their faces with disease, their eyes are blank, like a cat's eyes. Don't you think I know about them? Everyone knows the muledrivers, everyone knows what they are."

"I won't be like them, Mama, I swear."

"On the grave of your father."

"By the eyes of the sainted mother, by the gentleness of my own mother, who is a saint."

"It's a fine oath, Doro, but you don't even know the Church."

"I know my mother."

"Swear to me that you won't drink or smoke."

"I swear."

"Swear to me that you won't go with any woman who isn't your proper wife."

"I swear."

"By all that is holy."

"I swear."

"Go with God."

"Mama, I'll come back with money."

"When I was young, like you, I wanted money too. I could close my eyes and see lovely dresses. Silks, Doro, I dreamed of silks and pearls. I saw paint on my lips and perfume in my hair. My eyes were two nights of summer. I was dancing, eating persimmons and oranges. There were smiles, there was laughter. I wore ribbons in my hair and jade at my throat. I wore gold, I dressed in gold, I dressed in silver. I commanded the music, I led the dance.

"It was nothing, my little son, nothing. It was a lie. I pretended that I would live forever. And death is already speaking to me. Your father comes to lie beside me in the night: he is so thin, I hear his painful breath, I feel the coughing in his bones. What use is money now? I am an old woman, I know now that money cannot buy life or bring the rain.

"Bring back money, Doroteo, if you must. But I would rather have you home. There is no comfort in money. I am not the mother of money."

"Mama, what if we're hungry?"

"We've been hungry."

They carried silver from the mines near San Francisco del Oro to the refineries of Chihuahua, and then they bought store goods in Chihuahua and wine in Delicias to carry back to Parral, Canatlán, Santiago Papasquiaro, San Juan del Río, and the villages between. They were merchants and muleskinners, prey to bandits, winter, and the luck of the mountains; survival always surprised them.

Tomás Gallardo, who led the pack train, had inherited the mules, the burros, the routes, and the customers from his father, who had died with his belly filled with blood after being thrown from a horse. Tomás, a careful man, rode a mule that he had taught not to rear by whacking it in the head with the butt of his rifle whenever it raised both forelegs off the ground. At night, he made his own camp on high ground about thirty yards away from the main camp. He lit no fire and he slept with two loaded rifles by his side; if bandits were to attack the camp, Tomás would be able to fire down on them out of the darkness. He was careful to avoid ambushes of all kinds, including marriage, which he considered the worst of dangers; but he had a desire for a son, and he worked out that desire by taking young men under his protection. Doroteo was only the latest in a long succession of protégés, none of whom lasted very long; they either died on the trail or found the muleskinner's life too lonely and too full of hardship for their taste and went on to some more comfortable work.

For Doroteo, the protection of Gallardo was a burden; the man spoke constantly about the terrain, describing hidden canyons, passes through the mountains that could not be seen from a quarter of a mile away, solid rock trails over which a mule train could travel without leaving a trace, caves that appeared to have no entrances, caves with secret exits, box canyons that a man could slip out of without being seen, sudden draws and washes into which a man could disappear, streams in the desert, places for ambushes. It was his obsession, the only aspect of life that held any interest for him. He knew stories of men who had eluded entire armies in the wild mountain country of Chihuahua. He could point to places in the desert where a bandit had disappeared from the sight of a troop of rurales and turned up again riding behind them. He knew of the failures too: men who had died of thirst lying only a few feet from fresh water, men who had been shot to death in box canyons while they looked at the exits and did not see them.

He talked to Doroteo for days on end, leading him off the trail to show him a cave or a canyon or a waterhole. "It is how I live," he said. "A man can have one shot at me, maybe two, and then I'll disappear. A wolf couldn't find me in these mountains. Heraclió Bernal, Francisco Villa, Benito Canales, Macario Romero, Manuel Reyes—the greatest bandits couldn't find me here. I'm a magician, Doroteo, a wizard. I'm also a coward. That's the most important part—to be a coward. These drunkards who are riding behind us—Nono, Carpintero, Bisco Peines, Cabalgador, Emiliano Santos—they're all brave men. Not one of them will live to be forty years old. I'm a coward; when I die I'll be an old man. You know the difference between a coward and a brave man, Doro? Brave men are fools;

[33]

they want to die. Believe me when I tell you this. Don't listen to the songs you hear in the cantinas. No, no, listen to the songs, but think about them, use your head; they're all songs about dead men, aren't they? What do you think about that, Arango, what do you think about that?"

Gallardo was less adept as a merchant: he often bought goods that no one wanted; it was not unusual for him to have to sell cloth at the same price he paid for it; and his judgment of wine was so poor that he sometimes bought vinegar at the price of wine and had to sell it at the price of vinegar. When he complained to the merchants that he had been cheated, they answered by questioning his ability as a salesman, suggesting that it was his customers who cheated him. Gallardo didn't know who to believe; everyone seemed to be against him. He suspected that they were in league, passing messages up and back, conspiring. He devised ambushes for them: to a customer he related the death of a merchant, waiting for reaction; and getting none, he tried at the other end, telling the merchants of the deaths of his customers. But there were no clues, nothing certain. "They're too shrewd for me," he told Doroteo. "I'm a mountain man, I understand bandits; but these Spaniards, these thieves in the cities, sometimes I think the best thing is to shoot them, all of them, the Spaniards and the Chinese and the criollos."

Doroteo seldom spoke in answer; he nodded or smiled or made appreciative grunts. He feared Gallardo: the man bragged of riding animals to death, he overloaded the burros at both ends of his route, and he treated the men worse than the animals, cursing them, driving them, as if he dared them to finish the trip alive. When the animals balked, he beat them; when the men balked, he said, "The weapons, the shoes, the mules, and the food are mine. You can stay behind, but I take what's mine and you keep what's yours."

There was less money to be made with Gallardo than with any other pack train; no other man was as demanding or as cruel to the men who rode with him. Yet Gallardo had no difficulty finding men to work for him; everyone knew that to ride with Gallardo was to survive. On the trip before Doroteo joined them, the camp had been surprised in the middle of the night. Four bandits had come into the circle in which the men slept, moving quickly, coming upwind to avoid alarming the animals. They had gathered the weapons and stacked them before awakening the five sleeping muleskinners. Gallardo had waited in the darkness, watching while the bandits searched his men and herded them up against a rock to be shot. He killed two of the bandits, then moved from his position while the other two bandits emptied their rifles in the direction from which the shots had come. He fired one more shot, then he was silent. The bandits, who had taken cover after his first two shots, waited. Gallardo also waited. Several hours passed. The remaining bandits exposed themselves, moving slowly, trying to draw his fire without giving him a clean shot. Gallardo waited. Finally, the bandits stepped out into the area near the fire, ordering the other muleskinners to stand up against the rock, to prepare to die in retaliation for the deaths of their comrades. Gallardo waited until they had raised their rifles to execute the muleskinners, then he killed the bandits, using one shot for each of them. When he examined the bodies, he saw that he had shot three of them through the head and the fourth one through the neck. He stood over the man who had been shot through the neck, staring at the wound. "Forgive me," he said to the muleskinners. "Sometimes there's a bad cartridge." The men laughed as they searched the bodies. Gallardo took the rifles and cartridges and allowed his men to keep the money and whatever clothing they could wear or sell. They left the stripped bodies for the coyotes and the vultures, four dead bandits with their heads burst and their jaws hacked open, one of them still modest in his fouled underwear.

The mule train moved south out of Delicias, loaded with wine, strung out behind Gallardo like a knotted rope. They left the road when it turned east, taking the mountain trails, avoiding the big semicircle that reached out to Jiménez, saving six days on the way to San Francisco del Oro, where Gallardo expected to sell wine, oil lamps, lard, thimbles, galluses, and soap to the miners.

Snow fell in the high passes, lying on the trees, icing the trails. "It's like a telegraph wire," Gallardo said, "a message to bandits. But the lower trails are too exposed, they can look down on us like birds. This is a bad time, Doro. The burros lose their footing on the ice, the wolves will kill us for our blankets, a man could fall in the snow. I remember one time, we were crossing from Chihuahua to Sonora in the winter, and my father took the high trails because of the Apaches. What cold! I was a skinny kid, even skinnier than I am now. My father gave me his big boots and told me to wrap my feet in rags inside. It was lucky for me. Man, I never saw such cold; one driver's feet turned black, so they had to cut off his legs in the little hospital near the mine at Cananea. And he was a lucky one! One man fell from the rim of a canyon into the snow, and the wind was blowing so hard through the canyon that the snow closed over him right away and there wasn't even a mark in the place where he was. I was still young then and I wanted to look for him, but my father told me not to be crazy, that he didn't want to have to come back in the spring to see if the coyotes left something to bury. Those are the worst mountains in the winter. West of Casas Grandes it's all rock; there isn't even a place to get out of the wind."

"It's the truth?"

"You don't see us taking the high trails here; I learned my lesson, kid. The only thing to do in this winter weather is to stay away from the snow and move fast. If some wolves followed us out of Delicias, they're going to have trouble getting ahead of Gallardo."

They loaded the burros in the darkness before dawn and unloaded them in the darkness that came after dusk. They ran, steaming in the cold, cursing and poking the animals; someone was following them: a thick man with a great hat and tiny eyes; a thin, dark man full of white laughter; three Tarahumara boys carrying machetes, waiting for the opportunity to behead exhausted men in their dreamless sleep. They heard the laughter of the dark man, an echo in certain canyons, a faint warning brought by peculiar winds. Once, as they were poking the burros across and up the side of a narrow wash, they saw the forms of the Tarahumara boys against the sky, blankets flapping, machetes shining, their legs stretching in the long, slow strides of the deerkilling run. The tiny eyes of the thick man peered at them, sighting down the long barrel of his Winchester, discerning the vulnerability of their hearts. He was the one they never saw, for he dressed in white and rode a white horse, which was like the snow; he was the one they feared most.

At dusk of the fourth day out of Delicias they reached the Conchos a few miles west of the lake. There was ice in the river, and it was moving too fast for winter; they could hear the speed of it, like the applause of spring. It was too cold, they told Gallardo, too dark; they were tired, the animals were exhausted. He looked behind them, scanning the fading shapes of the hills, the peaks that softened into the dusk. They asked if he saw something —a fire? the flickering shape of a rider in the hills? He laughed. "I'm going across," he said. He turned his mule into the river, beckoning to Doroteo to follow.

For three hours they whipped and poked the burros into the river. They tied ropes to each other and to the animals, hauling the victims of the river onto the south bank. They stood in the water, they fell on the icy banks of the river, the wind froze the water in their clothes. The current turned Nono Rodriguez under and carried him downstream to the end of the rope. When they dragged him onto the bank, they had to pump his arms and put crushed pepper seeds into his nose to start his breath. Doroteo and Gallardo went into the water for almost every animal; Doroteo pulled on the lead rope and Gallardo poked the animal under the tail while Bisco Peines or Emiliano Santos pushed the beast or dragged it forward by one of its ears. The burros kicked and bit at them, pieces of ice crashed into their backs and shoulders, the temperature of the water entered their bones and became cold metal burrs in their joints.

When it was over, they built a great fire to dry their blankets, which they used to rub down the animals. Then they dried themselves and opened one of the casks of wine. Gallardo found a place that gave him a clear view of the camp and the river, wrapped himself in his blanket, and went to sleep.

Doroteo stayed with the men and the animals near the fire. While they drank wine, he ate corn gruel and chiles with dried meat. Then he wrapped himself in his blanket and his rubber poncho and went to sleep.

The argument had no subject; nothing was disputed. Cabalgador was playing his tiny guitar, singing softly; Nono Rodriguez was lying on his back, drunkenly trying to reweave one of the ropes that had broken during the river crossing; Carpintero was whittling tiny obscene statues out of pieces of green wood; and Bisco Peines and Mil Santos sat close to the fire, staring at each other, drinking wine out of the earthenware jars they carried for canteens.

"Fuck your mother," Santos said.

Peines took his pistol out of the holster.

Santos said, "You cross-eyed pussyhair, you better be careful or you'll shoot yourself another asshole."

"Take out your pistol and let's see what happens, son."

Still holding the jar of wine in his left hand, Santos unholstered his pistol and aimed it at Peines. He raised his wine in a toast: "Hey, Bisco, to the health of your whore mother."

Bisco fired first, a wild, half-serious shot that fell somewhere on the north side of the river. Before he could fire again, the clumsy slug from Santos's .44-caliber pistol tore a hole in his belly. The force of the bullet knocked him backwards out of his squatting position, bending him double, then throwing him over on his side.

Santos finished his wine before he stood up and walked around the fire to where Bisco lay. He kept his pistol ready until he saw that Bisco had dropped his weapon to use both of his hands to hold back the blood and intestinal gruel that pumped out of the hole in his belly. Bisco looked up at him. "Ay, God," he said, "it smells like your mother's cunt." Santos pointed his pistol at Bisco's head; then he changed his mind and put the weapon back in its holster. "It's not worth the trouble," he said, rolling Bisco over onto his back, using one foot, careful not to soil his boot with the mess that was oozing out around Bisco's hands.

They looked at each other for a moment. Santos smiled. "I did you a favor, man; your eyes aren't crossed anymore. You'll be able to see your way straight to Hell."

"I'll wait for you there."

Santos filled his jar with wine and went back to sitting on the other side of the fire. Carpintero resumed his whittling. Cabalgador picked out a new tune on his tiny guitar and began composing a song about the shooting of Bisco Peines. Nono wove his rope. Only Doroteo watched the wounded man, who had begun to wriggle backward, away from the fire, as if to escape the pain.

[37]

Doroteo said, "We should get some jimsonweed to put in his wound."

"There is none," said Carpintero. "It's winter."

"Let him alone," Santos said. "I want to see how he dies."

Doroteo looked up toward the place where Gallardo was hidden. The answer came down in a whisper: "Let him alone."

The others went to sleep; only Doroteo watched and listened. Bisco Peines died all night, vomiting blood, calling for his mother, calling for Christ and the Virgin, asking to die, at least to die quickly. He asked for water. Doroteo waited until he was certain that everyone was asleep, then he brought Bisco jars of wine, explaining to him that it would dull the pain. The dying man blessed him and took the wine. After drinking two jarsful, he said that he felt so much better he thought he might not die. Doroteo brought him more wine. Bisco offered his gory hand in gratitude. Doroteo drew back, then he saw the hurt in Bisco's face, and he gave him his hand to hold, maintaining the connection even after there was no more strength in the dying man's hand and he had to hold on to him as if Bisco's hand were his life.

Before he died, Bisco dreamed: he spoke to his mother and his sister, he gave flowers to a brother he had wronged, he held a cup of wine to the lips of Christ on the cross, he beheld the miraculous shroud, he danced with a woman called Milk, he was a fountain in a field of singing corn, he was a bird with brilliant eyes watching his own death, he was a god pouring his blood over the ashes of man.

When the others awakened, Bisco was dead and Doroteo was at the river, washing the stench from his hands. He came back up to the camp, ready to bury Bisco, but everyone said the ground was too hard. "Then we'll put stones in his pockets and bury him in the river," he said.

Gallardo shook his head. "We have to drink from the river."

"You want to leave him for the coyotes?"

"He's dead, kid. Pork."

"Nothing more?"

"I swear."

"He was a man."

Gallardo shrugged. "It's getting light; load the animals."

Doroteo left the pack train in Parral. While he was giving back the rifle, counting out the cartridges, measuring the rope, Gallardo asked if he was leaving because of Bisco Peines.

"Yes."

"I thought you were more intelligent."

"You could have helped him."

"A man who's gutshot is poisoned by his own shit; there was nothing to do."

"Still . . ."

"Still? Still what?" Gallardo looked into Doroteo's face. They were the same height, but Doroteo was heavier in the chest and shoulders. Gallardo seemed to be measuring him, as if he were considering a beating for the rest of his answer; but he only relaxed into a faint smile. "Arango," he said, "you have two faces, and the one I see now I don't like. After all I taught you and the way I treated you like a son on the trail, I think you would kill me if I gave you the chance. That's true, isn't it?"

"There were no bandits in the snow. There was no reason to push a man to the end of his reason. There was nothing but your damn greed. You killed Bisco. You killed him to save three pesos a day. That's true, isn't it?"

"Yes."

"Then I would kill you."

Like one of the merchants of ancient days, the boy walked south carrying his goods in a cloth bag, buying tortillas or beans to fit his hunger, imagining his profits, counting and recounting his orders in his head: needles for leather and needles for lace, a thimble for an old woman's finger, pins to mark the sweep of a long skirt, thread of gold, thread of blue, white thread and brown thread, black, green, red, yellow, orange thread, strong thread for leather and a tiny spool of silk to mend a communion dress, white buttons and black buttons, a card of buttons as big as eyes, two buttons smaller than children's teeth, hooks and eyes, button hooks to salvage the treasure of a lady's shoe, three vials of medicinal alcohol for the apothecary of Papasquiaro, a vial of rosewater and glycerine for the dying hands of a cowboy's mother, four pieces of white lace and a strip of black lace for the woman who sat laughing in the cantina of San Juan, eyeglasses for two farsighted men and one nearsighted man and three stumbling children, a large rubber bulb, two small rubber bulbs, a packet of snuff, a scissors, four forks, a long-handled ladle, and one set of teeth small enough to fit the delicate jaws of a grandmother of Spanish pretensions who had not been able to find teeth to match her gentility in Canatlán or San Juan or even in the dusty streets of Durango. He walked slowly, without fear, reciting the names and the wishes of his customers, proud to make the matching of eyes and hands, like the merchants of ancient days who unified the world.

Pablo Valenzuela came to Doroteo, put his arm around the boy's shoulder, and led him to his dark and cool store. He took Doroteo behind the counter and through the curtain into the back room to see the goods of poor men's dreams: rifles, pistols, cartridges, pots and pans, bottles, cheeses, harnesses, saddles, spurs, boots, needles, thread, yard goods, bins of herbs and bins of fruits and vegetables, machetes, lariats, chaps, hats, boots, lamps, scissors, eating utensils; loaded shelves, crates not yet unpacked, dust settled on shoes and metal plows, enough for Canatlán, enough for San Juan del Río, enough for the mountain people and the women who wandered the streets in their widow's shawls, enough for the children and the farmers and the barber and the butcher, enough for the cowboys and the muleskinners and the wagon drivers, enough for the field workers and the clerks and the potters who sat by their works in the damp shade of the market—enough, and more.

The boy followed the little storekeeper through the rows of shelves and boxes, through the smell of cotton dust and leather and the grease that covered the weapons. "You're rich," he said.

Valenzuela removed his soft brown hat and rubbed his hand over the freckled skin of his head. There were sweat stains in the hat, his fingers were marked with smoke stains, he was pale with age and the days of darkness passed behind the counter in his store. "No, no, no, Doro, not rich. In debt. I buy more than I sell. Every year I think the crops will be better, the calves will grow fatter. Every year I think the company stores will let go of the people's balls. And every year, what happens?"

"It goes without saying."

"So it's not a store I have, Doro; I have a warehouse, a debt. And that's not good to have a store with too much of everything. You know that milk turns into cheese after a long time, but cheese doesn't turn into milk."

"Well, what?"

"I have an idea. You see all these things? I sell them cheaper than the company stores, but how can people get to my store when they need something? Who will walk a whole day for a bar of soap? I want to send my store out to the people on the ranches. I want to compete with the company stores. You understand? I have lower prices, but the people are too far from me. I want you to take my store with you and go to where the people live. You can do it, I know, because I heard about the orders you take before you go to Parral and Chihuahua."

"The landlords don't like it."

"Are you afraid of them?"

"No."

"Then you'll work for me?"

"I'll need a rifle to protect your goods."

Valenzuela provided a horse, a burro, a good saddle, and a Winchester .30–.30, which Doroteo carried in his hand more often than in the boot. The routes were long and the orders were complicated; often he was away from home for ten days or more, living in the open or accepting the offer of a place on the floor of a customer's house when he could not avoid it. He washed himself and his clothing with a soap that killed fleas, but each time he accepted the offer of a night in a customer's house he arose itching, wondering which of the seams of his shirt and trousers had become hiding places for the fleas. It was easy enough to get rid of the ticks and the few fleas he picked up from the horse and the burro by washing himself in pine oil or rubbing himself with mint leaves when he could find them, but the hordes of fleas that moved into his clothes after a night as a guest could survive two or three washings; and once, after staying through a rainy night in a stable, he had to buy fleabane and stand naked, covered with pine oil, while he held his clothes and his saddle blanket in the smoke.

Worse than the fleas were the generous cooks, scurrying ladies who offered him carnitas or caldillos or even molé in return for credit or a little more rosewater in the bottle, a little more width in a wedge of cheese. He suspected that they were generous only with spoiled food: the fat on the carnitas always seemed to be rancid, the caldillos always had the slightly nutty taste of mold, and he never ate a gift of molé that had not gone over to the flavor of vinegar. After a while he learned to avoid the gifts: at breakfast he would say he had just eaten dinner; at lunch he pleaded an aversion to eating when he could not sleep afterward; and in the evening he claimed to be in a great hurry, having one more stop to make before he could sleep. He told one cook that he feared the dark and the next that he was allergic to the sun. Even so, he was sometimes trapped: a cup of rancid aguamiel caused him hours of vomiting and a meal of sick chicken sent him home to four days of enemas of maguey water.

He began to learn the signs of a poor meal to come: women who asked to taste a bit of cheese before buying were almost certain to give him a taste of their own curdled cooking in return; women who patted his cheek and spoke of his wondrous enterprise were leading him to the poisoned trough; and any woman who smelled unclean was sure to have food of similar quality. Eating utensils were another problem; he was never offered a fork or a spoon that did not have something of its history clinging to it. One morning, after dipping a filthy spoon into a bowl of atole served as a soup at dinner, he awakened with a nauseating fever that resisted morning-glory-root tea, maguey enemas, every known cure. The fever lasted almost three weeks, and when it was over, he could not eat anything but the thinnest soup or green tea.

Micaela cooked and ran the household. She administered the enemas and ground the maguey leaves and morning glory roots; but it was Martina who stayed with him during the weeks of fever, bathing him with cool water, feeding him sips of green tea and broth. She slept when he slept; and when

[41]

the voices of the fever spoke, she answered them, speaking calmly, almost in a whisper, as if she were not afraid. She became thin as he did, and the circles that sank his eyes sank hers as well. He thanked her, he made promises to her that he knew he could not keep, for he thought he was dying. When he was well enough to go into Canatlán for the first time, he borrowed money from Pablo Valenzuela to buy five yards of cloth to make a red dress for Martina.

He went back to his routes, traveling the trails, a salesman on one visit, deliveryman on the next. "Here comes Pablo Valenzuela's store! Bargains from Canatlán! I carry cheeses, I carry orange-colored cloth! Here comes Pablo Valenzuela's store! Pots and pans, pine soap that kills fleas! Bargains from Canatlán!

"Ah, little mother, how a woman of your talents could cook if only she had one of these copper pots! You could make miracles out of corn! And what soups, what stews! Well, if you have no meat, madam, you must have clothes to cover your thin bones. Look at these needles—sharp, huh? Careful you don't prick yourself! And how about this thread? Look at the colors! A rainbow, eh? A woman like you, with hands of silk—when you sew, you embroider, every stitch is a work of art. But not with a bone needle, not with thread that lacks color. It's a crime if you don't have what you need to show off your talents! What can I do? I'll have to make it a price you can pay. If I don't leave these threads and this needle with you, the rurales will be after me. Yes, yes, you can have credit. Pablo Valenzuela is a generous man. Half the price you pay in the company store and credit too. Whatever you need, little mother, anything. I ride these hills, I endanger my life for the love of my neighbors, to save you from the company store. How much do you pay for rice at the company store? Twelve cents a pound? I'll sell you better rice for half as much and give you credit too. Buy everything from Pablo Valenzuela, pay a free man's price, not one centavo more. Why so cheap? What's wrong? Nothing's wrong, little mother. Pablo Valenzuela loves you; we're all of the same race. Let the catzopines and the criollos go to Hell! Send all the landlords to Hell! Buy from Pablo Valenzuela!"

They bought. He sold out his saddlebags and the huge wicker baskets that hung over the burro's back. He took orders for a hundred or sometimes a hundred and fifty items, reeling them off out of his memory to Valenzuela, who darted from shelf to shelf, filling the wicker baskets. When there was more room in the baskets or the saddlebags, Doroteo picked things off the shelves at random and sold those too. He moved in a great circle out of the dark store, taking new orders with each delivery. Between them, the little bald man and the boy took the profit out of the company stores. They forced the prices down and still the company stores found their sales declining and their inventories rising. Unlike the saturnine clerks in the company stores who deigned to toss a packet of needles or a pound of wheat at the barefoot women who watched without comprehension while the marks were made in the old ledgers, the barrel-chested kid with the chino hair came smiling and talking, wide open, with his hat pushed back on his head and his shirt open at the collar. He asked them, he said he needed them and their business, and he never forgot their names or their orders or the names of their children or even the color of the hard candy that pleased their children most. Sometimes, when he had some luck on the trail, he had a deer or a rabbit or a wild turkey slung over the back of the burro, and he never failed to share the meat. He was an orphan among orphans, one of the mountain people even though his hair was chino and his jaw belonged to a Basque; Doroteo Arango understood the celebration of fresh meat: when there was a deer to be skinned and roasted, he watched the red flag go up to invite the neighbors, and his laughter was as real as theirs.

The landlords did not know him or his business; they were in the Capital or in Paris or in some other country. It was the clerks in the company stores who complained to the foremen who administered the haciendas, and the foremen who spoke to the sheriffs and the rurales about the problem of Pablo Valenzuela and Doroteo Arango. It was Valenzuela who first felt the pressure: his taxes were increased, the rurales came to look for stolen goods in the back room of his store, a Federal official from Durango came to inspect the weight of the packages of rice and wheat he sold, another came to see if there were mice in his store, and another came to examine the quality of the medicinal alcohol he sold.

Valenzuela worried. "One day," he told Doroteo, "they will come and offer me five fingers or five bullets. Then what am I going to do?"

"What can you do, little chief? If they're going to shoot you, make sure you sell them the cartridges. But don't give them credit."

The little man shook his head in mock despair. "Doro, Doro, what am I going to do with you? I'm in partners with a kid who's too young to be afraid of Porfirio Díaz himself."

"Why should I worry about Díaz? Does Díaz worry about Arango? When my father died, did Porfirio Díaz come to the funeral? When I was dying of dysentery, did he come to sit by my bed? Sir, I'm just a kid who sells pots and pans in the mountains; what does the President of Mexico care about me?"

"He won't be the one to shoot you, Doro. When I say Díaz, I don't mean Don Porfirio himself; there are men who work for him. It's all together; the rurales, the presidents of the municipalities, the inspectors, the tax collectors. You have to understand: it's the government, it's not like one landlord. They're all together."

[*43*]

"To Hell with them."

"Doro, do one thing for me: don't keep the rifle in your house. Carry it on the trail, but when you're home, hide it. If they find the rifle in your house, it's reason enough for them to hang you. Promise me you'll be careful with it."

The little man worried and Doroteo sold. They stayed in business. The taxes went up, the inspectors continued to come to the store, the foremen insisted that the people buy their goods in the company stores, and still Valenzuela made a profit on everything he sold. The little man complained that he was getting rich, like a landlord. They lowered their prices, and still they made a profit. Valenzuela made a gift of the horse and saddle to Doroteo. He told him that the rifle and the cartridge belt were his to keep. He gave him the burro.

The little man worried and Doroteo laughed. He went to rodeos and saw the rurales and the landlords watching him, sending the evil eye at him whenever he mounted a bull or a bronco. He caught the rurales following him on the trail. He won at the rodeos, he invited the rurales to drink coffee with him when he made camp, he laughed, he embraced the little man and clapped his back until Valenzuela lost his breath, he was going to be rich. Yet there were moments on the trail when he heard things moving in the brush. He noticed when the horse was nervous at night, and sometimes before he went out to sell his goods, he asked what the tonalámatl promised. He laughed when Pablo Valenzuela was with him; when he was alone, he often felt afraid, for he knew that pingos sometimes appeared in charro costumes, like those worn by the men he invited to his campfire to drink coffee. He examined the tails of black dogs, looking for scales or rattles. There were demons; perhaps they were also part of the government.

He decided to sell his soul to the devil. Others had done it: Heraclío Bernal, Francisco Villa, Manuel Reyes, Benito Canales, Macario Romero, even Ignacio Parra. They had gone to the Hill of the Coffer to stand in the cave where the Pope sat beside the Devil. They had passed the dogs of seven colors that stood guard at the entrance. They had cavorted with the jeweled women, lolling in their perfumed bosoms, cooling themselves in the folds of shining silk, sharing the icy wines that came out of the fires. Emerging, they were brave men; the dogs of seven colors licked their hands and sat at their command. And they left behind nothing more than their fearful souls.

Before he went to the cave, he came to my house in the saddle of the mountain to ask for advice. I could only laugh. "But I'm afraid," he said. "I hear noises in the hills. I've seen them, Popoca. They stay in the shadows and they move like birds. I think they can see at night."

[*44*]

"Who, little one? Tell me who you see."

"I don't know."

"Then why are you afraid?"

He wept like a child. I have seen it before, the Spanish fear, the gift of the coño priests. When a man believes this world is a mystery, he can do nothing but weep, for there is nothing he can know, nothing he can change; he surrenders to his religion of confusion and expects rewards. And what is left for such men? A darkness of sand and ashes; Heaven is for those who die willingly.

"I don't want to be afraid."

"You think this cave will make a difference?"

"I saw Manolo Reyes," he said. "It was near here. He was sitting by a fire butchering meat. I was only a child, but I knew he was not like other men. He wasn't afraid, he didn't hear things in the mountains, he didn't think about the shadows. Now I know the reason: Reyes went to the cave, he made the pact."

"I also know Manuel Reyes."

"Did he tell you about the cave?"

"You'll have to ask him, Doro."

He wept again. "Popoca, tell me what to say. Tell me how to get past the dogs. Please, Popoca; I'm afraid of the cave, too."

I gave him corn pollen to calm his weeping, and I told him what it was necessary for him to know. "A man is born with a heart and the possibility of a face. The heart must be strengthened by trial and the face must be made with thought and discipline. There are no secret ways, Doro; neither a heart nor a face can be found in a cave.

"Guard against illusions or your life will become nothing. Illusions will steal your heart, illusions will steal your face; you will be like a dream, which touches only the dreamer. When the ancient wise men failed, they asked themselves if they were not dreams, if the world was not a dream, if anything was real. And then they said that a man must have a face as real as a stone, which is how they rescued themselves from the danger of dreams.

"You were born on one day, Doro, and you were named on another. The tonalámatl tells that one is a good day and the other is a bad day. You are in the center, between the good and the bad, between illusion and the stone of Anahuac, which lies between the endless oceans. To make a face is to choose Anahuac; dreams have no faces, I wave my hand through dreams, the scrolls of my words dance through them as if they were air.

"Man is made of blood and ashes; we are as real as corn. Neither is death a dream, Doro. You will die. Everything dies, even the sun. And knowing you will die, what is there to fear?"

"The time."

[45]

"Knowing that death will come is real, Doro; expecting death is a dream. Go to the Hill of the Coffer, go to the cave, study illusion, look at the dreamed world, see if it has blood, if it has motion."

He arrived at night, as dreamers must. The access to the cave was guarded by silence, by tricks of light, by stones as sharp as broken glass. Doroteo climbed over moonlit rocks, stumbling into reflections, losing his feet in shadows, hearing nothing, not even the sound of himself falling. He was afraid, expecting the dogs. A fever came to him from the moon. He could not imagine the women, though he told himself of the richness of their powdered breasts, of the flesh curving into shadow. He saw instead the chairs upon the throne, the white robes and the red cape, the thin and suffered face and the face of leering expectation.

There were no dogs of seven colors at the entrance to the cave. There were no bejeweled ladies with perfumed breasts, nor was there a Pope or a Devil. The cave was dark and damp, decorated with the lubricious mold that grew and died on the blackest walls, rich only in the warm stench of the droppings of bats that hung in stillness or flew peeping and furry in pursuit of the gnats and wisps that swarmed through the night.

He would die; the world was not a dream. He laughed aloud: at the moment of death he would be afraid. There was such a moment, he thought; it was already there, fixed in a meeting of time and place. He laughed again: death would have to wait for him; he would not be the one to wait. He was not afraid, not yet.

It was the worst of summers: the clouds lay on the west side of the sierras, unable to cross, lacking wind, lacking motion, leaving their rain where they lay, where they died. The young corn, risen out of the earth, waited and withered. The cotton could not flower. There was no pollen, there were no seeds. It was the summer without marigolds, the year in which the roses died.

At the end of summer, Doroteo came home to cut grass and carry water, to save whatever could be harvested, to build shelters for the animals, to look up at the sun, to wait for rain. He had money for corn and cheese and oil. He had money for rice, but there was no rice. He came home to cut grass, for there was nothing else to harvest; only the grass grew, only the cactus bloomed; it was the summer in which no honey was made, the summer in which the bees died, the summer in which the people fell to dreaming.

The landlords came home too. They arrived in carriages, in gleaming carriages bearing beribboned ladies. They ordered laughter and singing, they ordered gardens and fattening steers. They came home to count the corn, to weigh the cotton, to feel the fruit as it fell from the trees. They came home to prowl the stables and to study the account books, to feel the udders of their goats and their cows and even the blunt teats of their pigs. They came home to stand in the dark rooms of their stores, men more grand and more luminous than the blocks of sunlight that fell through the doors, accountants with glorious wooden faces who came home to gauge their grandeur in the scribbled pages of the books of debt. They came home to learn of Pablo Valenzuela, to compare their clerks to Doroteo Arango.

The landlords visited Valenzuela in his store, polite gentlemen asking to see the quality of his goods, the size of his inventory, men with tiny beards and Spanish skin; accompanied by cowboys still stinking of the range, dark men with their fingers on Colt pistols, Winchester rifles, with the pale grease of cartridges still on their fingers. A captain of the rurales visited the store, a mountain man the color of iron ore, an assassin who had taken the five fingers. He spoke softly, though he addressed Valenzuela as if he were an animal or a child: "Two years ago, not even two years ago, I was at Temosachic. I didn't burn the church, Pablito. I argued with Carillo's man, with the governor's man, that's how much I wanted to save the women and the children. But what could one man do? To kill a few rebels, even to burn a town, that's necessary, but to burn a church with the women and children inside, that's not how my rurales work. I want you to know that, Pablito, I want you to know."

"I know about Temosachic."

The captain walked through the store. His spurs jangled. He looked in the cash drawer, he inspected the saddles, he checked the sights on the rifles. "You know how it all started in Temosachic? First, they didn't buy in the right stores. Then they didn't want to pay the taxes. Everything starts somewhere, Pablito; you understand me?"

"I pay my taxes. You can look in the records."

"I didn't start the fire at the church, but I heard them inside. It didn't please me, baldy. I had to go in afterward. Sometimes the fire burns the hands off and all that's left is an arm sticking up like a piece of green wood that didn't burn all the way.

"A lot of people died in Temosachic. Almost two thousand, perhaps

[47]

more. I think now that if I had gone there sooner, I could have saved the women and children. You know how? Some stingy son of a refucked mother started it, some bastard with a little store. Because of one greedy prick those women died, those children burned. And it was my fault, Pablito, because I waited too long."

The little man nodded. He was an old player of the game, one who paid his taxes, spoke seldom, lived simply, read in private, refused to join Masonic clubs, prayed softly, and did not drink. "I expect to die," he told Doroteo. "It's an old saying among people of our race that we are on earth only a short time. We should enjoy flowers, we should enjoy songs; perhaps it's all a dream. So I am not afraid. I knew my wife when she was a big mango. I was sorry for many years that we had no children. Now, I look at this life and I wonder. What can a man know, Doro? We come from a mystery, we pass through this life on the way to another mystery. Landlords and rurales and Federales and sheriffs and tax collectors and bandits don't frighten me anymore. Like a Spaniard, I have no hair on my head; like an Indian, I have no beard, not even a respectable mustache. What should I believe? What side should I be on? I only know that I am going to die.

"But you, Doro"—he had to reach up to put his hand on the boy's shoulder—"you're young, you should be careful. The landlords are not good businessmen, the country is selling itself off like slices of a cheese to keep its head above water. And this is a bad time for them, worse than two years ago. They'll be crazy. Just be careful. Listen to an old man."

Doroteo had nothing but a shrug for the little man's advice. "What do the landlords care about me? What do I care about them?"

"They're watching you."

"They should watch the girls."

"Money is their first pleasure. That's all they know about money, and pleasure is all they know about life."

The landlords stayed on the ranches that autumn. Their wives went back to the Capital and their children went back to their schools in foreign countries, but the landlords rode through the fields of dead corn and barren cotton, watching the progress of the drought, as if by their presence the crops would begin to grow without rain. But nothing brought rain, neither the arrogance of the landlords nor the mumblings of the coño priests, nor the prayers of the mountain people. There were floods on the west side of the sierras, yet the wind refused us even the hope of clouds. The people came to my house carrying butterflies and snakes, asking me to pray in the old way, and I told them to set the insects and the animals free, to feed their animals with water from the wells, to cut grass for food, to save their seed for the next summer, to practice virtue so that the next year, which was to be the Year of Wind, would also be the summer of rain.

Valenzuela advised his customers to save their money, to buy only food and no more than they needed. He advised them to eat cactus fruit and the soups and stews of roots and bones their great-grandparents had learned to cook when they were hungry. He sent Doroteo to advise them against buying on credit in the company stores, to remind them that there would be another year coming and that the debts they incurred this year would keep them hungry next year and the year after, that the debts were passed on to their children and their grandchildren. Valenzuela's taxes were doubled and doubled again. They were doubled for years past and years to come. He closed the store.

López Negrete came to the Arango house, bringing his escort of five cowboys with their rifles, with their pistols, riding on their great horses that were too slow for the range, too clumsy to cut a steer out of a herd, riding on their trampling horses, their warhorses, astonishing the earth with their heavy iron shoes, exploding the dust. The landlord rode at their head, dressed in black and gaiety, the leader of a parade, stiff in the saddle, a convention of angles rising from the bubbles of his belly and buttocks, an old prince in the shade of his own hat.

The landlord and his escort went inside to where the Widow of Arango and her daughter Martina sat in the dry shadows peeling cactus fruit, softly singing, telling each other a riddle song. The men entered jangling, wide walking, letting the leather slap: three cowboys carrying rifles, pop-eyed in the sudden darkness; the landlord; two more cowboys walking sideways. No one spoke. One cowboy put the muzzle of his rifle under Micaela's chin and forced her into a far corner. Three others spread the girl on the floor; the fifth stood to the side of the doorway, looking out into the sunwhite day.

López Negrete opened his trousers and positioned himself between the girl's legs. She did not move, but after a moment, he got to his knees and complained, "I can't enter." The man at the door said, "with your permission." He walked over to where the girl yet lay, placed the muzzle of his rifle at the entrance to her vagina, and forced the barrel into her. Martina let out a soft cry. The cowboy twisted the barrel of the rifle to one side, then the other, and withdrew it. "Now, sir," he said, "the gates of heaven are open." López Negrete lowered his trousers and lay down again between the girl's legs.

He wiped the blood off himself on the girl's dress when he was finished. "You should learn to move a little more," he told her, patting the inside of her thigh. "Ask your mother how to give a man pleasure. The men in San Juan used to give thanks to God for putting such an itch in her cunt." While he pulled his trousers up and buttoned them, the cowboys looked at him, asking. López Negrete smiled. "No, boys; the girl's too young and the mother's too old. Let's be practical. We're finished with her."

Micaela washed the girl and helped her to change into a clean dress, then she lay down beside her on the mat and stroked her hand and sang to her and wept with her. After a while, Martina slept. Micaela lay beside her, staring up at the boards of the roof, listening to the sounds of the chickens clucking streams, the goat pawing at some stubborn root, the voice of her child in the rasping breath that follows weeping. She waited for her sons, for her older daughter. There are no dreams, she thought; I am unable to awaken.

You have a wife, she told López Negrete, so you think there is nothing that can be done. But you have sons, sir. You have a son to marry my daughter. He laughed. It's a question of honor, she said, and a question of sin. What will the priest say? The priest knelt and kissed López Negrete's hand. Then think of yourself, sir, she pleaded, your family, your position. They were walking through the rooms of the great house, past velvet couches, walls hung with tapestries of scenes of the Inquisition, canopied beds, steaming kitchens, tables laden with roast pigs, young lambs and baskets of fruit, through turrets and cellars into a great hall in which cowboys danced with bleeding women to the tune of the gutstring harp played by the blind man who begged in the plaza of Canatlán. Then what of your reputation, she said, your dignity? He lowered his trousers and showed her two gray bulbs.

Doroteo picked up his rifle at the Franco house and went to the place called Two Watermelons or Camel Rocks to wait for López Negrete. Sooner or later, he knew, the landlord and his escort would pass by him on the road below. They would be three hundred yards north and almost a hundred yards below him, a long shot; but he had used the Winchester from that distance before. He knelt between the two rocks, sighting on the trail, plotting the elevation, the wind, marking his position to come back for the second shot after the kick, seeing a bird turn to whirling stone, a deer tumbled in midair, rabbits without heads or bellies, a snake rebounding.

An old man walking beside a burro came into view. The burro pulled a cart that lurched on wooden wheels, grinding on a wooden axle. Doroteo sighted on the man: not the head; the torso was a better target even in profile —errors in elevation. He exhaled slowly. Eject, load, sight. Exhale. Eject, load, sight, exhale. And still the man was walking through his sights, growing out of the leaf. Four shots? The kick had to be considered. Three. Two if the first shot missed and López Negrete spurred the horse. Two, surely two.

He drank water from a gourd and knelt on his blanket. His right knee hurt, his elbow sank into his thigh above his left knee. He coughed, calmed himself with visions of the fall of a bird, the little explosion, the separate feathers floating, thinking of the compensation in elevation shooting up, the curve of the bullet shooting down, waiting, measuring. He ate a tortilla. The smell of the rifle oil was on his fingers.

It was late afternoon when he saw the first cowboy. The sun was in the rider's face, off to his right, causing a slight halo. He moved slowly, looking up into the hills. Doroteo held the rifle across his lap, hiding the barrel behind the rock, not wanting the cowboy to see the reflection of the sun on the barrel. There was time. As the cowboy passed off to the left, Doroteo raised the rifle and sighted at the level of a rider, aiming at the place where López Negrete would enter his field of fire. He took two deep breaths to calm himself, thinking of the hawk, the hawk falling, the rabbit spinning, the somersault of the deer.

López Negrete. Doroteo inhaled, steadying his knee, the pivot of his elbow, slowly turning with the movement of the horse. Squeezing. López Negrete leaned, his right hand waved. Doroteo lost him in the kick of the rifle, found him again. The horse was running now. López Negrete had lost the reins. He held on to the saddle horn with his right hand. Doroteo took his breath, followed, led him, squeezed. The landlord's left foot came out of the stirrup. He tumbled backward and to his right. Doroteo fired again. The horse was gone. Two of the riders halted in front of López Negrete, shielding him, the others started up the hill. Their pistols were out, they looked for a target. The horses were rearing, slipping in the loose rock at the bottom of the hill, scrambling up under the spurs. Doroteo shot the horses, then he picked up his watergourd and his blanket and ran for the top of the hill. He heard the horses and the men screaming. They were shooting at him, but he could tell that it was only pistol fire, and he was well out of range. At the top of the hill he stopped to reload and empty the magazine at them, aiming in the direction of López Negrete, not expecting to hit him again, just firing and firing, pulling the trigger for the hope of it, for the joy, for the pleasure of the swing of the rifle in his hands and the manly caress of the explosion against his shoulder.

When the boy arrived at my house, he was full of dust and exhilaration. "I killed him," he said. "Popoca, he dishonored my sister, and I killed him." I gave him wine to calm him, and even though there was little water, I told him to bathe. He could not breathe without choking and he said he was sick. He asked for the mullein pollen to help his breathing, but I told him it was only his excitement and there was nothing to do but wait. His breathing became worse, tiring him, calming him, until he was able to lie down on a mat and finally to sleep.

In the morning, while he still slept, Antonio Lares came to tell me that a posse had been formed in Canatlán to look for Doroteo. López Negrete was not dead; he was at Santa Isabel de Berros with a bullet lodged in his shoulder and another in his thigh. Two horses were killed and one of the cowboys had a broken leg. The Municipal President had offered to send for Federal troops, but López Negrete had laughed at him, saying that it was foolish to use an army to chase a sixteen-year-old boy.

After Lares had gone, I awakened Doroteo and told him what had happened. He listened quietly, looking down at the floor, touching his hair, rubbing his eyes, chewing on his lips, nearly in tears, like a child listening to a punishment. I asked him if he understood what had happened, if he knew where he was going, what he must do. He shook his head.

"Think, Doro. Make some plan. They'll look for you here. They'll look in every house. What are you going to do?"

"Valenzuela's store is closed, López Negrete has two bee stings, no one can bring back Martina's honor, a posse is looking for me, who knows what will happen to my mother? I have sixty cartridges, an old horse, and the cinch strap on my saddle is tearing right in the middle before the place where I buckle it. What can I do?"

"Are you afraid?"

He stood up and went over to the corner where I had put his rifle and saddlebags. "No," he said. "I don't have any fear. I've just been screwed, that's all. When I started to work for Valenzuela, I didn't know what they would think about it, I didn't know there would be a drought, I didn't know anything."

"What are you going to do?"

"Be a rabbit. Is there any luck in being a rabbit?"

"No."

"Then what should I do?"

"Be a man."

"Well, Popoca, I think I'll live longer as a rabbit."

For a moment I was afraid for him; I have known so many men who lost their hearts and faces, men who lived in the hills, eating roots and unsalted meat, preying on woodcutters and miners, walking all their days, pretending that someone still hunted them, dreaming that they were still feared. They brought such a man to me once. A disease was growing in his liver; I felt it there, all lumps and strings. He had the eyes of a fever, but he was cold to touch. I asked him his name, the day and hour of his birth, and his name day. He could not remember. He was not an old man, but it had been so long since he had spoken, since he had even thought his own name; he was no longer a man. I do not know what he was—there is no word for such creatures—or what became of him, but I know that there are others like him in these hills, and I know that they eat dead meat.

I am an old man, and even though I still have a magician's fingers, there are so many lines in my face that I can no longer keep secrets. Doroteo looked at me and laughed. "You made a fool of an old man," I said.

"No, maestro, never."

It was my turn to laugh. "You're the maestro, Doro; you give lessons in humility."

I walked outside with him and waited while he watered his horse and saddled it. One cinch was torn, but the other one was still good. The animal was small and well built for climbing, even though it was old. We embraced, then he climbed into the saddle. His hat was on the back of his head and he was laughing.

"We'll see each other," he said.

"Of course!"

He rode north, heading for the high country near Las Nieves. We are always going north, thinking of it as the place of the Seven Caves, the Land of the Cranes; we believe that we will climb the hill that reverses time and see the Filthy Woman if we go north; we forget that north is the direction of wind and flint, of dogs and death. There is movement in the east, there are flowers in the south, there is rain in the west; yet we go north. It is not by chance that the color of the north is black.

5

The town of San Juan began at a stream on its western edge and grew to the base of a hill on the east. There had been no bridge across the stream for many years; wagons could not cross in or out of the town in the rainy summer, and in winter the chill of the water entered through the feet of the people and swelled their joints. The footbridge was built before the church, and the wide wooden bridge was completed before the kiosk was erected in the plaza. On the last street going east, bordering on the plaza and the municipal building, the hill was defeated by great stone steps, some of them two feet high, like the risers of a crude pyramid. At the top of the steps, facing the plaza, was the jail, built of adobe and stucco, fitted with heavy wooden doors and iron gates, and painted white, like the other buildings; a jail that would not intrude, a small and common jail to hold the shames of the community, which were expected to be the least of sins, the forgettable secrets.

There was quiet in the town; the houses had no faces, the stores had no signs, they were the mirrors of each other, white masks for the gardens and the bedrooms, hiding places for the revelations of mice and the placement of grinding stones. Behind the walls, behind the language, lay the soul and the sound of the race; the enclosures were a circle, as time is a circle, round as the sun, as the round of the sun, returning in all things and all people until the end of light when all secrets are known and die. The Spaniards and the Basques and the Frenchmen with their blue eyes imitating gods came to build the town, to replace dreams with promises, and were assumed into the circle, drowned in the women and the constant rolling of the grinder on the grinding stone, lost in the names of the parts of corn and the births of children; the houses encircled them, the town encircled the houses, the stream and the hill encircled the town; they dwelled in repetitions, they slept, they were.

No one came to visit Doroteo in the prison, which was dark and smelled of unused earth. He saw the sheriff, the jailer, and the other prisoners when he was not alone in the jail. Once, the rurales who had found him sleeping beside a mountain stream came to look into his cell and laugh. He listened to the town through the window of his prison room, the separate cell in which the dangerous prisoner was kept, the room with one high small window through which came only moments of the afternoon sun. He heard the town outside, the bells of the hours, occasional laughter, the calls of children, the uneven ring of horses passing on the cobblestones, the softer voices of evening, the violins, and the celebration of Saturday night.

The sheriff came in his purple shirt, resting his hands on the white handles of his pistols, to say, "I hear you had three shots at that son of a whore and you didn't kill him. Is that true?"

"I never shot from such a high angle; I didn't know the bullet would drop so much."

"Everything drops to the ground," the sheriff said; "it's one of the rules of science."

"Next time I won't miss."

The sheriff laughed, a redness appearing under the shiny brown of his cheeks. "To kill a son of a bitch like that takes a man."

"When I get out."

"You'll be an old man."

They laughed. "We'll see," said Doroteo. The sheriff talked about the law for fugitives. Doroteo leaned against the wall, squatting, looking up at the sheriff's hands and the roll of his belly over the gunbelt, gauging the strength of his mouth under the mustache, the clarity of his eyes. He looked for the death of the man, the blank eyes, the great shudders; but he saw only the fattening of the brown face, the belly expanding, future sweats and blushings, and the slow dimming of the eyes. The man would not bleed or lose the regularity of his breath; he remained solid, like a house, like the ground upon which a house is built.

A lolling rhythm settled into the days, atole at breakfast, the toilet, the long slow roll of the day, atole and beans at supper, the toilet, the blue eyes and the lean hands of the jailer, less and less water, the uneasy darkness, the needless hours of sleep, the contemplation of dreams, which had become the only life of his life. He had been given no sentence, he had not pleaded his case before a judge; no one had spoken to his sin. He languished, softening, dead and damp, staring at the bars sunk into the adobe above and below the small window, wishing himself changeable, narrow, smoke.

Soft music began Saturday nights in the plaza of San Juan, a gutstring harp, a young man warbling beside his guitar, one violin, a flute sung by a mountain man hoping for centavos, the laughter of the first girl, the whisper of her mother, evening wind in the dry brown trees. There were violins, big guitars, a trumpeter, a man who had been to Veracruz singing the resonances of his nose, duets and quartets and quintets, macaws and monkeys, sellers of candy and sellers of sweetcakes, the loudness of bad times, masking laughter; all of it lying on a bed of mourning, a rustling of dead leaves and hard seeds, the hushing counterpoint to the gaiety, to the expectation of seasons.

On Sunday mornings he listened to the bells and the babble of awe. He heard the priest intoning the litanies of sins and salvation, love and damnation, Christ and man, the Holy Roman Catholic Church and man, death, resurrection, and death. The sounds entered the window and settled in his cell, lying on him, as if he were sentenced to blindness. He jumped up, trying to see through the window, and he laughed at himself, knowing that no man can jump nine feet in the air. He laughed and jumped again, unable even to reach the ledge of the window with his hand. He jumped and jumped and jumped, until his legs ached, until he fell, until he fell again and again, until he lay on the floor of his cell, listening to the Latin Mass and damning the world that possessed the lock.

He jumped on Monday and Tuesday and Wednesday. He jumped like a monkey, he leaped like a cat, he tried to fly like a bird; he lifted his arms, he threw himself upward, he willed himself airborne, he fell. He took to exercising, raising himself up on his toes, flexing his legs, stretching, raising and lowering himself on one leg and then the other, heaving himself into the air. In two weeks, he was able to touch the window ledge. On the second day of the third week, he grasped one of the bars and held on until his hand cramped and he fell back to the floor. He tried to hold the bars with both hands, throwing himself against the wall as he jumped, bruising his chest and knees, scraping the skin from his hands. At the end of a month, he was able to grasp the bars with both hands and hang there until the pressure of the window ledge cutting off the circulation in his hands turned them numb and weak, and he fell. In two more weeks, he learned to take off his shirt, slip it under his arms and tie the sleeves around the center bar, creating a sling that removed the pressure from his hands; he was able to hang at the window for hours; he watched the first musician arrive on Saturday night, and he was still there, peering out of the tiny window, when the last mother led her daughter home.

He hung like a monkey, like a bat, like a child on its mother's back. He hung in anger, in a dreaming rage, seeing himself among the dancers, watching the frank eyes of a dark girl, or merely walking, climbing the steps, negotiating the cobblestones, on his way to the market or the plaza, moving to the instruction of his own will.

The sheriff sometimes came to visit him in the early evening, bringing Doroteo his food, watching him while he ate, seeming to count the spoonfuls, sneering as Doroteo pushed the poorly ground kernels to the side of the bowl, ending in amusement as he watched his prisoner wash his own spoon and wipe it dry. "How elegant you are, Mister Arango, using your own spoon! Did you learn to do that in the restaurants of the Capital? Would you like a cigar and a glass of brandy now that you've finished your meal?"

Doroteo squatted in the corner opposite the door, watching the sheriff, wondering whether it was possible to rush by him, wondering how fast the sheriff could get one of the pistols out of its holster and fire it. He waited for the sheriff to make a mistake, to close the distance between them, to cut down his time, to make it possible; but the sheriff was always careful: he set the bowl on the floor and stepped back to allow Doroteo to pick up his food, he leaned against the door while Doroteo squatted against the wall. There was no chance, no hope; at that distance, the .45-caliber slug would lift him up and carry him across the room, it would make him into beef and splinters. He watched and listened to the sheriff; he studied the roll of his belly and the bobbing handles of the pistols.

The sheriff spoke about the drought or whispered his hatred of the landlords, complaining as everyone complained. "But you're the sheriff," Doroteo said, wary of the man's fat cheeks and intricately tooled boots.

"Yes," he answered, pushing his hat back, rocking on the curl of his boots. "Yes, the sheriff. But my mother is not the sheriff and my sisters and brothers and cousins are not the sheriff. You think I'm a selfish man, like a landlord, just because I won't open this door and send you out to shoot that prick again. You think this is a good job? Tell me, kid, did you ever see an old sheriff? No. Never. And you know why? One night, I'll walk across the plaza to the cantina to tell some drunk to shut his mouth, and they'll carry me out with a hole in my belly. You know how many times I've been shot already? Six. Imagine! Six. Four times in the legs, once in the shoulder and once in the chest. The time I got shot in the chest, they thought I was going to die, but my Aunt Socorro brought that old Indian from Saddle Mountain and he saved my life. He's a witch, you know; but when you have a bullet in your chest, you don't care who keeps you alive."

"He's a friend of mine."

"So he tells me." The sheriff smiled. "You have a lot of friends, kid, even the sheriff of San Juan."

It was Doroteo's turn to laugh. "I call a friend a man I can trust."

The sheriff motioned to Doroteo to put the empty plate in the center of the room. "Did I tell you a lie? Did I open the gates and tell you to run and then shoot you in the back? What do you want, Arango? A saint? There are no saints and no virgins. If you marry a virgin, she'll confess to you on her deathbed—or yours—that she knew twenty men in her dreams before she met you. I, the sheriff of San Juan, am your friend, and that's the truth even if I kill you. Someday, if they ever let you out of here, you can ask your other friend, the witch, if those aren't the rules of friendship."

"Oh, it's very clear: I'm like the pig, whose best friend is the butcher."

"As you like, friend. What do you need me for? The Municipal President has such a deep respect and affection for your mother."

Doroteo did not respond, except by the change in his eyes, which became red within the brown, the eyes his mother called cinnamon. The sheriff drew his gun and backed out of the room without bothering to pick up the empty bowl.

It was two nights later that Doroteo made his discovery. He had just finished knotting the sleeves of his shirt around the center bar and settling himself into the watching position when he felt himself slipping. At first he thought the shirt was tearing, but the slippage stopped after the first small movement. He examined the seams of the shirt to see if any of the threads had ripped, then he checked the knot to be certain it was secure. Satisfied that it was neither the shirt nor the knot that had caused the slippage, he settled back to watch the plaza and think about what had happened. There was another movement, even more subtle than the first, almost imperceptible, so slight that he thought he might be dreaming. He waited, expecting more. But there was nothing.

The next night the slippage was repeated. He untied the knot, dropped to the floor, then jumped up again, this time tying the sleeves around a different bar. There was no slippage. He reached over to the center bar and pulled it toward him: the lower end of the bar moved, no more than a shiver,

[57]

but it moved. He lifted himself up higher to look at the place where the bar entered the adobe; there were a few grains of dried clay, like sand. With the handle of his spoon, he dug at the adobe; it crumbled; with each thrust of the spoon handle a few more grains of dried clay came loose. He kept digging.

Night after night, he hung in his perch, watching the plaza and digging at the adobe brick. As the dust accumulated, he blew it out into the street. When the lower brick was hollow, he began to work on the upper one, digging on the far side of the bar, so that it could not be seen from inside the cell. When he was finished, he planned to pull the lower end of the bar toward him, breaking through the shell of the brick and removing the bar to make a space large enough to wriggle through.

He took to sleeping closer to the door so that the jailer could only see a part of his blanket when he looked through the peephole during his nightly rounds. At his breakfast and dinner hours, when either the sheriff or the jailer usually entered the cell, Doroteo kept the shutter closed. "It makes the air less dry," he told the jailer. "Look at my lips from the dryness, listen to my breathing." The jailer advised him to pray for rain.

When the sheriff came to talk, Doroteo asked why so many criminals were caught, what mistakes they made, how the sheriff always seemed to know where to look for them. "It's the north," the sheriff said. "They either go to the house of a relative or they go north. That's where the money is. You know that; you've been to Chihuahua."

"And what if a prisoner went south?"

"It's too flat; he could never get away."

"And east?"

"There is nothing to the east."

"West?"

"Perhaps. If a man had a good horse, if he could cross the mountains, perhaps. I wouldn't follow a man who was going west; I would leave the job to the mountains."

"So every one of them goes north?"

"Didn't you?"

Doroteo finished the digging on Friday night. It was late and he was tired when the center bar at last felt like a loose tooth ready to be pulled out with a string. He waited through that night and the next. Shortly before midnight on Sunday, he snapped the bar out and wriggled through the window. He turned sideways and hung on to one of the bars while he curled his legs and feet through the narrow space. Then he let himself hang out to his full length before he dropped the last few feet to the stone walk.

For a moment he felt lost in the space of the empty streets; he started to expand, to become random in the opportunity: the directions spoke to him, beckoning, each with a promise of distance. He stood, feeling the movement of the moon, the going of the night, the slow explosion of himself into the world. He could not move except to spread, leaving a space in himself that was filled with giddiness. No single thing would settle in his vision; he wanted to sit, to slide down against the wall and wait, to let his life happen.

A nightbird sang, low and hollow, the clouded moon throat, the omen bird, death singing, proclaiming darkness, endsong. He looked for it in the trees and the parapets that were in silver and blackness around him, as if his own death were perched somewhere near, studying him with its shining eyes, its moons of the moon. The bird sang again, pronouncing his name. He contracted with fear, hardening into himself. The moon was moving; it was time, there was time, there were still shadows. He pushed his hat further back on his head, made a smile for his face, and sauntered down the great steps and across the plaza toward the bridge that led out of San Juan.

After the bridge, he walked up the long hill to the main road, past La Coyotada where the knife had been put under the bed of his birth, past the gully where they had found the bubbling corpse of the dead cow, past the fields where the corn had failed and the beans had browned before they bloomed, past the fertile spot where his father had died of his own blood; he walked out, away, beyond. He walked all night, moving south and west across the dry fields, through the dying orchards. He walked the moon across its arc, until the sun. In the morning, he stopped briefly at the house where Antonio Lares lived to ask his friend for the use of a pistol. They greeted each other with laughter and embracing; then Doroteo stepped back, presenting himself again. "Tonio," he said, "look at this face. Do you know it? This is the face of Francisco Villa."

The cactus softened, fell, and dried into sticks and plates of spines; the mountains had never been so naked. He found a rabbit lying in the shade of a rock: its nose and mouth were swollen and its eyes were blind with dryness. He lifted it up by the ears and cut its throat, then he put it on top of the rock and cut its belly open to clean it. There were six dead fetuses, rotted and crawling with worms. He threw the carcass away and cleaned his knife on a sharp edge of the rock, and then rubbed it with sand and rubbed it again and again. He found dead cattle and horses, lost on the way to water, fallen, unable to rise, dead in the sun, swollen and burst, stinking, putting off even the scavengers. Near Pommel Heights he found a small stream and made camp. The water came out in spurts and it was warm, almost hot, but it was clear and sweet when it cooled; he knew he could stay there for a long time, eating hearts of agave and nopal, waiting for the animals that smelled the water and came to drink.

It was colder in the heights; the winds, forced between the peaks, were multiplied by the compression into gales. The northern and western slopes were without vegetation, dustless, polished by the wind to their split bones. In the moments of calm there was a cool silence, nothing, proof that the world is imagined. The first long calm frightened him: he felt dead, weak, without the weight of speech. He shouted to the peaks, "My name is Francisco Villa!" The words sailed away, unheard, unspoken. He covered his ears and shouted again. He closed his eyes to listen more intently for an echo, which he told himself would prove that he was more than a dream. There was nothing; the words floated, less real than the wind. He babbled, he pulled on his tongue, he kissed the gourd of water, he licked his hand, he wiped his mouth, he ground his teeth. The sounds of his throat were heard in his ears—he was the container of himself, the beginning and the end, nothing. He lay against a wall of rock, looking into the cracks and tiny crevices of the peeling mountain. The sun moved, but it could not penetrate the crevices to enter the mountain. He poked into the shallow black veins with the end of a match, tracing the patterns, exploring the darkness, hunting a listener. There was nothing; he was alone, he was nothing. There was no movement.

He lay against the rock until his eyes lost their focus and he could not count the sounds of himself, the rhythm of his breathing or even the sound of his pulse. The perception of the place dimmed, failed. He stopped thinking, his hands and feet dissolved, the day mixed with the mountain and the time, without separations, without names, a blind block no longer waiting. He felt himself sailing into sleep, his eyes spinning, drifting up into the lidded darkness.

"I am Francisco Villa!"

He moved to another place and began again to poke the matchstick into the crevices. A small flat beetle emerged, gray and ugly. He poked it with the matchstick and it changed direction. He poked it again and it changed direction again. He picked it up with two fingers, holding it carefully, examining its brown underside, its nest of translucent legs. He put the beetle in his mouth and let it walk on his tongue before he ate it. The body was crisp, like something fried too long; the creamy innards were bitter; it was no longer a beetle, because he had eaten it. He laughed; no one eats in dreams.

The brief winter days went by quickly: he built snares for rabbits and badgers and set them near the stream; he found a cave in which to live, scoured it with fire, and built a fireplace of three stones. He moved the fireplace from one part of the cave to another, until he found a draft that would carry the smoke out. Then he built a spit and split rock to make a griddle on which to cook tamales made of corn grass, chiles, and meat. He made pots of clay and springwater, but they cracked when he put them in the fire. At night, working by firelight, he wove strands of maguey fiber into rope for a bridle and sewed rabbit skins into saddlebags.

The rhythm of his life became animal, the result of the circle of the sun; he was powerless, bound to his dreams. He sang. He thought of his mother, her darkening lines; he recalled conversations, words, the speeches of faces, the emphasis of hands, a fat woman of Tzeltin laughing with her eyes, Romualdo Franco weeping in the limp of his arm, Martina's shamed curtain drawing over the unknowing lights of her face, Gallardo's flat mask of fearfulness, Hipólito's sleep, and me, in whom he saw answers he could not yet decipher. In the repetition of conversations, he began to revise his answers, to plot the responses to the revisions and to answer anew, as if by invading his memory he could put off the stilling of life. Nothing was as it had been, yet nothing was new; he hung between, like smoke, like wind. Days went by, streaming, close and near, yet without substance. He studied the sun. He sat by the stream, watching the animals that came to drink, holding the pistol, holding the coiled rope, the knotted rope, waiting for the horse.

When the animal came, he did not know whether he should take it: the horse was small, but its back was short; it would hold his weight, if it would accept him at all. The hair was long over the pasterns, hanging and wild over the feet; the mane was knotted and hung with burrs; the horse was wary, turning its fleshy, mulelike head from side to side, watching and listening before it bent to drink. He guessed it was not a runaway, but a horse born wild, a true bronco, full grown, perhaps too old to break to riding. It would be better, he thought, to wait for another horse, a runaway or a young horse—if another horse came to the stream, if it did not begin to rain, if someone did not see the smoke of his cooking fire and send the acordada up the four directions of the mountain to encircle him and bring him back to jail.

While the horse drank, he opened the loop of the rope and prepared to throw it. When the head came up, he would step out, almost into the horse's path, and throw the loop wide and high so that the head came into the loop as it settled. He watched the animal complete its drinking, lift its head halfway, sniff the air, then turn, moving its hind legs around and stepping to the side, putting all four hooves into the stream. And there it stood, a wild, greasy stallion, sniffing at the edges of the stream for something edible, soaking and softening the horn of its feet. There was a good chance that the hooves were sand cracked—the horse was lame on all four legs.

He stepped out, whirling the rope to lay out the loop, then he called to the horse. It lifted its head and started toward him, startled but not running. He threw the loop easily. The head came in. Villa doubled the rope around his hands and prepared to lay back into it as the noose tightened. The horse reared. He gave it rope, holding on with his right hand, moving toward the animal, loosening his left hand grip to throw the rope over his back. When the horse came down, it backed away from him, like a cutting horse holding a calf. Villa put his back into the rope and drove backward with his legs. The horse screamed and reared again. He gave it rope, then jerked hard when it was at its full height. The forelegs came down. It reared again, and again he jerked it down. They fought for more than an hour; the horse and the man sweating and steaming, the man shouting and laughing, the horse screaming, reaching for him with its hooves, as if he were a snake or a wild dog.

After the horse gave in, he led it up and down the side of the mountain, walking off the lather, cooling it slowly; then he brought it back to the stream to stand in the water. He tied the rope to a solid outcropping of rock and went to have a look at the hooves. They were not as bad as he had feared: there were cracks on all four hooves, but they were recent, there had been no major deformation; he was certain that the hooves could be treated with soaking and grease, and the cracks could be clamped with nails. That night he went down the mountain to a place where he remembered seeing a dead horse. The carcass was half eaten, stinking and wormy, but it had been shod. He wrapped a handkerchief over his nose and mouth to protect himself from the stench, and cut the shoes and nails loose from the horn, which was still solid.

He split greasewood and collected the pitch in the shards of the pots that had cracked in the firing. Twice each day he led the horse to the stream, soaked its hooves for two hours, and covered them with the greasy sap. Wherever he went, he led the horse, talking to it, hand-feeding it whenever he came across a bit of corn grass or wild wheat. He split the leaves of prickly pear and fed it the pulp. He gave the animal food that he needed for himself. But on the sixth day after he had first put the rope around the horse's neck, he slipped the maguey-fiber bridle over its nose and met no objection. On that day he decided the horse was no longer wild; it deserved a name. He called it Yermo, wilderness, to return to the animal the life he had taken from it.

He lived without salt, he lived without words; whirled by the sun, according to the length of the days. The pots continued to crack in the fire; he ate with sticks and a knife; he chewed meat away from its own strings, tearing with his brown Durangueño teeth and the hardness of his fingernails. The spoon stayed in his pocket, except for the one time he was able to split the head of a heifer and boil its brains in its own skull; then he ate with a spoon and sang to entertain himself after dinner, and danced a polka, laughing and dreaming, circling the three stones of the fireplace, recalling the tailor's daughters, a woman in Chihuahua, a girl in Parral, taking them to his blanket, loving them as if they were an itch. The beheaded woman appeared in his dreams. She swam with him, she coveted his heart; she dressed in snakes, she held the earth. He danced with her, spinning on one foot, decorating her in the mirror light of the other.

There was no snow that winter, even at the highest elevations; there was nothing to melt in spring; there would be no irrigated fields. Villa collected corngrass seed and dug a series of small channels leading from the stream to a wide flat place nearby. On a warm afternoon he planted the seed in the flat place, working in the old way with a digging stick hardened in fire. He planted the seed deep and did not open the water channels for fear of frost. The wild kernels were small and hard, but they could be pounded into nixtamal; he could live another season, he could eat; he lacked only salt.

He stole cattle, drying the meat and hoarding it, making a saddle of calfskin, sewing himself a calfskin raincape. When he left the cave, he made a fire in the entrance to protect his store of meat and skins. He began to build a household: a bed of leaves and skins, a roasting pit, bags of rabbit skin and bags of calfskin, bladders for water, his stone griddle, a mortar and pestle, maguey needles, an awl of chipped flint, an obsidian scraper. It was a life. But he feared the silence, telling stories to the horse, then telling lies. He chose the words more carefully, sometimes passing a morning deliberating over the name of the shape of a woman's breast or the consistency of a piece of meat. He lay in his bed at night dreaming the names of the colors of the sky. He counted stars and gave them names that were not words, but sounds of their shapes and colors: eerah, no-oo, lalanla, ommna, tzo, cli, atlana. As their places changed in the sky, he changed their names. He felt himself settling, resting. His beard grew. On some mornings he forgot to chew the stinging roots to clean his teeth. He bathed the horse's hooves and rubbed them with pitch only when he remembered. He let the horse's manure pile up; he did not carry it to the corngrass field. Coyotes came close to the cave, howling to each other, without wariness. The horse complained. Villa slept and walked in speechless dreams.

In the back of the cave, where it narrowed sharply and began to lose its height, there was a sandy spot. He dug a deep hole in the sand and made a toilet. The cave dampened and the temperature rose; the walls greened, the skins began to rot. He felt more comfortable there, immersed, safe. Night after night he lay awake, trying to invent a word for the sense of home and self he now felt; the cave was now as much his as the pits of his body and the secretions of his eyes.

One morning, as he was spraying his urine into the hole, he thought he saw something moving in the dark puddle. He brought a piece of burning wood from the fire at the other end of the cave and illuminated the toilet hole with it. White worms had grown in the slops of his body. They squirmed below the surface, rising, fleeing the light, churning the thickness, feeding in it. He watched the worms for a long time; then he gathered the best of the dried meat, his rain cape, the few things he thought worth carrying in the calfskin saddlebags, loaded them on the horse, and left the cave. He rode west and south, into the highest mountains, looking for woodcutters, hunters, mountain farmers, people with whom he could trade: meat for salt, meat for a rifle, perhaps even a breechloader, meat for corn, meat for clothes, words for words. That night, when he looked up at the stars, he could not remember the names he had given them.

Then began the months of wandering: the days of no direction; the nights in which his house was no more than the fire that burned beside him for a warning, as if a warning could be a wall or a roof against the summer rains; the brushing of other men, passing words in the evening, the stories of other evenings, each and each, without the clasp of hearing each other, separate, sitting at the side of the fire, making trades of things—dried meat for a saddle blanket, calfskins for cartridges, cartridges and meat for a rifle— before sleep, before Villa rose in the middle of the night and led his horse to some uphill perch, doubling and redoubling, walking streams, losing them, whoever they were, losing himself.

Villa, Francisco Villa, no relation to the bandit, merely the grandson of Francisco Villa who farmed corn and beans and raised a few cattle in Durango, a nice old man with a tiny beard and a lifelong cough, a good man with bad lungs and fierce eyes; no relation to the bandit, merely the grandson of Francisco Villa who warned his dark-skinned wife not to count the days in the old way, who died before the first of his grandchildren was born, who left his widow debts and droughts to bring to the attention of Our Lady of Guadalupe, speaking heavenward to the Virgin through the medium of candlelight and candle heat; Francisco Villa, Spanish and Basque on the dead grandfather's side, Indian through the women, suckled at breasts the color of old wood or native copper.

No one knew him; he lied to muleskinners and woodcutters, trappers and gatherers of chiles, cactus honey, and wild wool. He trimmed his horse's hooves, he cleaned his rifle, he stole cattle and shot deer and rabbits. Packtrain drivers gave him salt in exchange for fresh meat, cartridges for jerky, fat tortillas for skinned rabbits. He circled north as the summer heat increased, visiting cowboys and the silent people who lived in towns beyond the range of the telegraph, isolated among the most isolated, leaving by moonlight, thinking always of the acordada and the prison of San Juan del Río. He hunted by the side of barefoot men who carried arrows in reed quivers, and he watched the dances of women who bared their genitals to the purifying light of fire. The clicks and swallowed sounds of mountain languages became familiar to him. The discoveries of peyote eaters and the dreams of jimsonweed eaters were told to him by signs and sighs and coruscating irises. He ate chía, atole, badger, snake, worms, ants, grasshoppers; he passed nights in the straw huts of feather workers and feather dyers; he longed for women with sunbrowned breasts and half-shaved heads. The thought of home nagged at him like a sore, calling him back to Canatlán, leaving him uncomfortable, itching, inspecting the corn from his wandered distance. He made a great circle to the east and came back toward home.

His second birth occurred on September twenty-fifth of their calendar, which is the twelfth month of the Tonalpohualli, the true calendar. The month is called Teotleco for the returning of the gods, who are led by Tezcatlipoca (Flint Knife, Carved Obsidian Knife, Enemy on Both Sides, The One Who Stole the Moon, The Smoking Mirror). The knots of Francisco Villa were cast. I read them with delight and then with despair.

7

He came to my house, riding a stolen horse, decorated with silver and elegant cloth. "I killed a man to take the horse," he said.

"There was no other way?"

"He was a rich man. He told me I was worth less than the horse."

"Wash yourself."

We heated stones and put them into the shallow water in the bathhouse. He steamed himself and doused himself with cold water, then steamed himself and doused himself again. After the third time, I told him to come out and put on clean clothes. He had nothing but what he wore, so I gave him a huipil to wear while he washed his clothes in the stream and spread them over cactus leaves to dry.

He brought me gifts: beef that he had slaughtered and dried, chía picked along the way north from Durango. I made tea of the chía and sat with him on the floor of the flowered room. I complimented him on knowing how to pick the seeds from the female lime sage plant. He made no answer. We discussed the rain, the blindness of Retana the tailor, the health of Micaela, Hipólito's gambling, the inability of Martina to find a husband, the recovery of López Negrete, the rain again, the chía again, more about his mother, and again the rain. His voice was soft and dry; there was a great distance for him to come before we could talk. I waited with him, talking away the time while he traveled toward me; and when he was close, I asked what he planned to do now that Doroteo Arango was dead.

"Sell beef," he said. "I'll go back up into the hills west of here. There's plenty of room in the Daffodil Mountains. Or I could go north to the Bear's Head or the Ruination Mountains. What's the difference? I'll be alone in one place or the other. It doesn't matter: I'd rather live alone like that than be a skinhead."

"Francisco, there are some dangers in loneliness."

"I know," he said. "I've met those people, the fugitives no one cares about anymore. I've shared my food with them. That doesn't frighten me."

"And do you know what happened to Quetzalcóatl?"

"Tezcatlipoca tricked him."

"No, it's more complicated than that. Tezcatlipoca was able to trick him because he knew that Quetzalcóatl was a monk, a hermit. He used his loneliness to trick him out of a kingdom. Imagine! There in Teotihuacán is the monk. He meditates, he prays, he writes poems, he gives butterflies to the sun. But he's alone, he speaks to no one, he never sees the world. Then Tezcatlipoca comes with his mirror and shows the monk his face. Quetzalcóatl is disturbed; his mind has been filled with flowers and song; he knows nothing else. Yet the real face he sees in the mirror is his; it must be his. He makes a mask of jade, he paints himself; the real world is so strange to a lonely man that he cannot bear it. Then Tezcatlipoca gives him maguey wine to drink, and the monk, who has never tasted wine, becomes drunk and ruins his life. In shame, having sinned with his own sister, Quetzalcóatl flees the place of the gods and puts out to sea in a paper boat. There on the limitless sea, he sets fire to the boat and rises to heaven in the flames. By his loneliness we were destroyed, for Motecuhzoma Xocoyotzin thought Cortés was the returning monk."

"What should I do?"

That's the place where everything I know fails me: if a life is predicted by the moment, if the calculation of the exact intersection of time and space tells everything, what is the use in thinking how to live? Which is the way of the world? If I reveal the future, is there a future? If a man knows how he will die, what is the use in living? How could the monk, who had the wisdom of a god, not know of the coming of Tezcatlipoca?

"When Motecuhzoma Xocoyotzin heard of the arrival of Cortés, he went to the wisest man in the world, Nezahualcóyotl, and he asked him what he should do. The wise man said they should play the game of fives to decide. Motecuhzoma lost the game, lost everything; the Weeping Woman laid with Cortés. Now you ask me what to do? Should we play the game of fives? I have the sticks and the marked stones; I'll draw the game here on the floor."

A boy, not yet eighteen years old, sat cross-legged on the earthen floor of the room of flowers, dressed in the net weave of a maguey fiber huipil, showing the pale of his bare legs, letting his eyes wander across the yellow roses, the asphodels, the jimson flowers, the red cactus, seeking some sign, the answer I would not give him. He touched the mustache that had begun to grow and thinly fall at the corners of his mouth. He smoothed his curling chino hair, so wild now after the bathing. His breath came dryly, cracking his lips.

"Popoca, please; I don't know what to do!"

"Here," I said, putting the obsidian mirror into his hand. "Look until you see your face."

He stared into the smoke, watching the forms appear and fade: the four

[*67*]

hundred rabbits of drunkenness, the shy moon, the ocelot, a young owl, the blackness of the right hand of the world, death's claws, sinuous birds, the swooping eagle, and finally his face—thicker, wearing a great mustache, hiding his eyes in laughter. The face appeared alone, it resounded through the black glass in the form of a hundred faces.

Villa put the piece of polished obsidian back into my hand and went outside. He dressed himself in the clean clothes that had been spread across the prickly pear leaves, mounted the dead man's horse, and rode down the side of the mountain, turning north, then west, wheeling the horse, north, then west again, changing and changing, as if he had not seen his face at all.

There was a time when everything was known: before the tlamatinime asked their questions, before Nezahualcóyotl wrote his poem in dispute of the certainty of the thirteen heavens, before Motecuhzoma Xocoyotzin misread the signs, before anyone dreamed that Tlacaélel had deceived us with his description of the hungers of the Fifth Sun. There was such a time. Now we ask.

It was said in the knots, in the tonalámatl, and again in the map of an unborn bird; or was I the one who sent him to Ignacio Parra? It was Jesús Alday who led him to the place where Parra and Refugio Alvarado camped. He made the introductions, acting like a salesman, telling Parra of the young man's horsemanship, his escape from prison, and most important, how he had killed a man to take his horse. To Villa he spoke of companionship in the hills, a rich life, fine horses, women when he wanted them, money enough to provide for his mother and his sisters, and freedom from the landlords. There was no danger, he said; Parra knew how to plan his moves, he was well armed, ruthless; the people protected him, gave him food, a place to hide or sleep or rest, whatever he wanted, for they understood that bandits were the allies of the people, the enemies of the landlords. Then he confided to Villa that none of these qualities were necessary or even important, for Ignacio Parra had certain powers, understandings gained in strange, brief sleeps, enabling him to see into the minds of the rurales, perhaps even to confuse their aim, if ever they came close enough to shoot at him. Alday talked for hours, never rushing his words, saying a sentence or two whenever their horses were abreast, lavishing longer expositions on Villa when they stopped to rest or water the animals. At the top of the tree line, Alday pointed to a small mesa surrounded by rocks. "That's Parra's camp," he said. Then he turned his horse and rode back into the trees.

Villa sat quietly, waiting, allowing Parra the first move. The afternoon sun lay beyond the camp, coming down into his eyes, forcing him to squint, hiding the detail of the rocks. He waited. The horse bent its head to look for grass. Villa tightened the reins. There was a breeze. He heard the sound of horses penned somewhere on the mesa or beyond it. Flies irritated the horse. Villa steadied it with the pressure of his knees. The sun lay long and red beyond the black rocks. Villa closed his eyes to slits, watching the rocks through a screen of eyelashes, seeing halos of light over the black wall of rock. His head ached. The light remained in his closed eyes, rolling upward, disintegrating into jagged shapes: reds and yellows, shades of orange, dots of blue, green, and violet. He waited.

A wavering black form came toward him. Parra—thin and young, barefoot, with a streak of white in his hair—strolled, unarmed, flaunting his ease. The deep vertical lines of his cheeks became arcs, and he showed his teeth in something like a smile. "So you're Francisco Villa," he said. "I was expecting a man."

"Then you won't be disappointed."

"We'll see."

Parra reached up, took the reins of Villa's horse, and led him through an opening in the rocks to the small mesa where Refugio waited, still sighting on Villa with a Winchester. Villa nodded to him. Refugio grinned, doffing his hat and bowing. His hair stood up, like oiled grass. "Welcome to the nest of eagles," he said.

Horses and mules stood in their own filth in a makeshift corral. Casks of water sank into a mud of leaks. Saddles lay along the fence; the silver decorations black with tarnish, the leather cracking, and the saddle blankets, stiff with caked dirt and sweat, lying across the seats. Four lean-tos made of gnarled sticks and crudely thatched with grass and rotting maguey leaves stood beside a roasting pit filled with ashes, bones, and blackened fat. Slices of fresh beef hung over ropes and sticks, drying in the sun. Piles of white gut and brown lung lay next to the slaughtering pen. Flies and bees swarmed over the gut, the drying beef, the floor of filth in the corral, and the open trench toilet. Bottles that once had held mescal, aguardiente, oils, sauces, and medicines; empty shell casings; the wreckage of boxes and sacks that once had contained wheat flour, beans, spices, cartridges, candles, and clothing; boots, one sandal; pieces of cloth, shards of baskets and hats; and tiny things, dead, shredded, or decayed beyond recognition—these lay like strewn leaves on the dirt. Over it all the flies and bees poked and buzzed, chewing and swarming, ringed with yellow or shining green in the last light. A breeze descended from the west, roiling in the rock-rimmed circle, blending the stenches of excretions and inedible flesh.

"It lacks a woman's hand," said Villa.

Parra laughed, but Refugio turned the rifle on Villa, saying, "Or maybe the hand of a nice hardworking kid."

Parra moved between them, watching Refugio while he spoke to Villa.

[*69*]

"We don't stay in one place too long. Maybe we'll come back here in a year or two. Then it'll be nice and clean and covered with good grass. Or maybe we won't ever come back here. When the rurales are after you, you have to be careful." He looked up over his shoulder at Villa. "Kid, you know what we do, don't you? We rob and kill. That's all we do. We don't clean up after the animals and we don't work in the field like peóns; we don't get on our knees to anybody. When things are good we get drunk and go with whores. When we run out of money, we rob or we steal cattle or mules. Sometimes we have to kill some people to get what we want; you understand? We shoot them, like you would kill a chicken. We don't even think about it. You think you can do that? Did you ever kill a man?"

"Jesús told you."

"Yes or no?"

"Yes."

Refugio said, "You never know if a man's dead or not."

"I knew."

"Nacho, I think he must be a witch."

"How did you know?" Parra asked.

"I shot him in the face."

Parra nodded, then asked, "Why in the face? Why not in the stomach? Or in the heart?"

"To be sure."

Refugio giggled. Parra waved at him to be quiet. "Tell me, how did it feel?"

"I didn't know his name."

"Could you shoot a man if you knew his name? Could you shoot me in the face?"

Villa looked down, studying the man, the aspects of his face, the sudden white streak that began at the forehead, the curve of bone at the corner of his eyes, the eyes themselves, white and dark, beneath the shining fluid, the long and narrow line of his nose, the breathing mouth framed in vertical lines of shadow, the sun-colored polished skin, the sweat and movement, the symmetry and singularity of the live and human face. He nodded. "Yes, I could do it."

Parra slapped his leg, laughing. "You're a liar, but you're welcome to join us."

They stole one man's mules, another man's wine; they emptied a store; they entered a landlord's house and took the silks and silver; they robbed wagons loaded with cloth and coaches carrying gold watches, rings, cash, and the incidental people who feared and stammered, straining to remember the faces of bandits. Whores embraced them, sapped them, danced them out

[*70*]

of rings and combs set with pearls, asked for the honor of feeling the weight of a bandit's pistol, cooled themselves with the touch of cold metal against their cheeks. Old women, their backs curling under black shawls, blessed them and called them warriors, accepting their gifts in upturned palms, grasping bread and silver with the same slow closing of knotted fingers. Two small girls, barefoot, half naked in limp and faded dresses, lacking even one button between them, held the horses of the bandits while they robbed a hardware store, and afterward accepted gifts of scissors, kettles, long-handled hoes, and a card of buttons for each. They killed no one, these bandits, living instead by threats, laughing and wandering, drinking mescal until they could not walk, until they rolled down hillsides, singing, pissing in the air, until the sun sickened them and they lay retching and stupefied, longing for water. They stayed in the houses of friends wherever they went, for they were the most generous guests, arriving with more food than they could eat, and leaving behind the tonic moment of rebellion, as if it were a tangible gift, a filling light given from one hard hand to another.

They lived too in the mountains, standing beside the Tarahumaras on the edges of the great Copper Canyons, nodding at the ancient prayers to the multicolored passing of the sun, trading salt and weapons for saddle blankets, jorongos, and wooden stirrups, mixing with the chorus of singers who stood outside the boundaries of the great ballcourt and chanted on the players, refusing to notice those who were broken by the weight of the stone and rubber ball. In the south, they sat at the Huichol fires, watching the wives expose their nakedness to the court of flame; then they moved north with the painted band, careful of the blindfolded children, the mysterious arrows, and the tasseled, dancing hunters, searching as the Huicholes searched, crossing invisible boundaries on the way to the abode of the flat, gray buttons of arrogance, the ignorant pride of those who yet made the Eye of God in the form of a turtle's belly markings.

Parra ate six times a day, and yet grew thinner, expelling blood from his bowels, sleeping with his belly in his hands to comfort his gnawed gut. He lay on straw mats in medicine huts, awaiting miracles from Condurango bark, peppers, arrowroot, Quassia broth, enemas of atole and honey, doses of cochineal and corn pollen, pastes of morning glory root and the honeywater of maguey. He vomited and he boiled, he wept orange tears and filled tubs with blue shit, but there was no cure, nor was there even relief except for a moment or two following enemas of atole mixed with jimsonweed or marijuana. He slept little, though he hungered for sleep; he drank mescal, though it was after drunkenness that he suffered most; what he lacked in physical strength he replaced with cold will, riding straight-backed and alert long after Refugio and Villa slumped in their saddles, nodding to the gait of the horses; he drove into fat whores while the blood ran down the inside of his legs and his face was the color of an old priest's belly.

He did not consider himself a thief, for he took nothing from those who were in need. He was a bandit, he said; the landlords were the thieves. He called them cannibals, explaining to Refugio and Villa that they lived off the flesh of other human beings. They were an inferior race, kin to vultures, believers in a dead god, without strength to endure the sun in the fields or the loneliness of the mountains, unable to bear children without screaming. Spaniards lacked blood, he said, and their hearts had no heat; he knew, for he had seen them dying on the roadsides, cold and dried out before they stopped breathing; a Huichol medicine man had cooked the arm of a Spanish woman and found that the skin had the consistency of grasshoppers and the flavor of pig—he spat the chewed flesh into the fire for fear of poisoning himself.

Unlike the Huicholes or the Tarahumaras, Parra was unable to see visions or even to hear peyote voices, but he sometimes ate Root of Gold and fell into a brief sleep from which he arose with his head full of new understanding. It was after eating Root of Gold that he shot the Municipal President of Canatlán; for then, he said, he knew there was no other defense of the land. Neither his brother's scheming nor his mother's tearful acquiescence could have any effect; the killing of the thief was the only response of a thoughtful and loving son.

They wandered, living out of saddlebags and straw baskets hung from the backs of mules. "We're like tortoises," Parra said. Refugio disagreed: "More like wolves, brother." Villa said, "No. I would like to be like a tortoise or even like a wolf, but I think the truth is that we live more like coyotes."

Parra laughed. "You only say that because of the way you sing."

Villa looked pointedly at Refugio. "No," he said, "it's the truth."

They reached for their pistols, but Parra stopped them, frowning and shaking his head. "We are what we are," he said. "And it's because of them, it's all because of them. So if you want to shoot someone . . ."

Refugio relaxed slowly. His hand trembled. It was not the first time he and Villa had come close to fighting. And there had been others before Villa: a cowboy with two fingers on his left hand who had ridden with them for almost a year, the fat kid from Jiménez, an Apache who had driven Refugio into rages by refusing to speak for weeks at a time, and an ex-Mormon who had traveled with them for only a week before he and Refugio had drawn their guns over a gold watch chain. Parra, who sometimes spoke of organizing an army of bandits, describing how he would capture ranches and raid towns, even cities as big as Parral, knew that Refugio's reputation made it difficult for him to recruit men; yet he said of Refugio only that he was willing to kill and that there were times when such a man was necessary.

Villa became more careful in the presence of Refugio, limiting his drinking to a few sips of pulque or a glass of beer, refusing the older man's offers of marijuana, saying that it caused his throat to constrict, giving him the terrors of a drowning man instead of the exhilaration the marijuanos promised. He watched Refugio, reading his eyes and the pitch of his voice. The man was more than twice Villa's age; his chest was thin, his belly was soft and hung over his belt, and his buttocks had gone wide and flat; but he was good with a gun and he could not be predicted; there was no comfort with him.

There was no comfort with Parra, either; he had become a talker. There were nights when he did not sleep at all, but lay awake watching the fire, telling Villa his life, his secrets of survival, the suspicions that allowed a man to grow old. He did not speak of his pain, even though he wore it on his face and in the occasional trembling of his hands. Only after he ate Root of Gold and had his moment of sleep was he calm and able to rest normally. He advised Villa to use it, showing him how to wash the root and make it into thin slices that could be easily chewed, for only when it was thoroughly mixed with spit did the root have the proper effect. "You'll see," Parra said. "Once you use it, you'll know why it's necessary."

Villa waited until Refugio was in Camargo, visiting an aunt who owned a small farm there, before he agreed to try the root. He and Parra had made camp on the edge of a bluff overlooking one of the streams that flowed into the Conchos. Parra told him to eat only a little atole for dinner to prepare his stomach to take in the root. "Afterwards," he said, "you can eat a spoon of honey, and then in the morning you eat meat or beans, whatever you want. But when you're going to eat the root, you have to have a clean stomach. It's good to shit first, too; that helps to give you deeper thoughts."

The preparation of the root lasted more than an hour. The sun had gone down, but the outline of the mountains remained in the west. A bird could still be seen against the sky. "It's better in the dark," Parra said. "We should wait." They sat beside the small cooking fire, watching the sky in the west, waiting. The horses and the pack mules were quiet, watered, staked, eating circles of dry grass. Below the bluff the stream ran evenly, washing speech over its surfaces, sighing hollowly at its smooth mud banks. They heard leaves, grass, the sputter of the fire, the first coyote of the night somewhere to the north, complaining to the moon. The mountains were gone, become the starless base of the sky.

The moon brightened. Cold light. They wrapped themselves in their blankets. Parra held out the pan of shredded root to Villa. "Chew it well," he said. "Don't swallow it until the root is as soft as cooked rice."

While Villa chewed the pulp of the root, Parra spoke to him, softly,

[*73*]

steadily, lulling and leading him out of the moment in which they sat, talking him on to a new intersection, one that is perhaps improper, as the end of the sun is improper, or perhaps nothing more than a dream in which the meeting of time and space are confused by sleep and only seem unlike the world. He led Villa to the farthest edge of the bluff and showed him the stream, which ran beneath the moon like a pouring of mirrors, flattering her, fickle, like the stolen bride herself. He asked Villa to listen to the stream, to sit counting the words while cool sleep began in his feet and in his fingers.

Francisco Villa walked beside the stream, approaching the place beneath himself. He was barefoot, dressed in white, carrying claws and ears of corn. There was a black, hairless place in the center of his head, an invitation. He rose out of his blanket, walked to the edge of the bluff, held up his hands before him like a swimmer, and dived into the black space in the head of Francisco Villa.

Beyond the hole was a place made of light, neither an inside nor an outside, but a mesh of beams: reds, oranges, crimsons, yellows, violets; colors of birds, flowers, and all the moments of all the seasons of suns. Each beam had the temperature of its color, like the suns that travel west, changing along the way, warming, cooling, coloring, light after light, ending in blue after red as they began in blue before red before yellow. Yet he was neither burned nor chilled, but held in the various lights that slid over him, smoother than water, beams of impenetrable air. He moved, and the beams moved with him; the direction was incomprehensible, there was only movement. At the end of the light he emerged into darkness and emerged again into the other darkness of that night during which he had leaped into the black place in the head of Francisco Villa. He walked beside the stream under the moon, listening to the water, watching the flattery of mirrors, until he came to a place where he could climb the bluff. It was steep, but he managed to climb without using his hands, walking wide-legged, with short, pulling steps. When he came to the place from which he had risen, he lay down. And there in the cold and starry night he awakened, damp and tired, wrapped in his blanket, his head resting on the hard rise of his saddle. After a while he got up and went to the inside of the mesa and hid himself in a nest of rocks while he coughed out the pieces of pulp, which were white and soft, like grains of rice boiled out of their form.

Parra waited for him. "How do you feel?" he asked.

"My feet are still cold."

"That's nothing. Did you have thoughts?"

"Only a dream; no more."

"The first time is difficult to understand."

"Should I tell you the dream?"

"No," Parra said. "If I understood it, you would always be at a disadvantage."

Refugio returned from Camargo leading a new horse, a big, mule-faced gelding with an enormous chest and long, heavily muscled shoulders. To celebrate the acquisition of the horse, he had bought a bottle of mescal. Villa took only a sip from the bottle. Parra and Refugio finished it off, drinking through the early evening and into the night. The mescal put them in magnificent spirits: they sang and laughed, telling stories of their own exploits and the lesser exploits of other bandits they had known. Refugio said prayers for the men he had killed. He and Parra tried to add up all the money they had stolen, the whores they had slept with, the criollos they had frightened. They examined Refugio's new horse, comparing it to other horses they had ridden, discussing the details of the animal: its hocks and pasterns, the slope of the croup, the length of the leg. They wandered around the campsite, arms around each other's shoulders, stumbling and laughing, looking for something to do, complaining that there were no whores in the mountains, blaming everything on the son of a bitch Porfirio Díaz, who was the father of every rural in Mexico, the big fucker who raped the poor with his five fingers.

The new horse stood quietly in the beginning; Refugio's voice was unfamiliar, the tones had no meaning, its name was not said. Refugio danced around the horse. "You can't fuck," he shouted. "You have no balls. What good is a horse with no balls? How can a great bandit have a horse with no balls? I can't trust you, horse. When the rurales come running after me, you'll lay down. I'll die because of you, because you're a priest, a goddamn horse priest, who'll turn me over to the rurales. You'll hang me. I'll dangle from a rope shitting my pants because you have no balls. Traitorous horse! Murderer! Assassin! You think I'm afraid of you, a horse with no balls? Look at these fists. I'll knock out your fucking teeth with my fists!"

He stood in front of the horse with his fists cocked, mocking the animal's size, making theater for Parra and for himself, clowning, finishing off the night with laughter. Then he landed a punch on the horse's jaw, and it backed off. Refugio followed it, driving the animal backward with jabs and shouts, forcing it to the end of the tether. He stalked it, punching and shouting. "Coward, cuckold, queer!" The horse moved sideways, circling at the end of the tether, pulling at the staked rope, trying to rear, unable to get the room to raise its legs. Refugio laughed. The horse began to whinny, letting its breath sound in little bursts, like terrified laughter. Refugio whinnied in return, still punching at the animal's face, working now, his breath coming hard, the sweat running, his feet dragging more and more, stumbling. "Faggot, faggot, faggot, faggot!" he screamed at the horse,

[75]

punching it, driving a fist with every word, rhythmic, raging. Suddenly, the horse charged him. He tried to keep his balance, holding his hands out, reaching into the air for something to hold on to. When he fell, the horse reared, pawing and screaming. Refugio rolled out from under the hooves and ran to his saddle. He took his machete out of the scabbard and went back to the horse, which now stood lathered and panting, the fear still showing in its widened eyes.

Refugio used the machete like an ax, chopping the horse to its knees, destroying one leg and then another. "Faggot! Get up and fight me now. Faggot! You have no balls. I can't stand a horse with no balls!" He struck it with the machete, slicing into its shoulders, cutting across its ribs, chopping the skin of its back and the thick flesh of its haunches. The horse screamed at a constant pitch, tossing its head, squirming on its shattered legs. Blood covered its hide in great blotches, like the markings of a gory pinto. The other animals pawed and whinnied, catching the terror and the smell of blood. Parra watched, drunk and dumbfounded, hunched over his own torso, his arms dangling, hung with empty hands.

"Enough!" Villa said. Refugio did not hear. Villa sat up and pointed the pistol at him. "Enough! Enough now!" Refugio turned around. The machete was raised over his head. Blood ran down over his hands, trickling into his sleeves. There were streaks of blood on his shirt, and drops of blood ran down his face like tears. In the firelight, no sign of anger could be seen in his face: his eyes were calm and narrow. "Mother of God, man," Villa said, "enough." Refugio smiled without showing his teeth, a cat's smile. Then he turned around, measured the horse once with his machete, and killed it.

They descended from the mountains to the plains of Papasquiaro. A small cut on Refugio's leg had become infected, and no mountain medicine would cure it. The infection spread. Refugio could not walk. They had to help him on and off his horse. They headed toward Sandias, where there was a curandero who was said to understand all forms of infection. On the way, Parra went off by himself to visit José y Maria Moya, a Spaniard who owned a ranch and a sometimes productive silver mine in the mountains northwest of Sandias. To pay for a favor done many years before, Moya arranged for Parra to steal a quarterly payment from the refinery in Parral.

The money was to be carried by a man on a piebald mare leading two burros, one of them very dark, almost black. They camped in a narrow draw at the top of a long straight rise in the trail and waited for the man. He came on the third day of waiting, a fat little man wearing a jarano decorated with paper pictures of St. Christopher. "Mr. Moya told me to expect you," he said when they stopped him. He raised his hands and smiled, showing

[76]

his teeth, which were white, unlike the teeth of people from Durango.

Villa and Parra searched the man and his saddlebags, but they found only forty-five pesos. "You have nothing else?" Parra asked.

The man continued to smile. "No, sir. Sometimes when I come down the mountain, I carry silver, but when I go up all I carry is supplies for Mr. Moya. Are you supposed to give me something for him?"

"No."

"Then I should go on," the man said. "Even though St. Christopher rides with me, it's best to arrive at the mine before dark."

Parra told him to pass. The man wished them the protection of God, then clucked to his horse, and moved on up the trail. He rode slowly, singing softly to himself, waving his head in rhythm to the song. "Something's wrong," Villa said. "He's too happy." Parra and Refugio agreed, but they did not know what to do. The figure of the man grew smaller, then disappeared around a curve in the trail. The burros followed, one and then the other, climbing along, the heavily loaded packsaddles swaying on their backs.

"The packsaddles," Villa said.

They caught the little man who was under the protection of St. Christopher and stripped the saddles from the burros. The money was there between the saddles and the saddle blankets, thousands of pesos in little packets spread evenly under the saddles. Villa asked the little man: "Are you also a bandit?" The man shrugged and smiled again, but with his eyes opened wide, making an idiotic face, full of fear and laughter. "I'm a poor man," he said. "My burros have saddle sores from so much work. My own buttocks are as hard as leather from the saddle and still I get sores from so much riding. It's not an easy life, sir. I have too many children and my wife is sickly. I would be a bandit, like you, but I have no courage—when I see the rurales, I start to sweat and my balls shrivel up inside my pants. I'm the victim of bad luck and evil spirits. I was the ninth child, so my mother said I was sent from the bottom of Hell where there is no luck. I have always had a hard life, sirs—when I was five years old, I lost the sight in my left eye; I have weak lungs and a liver that is going to be the death of me. What can I do? A poor man dreams of such a fortune. You can understand, sirs; it is widely known that you are not the sons of rich men. We are all the same, the poor victims of this life."

Refugio shot him in the belly.

"No!" Villa shouted. "No, no!"

Refugio shot the little man in the chest and again in the belly. He held on to the saddle horn, maintaining the obsequious smile until he began to cough pale blood. Villa took the little man by the arms and lifted him off the horse. He turned his head to avoid coughing blood onto Villa, who

[77]

lowered him gently to the ground. The little man's hat fell and rolled away. He looked over at it, trying to speak, but he could not make any words. Parra picked up the hat, tore one of the pictures from it, and put the picture in the hand of the little man, who looked at it for a moment, then pressed the paper to his heart. When he took it away to look again, the picture was crushed and bloody. Villa worked over him, trying to stop the bleeding by pushing pieces of the man's shirt into his wounds, but it was no use; the little man put the paper over his eyes and died.

"We should give Refugio's share to the widow," Villa said.

"Who was he?" Parra asked. "What was his name? Where did he live? It's impossible."

Villa looked at his hands. The blood was crusting, falling from the lines of his palms. "Mr. Moya would know."

"We can't go there," Parra said.

"Maybe there's something in his pockets. We can have someone read it for us." Villa knelt beside the dead man and searched his clothing. He found only a blue hummingbird wrapped in red twine.

At Villa's insistence they counted the money and divided it between them there on the trail. Refugio sat above them, watching the counting of the packets of pesos. When the money had been divided into three piles, Villa took Refugio's money and dipped it into the blood and intestinal oozings of the dead man. "A remembrance," he said, handing the bloodied end of the packets to Refugio. He turned to Parra: "I'm going up to Chihuahua until they've forgotten about this. If you want to meet again, I'll be at the place where the Root of Gold was discovered. We could meet there in thirty days, forty days, whenever you want."

"Forty."

"I'll be there too," Refugio said.

"You know what place I'm talking about?"

"Just tell me where it is; I can find it, buddy. I know this country better than you do. I know it even better than Nacho."

Villa stuffed his share of the money inside his shirt and went around behind Refugio to mount his horse. He rode up toward Refugio and reined in his horse. The animals brushed each other, became skittish. Villa put his pistol against Refugio's side. "Give me your rifle and both pistols," he said. As Refugio handed over the weapons, Villa dropped them on the ground. Suddenly, Refugio understood. "I can't dismount," he said. "You know I can't stand on my leg. You know I can't do it. You know." Villa spurred his horse and headed it down the trail. Parra followed. They heard Refugio cursing them, and they wanted to laugh, but it was too soon after the death of the little man with the paper St. Christophers. At the bottom of the trail, where it flattened out on the plain and crossed a main north/south road, Villa and Parra stopped to rest the horses. "I should have killed him," Villa said.

Parra shrugged.

"It was the right thing to do."

Again Parra shrugged.

They sat for a while without talking. The afternoon clouds were coming in over the mountains; the smell of rain was in the air. They put on their ponchos. "Where will you go?" Villa asked.

"I also have a brother and three sisters."

"Where are they?"

"They're well."

"I would like to go to San Juan to see my mother, but they are always waiting for me there."

Parra smiled. "Forty days," he said.

They separated, riding slowly, turning once to wave, then urging the horses into a trot. After riding north for an hour, Villa made a wide circle into the foothills of the mountains on the west and came back out onto the plain, crossing his trail only a mile from the place where he and Parra had separated. As the rain began, he was riding south toward San Juan del Río.

Villa camped on the hill overlooking the town. There were few lights: a dimness from the jail, the cantina still glowing, a candle in the marketplace to guide a sweeper or an old woman counting and recounting the bits of her day, lanterns at the bridges, and one house shining from every window as someone gave birth or died or celebrated or merely feared the dark. He drank some water from his canteen; the pebbles rattled. A light rain fell, like mist. The moon came and went, toying with his shadow. He touched his cheek, feeling his face on his fingers, his fingers on his face, that lonely perception. He reached inside his shirt to feel the money; there were fifty thousand pesos. Mist settled on his face, the moon blurred, he lay with fleas and dreams. In the pocket of his shirt, beside the tin spoon, was a blue hummingbird wrapped in red twine.

At dawn, he awakened and went to the edge of the hill to watch the beginning of the day of the town: before the farmers moved, a boy in white cotton and a red-and-black sash climbed out of a window and ran into the fields; the farmers were gone to their work before the crowing announced the animal day; the prisoners were herded out of the jail in a ragged line of unkempt hair and sour clothes; the baker opened his shutters; a girl in a sleeveless nightdress shivered, looked at the sun to estimate the day, and ran dancing across a courtyard; an old woman carried her tray of sweets to the plaza, walking the cobblestones as if they were the beads of a rosary;

[79]

church bells rang; the doors of the church opened, the priest peered out to see if anyone was coming to early mass, crossed himself, and closed the doors; a dog sat in the street to scratch itself; the nightbirds left the trees for darker roosts, and the daybirds came fluttering on the chill air to take their places; the smell of bread, coffee, and tortillas came on the air; the prisoners marched across the bridge and over the hill, eight men followed by the narrow figure of the jailer; doors opened everywhere and gave forth the clerks and merchants and wives of San Juan, and finally the Municipal President, tugging at his tie and combing back his hair with his fingers; then the doors closed and the town was quiet again but for the tardy roosters and the mumbling of the old women vendors mixing with the faint chatter of the birds. He wished to be there, one of them, a young man in his place behind some door, in the stern shoe of routine. Or if that was no longer possible, he wished to be anonymous, free to buy what he craved, the true owner of the fifty thousand pesos inside his shirt. Instead, there were fleas in his clothes and palpable stains in his mouth. He saddled his horse and rode in a great circle to the east, coming around the heights of the mountain to the house where his mother now lived, the old house in which they had washed his dead father, the old land that had never given them more than death and stunted corn.

Twelve years lying fallow had brought no change; the boundaries were still cheated by the slopes of the mountain; rocks fell, rocks grew out of the ground; the soil was a brown netting over the rock, waiting to be stolen by the wind or the rain, grown no richer in these dozen years than it had in the previous thousand; it lacked sweetwater and it lacked softness; the land was harder than a man—he had felt the plow break, he had seen his dead father; only the cactus prevailed.

Villa rode slowly across the farm toward the house, skirting the plowed patches, considering what had been done. He thought he would give his mother the money to buy an ox and a plow with two steel blades and cattle and chickens and goats to breed: money enough to make her rich for as long as she lived. He put his hand inside his shirt and felt the money, his mother's happiness, the security of his sisters, the start of his brothers. He came laughing to the old room, riding boldly so that the chickens flew and the goat was terrified at his coming.

There was no one to greet him in spite of the commotion of his arrival. He tied up the horse and went inside. The house was dark, although it was only noon. The Arango family, all but Antonio and Doroteo, sat near the cooking fire eating beans and drinking hot water flavored with myrtle. The girls were wrapped in shawls, Hipólito wore a jacket made of two pieces of unmatched wool blanket, Micaela huddled in the thinness of her black veil. His mother rose and came to the door. "You're so thin," she said.

She moved slowly, as if she had been sleeping. The fat of her face was gone; her empty skin lay in terraces below her eyes and beneath her chin. "And you're also thin, Mama," he said.

She offered no embrace. He took her hand and kissed the palm. "You call yourself by another name now," she said. He nodded. "Are you ashamed of your father's name?"

"No."

Hipólito and Mariana left their beans and started toward him, but Micaela waved them back to where they sat. Turning again to Villa, she said, "You must be ashamed of us to use another name."

"Mama, the rurales are looking for Doroteo Arango."

She led him to the center of the room, to one of the chairs that stood beside a small square of rough wood that had been set on legs, like a table. "Sit down," she said, taking the chair opposite him, folding her hands on the tabletop. "Tell me how you live, why you are so thin and your face is so hard. Tell me why your eyes frighten me."

"I live as I can, Mama. This has been a hard winter—the men I travel with were both sick, we barely stayed alive out there in the mountains. If my eyes are changed, it is because of what they have seen."

"Or what you have done." She looked over at Mariana and motioned to her to bring the beans and flavored water to the table. The girl came quickly, putting the plate and cup on the table and returning to her place.

"What have I done?" he asked.

"Do you steal?"

"Yes."

"And kill?"

"Yes."

"And you ask me what you have done? May God have mercy on us."

He said nothing. Her face was squeezed by a shuddering contraction; she closed her eyes. He smelled the bloody gas of her bowels from across the table. "You're sick," he said.

"No," she said. Then she got up and went outside to the toilet. Mariana whispered to Villa from her place beside the cooking fire: "Dysentery, worms, we don't know."

"Come here," he said. She shook her head. "Come here, I'm your brother. I haven't seen you for almost two years." She shook her head again. "Are you afraid of me?"

"Mama doesn't want it."

"And you, Hipólito?"

He shrugged. "Mama's sick. We try not to upset her."

"Martina," he said, but he could not even get her to look up at him. He saw how slowly she ate, picking the beans out of her plate with her fingers, crushing them one by one between her front teeth.

No one spoke until Micaela returned. Villa was not offered a plate of beans or even a cup of flavored water. He waited, not knowing whether to ask for food and water, afraid to be turned away. When Micaela returned, he said, "You *are* sick, Mama. Why don't you go to Popoca?"

"I go to a Catholic doctor—a man from Germany, where they have the best doctors. A person can't expect to be cured of a serious illness by a witch."

"But you went to him before."

"Now God punishes me. You understand? You should go to the priest and confess, Doroteo, if I may call you by that name. You should confess for what you did to Martina. God will forgive you."

"Let God forgive López Negrete."

Micaela closed her eyes and nodded her head wearily. She held her rosary beads, fingering them, praying under her breath even as she spoke. "Yes," she said, "him too. But he only committed the crime; it was you who made it public, who made your sister the shame of Canatlán. You are the one who put her in this silence. You are the one who made her eat like an animal, because you are a criminal."

"Mama, I would rather be the worst criminal in the world than see my family dishonored. Is that such a wrong way to think?"

"Look at your sister," she said. Martina had bent forward to lick the plate. She made soft groans as she ate.

"How could I have known?"

"You protected your own honor; you didn't think of her. You didn't think how she would be when everyone knew. I took her to the priest to ask forgiveness, but she couldn't speak, she couldn't confess. What could the priest do? I reminded him of what our Saviour said on the cross, but the priest said that she doesn't know what she is doing now. Then she knew; that is the difference. So I spoke of the shameless woman who knew Christ, and I asked him how we could dare to be the ones to cast stones at this poor child. He was sympathetic, he's a good priest, but he told me he could not change the rules of the Church—she must confess and do penance to be absolved."

"What does the priest say about López Negrete?"

"He confessed. And for his penance he gave to the Church two silver candleholders made in the mother country. His soul is safe. Only your sister is left to be condemned, because of what you did."

"Mama, he bought the priest. You want me to buy forgiveness for her?

I have a gun, Mama; it's even better than two silver candlesticks. C'mon, we'll go to the priest with her. If that's not enough, I'll take her to Durango to see the bishop. I'll make them wash her feet in holy water, and if they say one word against the purity of her soul, I'll send them all to Hell." He drew his pistol and laid it on the table. "Here," he said, "here is the Pope himself."

She crossed herself. "God forgive me for giving birth to you."

Villa took a packet of money from inside his shirt and laid it on the table. "I brought this for you. Use it to live in peace."

"It's stolen money," she said.

"Let the sin be on my head." He took the money and threw it across the room to Hipólito. "Take care of her," he said, looking toward his mother. "And take Martina to a priest. Give him a hundred pesos and he'll forgive the devil himself." Hipólito nodded.

Micaela crossed herself again. "Most Sacred Heart of Jesus, have mercy on us!" And turning to Hipólito: "Burn the money, put it in the fire. It's thieves' money."

Villa stood up. "Mama," he said, "I steal from rich men; I never steal from the poor. That's the difference between a bandit and a thief. The rich are the thieves." He picked up the gun and put it in his holster, preparing to leave.

"Your father did not steal," she said, speaking rapidly. "He was a good man, who worked hard to support his family. Every day he went into the fields. He worked in the sun, he worked in the cold. He went to the fields when he was sick, when he could hardly walk. He worked like a man. He worked every day of his life. He was a good man, not like you, not a thief or a bandit or whatever you call yourself. And he was a good Catholic too. He had years of indulgences, because he said Hail Marys in the morning before breakfast and at night before bed. He said Hail Marys in the field when he could hardly breathe."

"He's dead."

"Hail Mary, full of grace! The Lord is with thee; blessed art thou among women, and blessed is the fruit of thy womb, Jesus. Holy Mary, Mother of God, pray for us sinners, now and at the hour of our death. Amen."

"I carried him into this house and laid him on a table."

"O my God, I firmly believe that Thou art one God in three Divine Persons, Father, Son, and Holy Ghost; I believe that Thy Divine Son became man, and died for our sins, and that He will come to judge the living and the dead. I believe these and all the truths which the Holy Catholic Church teaches, because Thou hast revealed them, Who canst neither deceive nor be deceived."

"We put butterflies and ashes in his clothes."

"Hail Mary, full of grace! The Lord is with thee; blessed art thou among women . . ."

"We put fat tortillas and honeywater in his grave."

". . . and blessed is the fruit of thy womb, Jesus. Holy Mary, Mother of God . . ."

"You gave up life when he died, Mama; you took up the religion of widows; you married the priests."

". . . pray for us sinners now and at the hour of our death. Amen."

"Sainted mother," he said.

"Leave this house."

"It's not you, Mama; it's the priests who are speaking."

"I believe in the Holy Ghost, the Holy Catholic Church, the communion of saints, the forgiveness of sins, the resurrection of the body, and life everlasting."

"Keep the money," he said to them all. "It is a gift from a man who dressed himself in saints. Every peso you spend, you will be communing with saints. Amen and goodbye."

Hipólito and his sisters did not look up from the fire and Micaela did not interrupt the saying of her rosary as Villa left them in the dark room that smelled of wood smoke and beans and the emaciating sickness of Micaela's gut. After he was gone, they prayed together, kneeling before the colored picture of the Virgin and the two small candles that Micaela set out on the table. They prayed for their dead father, for their silent and animal sister, for their brother Antonio, for their brother and sister who had died in infancy, for each other, for all the good people of the parish. But they did not pray for thieves or bandits.

He came to my house in the saddle of the mountain, and when I saw how he was I gave him honeywater, I gave him tamales, I ground chocolate for him. He offered me money, and I shamed him by throwing it into the fire.

"You took money from my mother," he said.

"Yes."

"I have forty thousand pesos and she had nothing."

"It was necessary," I told him. "Your mother had to buy back her faith in the old ways."

He ate all that I gave him and he looked for more. I told him to clean his teeth, and when he was finished, I washed his face and hands and repeated to him the old admonitions: Swallow nothing given by inhuman beings, evil ones. Observe moderation in all things. Do not give your fluids to whores. Wash your body, your mouth, your hair. Ask who offers you food or drink. Or you will become nothing more than a tuft of hair and two old and tiny eyes, you will die by shriveling, your skin will hang, you will be a lock of hair, a strand of hair, nothing, without ashes.

"Cleanse me," Villa said. "I am afraid." He put the blue hummingbird on the ground between us. He said he had taken it from a dead man, and that he did not know why.

I told him that some people believed a blue hummingbird wrapped in red twine would keep away evil spirits.

"It's not true," he said.

"Because the man died?"

"Because of how he died," Villa said.

I put copal in the fire to make the moment. In the sanctified room I told him of the four Tezcatlipocas who were the children of Our Lord and Our Lady, and how one of them is from the North and has a mirror for a foot and is called Smoking Mirror and how another is from the South and has a shriveled foot and is called Blue Hummingbird of the South, Huitzilopotchtli, which is the name of War.

"Is it true?" he asked.

"There was once a great king who lived in Texcoco," I said. "His name was Nezahualcóyotl. He also asked what was true. He even asked if it was true that we live here on earth."

"And did he say it was true?"

"He thought it was enough to ask the question," I said. And when I saw that he did not understand, I asked him, "Do you ever dream questions about dreaming?"

"Then it is true."

"Only that we live here on earth. The other questions were not answered because of our destruction, because of the death of our race, because we have lost our language, because we have lost the sun of our skin. In the end, in the last days, there were so many answers. In Texcoco an empty temple was built to the greatest gods. In Tenochtitlán the furnace of the sun was stoked with blood. We are nearing the end of the eighth cycle since that time; perhaps it will be the end of this sun; there are predictions, counts. My great-grandfather foresaw the most terrible wars; you have brought me a blue hummingbird; those are signs. The end of this sun will be terrible: it will come with earthquakes, it will come with fire—that much is known."

"I didn't kill the man who had the blue hummingbird," he said.

"Yes, I know."

"I killed others."

"Ahuitzotl killed more than eighty thousand prisoners in four days, which is why the sun still lives."

"Is that true, Popoca?"

"Is it true that we live on earth, or is this only a dream?"

[85]

The shapes of the fire painted and repainted his face. He was thin, his cheeks were flat, he had lived like an animal, wandering as all of us had once wandered. There was nothing to guide him, no promise. His eyes were not certain; the color did not stay. I painted yellow squares on his forehead and sang to him. I washed him with smoke, I put his troubles in an egg, I proved him by the reflection of his face. Yet he said to me, "I am afraid. What should I do?"

What answer could I give? What hope is there for us? We live and we dream. There is light and there is darkness. I told him the ancient admonitions again. All that night I spoke to him of his face and his heart, and in the morning I began the history of the race, from the time we came up out of the Seven Caves to the finding of the eagle to the greatness of Axayacatl, Motecuhzoma Ilhuicamina, Ahuitzotl, Tlacaélel, Nezahualcóyotl and Cuauhtémoc, and I even told him of the end of us in the submission of the Weeping Woman.

After I had spoken all night and all day, he asked again, "What should I do?"

I put the blue hummingbird and a green snake into a cage made of sticks. Then I sprinkled them with blood taken from his hand and passed them through a perfumed fire.

"What should I do?" he asked.

I gave him salt and chocolate and reminded him that everything does not end on this earth, that there are other flowers more precious than the ones we have seen.

Retana the tailor had no talent for blindness: with his dimming eyesight he had sewed crooked seams, shirts with three sleeves and dresses without an opening at the neck; with no eyesight he sewed his fingers into the seams, he lined suitcoats with the palms of his hands, he made pincushions of his knees. His business faltered and died, the merchants took his furniture, the landlords took his house, his children lived hungry and nearly naked. He moved his family to an abandoned barn beside a dry well, a place with three walls remaining and a roof that neither Retana nor anyone else could see, for it did not exist.

The children stole purses, food, and clothing, and Retana begged in the plazas of Canatlán, San Juan del Río, Guadalupe, and Santiago Papasquiaro. They survived; they owned a horse, three goats, and a stolen cow; they cooked lizards and ate cactus. But in his blindness and poverty Retana became an arrogant man: he told everyone that he had been chief tailor to Maximilian, specializing in satins, lace, and gold braid, and that only a short while later, with the versatility of a true artist, he had turned to making the sober black suits of the great Juárez. When people asked why he had not become tailor to Díaz, he told them a lecture on the need for unity among the common men of this world. He earned a few centavos by his tales, and there were times when he spoke with such conviction of his contribution to the Independence that his audience collected a handful of coins for him. And once on a Saturday night in San Juan, he earned almost a peso by telling of the time he felt Carlotta's breasts while measuring her for a nightdress. "They were like silk," he said. His audience gasped. "You felt her naked breasts?" Retana shook his head, despairing. "She was just a woman, but my hands, they were like silk!"

Perhaps the thievery of the children was overlooked because of the foolishness of the father, perhaps the people who had known hunger and seen bones in the desert could not bear to think of the destiny of the children, perhaps the children were talented thieves; it is important only that they lived, only that they ate, only that they cared for nothing more than living another day; for it was to them that Villa went and was greeted like a son and a brother. They were not afraid; no further harm could be done to them on this earth.

Villa stayed with them for six days. The girls washed his clothes, the boys groomed his horse, they sat around him to listen to stories of the life of a bandit, they gave him a share in what they stole and what they found in the hills. The old man sat with him by the fire, picking fleas, smoking tobacco in corn husks, and telling his illusions: naming the colors and the shapes of things never seen, describing the sights of the world without light, the nipples of the Empress, the spearing eyes of Juárez, slaughters and glories, silk gleaming, the way velvet brushes the light, the fire mouths of cannon announcing morning, islands of flowers in a garden at the top of the world. Yes, said Villa to the visions, I am able to see the words. Then the tailor reached for whatever part of Villa he could find, a hand or a foot, and held it tightly, saying, "Stay with us here, Doro, and be the second father of this family."

On the day of his leavetaking, Villa and Retana talked all morning.

[*87*]

"Where will you go?" the tailor asked. Villa said he did not know. "And how will you live? Do you have a few cents to buy salt and corn?" Villa said that he would find a way. The old man shook his head. "You must eat," he said, reaching under his shirt and into his trousers, fishing down past his crotch to the insides of his thighs. He brought out a tiny cloth pouch gathered at the top by a white string. "I will give you half of what I have," Retana said, giving Villa one of the two pesos that were tied inside the pouch. "Go to see my cousin, Flor Anchado; she has a little store in Atotonilco. For a peso she'll sell you a good piece of salt and a bushel of corn."

Villa took the coin from the tailor's scarred hand; the silver was as warm as Retana's flesh. "It's not so easy for you to get a peso."

"It goes without saying."

"I don't know when I'll be able to pay you back."

"It's a gift."

Villa looked at the tailor's face: the wandering eyes, the fearful upward tilt of the head, the suncracked skin. Suddenly he threw his arms around the tailor and kissed his cheek. "Mr. Retana," he said, weeping, "Mr. Retana, Mr. Retana." The tailor pushed him away, but Villa repeated his embrace, clenching them together. "Mr. Retana," he said again. "Mr. Retana."

"What's wrong with you?"

"You are a saint, Mr. Retana."

The tailor tried again to push Villa away. "Don't be a fool," he said. "It's only a peso."

Villa took a packet of bills out of his shirt pocket and placed them in Retana's hand. "Here is a gift I have for you."

"It feels like money."

"Five thousand pesos."

"It's true?"

"There's enough to open a shop again, and even to hire a man to run it for you. I saw the place in San Juan, the old yard goods store next to Vega's market; it's empty now."

"Yes, the Widow of Torres died last year."

"Then it'll be yours."

"It's true?" Retana asked. "It's true that this is really money, these are really bills, pesos?"

"Yes. The money came from a silver mine near Sandias."

The tailor wept and kissed Villa's cheek and embraced him. They wept together, and when the children heard what had happened, they wept too. In the afternoon, Villa saddled his horse and prepared to leave. The children crowded around the horse, helping Villa into the saddle, then begging him not to leave. They said he was their sainted brother; they pulled his feet out of the stirrups and kissed them.

He lived like a rich man. He had a woven goathair saddleblanket, a gabardine suit, and a pistol that used the new center-fire shells. He wore soft shoes with leather laces and carried a tiny gold clock on a golden chain. His belt and saddle were carved like an ancient temple; the tops of his boots were decorated in three colors. He bought a pair of gold-rimmed eyeglasses and a soft hat. The load of his goods and clothing became so great he had to carry it in two baskets hung on the back of a burro that trailed his horse wherever he went. But he lived in the hills and cooked his own food. He moved in and out of Durango, Fresnillo, Zacatecas, and Torreón, living on the edges, staying for a day or two, then riding forty miles into the hills to be alone and safe.

In the cities people touched him, food came from unseen kitchens, and police and soldiers were everywhere, looking, measuring the price of his suit, his shoes, his slouch hat, guessing at the pistols under his coat, studying his horse. The cities were made of envy and impenetrable fear: the eyes of the women shone so that he could not see into them, the men had gambler's hands and alkaline faces, the children were old in their eyes and in the fall of their mouths and older yet in their legs, which were pale and had no muscle on them. Everyone walked; there were so few horses; there was so little of the smell of horses; there were so many dogs, thinner than country dogs, cowardly dogs, dogs that curled around themselves and trembled, there were even dogs without tails. So little grew in the city: the houses lay next to each other like the stones of a wall, without gardens, without grass; the cities had no flowers; neither was there space nor anything left to be taken; the only songs were in the plazas, and they were so carefully sung that they had no music. The cities smelled of dust and garbage and confusions of food cooking, but mostly they smelled of fallen smoke and the evaporations of black oil.

Mountain people came down to the cities to sell their wood and wool and brown pots and decorous cotton. They walked as if balancing on imaginary lines, precarious strollers looking too far ahead, stumbling on the routine rise and fall of the streets and walks. Theirs were the darkest faces, the most peering eyes, the revealed teeth. Otomis, Tepehuanes, Michis, Tarahumaras, Tecpanecs, Huicholes, Seris, Pimas, Yaquis, Tarascans, Coras, even Apaches speaking their unintelligible language to each other. And in the corners, leaning, were their nameless fallen, shaped like mud, darkly covered, waiting, the beggared children of La Malinche.

Good morning, Villa said to them, Good day, Hello, Speak to me, I'm Francisco Villa, Call me Pancho, I am one of you more than one of them,

Do not be confused by my gabardine suit and soft hat, Good morning, brother, sister, friend, I am no less lost in this city than you are, Good day, Hello. No one answered. Those who walked lowered their eyes, and those who had fallen put out their hands for coins. He sat on a street in Torreón, in that town of railroad smoke and cotton dust, and spoke to a woman who squatted, her children around her, all of them eating out of a brown pot filled with atole and chiles. "May I eat with you?" he asked. "I can pay. I have my own spoon." The woman's face was scarred, one eye was dead, her mouth did not cover her teeth, her neck was starved. "You are hungry?" she asked.

"Yes."

She pointed to the pot. "Take."

"Is that all you have?"

"Yes, but if you're hungry . . ."

"Thank you, little mama, but I have more than I need." He gave her two hundred pesos. "And I have this for you." She looked at the two bills and gave them back to him. "Please," he said, "it's a gift. For the children."

She smiled, showing the exposed roots of her teeth. "Everyone will think I stole the money."

Villa took the bills and put them in his pocket, then he searched through his clothes, finding smaller bills and coins, putting each one in her hand as he found it.

The woman counted the money aloud: twenty-one pesos, eighty centavos. Then she took the wooden spoon from one of her children, dipped it into the pot, and offered it to him. They sat together on the street, eating, like a family. He complimented her on the smoothness and flavor of the atole. She said that he did not have the sour smell of a Spaniard.

There were other women in the streets, other children, everywhere the fallen, everywhere the wounded. He saw them as if it were the first light: hands that could not close, eyes that could not open, legless, armless, fingerless, children, women and men, the mute, the deaf, the stones begging. He ate with them, he slept with them, they surrounded him, there was a miscreant world. They had nothing, they had debts, they lacked land, they were without seed, without horses, without plows. Whoever had a rooster did not have a hen, whoever had a cow did not have a bull. Their goats were dry, their sheep were bare. The sour water was for them; the white crust, the dead grass, the cracked land was for them. Nothing was for them, nothing and nothing more.

They were quiet, they were still, they sat in the sun, dust lay on them, gray on their dark brown legs, gray on their dried feet, their spread toes. Hats hid the men, shawls hid the women, dust covered the naked children.

[*90*]

Their eyes were black on yellow fields, their hair hung long and reddening, their lips were without color.

He touched them, he lifted up their children, he showed them laughter and the boom of one voice. Take this money, take this food, take this rifle, take these clothes, take from me, take what you need, take as I have taken; it is yours. For which they kissed him, for which they caressed his hands, for which they said his name.

And he saw that nothing changed: the poor were the poor in spite of him; his money and his food and his clothes were days in their lives. Nothing changed. There were so many. He could not sweeten the water or return their limbs or give them sight. He washed away the dust, and the dust came again. At the conclusion of his voice there was silence. He was neither grass nor rain; there are no wells of milk. The hungry ate and were hungry again. There was no limit, there was no end; the world belonged to the sour-smelling Spaniards, it hung at the end of a Chinaman's braid. He wept. When he arrived in Parral he had not slept for two days and two nights, for they had begun to ride with him, all of them, even the ones he had not seen; in his dreams he could not distinguish himself from them.

Hidalgo del Parral. The old priest gave us olive trees and vineyards. The catzopines came and destroyed the orchards and the vineyards. It was the law. Then there was a shout in the town of Dolores where the vineyards had grown, and fifty thousand of us, carrying axes, sticks, and machetes, followed the old priest to war. They executed him in Chihuahua and hung his severed head on the wall of the public granary of Guanajuato.

Hidalgo of the wild-growing vine, Hidalgo of the revolution, for ten years his head hung on a stone wall of the Alhondiga de Guanajuato.

The hotel had many conveniences: electric lights, sinks with hot and cold water, and a toilet room on every floor. The water boxes above the toilets leaked and sweated so that a man could defecate and wet down his hair at the same time. The water in the sinks sometimes came out in icy dribbles and at other times in gushing steam. But it was the electric lights that interested Villa most. He gave a twenty-centavo piece to the porter to explain to him how the lights worked.

"Well, I don't know if I should take the money," the porter said. "You want to hear about magic, and these lights don't work by magic. It's electricity, science. You understand technical information?"

Villa nodded.

"Okay, then I'll take the money." He put the coin in his pocket, sighed once, and began his explanation. "The whole idea of electricity is small, very small, everything in electricity is very small. Imagine a wick so small you can hardly see it. Now if you can imagine that, try to imagine a flint so small that no one can see it. Electricity is not so easy, eh? But you understand so far?"

Villa nodded.

"Good. Now these lights, they don't just hang there by themselves. They are connected to a very small tube. And these tubes are the longest tubes in the world; they go for miles, sometimes in the air, sometimes on the ground. And they are all connected up, like the roots of a giant cactus. You understand me?"

Villa nodded.

"Now comes the technical part. Inside these tubes is a special kind of kerosene. One drop is enough to light up a whole room. When you pull the string attached to the lamp, the little flint gives off a spark and the tiny wick inside the lamp catches fire. When you pull the string again, it cuts off the air and the lamp goes out. But the secret is all in the kerosene. I know, because one day I went to the place where they make this electricity and I saw them pouring kerosene into an engine as big as the engine of a train, bigger even. Ay! What an engine! Only the technicians in North America can make such engines." He pursed his lips proudly. "This science is very interesting, eh?"

"Yes. Thank you very much."

"Look, I'm busy now, but I can see you're a man who understands science. We'll talk some more, maybe tomorrow. For example, you know how the telegraph works?"

"Oh, yes, the little strings inside the wires."

"Of course, but do you know the difference between the dot string and the dash string?"

During the first days in Parral, he ate only food sold in the street: tacos, burritos, roast corn, barbequed pork bits, fried bacon rinds, and sweet churros carefully chosen from the great trays the women carried on their heads and then set out on rickety stands made of sticks tied together with twine. The other men in the hotel ate food sold in the street, but they also ate in restaurants.

There was a restaurant only two buildings away from the hotel that seemed to Villa to be most likely to have good food and clean plates, for it was not a secret place like many of the others: the front of the building was completely open, without doors or even a curtain of strings, and the food was cooked behind a counter that extended the entire length of one wall. He studied the place for two days before he went inside. There was a form for eating in a restaurant: one sat at a table, removed his hat, and waited for a woman with a white apron to come to his table with a large white ticket. While the customer held the ticket, the woman brought him pieces of fried tortilla, eating utensils, and a glass of water. Then the woman took back the ticket and brought a plate of food. At the end of the meal, the woman brought a small ticket for which one paid. Apparently the price was always the same, because the small ticket and the large ticket were always the same sizes. After this final transaction, one sipped coffee and picked his teeth.

Villa went into the restaurant, selected a table near the front and sat down facing the street. He removed his hat and put it on the far side of the small table, leaving plenty of room for the plates. The woman in the white apron came carrying the big ticket. She was fat and smelled of frying oil, but he was pleased to see that her hands were clean, wrinkled from immersion in hot water. He smiled at her. She frowned, picking up his hat: "This is not a campfire, mister. We don't eat with our hats on the table." She hung his hat on a peg and went back to the counter. "Thank you," he called after her.

The ticket was covered with words and lines, but he paid no attention to it. He had seen such tickets before: the markings meant nothing. When she returned with the bowl of fried tortillas, water, and utensils, he ordered his meal: "I want the soup and the yellow rice with chicken and fish."

"We don't have albondigas or paella." She pointed at the large white ticket. "Look. Order what we have."

"It tells here?"

"Fake! I'll bring you the meal of the day, if you can pay for it. Forty centavos. Sixty centavos with the filet of beef."

He gave her a peso. "Here, little sister. Bring me a good meal, but don't cook with anger, it makes the food bitter."

She brought the meal all at once: boiled suckling pig, cold beans and onions, hen soup, braised beef, rice with tomatoes, tortillas, refried beans, tripe; a series of little dishes and bowls lined up on the inside of her arm. He arranged the dishes on the table in the order in which he planned to eat them, lifting up each one to smell it before he gave it a place in the order. Then he took his knife, fork, and spoon out of the breast pocket of his suit and prepared to eat. The woman leaned over him and picked up the spoon she had set on the table: "What's wrong with this? It's washed in soap and hot water."

"I like my own, especially the spoon."

"If you don't like this place, you can eat somewhere else." She began picking up the plates.

Villa put his pistol on the table. "Miss," he said, "I'm just a poor country boy. Most of the time I eat what I cook myself over a campfire. It's a simple

[*93*]

life, but there are sometimes problems. Wolves smell the food and try to take it away from me. So I have to shoot them."

The woman put the plates back on the table and ran away to the back of the restaurant. Halfway through the meal, Villa felt something poke him in the back. A man's voice said, "Raise your hands, cowboy. Then stand up and walk out the door."

"What's wrong? I was only trying to eat a meal in peace."

"You threatened to shoot my wife; is that what you call eating in peace? Pig!"

Villa stood up slowly. The woman said, "I hope this teaches you a lesson."

"Yes," he said. "In a restaurant a man should sit with his back to the wall."

Out on the street the man clubbed him with the barrel of his rifle. Villa fell to his knees. He waved his arms, like a man in water, but he could not keep his balance. He fell forward onto his hands. The man put his foot against Villa's ribs and pushed him over into the dust. They threw his belongings at him: the slouch hat, the pistol, cartridges, utensils; everything landed in the street, rolling in the dust.

Two women who sold roast corn and tacos in the plaza came across the street and helped Villa to stand up. One led him to a bench in the plaza while the other gathered his belongings. They brushed the dust from his clothes; they looked in his face, his eyes, his ears. "Are you badly hurt?" the taco seller asked.

"No. I feel well enough, thank you."

"Well then, since you didn't have your meal, would you like to buy a few tacos, perhaps an ear of fresh corn? Food cooked by friends has the best flavor."

In the tavern called San Luis the men drank beer and tequila and rum and pulque when it was fresh. They stood in a row along the bar and gossiped or listened to the musicians who went from tavern to tavern earning coins for their songs. They laughed and argued and told stories of bandits and women, and sometimes they killed each other.

Every night after the sun, when the wind came up and the streets were long tunnels of dust, Villa went to the San Luis and sipped a glass of beer and listened as if he were in a school. In the old language, there are four hundred drunken rabbits, nine kinds of vaginas, five kinds of breasts, nine hells, thirteen heavens, and limitless names for the varieties of fear; he learned them as children learn the multiples of twenty.

He saw the pistols and revolvers that men carry, the knives that are hidden in boots or back of the neck. He studied the nerve of angry men,

[*94*]

the way that hatred leaps from one face to another, the suppurations of the wounds of a poor life. There was no one in the San Luis he trusted; they were like the blind snakes of spring.

On his fourth night in the town of Hidalgo del Parral, he watched two men draw their guns in anger. They lifted the guns out of the holsters at the same time, but one man hesitated while the other shot him. The force of the bullet bent the man in half; fluid burst out of his nose and mouth. But he did not fall. He raised his revolver and shot the other man. They stumbled in circles for a moment, like beheaded chickens, and shot each other again. While they lay dying, Villa looked at their revolvers: the first man had a .32-caliber revolver, the other man had a .38. Neither one had been sufficient.

In the morning, Villa went to the gunsmith's shop. He laid his Smith and Wesson .38-caliber revolver on the table in the little room where the gunsmith sat surrounded by springs and parts and bottles of oil and dirty cotton patches. "It's no use," he said.

"You want the forty-five?"

"Forty-five is not so much bigger than thirty-eight."

The gunsmith wiped his hands on a cloth. "Look," he said to Villa, showing him two bullets. "Your pistol fires a bullet of a hundred and fifty-eight grains. The forty-five uses a bullet of two hundred and fifty grains. You use twenty-one and a half grains of powder, the forty-five uses forty grains. You understand the difference?"

"If I had to shoot a man . . ."

"You were in the San Luis last night?"

"Yes."

"If you shoot a man with a forty-five, he won't shoot back."

"It's sure."

"With the Colt you can be sure."

Villa grinned.

On Saturday night in the plaza he spoke with a girl who read books and wrapped herself in petticoats. Her fingers were like soft candles, her feet were hidden in her skirts. He told her that he could read, she told him that she could cook. They sat together on a bench. She said the best fashions came from Paris, he said he was pleased with his gabardine suit. They spoke of electricity and the coming of a new century. She predicted marvels, he said he cared more about horses. He was from Durango, she had been to the Capital to see the building that was being made of glass. Mining and cattle were his interests, she was glad to be under the protection of the Blessed Virgin. He leaned toward her, thinking to touch her fingers. The wind blew across him, a breeze, without dust. Her face was remade by the

[*95*]

tension beneath her eyes; she seemed then of carriages and serving girls, Spain.

"What's wrong?" he asked.

Rising, she put her handkerchief to her nose, and in a moment she was gone, leaving only the scent of flowers and new fruit. The street musicians came and played for him. He settled his hat against the sarcasm of the spring winds.

They were called gladdeners. They painted yellow squares on their faces and drew flowers on their necks and arms, they stained their teeth with the red cochineal, they washed their hair in sweet soap and made it into patterns by halves, and they perfumed themselves with oils and incense and rose water. Rich men took them. Princes and merchants paid them for their laughter, for the petals opening, for the passage constricting, for the inventions of nights and flowers.

They were harlots, procurers, drunkards; their anuses itched, they used foul language. They were brazen, they sold themselves into slavery, they ate teonanacatl and became arrogant. They lay in the streets, they danced in the path of the rabbit, they licked the grinding stones and stepped over the places where the dead were buried, they wore skirts of snakeskin and coyote fur, they sold their youth for one green feather and a piece of gold; and when their laughter ended, they were women without children, they wept in the kitchens and the marketplaces of the old world; and when they died, they were without a direction, without bones. They pray to Xochiquetzal, the whore of Tezcatlipoca the Two Enemies; but she does not hear them, for she is like them, hearing only the sound of her own laughter.

The woman who stood beside Villa in the tavern smelled of rose water and sang laughter; her hair was long, shining, washed in rainwater and yucca, combed and combed until no interruptions marred its lights. She was clean; her clothes smelled of wind and hot, ironed starch. Her skirts were like the music, nodding from one side to the other: gaiety and color. She was younger than Villa; her eyes were dark and yielding. She called herself Socorro Riendo. Men smiled to hear her name, to think that help might come laughing; they put money in her hand and entered her.

She touched the handle of his revolver. "Forty-five is my mother's age," she said. "And my mother moves very slowly."

"I move quickly."

"May it please God, sir. And may you live long."

He laughed, he ordered a drink for her—a glass of pulque.

"Why is such a pretty girl still unmarried?"

"No one has asked me, sir." She winked; she cast her body to make him notice her breasts. "Are you married?" she asked.

[96]

"Oh, no," he said. "I'm the wrong age. I'm too old to be gelded and too young to be broken to the plow. Besides, I think it's not a good idea for a man to spend all of his time with the same woman; it causes him to sleep too much; you know what I mean?"

"It goes without saying." She put her hand on his chest and stroked him lightly, as if to reassure herself that he was still within her grasp, and at the same time to make promises. "Are you a cowboy?" she asked.

"No."

"A farmer?"

"No."

"A merchant?"

"No."

"I don't think you're a rich man's son."

Villa shook his head. "No, not a rich man's son, not anybody's son. My father died when I was a child and my mother doesn't speak to me. I'm not any of those things, but I have some money. So what do you think I am?"

"You're not one of those damned rurales?"

"No, they haven't offered me the five fingers. But if they do, you can be sure that I'll take the five bullets instead."

"Oh, what a courageous man!"

"Why do you make fun of me?"

"I make fun of everything. What else is there to do?"

She took him to an adobe room near the edge of the town. The dogs barked. She quieted them. A child lay sleeping. She kissed the child and smoothed its hair. Villa went outside to urinate. "You need to dig a new one," he said. "It stinks too much." She quieted him, reminding him of the sleeping child. They lay together on a mat; her clothes were hung carefully, his were thrown across a chair. She drew a blanket over them. There were fleas, the blanket was rough against their skin, the mat was coarse, the house smelled of wood smoke and pine oil, the child turned in its cradle and cried out but did not awaken.

Afterward, he did not want to leave. "I have money," he said.

"It's all right."

"You don't care about money?"

"There's always enough," she said. "When the cowboys are poor, the miners are rich. I don't have a bad season."

"Don't talk about it."

She laughed. "You want me to pretend I'm your wife? I'll grind corn and make complaints. Is that what you want? When you're inside me, I'll say my beads. Don't you think I know what a wife is? I had a mother, you know. She let herself get thin just to spite my father."

"I didn't ask for illusions."

[97]

"Then don't expect me to talk like a virgin."

He stayed with her until morning. She slept awhile, resting her head on his shoulder. He listened to her breathing and that of the child. Dogs barked in the distance. He heard the sounds of hunting birds. Fleas bit him, but he lay still, afraid to defend himself and so to awaken her. She stirred once, turning to him, pressing her breast against him, sighing, her breath floating over his chest. Awakening once, she invited him. He kissed her, he did not lie heavily upon her, for which she thanked him and said that he was not a boy but a man, that men are gentle.

"I like to dance," she said. "I like to dance."

"There is no music."

"I smell my own perfume when I dance. I am like a bird because I have skirts. My skirts catch the wind. I'm beautiful. I fly."

"I'll hire musicians," he said. "Tonight, we'll dance."

"No."

"I have money."

"The cowboys and the miners."

He went to the chair where his clothes lay. He found his money and counted out all but a few of the bills. Then he lay down on the mat again and gave her the money. She held it up, trying to make out the denominations of the bills by the faint light. "There are three thousand pesos," he said. "Stand up and count it if you want."

She put the money on his chest. "I don't understand," he said.

"I laugh at your money."

"Then keep it. You don't have to dance with me. Anyway, I'm leaving today for Zacatecas. I only wanted to be polite."

"You lie," she said.

"We both lie."

"But I also laugh."

He dug up the money he had buried, and before noon he was heading north toward Chihuahua. He entered the city in the early morning, joining that daily procession of servants and sharecroppers, the hunched and thin men who sat on rattling carts and spoke to the brown burros. They came with their children, who lay among the jute sacks, the nets of onions, curled in the young corn. The burros walked without rhythm on the cobblestone street, in the night-smelling air. The wagons clanked and thumped, the axles creaked in their wheels, there was an odor of earth and onions in the street.

On other streets the cattle were walking into the slaughterhouse, guided by the stinging ropes the cowboys swung, following the ox that returned; a row of them, a straggler there, and then the curly brown backs and white faces, like a jostling sea. The lumber wagons would come later, drawn by teams of mules, long and heavy with freshly cut pine, thudding, like a bass drum following on the manured streets. And finally, unexpectedly, the quick coaches would come in from the mines, hurrying, as if the white walls were spying, as if the light betrayed them.

He walked in the market, where the blues are drowned in yellows and the browns grow, where the air is rich with the smell of herbs, tanned leather, blood meat, and tortillas frying. He drank cold myrtle water. An old woman sold him a tamal and salted coffee. The shops were opening near the plaza, children were in the streets. He saw the banker and the dry goods seller, the sweepers in front of the cathedral, the shoeshine men with their unwaxed morning fingers, the mountain people emerging from their blankets, rising up out of doorways and the last shadowed corners. The clerks yawned, the sound of money began. He smelled cigarette smoke and dust. The trees were still thin, the light of the sun danced unmolested in the rich city.

A milk wagon passed him, and he waved to the driver as if he were a friend. He greeted the morning train from the north, saluting the engine and every hopper of coal and mysterious sealed boxcar that followed. He laughed to see Chihuahua born again of a morning: the city was a miracle; a man with money could buy anything, there was no end, the trains and wagons and carts came forever, the backs of the cattle clothed the earth. He paid a thousand pesos for a palomino stallion. Its name was Lucero, which he called the Morning Star.

This hotel was like the last; the men did not seem knowable, for they lay in rows of like beds, resting on like pillows, all of them waiting, hands folded behind their heads, dreaming like dreams, seeing the same smoke, so many views of the dead stream, the slow rise, the unlikely evanescence in the closed room. Their beards grew, they shaved; they stroked their mustaches into place. Each man hoarded something; for most it was no more than the next day's rent. Cowboys and miners—he thought again of Socorro, a girl dancing. He slept and ate meat in restaurants, keeping his back to the wall. He counted the days, watching the season go dry.

A man who carried a chicken under his arm, Isidro Yepa, came to stay in the hotel. He took the chicken, a great black rooster, with him everywhere, feeding it grain and gravel out of his hand, catching its filth in the same hand, cooing to it at evening, stroking the corners of its eyes to make it calm. In the afternoons, he took the bird to a quiet place outside the city and exercised it, putting its food on a flat board, forcing it to jump higher and higher to reach the food.

"Did you ever see such a bird?" he asked Villa.

"Never."

Isidro sat on the bench beside Villa, who had come to the plaza to watch girls. He was a tiny man, but he wore a tattered straw hat with a very tall pointed crown. The last joint was missing on the little finger of his right hand. Five small cloth bags were hung across his shoulders, each of them containing a different kind of grain. Sacks of gravel of various grades hung from his belt, bits of feathers were caught in the weave of his shirt and trousers, and he wore open shoes which showed his widespread toes and long, curving toenails. "People call me chicken," he said. "It's a nickname. Everyone thinks it's very funny. Here comes Isidro the Chicken, they say. They laugh because I live so close to my chickens. But on Sunday they'll stop laughing. This rooster, which I have named Victor, will earn a thousand pesos. You'll see, man; Victor is the most invincible chicken in Mexico. I trained him since he was a chick. His father comes from Spain and his mother is from the line of chickens in North America called George, which are the best hens. Victor is almost two years old, friend, and I never let him fuck even once; his balls are burning all the time. His only pleasure is killing. I fought him in Namiquipa, Bachiniva, and Sainapuchic. He killed twelve chickens in one hour in Sainapuchic, and one was a great chicken—Xolotl. Maybe you heard of him?"

Villa shook his head. "No, I'm from near Monterrey."

Isidro shrugged. "Well, you missed a great bird. Until the birth of Victor, Xolotl was the greatest fighting cock in Mexico."

"In this part of Mexico."

"As you say, but there were birds from Ciudad Juárez and even from Piedras Negras at Namiquipa, and they were afraid to bring them to Sainapuchic because of the reputation of Xolotl. Man, the owner of that bird was on his way to Chihuahua to win a fortune." He giggled. "But here I am in his place, because Victor is invincible." He massaged the rooster's legs while he spoke, moving his fingers with the grain of the feathers, smoothing them as he worked the muscles.

"You want to be partners?" Villa asked.

"Sure. Do you have ten thousand pesos?"

"Do you?"

"No, but I have Victor."

"I'll put in twenty-five hundred for half."

"Five thousand."

"Thirty-five hundred."

"Five thousand."

"Look, man," said Villa, "we can argue a long time, but all I have is three thousand five hundred."

They agreed that Isidro would take the first ten thousand pesos Victor won, and that they would split everything equally after that. Villa would bet for them, getting the best odds he could, considering Victor's reputation, while Isidro devoted himself to handling the bird. Afterward, it would be Villa's task to protect them from thieves and to pay off whichever officials demanded a bite of their winnings. Villa showed Isidro his Colt revolver and asked him to feel the weight of one of the cartridges. Isidro permitted Villa to feel the size and strength of Victor's thighs. They agreed that they would be rich.

They were always together after that. Villa helped in the training, holding up the flat piece of wood while Victor jumped and ate one peck at a time. He learned to stroke the corner of the bird's eye to calm it. Under Isidro's supervision he even massaged Victor's thighs. His main interest, however, was in protecting Isidro Yepa and his rooster from thieves and coyotes; he kept his hand on the butt of the revolver whether they were in the city or out in the exercise area in the hills, and at night he slept with the revolver under his pillow.

Isidro said it was bad luck to talk about their winnings, but he had enough faith in Victor to allow himself to speculate now and then on how he would live after he was rich. "I am going to buy two pairs of shoes and a chicken ranch," he said. "I'll buy the shoes on Monday morning and the chicken ranch on Monday afternoon."

"You won't fight Victor anymore? Oh, man, you could take this rooster to the Capital. Do you know how much money you could make? You could be richer than Terrazas."

"No, man; I don't want to take any chances with Victor. I'm going to buy him a hundred hens to fuck. He will sire a line of great fighting cocks, a line of kings. Thoroughbreds."

"With my share I'm going to buy a house right here in Chihuahua and open a business."

"What kind?"

"I haven't decided yet," said Villa. "There are many opportunities. Imagine this: a butcher shop that charged fair prices and was also a bank where poor people could come to borrow money to pay off the company stores. I could have a little restaurant in the front, and in the back I could sell ammunition and pots and pans and saddles and a few articles of clothing for men. I have it all worked out: I would sell so many things I wouldn't have to make too much profit on any one thing. And I wouldn't sell to the landlords or the foremen or the rurales, only to the poor people."

"A man tried to do that in Parrita, but the rurales came and shot his dog and burned down his store."

"I'm not afraid of the rurales."

They did not exercise Victor on Saturday; Isidro said he needed to store up his strength for the next day. This change in routine made them both nervous, but they tried not to show any change in attitude about the coming fight for fear the bird would be infected and lose his aggressiveness. They spent the day sitting in the sun and feeding Victor, who sat on Isidro's lap, filling his waiting hand with excretions. "It has a good smell," Isidro said, lifting a handful of chicken droppings to his nose. "I think he is going to have a very easy time tomorrow." He looked off into the distance, suddenly contemplative. "Ah, the chicken is a miraculous animal," he said. "No other animal is strong enough to eat its own shit."

In the late afternoon, Villa held Victor while Isidro worked on the spurs, cleaning them and honing the points with a piece of sharpening stone, inspecting the ties for weaknesses, drawing the heavy silken threads though his fingers again and again, looking for a rough spot that signified a break in the weave. After more than an hour of sharpening and inspection, he put the spurs back into the tiny leather case, satisfied that he had done his best for Victor's armament. "I spent fifty-three pesos for these," he said. "They are fitted exactly to Victor's spurs. They are just as if they were his own; the fit is so perfect that each little scale has its own place inside the band. They wouldn't slip, even if I didn't wrap them."

Neither of them was able to sleep that night. "Tomorrow at this time it will be a new life," said Isidro. "There can be no doubt about it, because Victor is the chosen of St. Francis of Assissi." He held up a small portrait of St. Francis. It had been altered to show a black rooster held in the bend of his arm.

Villa took out his blue hummingbird wrapped in red twine. "Touch this to his spurs," he said, passing the hummingbird over to Isidro. "St. Francis is a good saint for animals, but the Blue Hummingbird is one of the gods. And you know the gods are stronger than the saints—especially this one, because he is a wargod."

"The one from the South."

"Yes. You know about him?"

"Of course," said Isidro. "Why do you think Victor is such a great fighter? Look at his color. He's the color of the North, a god as strong as flint, an enemy. I ask St. Francis to protect him, but I ask the Enemy to help him kill."

"Very good reasoning, Yepa. I think I can sleep now."

Villa was awakened in the night by the sound of Isidro weeping. "What's wrong?" he asked. "Is Victor all right?"

"Yes, yes," he said, pointing to the bird, which slept beside him, its head buried in the feathers under its wing. "I was only thinking about tomorrow. Victor will not come away without suffering. I was thinking how the spurs catch under the skin and tear holes when they come out. You know, Pancho, sometimes they can catch a piece of the tendon and cripple. That

[*102*]

won't happen because Victor is a black bird, but he will suffer the spur galls, like any other fighter. He'll keep getting weaker because of losing so much blood. I give him little pieces of artichoke with his food to make his blood strong, and I'll give him corn pollen between fights to bring back his virility. But I can't help thinking of Victor as St. Sebastian—he gets all those wounds and I save him, and then there's going to be an end to the miracle and he'll be found in a sewer."

"Don't believe the lies the priests tell."

"Oh, Mother of God, don't blaspheme tonight!"

"Forgive me," Villa said. He turned over and tried to sleep, but it was too close to morning. He listened to the breathing of the other men and to the prayers and choked sobs of Isidro. The blue hummingbird was under his pillow. How strange, he thought, that the God of War should stand in the air to sip nectar, making himself vulnerable to the meanest hunter. He prayed to the Blue Hummingbird and to the Enemy for the life of Victor.

At dawn they took the rooster out to crow and to exercise its wings. Isidro gave it a few grains of corn pollen and a sip of water. Then they went to the pit to pay their entrance fee and to see what other birds were brought in to fight. Isidro studied each of the other roosters and commented on it to Villa: "That one is crossed with a pheasant; they're good jumpers, but the feet move the wrong way. That one's too heavy in the breast. A red; I never saw a red that could fight. There's a Dominique, but it's too small."

The judge explained to Isidro and to each man who paid an entrance fee for his bird that it would not be a fight to the finish: a man could save a badly wounded bird, and a bird that raised its hackles and showed white feathers was declared a loser and eliminated from the tournament. Only to the elegant landlords who came smoking cigars and wearing silver-trimmed charro suits did he speak differently. "The usual rules, sir," was all he said. And the landlords smiled, for their birds had been fed bits of raw meat and chopped egg from the time they were a few months old, and they had been massaged with mixtures of ammonia instead of urine to make their skin tough.

Villa gestured toward a group of men in charro suits. "How can you expect to defeat them?" he asked Isidro.

"Remember, friend, the men don't fight. In the pits, it's only the roosters."

The building around the pit was filled before ten o'clock. The raised benches were crowded, the electric lights above the ring were turned on, and the judge took his place in the high chair beside the wooden fence. There were no windows in the wooden building, and the air thickened with cigarette and cigar smoke, giving the room the ambiance of night. Twenty fighting cocks were entered in the tournament: a thousand pesos to the

[*103*]

winner; the rules of the judge were the final rules; the rurales who stood around the ring or walked through the crowd were the authority of the judge.

A slow and bloody fight began the day. Neither of the birds was able to rise; they tore each other down from the legs and breasts, the wounding of the legs slowing the spurs, drawing out the end. The birds fell and fluttered, met and fell, throwing blood and feathers, breast to breast in a dying stammer. There was no winner until the larger of the birds was suddenly dead, fallen into the calm posture of a nesting hen, but for its head, which lay in the dirt. There were whistles at the end, the few bettors applauded, the doors were opened to clear the air with day, and the next birds were brought into the ring.

Victor was in the eighth pair, pitted against a red cock with a poorly trimmed comb. Isidro whispered to Villa that there was nothing to worry about: Victor would go for the comb, the fight would be over in two minutes. "Bet," he said. "Take any odds."

Villa held up his money, moving into the crowd, making the circle, calling to the touts: "On the black, on the black." He gave odds and took odds; he did not argue. The touts took his money with smiles, showing their teeth. The brokers brought him to the landlords, who asked no odds and gave none, passing their money to the brokers, diffident bettors, more interested in their cigars or in the florid face of the amusing young man who pushed through the crowd waving his fan of pesos.

The fight started too soon for Villa; he had bet only seven hundred pesos when the quiet of the crowd drew him down toward the ring to watch the pitting of the birds. Isidro and the trainer of the red cock carried their birds into the smoked yellow light, holding the birds before them, mindful of the spurs. They stood in the center, two brown duelists dressed in shabby white, colored by hanging pouches and decorated sashes. Bending forward, they thrust the birds at each other, felt the rage, stepped back, withdrawing the cocks, shuffled once across the packed dirt, and cast the birds into the fight. With a rush of wings the cocks found their balance, closed, pecked, and went up together. Victor rose as if he could fly. At the level of the other bird's head Victor's feet whirred. A spur caught the red's comb and tore it open. In the instant of suspension at the height of the leap the spur caught the red's eye and then the neck. They separated, settling. The red turned and staggered, flapping its wings without effect, spinning on the vision of the remaining eye. Victor waited until the red cock fell, then he climbed onto the fallen bird and crowed once, holding the last note until it put the room into silence.

At the sign from the judge, Isidro leaped into the ring and gathered

Victor to him, holding the bird to his chest, stroking the corner of his eye, wiping the blood from his breast, unaware of the spurs, gladly laughing, walking on bird's legs, strutting. Villa collected his bets from the touts and brokers and went outside to meet Isidro.

"We made nine hundred," Villa said.

Isidro untied the spurs and wiped them with a rag, scraping the dried blood and skin with his thumbnail. "Bet more," he said. "Don't watch the fight, man; keep betting. And don't worry about the odds. Give two to one, three to one. You can see now that I didn't lie to you—Victor is invincible."

"Yes, invincible, but I don't think he's going to make a hundred thousand pesos for us, not today."

"Bet with the landlords. Screw them, that's the only way to do it. If some fucking landlord has his bird in there with Victor, he'll give you three to one, four to one, and for as much money as you want."

"There's no chance," Villa said. "He only fights four more times."

Isidro put the spurs into the leather case and took a bit of corn pollen out of a sack to feed to Victor. "You don't understand numbers, man. You take this four thousand and get two to one. That's twelve. Bet twelve even and you have twenty-four. Bet even again and you have forty-eight. On the last fight you bet even and you have ninety-six thousand pesos, plus you win the thousand-peso prize. That's ninety-seven. Pretty close to a hundred thousand, eh?"

"Fantastic."

"That's doubling, man. If you don't understand doubling, you can't make nothing in this world."

The second fight did not go so well for Victor. He was pitted against a jumper, a rooster that had been crossed with a pheasant, and he could not get enough height advantage to avoid the spurs. In the first flurry he was cut twice in the breast. The galls were not deep; Isidro had been right about the pheasant blood being good for elevation but not for galling—the spurs of the jumper scratched, they did not tear. In the second flurry Victor opened a deep wound in the other bird's upper breast close to its neck. There were no wounds in the next two flurries, but the advantage was shifting to Victor, for the deep wound in the jumper's chest was weakening it, causing it to lose elevation. The jumper staggered, its head rolled. Victor rose over it, cutting the head and neck, opening a second wound in the breast. The betting stopped. Everyone looked to the man in the silver-trimmed suit who had offered three-to-one and four-to-one odds on his jumper. He was expected to withdraw the bird. The man held a thin cigar. The ash grew. He spoke softly and continuously to the man who had trained his cock, discussing the fight, the qualities of the breed they had developed. There was a sapphire ring on the landlord's right hand. When the jumper lost control and staggered into the fence, he paused to watch. At the death of the bird he resumed the conversation.

Villa collected the money, sixteen thousand pesos, the landlord's offer of four-to-one odds. He rushed outside to tell Isidro: "We'll have a hundred and twenty-nine thousand, man. You're right about doubling, but four times is better. Imagine, if I could just get three to one on the next fight."

"Not now," Isidro said. "I've got to stop this bleeding." He had tied Victor to a stake, washed him, and was now preparing to dress the wounds. He cracked an egg, cupped the yolk out, threw it away, and mixed a powder of dried geranium root and maguey sap with the egg white in one half of the shell, stirring it with his finger until it became a thick brown paste. He lifted Victor's feathers with one hand and applied the paste to the wounds with two fingers of the other hand. The bleeding stopped immediately.

"Was it a bad wound?"

Isidro made a sour face. "No wound is good."

Victor won the third fight without taking serious wounds. The fourth fight was very quick: the other bird showed white feathers after the first flurry, and refused to lower its hackles although its trainer tried three times to pit it against Victor. The money doubled, but no more. At the end of the fourth fight, Villa had sixty-four thousand pesos.

The last bird to be pitted against Victor was a jumper, raised by the same man who had owned the other jumper, but the crossbreeding had been more successful in this bird: it had the elevation of a pheasant and the nasty feet of a Claiborne. In four fights it had taken only one serious wound, a long gash under one wing. A paste brought from Cuba had been used to close the wound, and it had worked well; the jumper appeared to be in near-perfect condition. Only Isidro claimed to be able to see any damage: "The cock is off balance," he said. "When he jumps, he'll favor one side; the points of the spurs will be turned. You'll see."

While they waited for the judge to call them in for the last fight, a broker came outside to talk to them. "Mr. Arrieto sends his compliments," he said. "He wishes me to tell you that he admires your ability to breed and train gamecocks. But he believes his bird is the best. He would like to bet with you."

"Does he offer odds?" Isidro asked.

"Four to one."

"Does he know that we have sixty-four thousand pesos?" Villa asked.

The broker smiled politely. "Yes, we have watched your betting. I am authorized to offer two hundred and fifty-six thousand pesos against your sixty-four thousand."

"Done," said Villa.

"Done."

Isidro adjusted the spurs, winding and tying the left spur again, rubbing clean a bloodied spot. It was almost evening, cooler, reddening; there was smoke on the wind. "We'll be rich," said Villa.

"Maybe," Isidro said. He gave Victor a sip of water from a small tin cup, and let him peck at the bits of corn pollen that were left. "Maybe."

"You said Victor was invincible."

"So are the landlords."

"That's why you need me, Yepa. With this Colt, I am also invincible." Villa patted the revolver. "It doesn't know the difference between a landlord and a skinhead from Sonora. Keep your confidence, man."

"It's a quarter of a million pesos, Panchito. I'm older than you, I know them better. They hang a man for stealing an ear of corn."

"You think Arrieto won't pay off?"

Isidro shrugged. "How should I know? I'm just a poor chicken farmer."

"You need to have faith, man."

It was time to bring the birds inside. Isidro threw his shoulders back and forced himself to smile. "Here comes the invincible Victor," he announced, "the chosen of the Enemy, the wings of the North." He went proudly into the wooden building, followed by Francisco Villa. The jumper was already there, standing in the center of the ring, a dark bird with a green tail, gathering in the light. The trainer squatted behind him, holding the jumper with the touch of his fingers.

Some bettors tried to touch their money to Victor's feathers as Isidro carried him into the ring. "Put it to him," they said. "Kill him," they said. "Don't let us down." Soft ten-peso notes stroked his feathers, coins were pressed against him. Victor did not struggle. The hooded eyes watched, the head did not move. Only Isidro felt the tremors.

Villa watched the ritual pitting of the birds, but he thought only about the money. After giving the first ten thousand pesos to Isidro, but adding on his investment of thirty-five hundred and splitting the thousand-peso prize, he would have a hundred and twenty-seven thousand five hundred pesos. "A fortune," he said aloud, "a great fortune." He considered marriage: the garden of a house, the smell of roses, the sound of bees in late morning, crystal and silver, cool tiles, a child with bare feet and braided hair, plush and leather, electricity, wasted food on white plates, evening through a window.

In the yellow light they began, in the smell of smoke and earlier blood, circling in the light brown circle, inside the red board circle, inside the circle of brown faces shouting, black and dark, decorated in red, decorated in red and green, on yellow feet, wielding steel claws, leaping to each other, frantic, running in the air. Blood from the jumper, and again, blood from

[*107*]

the jumper. The brown faces shouted, the touts and the brokers shouted. Across the ring, in half-light, shining silver on black, Mr. Arrieto smoked his thin cigar, and did not shout, and did not speak; he watched with steady eyes; once, he smiled, ironically recording the jeering of his name.

The jumper veered, leaning in the air, righting itself with flapping, cut, cut again. The birds flurried, feathers and bloodied galls rising. Mr. Arrieto removed his pistol from its holster, aimed carefully, waited on his moment, and fired. Victor was a soup struck by a stone, exploding. The brown faces fell silent. The shadows beyond the circle of light did not move. The smoke hung in dead streams, paling. The jumper walked over to the place where Victor had been thrown, pecked once at the pile of bloody feathers, and walked on, hopping slightly, favoring the wounded leg, bleeding, leaving dark spatters on the hard ground.

The judge pointed to the jumper. There was a sigh, the beginning of whispers. A man in gray stood at Villa's left side, a man in gray stood at his right. The broker was before him, holding out his hand. "You owe me two hundred and fifty-six thousand pesos," Villa said.

"Don't be a fool: the jumper is walking around and your cock is lying there like a stew."

The man in gray reached into Villa's pocket and took his money.

"You took two hundred too much," Villa said.

The man bowed his head, mocking. "For my trouble," he said. Villa tried to smile.

In a moment, or so it seemed, the wooden building was empty but for Villa and Isidro, who met in the ring where Victor lay. "Screwed," Villa said.

"Murdered."

"They took everything."

"I have seven pesos. You can have them."

"It's not worth the trouble," Villa said.

Isidro knelt next to the bird. "We've got to bury him," he said, looking for an unbloodied part by which to pick up the bird. "I can't do it," he said, looking up at Villa. "Will you, please?"

The lights went out. Villa tried to pick up the bird in the darkness, but his hands encountered only drying blood and torn intestine. "I can't," he said.

"I'll try."

Villa heard Isidro shudder. "You can't either," he said.

"No."

They went outside and cleaned their hands with dust. "What now?" Villa asked.

"I'm going home. And you?"

stores. It was a dusty army, dressed in uniforms that hung on the men's shoulders or pulled across their bellies. They dragged their feet in the dust. An officer rode behind them, directing them by gesturing with his sword, rousting them out of the shade.

"Do you still think we should have taken the horse?" Parra asked.

"Are you afraid of such an army?"

"A snake crawls in the dust too, but if it bites you, goodbye."

They argued back and forth, passing time, lazy in the shaded room of the café. Two soldiers entered and asked for water. The waitress ignored them. The soldiers stank of being too long in the saddle; their rifles were grimy with dust that had settled onto the oiled surfaces. The fly was open on one soldier's trousers; his pubic hair showed in the gap between the pieces of cloth. The soldiers asked again for water, and again the waitress ignored them. The soldiers insulted her, speaking the words softly so that she could not hear.

Parra leaned across the table and put his hand on Villa's arm. "Panchito," he said, "I feel drunk. It must be the powders. Help me to go home."

"You are drunk, man. Home is in the mountains."

"No. I lied to you. I didn't lose the money. I bought a house in Durango. There's a woman in the house, a very educated woman—she reads and writes. She'll know how to take care of me. Get me there, Panchito; I'm no good to you this way."

"The Root of Gold is better for you."

Parra shook his head. "I don't understand it anymore. I still knew enough not to let you take the fucking criollo's horse, but the root doesn't help me in the big things now."

"Maybe you shouldn't have killed him?"

"I only followed the rules."

"Well, okay, man," Villa said loudly, suddenly laughing. "Let's go to Durango."

They went as far as The Willows, arriving there after dark. There were soldiers in the street, and two thin recruits lay asleep in the hay of the livery stable, their rifles beside them, their hard-crowned hats covering their faces. The owner of the stable awakened them when he led the horses into the stalls. They compared the brands to the marks on their white papers and went back to sleep. The owner made excuses to his customers for the inspection: "There was a shooting at the San Romualdo ranch. Two bandits ambushed the foreman, and they think one of them was Ignacio Parra."

"Aiy, so many killings," Villa said. "It's dangerous to ride in this country, worse even than in Guanajuato where we come from."

"Oh, they didn't kill him," the stable owner said. "That's why the army is out; there's someone now who can tell them what Parra looks like. He's very young, you know, with a big mustache and chino hair. The wounded man says Parra has a jaw like brick. But who knows? For years they have been looking for an older man, thin, very handsome, but Indian in his coloring." He leaned close to them and whispered, "For my part, I hope they never catch him. Better bandits than this fucking army of worms and thieves."

"It's clear that you were never robbed," Villa said. "Once you've been robbed, it's a different story."

The stable owner gave them advice on where to eat and sleep in The Willows, and they paid him in advance for the keep of their horses. Crossing the plaza they fell to laughing over the confusion of identities. "But we have to go back," Parra said.

"No."

"The work is not complete."

Over bowls of atole eaten in a restaurant without a name or even a sign, except for the odors of cooking that came from the narrow entrance, they continued the discussion: Parra argued that vengeance was not done until the man was dead.

"What difference does it make if he lives or dies? Maybe it's better if he lives. He can tell others that there is a rule of vengeance."

"We failed."

"I won't go back, Nacho; they'll be looking for us."

Parra gave a soft laugh; the jessamine powder was beginning to work again. "You're not telling the truth about the rules; you're only lying because you're afraid."

"It takes a brave man to say that to Pancho Villa."

"Ignacio Parra is a brave man."

Villa broke the tension with laughter. He reached across the table and slapped Parra on the shoulder. "Whatever you say is okay with me. Do you think I'm crazy enough to fight with a man who has a jaw like a brick?"

In the morning they set out for Durango. Parra lolled in the saddle, slipping to the side, catching himself just before he fell, shaking his head furiously to rid himself of the dulling of the jessamine powder. He sipped water constantly, and every hour he dismounted to urinate. He complained of nausea; he said the sun made him feverish. "Panchito," he said, "if they should find us now, if they should find us on this road, Panchito, it would be worse than if you were alone."

"Never mind," Villa said, waving away Parra's fears. "I'm only worried about your stomach."

"It's better now. There's not so much black in my shit."

"Then it's worth the trouble."

[*112*]

Parra took a long drink from his canteen. "Panchito," he said, "I never found my mother. I don't want to die before I see my mother."

Eulalia lived in the little house in Durango. She ate berries and sang Spanish songs and was fragrant, like the pale flowers in the garden of the house. Ignacio said her name as if she were a honeyed delicacy, a morsel eaten, resounding on his palate: *Eulalia, Eulalia.* She sewed flowers on linen cloth, she waltzed to the music of lights, she wore silk: *Eh-oo-la-liya.* He kissed her name. He said he was in love, and that it was the first and only time of his life.

She wrapped him in her arms and in the rustlings of her silks. "How thin you are! How thin! My poor man. Ignacio, Ignacio. Oh, God, Ignacio." The face of the younger man seen over the shoulder of her lover said that he had tried, that he too cared for the life of Ignacio Parra. She smiled at the young man. Her teeth were straight, her hair shone, her eyes were darkened with interrupted sleep.

Parra slept, and ate unseasoned atole. He took the jessamine powders and drank yarrow tea. Eulalia cooked saffron rice and suckling pig; she mixed fruit into red wine. "The best fish are from the sea," she told Villa. "They're covered with hard shells and the meat inside is sweeter than anything you have ever tasted. The best of it is like heavenly chicken. This fish must be eaten within moments after its death or the subtleties of the flavor fade and the fish becomes ordinary."

"It's like that with snake meat," Villa said.

Eulalia shuddered. Her eyes became rapid. Villa apologized.

He said that he wished his hair were different. She touched scents imported from France to the pulse of her wrist and presented them to him as other worlds. He showed her his Colt revolver and asked her to feel the weight of a single shell. She cut flowers to put beside Ignacio's bed. Villa fed him atole from a brown bowl.

In the evenings, after dinner at the most Spanish hour, they sat in the main room of the house with the doors opened onto the night garden, and she told him poems, stories of walls of glass, jeweled chairs, courtly dancing, French kings, houses filled with books, and music played on great pianos. While Parra slept. And sometimes visitors came to sit with them: her sister, Serafina; Simón Ochoa, a cousin; Marta Paniagua, a woman with pale brown hair and gray eyes. They spoke of operas, carriages, the style of France, and the inability of the poor ever to be anything but the poor. Eulalia lamented her lack of a servant. Ochoa talked of foreign credits and the stability of the peso. Marta Paniagua praised green lands and damned the brown desert in which they lived. "There are no lawns in Durango," she said.

[*113*]

"Yes," said Serafina, "it is barbaric to be always living with sand and cactus and the dust blowing every evening so that nothing ever feels clean."

Parra slept. Villa sat the evenings through, not speaking, watching the sighs of the women, studying their long and opulent necks, the careful languor of hands washed in glycerine and rose water. He looked at their color in the varying lights of spring evenings, finding them pale, lacking reds, made of stale cream and shaded rooms. He listened to their talk and thought it must be dreaming, for they sat in such a tiny house in the shadow of the mountain of iron and let him buy their food and wine with money taken from the body of the foreman of the San Romualdo.

When they had gone, leaving behind the smell of Ochoa's cigars and the warmed perfume of the women, he watched Eulalia gathering the cups and glasses, darting at first, rattling spoons and painted china, wifely with her hands full, slowing in the later crossings of the room, passing before him and passing again, whispering to him with the casual touch of her dress, humming in her throat, a lock of hair falling out of capture, a bead of moisture forming on her upper lip or shining at her temple; then he went to the little room where Parra slept and he unrolled a mat on the floor and slept there beside his friend.

In time, Ignacio slept less; his body learned the drug, and he passed the mornings sitting up in bed, talking with Villa or listening to the dreamy woes of Eulalia. His eyes opened and were steady. He ate meat. The days went by easily, full of laughter and expectation. Villa tended to the horses in the early morning, slept away the heat of the afternoon, and sat through evenings of conversation in which no one ever addressed a remark to him. Parra kept a pistol under his pillow and a rifle at his bedside; Villa wore the Colt. In the small barn behind the house the saddlebags were loaded with cornmeal and salt, there was fresh water every morning in the canteens, and the blankets were rolled and tied. Eulalia did not question what she knew; she shopped for food in the mornings and for brilliantine and silk in the afternoons. "All money is the same," she said. "And we have enough for a servant."

After two weeks, Parra moved out of the small room and went to sleep with Eulalia. Villa rolled up the mat for the last time, moving to the vacated bed. The evenings became more lively with Parra there; he spoke his disagreements: "The French are good for nothing but making perfume. The rurales are worse bandits than the bandits, and Mr. President Porfirio Díaz is the worst of all the rurales. The rich will never be as good as the poor because they get rich by their lack of generosity. Landlords and pigs are the only beasts that will eat the flesh of their own kind. Political chief is just another name for usurer. This is an Indian country and it should be run by Indians, like Juárez."

Ochoa replied, "Let us be realistic, let us be scientific. If we followed your ideas, sir, the nation would be bankrupt. There would be no progress, no railroads, no foreign investment, our money would be useless."

"What good is money to people who don't have any?"

"The Indians, as a race, are destined to be poor. Juárez was an exception. And even Juárez, he was so frail his heart gave out. It's true of almost the entire race. Look at their women. Compare an Indian woman of thirty with a woman of white blood. You must be able to see; you have eyes. The race is physically and mentally inferior."

"My friend Francisco and I belong to that race, sir. Do you think we're inferior?"

Ochoa laughed until his oiled flat hair flapped. "Come, come, comecomecomecome. I don't see Indians in this room. I don't see any barefoot peasants eating with their hands. Your friend is so meticulous he won't eat with anything but his own utensils. For which, by the way, I commend him. And you, don't you have a mirror? Look at your features, the narrowness of your nose, the length of your face; you're an elegant man. And your friend—why, his hair is lighter than mine. Why do you call yourself Indians? And why do you both carry those enormous pistols wherever you go?"

"To protect ourselves from the likes of you."

Ochoa hooked his fingers in the pockets of his vest and expanded himself backward with laughter. "Me? Simón Ochoa? I've never used firearms in my entire life."

"I know your kind," Parra said. "You always carry one of those two-shot pistols in your sleeve. You shoot people in the back."

Then Serafina or Eulalia begged them to stop, to behave like civilized men; and Marta pretended she was near swooning, waving her handkerchief rapidly at her bosom until Simón offered to bring her a sip of brandy. Everyone apologized, but the evening terminated anyway; watches were consulted, plans for a busy morning were announced, the women claimed fatigue, speaking of the heat. They agreed to convene again.

Villa wanted to congratulate Ignacio, to laugh with him at Ochoa's belly and the softness of his hands; but Parra was gone, hurrying away with Eulalia on his arm, leaving Villa to listen to the other laughter. Later he heard their whispers, like hissing, through the wall. In the following quiet, he thought there were sighs, little screams of pleasure, imaginable rhythms. The smell of her was in the house, the oiled night was pumped through her. He asked for Serafina, Marta, the girl in Parral whose child slept. He asked for a dog to bark and for the horses to bang against the walls of the barn and for the nightbirds to roar, anything, until he heard the whispers again and he was able to sleep.

After another week they began to talk of earning more money, thinking perhaps they might open a store. Villa said he was the best of salesmen; Parra thought he would be able to charm the women customers; Eulalia said she would advise them in matters of style. They considered locations, whether it was necessary to face the plaza anymore; the town seemed to be growing to the east—that was where the future lay. But would a wise merchant put himself in the middle of so many stores? Maybe the opportunity was better to the south, near the new park. They knew only that they did not want to be in the area to the southeast of the plaza: "There's so much filth in the streets there," Eulalia said. "It makes me sick to walk in that neighborhood."

There were problems to be solved: whether to sell meat, how to keep it fresh. Was it better to have two stores, one for clothing and one for food? Should men's and women's clothing be sold in the same store? Did the saddlery belong with the food or the clothing, or should there be a third store if everything was not in one store? Days passed in imagining the business, and once they got so far as to discuss when they would be able to go safely into the streets again and whether they should continue to call themselves Ignacio Ramirez and Francisco Carbajal or return to their own names. They were in no hurry; it was the beginning of summer, hot and often raining; it would be better to start a business in autumn. They were satisfied; they could wait. Villa asked Eulalia if she thought Marta would be willing to stay with him, and she said, "Ask her. There's no danger in asking—you're the one who wears the pistol." Marta stayed that night, and the next morning she brought her clothes.

The wardrobe was filled. A chest was bought, and that too was filled, and its top was covered with jars and bottles of scents, emollients, night remedies and day remedies, combs, two sewing boxes, and a basket of unpolished silver jewelry. A square mirror was hung above the chest, and a long mirror was hung behind the door. Curtains were hung on the window, taken down when the room was painted, and hung again. Beside the bed she placed a night table to hold a blackening silver hand mirror, a lamp, a tiny silver chest filled with women's powders, and a Bible. Another table was brought from the front room to hold a metal washbasin, a pitcher, soap, towels, and washcloths. She asked for a clock and a trunk for her winter clothes. Villa laughed. "There is no room in this room," he said.

"Then we should have a larger room. Why do we have such a small room? We need more air, Francisco; this is summer. We should have a room with two windows so that we can get the breeze."

The bed was too narrow. "We're always damp," she said. "It makes our skin stick together. When you move in your sleep, it's like pulling hair." He said he liked it that way. She shook her head: "You are not a subtle man.

[*116*]

There are differences. By the differences things are increased: the hot next to the cool, the damp next to the dry. Would you like every meal to taste the same?"

"One meal is more delicious than any other," he said, reaching for the buttons of her dress, growling and laughing.

"Pig," she shouted, also laughing. "Savage, animal," squirming, feigning an attempt to escape.

He clamped his hand on her arm, holding her to a stop. The joke went out. Villa eased her down onto the bed, bending her by the manipulation of her arm. She sat, sullen, knowing it was not play. "If I'm such a pig," he asked, "why do you go with me?"

"Maybe it's a mistake."

"Why did you make the mistake? What do you want?"

"Did you ever think that I might have loved you?"

"You're not my wife."

"No."

"You called me a savage, an animal."

"Yes."

"Then you must be a whore."

"If you think so."

He released her arm and turned his back to her. "Do you know that I could kill you? I'm not afraid; it wouldn't be the first time."

"I'm sorry," she said. "I didn't know. I didn't know you. Sometimes a woman goes with a man for reasons she doesn't understand; she just goes. It's not scientific; Simón would never approve; I don't care. You asked me to stay with you; I came to stay with you. I didn't think you would hurt me. Now you call me a whore. I'm sorry."

He walked over to the window and looked out at the unpainted barn, the bare brown sand, the drying sand, the prickly pear on which the fruit had begun to grow, the high horizon. There were summer clouds holding light rain; the sunlight was colorless, stinging. "We could be married," he said. "If we had some land or the store was open. But without a store, without land, what could we do? If a man is married, he must have something to do. A cowboy can't be married. I don't know if I'm meant to be married; I was born on a bad day for luck and named on a bad day for marriage. There's something wrong with my nose; I snore all the time, even when I'm not sleeping. I don't know what to do. Why should a woman like you go with a man like me?"

She made a choking sound. He turned to her and saw that she was crying. "Please," he said. "Marta." He stroked her hair, and then he sat beside her and they wept together in the tiny room amid the wood and silk and silver things that she had brought to marry them.

[*117*]

There were days of planning, evenings in the sitting room, conversations, the first probes of intimacy, sleeping afternoons. They patched walls and arranged the garden, they lavished hours on bland rice and shellfish. Marta and Eulalia shopped and giggled in the kitchen, complained of the work, and won agreement from Villa and Parra that they would soon hire a maid. Simón raised questions about their ease, their method of raising money to open a store, and Ignacio parried with absurdities: his royal blood, his profits as a chief of the rurales, his inheritance, Villa's luck at gambling. It was the game of Mr. Carbajal and Mr. Ramirez, the gentlemen of means who could not read and never left the house: Mr. Carbajal who never was seen without his Colt revolver and Mr. Ramirez who never was seen without his Smith and Wesson revolver.

Parra gained weight; the bleeding stopped and the pain abated. To regain his strength he worked with Villa in the small barn, brushing the horses, cleaning the stalls, and spreading straw. It was only there in the barn that they spoke to each other outside the rules of the game they lived. And it was in the barn that they counted their money, taking down the dwindling bundle from the place under the roof beam where Parra had hidden it after he bought the house. At each counting they laughed. "Well, Mr. Carbajal," said Parra, taking hundred-peso bills from the packet, "now we have a little less than six thousand pesos to open three stores."

"What'll we do when it's gone?" Villa asked.

"We'll have to go on a business trip. I've been thinking for a long time about driving some cattle to the border and selling to the gringos. There's also a copper mine in Chihuahua that I've been watching. And Mr. Carbajal, I have not been to a bank since I was a boy."

"Nacho, I want to open a store."

"You'll be dead in a week. That son of a whore from the San Romualdo will walk into the store to buy a handkerchief and ten minutes later the rurales will be saying that you were caught in the act and killed on the spot."

"And if we stay here in the house?"

"Maybe one day you'll open the door and there will be a hundred soldiers outside."

Villa lay beside Marta, naked and sticky in the crowded bed. "My name is not Carbajal," he said, "and I am not a merchant or a gambler. And no one calls me Francisco. It's the same with Ignacio; he's not Mister Ramirez the gentleman. You're living in this house with two criminals, Pancho Villa and Ignacio Parra. We rob and kill. I've been in jail. Eulalia knows and she doesn't care. And you?"

"I knew."

"Everything?"

[*118*]

"Not your names."

"You knew about the foreman from the San Romualdo?"

"No. I saw the pistols. I saw that you were afraid to leave the house. If you were not bandits, why would you live so? Everyone suspects, everyone knew from the beginning. Simón says that it is only a matter of time before Flores finds you. And that's true, because Flores is not like the rurales or the army—he's a policeman, a hunter. Simón says that Flores keeps English hunting dogs to learn from them. Everyone knows that Flores has even taught himself to track by his sense of smell, like one of the dogs; that's why no one can ever escape him."

"Nonsense. He spreads those lies to frighten children."

"Simón swears it is true."

"Does Simón know our names?"

She thought for a moment. "No. If Simón knew there was a reward, the money would already be in his pocket."

"But he knows something."

She nodded. Villa looked away from her, out the window, seeing that it was the start of morning. They were often awake too early: she responded to his loud breathing, he awakened whenever he encountered her in the movements of his sleep, it was the season of heavy air, the bed was too narrow, they heard rain. "I want you to marry me," he said.

Marta stepped over him to the edge of the bed and stood slowly, with yawns and the stretching of her child's arms. She stood in the center of the cluttered room, turning, afraid to pace in the faint light. Her nightclothes were wrinkled, her hair curled with dampness; she fanned herself with a small white handkerchief. He waited.

"Now?" she asked.

"I don't think the priests get up so early in the hot weather."

"Francisco Villa," she said.

"At your service."

"Is that really your name?"

"Yes."

"How would we live?"

"Are you such a practical woman? How does anyone live in this time? Be realistic, be scientific, miss. We'll live as best we can. If we don't have bread, we won't eat radishes to give us an appetite; we won't be fools. Maybe we'll open a store; not here, but in Chihuahua or Torreón or Parral or somewhere in Sonora or Coahuila. And if we can't open a store, we'll have a farm or a ranch. I'll be a mule driver; I'll work in a mine or a factory. You don't have to worry yourself, Marta; I'll take care of us."

"And the day the rurales come?"

"Then you'll be a widow. What difference does it make? Sooner or later

[119]

every woman is a widow. My father wasn't a bandit; he left a poor widow. Bandits don't leave such poor widows; that's the only difference."

"And the children of bandits?"

"They eat."

She sat on the bed and put her head in her hands. He touched her back, he curled her hair in his fingers. "Marta," he said, "I want to marry you." She cried softly, the sounds no louder than breathing, but he saw the shaking of her back and the forward fall of her shoulders. He lay with his arms folded behind his head, watching the growing light, waiting for the first crowing. "The sun is moving again," he said. "The jaguar is gone for another day."

"I hate it when you talk like an Indian."

"It's not realistic, not scientific. This is not France, Marta. If Simón's Mr. Comte lived in Mexico, maybe he would think like an Indian instead of a Frenchman. Who knows? Maybe he wouldn't even hate our race."

"Not *our* race, Francisco. Look at your hair, look at the color of your skin."

"What do you think I am? One of those white Chinamen? Nacho is right; we're all sons of the Violated Mother. That's who you marry if you marry me."

She stood up and began her turning again. "You're so young, Francisco; why do you want to get married? I sleep in your bed now. I cook your food. Does the rooster have to marry the hen? I don't understand you, Francisco Villa; I don't know what you want."

"Peace. A happy house. Corn. Beans. Goats for cheese. A good strong table. Firewood. Children. To sleep without a pistol under my pillow. To go to the door without a pistol in my hand. A sweetwater well. School for my sons. One good horse. I don't want to be alone. A wife is someone to trust. What can a man make without a wife? He can't stop; there is no rest for unmarried men."

"And love?" she asked.

"Do you think there can be love unless there is marriage?"

She lay down beside him. They were cooler. After the long dampness her skin felt powdered, smooth. "Give me time," she said.

He sat up and looked out at the morning. "There is not much time," he said. "When I was a boy I used to add things up: every morning I would say that it was one day more, and now I wake up in the morning and think that it is one day less."

Afterward, in functions of the body, in the routine of the day, they seemed to forget. He tended the horses, she cooked, they ate, they slept for all the afternoon, and evening came with guests and dinner and the drawing room coffee, the cigar smoke, the politeness; and sleep again, and morning,

[*120*]

and the day following, functions and routines, words and meals, the spending of the days of summer. While the money dwindled, while the secret stretched its time and space, the two men waited, as if they were attending a dance, watching the softening of the lace and the tiring of the musicians in the late evening.

"We are kept in this house like prisoners," Eulalia said. "Why should we be forced to live like prisoners? We haven't committed a crime."

"You live on stolen money," Parra answered.

Marta looked to Villa. "Will we always live like this?"

He had no answer. They were in the garden, among the roses that were the center of the house. It was early evening, when the scent is heavy and the bees have gone to their hives. He broke off a rose, stripped away the thorns with his fingernail, and presented the flower to her. "Should I make promises?" he asked. "Should I lie to you?"

"Civilized men know how to use lies to make a woman comfortable," Eulalia said.

Villa answered softly, "I am an Indian."

"That again!"

He smiled, lowering his head and looking upward in humility, imitating the style of the mountain people. Only Parra laughed.

They arrived at compromises: Marta and Eulalia went more often to the markets and stores, buying pale summer dresses and rolls of ribbon. Serafina was allowed to bring her fiancé to dinner, and Villa and Parra were polite to him, listening with feigned interest as he told of the events of an apprentice cook's life and the dreams of a small restaurant of his own that sustained him through the washing of miserable pots and infinite piles of dishes. They agreed with him that a man of his talents, a prospective pastry chef and maker of French delicacies, should not be made to humble himself by stirring pots of atole and frying beans. They joined him in lamentations over the injustices of this world, but they did not ask him to cook. Marta invited her cousin Alma, a dark round pillar of a woman, to visit with them and to bring her husband, Abelardo, who was a foreman in a tallow-processing plant. Alma spoke in loud euphemisms of the ailments of women and her husband always had a faint odor of rejected meat, but Parra flattered the woman and Villa spoke intently with Abelardo of the price of mildly putrescent animal matter. They found it less easy to be comfortable with Simón's brother, a bank teller who mixed long French phrases into his conversation. Parra frequently baited him by asking for translations of the French phrases; and when the bank teller clapped his hands together and said, "Goodness, doesn't everyone know that?" Parra always answered that he didn't know, for he was only a poor Indian from the hills.

The women also invited real estate brokers to come to the house to

[*121*]

discuss stores that might be available either to rent or to buy, and Villa and Parra enjoyed themselves with them, saying that this store was too small or that one too far from the best business area. They even complained that some places were simply too cheap to be worth looking at. A tailor was also invited to the house to measure the men for suits. "Something befitting merchants, men of position," Eulalia said. The tailor looked at the pistols worn by both Villa and Parra and asked, "Just what kind of business do these gentlemen own?" But a glance from Parra was sufficient to end his sense of humor and send him to his tape measure.

Musicians were invited on Saturday night to play for their entertainment. A woman with a grandly powdered and displayed bosom and a man with a darkly tanned bald spot on his head came along to sing operatic duets. Villa squirmed and applauded loudly. Ignacio sometimes left the soirées early, claiming still to be weak from his recent illness. He always left when Simón was moved by the music to leap to his feet and recite his favorite poems by Musset or Vigny. Simón accused him of lacking culture, to which Ignacio replied, holding his hand over his belly as if he were in pain, "How can you say that, sir, when you know it is only that I suffer from a weak stomach?"

By midsummer they had less than two thousand pesos. "What do you think?" he asked Villa. "Do you want to go to the bank or would you like to sell some beef to the gringos? We need about ten thousand. Unless you're serious about the store—then we need forty, fifty, maybe more. What'll it be, brother, the beef or the bank?"

"How long before we run out of money?" Villa asked.

"Those bitches could spend it all tomorrow."

"How long do you think?"

"Two months, three; I don't know."

"Then we can wait. At least we're safe here."

Parra laughed.

Gaiety came into the house, as if it were the last season, the last month before a child is born, the last week of a great journey. The compromise went in favor of the women, who filled the house with guests. They poured wine. There was dancing in the cool rooms and in the garden, among the roses, brushing the marigolds. A shining horn was brought to sit among the violins. Villa played the guitar and sang "The Swallow" and "Little Darling."

Sing and never cry, my darling,
For singing enlivens the heart.

They all sang, even Simón and his cousin the bank teller, even Abelardo and his fat stone of a wife. They sang and danced and filled the house with flowers. They cut roses and marigolds and let the stems be long, for it was the heat of summer, the rains were ending, the flowers would not be so beautiful again; every morning they expected dust and the paling of the sun.

Villa and Parra discussed the possibility of leaving the horses saddled, which would enable them to leave more quickly in the event of trouble. "It would give us a mile," Villa said.

Parra thought about it. "You would leave them saddled all night too?"

"No, it would gall them, but I think we could saddle them in the morning and leave them saddled until we went to bed."

"And if the rurales come while the kid is exercising one of them?"

"There are always chances," Villa said.

They talked for a long time, examining the possibilities, weighing the advantage of that extra mile against the problem of a horse that was sore from too many hours under the saddle. "In the question of speed against distance," said Parra, "I always choose distance. The rurales will track you like dogs, and if you have to stop, you'll look around and find them all around you."

In the end, they agreed that it was enough to keep the saddlebags provisioned, the canteens filled with fresh water, and the loaded rifles in their boots. They changed the exercise boy's time to early morning, believing that the rurales were too lazy and too corrupt to come at that hour. "Worry about them in the heat of the day," Parra said, "when you're sleeping."

Villa shook his head. "How can I worry about them when I'm asleep?"

"It's not a joke, Panchito. I'm telling you something to think about."

So Villa no longer slept away the afternoons. He lay beside Marta in the narrow bed, talking, sometimes only looking at her, the valley of her waist beside her risen hip, the gradual disappearance of hair going past her ear and down her cheek, the miraculous fit of her eyes, the confluence of the pink skin of her lips and the pale flesh of her face. If she slept, he wandered through the house, listening at the doors, peering through the windows. Often he met Parra in the garden, and they looked at each other—two men in stockinged feet, bare chested, wearing pistols and gunbelts—and laughed.

Later in the afternoon they were more comfortable, sitting in the kitchen, drinking coffee or cool watermelon juice. But even then, if there was a knock at the door, either Villa or Parra went to meet the peddler or deliveryman; it was a rule of the house, the precaution that had first led the women to suspect them. Now it had become a joke: "There goes Francisco Villa, the great bandit," Eulalia would say, laughing, watching Villa hurry to the door, adjusting his gunbelt as he went.

The discussions of marriage between Villa and Marta persisted. In the afternoon, before a soirée to which a priest had been invited, he said to her, "We could be married here tonight. Think of the convenience, little one; you wouldn't even have to leave the house."

[*123*]

They were sitting at the small table in the kitchen. Eulalia and Ignacio were there with them, listening, amused, unwilling to mediate. Villa was unconcerned by their presence, but Marta complained, "Please, Francisco, not here; you're embarrassing me."

"Marta, I'm not ashamed to say that I love you. I would go to the plaza and stand up on a Saturday night and tell the whole city of Durango. If you don't feel the same way, tell me, please, because I don't want to go on misunderstanding you."

She patted his arm. "Don't pout, please. It's just not a good time to discuss marriage. Not here."

"Then we'll discuss it tonight with the priest."

Marta looked around for allies. "You see how difficult he is?" There was no response. "Well," she said, "is he difficult or no? You could at least do me the courtesy of giving an answer."

Eulalia said, "It's not an insult if a man asks to marry you."

Marta sucked in her lips and stared at her for a moment, nodding her head slowly, as if in recognition of some newly understood evil. "Very good. Then why don't you marry Nacho? We'll have a double wedding, and afterwards our husbands can rob the church and shoot the priests."

"Enough," Parra said. "You're not a prisoner here; the door is always open. It's certain that Francisco doesn't want to marry a woman who thinks of him that way. Or maybe he doesn't want to marry a woman who's willing to live with a man before she's married. You know, I've heard of men who would cut a woman's throat if they didn't see a little blood on the wedding night. I think you should be grateful to him for asking you."

"Stop it," Villa said, "don't talk about her that way."

Parra sat back in his chair, opening his eyes wide and showing the palms of his hands in mock surprise. Eulalia suddenly grabbed him by the sleeve of his jacket and shook him. "Did you hear the door? The guests are already here. Would Mister Carbajal or Mister Ramirez please answer the door?"

"You'd better let Francisco do it. Maybe it's the priest," Parra said, laughing. "If it is, he can arrange the wedding right there."

Villa stood up, still angry, but beginning to laugh. "Remember his vow of poverty," Parra called after him. "Don't pay too much." As he crossed the garden, Villa called back to the kitchen, "Prepare yourself, Marta." And to the continuing knocking at the front door to the house, he called, "Wait a moment, sir; I'll be right there."

He took a few seconds to brush his mustache with the back of his forefinger and to settle himself inside his jacket before he unbolted the door. A slim man in a white suit stood on the step. His face was long and cast with mournfulness. The outer corners of his eyes sagged. His mustache fell at the corners. Villa thought for a moment that the man might be a Chinese or a half-breed. Behind the man, across the street, was Simón or a man who looked like him, but he seemed to be waiting, not approaching the house, perhaps waiting for this guest to be greeted first. Villa smiled and nodded a preliminary greeting to the man in the white suit.

The man smiled and nodded in return. He wore a celluloid collar, which fit loosely around his neck. His throat jumped once before he spoke. "Good afternoon," he said. "I'm Jesús Flores, Inspector General of Police." Villa shot him.

Flores was lifted backward and thrown onto the street. Villa stood in the doorway, watching him, the feeble waving of his hands, the deadening of his face, the soundless opening and closing of his mouth. Flores coughed once, a fine spray of blood. His legs flexed, the movement of a frog; then he lay still.

The street was empty; white houses and pink, adobe walls topped with shards of broken glass, windows elegantly barred, fortress houses, flat roofs, stone walks, the hard-packed summer street, the unforgiving sun making its coarse shadows, an empty sky. There was no more. The other man had gone, if there had been another man. The silence made a vacant buzz, the sound of hearing. Where was the afternoon rain? In the empty street the body of Flores was foreign, a three-dimensional figure laid upon a flat scene.

Neither the flies nor the soldiers came, no winged shadows passed across the rutted, cracked street. The air had no odor. There was no wind. Where were the horses? Where was the afternoon rain? Blood seeped out from under the back of the dead man; it too seemed out of place, like a piece of dark cardboard laid upon the street, not part of it, false. Or the street was false and the dead man was true. They did not touch: the dead man was the only foreground, the white suit was so brilliant in the sun, it had the color of cold.

Villa slammed the door and bolted it. Parra was running toward him, coming across the garden, carrying the rifles in his hands, the cartridge belts hung across his shoulder. They could not find the women. Villa noticed the bees in the garden, undisturbed. He saw the roses. Durango, Durango. Were the women hiding? Parra saddled the horses. The guests would be arriving, the priest. Why was it not raining? There was neither dust nor rain. He looked for Marta, in the kitchen, in their crowded room. He called to her. In the barn, Parra was cursing, tightening the cinches and cursing. Villa looked in the kitchen again. A soup of albondigas was on the stove. The room was empty, the rooms were empty. He found his eating utensils, he found the blue hummingbird wrapped in red twine. Where was Marta? He ran to the barn.

Parra opened the barn doors and looked outside.

"Marta," said Villa.

"She knows what she has to do. There's no place for her with us."

Then Parra was up on the horse, the reins in one hand, the carbine in the other. His hat was pushed back, the bandoliers were strapped across his chest, his horse was dancing, more anxious than the man. And Villa stood, his hand upon the horn of the saddle, one foot poised for the lift to the stirrup. "The money," he said.

"Leave it for them."

"Yes, but they have to find it."

"Those bitches will tear this barn to pieces looking."

"Eulalia?"

"Be realistic."

Villa held the horse, waiting. Parra called to him again, urging him to mount, reminding him that he had shot the Inspector General of Police. Still Villa hesitated. The priest was on his way, crossing the town streets, the hem of his cassock touching the ground. Where was Marta? The money was waiting; he was waiting. The horse did not move. There was the blanket roll, there were the saddlebags with their dried beef, corn flour, baking powder, dry beans, salt, and matches. There was the canteen and there the waterbag. His eating utensils were in his pocket, the hummingbird was in his hand, held against the reins. There was no rain. Roses wilted from the outside, that was how the petals fell. The man had come in a white suit. He was so thin, the bullet had lifted him backwards. Flowers, Mister Flowers, Roses; Marigold was stolen by Two Enemy the Patron of Highwaymen.

Parra's horse was turning, backing. He came around and slapped Villa's shoulder with the barrel of his carbine. "If you stay here, they'll hang you." He hit Villa again with the barrel of the carbine: "Forget it, kid; a hanged man can't get married." Slowly, as if in sleep, Villa mounted. He had not yet found the stirrup on the right side when Parra slapped the rump of his horse. The animal jumped toward the open doors, running. Parra shouted, "Market Hill!"

The stirrup flapped against the side of the running horse; Villa concentrated on finding his footing. He turned the animal north at the cross street. Parra was behind him, holding the carbine out to the side, shouting, "Police, police!" Villa found the stirrup and the rhythm of the horse, leaning forward with it, urging, "Run, little one, run!" The horse stretched, the rhythm smoothed. He looked back at Parra and beyond him to the following riders—three, perhaps four of them, urging their horses as Villa and Parra were, running, less than half a mile between them and Parra. He expected to hear the whine of bullets, perhaps to feel one touch him. It was said that at such a great distance a bullet wound felt like a hard punch, nothing more.

Then they were out of town, riding north, passing long wire fences, the growing hills, sending birds to flight with their sound, keeping to the road, passing the little farms that feed the cities, feeling the hot wind drying them, expecting the dust. Parra drew abreast of Villa and rode apart from him on the other side of the road. He shouted the name of Market Hill again, and added, "Make for the arroyo. We'll wait for them in the arroyo." Villa nodded. There was sand on the road, the beginning of dust. They passed cattle grazing, sagebrush, the first stunted, thorny ocotillo pines, pale desert grass. Villa raised his eyes to the smoothing distance and gave himself to the running of the horse.

At the arroyo, they dismounted, tied the horses in a sheltered place, and climbed back up to the edge. They kicked footholds into the loose rock of the side of the arroyo, cached their canteens and cartridge belts, and waited for the police to come within range of the carbines. There were five. Villa chose one on the left, wanting the greatest angle to avoid the shield of the horse. He sighted on the man, studying his rhythm as he rose and fell in the sights. He raised the barrel slowly as the oncoming rider increased the angle.

"Too far yet for the carbines," Parra said. "You have to be sure when you're in a damn pit like this. Don't hit the horses. Once you force them onto the ground they'll have to stay and fight. Be careful, kid; you can't defend yourself out of a hole; the horses will come in over you. Goddamnit, Goddamnit."

Villa felt his foothold beginning to crumble. He kicked in deeper with his toe, and sighted again on the man. The angle was changing rapidly now; the man was filling up the sight, head to knee, neck to waist. Villa exhaled and squeezed the trigger. The man was hit, but he didn't fall. He reined in the horse and sat leaning forward over the neck of the animal, stupefied, but holding on. Villa couldn't see what the effect of Parra's first shot had been. The police were firing back, riding with the reins tied down, shooting like cavalrymen, missing wildly. Villa pumped the carbine and fired again, aiming as if at rising quail, shooting as the target entered his sights. He missed.

The horses were almost upon them. He could feel them in the trembling of the ground. Little pieces of the edge of the arroyo crumbled, bursts of sand poured. The horses were roaring, sweating; their mouths were streaming. He shot a man in the leg. The horses were coming, steaming out of the roiled dust. Villa crouched below the level of the ground and held his hands over his face, wedging himself against the wall of the arroyo. The trembling diminished, and he dared to look up. Stones flew and the dust was like a wall. He held his forearm across his forehead and squinted. The horses were retreating, running away. Parra was firing. "Shoot over their heads," he called to Villa. "Don't give them a reason to stay. Herd them, man; herd them back to Durango."

Villa wanted to stay in the arroyo after the shooting, but Parra insisted on moving north again. He repeated his fear of being trapped in a trench. "How did you like it when the horses were getting close?" he asked Villa. "It's not so easy to keep your head up; you feel like there's going to be a hoof in your hat."

"You saw me?"

"There's nothing to be ashamed of, kid; I was afraid too. Listen to me: I never met anyone who wasn't afraid of something. Horses scare you, holes in the ground scare me. What's the difference?"

"But you kept shooting. I heard you."

"Well, you know, I was a little off to the side. They were coming right at you. That's a big difference."

Villa put his arm around Parra's shoulders. "Thank you," he said. He pulled the smaller man toward him and embraced him. They walked down the arroyo together to the horses. Villa was weeping. Parra looked away.

He found me in a little valley where I often went to gather sage seeds to prepare chía. It was that changing time of year when it is necessary both to carry a parasol and to wear a fiber cape, the month of Teotleco, the month of the returning of the gods, who are led in their return by Tezcatlipoca. Naturally, I expected him to arrive in that month.

The look of a man was in his face, the look of a man was in the way his eyes had become set in his face. I told him so, thinking it would please him, that it would be a good greeting. Suddenly, strangely, he leaped from the saddle and fell on his knees before me and wept. I lifted him up and led him to my house, where I cleansed him and gave him food that had been prepared by a woman who knew the old ways. He ate slowly, questioning me about the food, which he did not know: frog tamales, white worm paste, waterfly eggs, turkey-egg tortillas in the form of a hand, beeswax tamales, chiles tipped with nipples, honeyed pastries, cocoa pastries, lizard pastries, amaranth sauce. All that afternoon and into the night we tasted the food and talked. I told him that I did not expect his weeping, that it was not in his days or his hours, but I confessed that the reading of the intersections was not always perfect, for there is so much to be considered in the meeting of the sets of days, hours, months, and seasons that no man's character can ever be completely predicted. There was also a question of the New Fire; he was born in the cycle that began in their year of 1871 and would end in their year of 1923.

He said to me that he was a murderer, and I asked him what rose and did not fall.

[*128*]

"Whatever goes to Heaven," he said.

"And do those who are killed in battle go to Heaven?"

"Yes," he said.

But he was not certain; we cannot see Heaven. So I said to him: "Death is man's invention, like time. For the rest of the world there is only day and night and the seasons. An animal dies in the day or the night, in winter or summer, spring or autumn; it has neither months nor hours nor years nor cycles of New Fire. Plants and animals have no time, they have only now. Time exists only for men; it is the invention of man, a dream. Death is also a dream, for it is no more than the passing from one place to another; if it were not marked in time, it would go smoothly, as day goes to night, for it is no more than a dream within a dream. The wisest of the poets has asked if this life is real or if it is only a dream, if we truly live on earth. In the dreams we know as dreams we never die. And who can truly know if they are the real and this is the dream or this is the real and the world we call dreaming is truly dreaming?"

He sat with his legs folded, like a merchant. He had gleaming eyes, brilliant eyes; there was a flash in his eyes. "Popoca, you are all saying the same thing: we must be realistic, we must be scientific."

I laughed. "How can we be realistic when we do not know what is real?"

"You've told me so many times not to be a dreamer!"

In the old time there were schools for thinking. The young men enlightened themselves with the pains of the body and the mind. They were like fingers without skin, they were perfect memories, each one was a book. I am the descendant of one who taught in such a school. I am many books, the keeper of books, but I am less than what was known, I am not all. To him, to this boy with a man's shoulders, I spoke as Tlacaélel spoke to the young kings. But so much has been lost; there are no schools. He is ignorant, I am ignorant. No man can be soothsayer, diviner, priest, teacher, and poet, not for all my years, not for all my concentration, not for all that I have read in the Book of Days. I spoke to him as my ancestors had spoken to the common people of the Empire, naming days and gods, practicing the medicine of physicians and the medicine of the Wild Dogs, saying the laws. But I could not tell him the meaning of poems, nor could I say the poems; the best of the words have been lost. The smoke survives, the mirror reflects; it is the words that disappear. I said to him all that I could say, that one day he would understand.

"How will I know?" he asked. "Will you tell me?"

"When the time arrives, you will no longer have to ask."

He was not satisfied; I knew that I had lost a part of him to this world he thought was real. Or did I misunderstand? I cannot expect to know, I am satisfied to ask; how could he expect more? I told him that it is certain the sun will die at the end of one of the cycles, but we do not know which cycle; we pray because we do not know, we dream because we do not know; out of ignorance we invented death and time, as if movement were not continuous, as if one heartbeat differed from another, as if blood were made of parts. He would not be satisfied; he stood up and paced the room, the innermost room of my house, touching the objects that were forbidden to him: the stones of Teotihuacan, the black mirror, the bloodied thorn, the wooden stone, the quetzal feather, the flint, even the gold serpent of Our Lord Who Rose in the East, the Precious Twin. I reminded him that death is only an illusion, a dream, which is what he came to ask.

"And suffering?" he asked.

"There is no suffering in death, if the dying understand that death is only an invention of man, that only the stopping of the sun is an ending."

"No," he said, "I was asking about the suffering in life."

"There are punishments."

"There are innocents who suffer."

"Why do you ask me this in the way of an accusation? I have never said that evil does not exist. No, I have never denied evil, I have never said that we are in control. Have I not pointed to the sun, the moon, the morning star and the evening star? What is it that you are asking? What is it that you want to believe?"

"I don't know," he said. "I know only that I'm not happy." Then he told me he was leaving and that it would be a long time before he came back.

"The three stones will be here," I said, "and there will be a fire." He embraced me before he went away. I went back into my house and put copal into the fire and burned a snake for him.

It was the dry autumn. They lived in the most cruel mountains, where there is no sand and every wall is made of stone and nothing lives but birds, yellow beetles, and the tough grass that only sheep and certain horses are able to chew. They descended to the foothills and high plains to find steers to butcher and hang in the sun to dry. Every day they had to walk the horses down to a valley to graze and drink. There was no rest. They gathered wood for the winter and stored mesquite beans and chiles, even though it was late and many were rotten and had to be thrown away. They went once to the lumber camp of El Vergel to buy cornmeal and balls of salt, but they did not stay long, for they thought they were being watched—the rurales hunted in the mills and lumber camps for men who were afraid to live in the cities or even the towns. They saw men in gray there in El Vergel, big men with silvered suits and the finest rifles.

When it became known that Refugio Alvarado was dead, other men asked to ride with Parra. Several came to live in the mountains that winter. One of them was Tomás Urbina, a young cowboy from the mountains near Canutillo. He was two years older than Villa, but he was very dark, with a sweet face, crossed eyes, and shiny skin that made him seem to be no more than a boy. His hair was long and straight in the style of the mountain people, and day and night he wore a great cape of rabbit skins sewed to a thick wool lining, for he suffered from the cold even when he sat in the sun.

On the night of his arrival Urbina said to Villa and Parra, "I want to be rich."

"And that's why you came here!" Parra said. "Look at us! Look how we live! You cunt hair! If you want to be rich, you should be a landlord, or maybe you should take the five fingers and get yourself a gray suit."

Urbina's eyes rolled. He looked from Parra to Villa and back again to Parra. "I thought . . ." he began. Then he huddled further into his cape and considered his words for a moment. "You know what they say."

"What?" Parra looked at him with cold eyes.

"Well, man, there's a lot of talk about gold. You know. For example, you're out some night with the cows and you sit around for some beans and a little coffee. You talk about pussy for a while, and then pretty soon someone starts talking about bandits and gold. There's a lot of gold that's been stolen. Millions, right?" He smiled; no smiles came in answer. "Well, I'm only saying what I've heard. But everyone says. Son of a bitch, I don't know how much gold there is in these mountains. I'm just telling you what I heard about the treasures that are buried up here. Maybe there's nothing, maybe it's all lies. But then I have to ask you one thing," he said, leaning forward, pointing at Parra with one finger, looking pleased with himself. "If you don't get any gold from it, how come you're doing this?"

Villa snorted, beginning laughter, then stifling it. "Why does the rabbit crawl into a hole in the ground?"

"To be safe from the coyote."

"Well," Villa said, "use your head. Think what we're doing up here."

Parra nodded. "He's telling the truth. You'd better think about it. Take a look at the hair on the coyotes and the rabbits before you decide; it's going to be a lousy winter. And I don't think you like the winter, little one. You're cold already; what's wrong with you? Is there something wrong with your blood?"

"No, there's nothing wrong. I had this fever when I was a baby, and the healer came and told my mother he could cure me of the fever but I would always be sensitive to the cold afterwards in my bones."

"You have pains?" Parra asked.

"No. Mostly swellings. But I'm not a cripple, understand? On the coldest

[131]

day I can use this gun faster than you." He showed them his revolver, a .32-caliber Smith and Wesson double action.

"It's not worth anything," Villa said. He took out his Colt and passed it to Urbina. "This is a pistol. You could shoot a man in the finger with this and it would knock him down."

Urbina examined the weapon carefully, taking out one of the cartridges and weighing it in his hand. "It's not a pistol, it's a cannon. It's too big, man. I've tried one of these; the kick is too much."

"Did you ever have to shoot a man?" Villa asked.

"No."

"Wait."

After Urbina, Sabás Baca joined them, and then Manuel Vaca Valles, José Solís, Juan Salas, and Martín López. They felt safe together, but eight men presented new problems: they could get enough meat, but they lacked cornmeal and beans and salt, ammunition was used up quickly, they had to move more often to find good grazing for the horses, they had no large pots in which to cook, and they dared not go into a town together because of their appearance, which was like that of a posse or a small army detachment. They made noise, they burned up a dozen armloads of firewood in a night. They drank and sang; they told stories and lied to each other and fell into arguments; they became the children of Ignacio Parra, obedient as to a father, but as restless as growing children anxious for their time in the world.

They were a family of thieves and drunkards, each one demanding what he most craved: a woman and money first; after that, whatever singularly pleased them: music, marijuana, the long night's sleep, a family on a farm, black cotton and real silver, heat, health. Only Villa could not say what it was he wanted, Villa who kept a handful of seed corn wrapped in his blanket and waited for spring.

Guided by Parra, they let out their secrets, the humiliations and the expectations that had sent them up the naked side of the mountain. He took their dreams and their shames as if they were raw wool, carding and spinning them, weaving the men together by the thread of their lives. He told them they would have to be closer than brothers. "There is no danger but betrayal," he said. "I'll kill any man I suspect, and you should do the same. But I'll pray every night that I never have to do it. That's why I want you to be close, to be like one man who would never betray himself. Talk, talk to each other all the time. Don't have even one secret. If your mother was a whore, tell your brother about it. That's how you make him your brother." They did as he asked, speaking in their country accents, formal in their intimacy, sometimes lacking the Spanish words, helping each other

[*132*]

to find the precision they knew in mountain words, listening and nodding compassion; and whenever a man could not help but weep, the others said to him that he was brave and that his weeping was a sign to them that he could be trusted.

SABÁS BACA

His mother wore long skirts and a derby hat, and she carried him on her back through the streets of Chihuahua while she sold rugs and sweaters, and then she carried him on her back while she walked home, following the rivers upstream to Santa Rosalía de Cuevas and on to Tutuaca to buy corn and salt, and then, like an animal bearing the sack of a child and the sack of her goods, she carried him up the last steep hills to their summer shelter. When he was older, he walked beside her and his brother rode on her back. It was the same journey four times every summer, thirty miles to the city of Chihuahua and thirty miles home. And every summer on every journey they carried no water and only a tiny sack of corn, and they were thirsty and hungry and afraid that somewhere in the mountains pumas waited for them and everywhere in the towns thieves counted their few pesos or measured the value of the rugs and sweaters held in the woman's arms.

Sabás and his brother were the sons of a priest who left the little settlement of Tutuaca when the youngest boy was two years old. Fourteen years later, another white man came to their house. It was winter, and they were living down near the river to avoid the snow. The man was older than the priest had been, and he was dirty and bearded and leading three sickly burros. He went into the house and drew the covering over the entrance. There was laughter. The man stayed a long time. When he came out, Sabás stabbed him in the throat with wool shears.

He loaded the body onto one of the burros and took it up into the mountains. His brother offered to help; but Sabás said that it was his own work and that no one, not even his own brother, could share in either the honor or the danger of having killed a white man. Sabás went alone. He walked through the snow for two days until he found the highest, most isolated place to which the burro could climb. He rested there for a while, lying between the burro and the dead man's body to keep warm. Then he took the white man's shovel and tried to dig a hole in which to hide him; but it was too cold, the ground was rocky and frozen, and the edge of the shovel hurt his feet when he tried to stomp it into the ground. He could not bury the body of the man. Instead, he gathered all the dry wood he could find and built a great fire and burned the body. The hands and feet burned away, the belly split and hissed, the head burst, but the main part of the corpse was only charred, cooked like the carcass of a big animal. He cut away the gut and whatever had been ruined by the bursting of the belly and ate the lean and salty parts.

MANUEL VACA VALLES

They had left the valleys to the catzopines. They had abandoned the corn-fields to follow Cajeme into the mountains, to make war, to defend themselves against the men who sold them to the henequen planters. Naked, hungry, having no more than bows and arrows with which to defend their last position, they had surrendered. The war was over, the Yaquis were defeated, Cajeme was dead; yet they remained in the mountains, for there was no other place; cotton grew in their fields of corn.

In this new place they learned to be hunters and scavengers again, like coyotes, like crows; they no longer prayed to the God of Corn, they loved the young deer, the armadillo, and the rabbit. It was a shameful time; men looked at the ground, children did not laugh, the milk of the women was thin, the dogs ran away. New gods arose, devils; the people beat the little drums and inflated themselves with dreams.

Manuel lived with his mother and four sisters. He was the oldest, twelve years, and he was the hunter, for his father was dead, one of the hundreds who had died beside Cajeme, a dead bowman, a dead runner, a dead teller of stories that could heal his children's wounds. The body had been lost, left behind in the losing flight; they had buried a stalk of corn in his stead.

The war had ended with the promise that the catzopines would not come again to take the people away to the henequen plantations or the tobacco plantations, but the soldiers came to the mountains, as they had come to the valleys and the hills, riding on their big horses, herding with their rifles and their long ropes, taking the young men and the young women as before.

They saw the horses when they were only halfway up the mountain. Manuel said to his mother to take the girls and hide in the twisting arroyo on the far side of the mountain; he was the man, he would defend the house, he would stand in the place of his father. She touched his arm before she left, as if to thank him, as if to tell him goodbye, as if to give him the courage to be as his father would surely have been. He told her to walk only on the hard places so that she would leave no trail. He reminded the girls to be silent.

While he waited for the soldiers, he felt good. He thought of dying. Perhaps he would be able to kill one of them first. He went inside the shelter and ate a piece of dried venison. Then he took his bow and arrows and sat by the fire to wait. From the little sack that his mother kept he took corn pollen and put it in his mouth, and then he drew a picture of the levels of the Upper World in the soft earth of the floor of the shelter.

Two soldiers and an interpreter came into the shelter. They stank of tobacco and sweat and horses. Manuel thought of his bow and his knife, but he could not move. The men were so tall, and they spoke in shouts. The faces of the catzopines were red, as if blood were about to burst from their pores. Their legs were covered with leather. They carried guns.

"Where is your father?"

"Dead."

"Where is your mother?"

"I live here alone."

One of the soldiers lifted Manuel to his feet, holding him by his hair, twisting it, raising him off the ground. "Where are they hiding?"

"I live here alone."

The soldier shoved his forefinger into Manuel's eye. He moved with such suddenness that Manuel barely had time to drop the lid. It was no help: the finger went through into the eye, cutting, tearing the eye loose. Manuel saw a terrible light, like a green sun.

"Tell him where they're hiding," the interpreter said, "or he'll take your other eye."

"They went to the twisting arroyo on the far side of the mountain."

JOSÉ SOLÍS

In Culiacán they were married, in the smallest church, in the least expensive way. She was a virgin, no more than a child, a fisherman's daughter, full of sharp Tarascan humor. Whenever she made a joke, she started to giggle; there was no sting in her. "You were born gentle," he told her when they were still courting. "I came down from the mountains and found you and the ocean, and you are as soft and warm as the ocean." She blushed, she giggled; he arranged the marriage.

He took her with him into the mountains to a stone house he had built along the river near San Juan de Camarones. The land was difficult: steep and rocky, eroded into a network of turning canyons, gullies, and washes. In summer, the sun was like fire on the skin; and in winter, when the sun had gone pale in the north, the snow crept down from the peaks and filled the canyons and washes. The rains were floods, the pines died near the end of summer. But the land was his, he claimed it, he did not fear that it would be taken from him.

A little bit of corn was all that he was able to grow. Often the first planting and sometimes the second were washed away; but he was tenacious, he planted again and again, burning the field, making holes with a stick for the seeds, building a mound around every stalk that rose. In the best of years there was enough.

He had two burros, a mule that ran like a horse, four dogs, and twenty sheep when they were married. She had needles and thread and four clay pots and an iron pan. He taught her to card and spin wool. She taught him to laugh and to live quietly in a house. They were together as much as they could be; whenever she could, she went with him to herd the sheep, shooing them along the riverbank to keep them from eating the grass down too far. They sheared the sheep together, and they went to San Juan de Camarones together to sell the wool in the spring.

She conceived in the late spring, predicting the baby's birth in winter. They were very far from a midwife and she was afraid that none of the old women would be willing to climb up to their house in the snow, so they made an arrangement with Tía Bienvenida, the midwife of San Juan de Camarones: when the pains were about to begin, José would bring her to the midwife's house to stay until the child was born and her milk had come in.

There were eight lambs in the spring, and six of them lived. José was pleased; he told his new wife of his dreams of a great flock. But there was bad luck in the winter. Wolves found his flock one night and killed a ram and two ewes. A week later, he heard the dogs in the corral area just before morning. He took his gun and ran out into the darkness, but two of the dogs were dead and a lamb was missing before he was able to fire the gun and frighten the wolves. Two weeks later, he lost another dog and two more ewes. The flock was reduced to twenty again; the year had been wasted, and it was only December. He could not depend on one dog to protect the flock; he stayed with them himself, sleeping at the edge of the corral. Day and night he was with his sheep. He wrapped himself in blankets and sheepskin, but he could not avoid the cold. He became irritable from lacking sleep, he kept the gun with him always, he saw his wife only when she brought his meals out to him.

When the pains began he could not take her to Tía Bienvenida, for there was only one dog left to guard the sheep, and one dog was not enough. He promised to help her with the baby. He knew what to do, he had aided in the birth of a dozen lambs; he would not be frightened; birth would not be strange to him as it might be to men who lived in the towns and cities. The child, a girl, was born dead, strangled by the umbilical cord. He buried the child and burned the cord, but it was no use; his wife said the death was a mark on his soul. She stayed there with him until the end of winter, but she did not speak to him from the time of the death until she rolled her few possessions into her blanket and went home to Culiacán. On that last day he asked her where she was going, and for the first time in more than three months she spoke to him. "Every day I pray to Our Lord Jesus Christ for the soul of my daughter," she said, "and every day I remind Him of your sin and beg Him to withhold his forgiveness from you now and in the next life and for all eternity."

MARTÍN LÓPEZ

The landlord instructed the foreman and the big Chinese in how to make the punishment most effective: the boy's hands were to be spread and he was to be revived if he fainted. "Lift him up! Higher!" the landlord said. "I don't want his feet to touch the ground. Suspend him!"

The Chinese held the boy around the waist, lifting him off the ground while the foreman made the knots around his wrists again. He was a tall boy, but thin. When they removed his shirt, the triangles of his shoulder blades showed in all their detail, making him seem more naked. He neither struggled nor complained, but everyone who had been assembled to witness the punishment could see the way the muscles crawled in his back.

It was a mild afternoon. There was no dust. The animals were quiet, except for the chickens, which wandered in and out among the people, poking their nervous heads and unreasonably clucking. The landlord wore an American fedora and smoked white cigarettes. The Chinese had a mustache that hung from his face. The seat of the boy's trousers had begun to wear through. His feet were bare; the toes of his right foot were twisted into a bunch and curled under the ball of the foot. He walked like a one-legged man, able to put his weight only on the heel of his right foot. Everyone called him Pegleg, and he did not mind the name, for he was a good-humored boy and he enjoyed the irony of the words, which actually meant "foot of elegance."

"Pegleg López," the landlord said, "you are being punished for stealing a pistol from the main house of this ranch and for refusing to confess your crime." He spoke loudly and very slowly, as judges do. "The punishment for theft is twenty-five lashes. The punishment for refusing to confess is to have your feet put to the fire." He nodded to the foreman, who nodded to the Chinese.

The boy turned his head from side to side, trying to see what went on behind him. "If you confess now," the landlord said, "and you return the stolen property, one part of the punishment will be cancelled." The boy struggled to see the landlord, who stood behind him and slightly to one side. The onlookers could not tell whether he was able to turn his head far enough. They listened for his confession, but he said nothing.

A muledriver's whip was used. The Chinese cracked it in the air several times before he began.

On the fourth stroke of the whip the boy's skin tore. After that, every lash opened another cut. The cuts crossed and pieces of flesh were ripped away. The bone was exposed. Water was thrown in the boy's face to revive him after the tenth lash and again after the fifteenth and after the seventeenth and the eighteenth and the nineteenth. At the conclusion of the whipping, the foreman brought two armloads of kindling and built a fire under the boy's feet. The calloused skin burst with cracklings that could be heard over the quicker noises of the small fire. The foreman wet down the bottom of the boy's trouser legs with a dipping gourd to keep them from catching fire. The boy hung from the post, bloody and still.

Two neighbors cut him down and carried him to the López house. Salt and urine had been prepared for the wounds and a paste of egg yolk and jimsonweed had been made to soothe the burns, but it was no use; his heart fluttered for a few moments and then it stopped. The people in the house knelt beside the body, crossing themselves and wailing. There was no priest to give him absolution, but they lit candles for him and put a rosary in his hand.

Martín stood in the doorway and looked out at the landlord, the foreman, and the Chinese, who stood together, laughing and smoking white cigarettes. The pistol was under his shirt, tucked into the top of his trousers. He touched the weapon through the cloth, feeling the shape of the handle, the hammer, the trigger guard. The pistol had been there for a long time; it was the temperature of his body, like a part of him, his. Someone called his name, asking him to come inside and comfort his mother.

JUAN SALAS

Every afternoon at four o'clock he went to the house of his sweetheart and sat in the main room with her and her mother and her aunt. They spoke of Verdi and Cervantes, electricity, oil, the advantages to the stomach of a balanced diet, the varieties of wine, the price of lace, Indian lassitude, the elegance of Cicero, the need for further foreign investment in railroads, Comte, and the civilization of Mexico under the presidency of Porfirio Díaz. He agreed, he drank coffee, he said all the French words he knew.

For one year and two months he courted Marie by courting her mother and her aunt. He grew tired of the aunt's rasping breath and the mother's whiskered moles. He did not like their coffee or their pastries or the strange bland sauces they poured over the food when they invited him to dinner.

He could not understand how Cicero could be a Roman and not a Christian, for everyone knew that the Pope himself lived in Rome. But he wanted to marry Marie, who told him with glances and sighs that he would not be sorry for his choice.

The mother and the aunt had their doubts about his suitability as a husband, and they delayed the announcement of the engagement because of those doubts. His youth was suspect. Juan had been arrested several times, twice imprisoned, and once sent to serve two years in the Federal Army. What were his prospects? How could a man with so little education expect to succeed in the modern world? Was he prepared to deal with science?

He answered as best he could: he was a clerk in one of the finest stores in the city of Torreón, he knew a great deal about guns and cotton, and he was as Spanish as Cortés himself. They nodded to his answers, but they did not announce the engagement. He pressed them, he asked for reasons for the delay, he had a suit tailored for him to improve his appearance, he put brilliantine in his hair. Finally, Marie's father asked to meet him. Juan went to the father's office, which was in a two-storey building across the street from the Municipal Palace.

Marie's father kept him waiting in the anteroom for a very long time, but Juan was not insulted; he had come to see a busy man—an attorney, a brother of the political chief of Torreón, an advisor to the governor of the state. When he did consent to see Juan, it was after six o'clock and beginning to be dark. The brother of the political chief sat behind a dark, heavy desk. The room was lit by two oil lamps. The light was yellow and wavering. Rows of books rested in glass cases, protected from the dust.

Juan offered his hand. "At your service, sir."

The man did not rise, nor did he offer his hand in return. His desk was covered with papers. He wore a vest but no coat. He was a medium man, neither fat nor thin; not tall and not short; ordinary, yet seated behind an imposing desk; his hair was thin, but he was not bald.

"I wish to marry your daughter, sir, because I love her."

"I'm prepared to offer you a thousand pesos to leave the city."

Juan smiled. "If this is a test of my sincerity, sir, I can tell you that my love for Marie is greater than ten thousand pesos or a hundred thousand pesos."

"Take the money."

"Thank you, but no; I want to marry her."

"When you go to work today you won't have a job, and you won't be able to find a job anywhere in the city of Torreón. If you stay in your mother's house, the taxes will be doubled and doubled again and again until she no longer has a house. The police will arrest you and you will be sent to the army, and the army will shave your head and send you to Tabasco to guard the tobacco fields. Take the money."

"You don't think I would be a good husband for her?"

"Don't be stupid!" He opened a drawer in the desk and took out the money, which he tossed across the desk to Juan.

"I could run away with her."

"I would have you killed."

"Then there's nothing I can do?"

"Nothing."

Juan reached down and picked up the money. The brother of the political chief of Torreón stood up and came around to the front of the desk. He put his hand on Juan's shoulder. "Very good," he said, "you're a reasonable fellow."

That night, before he left Torreón, Juan went to the house of the brother of the political chief to say goodbye to Marie, to whisper to her through the window where their real courtship had taken place, to cry with her for the cruelties of this world, perhaps to sing to her that life is not worth anything. He went around to the back of the house, carefully making his way through the twisted sagebrush and cactus. There was a light in her window, although the shutters were closed. He called to her in a whisper, as he had on so many other evenings. The shutters opened and she was there, his Marie. She beckoned him to come closer. He strained upward, grasping the wall with his hands, as if to find a climber's grip in the white stucco. Marie leaned forward and spat in his face.

Ignacio was their captain and their priest. "Do not be afraid," he said to them. "If you know you will die, you can never be humiliated. Isn't that why you came to me? You can never be safe again, you are bandits; the army is hunting you, the posses are hunting you, the rurales are hunting you; my name is your name. You've lost your other eye, Manuel; you have nothing more to fear. They've found the bones of the gringo, Sabás. They know who stole the gun, Martín. Your sheep have been eaten, every last one, José. And you, Juanito, you have murdered the brother of the political chief of Torreón. What can we do now, any of us? We're known. For me, I like it better this way; my choices are made."

"You think we'll die?" Urbina asked.

"You should be the least afraid, Tomás; it's warm in Hell."

Only Juan Salas was not satisfied. "What if I decide to leave?" he asked. "I don't think I like this life very much. It's easier for me to go into a store at night and take what I want and then sell it in the next town. I know stores. I like to live with a little comfort. What's the sense in risking my life to live like this? I might leave tomorrow. What would you do?"

[*140*]

Villa answered: "What could we do? We would give you ammunition and food and wish you a good life. This is not the army; we're not sergeants up here. And who knows? Maybe it would be better to go back and live in a town and have a job or work on a ranch. Do what you want, Juanito; we're all for you."

"Thank you very much," Salas said. "I've always heard that wisdom comes out of the mouths of babes. Do orders come out of the mouths of babes too?"

There was a long silence. "I would take orders from him," Parra said.

At other times, when he and Villa were alone, Parra spoke differently. He allowed the mask of command to slip; his body faltered, the shoulders fell, his neck bent; the pains had returned, he was bleeding again, the jessamine powders were used up, there was no corn to make into milky atole. The Root of Gold no longer helped, either. "The visions are strange now," he said. "I can't understand what I see. The last time I tried, I went to the house of a beautiful woman, but when I opened the door, I saw the head of a mountain lion."

"Did it attack you?"

"What does it mean if it did?"

"I'm not an interpreter of dreams," Villa said. "I was only curious."

"Something bad is waiting for me."

"Death. But I don't know that death is a bad thing. We have to be careful not to live on earth—you know what I mean? What we see is not everything; this could be the dream, what we see and touch. I don't know. I don't know what's the truth, what's real. I remember one time when I first left home, I was up in the mountains and I was just holding on, I don't know what for. Everything was going, fading. Then I saw a bug and I ate it, and everything came back; I didn't die. It was my last chance, that bug, and I took it. But I don't know whether I tied myself to the earth or I got away. I'm not certain; I don't know what it feels like to die."

"But if you saw a mountain lion . . ."

They were sitting on a crest of the mountain, looking down on the campsite where the others were cooking and bedding down the horses for the night. Parra wore a wool sweater and a sheepskin cape; Villa covered himself with a blanket. Parra's face was going thin again; there was gray in his skin—or was it merely dust? Villa thought he should wet a spot and rub it with his finger the way prospectors do with promising rocks to determine their content by the true color. "Nacho," he said, "I want to tell you one thing. We're still alive, man. Imagine that! We were betrayed by two women and we're still alive. We must be lucky."

Parra stood up and wrapped the sheepskin more tightly around himself. "Eulalia didn't betray us," he said, and walked down toward the campsite.

[*141*]

They spoke of it again the next day. Parra had spent the afternoon talking about pistols, explaining to them how the accuracy could be increased by reducing the amount of pressure required to release the hammer. He drew targets on pieces of sackcloth and tried each of their pistols to demonstrate to them how much the heavy triggers were hurting their aim. Sabás Baca's weapon was the worst: it took such effort to fire it that Parra was unable to hit the target at all. For contrast, he tore out a piece of cloth no bigger than a silver peso and hit it three out of five times with his own pistol.

A schedule was set up for each of them to go to Parral to a gunsmith who could be trusted not to call in the police or the rurales. Because Baca was the most in need, he was the first to go. Villa and Parra rode partway down the mountain with him. They stopped at a small arroyo to build a fire and boil coffee. After giving Baca twenty pesos, they sent him on his way with cheers and wishes of good luck.

"Baca's people fought the Spaniards once," Parra said. "But they were betrayed, and now the Tarahumaras have been quiet for almost three hundred years."

"A woman?"

"You're still talking about Eulalia."

Villa looked down into his cup. The grounds had settled into a semicircle around the edge. There was no pattern; nothing could be foretold from coffee grounds. He swished the last drops of coffee in the cup and watched the grounds settle again. There was still no pattern. "I killed a man, Nacho." He spoke softly, without looking up.

"Was he the first?"

"He was a man."

The fire was getting low, beginning to smoke. Parra gathered handfuls of sand and smothered the embers. "Why would they betray us? We took care of them, didn't we? They lived well with us."

Villa continued to look into the coffee cup. Suddenly, he threw out the grounds and went to his saddlebag to put the cup away. Returning to his place beside the dead fire, he said, "If it was Simón, why did he wait so long?" There was no answer. Villa went on: "There are two kinds of women who can be trusted. The woman who is married to you can't betray you without betraying herself. And a whore is in business, like a man; she knows who she is and how she keeps alive. Every whore understands the rule of revenge. But a woman who will live with a man without marrying him has no reason. She is neither one thing nor the other; she has no face."

"You've thought about this for a long time?"

"Since we left Durango."

"It was Simón."

Villa looked down and up, to one side and then the other. His head turned

in clicks, like a bird's head. He said his friend's name in a sigh—"Nacho"
—telling by the sound all that he feared for them. "Nacho," he said again,
trying to begin. Then he threw open his hands in submission. "I would
rather be your friend," he said. "Let it be Simón. Can it make any difference
now? The man is dead. But tell me, Nacho, why do you refuse even to think
it could have been Marta or Eulalia?"

"Because I have a face."

"Sometimes," Villa said, "it's not easy to be your friend."

"You came to me," Parra said. "I never asked you to be my friend. I live
in my way, and I can do it with you or without you. If you disagree with
me, you can leave. Do you understand me? We were betrayed by Simón;
the women loved us and that made them like saints."

Villa did not go back up the mountain with him. He followed the arroyo
in its slow descent until he came to a valley of dessicated mud. There, among
the slate-colored mounds that had once been the bed of trees, he dismounted
and lay down to sleep. Ancient dreams came to him: he saw Eagle Knights
and men in cotton armor, spearthrowers, and clubs edged in obsidian.
Armies moved upon a gray and arid plain; enormous phalanxes, driven by
the sound of drums and trumpets, marching to their own screaming voices,
met in a roar of death and settled into the earth. They came from the
horizons, the human squares of empires, and they died; and below them in
the earth horses appeared and erupted upward into steel and fire. He stood
among them, supported on one foot. His body was painted black, and there
were yellow stripes across his face. A woman stood beside him, her head
as round and luminous as the moon; he knew that all the spilled blood now
belonged to her.

It was more than a week before Parra thought they were ready. He drilled
them, he lectured them, he waited while they went to Parral to trade their
poor weapons for heavy-caliber guns, killing pistols. He cajoled them, swore
at them, begged them to have the discipline to follow his plan. They would
operate by ambush, he told them, not by charging, as in war. They would
be unseen at first, a voice, a shot, one direction and then another and
another. They would be a circle described by sound, only by sound, an
inescapable circle. No one would die, there would be no blood; bandits were
not assassins, they would live a long time.

There was no argument. He was Ignacio Parra; they followed. It was
Parra who would take the greatest risk, stepping out from his hiding place
and walking down among the ambushed men. Villa would follow. They
would go with drawn pistols, walking far apart, making their demands of
the surrendered men. The others were to stay hidden, to keep their rifles
aimed, to be six shields for the ones who walked in the open. It was agreed.

They practiced. They made assignments: who would fire at the man nearest to Parra, and who would fire at the next nearest; who would fire at the man nearest Villa and who would fire at the next nearest. They swore that they would not shoot at men who were compliant. It was not war; miners and muledrivers were not enemies—they went to steal, not to kill. Later, when they were stronger, more practiced, they would visit the Terrazas Ranch, they would look for the gray and silver rurales, they would make good their angers.

They rode down the mountain, northeast, up the river canyons between Cerro Prieto and Brincadero. The ground beside the river was flat and grassy; the muledrivers would take that route. It was the right place. They found a rocky section around a narrow in the canyon. Two draws led down to it. If the muledrivers were being cautious, following the river at a distance to avoid ambush, they would still come down through the draws to water their animals and let them graze. The rocks were charred by campfires, there was manure in various stages of drying; it was a common stopping place; they had only to wait.

José Solís the shepherd was sent away with the horses. He took them a mile from the river to graze beside a stream. The others waited, spread among the rocks at Parra's order, commanding both sides of the river, cutting off escape up either of the draws. They waited two days, eating dried beef without salt, listening for the sound of the muledrivers. Parra went from one to another, reminding them of the plan, the place each one had, the necessity of order. Parra would call out to the muledrivers. He would fire first. Then they would follow, shooting in the air, making the circle. He assigned them the numbers of a clock; they would describe a day in the order of a day.

On the afternoon of the third day they heard the muledrivers: the sounds came up the canyon, echoes dying, barely heard over the sound of water running against stone, then voices more distinctly speaking, "Burro, burro!" and the curses following. Villa and Parra were on the west side of the canyon; their voices would come out of the sun. They listened. The muletrain came close; they could hear the hooves on stone, the men walking, the packsaddles creaking, the braying of an animal responding to the sting of the long whip. "Burro, burro!" The whip, the braying, a jangling sound— something was loose, or a man with spurs walking. There was no scout, there was no one on either flank. They came around a jog in the canyon, five men walking, one on horseback, eighteen burros, twenty, twenty-one, a second man on horseback. What noise they made! It was a band coming up the canyon, a religious parade. The men on horseback were big, fat brothers dressed in leather. The walkers were kids and two old men. Under their huaraches their feet were bound with cloth to protect them from the

[*144*]

cold. They stepped carefully, avoiding the wet places, moving up the east bank of the river. Villa and Parra would have to cross the water to disarm them. If they stumbled, if there were sinkholes or deep mud, the muledrivers would defend themselves.

"Stop! We are bandits. This is Ignacio Parra speaking. Stop and throw down your weapons. We will not harm you. We are bandits, we want only your goods. You are surrounded. If you try to run or fight, we will kill you all." He fired a shot into the air.

They were all firing. The horsemen went down first, tumbling, pulling the wounded animals over with them. The men on foot drew their guns and fired into the sun or at the glaring rocks, seeing nothing, attempting to hide behind the burros, crouching, shot in the back, crawling in close to the wounded animals, pawed and kicked in their refuge, bloody, digging themselves into the tumbled-out goods and hardware and food of the burst panniers. Five men came running down out of the rocks, screaming, making themselves into a horde, firing at the wounded, stopping to take aim, whooping and running again. They ran among the wounded, shooting into their heads so that their faces and pieces of their skulls were exploded.

Both horses and seven of the burros were down. The floor of the canyon sloped toward the river. Blood ran down the slope, the river carried it away. The animals complained, kicking and pumping blood, but they did not try to stand. The bodies of the men lay in twists and curls. Baca, Urbina, López, Vaca Valles, and Salas began the looting, rolling the bodies over and around, taking their gunbelts and whatever was in their pockets. Baca looked in each mouth for gold teeth, hammering out the valuable ones with the handle of his pistol.

Villa and Parra came down from their places in the rocks and walked across the shallow river. It was cold water, deep enough in some spots to come in over the tops of their boots. They came together in the middle of the river. The men were laughing and holding up their loot for each other to see. Blood was on their hands, marking their clothes, shining on their boots, decorating their faces with dots and splotches and falling lines. The burros called and called, croaking and cawing; the horses whinnied like colts. Villa and Parra looked in each other's faces to give reproach and to see forgiveness, and they saw nothing; each man's face was fallen: Parra seemed to be having the gut pains again, Villa's eyes were drunk, the pupils too large for the afternoon sun. "I used to be a muledriver," Villa said.

Parra looked down at the river. The water was crawling up his trouser legs, past his knees. "We have to finish off the animals," he said.

Villa walked upstream to kill the horses. They were thin and old. The homemade wooden saddles had broken in the fall, and the splintered edges of the wood stood out like the broken bones of the men. He looked at the riders, trying to make out who they were, where they had come from. Not enough was left of the faces; the tops of the heads were gone, and Baca had split the jaws with his machete to inspect the teeth more conveniently. The blankets were the poorest kind, loomed in factories, and their clothing was undecorated cotton. One man was missing two fingers on his left hand. Villa thought how it must have pained him when he lost the fingers.

He killed one of the burros, then waited over the next; it was wounded in the belly, but the intestine did not seem to be torn. When Parra arrived, he asked him if he wanted to take the trouble to push the gut back in and sew it. Parra shook his head. "There are eleven left; that's more than we can use." He shot the animal.

"What now?" Villa asked.

"We take whatever we can use or sell. What do you expect? Do you want to get a priest to give them the last rites?"

"They were poor people, Nacho."

"Is this what I ordered them to do? What do you want? You want to kill those five? Go ahead. See if you get an argument from me. Bastards! Fucking cunt hairs! Sons of bitches! Do what you want. Shit in their mothers' milk for all I care."

"They were poor people like us."

"My stomach is killing me. Those fucking jessamine powders don't do any good. Oh, Jesus! Oh, Jesus Christ!" His eyes opened wide in pain, then closed into a squint. "I don't think I'm going to live too long, kid."

"They were poor people like us."

"You said that."

"Yes." Villa nodded his head slowly, as if to toll for them. The air smelled of blood and spilled intestine; the coyotes and the vultures would be coming. "We should bury them."

"The sand is too soft."

"We'll put rocks on them."

They dug shallow graves and pushed the bodies into them with their shovels. They piled stones on each grave, making small tombs. The bodies would be safe from vultures and coyotes, but the ants were already coming, walking down from the rocks in long lines, struggling back with their bits of flesh. Villa stepped on them, he scattered their lines with his foot, and in a moment they were back, the long lines of little red bubbles on walking sticks. He went from one corpse to the next, erasing the lines with his foot, coming back to find them walking over their own dead.

Baca sat on a flat rock smashing each tooth with the butt of his pistol, taking the gold and sweeping the pieces of broken tooth away with the side of his hand before he put the next tooth down. His arms were black with blood. Blood was spattered everywhere; there were clots of blood in his hair.

For every piece of gold that he smashed loose from a tooth he gave a little cry of exultation. Villa stood over him, watching the process. Sometimes the tooth did not break, but skittered away and fell into the sandy debris at the base of the rock. Then Baca leaned over, walked his fingers through the debris until he found the tooth, and began the process again, aiming more carefully at the flat part of the surface.

"They were poor people," Villa said.

"Yes, only two of them had gold teeth. But they had so much." He grinned, reaching under his poncho to take out four pieces of gold. They lay like strangely shaped nuggets in his hand, bright yellow on a surface of blackly dried blood and long streaks of tan at the creases.

"Is this what Nacho wanted?"

Baca put the gold pieces back into his pocket under the poncho and returned to his work, lining up another tooth, turning and turning it to find the flat surfaces. Again Villa asked, "Is this what Nacho wanted?" Baca continued his work, not answering. The tooth flew out to the side when he struck it with the pistol butt, and he leaned over to look for it. His head was bent, his neck was stretched out. Villa lifted the pistol from his holster. Suddenly Baca turned his face up to him. He grinned and reached for Villa's pistol. "Let me see that handle. This one of mine only has a little piece of metal. Look how the sides are chipping away from the hard teeth these fuckers have!" He took the pistol from Villa's hand and inspected the butt. "No, thank you, man; it's the same." He gave back the pistol and returned to smashing the teeth.

Villa climbed up the side of the canyon to a smooth and gently sloping place and lay down on his back to think about what had happened. He was tired from digging the graves and carrying the rocks. It was almost dark, getting colder; the sweat was drying in his clothes, a stiffening chill. The wind came down the canyon, following the turns of the river. There had been wine casks on two of the burros, the men were getting drunk while they still pawed through the panniers and searched the saddlebags, hoping for something more valuable than thread or tins of baking powder or printed cloth folded on squares of heavy paper. Solís had arrived with the horses after the men had been buried, and he had walked down the row of dead animals, touching them, shaking his head at the waste. He wanted to bury them, but no one would help; they only laughed and offered him cups of wine to make himself sensible.

On the other side of the river Parra sat in a curl, holding one arm across his belly, drinking wine, his head rocking, like an old woman soothing a child. López had taken clean clothes out of his saddlebag when Solís arrived with the horses, and now he knelt by the river washing the blood out of his shirt and trousers, rubbing the cloth, pounding water through the wet mounds with a smooth stone. The birds were overhead, floating in wide circles, black even against the night sky. In the distance, perhaps half a mile away, the coyotes were gathering, howling with anticipation. Villa wondered how they could smell death at such a great distance. Or did they watch the birds? He could no longer smell the blood or even the half-digested intestinal gore. He listened to the water running, rounding the stones, digging its channel, and he thought of the ants, silent, doing their work.

The bodies lay in the sand. They would not be eaten, they would be dissolved in themselves, carried off by the smaller things that burrowed in the sand, sliding between the wet grains, and they would be eaten by the blind white things that lay waiting in every man, hungering for him to be still. He did not know their names; three were only boys; perhaps they were a family: grandfathers, fathers, and sons. They had been the sizes of him and the look of him in the stages of a life like his. How long would the grandmothers, mothers, and sisters wait before they began to mourn? There was no set number of days; they would tell themselves lies at first, inventing bonanzas and then little disasters, animals lost, sickness, broken bones, the death of one, and finally the death of them all, lost somewhere in nameless rocks. And one woman or child, knowing the world, would dream of them eaten, dried, bones, scattered bones, dust. It would be her dream alone; she would tell no one, certain as she was that they also knew.

Parra called them together and led them upriver to a clean place to eat and drink fresh water. They built fires and cooked the meal and beans they had found in the packs. There was plenty of salt. When they rolled themselves in their blankets to sleep, they could hear the coyotes in the gaps of the wind, snarling as they fought over the flesh of the animals. The birds would take whatever the coyotes left. The scuttling things that lay in the river bottom would eat whatever fell to them.

They drove the animals upriver the next day, not crossing over until noon. Then they turned west for a while before they headed south to their mountain place. Near El Vergel they stopped while Parra sent Juan Salas into town to buy more jessamine powders from the apothecary and sacks of cornmeal from the general store. He came back with the cornmeal and the jessamine powders and two fat whores riding burros. Parra said to him, "You had better taste when you lived in Torreón."

"No, you don't understand me, chief. My dream was always to get my head between those big thighs and take deep breaths through my nose. That's how to enjoy a woman. What do you think Marie was like—some Spanish vine with thorns on it for hips? She was as big as a house; each thigh was as thick as a monastery wall. I used to dream of the smell of her on a hot night."

[148]

The whores giggled. The fatter of the two lifted her dress to show her thighs, which were dimpled with fat and truly as thick as a monastery wall, but with the shape of the trunks of oak trees. Groans of appreciation came from the men who surrounded her. "Oh, the whole mother! What handles!"

"Send them back," Parra said.

"Of course," Salas answered, "in the morning."

There was an echo of agreement. Parra looked around at his followers, who were still bloody and half drunk. "Pigs," he said, and walked away. Only Villa and Martín López followed him. They went over a little rise and made themselves a place to wait. The whoring went on all that evening and through the night. The women asked for money and received kicks and punches instead. They were made to dance naked while the men threw burning sticks at them and fired bullets at their feet. Baca scraped the insides of their thighs with a rough stone to make them more sensitive and Solís beat on their breasts with a thin stick. Every time one of the whores reached a climax the men applauded and whistled and poured wine on the shaking flesh. They sprayed them with semen and then licked it out of their crevices. Bets were made on who could bring them to orgasm. Urbina brought two small maguey plants and shoved the roots into the whores' rectums and demanded that they dance for him. Near morning, the men urinated on them and walked over them, demanding that they take pleasure in that too; and the frightened whores wept while they feigned their orgasms and begged for even greater pleasures. The men built a high bed of panniers and saddles and laid one of the women out on it, holding her legs apart while Solis brought a stallion to rape her. While she screamed and bled, they made jokes about the kind of children she would deliver. When they were finished with the whores, they chased them out of camp with curses and complaints.

During the night Villa confessed that he wished he were on the other side of the little rise that separated him and Parra and López from the whores. "I want the women," he said. "I'm aching from wanting them, but I'm also thinking of what happened to my sister. I don't know what to do. Nacho, I can smell them. My legs are shaking."

Parra lay with his head on his saddle. He had taken four of the jessamine powders. His eyes were closed against the irritating light of the fire. "Go ahead," he told Villa. "You think they'll know the difference if there's one more?"

"You don't mean that."

"No, I don't. It's not advice. But you have to decide who you are and what you believe. If I tell you, it's no good."

"Why don't you go over there?"

Parra sighed. "Because I'm sick to my stomach."

"What would you do if you weren't sick?"

Parra rolled over onto his side and covered his eyes with his hand. "Don't pester me," he said, yawning. "And don't expect me to make these choices for you too. Maybe I don't go because my mother took me to the church when I was a baby and I believe in Our Lord Jesus Christ and His Mother the Blessed Virgin. Maybe I don't like such fat, ugly whores. What's on my mind is mine."

"But you could stop them," Villa said.

A soft laugh came from Parra—not bitter, but worldly, without hope. He rolled over onto his back again, trying to find a comfortable position, a way to sleep. "No," he said. "I can kill them or I can let them alone, but I can't stop them. I decided to try to sleep. Maybe that's the wrong thing. Who knows? You think about it. Give me advice. I'm a sick man, the blood is running out my asshole; how can I think about two fat whores? Advise me, Panchito. Be my priest, tell me if I sinned." He closed his eyes. "I'm waiting. You don't mind if I sleep a little while I'm waiting."

Laughter came from the whores. One of them asked for another man, for wine; she challenged them to please her, to satiate her. Villa listened, imagining the sweat on the woman's face, the sparse curled wool of her crotch, the creases in the spread thighs, the rolling of her belly and her great breasts, the loosed folds of her cunt. It was her business, the way of her life, not a violation of her. She took money, lived by her pleasure and pleasuring, she laughed; he heard her laughing, teasingly asking them to step inside those legs again. Had they not beaten her, had they not humiliated her, he could have joined them. If she were not afraid. All women were afraid, even whores. There were other reasons; he could not think them. He lay shaking, with sweat running in his eyes and his mouth gone dry.

López whispered to him, "Me neither. Because of my brother."

"That's the reason, the true reason?"

"And I like to be in private."

"My sister was not a whore," Villa said.

"They say she was very beautiful. And a virgin."

"All the sadness of my life comes from that," Villa said. But after reflecting on the thought, he went on: "I say from the tragedy of my sister, but then I try to think to myself how that came to be. Those things don't happen to the sisters of landlords. They only happen to us. We plant the corn and harvest the corn, we plant the cotton and pick the cotton, we prune their trees and pick their fruit, and they kill our brothers and rape our sisters. Do you think it was meant to be that way?

"My mother used to talk sometimes about fate. I think she learned that from the priests. The world has its way, we have a place in our time, we have our days and our hours, but it doesn't say in the Book of Days that

[*150*]

we have to make them rich while they kill us. The priests are the ones who say that.

"I think sometimes maybe I'll go to live in a city, like Chihuahua or Parral, and I'll have a store and sell clothes and pots and pans, and I won't be rich but I won't be poor, I'll just be happy. I'll have a good store, like a man I used to know. But no credit. Those women are really hot; you can hear them.

"But you have to make some money, because that's the only way to keep them from using you like a burro. But I don't know. I think about those people who were driving these burros yesterday. They were from a family, you could tell that. And look what happened to them. Poor people, working, doing the work poor people do, trying not to be burros themselves. And now they're all dead. . . . You listen, you hear how wet those women are —loose, you know.

"So you live until you die, and you have so many tragedies. Your father dies, your mother dies, maybe you live to see your brothers and sisters die. It's from my sister that my sadness comes. If I didn't love her and think of her the way she was before, if I wasn't faithful to the memory of her when she was happy, I wouldn't think so much about life, and I would walk across that little hill and fuck those whores until their cunts sang cowboy songs."

He looked at López, whose eyes were closed, and at Parra, who had gone to sleep at last. The sounds of madness and pleasure came over the little hill. All night he lay there, sleepless, suspended between memory and the moment, trembling.

They began the trip up the mountain in the morning, riding slowly, hung over, tired, chilled even in the sun. The animals were skittish, the smell of blood was still in the air. At a narrow place on the trail that wound around the faces of the mountain, one of the burros bolted, lost its footing, and went over the side, rolling over and over, braying, the gray hide shredding on the rocks, while the pots and pans that had filled its two panniers clanked and sang and sent back reflections of sunbursts. All of them stopped to watch the fall, and then to look for someone to blame, Villa the muledriver or Solís the herdsman. But Solís was innocent, bringing up the rear, far from the fallen animal, and when they looked at Villa's face, they saw that it was he who assigned the blame and they who needed excuses. They moved on, cursing the burros, forcing the horses to the inside edge of the trail.

It was after dark before they had unloaded the burros and unsaddled the horses. The thin air left them feeling more tired and slightly drunk. Rats had found the camp during the week of their absence; almost everything they had left behind had been gnawed. The few sacks of cornmeal were opened, flowed onto the ground, soiled with rat droppings. Long shreds hung from the meat; the gristle had been chewed. The sacks of beans, like the cornmeal, had been eaten and fouled.

When it was fully dark under the spotted sky, the rats came again, fearing the small cooking fires, then racing through the light to the food. The horses and the burros reared, pawing at the scurrying sounds, but the rats were too quick. In the firelight they matched the color of the earth; only shadows moved, scratching across the open places, disturbing pebbles. Urbina and Vaca Valles went for their rifles. "I'll need a good fire," Urbina said. "I can't shoot them in the dark."

Parra shook his head, but no one saw him. It was Villa who ran up to them and grabbed the barrels of their rifles. "Don't be crazy," he said. "We're too close. You'll kill someone."

Urbina gave an angry laugh. "You don't trust my aim."

"The ricochets, man! You can't aim the ricochets!"

With shovels and machetes and rifle butts and pieces of burning wood, stumbling in the places the light did not reach, jumping back when the rats turned and leaped for their legs, they burned and chopped and crushed until the only shadows that moved were those that fled. They stopped to drink wine and to pick up the bloody carcasses by the tail and throw them into the fire. For every rat that died, they cheered; for every one that escaped, they cursed. They danced in the firelight, shadows themselves, sweating, keeping their feet moving for fear that one of the rats would crawl onto them. "They'll eat your eyes out," Baca shouted. "They'll chew off your eggs!" And when it was quiet and they sat around the fires, drinking wine or water, smelling the burning hair and the liver stench of the cracking innards, he said, "It's a shame to waste them. When I was a boy, we used to walk all the way to Chihuahua, miles and miles, all the way down the mountains into the city. And on the way, sometimes we didn't have any-thing to eat, and when we got near the city I would catch one of these rats with a stick trap. My mother cleaned it and skinned it and we cooked it over a little fire, just like you would cook a bird. It's delicious the way she cooked it, with sage and chiles sewed in the inside. The trouble with you mestizos is that you don't know how to live off the land; you're too used to begging from the landlords. A rat is a good meal when you're hungry, especially the back legs, the thighs." Everyone laughed. After that, they always called him The Rat, and he always responded to the name by smacking his lips and loudly sucking his teeth.

The food was destroyed; the filth was inseparable. They ate what they had taken from the mule train, and then there was nothing. There were no cattle ranches on the eastern slope of the mountain, the hunting was poor, and mesquite did not grow at that altitude. Manuel Vaca Valles said he would climb the mountain with a train of burros carrying trade goods and bring back cornmeal and beans from the other side. "They won't know the brands," he said. "It's not dangerous for me. And maybe I'll find Yaquis there; I could speak to them."

He took all but one of the burros—that one was for meat—and he climbed the mountain to the highest ridges, always walking behind the animals, poking them and whipping them up the drifts of fallen rock, around the sheer faces, changing directions, backtracking, driving the animals to the limit of their footing. At the campsite below, they watched his progress, shouting directions, possibilities to him. He climbed all day, and in the early evening, just ahead of the sun, he crossed over to the western slope and was gone.

Six days later he returned. One side of his head was shaved clean, wide yellow stripes were painted across his face, and his left arm was wrapped in a basket of woven maguey fibers and tied to the front of his shirt. They scrambled up the mountain to meet him, greeting him with embraces and eyes full of questions. Solís herded the burros down into the camp. The panniers were loaded with cornmeal, dried corn still to be ground, beans, sunflower seeds, chiles of all kinds: mild chiles, sweet chiles, burning mountain chiles, red chiles, green chiles, dried chiles. They helped him down the mountain, gave him a drink of mescal and another, and listened while he told of his visit among the Quatatl. He was weary from the long climb up the side of the mountain, and he was not yet recovered from his ordeal. His story came out in pieces, confused in the times of things and sometimes contradictory, as if he were dreaming, as if he had no sense. But this is what they understood:

The mountain descended very sharply on the western side. He had been forced to walk along the ridge of the summit for several hours before he found a place that the burros could negotiate. The sun was almost gone then, looking up at him from the horizon, partly screened by the great stands of pine trees on the slopes below. He managed to reach the shelter of the top of the tree line before darkness, and there he found a small plateau and a sort of open well that seemed to be fed by an underground spring. He watered the animals, staked them out to graze on whatever they could find, built a fire to last the night, and went to sleep.

In the morning, he saw nothing before him but trees; and leaving the burros still staked out in the little plateau, he climbed back up the mountain to look for a village or at least a trail among the trees. The belt of trees was no more than a mile wide. Below it was a wide stretch of barren rock, land so dead it did not even have the sparse touches of green made by cactus and mesquite. There might have been some sagebrush, but he couldn't be certain at that distance. Beyond the rocky area was a stretch of patchy, discolored land, perhaps a series of mesas rising out of the side of the mountain; then

[*153*]

another belt of trees; and far off in the distance the high desert continued without end, perhaps all the way to the sea that was said to be on the far western edge of the world.

Manuel made his way easily through the belt of trees. It was not so different from the land in which he had lived when he was a boy. These were not the white pines he knew, but the floor of the forest beneath the trees was thick with dead pine needles and dotted with the vines, sudden clumps of grass or sage and small hopeless trees dying in the shade of the great pines that he had known for most of his life. He was surprised only at the lack of game in the belt of forest. There were neither rabbits, nor mice, nor deer. The land seemed to have been hunted out; perhaps by packs of wolves or coyotes or families of mountain lions; but he saw no bones, no sign that animals had ever killed and eaten there. Before noon, he had cleared the belt of trees and entered the rocky area. The rocks were hard and often gray. Many of the rocks were more than eight feet high, obscuring his vision, leaving him with the feeling of a man lost. He navigated by the sun and the downward slope.

Halfway through the rocky area, he was struck in the arm by a projectile. The force was so great that he was knocked down. He thought he had been shot, but there had been no sound of a gun firing, and his skin was not broken where the projectile had struck him. He lay among the rocks where he fell, bemused, waiting for something more to happen. His arm was growing numb; he could not feel any sensation at all in his hand. No sound, no face came to answer his fear. The burros stopped, looking for something to chew among the rocks, found nothing, waited. A wave of nausea passed through him; he heard the sound of himself, blood and breath in their hurried patterns, nothing more.

After a time—he did not know how long—a net of woven maguey fiber was thrown over him. When he tried to struggle out of the net, it was slipped under and around him and pulled tight. He could not move any of his limbs. His arm was numb all the way to the shoulder. All day he lay in the net. He heard people taking the burros away, talking in a strange language that was neither Spanish nor Yaqui nor Tarahumara. He thought he made out a few words that bore some similarity to Yaqui: *ne, quata, tlatoani, nacatl* —I, stone, chief, meat. But he could not be sure; the people spoke quickly, and they were too far away to be heard distinctly; perhaps he was only imagining the similarities. He thought he had a fever. His muscles cramped. He could not move.

At dark they laid the first stone, placing it gently against his back. Then there was another placed behind his shoulders and another against his buttocks, and several against his legs. The stones were large and heavy; he

[*154*]

could feel them beginning to press against him. He struggled to turn his head to see who was placing these stones against him, building a wall behind him. Perhaps it was some form of protection for the night, or a ritual for the introduction of strangers. Then a rock was placed on his hip and wedged against the rock behind his back. Other rocks were placed on his legs and wedged there. The weight was uncomfortable. He was beginning to have difficulty breathing under the growing weight.

He was being crushed under the weight of the rock, not protected or buried, but crushed. Suddenly he realized who the people were—the Quatatl, the stoneheads, the slingshot people. His grandfather had talked about them. Long ago, as far back as anyone could remember, soon after the first Yaquis came up out of the earth, there had been a great battle between the Yaquis and the Quatatl. The arrows of the Yaquis had overcome the slingshots of the Quatatl, but not before many of the Yaquis had fallen. When the victorious Yaquis had at last stormed the camp of the Quatatl, they found their captured men wrapped in maguey fiber nets and crushed under the weight of great stones.

Manuel thought he was dreaming, dying under the weight of the stones. The Yaquis had chased the Quatatl into the high, barren mountains hundreds of years before, and the entire tribe had perished there. But the stones were still being piled on him. The pressure on his head was terrible. His entire body was being driven into the ground by the weight. He thought his ribs were going to crack. If it was a dream, he would appeal to them as in dreams. He came as a merchant and the right of merchants to travel freely was granted everywhere. *"Puchteca,"* he shouted. *"Puchteca, puchteca, puchteca."* It was a word known to all mountain people; like *atl,* the word for water, *puchteca,* the name of merchants, could be understood anywhere. He shouted it again, saying it slowly, one syllable at a time: *"Puchteca, nica puchteca, puchteca."*

The piling on of the rocks ceased. For a long time nothing happened. Manuel thought he heard them talking, whoever they were, but he could not be certain; his head was aching, filling up with rhythmic noises, something seemed to be pushing against his eyes from inside his head. He feared that he would burst. Then the word came back to him from outside the net: *"Puchteca, tinemi?"*

"Ninemi," he said. I live.

They lifted the stones from him, first from his head and then from his ribs and at last from his legs. Then they came around him to loosen the net, and he saw that they were wild people, chichimeca. They wore skins; their faces were painted. Some had long hair, waist-length hair, others had shaved their heads. Each one had a slingshot wrapped around his head. A few of them also had maguey fiber capes, crudely woven and dyed in turkey patterns. They wore huaraches of dried maguey leaves.

He asked them for water. *"Atl."*

One of them, who seemed to be the leader—an older one with a shaved head and a long cape—answered, "Agua?" Manuel smiled. The man passed him a gourd of water, and he drank.

A moment of privacy was permitted him while he urinated. Then they walked down the side of the mountain to the place in which they had constructed a few huts of sticks and maguey leaves. It was dark, but moonlit; Manuel could see the larger rocks, they guided him over the unseen obstructions. He realized that they had been in this place for a long time and that like his own Yaquis they had learned to see trails in the shape of the land itself.

He was taken to one of the huts and given sharply flavored atole to eat, a dipping gourd of very strong mescal to drink, and told to sleep. They were able to speak to each other in a mixture of Spanish and Nahuatl. He did not know whether to tell them he was a Yaqui, one of the chichimeca too, for there was history to think about, there was revenge to be considered. His arm had become very painful, but the mescal was dulling the pain; the cramps in his arms and legs and neck were receding; he slept.

In the morning, he examined his arm again; it was discolored from his shoulder to his elbow, painful, swollen, and useless. A man in leather leggins —his face painted yellow, his hair falling to his knees, decorated with red and yellow geometric designs and lip and earplugs of polished turquoise— entered the hut. He carried a woven sack and wore a mirror in the middle of his forehead, a large and perfectly polished piece of obsidian. The man gave Manuel roots to chew and rubbed his injured arm very gently with a warm and scented grease. All sensation left Manuel's body; his arm became supple, a thong hung from his shoulder. The man made a series of tiny incisions with a sharp piece of obsidian; the blackness of the wound oozed out of Manuel's arm. Suddenly the man jerked Manuel's arm straight, tied it into splints and wrapped it into the maguey fiber basket. Then he left him to sleep again.

A stench of feces permeated the village, and there was a strange chirping, peeping noise underlying all other sounds, as if birds or bats were locked into the straw of the huts to sing there. Manuel became aware of the sound and odor when he awakened again. His face was uncomfortably stiff and his head felt different, out of balance. He thought it must be the drugs, and he was not concerned, for the pain had disappeared from his arm and he was able to move his fingers inside the basket. He lay still, waiting, knowing that it was safest to be passive, to act the role of guest.

Toward evening, the man who had first spoken to Manuel and given him water came into the hut. They shared tubes of bitter tobacco and a dipper of mescal. The man was formal, but not unfriendly. He spoke at length about the village:

They were indeed the Quatatl, the people who had long ago been defeated by the Yaquis. In some forgotten time they had emerged from the top of a mountain in the north, but the harsh winters had driven them south, for even the rugged Quatatl could not bear the winters of their place of emergence. They had been aided in their trip by rodents, which had tried to help the Quatatl while fighting a constant battle against the coyotes, who were born of the surface debris of the earth and who were loyal to neither heaven nor hell.

At one time there had been many Quatatl, but they had endured a series of reverses that reduced them to three clans when the speaker, Mictzin, was born and named for his power over death. Since then, one of the villages had been destroyed in a landslide, leaving two clans. And only two years ago, an epidemic of lumps and fever had killed everyone in one of those villages. Now there was only one clan: eight men, eleven women, three old people, and five children. Marriage within the clan was impossible—the punishment for incest was to be crushed; marriage outside the tribe was considered adulterous, and the punishment for adultery was the same as for incest.

They had now begun to eat peyote, to find in it a dreamgod, to find in it the false pride, the haughtiness, the presumptuousness of the damned and the maddened. Mictzin said that he did not know what to do, that he believed there would soon be an end to the Quatatl. This was the last place that could be called Quatatlan. He too had begun to eat peyote, to expect in it the answer to the dilemma of the rules of the clan. He sat beside the bed where Manuel lay, and he wept.

In the evening, Manuel walked through the village. He saw the place from which the odor and the noise came. It was at the south end of the village, leaning against a stone wall, a giant cage made of hundreds of small cages, each of them held together with string of woven maguey fiber, made of nothing more than sticks. In each cage were at least two rats, and in some of them there were whole families of rats. The men spent most of their days rebuilding and reinforcing the cages, replacing the sticks and the maguey cord as the rats chewed through them.

The rats were fed pine cones and corn. Below the cages, the droppings and the chaff of their food were piled as high as a man's knee. The sticks of the cages were thickly encrusted with droppings, and there were fleas and beetles everywhere. The life of the animals in the cages was a hideous circle, for the rats ate the beetles and the fleas that lived on their droppings and their blood. Mictzin said the rats were sent to them by their god to provide food.

After eating peyote, the people of the village danced. Like the Huicholes, the women raised their skirts and displayed their genitals to the fire to prove their faithfulness, or if they were unmarried, to show their virginity. There was drumming and then vomiting and eating more peyote and drumming and vomiting and dancing, and then the people of the village sat silently around the fire until morning, when they all went to their huts and slept.

Manuel went to their fields with them to look at the corn and beans and chiles that they grew. Rat droppings were planted along with the seeds to honor their god, who had been good to them. The plants grew well, although the late-ripening chiles were sometimes bitter and the ears of the second crop of corn were always small. He agreed with them to trade the goods in his panniers for some of the food they had stored. They were glad to have the cloth and thread and metal cooking utensils, and he was glad to have the food to bring back.

Only when he looked into the obsidian mirror worn by the healer was Manuel upset, for then he saw that there were yellow stripes on his face and half of his head had been shaved. The healer explained to him that the shaving and painting were necessary to the cure of his broken arm. Manuel agreed, and he thanked the healer for his excellent work.

Mictzin came to his hut on the morning of Manuel's departure. It was he who had thrown the stone that broke Manuel's arm. He apologized for his act, explaining that there was no longer any way to recognize a merchant. Manuel smiled to show his forgiveness, and they went up the mountain together. They parted at the summit of the ridge, ceremoniously exchanging a hunting knife and a turquoise earplug. Then Manuel herded the burros over to the other side.

Juan Salas asked if the women were beautiful, and Manuel replied, "In their way. Yes, in their way they are very beautiful. They're like the songs that make you cry when you're drunk."

"Did you think about staying with them?" Villa asked. "From what you say, they would have welcomed you."

"They're dying," Vaca Valles said. Then he asked for water and for someone to help him to wash the yellow paint from his face.

The road near Guanacevi followed the contour of the mountains, turning and looping, seeking the gentle grades, skirting the peaks and the steep canyons; a troop of rurales or a regiment of soldiers could wait unseen around any of a hundred curves. At Sestin the road was flat, running straight across open land; but it was forty-five miles away, and they would have to ride all night to meet the coach.

They chose to wait near Guanacevi. "I'm dying anyway," Parra said. "Why should I tire myself with racing to Sestin?"

Villa asked if he felt sick.

"No. I'm just dying. You know, my mother named me for this saint who wanted to die to be with God. He was killed by wild animals, maybe lions. I think about that sometimes, the things the clergy does to us with the names they give. But I'm not like him, kid; I don't want to die, but I know what's coming for me. Look in my face, my eyes; you can see that I'm going to die."

"I don't see anything."

Parra said his gratitude with a soft laugh. "My eyes don't shine anymore, Panchito. They're getting dry, the skin is covering them up."

"You're only getting fat, Nacho. You forget: a light eater makes a good horseman."

Parra took a little cigar from his pocket, rolled it in his fingers, and lit it carefully. "I'm damned," he said, speaking out puffs of smoke. "Not the kind of damned the priests tell you when you make a mistake in the catechism; I am really damned. When I was living in the mountains, I met some people who walk in rows like ants and wear mirrors on their backs, and I walked with them and looked in their mirrors and all I saw was the night. There are other signs too: every time a woman cooks tamales for me they stick to the side of the pot; twice I've been in a house where ants swarmed; and about a year ago I was sleeping in the afternoon and I heard a strange noise that awakened me, a noise no one ever hears in the afternoon: a horned owl."

Tears came into Villa's eyes. "Maybe you don't know how to read the signs," he said. Parra did not bother to answer.

A shot stopped the coach, caught it fighting a hill, slowing for the curve at the top. The driver pulled the brake; the guard raised his empty hands. It was routine, the life of the times, the risks were understood, no one wished to die. From a distance the driver and the guard appeared to be relieved, even pleased, leaning back against the coach, legs outstretched. Parra touched Blue Star with his heels, and the animal went forward, stepping cautiously, testing its footing in the loose rock of the slope that led down to the road.

Villa did not watch the coach or Parra's descent to the road; he looked back in the direction from which the coach had come, expecting to see the dust of following horsemen or the silhouette of a rider moving furtively along the ridges, a vanguard, a sign of others who rode on the flank of the coach. They were prepared; the Winchesters, Sharps, and the new Mausers were loaded, lying across their saddles, shells in the chambers. He had calculated their firepower; they were capable of shooting more than five hundred rounds in the first minute of a battle, and there were revolvers and the magazines of the Mausers to hold the next minute while the Winchesters were reloaded. They were an army, the cavalry of Ignacio Parra, and while Parra walked his horse down to the road they looked to Villa for their direction. He could send them riding with a wave of his hand; the trigger of his rifle triggered theirs. They watched him, seeing nothing else; in this moment he was the master, all significance flowed from him.

The hills were empty. There was no dust, there were no silhouettes. He looked to one side and then the other. Had they been outflanked? Was the coach empty, or nothing more than the comfort of some fat man with his collar starched and white, the pedestal of his whiskers? Villa had heard of the shipment from a telegraph operator in Santa Barbara, a fat drunk with a salt-and-pepper mustache and small curled ears, who had expounded on the dangers of shipping gold by coach, the need for more railroads. "Mexico is still only half-civilized," he said. "As a technical man, one who works with the miracle of science every day, I see our backwardness in the light of modern times. We ship gold from Guanacevi and send our rurales who are themselves bandits to protect it from bandits. Ah, the blind lead the blind in Mexico. For all the foreign ideas, for all the foreign experts our president brings in, we are still a country of deserts and ignorant natives."

But there were no rurales. Villa tightened his eyes into the most distant focus. Nothing. A constant wisp of smoke rose from the mine at Guanacevi, ribbons of green marked the riverbanks, the stands of timber to the southeast were grayed with distance. He looked over his shoulder at Parra reaching the road, walking Blue Star to the coach. The driver's face was turned toward Parra; they were speaking. Blue Star was turned parallel to the coach, facing the rear. The door flew open, blue powdersmoke came out. Shots, the narrow crack of Mausers, and a gruff Winchester firing again and again. Parra twisted, jerked, dancing on the saddle. Blue Star collapsed. The coach was moving, the horses were running, whipped into panic. The door flapped open. The coach turned the curve and was gone. Dust was left, fading back to the ground. Parra lay half-covered by the horse. His hat was beside him, overturned. His blanket lay in the dust, a row of colors on the flat brown road.

"Don't let them!" Villa screamed, already mourning, clawing at his own throat with the sound.

Urbina was the first to move. His horse came scrambling down the steep side of the hill, with Urbina leaning back, balancing the animal, holding up his carbine, calling to the others, "Come on, boys! Get moving!" There were more horses, the sound of the stones rolling, pouring down the hill. They were urging each other, calling to themselves, "Let's go, let's go." The horses reached the road at a run, wheeling to the right, beginning to stretch. Urbina turned the curve with the others running hard behind him, bunching, running through the billowing dust, striving for the clear air.

Villa let his horse walk down to the road, turning this way and that way, picking its footing. He held the reins loosely, rocking with the movement of the animal. His body was tingling with heat and he felt a chill, as if he had just stepped naked into the hottest sun. He watched Parra, looking for movement, a sign that his death was only a deception. The dust settled, the air cleared. Villa dismounted and knelt beside the body. The blood was still, dying in the wounds. There was no movement, no heart; the face was destroyed, marred by two deep holes and crushed in the fall. Blackness was seeping into the skin.

He closed Parra's eyes and pressed his lower jaw shut; then he put his arms under Parra's, locked them over his chest, and dragged him out from under the horse. Villa sat on the road with the dead man's head and shoulders in his lap, and he thought of his father, who also knew that he would die, who also knew that death was coming but did not know when; and he thought that if they had not known the moment, their faces would have been surprised, their eyes would not have rolled white, their mouths would not have fallen slack.

After a while, he came to understand that Parra was dead, and he lifted the body off his legs and threw it aside.

The body turned in the air and came to rest face down.

Villa got to his knees and crawled over to Parra. He put the sprawled arms in place and straightened the legs. The movement had jolted the bowels loose. Villa gathered dust in his hands and covered the stain. Then he turned him over very carefully, keeping the arms and legs decent, and looked at the face. The dust adhered to the skin and made a gritty paste in the wounds. He took the waterbag and the blanket from Parra's saddle and washed and wiped his face. He straightened his hair and moved the jaw until the teeth met. It was the warrior's face again, cold and torn, but the nose was straight, a hard line, and the closed eyes were set apart from the line of his nose, as in all decent men. He could be prepared for Paradise.

The others came back. Two of them were wounded, but even they were uproarious with victory, remembering the sight of the horses falling, the disaster of the traces, the coach tumbling, the battered rurales crawling out of the smashed wood, bewildered, one of them pleading and then the rest losing their courage to the breaking of his voice, dying with squirms and bleating, conquered, humiliated, and finally dismembered to prevent this world from becoming the next. Urbina had been the maker of the victory, and he came back cheering, only to have the fever stifled by the sight of Villa on his knees beside the body of Parra, washing and washing, as if he could wash away the wounds.

They wrapped Parra's body in sarapes and blankets, for they had no white cloth; and they buried him with his weapons, with pieces of turquoise and jade and gold and silver in the most beautiful patterns. A dried branch was put into his grave so that it might bloom in the next world and give milk. He lacked only a dog to guide him, and that made them all afraid for him; they knew that the other world is not like this, and a man can easily become lost, unable to find the river even though he has something with him to pay for the crossing. It made them think of their own lives, of how they lived as wanderers, without three stones, land to work, and a pet dog.

Villa put the blue hummingbird wrapped in red twine into the grave to help Parra to be safe from evil and to guide him, if the bird chose to be seen in flight. He helped to lower the body into the grave and he wept, without shame for his tears, while the grave was filled with sand and stones and shiny slices of red sienna clay. Brother, father, friend, he said to Parra, capitulating on all of the old arguments, forgiving him everything but death itself. He continued to speak to Parra while a cross was made and put into the ground at the head of the grave, and one of the men who had served in a church said all that he could remember of those prayers for the dead.

Afterward, Vaca Valles was the first to come to him. "I'm going back to Sonora," he said. "There's a man there named Tatebiate who says we can go home to the Yaquimí River. He's in the Bacatete highlands now, and I think I know where to find him there. If not, someone will lead me to him, because I knew him when he still allowed them to call him Juan Maldonado.

That was a long time ago, before they put Cajeme up against a wall, but I remember his face. His eyes turned down at the outside corners and he looked like he had suffered for every one of us who died in Yucatán or the Valle Naciónal. If I go back now—well, I still have this one good eye, and I know the Bacatete valleys—I was born there. It could be something for my mother and my sisters."

Villa embraced him. "I'll miss you, Mano, but what you're doing is right." He held Vaca Valles tightly for a moment, feeling the life of him, certain that it would not be long before he was dead.

José Solís was next: "I've saved my money for these two and a half years, and I want to buy a little piece of land now and try again to raise a herd. Lalo Sebollas wants to go into partners with me, and I think that's good, because with two of us the problem that ruined my life won't happen again." Villa told him to look through Parra's belongings and take whatever he found.

"What about his mother?"

"Dead. He didn't know. It's not wrong for you to take the money."

Solís thanked him. "I'm not leaving because of you," he said. "A man can't stay in this life forever. Now that Ignacio's dead . . . Well, I don't want to abandon you, but this seems like a good time."

Villa gathered them all together. He walked a few feet uphill to speak to them. Someone said he was like Jesus preaching on the mountain, and Villa laughed, and then they all laughed, because he was wearing three cartridge belts and two revolvers and his rifle was slung across his back. He stood there for a long time, waiting for them to be quiet, looking at each of them, their dark faces, their great hats; some were scarred, two had fresh wounds; they were tired from never having a place to stop, and thin from weariness and from eating meat without corn or beans. As he found each man's eyes, the man became quiet.

"Some of you want to go home," he said, "and some of you have no home, and some of you are like me: you can't go home. Ignacio Parra had no home. He was glad to die. He had been in the mountains for so many years that you would think he had forgotten about growing things. Don't be fooled: he was like you, he was like me.

"Once, a long time ago, we stopped in a field, Nacho and I, and we saw an old man and his wife trying to bring in their corn. We picked the ripe ears for them and then we stayed until the small ears were ripe and we picked those too. And at night we sat with the old woman and husked the corn and scraped the ears. The sun was so hot it was scorching our hats, but we were happy. And then all the corn was picked and husked and scraped and we sat in the house with empty hands until we could not sit any longer and we had to go on.

[*163*]

"We were always going on to another place; and even when we stopped, we didn't plant anything or build anything. We didn't even have the luck of lizards that crawl under the same rock night after night to sleep.

"You came to us because you thought this was the way to become rich. You have had your hands filled with money, but you were never rich. This is dreaming. You were not rich, you were only dreaming, you were only imagining.

"If you stay here in the mountains and you live like a bandit all the rest of your life, the only home you will ever find is the one that Ignacio Parra found. And that is not enough—a man's grave should not be his first home. Listen to me now, let me tell you the truth. Go home. Learn how to live. Go home. Plant corn. Find yourselves wives and raise children. Then you'll be rich. Go home. There is a place for you. Find it. There is nothing left in these mountains but grief. Go home."

They drifted away, going to their horses, loading their burros, loading their baskets and saddlebags, rolling their blankets and tying them on behind their saddles. Villa stood on the hill to watch them leave, returning their waves of farewell, hoping for them. He stood on the hill until he and Urbina were the only ones left.

"It was all yours," Urbina said.

"There was nothing."

A wind came up, rattling the brush. Far apart, they had to shout to be heard.

"Do you have any money?" Urbina asked.

"A little. Not much. It went."

"You want a few hundred?"

"I have enough."

Urbina waited for Villa to come down to him. Villa waited for Urbina to come up the hill. The wind stopped, came again in gusts. Villa rubbed his eyes with his knuckle. The wind pushed at his hat. Urbina was wrapped in his rabbit-skin cape. He wriggled his feet in his new boots.

"I'm going to Las Nieves," Urbina said.

"It's a good place."

"I invite you."

"Thank you. I want to stay with Nacho for a while."

"I'll wait for you."

In the increasing dust Villa breathed through his mouth. From Urbina's distance he appeared to be smiling.

"You don't have to," Villa shouted.

Urbina went down the hill to where his horse and his two pack mules were staked out. He loaded the animals and came back up, sitting on his horse, with the mules behind. Halfway up the hill, he reined in the horse and called to Villa again. "The sons of bitches stole my rifle and two pistols. They didn't leave you anything but your horse. Can you hear me? They stole your burros, everything. You better come with me."

Villa waved goodbye to him.

Urbina wrenched his horse around and headed downhill, his little train moving with the shapes of the hill, like a snake. He sent stones falling, he made dust, he whooped to his horse like a herdsman. The rollings of the hill obscured him; there was only dust. He rounded the curve of the road. Villa stood with the wind and the grave and the hard land: crumbling rocks, pebbles, sand, gullies of the wind, brown stiff weeds, and green cactus that rose from nothing, without soil, without water, preserving itself with thorns, ugly and alive. He went to the place where Parra was buried and sat beside the grave to mourn.

The evening wind came and scoured his face with sand. The hills were shrouded in a mist of sand. Night came still and clear and cold. He looked at the shapes of the stars and the wounded face of the moon, and he thought of death and the pain of death. With a match, he made a small fire of twigs and burned his wrists.

He was ragged, gaunt; his skin was loose, there was madness in his eyes. I gave him a clean white cotton shirt and trousers. For his sake, I left my work in a dangerous time and tried to reason with him. It was the year 8 Rabbit, a year when the bad luck sign of the Rabbit is doubled. All that year, day and night, I prayed, piercing my tongue, feet, chest, ears, and the foreskin of my penis. I burned the scabs for incense and I wore the blood in my hair. People came to me for advice, frightened people, and I studied the Tonalpohualli and the Tonalámatl to read their calculations.

The next year was the catzopine century, and the people were afraid that it was the predicted end, for there had been years of drought and sudden floods, poor crops, rising prices; infants had died and there was true starvation for the first time that any of them could remember. I told them, as I told him, that the dangerous year was still a long way off. The year of their century was only 8 Reed, an ordinary year. The fire would not be extinguished until the end of 13 Flint Knife, as always, and the New Fire would be made on the first day of 1 Rabbit, as always. If the sun were to stop, if the predicted end in the upheaval of the earth were to come, it would be then, in their year 1923.

Villa picked up the old fig-bark paper on which I had drawn out the wheels of the years. He studied it for a moment, as if he knew what had been written, then he threw the paper down on the mat. "That's the old world," he said. "I live in another world, one where they have rifles instead of spearthrowers. I've been in the cities where they have electricity; you don't even know what that is. And there are trains. Have you ever seen a train? You, you're still afraid of horses. You should see a locomotive. Go into that other world and then come back and look again at your calculations."

It was not as if I had not heard such challenges before, but I did not expect it of him. I brewed amaranth tea and warmed some fruit tamales that a woman had brought for me, thinking that the severity of his hunger might be affecting him. I even burned copal in the fire, because I could see that the odor of the burned scabs was sickening him. While we ate, I told him the history of the four suns, how we had perished once in floods and once in fire and once in wind and once in the jaws of jaguars, how we have been giants and fish and monkeys, and how the calendar has always predicted these times by the cycles of the sun and the intersection of the cycles of the Morning Star. It has never mattered, I told him, whether it was the time of monkeys or giants or fish or men; the sun battles with the infinite armies of the stars until the sun comes to an end in a great cataclysm that changes everything. If this was a time of electricity and trains and rifles, what did it matter? How could these things affect the sun? They were not even acceptable sacrifices; they were nothing, the works of men, unreal, less than words.

He took out his pistol and shot a hole in the wall of my house. "Is that unreal?" he asked. I was ashamed for him; there had never been a weapon fired in my house before. I asked him if he thought that was magic, if he thought the monk could have been tempted by the simple act of making a hole in the wall of his house.

He replied, "Have you ever seen a dead man?"

"Many. Is that why you brought the rifle, to make a dead man of me? Are you threatening me?"

"This is not a rifle," he said, making his mouth disdainful. "It's a revolver."

"Well, you have upset me, Doroteo; I will grant you that much. Does that make you happy? Is that why you came here?"

He laughed. "The gun is magic. It even frightens you."

I made snakes appear on his legs. I made his legs crawl with snakes. He tore them from him frantically, throwing them against the walls of the house, and for every one he threw I made two more appear. He could not run, he could not even stand; they weighed him down, he was tangled in them. When I saw that he was giving up hope, I made the snakes disappear. He tried to kiss my hands to thank me, but I pushed him away, telling him to sit like a man and listen, to strengthen his face again, instead of behaving like a fool.

He was contrite, with tears and blushing and nervous movements of his hands, all the unspoken signs; but he said nothing. I was satisfied, however, and I spoke to him:

"It is very difficult not to be confused in this world. You see trains and electricity and rifles that can make holes in walls, and you begin to think that men and their things are important; you forget history and religion and thought. I don't blame you. The temptation is less for me, because I don't live in the world as you do; my life is concerned with history and poetry, perhaps to excess. I don't know the sweat of the fields or the clamor of the cities; a landlord has never humiliated me. In that I'm too much like the monk of Tula, I know; I know the dangers, I try to compensate for the dangers.

"There has never been a city as great as Tenochtitlán. And what is left of it, of Tenochtitlán? There has never been a structure greater than the Temple of the Sun. And what is left of Teotihuacán? There have never been such craftsmen as the Toltecs. And what is left of Tula?

"Would you compare the ugly houses bunched along the filthy streets, the ugly stores daubed with haphazard signs, the puny River Nazas of Torreón, with the great temples, the canals and causeways, the ball courts and palaces of Tenochtitlán? Would you compare the works of Porfirio Díaz with the works of Ahuitzotl or Motecuhzoma Xocoyotzin? Is there a locomotive that is not dwarfed by the great pyramid?

"Then think of it: Teotihuacan, Tula, and Tenochtitlán are ruins. And if we wait long enough, the great pyramid will be blown away by the wind. Think of it! If this earth is not a dream, what is it?

"There are twenty-two other worlds, and all of them are greater than this; none of them are dreams. You may pass through them, you may stay in them, you may be certain of them. Those worlds are all we can know, because they are unchangeable; and we can only know them through poetry, we can only imagine them with words.

"What is it you want to believe about this world, about the works of men? The ants will outlast your guns. If you add together the distances walked by all the ants of one great swarm in its history, you will understand that no locomotive will ever travel so far or work with such precision. And as for the power of your gun to destroy, would you dare to compare it to a flood or an earthquake or a hurricane?

"Be humble; you are only a man."

I gave him a butterfly to put into the fire and I cleansed him with an egg, and then I sent him away, for I had work to do. But I was not pleased with the visit. He had become presumptuous, like a Christian; he had become narrow and simplistic, like all the rest who were influenced by the Christian clergy. And while I have always subscribed to the philosophy of Quetzal-cóatl of Tula and opposed the ideas of Tlacaélel, believing myself that the sun has energies far beyond the powers of men to augment with their blood, it has always astonished me that we, at our most confused, killed men as sacrifices for man and the catzopines kill men as an act against them, as punishment. The conquest itself is ample evidence that gods are not influenced by men in great matters, perhaps not even small matters; the world is as it is, and perhaps the value of prayer is only to set our own faces and strengthen our own hearts. But to sit in judgment of men, to speak for the gods rather than to implore them, to kill men who are neither enemies in battle nor sacrifices, is an insane presumption.

The effect of this presumption upon the lives of the people has been terrible; the deterioration of the crafts has brought us back to the state of the chichimeca; the holding of land by a single man rather than by the state or the community has led to intolerable squalor and constant undernourishment; medicine is left to men who cannot recognize herbs in the ground and who deal with all problems by letting blood or cutting off limbs; the people are not clean about themselves; they are immoral; they steal; they wear wooden faces; they beat their children; they depend upon trains and rifles and electricity and sink to the level of animals. All of this proceeds from presumption; men have a small success—the invention of better weapons or the discovery of the horse—and they believe they are gods. The foolishness of a few then becomes the suffering of all the rest; it is madness.

None of this is new thinking. How many times has it been said? We said it to their priests in a courtyard in a great debate that followed by only a few years the death of Cuauhtémoc, and we have said it ever since. But they seem to be incapable of learning; men prefer to be presumptuous. We congratulated men who were about to die, and they make men their victims and pity them. We had wise men and priests; they have only priests. To lift men up is an enormous effort, for men are not gods and death is too distant. At times, I despair; I learned from my grandfathers and my father and my uncles; I studied with them, I sang with them, day after day, until I became a book to place beside the noisy books they put in my hands. But I have no one to sing with me, having chosen this monastic life, having chosen to be without a wife, without heirs.

In him I saw an opportunity. I read the Tonalpohualli for his calculations, I chose the hour of his naming; but it was not perfect—I could not choose the moment of his birth. That is why I teach him, that is why I calculated for him in his years the date 1923 when we would have to come to an end or begin again with the day 2 Reed and the New Fire. He would have power; I knew that. My only hope was to be in my time as Tlacaélel was in the time of Itzcóatl, Motecuhzoma Ilhuicamina, Axayacatl, Tizoc, and Ahuitzotl, or even to be as Nezahualpilli was to Motecuhzoma Xocoyotzin. I tried. I brought him to me, I spoke to him, I watched him, I was careful not to alienate him with demands, with arguments. I was one teacher among many, one word in a flood of words. I was also presumptuous, as bad as a mushroom eater or a Christian, for I thought my influence could be felt, I thought I could interfere with time. I flayed my chest, I pierced myself with twenty thorns, I considered putting out my eyes to teach myself again to be humble, to recognize that I too was only a man.

He sat for two days and two nights on the slope of the hill that overlooked his mother's house. In the great distance he saw figures moving, perhaps his mother, perhaps his sisters; he could not be certain. He saw his brother Hipólito coming in his direction to catch a goat that had wandered into the corn, and he thought he would run down the hill to speak to him, but the goat turned and ran back toward the house and his brother ran after it.

Villa stayed on the hill and watched, wishing for a moment close to his mother, to have her eyes look at him again with blessings; but there had been only two women outside the house, nothing had changed for Martina, nor could anything have changed in the way his mother thought of him. He had nothing to give them now, no gifts of money, no gifts of spirit. They were well but for Martina, they did not lack for anything: they had bought goats and milk cows and a team of oxen; there was an iron tank outside the house, a device to heat water; they had built a barn beside the house on the ground where the small corral had been; and there were three horses and a wagon with a cushioned seat and a sunshade for his mother and sisters. It was enough to have, a sufficiency of things. They had more than most people, he had given them that, he had done what a firstborn son was meant to do.

The wind changed on the third morning, suddenly coming out of the east, and the dogs caught his smell. They came running, barking and snarling, challenging, announcing a stranger. He thought of the time when they had welcomed him; he had been away so long; new dogs had been born and the dogs of the new dogs. He packed up and headed north.

The hiring hall was a wooden shack. It had been painted once, but the raw pine had soaked up the paint and left the surface unprotected; it had turned the color of dust, the wood had begun to shred, and the splinters curled. The hiring boss worked at a table in the center of the shack. There was a chair behind the table, but he did not use it, preferring to stand in front of the table, tapping the toe of one boot against the other, a small, expectant man dressed in a high linen collar and a workman's jacket.

"You're a big one," he told Villa, speaking with a tight-string voice. "What's your parentage?"

"My father is dead."

The hiring boss pursed his face in mock understanding. "So they say, so they all say. Well, it's convenient, isn't it? But what I want to know is what you're mixed with? Is there a Frenchman there somewhere? With that hair and that chest you could have a Basque in the family." He left the table and walked forward to stand close to Villa. His hair was oiled and scented. He touched Villa's chest, skimming him with his fingers. "Basque," he said, "definitely a Basque chest."

Then he snapped himself tense. "Name," he demanded, "full name." He ticked, to his table, to his pen, to his ledger. "Name."

"Francisco Arámbula."

"Make your mark here. Workday begins with the six o'clock whistle. Come late, lose your pay. Lose your pay twice in a week, lose your job. You make forty centavos a day, two pesos and forty centavos a week. We serve the noon meal, you pay twenty centavos. Six meals for twenty centavos, best bargain in town. Draw fifty centavos now, we take it out of your last week's pay."

On the first day, Villa carried two empty powder cans to a pool of water collected in the deepest shaft. All day he lifted the water in the two metal cans, carried it to a great metal bucket, and saw the bucket rise and come back empty, ready to be filled again. His hands blistered and the blisters tore. He shredded his shirt into bandages for his hands, and the bandages adhered to the fluids of his raw palms and fingers, deepening the tears. His elbows were ground by the burden of the full cans, and his neck was strained by the downward pull of his weighted shoulders. The unfamiliar walls and the low ceiling battered him, the rough timbers tore at his clothes and left slivers broken off in his skin. The water soaked through his boots and the skin of his feet caught and slid and was squeezed into fat blisters.

He laughed, watching the pool of water diminish in the yellow-lit night, thinking that he was a man and young, sure in himself and his power to master the weight and the water and the bending narrowness of the tunnel. He laughed to frighten the rats that paced on scratching feet, waiting in the darkest niches for grain fallen from the burros' feed bags or scraps of food lost in the dimness by the men. At noon, he was given a bowl of thick soup, almost a stew, of chicken, beans, carrots, and tomatoes. He saved a piece of carrot at the bottom of the metal bowl, and when he had finished eating, he threw the carrot into the darkness and let himself be amused by the sound of the rats fighting over it.

Afternoon came in a quarter of an hour. A whistle sounded, shrill, dying in the long reaches of the tunnels. Villa picked up the buckets and went again to the pool of water. It had increased again during his rest, and he worked faster, almost running up the length of the tunnel to the great bucket, enraged at the water, the increase in the pool, the failure of his work.

For a while, he did not feel the stinging of his hands or the blows of the walls against his hips and shoulders in the clumsy half-light. Then the dust was caking on his tongue again and the rags of his shirt were sliding against his raw hands, opening the sores of the morning. He walked slowly, lifting his feet high and setting them down carefully to keep from squeezing his blistered feet in the slide of his shoes. He tried carrying less water in the cans. He tried carrying more water. His arms trembled, he stumbled; the water spilled and rolled down the tunnel to the pool.

A foreman came to inspect his work, shining a bright lantern on the pool. "Good," he said, "good. The pool should be dry before quitting time."

"If we could bring the big bucket down here," Villa said, "we could fill it up here by the pool and then pull it up to the shaft."

The foreman said, "So you're an engineer," and snorted his derision. "Do what you're told."

Villa grabbed the sleeve of the foreman's jacket. "What's wrong with that?"

"Look at the floor of the tunnel," the foreman said, lowering his lantern. "You see where we laid the wooden track? You think we're so stupid we didn't think of your idea? The burros wouldn't come down this tunnel, the water warped the rails; we had to pull them up, what was left of them."

"A man could push the bucket to the shaft."

"No, Mr. Engineer, not one man—three. And one slipped and fell on the other one and the bucket rolled backwards before they could get the brake on. One was killed and the other one lost his legs. That's how much you know. Stick to your work. When a chicken tries to moo like a cow, you don't get milk and you don't get eggs either."

In the moments of the conversation the water gained and Villa had to run again to catch up with the flow. Each time he filled the cans at the pool he looked for the place where the water entered the tunnel, but he saw nothing. The water just appeared, as if by magic, and waited for him in the dark pool; and he carried it through the wan light, imagining the time, tuned to the whistle, lost without the sun.

The whistle blew and he climbed up out of the mine. The light of the late afternoon blinded him. He held on to the man in front, "Cover your eyes," the man said. "Look through the cracks between your fingers."

The miners washed in long wooden troughs of cold water, rubbing themselves with dark brown soap and balls of split cactus fiber, before they went to long empty rooms to lay their blankets or mats on the dirt floor. The man next to Villa looked at his bloody hands and said to him, "There are bowls of saltwater outside. Soak your hands or they'll be worse tomorrow."

"It's my feet that are worse," said Villa, holding up one foot for the man to see.

[*171*]

"An old man will come later to sell herbs. Buy wintergreen leaves from him. Wet the leaves and wrap your feet in them. And tomorrow, pal, keep your feet dry."

"I can't. I work in a wet place."

"Then go barefoot."

Villa looked at the man, as if to measure the value of his advice by the degree of his survival. He was only a few years older than Villa, tall and very thin, but not worn to strings like some of the others. Villa nodded to him and smiled. "They call me Pancho. For Francisco."

"Maclovio."

The man extended his hand, then he laughed, and they waved at each other instead. He brought two bowls of saltwater and sat beside Villa while he soaked his hands in the stinging solution. Later, he helped him to bind his feet in the wintergreen leaves, but he said almost nothing. When an old woman came around selling tortillas, Maclovio did not eat, and he advised Villa, "Save your money; it's better to eat in the morning. Sleep now. In the morning, wet the leaves again and rub them on your arms and legs for the pain."

"I don't have any pain there," Villa said.

"You will."

Within an hour they were all asleep, all the long rows of men lying on blankets or fraying mats. Long before the light, the first whistle blew to awaken them. They groaned, rolled onto their bellies, and got to their knees, beginning. One man, dark and thin, with long hair that spread behind him on his mat, did not get up. He drew his knees close up to his chest, curled his back, and cursed the whistle, the mine, the world, and even the mother who bore him. "Goodbye," he said to the awakening men around him, for he knew that a man who slept in the barracks in the morning would not sleep there in the night.

"He gives up," Maclovio said of the sleeping man, addressing his words in Villa's direction.

Villa was unable to attend the remark. He lay on his back with his eyes open, willing to get up, but unable to move his arms or legs. Maclovio unwrapped the wintergreen leaves from Villa's feet and dipped the dry leaves in water. Then he crushed the leaves in his hands and rubbed Villa's arms and legs. The muscles softened as they warmed, and after a while Villa was able to move. He thanked Maclovio, who said, "The water is the worst work, but it is not dangerous. Get a pick handle and hang the buckets on it. Then you can carry them on your shoulders. Make yourself into an ox with a yoke; only an ox can do the work."

He walked all day in his bare, blistered feet, filling the cans more carefully than he had on the first day, spilling less, slower, methodical, like the ant,

[*172*]

as dutiful as the ant. He sang sometimes; his voice was deeper in the tunnel, pleasing to him. At the midday meal of tortillas and a stew of pork rinds, tripe, and beans, he felt tired but not in pain. As the afternoon wore on and he lost count of the time, he felt watery, sick. He stumbled into the walls, he fell, the water spilled, the pool diminished more slowly. His toes were bruised by stones, the blistered skin tore open on the sides of his feet. Once, falling near the pool, feeling the water run by him, under him, downhill to the pool again, he thought he could not get up again. He lay there a long time; twitches startled his legs and his hands trembled. He touched his cheek to the earth and rested, allowing his eyes to close. It was quiet. His ears buzzed. And then he heard the rats somewhere along the walls, and he knew that they were watching him, waiting for him to sleep; in his defeat they would venture the invasion of him. He imagined the feeling of the claws scrambling over him, the teeth. He despised them—their eyes, their hairless scaly tails, their scavenger's teeth, the madness of them when they were about to die—and the hatred raised him to his knees, and then to his feet; and horrified, shuddering, he picked up the pick handle and the cans and went again to the pool.

At the whistle, he dropped the pick handle and picked up his boots and went blindly to the barracks, where he lay on his blanket in a thoughtless, wordless stupor. Maclovio brought him a cup of honeywater and held it to his lips. "Don't speak," he said. "This is the worst day. After this it will be easier."

Another man brought saltwater for his hands and yet another washed his feet and wrapped them in wet leaves. Villa tried to see their faces, but there were lights bursting in his eyes and water pouring through them; he could only hear the men pitying him, cursing the mine and the mine owner, wishing they had hired on at another mine, wishing they worked for a man instead of a devil, wishing and cursing and tending to the raw hands and bloody feet of the new man.

They rubbed him again with wintergreen leaves in the morning, and when he was able to move, eating breakfast with him, they asked his name and smiled at him and called him their comrade and their friend. He thanked them, and they said it was nothing, explaining how they had each survived because someone had helped them and how he would now be expected to help the next new man. This was a bad mine, they told him, but not as bad as some in Zacatecas and one in San Luis Potosí, and nothing at all compared to life in the Valle Naciónal on the tobacco plantations, or in Quintana Roo and Yucatán, where the Chinese foremen raped the women and beat the men on the henequen plantations. This was good work, they said: a man got paid, and if he was careful he could save fifty pesos in a year.

He walked with them to the entrance of the mine, where they gathered up their picks and augers and fuses and tamping bars and cans of black powder, and he took off his boots and went down to the tunnel and the pool of water. He felt better until he saw the pool; it was filled again, as it had been the day before and the day before that. Tears came into his eyes and overflowed, running down his cheeks, falling. He thought he must stop, for the tears were only more water to carry, and the thought made him laugh. When the six o'clock whistle blew to start the workday, he was still laughing. His hands were sore to the touch of the cans and the pick handle lay heavily on his bruised shoulders, but his eyes were dry and his head was full of the exhilaration of laughter; he no longer doubted that he would survive. At the noon whistle, he took his food from the bucket at the main shaft and carried it to a quiet place. He ate slowly, noticing that the food lacked flavor. After he had eaten, he leaned back against the wall of the tunnel and yawned.

They were paid on Saturday night, hundreds of them lined up before long tables, listening for the pay clerks to call their names, dreaming aloud to each other of beefsteaks and whores, farms and wives. Villa was among the last to be called. He took his two coins, one and a half pesos, and went back to the barracks. Some of the men were already asleep. A few gathered around blankets to play cards or throw dice. The Tarahumaras were spinning plum stones on a patch of hard dirt. Maclovio was stretched out on his blanket, lying on his back, his mouth open and shuddering with snores. Villa lay down and propped himself up on one elbow. He put the two coins on the blanket to study them; they were the value of his week of life, the name the mine had assigned to him: one of copper, one of silver, so light, so little; one of copper, one of silver, coins, measures, the worth of him; a piece of copper and a piece of silver, and they didn't even shine! He put the coins in his pocket and went to sleep.

There was a free breakfast on Sunday morning for the men who went to Mass. "It's a gift of the owner," Maclovio said, "for the love of God." He urged and prodded Villa into going with him to Mass, where they knelt and rose, knelt and rose, following the instructions of the bell. Villa grumbled softly all through the Mass, refusing to say the words. He could not understand why Maclovio had insisted on coming. When the collection plate was passed, Maclovio dropped a ten-centavo piece onto the plate, making it ring loudly while he scooped four other coins off the plate and slipped them into his pocket. "Thanks to God," Villa whispered. Maclovio crossed himself and kissed his thumb with a smack. On the way back to the barracks he gave Villa a twenty-centavo piece, saying that the Archbishop wanted him to have it.

"You're a heretic," Villa said.

Maclovio's long and bony face took on a more dour aspect than usual. "A man who works in this mine is more likely to be a martyr."

In the afternoon they walked down to Parral. Maclovio, who carried a small two-shot pistol, admired Villa's revolver. Villa did not respond.

They ate in the house of Sofia the Saint of the Miners. The old woman, who had lost her husband and all her five sons in the mines, served thick meat soups and cornmeal popovers for twenty centavos to those who could afford to pay. For those who had no money, she served the same meal at no charge, asking only that they pay the twenty centavos for their meals when they were able. She was fat and very old and her legs had bowed with the weight of her age and years, but the miners swore that she was the most beautiful woman in Parral, for her face was open, and although her skin was marked with more tiny cracks and wrinkles than could be counted, there were no deep lines of sorrow or anger in her face, only a gentle light that they said was the sign of her saintliness.

Santa Sofia served the meal at a long table in one of the two rooms of her house, moving from place to place behind the miners, filling their bowls or putting more of the popovers on the table before them. Heriberto Tacuiaé sat at the head of the table during all the meals. He wore a workman's jacket buttoned only at the neck and spreading open across his belly, and he kept his useless hands in his lap. Some said Santa Sofia fed him when there was no one else in the house, others claimed that he suckled at her ancient breasts, which gave honeywater and thick soup to heroes.

At the beginning of the meal, Tacuiaé lifted his hands out of his lap and laid them on the table for Villa to see. The fingers were of various widths and lengths and they curled around each other like the roots of a dead tree. "This is the result of loving one's fellow man in Mexico," he said.

Villa nodded and looked away, pretending to concentrate on the food in his plate.

"Don't hide your eyes," Tacuiaé said. "This is the work of artists. You see how the fingers have each become different? They planned that. They crushed some from the top and some from the side, and some they only broke into pieces. And then they put me in a dungeon in San Juan de Ulúa until the pieces of bone had grown together into these hands."

He lifted his hands off the table and dropped them in his lap. Villa continued to eat his stew and popovers. Santa Sofia said, "Tell him, sir, tell him why they did it to you. He doesn't understand."

"One night," Tacuiaé said, "when it was so hot in the mine that we couldn't breathe, I said to the men who were working with me at shoveling ore into mine cars, 'We have to go up to the top and get some air or we're going to die.' As always, they were afraid, but I said to them, 'If you don't go up now, you're going to die down here. At least you have a chance if you go up now.' I don't think they believed me, but what could they do? They were gasping, they knew they would die down there. So we went up, and when we got to the top, the foreman told us to go back down. But we couldn't; we needed to breathe. I stepped forward, I was the spokesman, I told him that we couldn't breathe down there anymore and we had to be allowed to go to the barracks to rest for the night. He said that he understood, but we could see by his face that he didn't mean what he said; he was only afraid of us.

"We went to our barracks. Some of us wanted to run away, but what chance was there? Where could we go? We were so far from home. The rurales came before morning, a whole troop of them, gray, the color of that terrible dawn. The foreman came with them, pointing to me. That's when they did this to my hands. They smashed them with the handles of their pistols and the stocks of their rifles. And all the time they were holding me and doing it to me I kept struggling to get free, and I did not faint or cry out even once. I was a man."

"Yes," said Maclovio. The others around the table, strangers and old friends alike, also said, "Yes." The old woman wept.

"Sofia, Sofia," said Tacuiaé, reaching out with his eyes and the pitch of his voice to comfort her, "please don't cry, Sofia. I don't tell this to upset you, but to tell these young men what can be done, what must be done."

On the way back to the mine Maclovio told Villa: "The old cripple was lying. He gives good advice, but he lies about himself, all of the Liberals are liars. His real name is Juan Melos Alvarez. The brake gave out on a mine car and it smashed his hands against the car in front of it. I don't know how it happened—the bumpers should have kept the cars apart. Anyway, the doctors wanted to cut off his hands because they were afraid of gangrene, but he wanted it like this. Liberals are all crazy. Everyone knows that, even Sofia."

"Then why does she keep him there?"

"I told you she was a saint."

Villa carried water from the pool on Monday and Tuesday. On Wednesday, he was moved to loading ore into the mine cars. The work was hard, but there were other men to talk with, the light was better, and sometimes they rested for an hour or more, waiting for the dynamiters to loosen more rock. Several times during the day Villa wondered who was carrying the water from the pool at the end of the tunnel. He saw the man in the barracks that evening. He was older than Villa and much smaller. His face was streaked with blood from rubbing his eyes with his hands, and his feet were raw, for the blisters had burst and the skin had blistered again and burst again. He had not spread his blanket before he lay down. The dirt of the floor adhered to the raw flesh of his hands and feet, muddying the wounds.

Maclovio and Villa lifted up the new man while a third man unrolled his blanket under him. They brought bowls of saltwater for his hands and they washed his feet and wrapped them in wintergreen leaves. They told him not to try to speak. They told him that they knew, they understood. "Mother of God," he said, "Mother of God, what have I done?"

They awakened him in the morning at the sound of the first whistle. Villa brought him coffee and tortillas and Maclovio rubbed him with the wintergreen leaves, but the man could not get up. They rolled him over onto his belly and lifted him onto his knees, but he collapsed. Again they lifted him and again he collapsed. Villa stepped over him, planted his feet on each side of the man's hips, put his hands under the man's arms, and lifted him to his feet. There was nothing left in the man. He could not stand, he could not speak, his arms dangled, his eyes remained closed, his jaw hung. "It's no use," Maclovio said. "Put him down. They have another one, they always have another one." He reached into the man's pocket and took out the fifty-centavo piece.

"For your services?" Villa said.

Maclovio hissed to the woman who sold coffee, to attract her attention. She nodded to him and held out her hand. He tossed the coin to her. In response to the puzzlement on Villa's face Maclovio said, "The hiring boss and one of the foremen will come later and throw him out. If they find the fifty centavos in his pocket, they'll take it back, but if they don't find any money, they can't take it away from him. The coffee woman will pick him up outside the gate and take him to her house. She'll use the fifty centavos to feed him until he's well."

"What if he dies?"

"I'm not God," Maclovio said. "I do what I can."

It had been a long time since Villa had begun working in the mine: a month, two months, perhaps three; the time did not seem to matter, there were no seasons in the dark. He was tired of the work, afraid of the sullenness that was forming in him, wishing for something to happen to change the routine. Marta was often in his thoughts and so was Ignacio: the bed and the grave, resting places, thoughts of a weary man. And what of his mother and Martina? Were they well? Better? Did the wagon ride smoothly and did the arch of cloth give them comforting shade? Was the corn in its season? Were the cows full of cream? Did cotton grow and dogs bark and horses run? Was the water hot for bathing? Did they ever speak his name? He thought of them often, seeing them in the blank spaces of the yellow-lit walls, hearing their voices in the silences between the end of the

[*177*]

tamping and the roar of the black powder exploding. More and more he thought of other places, other times.

In such a moment the rock fell.

It tumbled off the cart, a jagged, formless piece of stone weighted with silver and lead. In the surprise of the pain Villa let out a noise of fright. Then he laughed and picked up the rock and put it on the mine car again. His foot was numb for a while. Later, it felt cold. A sensation of many needles followed and, as he expected, that also subsided, and he limped through the day. It was a deep bruise; his ankle ached, the bones in his foot were sore. When he undressed that night he found some blood in his boot, but not so much that it worried him. The pain was worse the next morning, but he rubbed oil of turpentine on his ankle and foot and went to the mine. On the third day after the injury his foot seemed to be better. He limped, but he thought it was more from habit than from pain. He rested on Sunday, lying on his mat with his foot raised to let the swelling flow out of it.

On Monday morning, his foot was swollen so badly that he had difficulty getting it into his boot. Maclovio and one of the old women who sold coffee advised him to keep using it, explaining that the day of rest had allowed the swelling to increase. "Walk, walk," the coffee vendor said. "When the blood stops, the wound gets worse." Villa walked and worked, lifting and loading rock, following the mine cars. Several times during the day he had to drop large pieces of rock to keep from falling; without being able to put his weight on his left leg he could not balance himself.

He could not get his boot off that night, but he was not worried, for as everyone knew, the boot acted as a bandage to limit the swelling. On Tuesday, he could not walk without holding on to something to keep his balance. A foreman saw him holding on to a mine car, hopping along behind it. "Everyone who works here must have two legs," the foreman said, "unless they are mules. Then they must have four."

"I had an accident," Villa said. "It's much better now."

"We don't hire cripples. You get full pay, boy; give us the use of both legs for it or get out."

Villa held on to the mine car with both hands and began walking behind it, setting his feet down one after the other. The first few steps filled him with nauseating pain. He was sweating, but there were long streaks of cold in his neck, leaping from there to his back and his face. He walked, step after step, holding himself up by the strength of his arms, rocking with the waves of pain that came from the rise and fall of his foot, the breathing pain.

"Come over here," the foreman said. He stood downhill from Villa and off to the side of the track, a thin man with high laced boots and a brown felt hat, narrow, narrow everywhere, guarded by his pistol and his knowledge of the mine.

"What for? I've got to get this ore up to the main shaft."

"Come!"

"What for?"

"You son of an Indian bitch, do what I tell you." He put his hand on his pistol.

Villa called to the burros to halt, pulling on the handbrake as they slowed, fixing the brake to keep it from sliding loose. He turned on his right foot, holding on to the edge of the mine car with one hand. His left leg buckled on the first step and he fell forward onto the tracks. He put his hands out to catch his fall, but they slid in the warm rotting manure between the ties and he stretched forward full onto the tracks.

"Get out!" the foreman said. "Get yourself up out of the shit and scram! If you ever learn to walk on two feet you can come back."

"Tell me your name, sir," Villa said, begging. "When I'm well, I want to apply to you to get my job back."

"Luis Ochoa Bello, Don Luis."

"Thank you, sir. I'll be back to see you when I'm well, I promise."

The foreman went down the track into the mine to find someone to work the ore car. Villa got to his knees and crawled up the slope of the hill until he found a piece of timber that would serve as a crutch. He was slick with manure and he was weeping, saying the name of the foreman again and again, as if to ensure the promise. It was a long way to the entrance of the mine, and he moved very slowly, stumbling, resting against a wall, in pain, stumbling forward again, his hand taking splinters from the raw crutch, sweat in his eyes, the manure stinking and shaming his chest and knees, faint but for the sight of Don Luis Ochoa Bello dying in an open place, in the sun, with his blood congealing in his hands, drying dead, as brittle as kindling sticks, as old as sand. When he reached the surface, he went to the water trough and sat on the edge to drench himself clean. He rested awhile and then he went to the gatehouse to get his pistol.

The old woman who sold coffee took the rag from her hair and gave it to him to bind his hand against the splinters. She gathered maguey leaves and tore and folded them into a pad to put between the end of the piece of timber and his armpit. "The foreman threw me out," he said to her, touching his pistol, "and now I'm going to do a favor for him."

The old woman was full of nods and shrugs, attending meanwhile to tying the maguey leaves securely onto the top of the wood. "Will that heal your foot?" she asked.

Her fingers were like turkey feet. He saw in them that she had never rested, not in all her life. He saw in the thick nails and the hard scrawny fingers that she had been neither a girl nor a woman, but only a working thing, always old and turned away from the pale roses that are so becoming

[*179*]

to the soft women of Parral; and he put his fingers over hers, feeling even in his own horned skin the indelicacy of her hand, and he said to her, "You're a good woman."

"There is no justice," she said. "We do for each other what we can."

"These are the hands of a good woman," he said.

"I can put them in fire."

Tears ran down his cheeks. He squeezed her hand. "Is your foot so painful?" she asked, turning her parched face, her mouth of broken teeth up to him.

"No, mother. I cry for you."

"Too late," she said, "too late. Think of the living."

"The young."

"Yes."

"My tears are for you, mother."

"Then you're a foolish man who will die before his time," she said, and she jerked her hand out from under his and walked away from him, dragging her feet across the coarse ground.

For the rest of the day he walked down the hill. Once, he fell and rolled, losing his crutch. He lay there for a time, a thoughtless thing, turning slow, cooling, grays and pales, all soothing, in a humming sleep. The ants found him, coming in their long lines, entering his sleeves and collar. He felt them crawling, their feathery legs, and he permitted them, for he no longer cared. He permitted the first of the stings, and more and more. They hurried into his sleeves, they crawled in his hair, they ate his flesh, and he permitted them, wishing himself numb, until he could bear the stings no more and he rolled up the hill, crushing them inside his clothes, letting the sting of them drive him to his lost crutch. He brushed them out of his hair; he got to his feet again, supporting himself with the crutch, and like an old man, lame and hopeless, driven by the ants, he made his way down the hill into the town of Parral.

He slept beside the river with his left foot in the cool water. In the morning, the swelling had diminished, but the skin was discolored from the bottom of his foot to his ankle. A man with warts on his face and neck offered to give Villa five pesos and a pair of huaraches for his boots. Villa took the money; he had eleven pesos. For fifteen centavos he bought coffee and two thin tortillas. Then he was left with the day. He lay on the grass in the plaza until the sun heated his foot. The church was cool, but the priest told him he could not put his leg up on the pew. In the afternoon, he lay in the shade of an empty house, and again that night he slept with his foot in the river.

The next day was the same, and the next. His beard grew, his clothes were filthy, there was dirt and straw in his hair. Every day the swelling in his foot was less, but the discoloration did not change and the pain did not diminish. His body ached from lying on the hard ground, his joints were stiff from the river dampness, he could not think beyond what he felt: pain when he lay down, pain when he stood up, pain when he walked, pain that renewed itself with every movement.

Villa went to the river and waited there on the bank until dark. He put his foot into the water, felt the comforting chill, and slid down after it. The sting of the sores faded, he was comforted, he felt clean. He pushed himself forward with his hands, sliding easily on the riverbottom, deeper, up to his waist. The water washed into the place under his arm that had been bruised by the crutch, cooling there, soothing there. He lay back and let the water cover his face. The silence lulled him, the weight of the water protected him. There were stones in his pockets, a twig was tied to his belt, he lacked a dog, but he carried his pistol. He opened his eyes and saw the moon through the water, like a glowing above him, a glimpse of Heaven. Then his chest began to hurt and his head became heated with pressure. He sat up out of the water and breathed.

The water had been too shallow. He pushed forward into the river, seeking the deepest place, and there in the center he lay down again, and again he was soothed and lulled by the protecting water. Again he opened his eyes and saw the glimpse of Heaven, the light without heat, the stolen woman awaiting him. But his chest burned and the pressure in his head became unbearable. He scuttled across the bottom of the river, looking for a deep place, a drowning place, but it had been too long since the thaws and the spring rains; the river could not contain him. He dragged himself to the riverbank and lay there shivering and sad, failed, waiting for the sun.

The thought of death came again during the night. It spoke to him of the pistol. He examined the cartridges to see if one was dry, but that too failed him and he lay in the mud of the riverbank, looking up at the sky, cursing that starry beast who had chosen against him, leaving him alive and in pain. For the rest of the night he could not sleep; instead, he questioned his courage and his belief in death the reliever. There were no marigolds. He made a ball of mud into the shape of a skull and threw it into the river. Somewhere there was a sea into which the Precious Twin had sailed and out of which the catzopines had come. He, Francisco Villa, had neither risen in fire to become sinuous birds nor returned to the land with steel and thunder to ride conquering across the navel of the universe. He lay in the mud and he was cold, and the pain in his foot was tied to him as surely as his bones.

Like a beast, he rose from the mud in the morning; his back shone with brown and green slime, he staggered on one leg and a crutch, his hair and beard were tangled in filth. Death had failed him; now he knew only to look for work. He sought some endless task, as the water had given him in the mine—a repetition, a work of despair, without promise, a dying peace. And he found such work before the morning ended, a gift to a cripple from a stonemason. This is the hammer and this is the rock; break the rock with the hammer; break the broken rock into smaller rocks. Sit or stand, do the work however you can, and if you work well I will give you half a peso for this day and one peso for every full day that you work. Take the hammer; there is the rock; work.

At the end of the week, the stonemason, Santos Vega, said, "I never knew a man to work so hard."

"I like to work."

The conversation was ended, but Vega would not have it so. "Has your leg always been that way?" he asked.

Villa looked at him for a moment, deciding whether to speak. The man had been fair: he had paid him at the end of every day and he had even given him food and a pair of thick leather gloves to protect his hands from the sharp rock. It was his face that Villa did not trust; Vega had a thin line of a mustache and a long Spanish jaw, and his eyes were green and marmoreal, night eyes. "I hurt it," Villa said.

"And the doctors can't fix it?"

"I haven't been to a doctor."

Santos Vega was incredulous. "That's madness! I've seen the pain in your face, man. The way you looked when you came to work for me, like some monster that came up out of the river. You have to see a doctor right away!"

"Will I have to lose my leg?"

Santos Vega's face closed. "I'm not a doctor. I can only give you work and fair pay for it. No more advice. Find your own way."

Villa worked six days, a week of brooding: the pain was worsening in his leg and the stench was there again. He could not hobble up the hill to wash his clothes in the dark after the women had gone home. He needed a change of clothes. He needed a place to sleep. There was not enough money for all that he needed and for a doctor too. He smashed rock, he wore the hammer thin. He lived in a fever, often dreaming out the day while he crushed rocks, forgetting to eat, surprised when Santos Vega touched his shoulder to tell him the day was done.

On Sunday he went to the house of Santa Sofia. It was early, and she came to the door in her robe, older yet without her corsets, crouched, fat, with her white hair hanging in one fat braid. She invited him inside to eat breakfast. Tacuiaé was already at the table, little sticks of a man in a sleeping gown stained with food. They drank coffee and ate tortillas and figs. "You have gangrene," Tacuiaé said; "I know the smell."

"Will I have to lose my leg?"

"It can be cured," Santa Sofia said. "There are two women who live at the high end of the river who have cured gangrene before. They are very old; they were old when I was a child, and that's not a trick of memory, for I remember that their hair was white even then. They're not witches; they use roots and herbs; they cure the natural diseases; they know nothing of dreams or omens. Say to them that I sent you. Their names are Celia and Sara. Call them aunt, show them respect. When you've finished your coffee, go to them; they live in an unstuccoed house with two circles of marigolds growing in front of it. Give them money if you can; they won't ask for it."

Santa Sofia walked to the door with Villa at the finish of the meal. He pressed a half-peso into her hand, thanking her: "It's little to give, but I don't have much." She knelt before him, holding on to his hand for balance until her knees touched the ground. Before he could lift her up she kissed his swollen foot.

Villa walked all the rest of the morning and into the afternoon, climbing the long hill beside the river to the house where the old women lived. He arrived in the heat of the day, feverish and sick, wondering whether he could go on, hoping the little house with the circles of marigolds was their house. He looked down at the town below, the nests of houses, curving streets, green patches of the plazas, great gray churches, long roofs of stables, houses following up the hill, thinning as the land climbed, beginning gardens. Above him, where the hill began its longer climb into the mountains, there were few houses; he saw cattle grazing, eroded fields, a long stretch of whitened alkaline soil curving off to the south. There were other houses above, perhaps other marigolds growing in circles; he wished for this house surrounded by a fallen stone fence, protected by the noise of ducks and chickens but not by dogs, to be the house of the old women.

Around the marigolds and on both sides of the house was a tangle of plants: geraniums, yellow radishes, sage, amaranth, chiles of all kinds, strangely shaped and colored squash, jimsonweed; and in a great bed of sand were dozens of varieties of cactus. Around the house were cypress, sweet gum acacia, and various kinds of pines. He went through the gate, pushing by the crowding chickens, chasing back the geese with his crutch to keep them from biting his legs.

A woman opened the door before he knocked. She was older than anyone he had ever seen, a tiny, bent thing, compressed by age into a packet of lines and splinters. "Aunt Sara?" he asked.

"No." The voice came through a reed, traveling from some distant place or time, thinned and hollowed in the journey. "I am Celia. Sara is too old now to come to the door. She no longer walks."

"Santa Sofia sent me, with your permission."

Aunt Celia looked him up and down, stopping a moment at his foot, studying it. "Come in, poor little one, come in. We shall make your one foot as well as the other. Come in."

The main room of the house contained a simple kitchen and fireplace, several wooden benches, two narrow beds, and a couch on which an old woman no bigger than a child lay smiling. "Forgive me for not rising," she said in a voice more distant and hollow than Aunt Celia's. "I am very old and I have not left my couch now for many years. But do not be concerned because there are not two of us to care for you. Celia still consults me on the most difficult problems."

Villa bowed to her; he did not know what else to do. Aunt Sara smiled at him. He thought there was something shy or even coquettish in her smile. "Go with Celia now," she said. "Run along, like a good boy."

He followed Aunt Celia into a second room. There was a table in the center, and all four walls were lined with shelves filled with bottles, jars, and sacks. Light entered the room from windows in the roof. "We are not witches," Aunt Celia said to him. "Everything we do is natural. We use powders, balms, ointments, infusions, and poultices. If you wish to be cured by prayer, you must pray for yourself. Our work is natural, not supernatural. Every one of our medicines is labeled. Can you read? If you could read, you could tell what is in every jar or sack by reading the label. We are able to write, Sara and I; we have studied and catalogued all of the substances in this room, and there are nearly a thousand." She put her head against his arm and giggled. "But some of them are utterly useless."

She took a moment to catch her breath after the laughter. When her breathing became regular again, she said, "Sit up on the table now and let me examine your wound." After studying Villa's foot, she said, "It will have to be cleaned. Stay right there while I heat some water."

Aunt Celia lit a fire under a pot of water on a kerosene stove, then she mixed an ointment of turpentine and jimsonweed and spread it over the swollen area of Villa's foot. Almost immediately, his skin tingled. As the tingling subsided, his foot grew numb. She brought a sharp knife, like a razor but smaller, and with two quick strokes cut a deep cross into his flesh. Pus and blood were expelled in a burst. With a stick, she lifted a white cloth out of the heated water and threw it over the opened wound. She removed the cloth when it cooled, and replaced it with another cloth, hotter than the first. Villa felt nothing.

She put more jimsonweed and turpentine into the wound, and then she propped it open with four little hoops of bamboo cane. "This will pain you later, but you won't feel anything now," she said, sprinkling salt into the open wound, dissolving it in hot water, allowing it to be absorbed for several minutes, and washing it out with urine. Finally, she closed the wound, covered it with a poultice of charcoal and nightshade, and wrapped it in white cotton cloth.

She gave him a bottle of turpentine, instructing him to "keep the bandage wet with this turpentine. It will keep the odor from bothering you and it will help the medicine to be more effective."

"Am I cured?" he asked.

"No. Oh, goodness no. You must come back tomorrow and we must clean the wound again and again until all the sickness is gone. It won't take too very long, a week or two. Meanwhile, you must take something for the fever."

She gave him an infusion of sand-tomato root and red maize, a bitter fluid that he tasted and then drank off in a gulp. He thanked her, and she reminded him to come back the following day. There was no discussion of money. She turned to cleaning the bloodied table. As he passed through the outer room, Aunt Sara awakened from a dozing sleep and lifted her hand out from under her crocheted wool cover to wave to him. Her hand, at the end of an arm no thicker a man's thumb, was enormous, studded with lumpy knuckles and heavy, curved fingernails.

Villa suffered more than ever that night. The incision burned and throbbed. He was dizzy, he vomited, his thoughts floated out of control, becoming monsters, physical beasts that flowed from shape to darkness to shape; faces oozed through his vision, the colors of mixtures of fruit preserves pouring. He bathed his face and chest in the cooling river water, he chewed mint leaves; he could not awaken to the reasoned day, neither could he sleep; he expected to die.

The morning light anchored him to the hard shapes of hills and houses. He washed and went to a half-built house to crush rocks for Santos Vega. The pain lessened by midday. He ate and drank honeywater. When he told Santos Vega in the late afternoon that he was leaving early to climb the hill to the house where Sara and Celia lived, the stonemason said, "Some people believe in them. They were called the Widows of St. Castulus, because people thought they could have cured St. Sebastian himself. But they are not pious women; the priests have told everyone. The medical doctors also oppose them. No one goes to them now but the very old and the hopeless cases. Even the country people don't go to them anymore. There's something wrong with those women; they've lived too long. It's not natural."

Aunt Celia opened his wound and cleaned it and bandaged it again. She said little, except to tell him the names of the herbs and roots she used along with the salt and charcoal and turpentine. She gave him amaranth root for his fever instead of the infusion of sand-tomato root and red maize, because she thought it was less likely to make him sick and full of unhappy dreams.

After each treatment the numbness wore off more quickly and the pain was greater. She apologized for the pain, explaining that she was no longer able to afford coca leaves, that he would have to make do with jimsonweed for a few days more, for another week, until the wound was clean and the blood came freely.

The swelling went down, and he was able to put a part of his weight on his foot. Celia appeared to be pleased when she removed the bandages. The green and brown fluid was still there, but there was less. The wound bled. The charcoal and turpentine defeated the stench. He believed he would live.

Santos Vega and others continued to advise him against the old women. A priest came to visit him while he crushed bricks; Villa told the priest he was not a religious man. "I don't go to church, priest. I don't confess, I don't kneel."

"You've learned that from those heretical old women," the priest said.

"The women don't talk about anything but curing wounds."

"My work is curing souls."

"If a rock falls on my soul, I'll call you."

"Your employer is a religious man, my son; I'll have to speak to him about your unbelief and your insolence." He waited for Villa to look up from the rocks he was smashing with the hammer, but Villa continued his work as if the priest were not standing beside him. "You don't care if I speak to Mr. Santos Vega?" the priest asked.

"Why should I care? Why should he care? I smash the rocks for him. There are burros that haul the rocks for him. Speak to him about the burros, too."

The priest spoke in whispers with Santos Vega, who came to talk to Villa after the priest had gone. "You're making trouble for yourself by going to those old women," he said. "But that's your business. All I ask is that you don't make trouble for me by insulting priests."

"Tell me, sir, do you believe in the holiness of the priests and the infallibility of the Church?"

"You put my soul in jeopardy."

"I won't tell anyone. But for me, for my sake, so that I know how to live, answer the question, please."

Santos Vega picked up the hammer and put it in Villa's hand. "Work," he said, "I'm not paying you to sit around like a politician."

On his thirty-eighth visit to the old women, Villa walked up the hill without his crutch. His leg was weak and the toe was turned in more than ever, but there was no pain. The incision had been closed for three days, the swelling was gone, he had no fever. "You are cured," Aunt Celia said upon completing her examination. "The treatment is over. If you come here again, you come as a visitor, a friend."

"I have twenty-five pesos to give you," Villa said. "It's not enough, but it's all I've been able to save."

She took the money and tossed it onto a shelf behind her. "You won't be coming back," she said.

"No."

"Because they say we're witches, heretics, evil women, friends of the devil, the devil himself dressed up like two old women. The priest told you that, didn't he?"

"And others too."

"Do you believe them?"

"I believe that I can walk on my left leg."

Aunt Celia smiled at his reply. She took him by the hand and led him out into the main room where Aunt Sara lay sleeping. "Sit here," she said, drawing him to one of the small benches. "I'll awaken Sara. We want to talk to you. Now that they've accused you, we must tell you everything. They will say you have a compact with the devil; you must know how to defend yourself."

The tiny woman on the couch was awakened with difficulty. Her flat eyes rolled upwards, the lids closed. She raised one of her enormous hands, groping; the hand fell of its own weight, dangled over the edge of the couch. Aunt Celia brewed a cup of sage tea and brought it to Aunt Sara, holding it to her lips while she drank. The fingers of the dangling hand opened and closed, as if pumping life or wakefulness into the old woman.

Aunt Sara's eyes opened, held steady, looked around the room and returned to studying the cup before her. The great hand was raised, groping, finding the cup, encircling it, the fingers overlapping. "Francisco is here. I've told him we would explain ourselves, dear. It's necessary, you know; the boy is accused of consorting with the devil."

"Will he understand? Is he educated?"

Villa sat stiffly on the bench, wishing to leave. The women studied him: the one on the couch, whose eyes he now realized were blind, and beside her, not much taller than the arm of the couch, Aunt Celia, nodding, moving her lips prior to speaking, as if to practice the words or the act of speaking.

"Whether he understands or not, we must tell him."

Aunt Sara settled the cup on her breast, the hand relaxed; she sighed. "God does not exist," she said.

Villa shifted his position on the bench, squirmed, rubbed his nose with his forefinger, wet his lips, waiting for the women who waited for him. No

[*187*]

one spoke. He heard himself breathing, the air faintly echoing in the hollow of his mouth. It was for him to respond, he could not outwait them; the old women were centuries, stretched in time; he was two decades, hurrying. "The priest was not lying," he said.

Aunt Celia tilted her head, cheerful in the gesture, the stiff-necked and feeble cat remembering the kitten. "Did we say he was lying?"

A finger of Aunt Sara's enormous hand raised up to call their attention to the words she was about to speak. "The devil does not exist, either."

The sight of the old women, so compressed, speaking from such distant origins, softly overturning the world, frightened Villa. "Then what is there?" he asked.

"Truth," Aunt Celia said. "Science. The world. Man. The greatness of our race." She gathered her breath. "As you may have surmised, Sara and I are sisters. We were born two poor Indian girls in the mountains of the State of Mexico; Sara first, then five more, and ten years after Sara, I was born. We lived, but we did not live well. It was a poor village, too high up for good corn, existing on maguey and whatever grew wild in the mountains. Our mother died and our father went away, leaving us small and sickly, perhaps to die.

"The priest who visited the village heard of our misfortune, and he came to visit us. What a good and gentle man he was! He brought us sugar candy and sacks of ground corn to make atole or tortillas, whatever we desired. He came often, he took care of us. I don't remember how long it was—a year, perhaps more. Then one day he came with a wagon and took us away, down the mountain to a convent school, where we lived and worked and studied and devoted our thoughts to God and the Church.

"We learned to read. We studied the lives of the saints, we read the works of the great doctors of the Church. Sara and Celia, two Indian orphans destined to be married to the Church. But there was something wrong; we became disillusioned—the Church acted only in service of the Church. Good people, we decided, served not the Church but God Himself. We left the convent and went to live in the mountains from whence we had come, there to be with nature, to help the poor and unfortunate of this world, and to worship God. It was the sweet time of our lives: we were happy, useful; we did not consider ourselves sinners.

"War came, and more war. We nursed the wounded, we comforted the sick and the many who were bereaved. Sara and I traveled with armies, two women dressed in white, two very strong women who cried only in the night and in private. One war was followed by another. We saw the limbs of men torn and broken, we saw the dying and the dead, we heard the sound of executions, the drumming, the cries of the condemned, the sound of orders, death itself. We lived with death; we saw women murdered, children muti-

lated. Could this be God's world, we wondered? We came to believe that
God had abandoned the world, and we wept for that loss, that terrible loss,
the loneliness.

"But God had made the world, we knew; he was the power and the glory,
we had been told; he was all-knowing and almighty, we had been told. We
knew what had been said of God and we knew the world as He knew it,
as He made it or permitted it to exist. God must be mad, we thought, or
evil; or God did not exist. We chose to believe the most hopeful way: in a
world without God, man could perfect himself. Perhaps man was in such
a process. We turned to the study of our ancestors.

"Nothing mattered to us but our studies. We left our home and came up
here to Hidalgo del Parral to live and study. We supported ourselves by
curing people of their simple illnesses, accepting money or food or livestock
for our work. In the language of our ancestors we learned the science of our
race: the herbs, roots, animal substances, and minerals that control the
health of the mind and the body. The jars you saw in the inner room are
marked in the ancient language, for there are no words in Spanish to name
the varieties of medicines. What do the Spaniards know of Xoxotlatzin, Uei
Patli, Mamaxtla, Ichcayo, Acaxilotic, Iceleua, Chichipiltic, Tenxoxoli?
They do not know enough not to eat Tochtetepon. Only in us, in our race,
is there hope for the perfection of man, for we were the beginning, the first
scientists.

"In that way we lived happily here. The people came to us to be cured,
but we did not speak to them; the priests left us in peace to pursue our
studies. Unfortunately, the news of Sara's blindness brought a priest from
the town to visit us. He said he wanted to pray for the return of her sight,
but in our grief we could not deal with him. We told him to go away. We
shouted at him, we told him that God did not exist. That was the beginning
of our trouble: the priest cursed us, he told everyone that we had knowingly
separated ourselves from the mystical body of Our Lord Jesus Christ. We
were excommunicated, damned by the Holy Roman Catholic Church to
endure the worst tortures of Hell.

"It only amuses us. What do we care for a Spanish condemnation? We
are of our own race, descendants of the rulers of the greatest city the world
has ever known; we are the recipients of the minds that built the pyramids
of San Juan Teotihuacán; ours is the blood of the first people to understand
the sun, the moon, and the stars. We are proud. And for that they call us
heretics, they say we are in league with the devil himself, a devil who will
soon be here. The devil is a Spanish dream, the whip of the Church; this
world belongs to us, the Indian race. That is the gospel, that is the truth;
men are gods."

She was trembling, there were bubbles of saliva on her lips, her eyes flickered, fire and dullest sand; her sister's great hand lay open on her bosom, the cup had spilled. "Now you know, not everything, but you know," she said. "Enough. Your wound is cured, you are initiated into the visible truth." She laughed, a breathless cackle. "You have been with the devil." Villa opened his mouth, as if to begin a disagreement, but she quieted him with a flutter of her hand. "Go now," she said. "There is nothing more for you here. Go now. The light is failing; you musn't fall."

It was a surprise that Celia died before her older sister. Some people said it was a heavenly punishment, for they reconstructed the deaths in their minds, realizing the loneliness of the blind older sister on her couch, hungering for what little she needed to eat or drink, perhaps calling to Celia, begging her for food or water, eventually knowing in her darkness, perhaps by the deathly odor, that her sister lay dead on the floor of the room.

The priests spoke against the sisters, describing the loneliness of the death of the unforgiven. No one was to bury them, they said; the house was to be left for a reminder of the sins of heresy and apostasy and the punishment that was invited by sin, a punishment that only began on earth.

Santa Sofia came to visit Villa at his work to tell him of the sisters. He wept for them there among his hammers and crushed stones; the tears muddied the powdered stone that lay on his cheeks. The next morning he rented a horse and wagon and drove it to Santa Sofia's house. He and Sofia carried Tacuiaé out to the wagon and propped him up on the seat, and then they drove up the hill to the house where the dead sisters lay. Santa Sofia covered her nose and mouth with a cloth and went inside to prepare the bodies while Villa dug a grave beside each of the circles of marigolds. He carried the bodies out and laid them in the small graves. They had no weight, even wrapped in white sheets and covered with the draperies that had hung over the front windows.

"Go inside now," Tacuiaé called from the wagon, "and empty the jars. Destroy everything. Bring out their books to bury with them."

Villa asked why; he wanted to know what good it would do to destroy the work of their lives. Tacuiaé would not answer. "Do as I tell you," he said. "Later, when you least expect it, you'll think about them and you'll understand."

Santa Sofia gave Villa a cloth to cover his nose and went inside with him to empty the jars. It took them a long time, for there were so many jars, and so many pouches, which took longer and were more difficult to empty —the herbs sticking to the leather. The floor was covered with herbs and roots and the dried flesh of animals. They waded in the debris, mixing everything. When it was done, they carried out the books and laid them in the graves. Villa expected Santa Sofia to pray over the bodies, but all she said was, "Merciful sisters, we shall miss you."

He filled the graves, and instead of crosses they transplanted circles of marigolds to stand at the heads of the sisters. "Thank you," he said to each of them as he finished the planting; then he helped Santa Sofia into the wagon and drove down the hill. They stopped once to look back at the house: the chickens and ducks walked in the yard, scratching in the earth, endlessly garrulous, limited to their hungers, pecking at the varieties of plants that grew around the house. The flowers of the garden of herbs were browning, feathering their seeds for the wind. The vines mingled, the roots intertwined, the names were lost.

The year 1900 in their calendar arrived in the month of Tititl, the time of foul weather, the feast of Tonantzin, the ritual beating of women with bags of straw, the ceremony of Llamatecuhtl: wearing the face that looks in two directions. It is also the time of their god of two faces—a coincidence, surely a coincidence; Quetzalcóatl did not cross the sea in his paper boat, he rose in flames, he became smoke, he became the most beautiful birds, the most beautiful flowers; he has not returned.

Their date is presumptuous, false, a dream. The sun was in the sky before men were on earth; nothing can be counted from the beginning, because the beginning is not known. Only the cycles are true, only the cycles can be observed. They deny the truth of mathematics and the plain face of reason; men do not precede their gods.

They celebrate their date with drunkenness; they mock themselves.

Perhaps they lost their faith in Mexico; they are poor conquerors, perverted in the first generation, thereafter dissolved. It was useless for them to intermarry, as it was useless for us. The end of conquest is always the destruction of both the conquerors and the conquered. We have seen it in our own empire. The admixture of the sun and the night is an angry grayness, an infirm world, a struggling world, a world desperate to clarify its nature. War begets conquest, which holds the seed of rebellion, and rebellion is the beginning of war, which begets conquest.

Finally, everything falls; the sun ends and is not reborn. Then the wisdom of historians and the errors of emperors are the same; life on earth is nothing but a dream, only a dream. Why do we live on earth?

Villa learned to mix mortar and to lay stones in straight walls; he became a craftsman. Santos Vega was pleased: he paid Villa three pesos a day and then four, he allowed him to hire men to follow his instructions, he gave Villa retaining walls to build and then the walls of houses. The business prospered; Villa earned five pesos a day and then ten; he lived in the Hotel Fuentes in a room of his own and he had a woman to wash his shirts. He bought a horse and a silver-trimmed saddle. His hair gleamed with oil. Every morning he ate eggs with cream, and in the evening he always had meat. At night he danced with the flowering virgins and lay with the most delicious whores. He carried a watch on a thin gold chain, he permitted children to shine his boots, he was generous with beggars and the sorrowful gliding women who carried trays of sweetcakes on their heads.

When he felt strong enough, he went to the house where Socorro Riendo lived. The child who had slept through their night was a small boy, sitting in front of the house, tracing lines in the dust. It was early evening, the sky promised heat and rain, the light was orange, reflected, without a center. Villa went inside the house without knocking. Socorro stood before a small round mirror, painting her face for the night.

She saw his face in the mirror. "I should have taken the money," she said, going on with the painting, darkening her eyebrows.

"Shall we dance?"

She laughed, and he took it for a sign of welcome. He laughed too, opening his arms to embrace her, expecting her to turn around and accept him. She continued the painting. Her hand was steady. She moistened the brush with spit.

He let his arms fall. For a moment he could not think what to do. He watched her eyes in the mirror. She was making them tense; without the darkening paint they were softly brown, understandable; she invented herself, she played at being Socorro Riendo. He thought then that he knew something about her. "Is your house still full of fleas?" he asked.

"Didn't you take some with you?"

"Does a woman with fleas also dance well standing up?"

She wiggled her buttocks in response.

"No, sweetie," he said, "that's not dancing. I'll have to put fleas in your shoes."

She turned around abruptly, thrusting her face at him. There was a red scar on her cheek reaching down to the corner of her mouth. "I can still dance on my back," she said. "Give me two pesos and I'll dance all night for you."

"For that I'll need my strength; we better eat first." He shook his head, laughing. "I'm a working man now. I build walls out of stone. I can't live the way I did when I was young. I have my routine. Let's eat. Then we'll dance."

"Not here," she said. "Go and eat and come back."

"Why not here? The boy won't know. Tell him I'm his uncle."

"Stupid," she screamed. "There's nothing to eat, not even an onion! I'm ugly, can't you see? Are you blind as well as stupid? Nobody wants an ugly whore. So get out of here! Go fatten yourself; I have work to do."

He opened his arms again to her, and this time she entered his embrace. She laid her head against his chest and wept. The paint ran down her cheeks in watery gray lines. Villa took out his handkerchief and reached out to dry her tears, but she pushed his hand away, took the cloth from him, and wiped her face with it. "You don't have to touch the scar," she said.

"If a man did that to you," he said, "tell me his name and I'll kill him. I'll do it slowly. I'll gutshoot him or I'll hang his head over a little fire the way the Apaches do. Please, tell me his name, let me do this for you."

"It was an accident," she said. "I fell."

"If that's what you want."

He led her outside and lifted her up onto his horse, put the child behind her, and led them down into Parral to a restaurant. She did not want to go inside with him, protesting that he should not be seen eating with a known whore. He slapped the holster on his hip, saying, "This makes you the most respected woman in Parral."

"And what about you? When they see you with me they'll say that you're a fool."

He slapped the holster again. "That's possible, but they'll only say it once."

After dinner he bought corn and oil and chiles and meat and cheese to carry up to her house. The next night he moved his belongings out of the hotel and into her house. All the money he earned he spent for her and the child, buying hens and then a rooster, two milk goats, a pregnant sow, four turkey chicks, and clothes and shoes and cooking pots and cheese pots, an indoor stove with a flue that went up through the roof, and glass windows and a wooden door. He bought a bed for them and a closet with drawers to stand against the wall. On Sundays and in the early part of the evenings he built stone walls to make another room. Behind the house, on the rocky sloping ground, they planted corn, squash, tomatoes, onions, and beans. He planted rose bushes on either side of the front door. He built a chicken house and a pen for the pigs and a shelter for the horse.

"Are you happy?" he asked her.

"Yes."

"Then tell me the name of the man who hurt you."

"It was an accident," she said. "I fell."

He finished one new room of the house and began to build another. The corn grew, small green tomatoes appeared, they picked the first of the onions. Socorro fed the chickens and the pigs; the boy collected eggs and learned to sit a horse. A stray dog stopped to drink the water that had been set out for the pigs; the boy fed it once, and the dog stayed. Socorro confessed that her true name was Julia Celís and that she was the daughter of a carpenter from Santa Rosalía. Villa told her about himself, his sister, Ignacio, Urbina; he talked night after night, lying beside her, remembering, saying everything that came up out of his memory, laughing often, melancholy only when he spoke of the death of Parra or the deadly staring quiet of his sister. He told her his life, all but the time he spent in Durango living with Marta, and finally he spoke of her too, but casually, describing in vague terms the woman he still remembered so well.

Socorro asked if he thought Aunt Celia would have known how to erase the scar on her cheek. "Yes," he said, "I think she could have done anything, but I don't believe she would have erased the scar. Aunt Celia and her sister were very brave women; they were not the kind who would think your scar was important. It's not a sickness, it's nothing."

"The scar brought us together," Socorro said.

He leaned over her to kiss the red line, but she turned her head, giving him her mouth.

They lived together through the autumn and the winter and into spring. They were a family. The boy said that Villa was his father. Socorro walked and worked beside Villa as if she were a wife. They were carpenters and stonemasons and shepherds and farmers together. There were three rooms in the house, and it was rich with chairs and tables and beds and even a sofa that the child was not allowed to sit on. Villa chopped wood, the boy gathered kindling, Socorro cooked. They listened to each other, they told stories to the boy, filling his dreams with giants and saints and jaguars. They were grateful to each other, the family of Arámbula or Villa or Riendo or Celís.

At night, after the animals had been herded into their pens and the chickens were asleep on their roosts, when the dishes had been washed and the child had been put to bed, Socorro came into the bedroom to unwind her hair and touch herself with the oils of flowers. She slept naked to be ready for him. "It's an easy life," she said. "I remember when I was alone."

He brought her a ring and asked her to marry him. She declined, giving no reasons. She wore the ring on a piece of ribbon tied around her neck.

They had no children together, for she had learned after the birth of her son to use stoneseed and wild yam to make herself sterile. He did not object, but he told her that when they were married, he expected to have two sons and at least one daughter. She agreed; but they did not get married, and there were no children.

Santos Vega came once to their house to eat with them. Socorro cooked chicken and rice in the Spanish style, coloring the rice with saffron instead of tomato. It was to please him, she said, because he was more like a Spaniard than like an Indian; he was an owner. Villa argued that Santos

[194]

Vega was not like other owners; he was a good man. But when he arrived, Socorro looked once at his eyes and never looked at him again. Nor did she speak to him, except to offer more food. Villa made jokes, he told stories about the men at the building sites, he teased the child with riddles to make them all laugh; but they ate quickly, and Santos Vega went home before dark.

Only once did they argue: Socorro bought a gourd of teshuina from a Tarahumara who came to the door. When Villa came home she lay on the sofa in a drunken sleep. He slapped her face and sent her to bed. The boy complained that he was hungry, and Villa cooked for him and washed the dishes and put him to bed. Then he went into the room where Socorro was sleeping and beat her until she was sick. He opened the window and hung her outside like a rug while she vomited. She swore she would have her revenge for the beating and the humiliation, but in the morning she laughed and thanked him for helping her to expel the poison the Tarahumara had sold her.

At the end of the gentle season, before the coming of the summer rains, hurrying, he completed walls for Santos Vega and worked the garden for his family. Without a plow, he turned the soil by hand, the boy beside him, chattering, breaking the sandy clots with a stick. Every evening he turned another square of land, working in the cool dusk, talking to the boy, teaching him the laws of corn and beans, what the weather meant, how to read the clouds and the color of the sky. At planting time, Villa made the holes with a stick, dropping in the seeds, five for each hole, and the boy followed him, covering the seeds, building a mound over each hole to make a house for the young corn.

The evening meal was late in that season; they fed the chickens and the pigs in the dark, carried water up from the well, brushed and bedded the horse, and went inside to sit in the circle of the lantern, tired, pleased, seasoning the meal with laughter.

What grinds like a metate and has a piece of leather inside?
Your mouth.
What is black and writes with liquid lead?
The snail.
What is slender, red, and bites?
An ant.
What flys through the air, clapping its hands?
The butterfly.
What has a small, wrinkled face and kicks?
Your knee.
What has a white head and holds a green feather?
An onion.

[195]

The boy giggled; he kissed Villa's cheek, he lay his head against his mother's breast. Before the meal was over, he fell asleep, and Villa carried him to bed, a slender child, with long black hair hanging straight, shining. Villa held him cradled in one arm, and with his free hand, he held the child's fingers, laughing at the soft wrinkles, the tiny fingernails, black-rimmed even after washing. He lifted up the warm fingers to his mouth and kissed them, then he squeezed the boy close to him in praise of innocence, and gently lowered him to the bed. Sometimes Villa stood over the boy for a moment or two before going out of the room, enjoying the paternal thrill, tears brimming in his eyes, loving the smoothness of a face in true repose, the exact closing of faithful eyes.

Socorro had cleared the table when he came out. Sometimes she brought little bowls of custard or cooked fruit, and always there was chocolate sweetened with vanilla and thickened with goat's milk. They talked while the chocolate cooled: the progress of the building, the progress of the garden, how the boy was growing, whether the rains would come soon enough. He told stories of the men who worked for him; the weaklings and the fools, the ambitious ones who made crooked walls in their haste and the simple one who let the cement harden around his hand. She said what the women said at washing or in the market, reporting a coyote in the neighborhood, a daughter shamed, a heart stopped, the cost of rice, the quality of cotton, the colors of thread. They declared their happiness, and went to bed.

On some nights they opened the window and looked at the stars. He likened them to bandits; she said they were jewels. Breezes came. They heard the animals in the pens, shifting, grunting, signifying simple dreams. She lay close to him, the exciter, beginning with sighs, laughing and weeping when she was pleased, drying them with a cloth, then the first to sleep.

Santos Vega told him in whispers: a woman had betrayed him, the police were asking questions, comparing him to the bandit Pancho Villa. "I told them you were working on the other house near the Plaza Juárez," he said.

"You're sure they said it was a woman?"

"Yes, yes, a woman. They described you exactly: chino hair, the jaw, the way you always breathe through your mouth."

"A woman from Parral or a woman from Durango?"

Santos Vega was exasperated by the conversation. He hopped on one foot and then the other; his body jangled. "It's not important, man! If they think you're this bandit, they'll hang you."

"Sir, if someone betrays you, it's right to shoot them, isn't it? Even if it's a woman?"

Only then did Santos Vega become calm. Like Villa, he stood quietly,

[*196*]

seeming to reflect upon the situation; now it was complex for him too. "I don't know what you've done," he said, "but you were always a good worker. One day, I thought, you would be a partner in this business. Look, you're going to need some money. I have about a hundred pesos here; will that help?"

Villa threw his arms around Santos Vega and hugged him to his chest. "Don't worry about me, old friend. And don't be sorry for me. I thank you for the money, but you keep it, please. Francisco Arámbula always needs money, but Pancho Villa . . ." He led Santos Vega to his little open buggy and lifted him up onto the seat. The man had no weight, like the child of the evenings. There were tears in the tight Spanish eyes. Santos Vega took off his hat to mop his forehead and, incidentally, his tears. Villa looked at the small skull, the black hair oiled and combed in streaks over the naked places, and it made him laugh. "Goodbye, Mr. Santos Vega; you're the only good employer in Mexico."

Santos Vega drove off, sitting very rigidly, looking straight ahead, holding himself as employers must, holding back. Villa was surprised to find his vision clouded, tears in his eyes too. He took the Colt out of its holster and gave the cylinder a spin to be sure it was loaded—a gesture of return, change, a new season of his life. The horse was there, waiting, a stocky, strong horse, not for the long runs, but good enough. He had a rifle and fifty rounds, a poncho for the rain. Where would he get eating utensils, a canteen, coffee, salt, a pan for frying? Was he to grind wood for flour and suck maguey leaves and eat unsalted meat again? Urbina would take him in, Urbina would help him through the first days.

A workman, Eleuterio Soto, stood beside him. Villa looked his annoyance, but Soto would not go away. "Take me with you," he said. "I know who you are, and I'd rather take my chances with you than spend the rest of my life with these fucking stones."

Villa examined him: a young man, more like a boy, shirtless, wearing huaraches, the straps of his stone-dust-grayed overalls loose on his shoulders. He had a farmer's face: a fat nose and open eyes that were prepared to weep over diseased corn or the lack of rain.

"You know how to use a pistol?"

"Better than a trowel," Soto said.

"It's not a good life; you live like an animal, sometimes a rabbit, sometimes a wolf; the wolf doesn't live much better than the rabbit."

"Take me with you."

"The rurales will be looking for us."

Soto smiled, shy but pleased, like a boy who had been embarrassed by winning a prize. "They're already looking for me."

Villa put his arm around Soto's shoulder, and they walked together to the horses. "Why didn't you say that in the beginning? The only decent men in this country are criminals."

They tightened the cinches and prepared to mount the horses. "I haven't committed any crimes," Soto said. "Everything they say about me is a lie."

Villa smiled. "Yes, I understand. It's the same with me."

11

He sat among the flowers, as his mother had done when she came to me still smelling of birth. He thought of her, he feared for her; his eyes protruded, they were vulnerable. Eleuterio Soto was with him. They were tired and filthy, they smelled of the sweat of men and the sweat of horses. I sent them out to wash, I gave them white clothing and I blessed them and cleansed them. While Soto carried the egg outside to bury it, Villa asked about his mother.

"Dead," I told him.

"Why is she dead?" he asked, as children do, expecting an answer, names, as if death were days or the parts of corn.

I spoke to him for a long time, not to comfort him, but to assuage his anger against her. I do not know what I know about death, I told him, and that is not a riddle for a child. In the time when we believed that the earth was real, in that time of certainty, it was possible to answer his question; ideas were thought to be true, as things were thought to be real. Then the questions were asked, the poems were written, the discussions were begun. I told him the poet said it was not true that we came to the earth to live. I told him the body is a flower that blooms and withers. I sang the ancient songs.

He listened, his eyes were round, like bubbles; his face was foolish; his grief had been confused. I sang the poems again. He was not comforted, he could not understand that everything cannot be understood. "Death itself," I explained to him, "can be seen. Life is movement, death is the end of movement. What is blood, what is heart, but another way to say movement? Death is without movement. Eventually, everything stops, the sun stops, everything dies. But is that only here on earth? I do not know; it is not known. If you want answers, Francisco, if you cannot abide the truth of not knowing the truth, go to the priests in their black dresses. Kneel. They will answer every question for you."

He sat for a long time, staring at me, reading my face to find the deceit that he now seemed to expect in everyone. His eyes narrowed, the color changed, reddening. He screamed at me, like an animal: "I want to know!" I saw his teeth. He threatened me.

"Do not raise your voice in my house," I said.

He rose as if to attack me. His hands worked, grasping air; then he fell forward onto the earthen floor and wept. I lifted him up and showed him the black mirror, offering visions of Heaven if he chose to see them; but he saw nothing, the mirror was filled with smoke.

Soto came back with soiled hands. He understood nothing; he had broken the egg; I feared for them.

They laid Micaela out on a long table and surrounded her with white candles. She lay in her widow's dress, the rosary in her hands in the open house amid the fluttering candles, pale, the shell of a dead heart, paler still, dead among her children, flesh upon a table for her last evening, lost, gone, echoing. All around her stood the priests, the mourning children, the mourning sisters, brothers, nephews, nieces, cousins, the mourning candles flickering, dying pale, wax.

In the town of San Juan del Río Doroteo had stood in the shade watching the children eat sugary skulls. They walked in the sun, chewing, crunching. They played on the high stone steps, clambering over the rises, the white skulls dangling, half-eaten, the sugary tidbits falling into the cracks between the stones. The ants would come. Micaela was inside the store. He heard her laughter, the sound of her skirts, the heels of her only shoes evasive and quick on the board floor of the grocery, the basso laughter of the expectant merchant. Doroteo chewed his thumb, tasting the salt of himself. Saliva ran from the corner of his mouth. Micaela came out in skitters, as if she were dancing. Her skirts swung wide, her face was animated with laughter, dazzling as she came through the shaded doorway. Then she saw him there, half crouched against the wall, his eyes upturned, showing white, the saliva running down his hand, wetting his chin. Her smile faded. She reached into her woven bag and took out a small object wrapped in newsprint. "Take it," she said. "It's for you." Inside the paper was a tiny white skull. He licked it once to test the flavor, then he popped it into his mouth. The sugar captured his senses, sending him running, spinning with joy. When the skull was eaten, he kissed her, and she said he tasted sweet.

Villa lay in the field downwind from the house, resting on the plowed ground, spread across the damp leaves of the fallen corn. It was the field in which his father died. Was she cleaner? he wondered. Were her nostrils

[*199*]

clear? Did they have to pick the jellied clots out of her throat? There were too many horses around the house; the barn was full. He saw the dogs skulking, the bent necks, fallen tails, shadows across the doorway. The posse was there. He lay with the barrel of the carbine beside his cheek. Soto was behind him in the foothills, holding the horses. The priests were burying her; she would not have a stick or a gift or anything to eat along the way. The house had a water tank and a barn; he had bought them a buggy and given them money for seed and horses and pigs and goats, but she would be buried in a widow's dress with nothing to comfort her but the droning Latin of the priests.

He could not speak to her; he did not know what to say; if she had forgiven him, if she had not. The wind was up. He heard the rustling leaves of the standing stalks, the dead whispers. Dear Mother, sainted Mother, lost Mother; dead, she left the world and all its cares to him. He lay his face against the bosom of the earth and wept.

Before morning, when the breath of the day still lay frozen over the fields, he and Soto rode east up into the saddle of the mountain and then turned north. "I don't know what she thought of me," Villa said. Soto told him, "You were her firstborn son; she loved you." Villa rode on for a while. It was so; women loved their sons. They taught them, sometimes with disapproval, but the truth is that women love their sons. "Do you think she forgave me before she died?" he asked Soto, as if his answer could be the sure truth.

"She prayed for you."

"But not with the priests."

"The last prayers are always alone," Soto said. "You can be sure of that."

"God willing."

Soto looked at Villa's face to see if he was expected to laugh. There was no sign; the eyes were without light, the long cheeks of his face were flat and darkly bearded, the jaw had no thrust. Soto made no response.

They rode north through the wintering cotton fields, the long rows of dry bushes and hardening soil. The last of the weeds were dying. There was no grass for the horses. They bought feed in the mining towns along the way, climbing the hills to Dinamita and down again to the rail-crossing town of Bermejillo, up out of the great plain irrigated by the Nazas and the Florida, west of the dry lakes, into the corn land and the cattle land, moving from stream to stream, guided by the sweetwater, picking up Urbina in Jiménez, going north again to camp outside Santa Rosalía.

The weather had already turned in the high places northwest of the town: water froze at night, the horses needed to be blanketed, much of the day had to be given over to collecting firewood for the night. Urbina complained of pains in his bones, swellings in his knees and one of his hands. Villa told him to sleep closer to the fire and to eat less salt. Urbina said he wanted to live in a warm house, like a rich landlord. He wanted enough to drink, two wives, a good place for his mother, chocolate, little pieces of pork roasted on a spit, a bed with a canopy, electricity, and music all the time. They planned to rob the bank in Santa Rosalía; Urbina said it would be full of money on the next-to-the-last day of the month.

Soto said he was afraid. Villa and Urbina comforted him with scornful laughter. He tried to pretend he wasn't afraid, hoping to avoid their derision, but he couldn't control his bladder; every hour he walked away from the camp to urinate. They called him the river of fear. They said his sweat had a sickening odor. He made promises to them, he swore his courage on his mother's soul, but he could not control his bladder.

It was warmer at the level of the plain; the horses walked more easily on the thawed ground, the men felt the late-morning sun. At the first tavern, Urbina bought two glasses of tequila and Soto emptied his bladder, while Villa waited outside with the horses, pacing the length of the hitching rail. Children came to look at him, the stranger. Women wrapped in their winter shawls passed the pacing man and his three horses, glancing, fixing him in the flash of curiosity, and hurrying on. An old man, the driver of a squeaking, broken wood cart, waved to Villa. His face was covered with a long white stubble of surrender and his eyes were askew, maddening the cheer of his face. "Long live bandits!" the old man shouted. Villa moved around to the other side of the rail and stood between the horses. "Kill the rurales," the old man shouted. "Fuck their mothers!" Villa pulled his blanket higher around his shoulders and hid his chin in the fold. The old man passed.

Villa went into the tavern to fetch Soto and Urbina. They were standing at the bar, leaning, each one with his head in his hand, silently drinking, staring down at the wood of the bar, as if they could divine the day in the grain of the wood. "Midday," Villa said.

"For my rheumatism," Urbina answered, grinning.

Soto looked around, dog eyes in his round face, not speaking. "That won't help your bladder," Villa said. Soto looked down at the bar again. Villa turned and went back out into the street. Soto and Urbina followed him, walking slowly and with uneven steps. Soto had difficulty mounting his horse, missing the stirrup with his foot. Villa gave him a boost up across the saddle, where he lay for a moment, parallel to the blanket roll. Urbina giggled through his nose.

They made jokes on the way into the center of the town, arriving with laughter, loud, three cowboys hiding in the innocence of their commotion. Soto wanted to graze his horse in the grass of the plaza; Urbina wanted to take his horse into the church to have it baptized; and Villa argued crazily with them, explaining that drinking holy water made a horse's belly swell and that the grass in town plazas was fertilized with dog manure, which caused horses to bark and chase rabbits. They tied the horses to the rail in front of the bank, preparing to go in. Soto and Urbina urged Villa to come inside with them. "I can't go," he said. "You have to know how to write."

The answer gave pause to Urbina, who stood on the steps of the bank, scratching his testicles while he pondered the problem. Suddenly he brightened. He pointed at Villa. "But you can count."

The game lost its humor for Villa. He saw people behind them who seemed to be drawn to their noisy laughter: women in long dresses and feathered hats, men who could be police, older men with the disapproving faces of the rich, merchants in their round hats, cowboys and bookkeepers, clerks with garters on their sleeves hurrying in the cold. They were looking, seeming to study the faces of the three loud men, who could be cowboys to be forgotten or thieves to be hanged. "Get going," he said. The laughter ended.

Villa stood between the horses, half hidden, slapping them away when they began to press him between them. He watched the bank and the street and kept his hand on the stock of the carbine slung loosely on his saddle. A long time passed, longer and longer still. He pretended to fix one of the cinches, thinking it would look suspicious for a man simply to be standing between two horses with his hand on the stock of a carbine. Customers went into the bank and customers came out. The lunchtime closing hour was nearing; shopkeepers were pulling down the shades in their windows, closing the shutters and doors; quiet was beginning in the town. Villa could not imagine why nothing had happened inside the bank. If Soto and Urbina had been killed, he would have heard shots. If they had not been killed, why was business continuing? It was as if they had gone through the door and disappeared. Two more customers came out of the bank, men in striped shirts and white collars, clerks, perfumed and pale, chatting as they descended the steps. Villa could bear it no longer; he went inside the bank.

Only one window was open; and there was a long line of customers waiting, among them Soto and Urbina, who stood, drooping, patiently moving forward as each customer finished his business and left the window. Villa counted eight customers still in front of them and three behind. He stood at the writing counter, pretending to look at one of the forms, waiting for Soto or Urbina to notice him. He could see Urbina's eyes, more crossed than usual, the control gone in drink; but Urbina apparently could not see him. Soto's wide-brimmed straw farmer's hat was pulled low over his eyes; he appeared to be asleep where he stood. Villa put the form back in the rack at the back of the writing counter and went outside again—eventually Urbina would reach the window.

The customers came out at regular intervals. After the sixth, Villa untied the reins of the three horses and looped them lightly over the rail. He moved around between the horses again and held the stock of the carbine, ready to use it. There was little time now; he no longer bothered to pretend he was fixing cinches. The seventh customer came out. The guard appeared in the window of the door as he lowered the green shade. The door opened again to allow the eighth customer out. The guard held the door for him. He remained there, a square man in a gray uniform with golden epaulets, his left hand on the door handle, the gun hand hanging free. When Urbina and Soto reached the window and drew their guns to frighten the teller, the guard would be behind them; they would not see the gun that killed them.

Villa pulled the carbine out of the boot. As if he were shooting at quail rising, he threw the gun to his shoulder, sighting on the lift of the barrel, squeezing the trigger while his eye was still frantic. He shot the guard through the head. The eighth customer, coming down the steps of the bank, froze at the sound of the shot. He and Villa stood ten feet apart, as still as the afternoon, caught in each other's eyes. Villa could see every detail of the customer's face: the lines radiating from his eyes, the white hairs of his little beard lying neatly, the long Spanish chin, dry pink lips, mild eyes, the faint weakness of one eyelid. He turned the rifle on the customer, sighting on him, raising the barrel the length of his body, adjusting his aim, ready to lead him if he turned. He passed the feeble crotch, the little pouch of belly, the shallow chest, the folds of neck crowded by the collar, the trembling mouth, and settled on the eyes, splitting them in the convergence of the sight. The customer turned to his left, square as a soldier turning, then he ran. Villa followed him, leading, sighting at the level of his eyes, moving just ahead of his nose.

The old man disappeared from the sight. Villa opened the other eye to look wide, and saw the customer tumbled on the stone walk, crawling. He turned toward Villa and raised the palms of his hands. Blood was filling in the lacerations. The sleeves of his coat were torn. He reached across with one hand to hold his elbow. The pain was signed on his forehead.

"Get out of here, old man."

There were noises in the street; people running, the slamming of shutters. Urbina backed out of the door of the bank, a canvas bag in one hand, the pistol in the other. He turned and came running down the stairs. Soto was behind him, firing twice into the ceiling of the bank before he closed the door and ran for his horse. Villa threw the reins up to them as they mounted their horses, and for a moment he stood alone in the street, holding the carbine, watching the horses wheeling on either side of him. Men with drawn guns were running down the street, heading toward him. He fired at them, missing, sending them into the safety of doorways. Urbina and Soto

[*203*]

turned the corner at the church. Shots came back from the doorways, the quick cracks of light pistols. Villa mounted his horse, lying over on the left side away from the gunfire, and rode for the corner.

At evening he was back in the hills again, waiting at the old campsite, huddled in his blanket, afraid to build a fire. A rider came up the last hill, framed in moonlight, a black shape leaning over the horn of the saddle, his head bent so that the brim of his hat pointed straight up. It was a farmer's hat, frayed at the edges, with pieces of straw sticking up everywhere, like stalks in a winter field. "Soto," he called, "Eleuterio Soto." The rider did not raise his head. The horse continued climbing, picking its way through the rocks in the uncertain light.

Villa helped Soto down and laid him on a blanket. He didn't appear to be wounded, but his limbs were flaccid and he refused to speak. Villa left him while he cared for the horse. When he returned, Soto was asleep. There was nothing else to do; he covered Soto with a blanket and went back to watching the slopes of the hills. He saw coyotes, dark birds, the scurriers of the night. The moon passed, dressed in clouds. Soto spoke in his sleep. The horses let out long shudders. Between the near sounds the silence was perfect.

He sat there all the night, with the blanket across his shoulders and the carbine cradled in his arms; and he was glad when the stars faded and the known sounds of the day began. When Soto awakened, they talked awhile, and then they built a small fire of twigs and made a breakfast of dried meat, coffee, and tortillas warmed in the ashes of the fire. Soto said, "Urbina turned south and I kept going east into the mountains. The posse chased me until sundown. When they turned back toward Santa Rosalía I just followed them. Sometimes I was close enough to hear them talking, but they never looked back. The safest thing is to stay behind them, then you always know where they are."

"Was it a big posse?"

"I counted twenty-three."

"That's not enough," Villa said. "Some must have followed Urbina."

"Do you think they caught him?"

"He has that rheumatism. Sometimes he can't ride so well because of it. Maybe he had to hide somewhere. We'll wait until tomorrow morning for him."

The day passed. They cooked before dark, then settled in their blankets to wait away the night. Soto slept for a while, awakened at an unsounded noise, and then sat beside Villa to watch the moonlit fall of the mountain for the sign of a man riding.

Villa said: "He was not a bad man; he took me in when I needed him. He lied for me, and that is why I trusted him.

[204]

"I think we lost him because of a mistake, my mistake and his mistake. The tequila was my fault; I shouldn't have let him stop in the tavern to make himself stupid. And his mistake, that was even worse: he dreamed that three men could capture a town. One blow, one terrific blow, that should be the rule. The way to live long is to choose something alone, be decided when we go, and then give everything at once. We should have known; this lesson cost too much—Urbina was not a bad man; cross-eyed and greedy, but not a bad man."

Before morning Soto fell into a deep sleep again, snoring and speaking out in his dreams. Villa arranged the ashes of the fire into an arrow pointing southwest, then he saddled his horse and rode north toward the Río Bravo, for he had heard that on the other side of the river everyone was rich, even the wives of sharecroppers slept on silken pillows and decorated their hair with silvered combs and ropes of pearls.

He wandered north, rolling up like a warm wind, choosing the valleys of passage, sliding through the towns, around the houses, unheard, unseen, but moving certainly in his own direction. In a little charreada outside Delicias he won twenty pesos riding a bull, at a cockfight near Santa Ysabel he turned the twenty pesos into forty-five; but a widow who sat with her children in front of the market in Chihuahua begged him to give her a peso and he gave her twenty because it comforted him. He swam and fished in San Bernabé Lake, stole two mules in Bustillos, and led them north into the ranch country. On the Terrazas Ranch he butchered cattle, dried the meat in the winter sun, and carried it south to the lumbering towns to sell to camp cooks and the managers of the company stores. He bought salt, corn flour, and cooking oil and carried it down into the Copper Canyons, selling it to the Tarahumaras and the prospectors who wandered the greenwater tributaries of the Urique, the Papigochic, the Conchos, and the Mayo. From his trading he filled a sack with flakes of gold. He camped each night in an inaccessible place, a natural tower or a tiny platform among the broken edges of the mountains, sleeping soundly there, letting the horse and the mules do his watching. He wandered away the winter, and in the early spring he sold the mules in Casas Grandes and took the road north to Palomas, crossing the border there to Columbus, New Mexico, at the end of April, which is the time of the long fast and the hope of the new corn.

The town lay at the foot of a round hill. To the west the mountains hid behind a brown haze of dust, to the north the land dipped and rolled along the base of a chain of sawtooth mountains, and on the east a long stretch of deadly waterless land led to the river and the great northern pass. He saw the town first in the afternoon in the harsh wind, when the streets were empty and the sound of creaking metal was all that came to a man passing the rows of barracks, mess shacks, stables, and officers' houses, riding up the road between the customs house and the tan square of the railroad station, crossing the tracks, turning east on the first street, then north at the Commercial Hotel to the block of stores, the silk and silver treasures of the rich.

The streets were made of hard clay dusted with sand. The town smelled of manure and alkaline powder that did not settle out of the wind. Soldiers passed on their high-tailed horses, their lustrous, white-hocked horses. They sat as if on parade, the reins in one hand, the other hand upon a hip. Their hats were tilted, their boots were shined, their spurs were polished; each man wore a single bandolier across his chest. The soldiers' faces were red, they squinted their eyes in the wind.

There were women in the streets, hurrying from store to store, dressed in long skirts and bonnets that hid their hair. They pulled children along with them and carried packages wrapped in brown paper and tied with rough twine. Businessmen in dark suits and white shirts stood in the streets. They kept their hands in the pockets of their trousers. They wore thin neckties that hung down to their waists. Some chewed tobacco and spit streams in the dust. The spittle did not mix with the dust but lay on it in dark globes.

Mexicans walked between the businessmen and the soldiers and the women in their bonnets. They were barefoot or wearing the poorest huaraches. The women wrapped their heads against the wind. The men wore farmers' hats and faded blue shirts and trousers. They did not raise their heads; only their eyes lifted to see who passed. They walked slowly. They did not speak. The men removed their hats for everyone, even the soldiers who passed them blindly on their high-stepping horses, as if on parade.

Villa tied his horse to a rail near the drugstore and walked along the rows of stores to look in the windows. They were richer than the stores in Torreón or Chihuahua, profusions of canned goods, sacks of beans, flour, potatoes, and onions. There were crates of eggs, slabs of bacon, fresh-killed chickens, cleaned tripe, and strips of dried beef. Bolts of cloth lay one upon another in disarrayed mountains of reds, blacks, browns, whites, and prints, checks, patterns of flowers and dots and stripes and squares and mixtures of every kind. He passed barbers and gunsmiths, saddlers, feed merchants, bootmakers, assayers, bankers and cattle brokers, bartenders, bakers, waiters, and tailors. It was a town of hundreds with enough goods for thousands, a rich and dusty town, hostage to the wind.

He sold his pouch of gold flakes in the assayer's office for two hundred and six dollars. A man with a pale bald scalp counted out the money and explained in Spanish that each dollar was worth two pesos and that he could have his choice of pesos or dollars in payment for his gold. Villa took the dollars and went to the barber shop. The barber, who was sitting in a chair tilted back against the wall, said that he was too busy; he directed Villa to the Mexican barber two blocks west and one block south. "I have dollars," Villa said in Spanish. The barber directed him again to the Mexican barbershop.

"Son of a bitch," the Mexican barber said in his best English accent, and then returned to Spanish to continue his discussion of the American barber. "He says we have lice in our hair because of the grease we use on it. That's how he stays in business. The gringos won't come to me and he won't cut hair for the Mexicans. It would be all right, but the gringos have the money and the Mexicans have the hair.

"Look at yours, for example; it must be almost a year since you cut your hair. How can you wear a hat over so much hair? Thank God it's clean. If so much hair was dirty, I would send you to the baths first; it's the only thing to do with cowboys. Are you a cowboy? What ranch are you from?"

"I'm a woodcutter. I sold my wood in Guzmán and came up here to look at the Americans. They say that all the Americans are rich."

"Sure. The gringos are rich because we do the work for them, us and the blacks. The whole country is this way. I have been to California to see it there too. All rich people in America have blue eyes—it's a rule. All poor people are black or toasted—that's also a rule."

"Who makes these rules?"

The barber clipped and combed, cutting a part into Villa's hair, mumbling that he would have to charge more for so much hair. "Books," he said in answer to the question. "The rules are made by the books."

"Books don't make rules."

The barber came around to the front of the chair and waved his comb in Villa's face. "You think I don't know what I'm talking about—you think I'm just a foolish barber who only knows about hair. Well, Mr. Woodcutter, if you see a rich Mexican in America, you ask him who makes the rules."

Villa closed his eyes and let the barber continue his work without interruption. While the barber stropped the razor before shaving his beard, Villa said, "I'm not a woodcutter, I'm a prospector. I just changed a little bit of gold for dollars in the office on the main street. Now I want to buy some supplies to go back out into the mountains. Is there a store here where they won't cheat me?"

"Ravel," the barber said. "Ravel the Jew is the only one to trust. He doesn't like Mexicans, but he doesn't like gringos, either. They're hard men, Ravel and his brothers; they don't sell on credit and they don't give anything away, but you can trust them, because you know they're sons of bitches. In America, the only ones to do business with are the sons of bitches. The other ones put stones in the cheese to increase the weight, and then they sell it to you at a good price for cheese, which is a poor price for stones."

"And the gringo barber," Villa said, laughing, "isn't he a son of a bitch?"

"No, he's not a true son of a bitch; his mother likes it."

It was early evening when Villa left the barbershop. He smelled of sweet oils and his hat seemed too large; he held on to it in the wind. On the main street some of the stores were closed, music and singing came from the taverns, soldiers walked in the street, some of them already staggering. Ravel's Mercantile Store was still open; the lanterns shone yellow in the windows and there were customers inside, examining cooking utensils and picking through piles of denim overalls. Villa stepped up onto the board-walk and looked in at the great array of merchandise; it was the store he had dreamed of in Durango, a store of sections: one for clothing, another for cloth, and another for utensils, and yet another for saddlery, and in the back a section of rifles and ammunition, and off to one side a section of spices, salt, beans, flour, and dried meat. Clothing, utensils, weapons, and meat hung from the walls; rows of bridles dangled from hooks; hats were stacked on shelves; the counters were filled with spices and boxes of ammunition, underwear, and spurs; great scales and small scales stood side by side on the counter tops; and all around the store the shelves reached to the ceiling.

The smell inside the store was so wonderful it made him dizzy: leather, spices, cotton dust, meat, gunpowder, and crude oil, the blended odor of plenty. This was not the dry, dusty smell of Valenzuela's little store; it was the moist smell of dreams. He walked among the tables, touching the cloth, the cool buttons, the heavy utensils, the carefully oiled metal of rifles, the soaped and oiled leather.

A small, thin, very neat man moved away from a group of people at the spice counter and came to Villa's side. "Good evening," he said in Spanish. He was of the size and bearing of a young man, but there was a large pink inflammation in the corner of his right eye and the flesh around both eyes was dark and wearily fallen. His hair was thin, his mouth was tight; he did not smile. "Sam Ravel at your service."

"I want a suit," Villa said. "And a white shirt and a long tie. And a pair of low shoes in two colors of leather. And an American hat."

"There are seven-dollar suits and twelve-dollar suits and thirty-dollar suits—which do you want?"

"I don't know," Villa said. "I want to compare them."

"That's what I would do," Ravel said, and for the first time his mouth softened at the corners.

The seven-dollar suit did not have a vest, and the thirty-dollar suit was too thick for the coming summer; Villa chose a brown wool suit for twelve dollars. Ravel was disappointed by the choice, and he showed his feelings in the pursed curve of his lips. Villa asked what was wrong, and he answered: "I thought you were a smarter man; the seven-dollar suit is all you need. That's what I wear. In the other suit you pay five dollars for style, and the style will change before the suit wears out."

"It's the vest, my friend. An American, like you, doesn't need a vest. But a Mexican country boy needs vests and perfume and shoes made of two colors of leather."

"For what?"

"I don't know yet. But I think that on this side of the river a man who carries a Colt pistol should hide it with a gold chain across his vest."

"A gold chain will cost you twenty dollars."

Villa made an innocent mask of his face. "Maybe a friend will give one to me," he said. "A man never knows where he is going to meet a friend."

Ravel's speech quickened. "I'm not only in the mercantile business. We deal in cattle too, all kinds of cattle. Some of the cattle we sell aren't even branded because they come off the big ranches. They're not stolen, you understand, just not branded, because the ranches are so big they can't brand them all; especially some of the big ones in Mexico are that way. We buy them here, fatten them, and drive them to El Paso or load them onto trains right here at our own loading platforms. Our prices are good, sir, very good. We'll pay in dollars, pesos, or gold."

"And if they're branded?"

"It spoils the hides, so we pay a little less. But there's no need to worry, our prices are still good, and we'll buy as many as you can deliver. No change in the price, whether you bring in one or one hundred thousand."

"Well, that's good to know," Villa said. "I'm just a poor prospector now, panning a little gold out of the streams wherever I find it. But if I should ever get into the cattle business, I'll know where to sell my beef."

The clothing cost nineteen and a half dollars. Ravel included two pairs of socks and a suit of underwear as a bonus. "And stay in my hotel tonight," he said, "as my guest. You know the Commercial Hotel? It's the best in town."

"You must be a rich man," Villa said.

"No, no. I'm only a shopkeeper, a middleman; I make other men rich."

He rode along the railroad tracks, close by the border, stopping at Malpais and Potrillo to eat and sleep, arriving on the third day at the sight of the Rio Grande and the wide pass between the Franklin Mountains and Mount Cristo Rey. He smelled the city long before he saw it, for the wind was out of the southeast and it carried the fumes of the stacks of the customs smelter out over the desert. There were groves of pecan trees and cottonwoods, fields for corn and cotton and onions, and the three great stacks of the smelter beyond, trailing smoke like pennants in a breeze. He followed the tracks past the smelter to the edge of the town. The salt cedars of the desert gave way to oaks and elms, staunch and budding, guardians of the hills and greening lawns and colonnaded houses. He turned south into the business district, passing the green plaza and buildings of six, eight, ten storeys and more; red brick and whitewashed buildings, straight up, without balconies, without ironwork. The streets of the business district were crowded with carriages and trolleys, men in suits, women in long dresses with feathered hats. There had never been such a city since the destruction of Tenochtitlán; he sensed his fortune there.

Beyond the main streets, closer to the river, the buildings were older, lower, the homes of Mexicans. He heard Spanish again in the streets and saw barefoot children, widowed women, street vendors, burros pulling carts, balconies along the second storeys of the buildings. It was a rich Mexico; there were oranges and bananas in the stores, the vendors sold burritos fat with meat, and enormous ears of roasted corn. The stores were so full of clothing and furniture they seemed to overflow onto the street. There were signs on everything: in the windows, over doorways, hung from the sides of buildings, attached to crates and tables, protruding from piles of fruits, vegetables, and clothing, dangling from tables and chairs. Men shouted at him to buy, to get the bargains now, to take advantage of them and their bad luck, to get what he wanted at half of what he ought to pay. Everything seemed to be a bargain. The streets were nearly impassable; he saw people he had never imagined: men with fifty hats piled on their heads, girls carrying crates of lettuce and tomatoes, a blind man with thimbles on his fingers blowing into an ocarina and tapping out a rhythm with his thimbles, beggars of all ages, varieties and deformities, priests, nuns, men with long white beards and somber black hats and coats, cowboys, a juggler, fiddlers, trumpeters, harpists, mountain women wearing derby hats and carrying children in their shawls, carpenters, painters, a stretcher being loaded into a white ambulance, mutes speaking with their fingers, drunkards sleeping in the gutter, one with a filthy pillow under his head, a Chinese walking six ducks on a string, women as pale as the inner dough of rolls dressed in jewels and feathers and striped silk, a general, two men in buckskin, a flock of Mormons dressed in dark brown skirts and flowered bonnets, three men in top hats, four men carrying a pane of glass as tall as a house, a dwarf accordionist, three trained dogs walking on their hind legs and wearing conical clown hats, and a man with ten-foot-long legs wearing signs on his chest and back.

He put his horse in a livery stable and rented a room in a small hotel off the main street. After washing, he changed into the clothing he had bought from Sam Ravel and went out again into the street. The excitement caught him; he scurried, like the others, up one street and down another, crossing between the horses, running to avoid the carriages and wagons. The signs slid past, voices came by in waves, some calling to him, others going across and beyond him. He looked down, he looked up; something seemed to be going on everywhere, the buildings shook. He caught a lamppost and held on. A child in a torn dress taunted him, insisting that he was drunk. He focused on her knees, the knobs, the streaks of dirt, colorless threads of her dress hanging. "Take this," he said, giving her a dollar. "Wash yourself and put on clean clothes." She lifted her dress to show a hollow triangle, a vagina still in the form of an unripe bean. Then she grabbed the money out of his hand and ran away. He held on. A boy began to shine his shoes, another dusted him with a filthy broom. Their hands were held out to him, tiny, lined with black grime, grasping. The ocarina player was nearby; he could hear the rasping of the thimbles and the hollow song. Villa saw a tavern and ran to it, holding his hat, bursting through the louvered doors.

There it was cool, there it was dark; he entered, slowing, his own thump the peak of the sound. He saw that the light was red, leveling shapes, reducing reflections to glowings. Women were known by the silhouettes of skirts, by the bulk of hair; a guitarist by the round body of his resonance. Bottles, glasses, water running, urine, oil, the flavor of bitten coins; in this town or that, haven; the death of flowers, the deafening of song, without night or wind.

He sat, coming to the end of a spinning, holding on to the round rail, another in the row of toasted copper faces, one felt hat in the row of straw. The faces were burnished by the low light, the eyes were dim, without definition. "Beer," he said.

The head of the man, bulk above the shoulders, a darkness and mustaches between him and the light, said, "American or Mexican?"

"From the Moctezuma Brewery, sir!"

"Ice cold?"

"It's not good for the throat."

"At your service," the bartender said.

Villa sipped from the glass, bought an egg, and busied himself with cracking, peeling, and salting it. He picked a piece of eggshell out of his mouth and flicked it into the trough under the bar. The color of the shell was rose in the tavern light. The shell stuck to the tile of the trough and was not carried by the water. He studied its position between his feet, thinking he might pour beer on the piece of shell to wash it away. Or spit. His mouth was not so dry, the dizziness had passed. He sucked saliva, gathering it on his tongue. There was a woman beside him; her red hair redder in the light. "Good evening," she said. Her teeth were the color of the eggshell.

"Will you have a drink with me?"

"Bourbon."

The bartender was pouring.

"You live here in El Paso?" he asked.

"Here and there. And you? I see by your clothing that you are not a man from this neighborhood."

"I'm from Coahuila. I have a little ranch there, not so far from Ojinaga."

"Give a dollar to the guitarist. I like his music. He plays zarzuelas better than anyone on the border. And that's the truth. He has the soul of the mother country."

"I'm a Mexican," Villa said.

"But your soul . . ."

". . . is Mexican. I'll give him two dollars to play 'Jesusita en Chihuahua.' "

"He knows only songs from Spain."

"Then let him starve. And you, are you a catzopine too?"

She reached down the bar for one of the candles burning in a red glass. "Look at my face," she said, holding the glass at her breast.

The light spread upward in an elongated circle, casting long ghostly shadows; it illuminated her days, her years, the marks of bourbons and mornings; her face was filled with all the ribbons of her life, shreds and pockets, spaces, as all meat ages. The face belonged to a woman who should not have come down from the mountains, a woman who was created for the lean days and the sun. He leaned forward and kissed the line of her jaw, the weakest place, and then her eyes, the darkness surrounding the darkness.

The guitarist played a chord, another, strummed once, and let the sound fade, seeing that no heads turned and no dollars were offered.

"You are not a city man," she said.

"No. I'm dizzy here."

"You're a horseman."

"This city is a madness; it lacks the order of the hills or the towns. No one can live here."

"I was born in the city, in Juárez."

"Forgive me."

The bartender brought another bourbon, another beer. Villa paid, leaving one beer beside the other, while the woman drank the bourbon. "You are too young to do that," he said.

She smiled: rose teeth, deep red tongue, rouge on her lips. Yet shy, with apologies in the crinkled darkness of her eyes. "You are too kind."

"In the old days only old people were permitted."

"I'll be an old woman soon; tomorrow, next week."

"It's a long time," he said, "but a willing heart goes all the way."

"Sure, and the best broth is made from old hens."

"Well," he said, laughing, "with love and wine you can drown all your sorrows. And dancing makes the cripple swift. Come with me, come dancing."

They slipped out of their seats together; she put her arm in his. "To a hungry man a taco is a feast," she said, and they went out together into the street.

Her name was Filomena. She led him through the streets of El Paso, across the border to Ciudad Juárez, into dance halls and gambling palaces, a guide pressing herself close by him, touching hips and breasts, a dancing partner tiring easily, a woman of gay words and darkening eyes, perfumed, red, toasted, full, a woman of weight, a woman of curled hair and great thighs that trembled at the end of dancing. She held him closely, she kissed his hands, she touched his forehead and called him a boy, no more than a boy.

He took her in the room of the hotel, once, and again, until she wearied of him, calling for night, for morning. He incited her, he wore her weak, and again. Her eyes closed, dark ponds, night, flint, a woman sleeping in the rain. "Why?" he asked.

"Because I am old."

"Filomena."

She was asleep.

She lay on her back, a wet and souring woman. Her mouth was open, gurgling air. Villa lay down beside her. In the cold room, in the unclad room. He rose, covered Filomena, and lay down again. The building creaked, mutters in the wind. He rose again, took his pistol out of the holster, and put it under his pillow. The sun lighted the faces of the houses in the west, comforting him; he slept.

A man with a blind white eye came in the afternoon to awaken Villa. "It's time to check out," he said, "or pay for another day." Villa pointed sleepily to the chair where he had left his trousers, telling the man to look in the pocket.

The man laughed. "Wake up," he said. "You're dreaming."

Then Villa saw that his suit was gone, and his shirt and his new boots, even his underwear, everything he had bought from Ravel's store. He rubbed his face, as if to wipe away the fog of sleep. His beard sounded scratches on the calluses of his hand. The holster was still there on the nightstand beside the pitcher of water. He felt under the pillow; the pistol was there. "I have nothing." He shrugged. "I can't pay."

"Filomena," the man said.

"You know her?"

"She promises everything, but when you get her in the room she fucks like a dead sheep. Filomena one time we call her. She looks for strangers."

"Where can I find her? She didn't even leave me money to buy a taco."

"Can you find the sun at night or the stars in the day? Your clothes are sold by now, and she's taken the money and gone to another town. Don't you think she knows you'll be looking for her? She's not a young woman; she knows how to take care of herself."

"I'll get dressed and be out of here in a little while," Villa said.

"You want a job? There are hiring bosses in the neighborhood. They're looking for mineworkers, muledrivers, dynamiters, laborers for the smelter."

"What's the best job?"

The man fixed Villa with his one eye. He forced a smile. "How do you want to die?"

"Of old age."

"Then learn stubbornness from the mules."

There was no rain. There was no corn. There was no grass. The Bravo turned to mud, like the Conchos and the Nazas and the Yaqui, and the Verde and the San Juan, the Ramos, the Santa Maria and the Oro, the Casas Grandes and the Urique, the Papigochic, the Mayo, and the San Miguel. The lakes dried up. The fish died. The people lived on cactus fruit and mesquite beans and the honeywater of the maguey. The cowboys split prickly pear to feed the cattle. The sheep ate the roots of the grass that would have saved the land. The wells were dug deeper. There was no water for washing; there was not enough to drink. The deer ate the trees. The rabbits descended into the towns, and the snakes and the wolves came after them. It was the first summer without rain, the first winter without snow. The people consulted with the magicians, who consulted with the stars and found them dry. Women were beaten with bags of straw, but their tears brought no rain. In the mountains, between the villages of Carichic and Nonoava, three children, carried up from a city, were slowly sacrificed in the hope that the tears of their final moments would inspire the rains of Tlaloc. Neither those fearful tears nor the remorseful tears of their tormentors affected the skies. There was dust for breakfast and dust for dinner. Onions grew to the size of beans and beans grew to the size of peas. Tomatoes were no bigger than berries. The male corn had no length, the female corn had no flower; the husks were brown, the ears were sticks; there was nothing to eat.

In this dry and dying time Francisco Villa returned to Mexico. He was older, a man grown, a man grown wary. He wore a Texas hat and carried two pistols. For two years he had followed mules and burros and thick-legged horses. He had been to Deming and Mimbres, Bisbee, Douglas, Yuma, Silver City, Tucson, Indio, and Phoenix. He had driven a team of mules to the heights of Flagstaff, skidding and bouncing along the snow-covered rims of the rising land; and he had seen his burros die of thirst and snakebite in the shimmering dream of the Mojave. The color of his eyes darkened; the red was always there.

He rode with men who could speak English. They offered to teach him the words, but he declined. "There is too much growling," he said. "No one can sing in that language. It's not good for making jokes or seducing women." He bought a guitar and sang to the mules and the white-nosed burros and the horses with the great hooves that boomed on the hard clay and packed sand of the red-and-tan roads. He was twenty-seven years old and the world did not please him; he went home to Mexico.

"When I was coming back, I wondered how long I had been gone, and I could not think of the time; it seemed like one day."

"What made you come home?"

"Discontent."

They were in Soto's house. His mother had cooked for them: a thick soup of meat, chiles, onions, and bits of tomato. There were no tortillas; it was better now to slaughter cattle than to eat corn. Mrs. Soto worried about the crop. She twisted one hand in the other, she fondled her beads, she chewed the corner of her lower lip. "Are they all rich on the other side?" she asked. "Did you hate them?"

"The drought is there too," Villa said, "but they get food from the north; their country extends very far north."

"So they are rich," Eleuterio said. "You hated them because they're rich."

The small cooking fire burned, crackling less now near the end; a plow leaned against the wall, a harness hung long and soft with age, nearly empty sacks of corn and beans were lined up on a board like fallen stockings, brown clay pots sat on a tilted shelf, and all along the walls clothes, hats, bedclothes, stockings, petticoats, and belts were thrown over pegs driven into the brick. A small altar had been constructed in one corner. The Virgin of Guadalupe looked out upon the room; beside her were two tarnished candleholders, and above the gentle face of the Virgin, carved in oak and stained the dark color of pain, Christ suffered on a cross surrounded by rows

[*215*]

of red, yellow, pink, and purple woolen yarn. A red-and-gold yarn tassel hung from the bottom of the cross. The crown of Christ was made of real thorns. His eyes were tiny pieces of turquoise. Tears of dark brown blood ran from the wound in his side.

Villa ate slowly, using the metal spoon he carried in his pocket. "Marvelous," he said, "delicious. Mrs. Soto, you are the queen of cooks, the empress."

Mrs. Soto smiled modestly; the worry in her eyes was not dissipated. Eleuterio said: "They own the mines, the ranches, the oil fields. I've heard it all, Panchito; the railroad workers talk about them, the way they work their swindles, the way they take the best jobs. I tried to get a job on the National. It's no use. We sweat and they get paid. They have everything, man. You should see their houses! They put a white fence around everything. They eat only from gold plates. It's a crime!"

" 'Poor Mexico,' that's what the President says, 'Poor Mexico,' " Mrs. Soto repeated, " 'so far from God and so close to the United States.' "

Villa licked his spoon clean and put it into his breast pocket. "You look different, Eleuterio; you no longer have a farmer's eyes. Maybe it's better to think about corn and rain than to worry about the landlords and the bread rolls?"

"There is no rain and there is no corn."

"I know. I've seen the fields. What can we do? It's not their fault if it doesn't rain. It doesn't rain on the other side either, believe me. They also have deserts and alkali water. Their cattle die too. They're not all rich: some of them work in mines and some of them are poor farmers. Like us. Some of them are even servants to the other ones. There are rich and poor everywhere; I've seen that, I can tell you the truth.

"But it is true that there are more rich gringos than poor ones. In that they're very different from us. But you can't really compare, because the whole country is different: they have electricity everywhere, even outside the cities, and their railroads go to every town. Machines are what make them so rich; they use machines for everything.

"This is why I have trouble making a comparison. It's not that the people are rich, the whole country is rich; the people are different. They're afraid of dying—that's one of the first things you learn about them. But when one of them dies, there's very little mourning; they just hurry up and bury him and that's the end of it. Sometimes I would watch them working with their machines and think how much like the machines they are. They're always the same, the gringos, like machines. They start in the morning and they stop at night, they work and work and work; and that's what they want, that's what they like. So the answer is yes, they are rich, but the answer is also no, because they live a poor life, even the richest of them.

[*216*]

"The thing the railroad workers say puzzles me, though, because it sounds too much like they're speaking for the landlords. Do they mean to tell us that Terrazas is a good man or that Pablo Martínez is a good man or that the Creel family is kind to the poor? Should I believe that the gringos sent López Negrete to attack my sister? No, friends, that can't be the truth. Remember, when the coyote steals chickens, he dresses himself in feathers."

"You defend the gringos," Eleuterio said.

"Is that what you think?" Villa combed his mustache with his fingers, rubbing away the stiffness left by the broth. "Well, I think you defend the landlords."

"Francisco Villa, if I hadn't sworn you were my brother . . ."

Villa laughed. "The truth hurts, kid; you see how the truth hurts. Now listen to me: the gringos rob us a little and the landlords rob us a lot. You can't go to Wall Street in New York City and steal back from the gringos what they take from us, but the landlords are not so far away. You understand?" He nodded toward Mrs. Soto. "I don't have to explain to you."

"You can speak in front of my mother," Eleuterio said. "She used to be a maid. She was stealing from the landlords before we were born."

Mrs. Soto nodded proudly. "I stole food for him when he was a baby. The child of the richest person in Mexico didn't eat any better than my son."

Villa leaned over and kissed her hand. "A loving mother is a saint," he said. He turned to Soto. "I met a man in Columbus just across the border from Palomas. He says he'll buy all the cattle we can deliver. If it's not branded he doesn't care, and if it is branded he doesn't care what brand it carries. He says he'll pay good prices, and if he doesn't, we'll find someone who will. Now don't you think it's fortunate that Mr. Creel and Mr. Martínez and Mr. Terrazas are so generous that they are willing to give us a few of their cattle to sell in Columbus? It's almost a miracle."

They gathered themselves in preparation of laughter. Stopped. Held the moment, having seen reflections. Their mouths were left with lips parted, the openness begun. Then came the slow closing down. Beside the gold the corpses lay. Mrs. Soto crossed herself and took up her beads to pray away the other side of the vision. Eleuterio looked up at the ceiling of the house. A mist lay on his eyes. The long poles were so thin, the boards painted with pitch were so uneven; a roof of thatch might have been better, tile was beyond expectation; it was a roof against neither the rain nor the sun; a poor roof, an accident, spilling light or water, neither Spain nor Tenochtitlán nor the ancient known hills. Soto and his mother turned to Villa, who sat heavily, looking down at the roughly cut planks of the table, the wood rubbed smooth by pots and plates and leaning arms, the thousand planes, the crags of the axe aged into hills.

[*217*]

"The mines are more dangerous," Villa said. "And we all know this life. My father died between two rows of corn. He was a young man when he died, choking on his own blood. I carried him to the house."

"Eleuterio's father also died young," Mrs. Soto said. "He died by fever. It burned up all his flesh, and when we buried him he was no heavier than a child. I remember I said to my sister how I was surprised that our bones weigh so little. The priest heard me and said that I must tell that in confession; it is a sin to speak of the dead that way, forgetting the immortal soul. But he was so light, there was so little of him; I have never forgotten, not in these many years."

"We'll be careful," Villa said.

"You'll take no chances," Mrs. Soto said. "Swear."

Villa nodded. "On my mother's grave."

Mrs. Soto asked no more. She cooked the coffee Villa had brought for a gift, and served it to them. They went outside, each in turn, and when they came back Eleuterio smoked and then they put out the mats and lay down to sleep. In the morning, they set out for Jiménez. There were rumors that Urbina was living there again and that he had three horses, a small barn, and a house with electric lights.

The house was not grand and Urbina was not rich: he had a horse and two burros stabled under a lean-to, and there was no electricity in his house, although he often spoke of his admiration for the powers of electric lights. He lived meanly, in the way of city people, trading and bargaining, arranging his debts to take on more debts, squirming, an empty-handed merchant seeking to make something of nothing. He embraced Villa and then Soto, who said to him, "We thought you were dead."

The lights of greeting left his face; Urbina said, "There was less than a hundred pesos in that fucking bank. Nothing. For two years I've been thinking that you were both dead for nothing, a hundred pesos."

"A hundred pesos?" Villa attempted the look of an inquisitor, but he could not hold back his good humor. His brow was furrowed and his mouth was laughing.

Urbina's eyes crossed—his expression of innocence or surprise. "Ask my mother. Come inside and ask my mother. I laid low for almost a year after the bank. We had no money, we almost starved. She washed clothes, I was afraid to go out of the house. It's true, man; I was so scared I used to wait until dark to go out to shit. That's not so bad in winter, but in the summer you have to wait a long time. I pissed in a gourd, but you can't shit in the house. It was terrible. One time I ate something bad and I had to shit all the time; I used to run out of the house carrying my rifle in one hand and opening my pants with the other."

"Poor little Tomás," Villa said. "All that time I was living on the other side, like a rich bread roll, like a king, with women, with the best food. In these last two years I had more women than the Bishop of Guadalajara."

"Please, man; my mother will hear you."

"Tell us what you did with the money," Soto said. "I saw you putting money in the bag, and I heard that the bank said it was more than five thousand pesos."

Urbina opened his arms, showing his palms. "Look at me, look at my house. Is this the house of a man with five thousand pesos?"

Soto looked over Urbina's shoulder, trying to see into the house, but the contrast between the sunlight and the darkness of the house made it impossible. "You know the old saying," he told Urbina, threatening, "believe nothing that you hear and only half of what you see. Maybe you spent the money. Or maybe you hid it somewhere. Maybe it's buried in the floor of your house, or maybe your horse is standing on the place where it's buried." He turned to Villa: "He stole from his friends; we should kill him."

"No," Villa said, "no. I don't think a man should shoot his friends, not over such a little bit of money." He pushed his hat back and ran his hand over his hair, smoothing the tight curls, grooming himself with his own sweat. "Anyway, it's not so easy to shoot a friend. Forget it, man."

"Don't worry yourself; I didn't ask you to do it."

Urbina was astonished. "You could shoot me, your friend?"

"Yes. If I had a pig that ate everything so that there was nothing left for me, I would have a choice between starving and eating pork tidbits."

Villa reached out and put his arms around their shoulders, drawing them to him as if they were his children. He embraced them and patted their backs and laughed, telling them how they needed each other. "Listen to me," he said. "A year from now we'll be so rich that five thousand pesos will be like a joke. You'll put that much in the collection box on Sunday." They laughed with him, and went inside the house to plan the first delivery of cattle to Sam Ravel.

Mrs. Urbina sat upon a wicker chair, rolls of dark brown polished stone piled on spread knees. She wore a madwoman's hair, dead, chopped, fallen in dirty streaks. "We are innocent," she said on seeing the false humor of Soto's eyes. "Oh, Mother of God, preserve us for we are innocent. Holy Mary, Mother of God, pray for us sinners."

"We are your son's friends," Villa said.

She looked from him to Soto, the telling of her eyes concealed in the surrounding flesh. "What are the three theological virtues?" she asked, speaking rapidly, clipping the words. "Which are the seven gifts of the Holy Ghost?"

[219]

"I never learned the Catechism," Villa said.

Soto shrugged. "I forgot."

Mrs. Urbina laid her forefinger on her lower lip while she thought about them. Her chin was lifted, revealing the round rings of her neck. She put her finger down after a moment and said with sweet concern: "You're Masons. Oh, my dear Jesus, I see before me two boys who have chosen to live without knowledge of the Divine Tradition. How shall I bring them to Grace? How shall they be saved?"

"There is no need to worry yourself," Villa said. "We are going soon to see a man called Ravel on the other side of the Bravo, and we are certain that he will save us all."

She rose from the chair; an air of beans surrounded her. "Take my son with you. Let this man also teach him. Lead him to confession and then to contrition, I beseech you, for I am afraid that I have become the mother of a Mason. We must defend the Church. We must defend ourselves against revolution and incest."

Urbina was rolling his clothes in his blanket and filling his saddlebags. He gave his rifle and a bandolier of ammunition to Soto to carry out for him. The house was not clean, the clothes were not washed, the mats were not swept, spoiled food lay in the corners of the house, the insects of the night walked in the dark seams of the walls and the places where the walls joined the floor and the ceiling. There were fleas; there was no scent of pine oil or marigolds. The floor was high and very black. It had not been swept, it had not been shoveled.

"Pray for us," Villa said.

Urbina kissed his mother's hand. "Go with God," she said to him and again to all of them as they went out.

That night, when they were camped out in the dry hills, Urbina said, "You must forgive my mother. My father is dead, or maybe he ran away; I don't know. And I'm the last of the children to leave home. She's an old woman, a great-grandmother. She doesn't know what to do. I don't think she expected to live so long."

"Our mothers are all saints," Soto said. "They're without sin. There's nothing to be ashamed of. Don't ever apologize for your mother."

They looked to Villa for confirmation. He sat with his back against a rock, staring at the hot yellow deadwood fire, drawing them with his silence. The fire burned quietly; there was no sap in the wood. They had passed dried up streams all afternoon, they had ridden across a river turned to sand. They had canteens, but the horses would need water in the morning. Perhaps there would be water in the Conchos or the San Pedro. They could not expect to go as far as Lake St. Bernabé without water. Villa said, "We are all the sons of widows."

* * *

The cattle had been left to roam, to find forage and water or to die. They were dusty, like sheep; they ate the grass down to the roots, like sheep, and the sour dirt poisoned their stomachs and blocked their intestines; they died of starvation, they died of vomiting; they gored each other at the waterholes, fouling the water with their wounds. The scavengers thrived. There were not enough scavengers; the bodies of the dead cattle swelled, burst, dried, became leather. The carcasses were the breeding places of wasps; reptiles lived in the visceral darkness. The ordinary scavengers chose their portions from the freshest meat.

They picked up strays, making a herd, driving them northwest. The cattle moved easily. Weary, they did not balk. Fearing starvation, they feared nothing else, neither snakes nor thunderclaps nor the sound of the men hunting rabbits and deer along the way. Their eyes were yellowing, distended. They had the listless ears of milk cows. They would not run, there was no grazing, they walked. But it was too far. Villa had miscalculated the drought; the weakened animals could not endure the walking days; for every three they added to the herd, two died. Every morning, some animals would not rise. Villa, Soto, and Urbina learned to tell from the tongues which ones should be prodded and slapped with the rope and which should be left to die, mooing in the sun.

On the range the cattle died, and in the towns there was no meat, in the sharecroppers' houses there was no corn, there was no meat, the eyes of the children were reflections of the eyes of the cattle. Every morning Villa looked at the cattle dying, and in the distance he could see the earthen houses and white churches of villages, above the carcasses bells tolling and the wispy smoke of cooking fires. He chose the weakest ones at the end of the day and drove them their last miles to the near houses. "Hello, hello," he shouted, with the dogs barking and the dying cattle spitting long strings of thick mucus and the man inside the house clutching his machete or his hoe, cowering, with his family around him, his children weeping at the sight of the armed man. "I bring you the gift of one dying steer," Villa shouted. "Take it. Run up the red flag for your neighbors. Feed your children." But they did not come out of the house to take the animal. The dogs barked. He saw eyes in the doorways, in the dark squares of the window holes, and he knew why they were afraid. He begged them, the salesman again, with promises and innocence in his voice, calling the litany of his wares then, the litany of himself now. "Don't be afraid, not of me. We're of the same race, country people, the underdogs of this world, the hungry. I steal cattle, I give you what will not survive the trail. I make you the market for what will not get to market. Take this steer. You have no corn, then eat meat. Slaughter it, dry what you cannot eat, use everything, the tripe and the brains and the

[221]

tongue and the kidneys, and even the bones, eat the marrow of the bones. Make soup of the tail, chew the hide, stew the blood. Take this steer, live from it, let your neighbors live from it. Don't fear me, not me. I am nothing but a thief, a cattle rustler. My name is Francisco Villa, Pancho Villa. I am a gypsy, a bandit, the victim of the rich, hunted by sheriffs in Durango, Parral, Santa Rosalía, in the very district of my birth." Then the man came out, blinking in the light, carrying the machete or the hoe, calming the dog so that Villa could dismount. "Take the weakest," Villa said, "and let me take the others to the next house." Often the man would leave the animal for his wife to slaughter and walk on with Villa to the next house and the next, pointing out the houses that lay hidden in valleys and canyons, leading the way, announcing the gift of the armed man: "Hello, cousin; hello, brother; this is the bandit Pancho Villa, one of our race who has stolen cattle and gives away the weak ones." To their gratitude Villa said: "If I gave something of my own, I would expect you to thank me, but these cattle are not mine, they are yours, cattle born in this district, left to die, to feed the vultures. Better to feed people than vultures." He saw them swallowing saliva while they spoke, in the moment of their gratitude. He saw children lick the blood of slaughtered animals. He saw them chew the raw meat, which was the color of their lips, the color of their tongues. And he saw some who could no longer eat: children without hair, old women who had lost the will to sweep away the flies that walked the crevices of their skin. They were like the cattle that could not rise to another day: of the same eyes, of the same feeble, dying sounds, of the same knowledge. He touched them, giving them his hands to feel, the strength to suck into themselves, but they did not respond, they did not know. Dust had begun to collect on them; he could not feel them through the dust. Each night he rode back to the place where they had made camp, and he ate and lay down to sleep and was unable to explain to the others why he delivered the dying cattle to the sharecroppers, for they knew that he found no comfort in what he did.

He gave away four hundred head of cattle and twelve hundred more died on the way, so that when they rounded the herd into a narrow place and bedded them down in the dust-naked hills across the border from Columbus, they counted fewer than seven hundred, and some of them would die before morning. Then Villa went across the border and came back with Sam Ravel, who walked among the resting steers with a lantern, inspecting the weight of their haunches and the fat of their sides, noticing every patch of fallen hair, every missing tooth, every yellowed eye. "A dollar a head," he told Villa, "a dollar a head for every one that comes across the border alive and walking."

"Five," said Villa.

"They're mangy, underweight, stolen cattle. A dollar a head."

[222]

Inside the lantern the flame wavered, throwing light on one face and then the other, weaving shadows through the glass, controlled by the wind, like the land and the days, sculpted and dressed by the wind. Villa was taller than Ravel; his hat loomed darkly; he had not shaved for many days; he smelled of dust and of the dry trail, though he rubbed himself with sage and washed his mouth with stinging roots. "You told me once that the brand made no difference," Villa said. "You promised me."

Ravel's shirt appeared orange in the light of the lantern. He wore a long, dark coat and a black derby. He spoke Spanish quickly, nervously, saying some words like a Frenchman, phlegm in the *r*'s. "Yes, yes, and I hold to it. What difference does the brand make? Who would care about a herd of dying animals? Look at them! Half-bald, the skin full of sores, every bone showing. What do you expect me to do with such animals?"

"Buy them. I brought them here for you to buy them, because you made me a promise."

"To buy them at all is a gift. But five dollars? You may as well rob me."

"I've considered that," Villa said. "But for the sake of my conscience I would prefer that you robbed me. I'll sell them to you for three dollars a head."

"Fifteen hundred for the lot."

Villa threw up his hands. "What can I do? I have to let myself be robbed. It's two hundred and fifty miles back to the slaughterhouses in Chihuahua; you use the distance better than most men use a gun."

Ravel counted out the money, and at the end he and Villa shook hands. "Now wave the lantern," Villa said, "and your cowboys can drive them to the United States. Go ahead—we saw them come across the border with you; eight soldiers riding on army saddles and wearing parts of their uniforms. Urbina is cross-eyed, but he knows where to look for nervous men."

"I was carrying a lot of money," Ravel said. "I heard that you had seven hundred half-starved cattle, and I brought fifteen hundred dollars. That's more than they're worth, but I wanted to start our business off right."

Villa embraced the smaller man, leaning down to meet him, laughing and patting his back with both hands. "It's good that we trust each other," he said.

Ravel laughed too. "From now on we'll be partners." Then he waved the lantern and the eight soldiers came riding, holding their short cavalry rifles at the ready. Villa was gone when they arrived, riding south with Soto and Urbina, keeping low on the hillsides, hidden from the moon.

They spent the money on Texas hats, horses, and whores. In a month they were in the hills again, stealing strays, driving them north. As the drought worsened, the cattle were less able to make the long drive. They moved four miles a day instead of six, and the thin, dying creatures fell at the end of

[*223*]

four miles, lying on their folded legs, rolling over in the effort to rise, dead there, refusing another day. Villa left more animals with the sharecroppers along the way; he dared to drive animals up to the edge of a town and give them to the first man he encountered, asking him to share the meat with his neighbors. It was not so difficult to give them away, for the people seemed to expect him. "Yes," they said when he told them his name, "we recognize the slouch hat." Old women blessed him and called him son, healers gave him herbs and advice against evil, men spoke to him in whispers about the proximity of rurales or the passing of a troop of Federal cavalry. Children appeared in the desert to tell him of shorter routes or to warn him of bad water. When he had no animals to give to them, he gave them money, and when he had no more money he gave them salt or baking powder or a dollop of lard to carry home in the cup of a yucca leaf.

At a shack, a place less than a house, made of piled firewood and a few logs for support, he met a young woman and her two naked children. He had four steers with him, animals he had herded up from their camp along the Santa Maria River to give to people who lived in the western part of the valley on the way to Galeana. "Leave them with me," the woman said, "and I'll fatten them and sell them for the price of a house."

"It's too late; they'll be dead in the morning."

"When my husband left me, they said my child would die, but I raised this one and gave birth to that one, and I did it alone. To keep four steers alive will be easy."

"There is no water."

"There is water," she said. "If I show you the water, will you let me have the cattle?"

He dismounted and tied the horse to a mesquite bush. She waited for him to finish, then she began walking rapidly toward a low hill behind the shack. Villa followed, having difficulty keeping up the pace. He had been in the saddle for thirteen hours; the joints at his hips were stiff, and there was no tension in the muscles of his legs; he walked uncertainly, dragging his boots among the rocks. She was younger than he and comfortable in that place. He watched the grace of her feet, clad only in huaraches, slipping between the rocks. She was a woman without softness. Her legs were lean and dusty; the muscles of her calves bunched and rolled, carrying her on her toes. She wore a thick skirt, torn at the hem, and a poncho woven of uncolored wool.

They came to the top of the little hill and she stopped there, waiting for him to climb the last few feet, a figure at the crest, there for the breeze to take her skirt, to make her graceful in silhouette. "There is my water," she said, pointing down to a wide green arroyo cut by a narrow stream that came out of the rock, spread for half a mile, and went underground again. A dozen sheep grazed there, guarded by two dogs, penned by the sloping sides. Corn grew in rows along the sides, beans grew on terraces cut into the rock. The ruins of a log and adobe house lay at one end of the arroyo.

"Last winter, the water dried up," she said. "That's when my husband left. I told him it would come back, that I knew because my mother, who once lived in that ruined house, had told me. But he had no faith, no optimism; he could not balance himself in the world. He went to Cananea to work in the Green Company Mine. That was more than a year ago. A week after he left, eight days to tell the truth, the water began again, sweeter than ever, sweeter than when we first came here fifty years ago. Come down with me and taste it, taste the sweet water."

She walked down a narrow trail cut into the side of the arroyo. At the bottom, she kicked off her huaraches and ran across the grass to the head of the spring, where she knelt and cupped water. Villa knelt beside her. The water was sweet and cool, without the coppery flavor or the faint rustiness of much spring water, pure. He drank and drank again, splashing the water into his face, washing it over his eyes, cooling them, letting the water run down his chin, anointing himself with it. When he had finished, he turned to tell her of the pleasure of the water and he saw her no longer in her torn skirt and wool poncho, but naked, lying on the grass, open to him. "For the gift of the cattle," she said, "if it pleases you."

The sun, low-lying, red of dust, painted her. She became beautiful. She receded from him, like a scent passing through smoke, losing its definition. He stared at her, seeing the submission of her knees, the beckoning of her upraised arms. The combs in her hair were spindles, the sun had dressed her in a second skin. He knew then that she had never had a husband, he divined the death of her children, the empty cradles, the sound of weeping. She lowered one hand and placed it between her thighs. "I am the mother of my children," she said. "Do not be afraid; I am not afraid."

"No," he shouted, saying it as a sob, falling to his knees beside her.

"Then you must speak to me," she said, her voice mixing with the sound of the lambs, bleating and bleating in the growing darkness.

"I protected my sister, not myself. There was no father, no teacher. I cared for my mother. I saw her dead, surrounded by candles. I saw her in the room, dressed in a shroud, lying on a table between the white candles, the wax burning. I saw my sister there beside her in the light of the white candles, silent as always, my sister of the downcast eyes. I saw them in the same room, a distant room, the room of the house where I was born, my mother and my sister lighted by the burning wax of the white candles. The priest was there, a figure as dark as my mother's shroud; I saw him. I saw Ignacio Parra, I saw the man with the bloody paper saint, I saw the man in Durango, the man in Santa Rosalía, the man lying in the street, the men lying in the dust. I saw my father, his blood stilled, soft stones on my finger.

I saw them all in the room of the house where I was born, in the light of the candles, the bone-white candles."

"I am the mother of my children," she said.

He went to the place where the stream came out of the wall of the arroyo and dipped his hands into the soft mud under the water, gathering it into one hand, squeezing out the water. She lay there in the same place waiting for him. He put the black mud into her mouth.

Everywhere the gossip was about Cananea. They heard it in Guzmán and Galeana and Pearson, all the way south, the length of the deep dry valley. The news had crossed the mountains from Sonora, brought by merchants, writers, and woodcutters, by shepherds and cowboys, and by the roaming Yaqui hunters. In the taverns and whorehouses of Namiquipa and Bachiniva, in Madera and La Junta, in San Andrés and Palomas and Santa Ysabel, in every town and along every river and railroad spur the talk was only of Cananea. The hungriest people, the wounded of the leanest years in memory, abandoned thoughts of their own troubles to describe what they had heard about Cananea. They said the names of the leaders: Manuel Diéguez, Esteban Baca Calderón, and the Yaqui, Huitemea. Twenty-three dead, twenty-two wounded, fifty imprisoned, the leaders sent south to the prison at San Juan de Ulúa.

They walked up the long road between the mine-car tracks, under the trestle, heading toward the plumed stacks, a mile of them, two miles, pairs and threes and fours and men alone, carrying their picks and tamping bars and shovels. Diéguez and Baca Calderón and Javier Huitemea, the speakers, the discoverers, walked at their head, and the men came behind, a loose body along the serpentine road. It was a strike, not pleading as sharecroppers must, but a demand that the Mexican workers be paid as much as the North Americans. Two thousand men, the Mexican miners of Cananea, arrived at the lumberyard on their way uphill to the town and the offices, and there the North Americans met them with rifles and pistols. The first miners fell: two dead and twenty wounded, and then the others came forward; having no weapons but the stones that lay around them, they threw the stones, propelling them with rage. Then the North Americans fell, three of them, and the others ran up toward the town, reloading and firing as they ran, putting the distance of rifle fire between themselves and the miners.

While the North Americans fled to the town, the miners set fire to the place where they had fought: five stacks of lumber burned, and the office of the lumberyard and the granary and the hayloft. The flames rose a thousand feet and the smoke darkened the desert. They were burning

Cananea. Then the North Americans in the town understood that the miners had no weapons but fire and stones and they took their courage from that and they went back into the streets with their rifles and their pistols and killed whomever they saw with a stone in his hand or a miner's tool on his shoulder. They killed according to the color of a man's skin and the angle of his eyes. They killed and killed until the miners fled to the hills beyond Cananea, and then they called for more North Americans to come across the border.

On the second day the North Americans of Cananea and those who had come across the border to hunt with them went into the hills to kill the strikers, to take revenge upon the victims of the first day. The North Americans walked the town like wolves, and the strikers hid themselves in caves and canyons and the most inaccessible places of the hills beyond the town. Then the governor of Sonora came and with him the rurales and the Federal troops. The town was declared under the law of the military. The North Americans went home, the dead were buried, the wounded suffered in the midsummer heat, the fires of the smelter burned, and the stacks were plumed. The leaders of the strike were sent to prison, the Yanquis and the Negroes and the Chinamen continued to be paid more for their work than the Mexicans, and the week of life of the Liberal Club of Mankind of Cananea, Sonora, was ended. But in the taverns and the stores and the barbershops, and along the rivers and the railroad tracks, in the thinnest newspapers and the quietest meetings, in the railroad workers' shacks and the miners' dormitories, men spoke of Cananea and what was possible. Villa and Urbina and Soto listened to the stories and counted the dead and the imprisoned and the fugitives and concluded that nothing was possible. They set out from San Andrés, rounding up strays, keeping the best of them, giving the rest to the poor along the way. Feliciano Dominguez, Antonio Sotello, José Sanchez, Panfílo and Cesáro Solís, Bárbaro Carillo, and Pedro Aprisco rode with them.

Now they traveled closer to the towns, and they drove their growing herd along the rivers and streams where there was still grass. They entered the herds on the Terrazas and Martínez ranches and cut out the fat steers and cows with calves. Six men rode the flanks, scouting and gathering strays; one rode ahead and four drove the herd. They also had a wagon; it was old and the wooden axles had to be greased every day, but they could carry a variety of food and clothing and three cases of ammunition. The threat of rurales and posses, even the posse of cowboys that roamed the Terrazas Ranch, no longer frightened them. If it became necessary, they could stand and fight. "We have firepower," Villa told them, "a hundred and fifty, two hundred rounds each. If we're attacked, we can defend ourselves from cover. If we choose to be the attackers, we can destroy a troop of Federals with one terrific blow. We could conquer a town, Namiquipa or Pearson. There is no reason to be afraid."

At night, around the campfire, they discussed the methods of small wars. Soto, who had been in the Federal Army, spoke of crossfire and cavalry charges. He made diagrams in the dirt, describing sieges, skirmishes, flanking movements, the advantages of firing from a prone position. He said they needed an artillery piece. The others laughed, but he described a demonstration he had seen of a small German cannon, the distance and accuracy and the size of the shell holes, and he quieted their laughter. Feliciano Dominguez, who had been in the rurales for almost a year, disagreed with everything that Soto said. "The best method," he said, "is to fight man to man, to choose an opponent and kill him, then to choose another and another. Cavalry methods are useless for such small numbers. It is all chance. Better to pick a target and kill him, and then go on to the next. And even better when you have two men with the same target. Imagine, if Bárbaro and I pick Villa for a target and concentrate on him, what would happen?"

"He would kill you both," Urbina said, and everyone laughed.

"No, no, be serious," Villa said. "Feliciano knows what he's talking about. There are different problems, different answers. You don't plow a lake or bathe in a cornfield. When there are few, we'll use Feliciano's way, and when there is a troop to fight or a town to take, we'll use what Eleuterio learned from the army." Then he assigned them to pairs and showed them how the pairs could turn to the left or the right and become two rows.

At the end of every discussion, when the flank riders came in and the men who were to replace them were finishing up their food, preparing to go out, Villa spoke to them about the necessity of avoiding the rurales and the posses and especially the army. "It's good to be ready," he said, "but the best army is still going to lose some men. Why should we take that chance? It's better to avoid trouble. The mountain lion doesn't attack bulls, it eats rabbits."

"Oh, you're only talking," Panfilo Solís said.

Villa looked at his companion: a sixteen-year-old boy with earnest eyes and an armory hung on himself—two bandoliers across his chest, a cartridge belt around his waist, two pistols and a hunting knife. "Are you a bull or a lion?" Villa asked.

"I'm not a rabbit."

"We'll see. When the time comes, we'll see. For me, it would be fine to be a rabbit, to eat pine needles, and—" he giggled—"make lots of little rabbits."

Panfilo stood up. "Maybe I'm riding with the wrong man," he said. His

[*228*]

brother, Cesáro, who was four years older, reached over and slapped him on the leg. "Sit down and be quiet, Mr. Puma, or I'll take down your pants and whack you on the ass with a stick."

The boy reached for his pistols, but before he could get them out of the holsters, Urbina, who was sitting on the other side of him, grabbed his ankles and tumbled him onto his back. When he recovered himself, he saw that Urbina and the others, even his own brother, had drawn their guns. "A boy who would shoot his own brother is no good," Urbina said. "I'd shoot him now, but I don't want to frighten the herd."

"Maybe we should hang him."

"There isn't a tree for ten miles in this fucking desert."

"Cut his throat."

"Use that sword he carries."

"No, it's too easy for him," Soto said. "Let's bury him in an anthill. I'll get some honey from the wagon."

Urbina agreed: "A boy who would shoot his brother deserves the worst. Anyway, I would like to see that. I've heard about it, but I've never seen one. They say the ants eat their way in through the eyes and the nose. Be sure to smear a little honey in the nostrils, Soto, because that would be very funny to see ants walking in and out of his nose, especially a snot nose like him."

"You want to do it now or in the morning?" Soto asked.

"Now, let's do it now; we don't want to waste the morning. You know, sometimes it takes the ants two or three hours to finish them off."

"No, Tomás, we can't do it now: the screams will stampede the cattle and we'll be up all night chasing strays because of this prick."

"We'll sing while we bury him; the cattle will think the screams are just another chorus. After a month of your lousy voice, they'll probably be glad to hear a new song."

Dominguez and Pedro Aprisco, who had just come in from riding the flanks of the herd, ate, scraping their tin plates with their spoons. Villa sat on the far side of the fire, picking his teeth with a thorn. The boy sat where he had fallen, following the speakers with his eyes, afraid even to move his head. Whenever there was a lull in the discussion, he looked over at his brother, who sat with his pistol in his hand, resting his forearm on his knee. His face was stolid, dark; he gave no sign of compassion.

"I wouldn't have shot him," the boy said. "You know that."

"Listen, friends," Urbina said. "The puma speaks."

"How do we know that?" Soto asked. "You went for your gun. If a rabbit goes for his gun, maybe he's bluffing, but a mountain lion is a killer; everyone knows that."

"Cesáro, tell them," the boy pleaded.

[*229*]

His brother did not answer. Dominguez and Aprisco ate. Villa picked his teeth. The fire burned dryly. The boy's face was wet. "Oh, my God," he said, "you're going to do it." And all around him the men nodded, even his brother.

"We'll, I'd better get the honey," Soto said. He got to his feet and started toward the wagon.

Bárbaro Carillo, who had been quiet until then, called out, "And don't forget the shovel. We can't dig such a deep hole with a fucking machete."

"Oh, don't do it, please," the boy pleaded. He put his hands together, as if in prayer, and then he rose to his knees and crawled to them, looking in one face and then another, showing them his eyes and the tears that ran onto his cheeks. "I'm a rabbit," he said. "No one is more a rabbit than I am, no one is more afraid. Please don't do this to me. Mary, Mother of God, please don't let them do this to me. I'm only sixteen years old. I'm too young to be a rabbit. I'm not even a full-grown rabbit. Look at my teeth, look at my ears. I'm only a baby. Oh, God, I'm only a baby."

When he came to Villa, he said, "Would you do this to me? I know where you go at night with the sick cattle. Everyone knows. They talk about you everywhere: Pancho Villa, the one with the slouch hat, who comes like a gift from God with meat for the poor. Would you do this to me? A boy, a poor boy, a poor rabbit, a poor little rabbit."

"Take your horse and go out and watch the herd," Villa said. "But understand two things: if you reach for your gun, you have to use it; no one knows that you're playing a boy's game. And when you're with us, you're one of us. We don't fight with each other, we don't threaten each other; we're together. When I was a boy, I traveled with a mule train, and I saw one of the drivers shoot another one. The man took a long time to die. He gave me his hand. I held his blood in my hand. I don't want to feel your blood or your brother's or Urbina's or Soto's or my own. If you reach for your gun, you betray us; do you understand? Now take your horse and go out there on the edge of the herd and think about what I said to you. If you're still there in the morning—well, if you're still there we won't talk about this ever again."

The boy took Villa's hand and leaned forward to kiss it, but Villa withdrew. "Don't be an old woman," he said.

After the boy had gone, Urbina moved around the fire and sat next to Villa. "Don't think you've made a friend," he told him. "No one likes to be forgiven. It's an insult, especially to a boy who's worried about whether he's going to grow up to have a pair. You can never trust him now."

"I trust you," Villa said. "Soto and I trust you and we forgave you."

"That's different. You only admitted a mistake."

"Tell me the truth, Tomasito; would you have buried him?"

[*230*]

Urbina looked away for a moment. He appeared to be no older than Panfílo; his hair was still too long and as straight as a baby's first hair. There was no sign of a beard on his dark skin, and the hair of his mustache grew only above the corners of his mouth. When he looked back at Villa, his eyes had crossed. It was an innocent face, slightly comic. "Yes."

"The truth."

"Yes." Urbina smiled, showing his teeth. "And you should be glad for it. You're too kind, brother; you need to have men around you to do what has to be done. Leave these things to me."

Villa picked up his eating utensils and went to his blanket to sleep. He loosened his belt and the top button of his trousers and covered his eyes with his hat. The night was warm, but he covered himself anyway to shut out the insects. On the edge of the herd Panfílo was riding, slapping his chaps with a coil of rope and singing steadily, thoughtlessly, providing the background of noise the cattle required. Villa went to sleep to the sound of the boy, and when he awakened at dawn the voice was still there, pale, hoarse, but still singing of the same lovely girl of Tehuantepec.

They drove the cattle north, avoiding the rurales and the posses and the Federal troops, but they lost animals to Loco Weed and quicksand and the snakes that could not escape the herd and chose to kill before the hooves crushed them. In one night near the town of Guzmán they lost forty-three animals, including Bárbaro Carillo's horse, all of them paralyzed by the pale purple flowers that no one had seen in the dust, in the bluing darkness of the end of the day. The meat was poisoned, lost; even the scavengers would avoid it, leaving the bellies to swell until they were entered by the ants. Nor could they eat the meat left by the snakes. And when a steer or a cow walked into quicksand, they learned to leave it to drown, for there was no way to keep it calm and afloat while they dragged it out; the effort only exhausted the horses, and in the end they always had to cut the ropes.

Ravel paid five thousand dollars for the eight hundred and fifty cattle delivered to him at the border, nine hundred and ten pesos to each man who had worked in the long drive that began at San Andrés in the beginning of the second summer of the drought. It was August, another crop had failed; but there had been a few days of light rain in the mountains. Trickles appeared in some of the dried-out riverbeds; the level of the water rose in the wells: inches, drops—but more, not less, for the first time in two years. The people took hope from those small signs. They said that the world was not meant to end in drought, for it had not been predicted; the fifth and final sun would die in earthquakes and in fire.

With the coming of new grass the herds were counted again, the thefts were known. Troops of rurales were sent into the countryside with instructions to destroy the habit of rustling, to eradicate it, as the Spanish Church

[231]

had eradicated the sin of Mexico. The priests blessed them and sent them out as crusaders, men who would enter Heaven by the sword. And they did their work, they killed the cattle thieves and the mothers of cattle thieves; they hanged them at crossroads and in the plazas of the towns; they killed their children, they killed their horses; they left them spilled upon the fields, upon the hillsides; they left them hanging, frightening the birds with their swinging and twisting, with the stiffenings and dyings of their limbs; they mutilated them and fed their organs to the dogs.

There was no one in Mexico who could escape knowing the work of the rurales. In every town that Villa visited, in every store and tavern, he heard of the hangings; in the whorehouses, in the shuttered afternoon rooms, the women whispered the names of the dead and described the intimacies of the killers. Villa began to avoid the towns. He took only unbranded cattle. Three men drove the herd and eight rode as scouts. Each man gave his word to the others that he would fire at least one shot before he surrendered. They trusted each other, they rode with their rifles across their saddles to keep the promise. When they met Ravel at the border, it was winter; they could see the snow in the mountains, they could see their own tracks, the swath of the herd. This will be the last herd, they told Ravel; the drive is too long, there are too many rurales, too many opportunities; there will be no more herds after this.

"The rurales have other things to worry about," Ravel said. "In Coahuila, in a little town called Jiménez, there was a revolution, the beginning of a revolution. Maybe you heard about it. Thirty men of the Mexican Liberal Party attacked the town; a boy named Almaraz was killed. They held the town for two days until the rurales came, and then they killed a captain of the rurales before they abandoned the town. That's the kind of trouble the rurales are going to have from now on. The Liberals are in El Paso now, Flores and Sarabande, planning—strikes, attacks, uprisings. Don't worry about the rurales. But I'll give you some other advice: keep your money in dollars or in gold, not in pesos. Once it all begins, the pesos won't be worth anything, not the paper ones. You sell cattle to me, keep your money in gold, and when this is all over, you'll be able to buy the Terrazas Ranch."

"The Porfiriato will end when the President dies," Villa said. "And then Corral will be the President, and he's worse than Díaz; ask the Yaquis about him. No, there will be no more cattle; it's too dangerous. And there won't be any revolution either. I know the Liberals better than you, I know them since I was a laborer in the mines. They talk, that's all, talk. It's a trick by the Masons. They're always together, the Liberals and the Masons. Priests, Liberals, Masons, Porfiristas—they're all the same. I take good care of my horse and I clean my carbine with an oiled patch every night before I go to sleep."

"What about the success in Coahuila?"

"Ravel, with these ten men I could take that town and hold it for a week. Yes, we've thought about taking a town. If it was the right town, there could be a lot of money in it. But not like those Liberals. Do you know the truth of what happened there? They took an unarmed town by surprise, then they sat there on their butts for a day, and the next day the rurales came and chased them out in ten minutes. No, Mister Ravel, there will be no revolution and there will be no more cattle, not for a long time."

The wind blew steadily out of the northwest, a high, cold wind that did not carry dust. Ravel walked in small circles, his hands clasped behind his back, his sharp nose leaning down into the collar of his dark, narrow coat. He had wrapped a scarf around his head and under his chin and pulled the derby hat down over the wool. "There are always revolutions in Mexico," he said. "The scientifics—and it doesn't matter what you think of them— are right: the people can't govern themselves. They can't read, they can't write, they don't know the first thing about politics. So you have generals. First one general and then the other. After the Porfiriato, you'll have the Corralito or the Florecito. They kill one another, but in between they eat up the country. The newspapers say your Porfirio Díaz is a great man and Limantour is a financial wizard, but listen to Sam Ravel: on the day Díaz dies, if not before, the whole country will come apart. It's held together with string, the string they put around your neck when they hang you from a tree." He paused to laugh at his joke, but ruefully, lifting up his face to show Villa that he took no pleasure in it. "I'll tell you what," he said, returning his face to his collar. "Leave that damned country. Come to the United States—I'll fix up the papers—and work with me. I'll buy a ranch and you can run it. We'll be partners. What do you think?"

"I was born a sharecropper," Villa said.

"No, no, no," Ravel insisted, pacing, gesturing with both hands, caught in the light of the idea. "We'll be partners. We'll own it together. You have to understand the difference between ownership and a sharecropper's lease." He described the law and the papers and the way the money would have to be divided. He wove the offer into the history of Mexico, the hopeless situation of the poor. He described his own life, coming across the ocean when he was a boy, dreaming, finding an open place, an opportunity, and always he returned to politics, to history. But Villa was not hearing. The cattle were delivered, the drive was over, the days without dust were coming, there was rain. They would give the wagon to some sharecropper with rags wrapped around his huaraches to keep his toes from freezing, and as they went south they would give away the steer hides they wrapped about themselves in the northern winter nights. The ammunition would be packed on mules that could run like horses. They would be light again, they would run, twenty miles, thirty miles in a day. They would run to water, with their faces uncovered and the dust behind them. The cattle were gone, the long string they left behind them for the rurales to roll up into a noose was gone. They could sleep now, they could wash and sleep and eat food cooked by a woman. They could clean themselves with pine smoke and turpentine and rest without the sting of fleas and the festering of ticks. They could plant corn and dance and be like the new season dreaming.

Villa waited until Sam Ravel had finished speaking, and then he looked at the man's eyes, the darkness surrounding the fever, the pink weakness that seemed always to be growing in the corners, as if for a sign, and he said softly to Ravel's expectations: "No. There is no way. I want to do it, what you say. I want to have a farm and a family and live like a human being, but there's no way. I'm a bandit, not a farmer or a cowboy. I hear that you can get five hundred pesos for helping the rurales to hang me. A man I used to know in Parral, Claro Reza, is one of them now; he sent word to me. What do you think of that, Mister Ravel? My hide is worth as much as fifty of your cattle.

"No, it's impossible, Sam Ravel. You're a good friend. You keep your promises, you pay fair prices. I'd like to be your partner, but I'm not a cowboy or a farmer anymore. I'm like the burro. You know, the burro isn't born mean and balky, it's experience that makes him that way. I wasn't born a bandit, but there's no way to change now."

"I'm sorry," Ravel said.

Villa slapped him on the back. "That's life, Samuel. And one more thing: everything you say about Mexico is probably true, even the history part, but I don't like to hear you say it. I'll be seeing you, friend."

Villa took his money to Chihuahua and let himself be lost in the city. He bought a house on Tenth Street, a small house with a small stable behind it, and he sat there through the end of winter and the spring and the hottest days of summer before the rains came. He patched the stucco and white-washed it. He made a tile floor and he put mortar around the windows to keep the wind from entering his house. He made a garden of roses and marigolds and oleander bushes. On Sunday afternoons he went to the bullfights. But more than anything, he just sat in his house and thought about what he would do. When friends came to visit him—Soto or Urbina or Aprisco or Claro Reza—he told them he was not hiding, not afraid, just waiting, thinking of what to do. At the end of summer he began to go out in the afternoons, walking around the town, watching the carpenters and the masons and the dairymen and the ranchers who sold their beef to the slaughterhouse. He asked questions, he was polite, he was not interested. At night, when he was not sitting in his garden watching the stars, he went to the taverns; but he did not like the taste of liquor and the effect disturbed him, so that he only sipped at a glass of beer and listened to the music and the gossip until that bored him. Then he went to the whores, who also bored him. On most nights of going out of the house, he came back early, so that he could awaken at dawn and hear the roosters and the sounds of the carts coming to the market and go outside when the sun was becoming full and the opening of the flowers could be seen.

He heard stories of the mill workers' strikes, the Circle of Free Workers and how they died. The gossip came up slowly from Orizaba in Veracruz, the way the railroad workers carried the ideas of the Liberals, the formation of the circle, the demands of freedom from the company store, better pay, shorter work hours. Then the closing of the mills and the workers at the White River Mill asking for their jobs again, the mediation by the President himself, and the first massacre in the streets, the soldiers firing from the parapets and balconies of the mill, the bloody streets, the stones thrown and answered by fusillades. So much was made of the wild day, the burning of the company houses, the end of the organizer of the Circle of Free Workers, the madness in the streets. There was a hero, a lieutenant of the rurales who would not order his men to fire upon women and children, and there was the execution of the hero, the execution of his men, the martyrdom; no one could remember his name, no one could remember the names of his men; it was not certain how many there were. Nor did anyone know for certain how many of the strikers were carried off to the boxcars that became their prison, the place of their quick interrogation and judgment, the place where they waited to be taken ten by ten to the wall. Two hundred, four hundred, a thousand. The greatest anger was the anger of the women, both the women who worked in the mill and the wives of the men who worked at the looms and spindles, for it was the women who knew the prices in the company store, and it was the women who spent the days with their ragged children, their begging children. It was the women who knew best the wind of empty bellies, the sound and the smell of it, and so they were the most angry. They were the looters and the throwers of stones and the inciters of revolt. When the troops fired on the women and their children, they left their loot in the streets and ran, those who could; the others died, the others were carried, bloody and condemned, to the railroad boxcar prisons to await their execution.

It rained on the last day of the confrontation, after the women were slaughtered, after they left the salvage of their burned houses in the streets. The generals came and looked at the loot gathered by the soldiers, piled in front of the entrance to the mill, below the clock tower. The owners of the mill, Germans and Spaniards, also came and stood under black umbrellas in the rain and watched the collecting of the clothes, the imprisoning of the wounded, the piling of the dead on the horse-drawn wagons.

The people fled to the hills, hiding in caves and canyons. The soldiers hunted them. It was like Cananea, but so many more were dead. It was like Cananea, except that it rained in Veracruz and the streets turned to mud and the dark pools that signified the wounded were washed away, while the generals and the owners looked on from under their black umbrellas. It was like Cananea, for nothing was gained; worse than Cananea, for the White River Mill remained closed after the dead were buried and the fugitives were hunted down in the hills, and there was no work in the town and nothing to eat and the people of that little place outside Orizaba were more terrified and more hungry than they had ever been.

The stories were told in the taverns and in the plaza where the Freemasons sat in the shadow of the cathedral and preached an end to tyrannies. Villa listened; and often in the chill of the evenings, with his blanket wrapped around him, he dozed, lulled by the whisperings of philosophers and travelers, those who promised new worlds and those who spoke of worlds they had seen: St. Louis, Kansas City, Chicago, Denver, Los Angeles, Dallas, San Francisco, Houston, New Orleans, San Antonio—names, tales of automobiles and tall buildings, rich cities, cities of machines, impossible places, songs, dreamy sonorities. He slept there until the conversation abated; and, awakened by the quiet, he walked back to his house, passing through the windwashed streets, glancing into the windows of the low houses, where the children still played in the last warmth of the fire and the men slept in their chairs or drank beer and the women sewed by the light of oil lamps. He saw them through windowpanes, through distorting glass. Sometimes he paused too long at a window and the eyes inside caught him, showing him a woman's fright or a man's rise to anger; then he hurried back to his house, looking straight ahead, like one soldier marching in the dark.

Pedro Aprisco came one day and said to Villa, "You look alone in this house. You need a family. Come home with me."

"I'm not lonely," Villa said, "just thinking about what to do." But he went with Aprisco to San Andrés, to the little ranch outside the town where the Aprisco family tried to raise cattle and tried to grow corn, paid too much in taxes, and lost their chickens to coyotes. The Apriscos lived in a great, crumbling house left to them by the Juárez government. It had been a rich house before the division of the land. Now the property no longer included the Santa Ysabel River, and the only water came from the stream at the bottom of the Arroyo Durazno, a deep cut in the land that swallowed up cattle and offered fresh water only in the winter and spring. The sides of the arroyo were steep and dry, crumbling, like the walls of the house, falling to the wind.

"This is where they had the stables," Pedro said, leading Villa around the house before they went inside. "My grandfather used to say that there were a hundred horses and twenty men to groom them and exercise them. But he had two horses and no carriages and no one but himself to care for the little he had, so he took the wood of the gates for firewood, and when they were gone he chopped the poles out of the roof, and after that he burned the wooden mouldings of the doorways. Then the roof caved in and the rain collected in the stalls and the bricks at the bottom turned to mud again and the walls fell down. It was still a good garden when I was a child; there had been so many years of manure on the ground that vegetables grew like magic: tomatoes almost as big around as your head, giant onions. I remember them. Now, nothing grows there; I don't know why. Every year the soil got harder and harder. You have to make holes with a pick to put the seed in."

They went around to the front of the house. The stucco was peeling; what remained was streaked, blending with the color of the adobe underneath. The wooden doors were bleaching in the sun; there were splinters where the carved scrolls and flowers had been. Small black pigs scoured the shaded places against the walls for whatever lay there, for whatever softened in the dark crevices. "There were trees here," Pedro said, waving his hand to indicate the entire front of the house. "They used to bring water up from the river for them, but we have no river and there is not enough water in the arroyo and no one to bring it from there. Every year the trees had fewer leaves. The limbs turned hard and twisted. In the moonlight the trees looked like ghosts. My mother cried when she saw them. I remember when we cut down the last of them; we had firewood for a whole winter.

"It was a great house once. Sometimes I'm sad when I think what has become of it. I've thought of building the stables again and planting new trees beside the stumps, but my grandfather, who is an old man and very sour, says that it is useless now; these are no longer days of growing and making of good things. Everything comes from factories. Nothing is left to make the world good to see. There are only machines, so what is the use?"

"Is that what you believe?"

"I don't know," Pedro said. "He's an old man, he knows how to put value on things. What he says about the machines is true. Only my sister Liviana argues with him; she has bad manners."

"The world changed before your grandfather was born," Villa said.

"I'll tell Liviana that she's found an ally." Pedro took Villa's arm and started toward the entrance to the house.

"It's not so simple," Villa said, hanging back, putting the weight of himself into his arm. "The grandfathers are also right; it's getting worse, it's getting more difficult, it's not a good time for any of us; even the weather has turned against the poor. Do you remember when I sent you to the store to buy food? Do you know the cost of a blanket? Think about it, kid; ten years ago you could buy a shirt for two pesos. Now, it costs four or six. Ten years ago, a woman earned a peso for sewing a shirt. Now, the same woman works in a factory and earns a peso for sewing twenty shirts. Where is all the money going? To the Spaniards and the Chinese. For our race there's nothing but hard work and drought. The Chinese and the catzopines are allied against us. Ask some of the Yaquis who know about the plantations; the catzopines are the owners and the Chinese are their overseers."

"And the breadrolls?"

"It's the difference between locusts and pigs: they both eat the grass and the corn, but the pigs give you something in return. The North Americans are pigs, but they give us railroads and electricity for what they steal. The Chinese and the Spaniards just steal."

"I hate them all," Pedro said.

"Like me," Villa agreed, and allowed himself to be led into the house.

The rooms were empty, scrubbed, as if it were the first week of new residents in an old house. Light came from the patio, but the rooms were cold and quiet, a lull in the wind. It was a house without children, at the end of generations. "They left us an empty house," Pedro said. "They took everything but the walls; they removed the windows, the glass doors, the chandeliers, everything that could be carried. We never had the money to buy furniture. When my mother was born, they were still sleeping on mats and living in two of the rooms. There were some good years around the time I was born; we bought tables, beds, glass windows. Those were the last good years. We had a dream that when the railroad came through San Andrés we would get rich somehow; no one knew exactly how, but we had that dream. It worked the other way; after the railroad, after the workers left, the prices went down for beef and milled corn and everything else that we could grow here. The drought was only the last blow. If I hadn't brought home eight hundred pesos from Sam Ravel, I don't know what we would be doing now. We're all grateful to you for that."

"If the rurales had hung you from a cottonwood tree, would your family be grateful to me for that?"

"But they didn't."

"Well," Villa said, "at least I gave them the opportunity."

They went into the patio, a square of green and winter flowers, yellow, orange, cinnamon, red. Villa walked to the edge of the garden and leaned down to touch the leaves. Eulalia's garden had been so much richer. He looked around at Pedro. "I always wanted to own a ranch," Villa said.

[238]

"And then there was a time when I dreamed of having a store. I used to think all the time about the store, what I would sell there." Suddenly, he laughed and slapped Pedro on the arm. His voice rose to coarse good humor: "Come on, let's meet the Aprisco family. You think I rode all that way with a suit and tie just to talk to you?"

Aprisco took him to the dining room, where a fire burned and gave the smell of life to the air and the long wooden table was set with white napkins and silver spoons around brown plates. The family entered: the dark and tiny grandfather, with his white beard as stiff as stone; a round mother carrying a pot; the father, a square, somber face atop a body bulging at the belly like a gourd; a sister and her husband who slid into the room quietly, staying against the walls, settling into a corner, fading; a boy of twenty bent over a short crutch, swinging a stiff leg, walking in halves of pirouettes; two women in mourning dresses who held hands; and Liviana, a girl as big as a man, yet a girl, with a girl's walk, light, but not gliding as women walk, a girl, green-eyed, and with a sun-washed face more open than the face of a child.

It was a meal of formalities, a celebration in a room with the shutters drawn closed and the red-and-yellow light reaching up from the fire, the candles, the oil lamps suspended from the walls. The mother brought tamales of four kinds: chicken, beef, pork, and amaranth and chile. She carried in a fish taken from the Lake of San Bernabé, a great bass stuffed with nuts and sage and water herbs and baked under a blanket of onions and mountain chiles and sweet red chiles. And there were also pork in mole sauce and beans refried and dressed in goat cheese. She served them chocolate, she served them yellow custard and brown caramel sauce. There was salt, there was flavored water, there was water bread, for each of them two small loaves split in rising and twice encrusted. "It's a feast!" Villa said. "Magnificent!"

"My house is your house," the father replied, "and I say that because it is true: if not for your generosity to my son, we would not be eating such a meal. Before he came home from the north we ate weeds."

"He took risks for the money," Villa said, looking down at his plate. "It was not a gift. The rurales hang cattle thieves."

There was quiet at the table. The women in black crossed themselves, the mother crossed herself. Above the table, between the shuttered windows, Christ hung on a wooden cross, a silver figure blackened with age. From the opposite wall the Virgin of Guadalupe saw him with beatific eyes, his dark mother blessing him with roses. The women looked at Christ and at the Mother of God in her face of flowers, crossing themselves, touching their thumbs to their lips, kissing.

"We've never had a real bandit in the house before," said Liviana. "Only

[239]

my brother the apprentice. Tell us how many people you've killed. Do you enjoy it?"

Pedro banged his hand on the table. "He's not a bandit. How can you be so damned ungrateful? He's a man who helped us." He would have gone on, but Villa put a hand on his arm to quiet him.

The room was silent; everyone looked at Villa, awaiting his defense, prepared by the rules of hospitality and by the smell of the food in the serving plates to nod to his lies. "I am a thief," he said. "There is blood on my hands. If it pleases you, Miss, I'll leave your table."

"Oh, we've hurt his feelings," Liviana said. "I would have thought it impossible. My brother told us about a different man, how you behaved in taverns, how loud you are on the range, how much you laugh."

"This chair is not a saddle; your house is not a tavern."

The grandfather rose to his feet, pushing his chair out from behind him, using the sound of the wood scraping across the tile floor to gain the attention of the others around the table. His hands trembled, he pulled his beard, he was so tiny, so thin, bones inside gray cloth tubes and a yellowing shirt. "I am a Freemason," he announced. Everyone around the table nodded, and he sat down.

"You are Catholic," one of the women in mourning clothes said to Villa, and the other added, "We are all Catholic."

"I was baptized."

"St. Francis was one of the greatest bringers of the true faith to the world," the first woman in black said; and the other added, "It is the name of missionaries, blessed."

Liviana said, "Mr. Villa is also a missionary; he's taught our Pedro to be a bandit, he's inducted him into the Order of Thieves and Assassins."

"And you didn't hesitate to put the food earned by thieves into that cow face of yours," Pedro said to his sister, and then, turning to Villa, "Forgive my sister—she has bad manners. When a woman has no suitors at her age, she can only look forward to life as a spinster. For some women that means a life of sweetness and giving, perhaps entering a holy order. For others the prospect of being a spinster turns them bitter, like chiles in the wrong season."

Then the father spoke. "Let's eat," he said.

"Hurrah for the simpleminded," the grandfather shouted. "Sometimes they are the only ones with any wisdom at all." He reached for the platter nearest to him, the fish, and lifting it with great effort, lowered the platter onto his own plate. "Ah, what a fish!" he cried, "an old-fashioned fish!" Onions and tomatoes and chiles flew over the table and onto the floor as the old man attacked the center of the fish, cutting out great chunks and stuffing them into his mouth. The mother watched him for a moment—her eyes were filled with the saddest surprise—and then with a shrug she began passing the other platters. Villa filled his plate with tamales, beans and pork, salted his food, broke open his bread, took the knife, fork, and spoon out of his breast pocket, carefully wiped them with his napkin, and began to eat.

Only Villa and the old man ate; the others watched, affronted by his rejection of their eating utensils. It was Liviana who finally spoke: "Mr. Bandit, how can you trust our food, if you can't trust our utensils? Do you know how you've insulted us? Do you care? Are you such a . . ." She was interrupted by the old man, who reached over from his place next to her and put a forkful of bony fish into her mouth. Everyone laughed while she picked the bones out of her mouth with her fingers, hiding her face behind her napkin and depositing the bones on the side of her plate. She did it all with great delicacy, holding the bones with the tips of her fingers, raising and lowering her hand with a graceful sweep. They laughed louder for her efforts. "Miss Aprisco," Villa said, "you must not trust the utensils either, or you wouldn't be eating with your fingers."

Liviana shook her head, unable to speak for fear of choking on the bones.

"But even when you eat with your fingers," Villa said, "you're the most beautiful young woman in Chihuahua."

The course of the meal that most interested everyone had been served: the women in mourning clothes put their heads together, the mother and father exchanged glances, the sister touched her husband's arm, Pedro giggled, Liviana smiled through narrowed lips that showed the ends of two white bones, and the grandfather declared, "My Liviana is still part of the damned Church; look how she picks clean the bones of a poor fish!"

"God forgive him," the women in black said in unison, "for he knows not what he says. Mary, Mother of God, forgive him now and at the hour of his death."

The grandfather cut off the tail of the fish and tossed it at them. "Crows. If Juárez hadn't thrown out the damned creoles and their clergy from this land, you'd still be walking barefoot behind a plow or wiping the cheeks of some blue-eyed brat. The Church and the machines, this country goes from one plague to another."

No one answered the old man. Pedro whispered to Villa that it was useless to engage him in argument, because once the old man was set in motion he was like a stone rolling downhill; he could go on for hours, gaining speed until suddenly he stopped and fell asleep. So the meal went on mainly in silence, the conversation limited to offers of more food or chocolate or flavored water. At the end of the meal, after the custard, after the coffee with chocolate and cream, at the beginning of sighs and drowsiness, Villa told the mother, "It was the best meal I ever ate."

"Hah!" the old man grumbled, "how these bandits lie! It was nothing but fish."

After dinner, when the women were in the kitchen and the men had retired to their bedrooms to sleep, Villa went to the room that had been the salon and stood at the window, looking out at the brown, unplowed hills that rolled down to the river. It was poor land, but not useless; corn would grow on a hillside, tomatoes needed sticks on a slope, onions were comfortable anywhere, beans were a problem, plums and figs grew as well on a hill as on a plain once the saplings took root, but corn was best, corn could grow up the side of a mountain if there were no heavy rains. He felt the old man at his side, looking out the window with him, barely tall enough to see over the angled cut in the adobe. "You think I'm just an old fool," said the grandfather, "because I don't grow anything on my own land. Well, you're not so smart for a big bandit. If I plant corn on those hills, the political chief of this district will double my taxes. And if I can't pay the taxes, his in-laws will be living in this house and I'll have to move into a cave in the Blue Mountains, like my own grandfather. Oh, the bastard, the son of a bitch, the cuckolded prick, how I hate him! For thirty-five years I've hated him, and I hated his father before him. But they're kings, young man, the bastard kings, godforsaken cunts that they are, even Juárez himself couldn't get rid of them. Have a cigar."

"Thank you, no," Villa said, making the sign with his hand before his mouth, twice denying the taking in the gesture. "I don't smoke."

"How can a man not smoke?"

"Sir, there are no cigars in the hills; I never learned the habit."

"I hope I die before they do it to me," the old man said, watching Villa's face over the lighting of the cigar.

"I can understand."

"You don't know what I'm talking about," the grandfather accused.

"Eviction, sir."

The old man laughed. "You're good people, Mr. Bandit, very ready. Ordinarily, I don't take to people with your kind of hair, but I make an exception for you. Say, what do you think, Villa, you want to marry my granddaughter?"

"Horses and women of good stock."

"Well said," the old man told Villa with a slap on the back. "I'll arrange it."

But there was no marriage; it could not be arranged, not then, not even by the old man. Liviana made demands: a house with running water, a business or a piece of arable land, some proof of a possible life, some life from which they could not be evicted. "I went to the Church school," she said. "I can read Spanish and Latin. I will not consent to life in a shack with

[*242*]

a husband who could be hanged any day of the week in any town in Mexico. Why should I choose to be a poor widow?"

"God will provide," Villa said.

She mocked him in return: "God has already provided me with the opportunity to marry an unlettered criminal with chino hair and noisy breathing. Any greater generosity would be unbearable."

"God rewards the pious."

"Impious women are weak spirited and given to marrying men without prospects, even to marrying criminals."

He loved her for the sting in her words, for the spirit she brought to life. He asked her why she demanded so much, why she took no risks in choosing a husband, whether she had any sensation of love, infatuation, adventure; and she replied stolidly, teasing him, "A horse that won't pull a wagon doesn't deserve any oats."

"I'll be a businessman," he promised her, "a successful businessman."

"I'll wait," she said.

She gave him only barbs, she treated him to spurs and lashings. When he reached for her, she withdrew, making a game of them, a dancing game of forward steps and backward steps, of spins and turns with never an embrace. She practiced with the old man, who gave her the tricks and calculated crudeness, the sudden fancies and unexpected turns of age. And Villa could do no more than sit in his solitary house contemplating the fullness of her white blouse and the flat certainty of her face. "I love your sister," he told Pedro, "and I don't know what to do. She's difficult. She doesn't listen to her parents, you can't win her with singing songs under her window or dancing around in circles in the plaza on Saturday night. I think she wants a rich man. Maybe she has her eye on some rich creole, the son of a political chief or a judge? I don't know; with her marriage is like a business. She's too proud. She's just a girl and she's as crafty as an old man. She has no heart and I love the softness in her eyes. She's just a girl and I'm almost thirty years old and she drives me like a mule. It doesn't make sense."

Whatever Villa asked him about Liviana, Pedro always began his answer by saying, "She's my sister and I don't want to talk against her." Then he could say, "But why do you choose her? She's been a problem all her life, even when she was a little girl. Only our grandfather can talk to her, and they do nothing but argue: they fight about the machines and the political chiefs and what to plant and whether the Juárez government was any good because it gave him a house with no water. They fight about the Church all the time; she says there are good priests and bad priests and he says they're all bad. She tells him that Freemasons spend eternity in Hell and he says the Church is a worse boss than the landlords. The only time he can get her angry and make her cry is when he tells her that Our Lady of Sorrows is a fake, that Juan Diego was nothing but a servant to the creoles, a traitor to his own race. Then she screams and cries and tells him his soul is damned."

"She would be a good wife," Villa insisted. "She has spirit, which is as important in women as it is in horses. Would you have a mare without spirit? There have always been women who thought it was their place to gladden the lives of men. Those women have no spirit; they paint their faces and perfume themselves, but they have no spirit; they become bitter, their children are bitter, their houses are bitter, they turn to bitter weeds."

Pedro shook his head. "My sister is twenty years old and she talks like an old man, but the things you say sometimes are ancient, from the hills, from Indian Mexico."

"We're all Indians."

"Don't tell Liviana."

"She loves her machines, but she has the soul of our race. I've told her that many times."

"And what does she say?"

"She makes jokes, she teases me. And I tell her that one day I'll take her to the mountains, to the Tarahumaras or the Apaches or the Otomis or the Huicholes, and she'll see that her náhual, her second person, is Indian. That's who teases, that's the way the race is; the mountain people are the best at teasing and at making jokes, they pretend to be old men, they juggle sticks with their feet, they paint themselves to be something different. Liviana does that; she's a gentle girl who makes herself into a difficult old person."

"Then let her go."

"I have plans to start a business," Villa said. "Don't say anything about it to her. When the business is successful, I'll tell her."

Although his smock was bloody and there were pieces of raw meat caught under his fingernails, the butcher of Second Street was said by the cooks and serving girls to be the most charming merchant in Chihuahua. He was tall, unmarried, successful, and the most gracious of flirts. When he left the shop, he dressed like a North American rancher or mining engineer. He was a bit awkward on his feet; he seemed always to be stepping on his own toes, but when he was on horseback, well, a gentleman is one who sits a horse well.

It was the best business, the most profitable: Soto, Urbina, Aprisco, and the others stole the cattle, choosing only the fat ones without brand marks, brought them to the slaughterhouse, and carried the skinned and cleaned quarters of beef and edible innards to the shop on Second Street. Villa paid the rent, the price of rustling and of slaughtering, and kept the rest for himself. In three months, he had the busiest shop in Chihuahua. He hired an assistant, Victoriano Saldivar, who had been an apprentice in one of the other shops; he spread sawdust on the floor, bought a machine for making thin slices, and had wrapping paper printed with a picture of a puma, the sign for his shop, the sly and undeniable beef eater, the beast that took the choice parts and left the rest for the scavengers.

With the luxury of an assistant, he was able to spend less time in the shop. He went to bullfights and rodeos, and often he went to the small building on the outskirts of the city where he had seen his fortune disappear at the cockfights. He bet more carefully now, and often he only watched and listened to the gossip. The role of businessman pleased him. He bought a pocket watch with a gold chain that hooked through the buttonhole of his vest, he gained weight, his arms softened, the little ring of fat about his waist made him laugh with well-being. He went to the barbershop in the afternoons, emerging clean shaven, with scented talc on his cheeks and sweet oils in his hair.

He married Liviana in the summer, in the middle of the morning, after the rain, amid flowers and silk, kneeling, with Christ and Our Lady of Sorrows looking on, and all around him Apriscos and Arangos, even his silent sister, who blessed the day with the long-unheard sound of her laughter. He married Liviana dressed in white, his bride of prayer and promise, who directed the placing of flowers and touched her husband at the time for him to rise and the time for him to kneel and led him in the sign of the cross. They stood and knelt and kissed in the softly broken light of the holy pictures that the Church placed between them and the sun, in the cool light, the unmoving light, the weakened sun. Her eyes were clear, her mouth tasted of cloves. Afterward, they feasted in all the halls of the old house near the Arroyo Durazno. He danced with her to the beginning of the music and to the end, and all day she promised him by the dampness at her temples and the pulse in her neck that there would be a night. "I can feel my blood," he whispered to her.

"Marriage is holy," she answered, pronouncing it a lie with the slowness of her words. "Even Freemasons and bandits believe in the holiness of matrimony. Surely you must be thinking now only of the heavenly aspect of our union. Surely you must."

"Can there be anything else?" he asked.

"Some men are animals."

"I have promised our wedding night to the Church."

They laughed and turned a dancing embrace, wheeling and skipping along the rooms, their feet applauding on the tiles of the corridor, turning and turning, seeing each other, the party of the rooms, the roses of the garden, flowers in the real sun. They ate and drank chocolate and danced out the day, she in her long dress and he in his wedding shirt, in their new cotton and glossy silk, in their embroidered day, in their day of trumpets and bright colors, in their day of lights.

The early evening train took them to Chihuahua, a wedding party rich in aunts and cousins, a congress of friends carrying gifts of pots and chairs, skirts and bridles, knives, ribbons, thimbles, spices, shirts, flowers, ladles, blouses, and holy pictures. They boarded to music, filling up a car, singing, eating cinnamon and sugar, opening and closing the windows as the wind changed the direction of the smoke. Soot fell on the white wedding dress. The plush seats dampened them with sweat, they sang and drank cool mint water from gourds. The drunken men shot at birds, rabbits, a coyote, as the train passed the animals, going slow, riding the great half-circle of rails to Chihuahua. They shouted, they poured wine over the head of a somber man in a striped suit and a flat straw hat. He moved to the other car, as all the other passengers moved. The car became theirs, the second house of the wedding feast; they danced in the aisle, stumbling to the uneven sway of the train, bruised by the seats, all laughing, the young women, the cowboys, the curious children peering, the excited children flying in the aisle, the bride in white, the groom in his beautiful tasseled hat, the whining puppy on a red string, the chickens in a festively painted crate, the young she-goat with the tiny silver bell.

From the train station they made a procession of stragglers to the house on Tenth Street. Francisco Villa and his wife rode in a carriage driven by his assistant, Victoriano Saldivar, and all the rest followed on foot, except for a tiny girl who rode astride the back of the goat. Children, guitarists, dogs, delivery carts, the life of the streets, became part of the procession, walking with them for a block or two, singing or barking, running alongside the carriage or dancing around the musicians. They moved slowly, heavy with eating, some of them drunk, finishing the day as the town grew cool in the reddening light and the wind lifted up out of the west. At the end, they put the gifts in the house, even the chickens and the she-goat, and everyone kissed the bride before leaving. Then the musicians gathered on the street in front of the house and softly sang.

Villa carried the animals outside, the chickens and the puppy and the she-goat with the silver bell. The house was quiet but for the singing faintly stealing in through the shutters and the closed windows. Liviana sat on the chair in the bedroom, the white of her dress luminous in the darkness. He lifted the globe of the oil lamp and struck a match, but he saw in the light of the match that she did not want the lamp, and he let the fire go out.

"The house is clean," she said.

"I hired two women to clean."

"It's a man's house; it smells of leather."
"I never brought another woman here."
"Yes."
"Are you afraid?"
"Tired. And you?"
"Happy."
"Content?"
"You are more than I expected."
"I wanted a man. I waited."

The bed was narrow, set on an iron frame. They heard the singers, the rustle of clothes falling, the bell of the she-goat, the lonely puppy. The cleaning women had scented the sheets and they had put a pitcher of water, a bowl, and towels beside the bed; veterans of marriage beds and child beds, they would be there again in the morning to clean and nod to the success, fat inquisitors, old with nostalgia. Liviana touched the bowl and the towels. "The cleaning woman," Villa said. She made a sound, not words.

He was shy with her, silent; he did not know the decent words. She cried out once. He touched her lips with his finger and reminded her of the singers outside the window. She spoke only in her throat. Then she bled. He did not know in the darkness until he smelled the blood; then he wanted to give her the towels, but she whispered to him to go on, to finish.

They heard the singers laugh, a joke among themselves, drinking, passing a bottle perhaps, singing again, the same songs in soft male whispers. She washed and lay with a towel between her legs. He saw the form of her in reflections, the damp outline of her returning a light that had no source. The silver bell sounded and the puppy cried, lost in the new place. She said she heard the sounds. He lay with one hand on her waist. She said she felt his breath on her neck. He told her that he had often dreamed in the worst days, when he slept in cold rain or lived in fear. Sometimes the dreams were of dying in fire and sometimes the dreams were of losing the warmth of being alive, but there were also nights alone when he forced his dreams and saw himself in solid rooms beside a woman with a girl's face, one who had been waiting for him, wife, mother to his children, saint and confessor, a woman more than flesh, a true woman from whom his life would rise again, new and hopeful, full of sun and certain days, a happy life on one piece of land, a little country of his own rich in the smell of earth and corn, warm rains, cut grass, horses, serenaded by cattle feeding and the voices of children at their games; all of this emanating from the center of the certain woman, the true woman who was devoted to beginnings and forgetting, for he had now done so much to be forgotten: he had made death, he had taken the boots of bloody men, he had stolen, cheated, lied, wounded his sister, caused pain to his mother, failed her at her death, lying instead in the furrows, like an animal, the killer too bloody to enter the sacred house of his mother's death and his sister's wounded silence; he had destroyed more than he had built, he was unclean, he did not know where to go, how to wash, what prayers to say for the sake of his soul; and now he lay in the house of his fashioned dreams and looked to her, Liviana Aprisco, the wife of Villa, to be the source of forgiveness, the beginning of the third season of his life. He held her gently, his luminous wife, this woman of marigolds and roses.

12

They destroyed his business with papers, with laws, with symbols. First they told Urbina they would not slaughter unbranded cattle, and when Villa sent him to buy branded cattle from the small farms, he was told that only cattle accompanied by the proper papers could be slaughtered in Chihuahua. A man who could not read went to another man who could not read, and together they went to the farmers who also could not read, and they discussed the papers that had to be made for the slaughterhouse. They were helpless; the red ink and the black ink that were the writing of Mexico had not been used in four hundred years.

Villa went to see the administrator of the slaughterhouse. He stood in the long, dark office, in the narrow room, among heavy tables, among the signs of the conquest, the thick pieces of wood carved as if they were stone. The room smelled of leather and oils, incenses to mask the death smells. The administrator sat behind his desk, a narrow man and heavy in his movements, a man of the room. He sucked in his lips as bitter women do. Below him, on the main floor of the building, the cattle hung by their hind legs and were carried along on a pulley to the man who cut their throats, quieting them, sending the blood into the vats that rolled on to the sausage room. Children gathered to watch. The struggles of the cattle threw streams of blood, spattering the children, drenching the man with the knife, dressing him in blood, adorning him with clots.

"There are laws," the administrator said. He smoked thin cigarettes, holding his wrist in a Spanish turn. "Health laws, ownership laws. We're a civilized people."

"You ruined my business."

"The finest cattle are available, sir. The Terrazas, Martínez, and Creel ranches supply us with fat, healthy animals, which we prepare for the meat markets of the city. You have the advantage in buying our prepared beef of being able to choose the parts you want: so much ground meat, so much roasting meat, brains, tripe, sweetbreads, as much as you can sell. But when you bring in your own animals, you have to sell what the animal gives. The meat gets soft; it stinks when you don't sell it right away. So you see, Mr. Pentira, we are not ruining your business, we're helping it."

"And the prices, what about the prices?"

"The same for everyone, wholesale. The best beef at the best prices; that's the way we do business."

Villa had dressed himself in his wedding suit, all but the embroidered shirt, all but the joy. He felt the tie against his throat, the constriction. The trousers were too tight, his left foot was twisted in the boot; the leg ached from standing in the room, from standing in the shop, from sleeping poorly in anticipation of the visit, the muscles were too hard, too full of blood. He scratched his crotch, rearrangingly. "You ruined my business," he said.

The administrator did not answer.

Liviana had asked him not to wear the pistol; businessmen did not carry pistols, and she had married a businessman, not a bandit. There were other ways: talk, reason, even argument. She would read the papers for him, she who could read Spanish and Latin too. Merchants went unarmed; it was the rule, they had always been welcome. In the dark room he felt for the pistol, the white handle, the weight, the sound and the shock; and he found nothing, his hand closed on a habit. "You ruined my business," he said, and the administrator said nothing. Lights came into Villa's eyes, streaks of moon, blindness. He lost sight of the administrator, so far away, in darkness, obscured by the lights. His head ached, the side, the back, somewhere behind his eyes, deep, a pulse, out of tune with the lights, out of tune with the blindness. She had been wrong, an innocent; men carried guns; he had trusted her eyes, the certainty of her, a woman, a girl, adjusting his tie, the perfume of morning, dressed in promises. "You ruined my business," he said.

The administrator did not answer. Three men in gray entered the room; one of them seemed to be Claro Reza. That one—Villa could not see him —whispered, "Smooth, be smooth, Pancho. Use your head." He took Villa's arm and led him out of the dark room.

"He ruined my business," Villa said.

"Be smooth," Reza told him. "I'll take you home."

The business was no use to Villa anymore. He sent Saldivar, his assistant, to the slaughterhouse to buy meat, and Saldivar came back with the poorest

[249]

cuts; the last choice was left to the newest customer. The women who had patronized the store on Second Street went back to the butchers they had known before. The few who remained as customers bought little, haggled over prices, and demanded credit. Villa went to the store less often; sometimes he did not appear for a week or more. He stayed home at first, passing the days with Liviana, visiting friends with her, going with her to the shops around the main plaza. Then he went to Jiménez to see Urbina, and south to visit Soto, and the three of them went to Juárez and Columbus, where Sam Ravel offered to buy cattle from them again.

When he came home after a long trip, Liviana demanded that he bathe before he embraced her. She asked what money he had, he asked what friends she had seen; they spoke of relatives and the price of corn; they were no longer lovers. She had begun to gain weight, she had begun to keep accounts in a long gray book. He felt the loosening of her belly, he complained of the unhappiness of her breasts. She asked him to shave more often. They slept in the same room, the same bed, but there were no musicians outside the window. He interrupted her sleep with snoring.

"They tried to cure me, the way I breathe," he said to her in the middle of the night. "We went to a healer. He made it better, but it cannot be entirely cured."

"Don't sleep on your back."

"How can I keep from turning over when I'm asleep?"

"How do you sleep when you're in the hills?"

"Alone."

He went away again, each trip longer than the one before, each trip more expensive than the one before. Saldivar sent them very little in profits from the shop; he was pressed to pay the rent, the slaughterhouse refused him credit, his customers demanded it. Liviana kept the accounts in the long gray book. There were taxes: a collector came to the house, another came to the store. They could not afford bread, the quick patting of tortillas was heard in the house. They ate the meat that was not sold in the store, the dark brown meat that the bargain hunters rejected. The old woman who washed the steps went to another house. Liviana mended her own clothes. The grandfather came to visit and put a fifty-peso gold piece in Liviana's hand when he kissed her cheek in farewell. Liviana wept. "We're taking charity," she said.

"Did you beg?" Villa asked.

She threw the coin at him.

Villa delivered milk, cut wood, poured mud and straw into adobe brick forms, broke horses, rode bulls for money in rodeos. When everyone in Mexico was talking about the grace and courage of Gaona of Guanajuato, Villa borrowed a traje corto, a cape, and a muleta, and tried his luck in the

[*250*]

little wooden bullring at Delicias. The suit was too small, leaving his arms and legs bare in adolescent places. He did not dominate the bull, he dared it, pulling it by the tail, twisting its horns until it bellowed and fell. And in the killing, he missed the heart again and again, hacking the hump bloody, forcing the blade into the lungs so that a pink froth poured out of the bull's mouth. The audience applauded with laughter, saying that he was twice as brave and half as smart as the bull. He shouted back at them, calling them cowards and professors of dishwashing. In the end, he had to wrestle the bull to the ground and roll around with it in the bloody sand until he was able to sever its spinal cord with a dagger.

For his day of humiliation he was paid twenty-five pesos. He paid five pesos to the wisemonkeys who attended the bullring, ten to the peones who placed the banderillas and attended him in the ring, five to the picador, and five more to the man who loaned the suit to him. Liviana laughed at the accounting. "Do honest work," she said.

Villa's ribs were bruised, and a wide laceration that began at his scalp and ran down the entire side of his face was turning into a hard scab, stiffening his face and causing him difficulty in speaking. "A butcher shop is honest work."

"That's gone. We'll have to do something else. There are other kinds of shops."

Villa lay on the bed. He was fully clothed, his boots left dark marks on the pale green bed cover. Liviana sat in the chair at the foot of the bed; Villa's eyes were nearly closed as he looked down the length of his body to her. "They own everything," he said. "Wherever you go, whatever you do, it all goes to the company store. This is no country for an honest man. My father was an honest man, your father is an honest man; what does it get them? Your friend, Don Perfecto, he's going to change everything with his liberalism. What does it get him? They're killing him with taxes; he admits that to you; every month they make a new tax for Perfecto Lomelí the Liberal. You know the trouble with Liberals? They're like my old friend Maclovio Herrera; they attend all the funerals."

"And President Juárez?"

"Was the father of Porfirio Díaz," said Villa, fingering the side of his face, the scab that had become as hard as dried plaster. Pieces of dried blood came off in his fingers. He looked at the dark clots that turned to powder between his fingers, and he let out a grunt of disgust. The backs of his hands were cut, the skin was gone from his knuckles. He held them up for her to see. "Some wives would weep," he said.

"The bull is dead; let the cows weep."

Villa let his hands fall. "Oh, what a lot of salt I brought into my house. I can remember times when I was with Ignacio in the mountains that even a pinch of salt would have made us happy, and now I have so much salt that I can't keep it out of my sores. I feel the sting in every cut. Pity the man who gets his salt by marriage."

"When you marry a woman you make promises, you don't let her go hungry."

"Did I know that angels had such appetites?"

Liviana stamped her feet on the tiles. She screamed at him: "You try to make a fool of me. That's all you want, that's all that pleases you—to make a fool of your wife."

"What do you want?"

"A thief is a coward. I want an honest man. That's what you promised me. I see honest men in this town and in my own town. Look at Don Perfecto! He has as much trouble with the landlords as you, and he takes care of his family. Without stealing."

"Liviana, I bought this house with cowardice. I paid for the wedding with cowardice. Because your brother was a coward, your family survived the drought. Cowardice is good to you, Liviana; don't be ungrateful. And as for your Don Perfecto, I think he's not so brave. He was born rich; the government takes a little of his riches from him to teach him how to be a good landlord, like the rest of them. It's not so easy for me. In some towns they would pay a reward for my head. In Durango and Parral and Santa Rosalía there are people who would shoot me on sight. They would chase me with posses, with troops of rurales, with armies. You have an angel's face, Liviana; I hope you never see a man who's been shot."

She rose and paced the floor, the leather of her heels sounding on the tile. "How can we live?" she asked, looking heavenward, folding her hands as if in prayer.

"I'll make a trade with Terrazas. If he won't let me sell a few animals a week in my butcher shop, I'll have to sell a thousand a week to the Jew from the other side. What else can I do? He invites me." Villa laughed. He laughed until the bed shook and the hard walls of the room turned it into a hall of laughers. She stepped back from him, shrinking from the sound, holding her hands before her, palms outward, the fingers curled. "Come here," he said, holding his arms out for her.

"Oh, no, Francisco, you're hurt. When you're well again."

"You married a man," he said.

She boiled water for chocolate, but there was not enough for two cups. She scraped the can to thicken the dark water in his cup, but it was not enough. With a can opener she cut off the top of the can and scraped the corners with a spoon. She loosened the powder in the seams with a knife point, but the chocolate mixture in the cup remained thin, pale in the spoon.

She added milk and cinnamon. The mixture thickened and cooled. Then she poured it back into the pan and heated it again. A thick skin formed. As she skimmed it off with a spoon, the mixture thinned again; the chocolate was wasted. She put the lid back on the stove and sat down at the table to look at the mixture in the pan. The skin formed again. Underneath it the mixture became thinner and thinner, it became like the flavored water sold on the streets, it became the color and the texture of poverty, the mean and dreamless life, the days that fell to dying. She hungered for luxury: silk, perfume, the fluff of new wool, the clean corners of cotton never worn, unmarked leather, the wine of another province, the flowers of another season. There was cornmeal on the shelf, there was lard, there was even white flour. She had a box of salt, she had herbs and chiles and bacon and bags full of beans and cheese wrapped in porous cloth. But there was no chocolate, and the edges of her blouse had been washed soft, worn out of their will. She put her head down on the table and wept.

Villa came from the other room. The scab had been torn, there were blood marks on his shirt, on the neck and on the shoulder. He stood over her for a long time, but he did not know what to say. The pan was there, the can of chocolate was there, torn open, scraped clean, the seams split by the knife point. He went back into the other room and put on his boots and his riding jacket and his soft Texas hat. He packed his saddlebags, rolled his blanket, hung the cartridge belts over his shoulder, and strapped the revolver to his waist. He picked up his rifle and went into the kitchen again to get his eating utensils.

"You blame me," she said.

"Never."

He took the knife, fork, and spoon out of the basket, and put them in the breast pocket of his coat.

"Where are you going?" she asked.

"To buy chocolate."

They trailed the herd, sixteen men masked against the dust: cowboys and farmers, two Tarahumaras and a Yaqui, one who had been a Mormon, one who had lost four fingers in a copper mine, one who ate no meat, one who smoked marijuana all day and into the night. For nine days they lay back on the outskirts of the herd, men in the style of wolves, living without fire. There was no wagon to feed them, there were no pack mules to carry their pleasures; they ate atole, herbs, berries, and fresh honeywater drained from the heart of the maguey; they softened tortillas in water and wrapped them around strips of dried beef and mountain chiles.

There were six thousand cattle; it took them half a day to pass through a narrow place. The ground turned to dust wherever they passed; their

[253]

manure could be smelled for miles; the sounds of their hooves and their constant mooing were like low tremors in the earth, layers of deep sound that Villa and the others felt in the bone of their skulls and the hollow pockets under their eyes. Twenty men attended the herd, nineteen cowboys and a boy who cooked and drove the supply wagon.

Villa told the Yaqui, who spoke more Spanish than either of the Tarahumaras, to listen to the conversation of the cowboys. The Yaqui removed his clothes, rubbed himself with sage; and out of one of his deerskin pouches he took a handful of pinacate bugs and rubbed them on his arms and legs to make himself stink, to ward off the stings of snakes and scorpions and the inquisitiveness of dogs. Naked but for a cartridge belt across his chest and the rifle in his hand, he stood before Villa. "I could kill them all," he said.

"Just listen. We'll take the cattle later. Let them do the herding, let them work for Terrazas. Just listen. Learn what they say, remember what they say, tell me what they say." Villa pointed to the campfire at the foot of the hill almost a mile away. "Don't go near the cattle, brother, stay downwind. The pinacate will upset the cattle." The naked man set off down the hill. Villa and the others watched him. He ran easily, lightly, choosing his steps in the moonlight.

While the others slept, Villa and Urbina waited for the Yaqui to return. Urbina was wrapped in his sheepskin and wool cape. "I can't last too many more nights without a fire; the fucking wind is freezing my bones. Prick! Fate leaves me with aching bones and he runs naked. Prick!"

"I like to hear you complain," Villa said. "I think of Nacho. You remember those days?"

"Better Pancho Villa."

"Nacho was a good leader."

"He was too serious," Urbina said. "It wasn't his fault; it was all the fucking trouble he had with his belly. They killed him because he was too serious. I've thought about it a lot. The sons of bitches are serious; they can predict a serious man, they can trap him."

"And I'm not serious, a married man with a house in Chihuahua?"

"Bandits can't be married."

"Go to sleep, Tomás; it's good for your bones."

"You don't like to think about the truth."

"I don't want to kill an old friend on such a cold night."

It was the middle of the night when the Yaqui returned. He rubbed himself with prickly pear fruit to neutralize the odor of the pinacates before he put on his clothes. "I'm sorry there's no fire," Villa said.

"I ate some little chiles to be warm from the inside," the Yaqui said. He sat down on folded legs and told what he had heard: "They will drive them up the Santa Maria River, slowly, watering them to add to the weight. When they go around the lake and through the valley between the San Blas and the Santa Maria ranges, they'll turn to the east along the railroad to Ciudad Juárez. There are troops along the railroad. I don't know how many; they didn't say.

"I saw thirteen in the camp, and I saw the boy come and go, the boy who cooks and drives the wagon. Six are riding the herd now, but they are not singing. One is asleep in the saddle. I saw only one, the one who was asleep. His horse was eating sage, its neck was bent, and the rider was asleep in the saddle. He was in a deep sleep, facing the wind; I saw him."

"The day after tomorrow," Villa said. "We'll take the cattle at night and drive them west across the ford the next morning. There's a low pass in the San Blas Mountains north of the ford. We'll take them west through the pass and up around Lake Guzmán to Palomas. The day after tomorrow."

The Yaqui nodded. "I'll sleep now," he said.

Villa thanked him, and then he unrolled his own blanket and lay down to sleep. The moon watched him. He could not sleep. He took his canteen and went up the mountain, climbing through the cold shadows. The Root of Gold grew there; they had been using the bark of the root to clean their teeth and freshen their mouths. Villa uprooted one of the plants and sat down on a rock to prepare it. When the bark and the brown core were removed, he shredded the remaining root and put it in the cup of his canteen to soak, then he emptied his bowels and washed his face with cool water. The moon watched him eat. He lay down and the moon lay beside him. She kissed him. She sang to him with golden bells. He touched her neck, the bloody stump. "The twenty are mine," she said. "They follow me."

"I loved my mother," he said.

The moon laughed. "You are my lover," she said.

He embraced her, he embraced the golden bells. The twenty who were hers were also his. They sat in a row, observers, waiting, twenty rabbits. Then the light came and the moon fled, taking the twenty with her, drawing them with her into the western darkness.

When they gathered again to eat their meat and tortillas, which the Yaqui and the Tarahumaras called tlaxcalli in the old way, Villa instructed them in what to do. "I saw the right way," he told them to make them agree, for they all knew it would be easier and safer to kill the twenty men.

He sent the Yaqui, the two Tarahumaras, Soto, Urbina, and Aprisco ahead to surprise the men who rode the edges of the herd. They went down the hillside together, three of them naked, rubbed with herbs and pinacate bugs—they would cross to the far side of the herd—and three in riding clothes, with mud on their buttons and dark cloth tied around their cartridge belts. The naked men were silhouettes, darker than the sand on which

[*255*]

they walked. At the bottom of the hill they began to run in long, smooth strides, upright, gliding, deer hunters in the style of deer.

One man was left with the horses. Villa led the others across the face of the hill toward the campfire. They walked carefully to avoid dislodging loose rocks; they did not speak, they did not wear spurs. When they were above the campfire, they spread into a half-circle and moved down the hill. Now the rifles were cocked. Now they saw the men around the fire, the boy beside the wagon, scraping pans, washing them in the river, the horses staked and unsaddled. One man held a guitar. He touched the strings now and again, but he made no song; there was no melody. One mended a stirrup, pushing a piece of leather thong through the holes with an awl; another whittled a piece of white pine, cutting indolently, mindlessly, throwing the chips toward the fire; some lay in their blankets, sleeping or watching the sky or looking emptily into the night; some smoked; they passed a bottle of sotol, taking small sips, without hunger for the liquor, social, sleepy men, drinking after the long day, before the next long day. The leader could not be identified; they seemed equal, weary, thirteen men and a boy, resting, without wariness, without fear. South and west of them the herd made its low night sounds; the animals had been to the river, they had eaten the grass, they folded their legs and slept.

The moon is the leader of the stars, of the armies of the north and south; she is the matricidal lover of the night. A woman stands at the crossroads between heaven and earth; she weeps. They are all in the night, the night of nine levels, the night of mice.

"Here comes Pancho Villa! Raise your hands! Stand up! Raise your hands! Raise your hands!"

They stumbled, caught in their blankets, like men suddenly awakened, turning from one shout to another, spun by the sounds. It was the boy who ran, kicking through the shallow water of the riverbank, sending up the water to reflect the fire, ringing himself in the broken mirror. It was the boy who set off the Winchesters, the barking of wild dogs.

Villa screamed at them to stop; it was not what he had seen.

The barking ended. A man lay in the fire; his shirt was burning, his hair was burning. The sound of the cattle was like a great horn moaning. They were rising, lifting the water and the grass; the legs were unfolding, the chewing had stopped. There were men among them, riders singing. The boy lay in the river, half floating, slipping into the current. All the men lay dying. One whistled through a hole in his throat.

Bárbaro Carillo asked, "Should I finish them?"

"The cattle," Villa said.

"No. Like bulls, with the dagger."

"Then hurry up."

With one hand Carillo held the back of a man's hair, pulling forward, stretching his neck. With the other, he jammed the point of the dagger into the base of the man's brain, working the edges of the dagger back and forth to sever the spinal cord. The body collapsed, the hair was jerked out of Carillo's hand. He went on to the next. He was quick with most of them, but several times the point of the dagger struck bone and slipped to the side; then the sudden convulsion of the man pulled him away and Carillo had to begin again. The others watched him. Carillo made jokes, speaking in the language of the bullfight. "Oh, son of a bitch! Another pinchazo!" he said, slapping himself, laughing. At the end, José Sánchez cut off the ear of one of the dead men and threw it to Carillo. Everyone laughed, everyone applauded. Carillo took a turn around the fire, holding up the ear, careful to step over the bodies as he danced and turned to the sound of their applause.

They pulled the burning man out of the fire and threw sand on him to stifle the odor of his flesh. Then they threw more wood and dry brush on the fire to light the campsite for the scavenging. They took the weapons before they smashed the teeth to pick out the gold. Finally, they took the boots and the hats and the unbloodied blankets.

While the nine men robbed the thirteen dead, squabbling over the communal four, Villa went to the river. The body of the boy was still there, turned now, the feet pointing downstream. If the coyotes did not come in time, the body would float downstream to the lake. There, standing in the mud, he took the boy's arm. It was dead; Villa's fingers reached all the way to the bone. The sensation of the flesh without resistance sickened him, but he held on, walking backwards in the mud and shallow water, dragging the body up onto the bank where the coyotes and the vultures could clean it.

"This is not a victory," Villa said. "You deserve nothing, not even what you robbed from their bodies, not even what you pried out of their teeth. I told you that I saw an army. They would have come with us. They were poor men of our race, twenty cowboys. What good are they to me now? If the rurales find us or the Federal troops find us, you'll regret every man that was lost here tonight. You're all very brave when you shoot boys or sleeping men, but if the rurales come, your pricks will shrivel up with fear and you'll wish you had listened to me."

The Yaqui came back, riding a horse, wearing another man's hat, two gunbelts, and leather leggins below his naked thighs. He still stank of pinacate bugs. His left arm was bloody but not wounded. "He struggled," the Yaqui said, "and I cut the throat."

"Was he asleep?"

The Yaqui showed his teeth. "Now he sleeps."

"Watch out for the herd."

"There is nothing to drink? I want a drink."

"There was only enough for thirty-six."

The Yaqui looked puzzled. He pushed back his hair, sweeping the roughly cut black bangs out of his eyes. "Tacea," he said, his own name, nothing more. Suddenly, he began to laugh. "Chief," he said, nodding to Villa, wheeling the dead man's horse, kicking it with the dead man's spurs, heading back out toward the herd.

Villa watched the others come in, each man alone, each man on a new horse: Soto, Urbina, the Tarahumaras, and finally Pedro Aprisco. He did not speak to them. They talked softly with the others, ate, and went back out to the herd; all but Pedro Aprisco, who took his plate of beans and bacon and went up the hill to sit alone. Villa went up and sat down beside him. Aprisco continued eating, chewing with the vacant solemnity of a cow. Villa took a tortilla out of his hand and scooped some beans out of his plate with it. "My brother-in-law, too," he said.

"No, man; I tried to do what you asked. I showed him the rifle, I made him dismount and stake the horse. Then I put the knife to his throat and stood there behind him, waiting for the signal fire. When the shooting started, he jumped and I jumped; the knife cut him open. I thought he would fall down, but he didn't, Pancho. He turned on me and started to run at me. The blood was coming out of his throat and he was hissing like a snake. I ran from him. Oh, God, how I ran! But he kept coming, man. He wasn't running, but he kept coming after me. When I got a little bit ahead of him, I turned around and hit him with the rifle. Then he fell down. Then he didn't chase me anymore."

"Carillo always puts too much lard in the pan when he cooks refrieds."

Pedro looked up from his plate. In the darkness Villa could not make out his expression, but there was the sound of betrayal and sadness in his voice: "You have nothing more to say?"

"I don't believe in ghosts. And I didn't kill him. I didn't kill anybody. I saw an army. Thirty-six. Instead . . . You smell of blood; you should wash yourself. That kind of blood stains, like cochineal."

"You've done it too. Liviana told me. Everyone knows."

"Yes."

Villa lay back against the side of the hill. He put his hat on his chest and folded his hands under his head. It had been the same with Parra, with the mule drivers beside the river, caught in the canyon, dying in the crossfire. Sooner or later the rabbit entered the house, the pots cracked, and the luck of a man threw him into the circle with the ants; and Christ would not help, a man could not be extricated, a man could not save himself from the ants.

He spoke aloud, muttering, falling into sleep. The boy heard him, but he did not answer. Down below, around the fire, the men were singing, a slow waltz, three guitars, eight voices, a slow waltz sung in unison over the lowing of the herd and the coyotes announcing the dead. The bodies had been dragged away and thrown in a pile. New owners wore their hats, new owners wore their boots. While they sang, the new owners exchanged hats, passed boots from one to another, looking for the right fit, matching themselves with the dead. They sang, the slow waltz, the song of the face of the girl with the lovely mouth. Villa thought of corn, of great fields in days of sun and soft rain. He was the son of an old woman who hid behind the whitewashed walls of an empty house. He could not remember his mother's name. He thought and thought, but he could not remember her name. When he called to her there was no sound, she did not turn to his voice, the sun was brilliant on the white walls. From inside the walls one word was returned: *Temictiani.*

In the morning, he asked Tacea if it was a real word.

The Yaqui nodded.

"I only dreamed the word," Villa said. "In the dream I thought it was my name."

"There is no such word. I made a joke."

He did not visit my house when he came to San Juan del Río; he traveled now with an escort: twenty-three men, cowboys, farmers, miners, mountain people; some had been soldiers, two had been rurales, one understood artillery, one had learned to be a telegraph operator. They wore boots and spurs, like catzopines; they rode the best horses, big, long-running animals. The rurales hunted them; their names were known.

When they arrived at the house across the river from San Juan, Antonio Arango met them with his rifle pointed. His wife and his brother and his silent sister were behind him, hiding in the darkness of the house. "Rob the rich," he said. "We have nothing. Leave us in peace." The dogs barked. Twenty-four horsemen lined up in rows in front of the small house: six and eight and five and two and three. The horsemen wore cartridge belts and buckskin leggins. They did not speak. Arango looked from one face to the next, pointing the rifle, moving it as his eyes moved.

Villa came around the rows from his place in the back. "Don't be afraid," he said. "It's only me, your brother."

Antonio did not lower the rifle.

"I was born in this house," Villa said, throwing his leg over the horse, dismounting.

The brothers looked in each other's faces. The dogs approached Villa, sniffing at the stranger. The men on horseback touched their weapons, shifting in the saddle, causing the horses to change their footing. In the dark of the house there was silence. The brothers looked in each other's faces;

Francisco the taller, redder, toasted and windburned, heavier, dark at the jaw, standing with his left foot turned in. Antonio's eyes wavered, looked the length of his brother: the soft hat, short dusty jacket, belts of cartridges, the pistol, the desert-scarred leather, the finish worn off the boots, the toe turned in, awkward. "I remember when that happened to your leg," Antonio said.

"A worse thing happened in Parral. They wanted to cut off my foot."

"Really?"

Villa nodded. He deliberately turned the toe of his left foot outward, leaving a mark in the dust. "It was a bad time to be without a family."

Antonio opened his arms, pointing the rifle up and away from his brother. They met and embraced. "Brother," they said, "brother." With their arms round each other's shoulders and tears running on their faces they went into the house. Martina, the silent sister, said, "Welcome," and Villa wept aloud for the joy of being home.

He stayed there that night, sleeping in the house while the twenty-three men camped out in the yard. In the morning, he told his family that they were going to Chihuahua. There was a house for them, there was an easy life awaiting them; they were rich. But Antonio said that he and his wife would not go: they would not live on stolen money. Villa answered him with laughter: "Stolen money! Tonio, I steal a few cattle. I take them off the open range. They have no brands, nothing; they run wild. Is that stealing? If you want to talk about stealing, talk about Terrazas; the great Don Luís Terrazas stole the state of Chihuahua!"

They left in the afternoon, a family called Arango and called Villa. They rode in a dirty and torn buggy and in a flat wagon with wooden axles and no sides to contain its load: three small boxes of private belongings, and the mats, the table, and the four chairs of their house. Their chickens also rode on the bed of the wagon. The pigs rode in the buggy, and the two goats trailed behind. Twenty-three armed men escorted them, riding the hillsides and the stony ridges above the road, the little army that came at night to rest and eat food cooked by women. On the fourth morning, Mariana and her sister-in-law knelt in the dust beside the buggy and wept to God because it was Sunday and they had no priest to lead them in the Mass.

They were a family, although they had two names and they lived in two houses, one on Tenth Street and another two blocks away on Eighth Street. Hipólito took the name of Villa; the others hesitated. All of them went often to visit Liviana's family, riding the train to San Andrés, making a party of the trip, carrying jars of mole, fresh-baked wheat bread, and three or four chickens in a crate, fat hens to be killed and plucked in the open yard behind the house, fat hens to be filled with herbs and washed in lemon or to be boiled in salt water and soaked in mole. The passenger car of the train steamed in summer and in winter it was the last resort of flies, but there was sometimes singing and there was always a barefoot man with a gourd ladle and a kettle of juice to sell to the people in the green plush seats. The family of Chihuahua went on the train to visit the family of San Andrés— all but Francisco, who rode cross-country in the company of four or six armed men, his escort, racing the train, cutting across the big curve, sweating the horses on the way west.

Then there were days in the great ruined house: the yard was littered with fish bones and feathers; the horses drank in the arroyo and at the river and grazed in the grass that did not belong to either family; the children played with dolls and wooden toys; the men practiced shooting and riding, roping the same tired calf again and again; the grandfather held forth; and Liviana disputed whatever was said. There was chocolate and fresh meat, all the water was cool and flavored, the men smoked cigars and drank pulque and even brandy, there were flowers in the patio and in the house, the dust receded in the cool house, blown away by laughter and the sweep of embraces; there was light in the rooms.

They brought water and straw and good clay to the yard behind the house. They built wooden forms and filled them with the builder's mud to make bricks. And after the sun baked the bricks, they stacked them one on the other, cementing them with mud, rebuilding the stables, making an estate again of the ruined house.

Neighbors came on these full days, visitors from the town, sharecroppers from the nearby ranches. They brought their children for the food, they took home the scraps, they filled their clay pots with gifts from Pancho Villa. "My house is your house," the grandfather and Villa said to the thanks of the neighbors, for they wanted them to have the comfort of guests, they did not want them to eat the cold food of charity.

It was also a house of complaints; no one feared to condemn a landlord in the presence of Pancho Villa. "You make them feel safe," the grandfather said to Villa. "You give them courage."

"Of course, old man. Why should they worry when I'm here? The landlords want only to rob them."

The grandfather was amused. "Do you think yours is the only life they want?" he asked. "Tell me. Tell me if there aren't other ways to kill a man. Tell me that you can't starve him to death by raising the rent until he can either pay you or feed himself and his family. Tell me that a landlord can't squeeze a man to death like those jungle serpents. Ha! You're nothing but a bandit, Pancho, a damned bandit. How could I expect you to understand the problems of decent people?"

"Do you believe that?"

The old man shrugged and walked in circles, appearing to be deeply considering the question. "Yes and no," he said. "Maybe yes and maybe no."

"Very clear, sir."

"If I thought you were nothing but a thief and a murderer, as some people say, I wouldn't have allowed you to marry Liviana. On the other hand, you don't live an ordinary life; how can you know? For you there's always the gun—yes or no, live or die. But look at the people who come to this house —can you understand what is happening to them? How can I explain to you?"

He walked in circles again until he found the words he wanted. "We're planning a rent strike; I want you to protect us."

Villa shook his head.

"Why not?"

"Because they'll send the army."

"You're afraid!" the old man accused. He put his finger in Villa's chest. "You're afraid."

"Listen to me, little grandfather: one man can run away from an army, but it takes more than one man or a hundred men to fight an army. I can't protect you. The only thing I can do is die with you. If you told these people who come to your house that I could protect them from an army, you lied to them. You better tell them the truth, or you're going to have a lot of blood on your hands."

"A bandit is nothing but a bandit," the old man said. "I should have known."

People milled through the house, the patio, the area where the stables were being rebuilt. Most of the women were in the kitchen, making food and gossip, seasoning the food with peppers and sins. The men wandered; they wore the saddest faces; they were mostly thin, leaning on their feet like old horses; they chewed and chewed: one had seen columns of fire at the eastern sea, another sprinkled water on the faces of his children every night so that the coming earthquakes would not stunt their growth, another swore that rabbits were entering the houses in his neighborhood, and there was also talk of Tata Porfirio and the fireplace stone that had exploded with its promise of violent death.

"Cananea," Villa said, "Río Blanco. The Liberals and the Freemasons work well. You can do the same thing for your friends, grandfather. And if you really want to help them, get the women and the children together in the church so that the Federals can set it on fire. Tata Porfirio will send you five medals, one for each of your fingers."

The old man called Villa a coward and turned his back to him, walking away slowly, strutting, daring, a frail figure in black and silver, shrunken, the size of a child, the tight trousers revealing the bend of his knees. Villa went to the kitchen to find Liviana. "You better do something about the old man," he told her. "I think he's crazy, too old. He gives these people food, and they listen to him about rent strikes and his Liberal ideas. He buys them with that. He shows them the silver on his suit and they see his fancy boots and they think he must be right because a rich man is always right. Well, I'm telling you, he's going to get them all killed."

"Is it better to die for stealing horses?"

"You speak very bravely for a woman who doesn't like the taste of beans."

"If everyone was a thief, my dear husband, there would be no one left to steal from."

"These are country people; they don't know what he's doing to them."

"Let us be scientific," she said, "let us be realistic. These Indians can't think for themselves; a strong man must lead them to progress. Meanwhile, they don't need to have shoes or bread. Let them pay the rent. Let the Spaniards and the foreigners be rich, because they're scientific, they're realistic."

"Don't mock your husband."

"Don't insult my grandfather."

"He's a fool, worse than that Lomelí. He shouldn't have started this business about a strike."

Liviana laughed. "Pancho, Pancho, my poor Pancho, don't you know it's not my grandfather. There's an organizer who comes here to make speeches, a man from San Luis Potosí. He calls himself Azcatl, because he says we're all like ants and we must work together like ants, if we want to have a strike, if we want to succeed."

"You've seen him?"

"Yes."

"How many legs does he have?"

"Now you're the one who's mocking," she said.

He put his arms around her and clasped her to his chest. She smelled of chocolate and corn and wood smoke. "Sweetheart," he said, "life of my life, Liviana." She relaxed, leaning against him. He saw the sign of a smile on her cheek, satisfaction. "Remember one thing, please, dear: the Porfiriato steps on ants." She pulled away from him and ran back toward the kitchen. He swatted at her buttocks as she ran, calling to her, "Hurry up, hurry up, get in there. A woman's place is not in politics; it's in the kitchen."

Azcatl came to the house of the Apriscos. He stood on the stump of a tree in the yard of the house, in the shadow of the rebuilt walls of the stables. The people came up from the town to listen. They came on the backs of burros; they came in carts of rough wood, hauled like sacks of onions, like chunks of beef; they came on bare feet, their children beside them, their babies hung from their backs in shawls of dark cloth; they came in the sun, wearing tattered hats with small tassels hanging, wearing dark cloth over their heads and wrapped once across their throats; they came in soft cottons and the mesh of cactus fibers, in heavy skirts and white trousers, in striped shirts and embroidered blouses; they came with machetes and the oldest of rifles, with glazed bowls and gourds and tin canteens; and they came in the rough and dusty clothes of cowboys, with their hats shading them and their buckskin pants flapping; they were hungry, toasted, the thin parents of children made of spindles and stone; they wrapped their noses and mouths against the dust and their eyes looked out from behind the guardian nets of eyelashes. They crossed themselves and sprinkled water on their faces; and there was not one of them who did not carry the image of a saint, of the sorrows and roses of the mother of gods.

They stood in the yard where the wind blew, and they ate and drank the gifts of the family of Apriscos. Some sat in the dust. Women ate tortillas while their infants nursed. Some children slept after the long walk, curled in the dust, resting their heads on the thighs of their mothers, lost in the safety of skirts. The men were on parade, brave and barefoot, circling the women, dangling the curled horns of their hands.

In the early afternoon, the sleeping hour, Azcatl took his place on the stump. He wore city clothes and city shoes. The wind took his long black hair, making stripes on his face. He shook it into place after every gust, he combed it with his fingers. He was thin, thinner in the dark striped suit and black shoes; the skin of his face was like a skull's glove; his eyes shone, his eyes had no light. He coughed, he emptied his throat of coughing before he spoke:

"Brothers and sisters, Mexicans, lawbreakers. I come here to ask you to break the law again. You've broken one law by coming here; I ask you to break another. Because you have a choice: to break the law and be human beings or to adjust your lives to the law, and then to live, at best, at the very best, as domesticated animals.

"The law chains us, the law enslaves us. To break the law is to be free!

"And what is the law anyway? The law of the fugitive! The law of the landlord! The law of hunger! The law of confiscation!

"What do you have here? Ask yourselves. Think of the rents you pay, the rents that go up year after year to support the landlords in their rich houses, to send their sons to foreign lands, to send their wives to the Capital, to keep Don Porfirio in silk hats and handsome carriages. When there is drought, the rents go up. When there is plenty the rents go up. Every year they take a little more and a little more. That is the law! The law takes! The law is a thief!

"I ask you to be unlawful, to break the law, to put bread in your mouths and milk in the mouths of your children!

"The law humbles, the law makes us effeminate; breaking the law strengthens, breaking the law frees.

"A revolution is coming, brothers, and soon. All over Mexico our brothers are preparing to break the law, to vote with their guns and their knives, to free themselves and their children forever, to end the confiscations and the slow starvation of the high rents and the exorbitant prices of the company stores. Brothers, the revolution is beginning in the mines and the fields and the open ranges. The revolution is beginning in the cities and in the mountains. The teachers are ready to break the law, the students are ready, the women are ready. What about the men? Are the men ready for freedom, are the men ready to be men?

"But do not tell me so easily that you are ready. Tell me the truth. Tell me that you are ready to fight for your liberty! Tell me that you will fight until death against the laws that have made us all slaves! Tell me! Shout to me! Are you ready?"

"Yes!" they shouted. "Yes! We're ready!"

"Then strike! Begin with the strike! When the landlords raise the rents, strike! Pay them nothing! Eat what you reap! Show them guns and machetes when they ask for corn and cotton! Show them that you're men! Show them! Break the law! Strike! Strike!"

They applauded him, they took his words for a gift, they answered him with promises. He stepped down from the stump into their hands, lying in them, in the bed of their hands, held in them, praised by the touch of them. Villa asked Liviana to bring him into the house. "I want to hear him more," he said. "I thought he was speaking to me, and I want to know, I want him to explain."

He waited in the patio until the others had gone and Liviana and her grandfather led Azcatl through the house to the open place. There were spring flowers, the light was soft, falling roundly over the walls of the house; it was quiet now that the neighbors had gone. The last of the carts, the last of the burros, had disappeared down the hill that led to the town. The two aunts in black dresses fled through the house. Azcatl came on the arms of Liviana and the grandfather, held between them. The pockets of his suit were stuffed with food, two cheeses were suspended on a string hung over his shoulder. He chewed something; the tight skin of his face revealed the chopping and grinding of his jaws.

"This is my husband," Liviana said, "Pancho Villa."

Azcatl pushed the food into his cheek. "The bandit?" he asked.

"The lawbreaker," Villa said.

"The first stage of the revolution," Azcatl said. He sucked the lump of food into his mouth and swallowed it. "Destruction of the existing order, the tearing down of the repressive social structure. Very important."

"Who do you work for?" Villa asked. "Will you be here when they have the strike? Will you break the law too?"

Azcatl smiled; the skin of his face was formed into rows of lines. "I've already broken the law. In my way I'm more of a bandit than you. I don't steal and I don't kill, not yet I don't kill, not until the time comes. I go from one town to the next; I'm a teacher; I tell the people about liberty. You heard me. I broke the law by telling them, and they broke the law by listening to me. We're all lawbreakers now, Mr. Villa. We're all brothers."

"Who pays you? Who do you work for?"

"I'm glad you're interested. I wanted to talk to you or your grandfather about that problem. For a while, I was paid by a Liberal club in the United States; they sent me ten pesos a week to cover my expenses, but since I've been traveling out in the hills in these small towns I haven't had a chance to collect my money, my money for expenses—you know, for a train ticket, a taco here and there, a pair of shoes, a clean shirt. Look at these shoes I'm wearing, just look at them." He lifted up his trouser leg so they could see his thin black shoes. They were laced with white string. The soles had come away from the tops along the outside. "How can a man go around wearing such shoes? Stones come in through the hole in the side. Dust collects under my stocking. Imagine what it will be like in winter! Besides, it's an embarrassment; a man like me, a teacher, a graduate of the college of secondary school teachers, a fluent speaker of the French language, should not appear dressed this way."

"What do you want?"

"Fifty pesos."

"After the strike," Villa said. "If you live through the strike, I'll give you a hundred pesos."

Azcatl sneered, turning away from Villa, avoiding his eyes. "Not me," he said. "I have work to do. There are a hundred towns to visit, a hundred strikes to start. My work is too important for me to stay here and wait for these people to get ready to strike. When the time comes, if there's enough advance information, we'll send someone to help with the political education of the strikers. But not now; I can't wait."

"Where do you live, Mr. Azcatl?"

"Now?"

"Yes," Villa said, "now. Where is your home? your wife? your mother? Where do you stay?"

"The revolution is my home."

Villa reached into his pocket and took out a handful of gold pieces. He opened his hand and held out the money to Azcatl. "Take your fifty pesos," he said. "Then ask Pedro to drive you to the railroad station. Get on the train and go where you're going and never come back."

"As you like," said Azcatl, taking the coins out of Villa's palm. "As you like. I didn't mean to offend you. I didn't realize you were opposed to the revolution. If I had, sir, I can assure you I wouldn't have come here to your grandfather's house."

"He can come any time," the old man said to Villa. "My house is his house. He is as welcome here as you are."

Villa looked at Azcatl. "You understand?"

"Yes, sir. I won't come back here, I promise. You have nothing to fear. I thank you for your hospitality, for your gift of money to the cause of liberty. And I know I should leave it at that, but I can't. Let me ask one more favor of you, which is to tell me how I have offended you. It's important to our party. What is it that I said or did that offended you?"

"Nothing."

"Tell him," Liviana said.

"Anything to please my dear wife," Villa said. "Your name is wrong," he told the revolutionary. "In the mountain languages Azcatl doesn't mean anything. It's the word for all ants, not for any ant. Nothing is called Azcatl, nothing but you. So why did you take the name? To trick the rurales? No. To trick us. You wanted us to think that because of your name you came up out of the ground, like the ants and some of the first people. You wanted us to think because of your name that you were part of a great family of workers, like the ants. Well, you haven't fooled me. Every ant has a name that tells what it is. Your name is Icel Azcatl, which means the Lone Ant. It's the big red ant that you always see walking by itself. Icel Azcatl; it's not like any other ants: it lives alone and works alone; it's the only ant that has no sting and no sweetness to eat. Goodbye, Mr. Icel Azcatl, goodbye."

Liviana and the old man saw the anger overtaking Villa; they had learned to read the color of his eyes and to listen for the constriction of his throat that caused the words to come in pumped spurts. They said nothing. The revolutionary went to the front of the house and waited there with his cheeses and his city clothes while Pedro hitched up a horse to the light wagon. Villa stood on the other side of the great wooden doors, listening, giving the appearance of a man who would not tolerate even one more word from his antagonist. Liviana and the old man waited until they heard the wagon going down the hill toward the town, then they spoke their reproach. The old man told Villa that he was uncivilized, a violator of the rules of hospitality. Liviana said that he was an animal, a preying beast more at home in the mountains or the desert than in the world of human beings. They said that he disgusted them, that his habit of eating with the knife and fork and spoon he carried in his pocket was the rudest thing they had ever seen.

He listened to them for a long time. He listened to all their accusations, and he made no attempt to answer. The voices were like the sounds of hungry birds. The old man looked like a hopping goat, Liviana's face thickened and her lips turned pulpy and dark. They criticized his upbringing, they criticized his youngest brother for his profligate habits, they criticized his sister for her blank sadness, they criticized all of his sisters and brothers for being parasites. He was selfish, they said, a selfish simpleton who repeated himself like an Indian when he spoke. They talked and talked, and when at last they were quiet, he said to Liviana, "You eat too much chocolate; there are pimples on your chin, there are red blotches, there are pustules on your chin. I do not like to look at them."

Liviana put her hand to her face. Villa laughed.

"Shame," the old man said, "shame."

Villa opened the door and stepped over the stone threshold. He looked back at Liviana and the old man. She had not taken her hand from her face. The old man was close beside her, narrow in black and embroidered white cotton, the owner of a thin and pointed beard. "Shame," he said again, looking his distaste at Villa.

"With women and horses it's the stock that counts," Villa said. Then he pulled the door closed to shut out the answer that would have come from the old man.

He went to the yard where the stables were being built and called Soto and the others together. They saddled the horses and left that evening, heading north toward the Nesting Mountains, riding slowly along the arroyo, keeping the horses at a walk. There was no reason to hurry. They loafed, starting late in the mornings, stopping to hunt for deer or wild turkeys, making camp before the sun went cool. Villa spoke very little, and then only to Soto. He confessed that he did not feel any longing for his wife. One woman was like another, he told Soto; whores were no good, but one woman was like another. He made the same confession every day. On the fourth day, Soto made a comment; he said, "You married late, brother."

In March, the wind was more than they could bear; no barricade they could erect would contain it. The horses were restless, frightened day and night, refusing to crop grass. The men had to wear kerchiefs over their faces whenever they went out of the caves. They could not endure the wind; they abandoned the caves and went down to the towns. Villa, Soto, Urbina, Aprisco, and the Solís brothers went to Chihuahua. The wind was also

[268]

there, but they lived in houses. After a few days, Urbina went on to a small farm near Santa Rosalía. The others stayed in Chihuahua, an escort for Villa, who lived again with his wife in the house on Tenth Street.

Liviana was not a docile woman when they were together, but when he had been away she lost her gentleness entirely: her embrace resisted, she was hard ground, a woman dressed in starch. If he sought to seduce her, she drew away, she moved along the wall following the farthest corners; if he sought to conquer her, she did not deny him anything, but when he touched her mouth he found her teeth cold and clenched, the sign of her will. "There are other women," he said.

"Go back to them."

"I haven't been with any other women."

She made rueful sounds that could have been mistaken for laughter, peckings of breath. He was a poor husband, she said. He demanded to know why they had no children; he asked for his sons. She answered that sons must have fathers. They were neither lovers nor enemies; they lived in the same house, friends in dispute. She presented her breasts, she gave him chocolate, she opened her thighs; they rocked the iron bed, the tiles of the floor sang, the bedsheets whirled, the wall was chipped; she slept at the edge of the bed only one step from the cold tile floor.

"You were different when I worked in the shop," he said.

"We were a family."

"You're my wife now too."

"No," she said, "not your wife, something else. A wife is every day of your life, like your food. A wife makes a man strong; what am I to you? This time you were gone for a season, the next time it will be a year. When you come back to this house, you're a stranger: your hands are different, you wear clothes I've never seen before, the size of you is a surprise, you smell of deer or cattle or smoke under the dust; I don't recognize your smell, I don't recognize the feel of your hair or the strength of your arms; the way we fit is not the way I remember us. I'm always a widow with a new man in my bed; I feel shy, I'm afraid of you."

"You could run away."

"You could stay home."

After a week, he was more comfortable with her. After two weeks, he did not know how to live the days: he had no land and he had no work; he was neither a shopkeeper nor a farmer; he had no place; he came from another town. He paid a thousand pesos to Claro Reza to warn him if the police or the rurales knew he were in the city. He visited his brothers and Martina in the house on Eighth Street. Antonio worked in a dairy; when he was not away at delivering milk, he was asleep. Hipólito gambled, winning at cards and dice, losing at horse races; he was slim and perfumed, the darling of

[*269*]

the whores. Martina sat in the patio of the little house, resting on folded legs, a stalk among the dried flowers. In the evening, Antonio's wife went into the patio and brushed the insects from her hair and the folds of her skirt and led her to the dinner table.

With Eleuterio Soto and the Solís brothers, Villa built three more rooms onto the house on Tenth Street. The front was wide, touching the houses on either side, and the new rooms that led back from the street were the beginnings of the enclosure of a patio. In the beginning of April, Urbina came up from Santa Rosalía, bringing eight others with him. Feliciano Dominguez came in the next day, and the day after that the Yaquis and José Sánchez arrived, bringing ten more with them. Bárbaro Carillo and five more came to Chihuahua on the first day of the second week of April. Luis Beltrán was the last to arrive, coming with seventeen old men like himself, all of them with gray whiskers and pictures of saints on their hats. They arrived on burros and mules—five came together in a cart—for Luis had told them that Pancho Villa would give them horses and new rifles and make them rich. Villa scattered them over the city, he sent them to rooming houses and hotels, and a few went into the hills near Millas north of El Fresno to wait. There were fifty-two; they could go to the big mines, they could take any herd, they could conquer whole towns. Soto, Urbina, and Villa sat in the newest room of the house and counted the value of the towns and mines and herds of Chihuahua.

Liviana did not enter the room where the men sat all day speaking of cattle trails and the wealth of mines. She sat in the kitchen of the house. She ate prickly-pear fruit and soothed the sting of it with chocolate. The flesh of her cheeks thickened, the view into her eyes narrowed, they were no longer child's eyes. She went sometimes to the house on Eighth Street to visit Martina, who still sat out her days among the dead flowers.

The soldiers came back from San Andrés on the morning train: two carloads of men and eight cars of horses. They had two small pieces of artillery and an automatic gun. Their return was seen by two of the old men who came with Luis Beltrán. They had gone to the rail yards to steal melons and bolts of cotton cloth, and instead they saw the soldiers arriving, more than a hundred men with the odor of exploded powder still on them. The graybeards watched the unloading of the troops and the horses; they saw the quiet of the men, they saw the nervousness of the horses and the tenseness of the men with them; and they reported everything they had seen to Luis Beltrán, who went to the house on Tenth Street to tell Pancho Villa.

Villa sent Liviana and Pedro to San Andrés by train. He put ten men on the train with them for an escort and took all the others overland with him.

They rode the distance in two hours, spurring the horses uphill, gathering them, pushing them to maintain their gallop through the narrow places; and when they came to the town, they saw that it was too late, the ride had been useless, a waste of the horses; they saw the women weeping in the streets, the bodies hanging from the poles and the trees; they saw the fire in the granary and smelled the charred corn, the charred wheat, the charred flesh.

The soldiers had been gone since early morning, and the people had not put out the fire, they had not cut down the bodies of the hanged, they had not buried the dead. They wept, they chased the children from the streets where the bodies hung from the trees and the poles and the dead lay in the hard dirt. They chased the dogs, they chased the birds with stones. The women beat their chests and threw water on their faces.

More than ten had been hanged. Their trousers had been cut from their waists; the cloth lay in rolls about their ankles. The bellies of some had been cut open; their entrails hung like strings of bloody spittle, reaching down to the street. The soldiers left them naked to show their shame, the way they fouled themselves, the way their organs hung sticky and shrunken.

Villa rode down the row of hanged men: the grandfather was not among them. He walked his horse through the street, looking down at the women, pausing at each body to inspect the face: the grandfather was not among them. He saw men who had come to the Aprisco house near the arroyo. They looked older; they had been dead since early morning. He spoke to the women, calling them by their names, but they did not look up. He saw their bare feet under them, behind their skirts. He saw their hair still in fat night braids. He asked for Grandfather Aprisco, but they did not look up; they wept, they were mute, they heard the birds on the air and threw stones, they heard the nails of the dogs on the hard dirt and threw stones, they did not hear the horse or the man who called their names.

Villa and the men who followed him tied up their horses in a place upwind of the granary and went down to the well. They wet their clothes and put wet kerchiefs over their faces to protect themselves from fire and smoke, and then they walked back to the big stone building. Eleuterio Soto said he would enter the building. He removed his cartridge belts and covered himself with wet ponchos. Smoke came out of the windows of the granary; smoke and little tongues of flame came through the tiled roof. Soto tried to open the small door, but the handle was too hot for him to touch. He went to the large doors, the wagon doors, but they were bolted from the inside. For a moment, he did not know what to do; he paced from door to door, looking for a place. Suddenly, he rushed at the small door and attacked it with his foot, driving the heel of his boot against the lower panels. The wood split. He kicked again, and his boot went through. When he pulled his foot out, flames followed, crawling up the outside of the door.

He came back to where the other men stood. "It's an oven," he said. "No one can go in there."

Three small boys came out from behind the bank building and stood with the men to watch Soto. Villa caught one of them, a small boy in a faded red shirt and dirty white pants that dragged in the street. He held him by the shoulder, squatting in front of him to look at his face while they spoke. "Who's in there?" he asked the boy.

"People."

"What people?"

"My cousin Felipe and some others."

"An old man?"

"Yes."

"What did he look like?"

The boy shrugged, and Villa let him go.

It was near the end of the day; the train was due. Villa went to the little station house to wait for Liviana. Soto and the others cut down the hanged men and covered them with sheets and blankets from the dry goods store. A doctor in a black frock coat walked through the main street of the town examining each of the corpses. He was followed by a fat woman in a white dress who wrote down the names of the dead men. The roof of the granary collapsed, sending a thunderous wind through the town, spreading smoke and ash everywhere. People came out of their houses, threw water on the burning ash that fell near them, touched the wet ash to be sure there was no danger, and went back inside. An old brown dog with an upcurled tail sat on the edge of a blanket that covered a hanged man. It raised its head once and howled, then it lay down beside the man.

The doctor went to the station house where Villa waited. He was a tall man with hair that grew back thickly from the middle of his scalp. "You're Pancho Villa," he said. Villa reached for his pistol. "No, no, my friend; I'm a doctor." He spoke with a strange accent, as if there were a piece of soft food in his mouth.

"What do you want, Mr. Doctor?"

"We have to bury these people or burn the bodies; if not, there is a danger of disease."

"Are there so many?"

"Twenty-five," the doctor said. "And more in the granary."

"Poor things," Villa said.

"You're crying," the doctor said, astonished.

"Why does that surprise you? Even the dogs are crying."

"Forgive me," the doctor said, bowing slightly. "I was not thinking. I was only concerned for the health of the town. These people must be buried or the bodies must be burned or there will be disease. Will you help me?"

Villa shook his head. "Let the priest attend to that."

"The priest was with the soldiers."

Villa slumped against the side of the station house. His hat was pushed forward, tumbling over his face. He caught it with both hands as it fell. "I should have known," he said. "The priest. I know that priest, sir. He prayed for me at my wedding. A good priest, they told me. But I saw that he was a fat one; he likes cheese and sweet cakes, he drinks coffee mixed with chocolate. At my wedding, he drank too much and fell asleep. We all laughed at him and said what a good priest he was! Now I have to kill him." He looked over at the doctor. "Yes, tell the boys to bury those poor ones. Tell them Pancho Villa said to do it."

Eleuterio was behind the doctor, standing quietly, the rifle cocked, listening, watching the doctor's elbows, prepared to race the sudden movement. When the doctor went back to the main street, Eleuterio went with him; the doctor in his frock coat walked with measured strides, with stiff shoulders; the man in the wet ponchos lumbered, the plowman's walk, the wide-set walk.

The women put the bodies in rows, they dragged them, they straightened their feet and closed their eyes and wrapped sheets and blankets around their wounds. The dead were in two rows. The women folded their hands on their chests, working quickly, preparing the dead as they always prepared the dead. They pulled up the trousers of the hanged men and tied them with their string belts. By their work they made the dead appear to be in order again.

Soto and Urbina went to the church and brought the priest out into the street, to the rows of orderly dead. The priest looked for a smooth place in the street, brushing away the pebbles with his foot. He pulled up his cassock and lowered himself, one leg at a time, to his knees to pray. The fat of his belly and buttocks swelled the lower part of the cassock. He prayed, the quick Latin resonating in his nose. The women gathered, watching; they did not kneel. The priest's hands were clasped, his head was lifted up to Heaven. Soto crushed the priest's skull with the butt of his rifle. The women crossed themselves. The cart came to take the bodies to the cemetery. The women loaded the dead onto the cart, stacking them like wood. They stacked the priest among the others. A woman pulled up the hood of his cassock to hide the wound. A drummer and two horn players walked behind the cart. They played loudly in measured beats, like a war song. The women followed, hiding themselves in their shawls, weeping. The children came last. They did not know the name of the song. Everyone walked slowly; they were all in rows, all in order, honoring the Liberal sharecroppers of San Andrés.

When Liviana arrived, Villa took her directly to the house near the arroyo. He told her that he did not know about the grandfather. There had been shooting, executions, he said, but he did not know about the grandfather. She saw in the light of the lanterns that he had been crying. She touched his eyes with her small handkerchief. "How macho!" she said, with a laugh that ended in sobbing. Villa held her against his shoulder until someone brought a buggy, and they rode slowly up the long hill to the Aprisco house.

They found the old man in his bedroom, sitting in a chair with his face to the wall and a rosary in his lap. "Thank God," Liviana said.

The old man said nothing.

Villa went across the room and stood by the grandfather's chair. He saw that the old man's shirt was open at the collar and the top buttons of his trousers were opened. He had wept some time earlier in the day; the strings of mucus had dried in his mustache. "You were lucky to get away," said Villa.

The old man did not move, he did not speak.

Liviana came and knelt beside him. She laid her head on his leg, as she had when she was a child, but she suddenly jerked herself upright, she pushed herself away from him. The old man's leg was wet and stinking, his bladder had failed. Liviana put her hands in her hair. She made claws of her fingers, she cut her skin. "Oh, my dear grandfather, my poor grandfather, my dear, my darling, my old darling!" She wobbled on her knees, she wailed. Her face was squeezed with grief, her mouth was crushed. Villa lifted her up and carried her from the old man's room.

He carried her to a bedroom where they had slept before, and he laid her on the bed and covered her with a rough blanket and begged her to sleep; but she would not, she asked first to know what had hurt the old man, how he had been wounded. The father came into the room, the unseen father, the shadow between Liviana and the old man. "I saw it," he said. "I saw him come riding up the hill. When the shooting started in the town, I ran outside to look, and I saw my father come riding up the hill on Sweetwater, the big mare. He lost his hat, the big hat with the silver on it."

"He ran away," Villa said.

The father nodded. His eyes were dark and deeply circled, owl eyes but for the sorrows of them. Villa had not understood his eyes before. The father looked away, around the room, at the floor and the ceiling, at each of the walls and the corners of the walls, before he showed his eyes again to Villa. "He should have died there, Francisco; but it's always been like that with him, he has no luck."

[*274*]

Liviana said nothing, she tried to sleep. In the middle of the night, she awakened and gave birth to a dead child. She tried to hide it in the sheets, but Villa was awake, watching her. He saw that the child was no larger than a man's thumb.

13

There are omens.

Because I know the omens, some say that I am a sorcerer. They put a knife in water when I am near. It is not true; I am not a sorcerer; because I know the omens, they say that I am a sorcerer. It is not true.

There are omens. I learned them from my father, who learned them from his father. They have been known since ancient times. There are omens of the person, there are omens of the family, there are omens of the world. The day of birth is an omen, the hour is an omen. The day of naming is an omen, the hour is an omen. It is true, it has always been true, it cannot be changed.

There are omens of the night and the day, of the house and the town and the field and the forest. When an animal is heard in the night and it is like the sound of a woman weeping, the one who hears will die in war or in sickness. He will die like a slave. His children will suffer. Disaster will linger in his house.

When the horned owl hoots, death comes soon after. If it stands on the roof of a man's house and hoots, the house will be defiled; waste will be thrown in the doorway, strangers will urinate in the yard, strangers will defecate in the yard, the house will stink, weeds will grow, salt will appear in the soil, the walls of the house will crumble, the house will lie in ruins.

The screech owl and the weasel bring sickness, they bring calumny against one. A rabbit in the house brings ruin. Ants appear in one's house by the wish of dead enemies; they signify the coming of death, they signify that the wishes of one's enemies will come true. There are other omens: the severed head, the tiny girl, the night axe, the giants, the red spider, the tamal that sticks to the pot, the creaking roof beam, the broken grinding stone. All these are omens of the person, of the family. Even the warning of the coyote seen in the day is only an omen of the person, an admonition from Tezcatlipoca.

Of all the omens, one is the worst, one is an omen of the world: citlalin popoca, the smoking star; it is the sign of war, of death and hunger. Even its tail, citlalin tlamina, is a dart that always ends in death, that always strikes a living thing and turns it into a poisonous worm. On the second night of the month of Tóxcatl, the beginning of the rainy season, the omen appeared. Every living thing was afraid. The people hid in their houses, the cattle would not lie down in the fields, the coyotes called in a strange voice, the birds awakened and complained to the cold, smoking light that disturbed the sky. I put a mirror upon my head to protect myself from the dart and went outside to study the omen and to remember what Nezahualpilli had said to Motecuhzoma.

The *Chronicles* say that the Emperor met with the King of Texcoco to ask his advice about the smoking star, and Nezahualpilli told him it was the sign of catastrophe: death, misfortune, the ruin of everything the Mexica had built, the loss of all they had won in the wars, the end of the Empire. He also foretold his own death by the sign of the star. The Emperor mourned his fate and the fate of the Mexica. He begged Ometéotl, the Lord-who-invented-himself, to tell him some reason, to explain why the destruction would occur during his reign. Then the Emperor wept and kissed the hands of the King of Texcoco, who had been his friend and ally and the wisest man since Tlacaélel. Ten years later the catzopines arrived. First they took her, La Malinche, and raped her and made her their mistress, and then they raped the Empire and made it their mistress; we all lived in a destroyed land, the descendants of La Malinche, the bitter sons of a raped woman, the orphans of the catastrophe predicted by the smoking star.

We were deceived, we deceived ourselves. We looked at Cortés and we thought he was the Monk of Teotihuacán returning from Heaven. We thought, and what fools we were, that he was the sign of the end of evil in the world; Quetzalcóatl, who had brought man back from the land of the dead, had returned to give goodness back to man. But if Cortés was a god, he was a god of Mictlan, the place of the dead; he was Mictlantecuhtli, the Lord of the Place of the Dead; we called him *temictiani,* the killer.

So the end was prophesied and the end came. How did the few destroy the many? Do we truly live by the will of the gods? In the schools, the wise men, those who could teach a man how to have a face, debated the question. The poet had asked if our lives on earth were merely a dream, the poet had asked if we should not see the world as it was. The wise men debated. There were gods, there had to be a beginning, Ometéotl, the one-who-invented-himself. If Ometéotl had invented himself, he could also have invented his sons, he could also have invented Coatlicue, the mother of his sons. They debated: if a god had the will to invent himself, he had the will to invent everything, the world was the will of the gods. Then what was life on earth?

Empires are made by soldiers, who invent nothing. Wise men and poets and sculptors, even the historians who write out time in red and black inks, are inventors. But empires are made by soldiers; the symbol of empire is the eagle, not the quetzal. It was told to me by my father, who was told by his father, who was told by his fathers before him, that the few were able to destroy the many because the many were beholden to soldiers, who invent nothing. Is it true or are omens true? I listen to the wisdom of my fathers, but I also know that there are streetcars in Tenochtitlán. Did Ometéotl destroy the Empire? Then I must ask the question Motecuhzoma asked: why? If he destroyed the Empire, he must also have built the Empire; why did he build what he intended to destroy? Of all the gods, Ometéotl—the one who is two, the one who invented himself, the one we cannot imagine —is the most difficult to understand.

In the calmécac the wise men taught and debated with one another. Had there been time, perhaps they might have learned the answers to all the questions. They spoke to each other, they learned from each other. I am alone, without an heir or even a student; Pancho Villa is a soldier. What shall I do? I have seen the most disastrous of omens, the nation is terrified, the end of the world is predicted; and I have no one to tell what was told to me, I have no one who will be heir to my questions.

When the smoking star appeared in the sky, the people came to my house, they sent delegates to my house. Was it time to scream and pat their mouths? they asked. Was it the end of the world?

I asked questions in return: What is the end of the world? If life on earth is a dream, and one awakens, is that the end of the world? If life on earth is real, and one dies, is that the end of the world? If the world ends, and one continues to dream, what will he dream? If the world ends, and one continues to live, how will he live?

Because I answered their questions with questions, they laughed at me, they went away in disgust, they said I was good only for curing warts and getting rid of fleas. A few said that I was a sorcerer who would not reveal his secrets, and they made threats; but I laughed at them, asking what secrets they would learn from a corpse, asking if they intended to eat my flesh to learn to be sorcerers themselves. And there were also a few who truly wanted to know, and to these I told the history of the suns, to these I spoke of the end of days, the end of counting, the death of time.

Four times the world has been destroyed: after the flood, men were changed into fish; after the fire, men became birds; after the wind, men became monkeys; and when the world was the place of giants, the jaguars came and ate them. This is the Fifth Sun, the last world, and it will be destroyed in earthquake and fire.

An old woman came forward from the group who sat in my flowery room, and she said, "The order of the worlds is not as you say. Tezcatlipoca was the first sun. He made a world of giants, but Quetzalcóatl defeated him in war, he struck him with his staff, and Tezcatlipoca fell into the water and emerged in his disguise. Then the jaguar Tezcatlipoca devoured the giants, then the world had no sun. After that came the wind, and then the fire, and then the flood."

A sheepherder from the north, a cowboy on one of the ranches, came forward. "This is the fourth world," he said. "It will end in madness, in tumbling, in endless tumbling." And another, a widow peering out from her black shell, a lover of the Spanish clergy, made the sign of the cross, and said, "This is the only world. After this world, there is only Heaven or Hell." The dispute ended when a peyote eater, perhaps a Huichol (I did not know him), stood up and told in the arrogant way of the peyote eaters that he had heard the words of Mictlantecuhtli himself, that they had come to him on the cold, hellish wind of the north, Mictlampa ehécatl, that he alone knew the future of the world. We were curious, all of us in the room; we asked him to reveal what he had heard. He took his orange and black and white and yellow bag from his shoulder and overturned it. The brown knobs, the gritty, bitter, nauseating knobs, tumbled onto the floor. "There," he said, "there is the truth." Everyone laughed.

I did not tell them the name of the year, I did not show them the calculations, according to the day count. They would not have been comforted; they were unable to know that the end of the world could not come for thirteen more years, they were unable to know it was yet thirteen years before the end of the cycle, before the moment of darkness that precedes the lighting of the New Fire.

For a long time afterward I stayed in my house. I saw no one, I lived among flowers and incense fires, I ate nothing, I pierced my tongue, my arms, my legs, my penis; I thought. In the obsidian mirror I saw the shards of a cooking pot. Every night I heard the woman weeping, her voice multiplied by the hills. The truth is that I am the last of my time, the truth is that the world ends in many ways. I stay in my house and ask questions that I cannot answer. The smoking star is the prophecy of war, famine, disease, death, ruin, the fall of empires; the omen is known. But is it the will of the gods or the will of men that the star prophesies? What is told? Do we truly know the names of the gods, the order of the worlds? If I am the only one, I am merely arrogant, like a peyote eater, like a mushroom eater. If I am the only one, I am a dreamer, I have no face.

If the gods are implacable, what was the purpose of blood?

Ometéotl, the Creator, is the god who invented himself.

A trolley runs in Tenochtitlán.

Villa came home to Tenth Street smelling of beans and the sourness of a winter on the range. His hair was a thick and greasy pile, his face was stained dark by the sun, everything about him was scuffed and thin. He slumped in the saddle, swaying with the walking horse, looking down over its neck, like a cowboy worn out by the winter. Soto and Urbina rode beside him, José Sánchez and Pedro Aprisco rode ahead, Bárbaro Carillo rode ahead of them, the Solís brothers followed, and the Yaquis followed them. It was early evening; the shoppers were finishing, the workday was finishing, the market was closing, carts and horses moved in the streets; the walks were busy, a murmur ran in the streets, a sigh in the evening air; and the shoes of the horses and burros made their hollow tapping on the cobblestones. The dusty men coming in from the western hills went unnoticed, ten horsemen spread the length of two blocks, all loose and leaning, resting in the stirrups, ten dark men on walking horses in the first free breeze of evening. They were the color of the night, they were no thicker than the wind.

When they came to the house at number 500, the Solís brothers went to the far end of the street and the Yaquis waited at the near corner. The others rode slowly up and down the rows of houses, studying the windows and the doorways, looking for shadows in the lamplight, looking for the reflections of iron washed in oil. Pedro Aprisco dismounted and went to the door of the white house. Villa, Soto, and Urbina waited to one side, holding their horses close to the walls of the houses, making a narrow angle to the door. Pedro knocked at the door.

A voice from inside asked, "Who is it?"

"Pedro Aprisco."

The horses steamed lightly in the growing cold. A woman passed the street at one corner, calling the name of a child, scolding and pleading, bent, holding the wrapping of her shawl close against her throat. The evening train from the south was somewhere in the distance, making its slowing entrance. The lamplight brightened in its comparison with the sky. A door closed somewhere, slamming: a careless, comforting sound.

"It's too long," Soto said, drawing his rifle out of the boot.

Villa gave a soft laugh. "You don't know women," he said.

The door opened. "What time is it?" Pedro asked.

"Time for the rooster to come home," Liviana said. Then she threw the door open wide and embraced him, patting his back, raising puffs of dust out of his jacket, looking over his shoulder for her husband, who was dismounting, giving the reins to Soto, hurrying across the cobblestones to her.

Villa kissed her and embraced her and kissed her again. He stood with his arm over her shoulder and waved to the men in the street, thanking them, calling them boys, his boys. "Bathe," Liviana whispered. "Bathe, and after you bathe . . ." Villa kept waving, smiling, watching them turn the horses, and Liviana continued to whisper the bargain, the promise. When the men were gone and his horse had been led away and the street was empty and quiet but for the woman still calling her child, Villa went inside the house with his wife.

Liviana took him by the hand, leading him to one of the lamps in the sitting room. "I have to see your face," she said. "You sound like my husband, but you smell like somebody's goat; I have to be sure. Let me see now: the chin, the eyes, the hair; it must be my husband." She sniffed him once and screwed up her face. "But it can't be. A man who smells like that could never get a wife."

He felt her shoulders, her arms; he put his hands around her waist, he took her breasts in his hands. "A horse and a woman should feel good."

"You want to see my teeth?" She was giggling, the girl was in her eyes; she walked prancing.

He lifted her up, he danced with her held in the air. "Liviana, Liviana, Josefina Liviana, I love you; how I love you!"

She sent him to wash. She brought hot water, towels and clean clothes. She brought the sweet oil he had left in the bedroom. She brought chocolate for him to sip. All this as if he were a guest, as if a prince had come to her house. She attended him and took him to her bed, with sighs and whispers and the laughter of pleasure, and then the tears of loneliness relieved. And he too was sad afterward, thinking in his bed, beside his wife, of the nights in the Nesting Mountains, the long drives north, the distances that appeared to have no end, the farther mountains. He told her of the moment before they entered a bank or a mine office, of the lights that floated in his eyes, the blind holes that came into the world.

"My grandfather died," she said.

"I heard."

"The priest was made a martyr; they say now that he died for the people."

"I heard that too."

"It's best that my grandfather died; he was a coward."

"No," Villa said, "he was too old, only too old."

They praised the grandfather and wept for him. Before they went to sleep, Liviana cooked a supper of sausages and eggs and brought it in to her husband. She sat at the foot of the bed, weaving her hair into braids, watching him eat.

In the doorway of the house, propped against the narrow inset of the walls, Tacea and Atme, the Yaquis, sat and slept. They were covered by their soft straw hats and thick brown blankets. Beside them, hidden in the blankets, were two Winchester rifles. They were loaded with bullets dipped in the poison Tacea bought from a Pima medicine man.

In the middle of the night Liviana awakened. She did not cry out, as if awakened by a dream, nor did she leave the bed; only her breathing changed, quickening. Suddenly, Villa was awake and turning, grasping for his rifle. She patted his cheek and kissed him. "You taste like eggs," she said.

"Is something wrong? Do you have to use the toilet?"

"No. I just woke up."

"Are you disturbed because I'm in your bed? You must be used to sleeping alone."

A clump of hair rose from one side of his head. It looked solid, like a strangeness in his skull. She smoothed it with the flat of her hand. The clump rose again. She made a comb of her fingers and broke the clump apart. Then she smoothed it again, and it stayed. "Go back to sleep, Francisco. I saw in your face how tired you are. Go to sleep, rest; you need to sleep."

"I never sleep well. I always wake up in the middle of the night. If I'm alone, I move to another place. If I'm in the mountains, I move up so I can look down on the place where I was sleeping. If it's cold, I move to keep warm. If it's hot, I start riding in the middle of the night so I can rest when the sun comes up. I never sleep the whole night, not since I was a boy."

"It's not healthy," she said.

"Yes, I know. Sometimes I'm sick: my stomach swells up and I suffer pains in the back of my head."

"Do you want tea? I can make green tea or cinnamon tea."

He sat up and leaned against the headboard. "No, not now. I'm not sick now, I'm home with my Liviana; how could I be sick now?"

Liviana sat up beside him. They were quiet, sitting stiffly, staring into the darkness of the room. Only Villa's breathing could be heard, the windsound of air in his dry throat. Liviana began to laugh. "We're so funny sitting here," she said, "like two old ladies in church."

They slid down in the bed. She rested her head on his arm. She was turned toward him, her hand lay on his chest. "When you're gone a long time, like this last time, I forget your size, I forget that you're almost a giant."

"It's good to be big; I can always get a job in the mines. They can pay me less than it costs to feed a mule."

"Do we need money?"

The uncertainty in her voice made him laugh aloud. "No, little girl, we don't need any money. Did I forget to tell you? We're rich. We're not as rich as Terrazas or Creel or Martínez, because I left them a little something to provide for our future, but we're rich."

"How much do we have?"

"I don't know. Enough. Ten thousand, a hundred thousand, it makes no difference, I can't do anything with it. We can have chocolate instead of myrtle water, that's all. You can have new dresses, we can build more rooms on the house, but that's all. We can't live like rich people; the day they notice me is the day they'll hang me. Do you understand? I sell more of Terrazas' cattle than he does. I take as much out of the hills as the American Smelting and Refining. But if I raise my head, little girl, you'll be a widow. So we're rich, but we're also poor. The boys who ride with me and live with me up in the mountains are also rich and poor. A thief can't keep what he steals; a thief can't be a rich man, he can only be a thief."

"Then it's worth nothing."

"Well, I don't know. Three days after your grandfather died, the news came to us. We heard how they made a martyr of the priest, how they prayed for him. We heard how they spoke ill of your grandfather. They said he was a coward, a man who couldn't finish what he began. They said he was weak. And who said those things? Who was the slanderer? A foreman on the Terrazas Ranch.

"We talked about it in the camp: Pedro, Eleuterio, Tomás, your husband, we all wanted to do something in the name of your grandfather, to avenge him, right? When I spoke to them, they were ready to do what I wanted. I heard no arguments, no complaints; they did not renege, they went with me that night to the Terrazas Ranch.

"We chose the closest compound, one with a little town next to it, a company town, to be sure, but a town with a bank and stores and a church. We rode in at the rest hour, all of us, coming from every side, and we dealt them one terrific blow. Carillo found the foreman and put a rope around his neck. He made him run behind his horse to the center of the little town. We hanged him, and then we cut off his pants so everyone could see his shame, so they wouldn't be afraid of a foreman anymore. Then we went into the big house. I rode Star Two through the main doors and into the rooms. The men followed me. We destroyed everything: the windows, the tables, the furniture, the rugs; the horses shat and urinated in the house. We put dynamite in the fireplaces and blew them up so there would be no warmth in the house for the rest of the winter. And some of the men found the women of the house hiding in a food cellar. We let the servant women go, but the rich ones had to be shamed. We raped them."

"Did you?"

"No. Because of my sister."

Liviana thought for a moment. "I believe you," she said.

"When we finished in the house, we went back into the town. The people were hiding, they were afraid of us, the bandits. We all sat there on our horses in the center of the little town; we didn't know what to do, we didn't know how to tell the people that we were their friends. A merchant came out in his little round hat with no brim and his striped shirt with the white collar and the fat tie knot. He took off his hat and held it over his heart while he made a speech of gratitude. He said he was speaking for the poor suffering people of the little company town. When he finished the speech, he stood there smiling, with his teeth showing and the hat still held over his heart.

"I said to him, 'Sir, on behalf of all the poor people you speak for I want to make this little gift,' and I shot him through the hat. We all laughed because we knew what a liar he was, how he sold his goods for such high prices and shared the profits with the landlords; we all knew what kind of man he was.

"He didn't die right away; he crawled around on the street, making noises and rolling over and over in the dust. I got down from my horse and took my rifle to finish him off. Then I saw the light of the sun in one of the store windows and I knew what had to be done to show the people we were on their side. I told Soto to finish off the merchant and I went over to the store and smashed the window with my rifle. It was a bakery, with bread and sweetcakes in the window, so I was careful not to get glass in the food. The next store had shirts and dresses and rolls of cloth. I smashed that window too. I smashed open the hardware store and the feed store and the grocery store and even the tavern. Then I stood in the street and called to the people: 'Come and take it! You earned it. You paid for it a hundred times!' A few came out from the row houses, a few young boys. I kept shouting. Finally, they all came out, the whole town. They cut themselves on the glass, they shouted and screamed over the dresses and the hoes and the steel points for the plows. But they were all laughing, and we were laughing too, and the damned foreman was hanging from the big tree near the well."

Villa began to laugh, as if the excitement of the moment were there in his bedroom. Liviana also laughed, but he could tell by the tightness and the broken rhythm of the sound that she was afraid for him.

There was never a night in which he did not awaken, brought out of sleep by a sound, by Liviana shifting in the bed, touching him or moving away, curling a leg or turning her head; or if Liviana and the night were still, the time in him came to the end of sleep and his eyes opened to the dark morning of his own round of days. She awakened with him sometimes, feeling him roaming in the bed, sitting or stretching to the morning, but more often she slept or pretended sleep. Then he walked the house, inspecting the dark rooms, sliding along the walls, studying night in the garden: the moon-eyed insects, the slithering things that ate the earth, the modest flowers. He went on to the small stable or the chicken coop, passing the animals on their folded legs, the birds with their buried heads, leaving them in their sleep, the routine of his night the routine of their night. Then he opened the front door and saw the Yaquis or the Solís brothers or two of Beltrán's old men sitting in something less than sleep, greeting him with the muzzle of a rifle, whispering that the night was quiet, it was safe to sleep, the house could not be entered. Finally, he went back to the bedroom and wiped his feet and returned to the bed to lie with his thoughts, to think of next year or next month, to find nothing, to see nothing, to wait for the police or the army or the rurales, to see nothing, to begin the remembering that always lasted until the morning.

With Soto for his foreman, he built the house, completing the square around the garden, making a portico between the rooms and the garden. Behind the house, he began a series of small houses, the start of a compound, a place for his escort, a ranch inside the city. An entrance to the compound was made on Eighth Street, and two men also slept there in the doorway every night.

The families moved into the compound before the row houses were completed, living without windows, behind unstuccoed walls, sometimes without doors or any furnishings at all, sleeping on mats and eating from dishes that rested on the floor, as they had in times past, in the houses of their birth, before they came to the city. The women helped with the cooking and the washing: great pots were bought, washtubs were bought, ropes were strung between the main house and the row houses, and in the afternoons the clothes hung on them like flags. Children played in the quiet of the wide yard between the main house and the row of small houses. They ran on quiet feet, girls in shifts with long hair flowing, tiny boys, half-naked, decorating themselves with mud and the soft foods infants eat. The sun was brilliant on the white walls, casting hard shadows, silencing. They sprinkled water in the yard to sink the dust. They moved the stable to another place, keeping only the chickens and three milk goats in the yard. They hung the rifles on the walls; they lived at ease, as if it were a secret house. When Villa circled the yard at night, keeping close to the walls, the dogs did not lift their heads, the children slept, the doors remained closed.

Liviana was comfortable in the house; she talked often with the other women, she bought presents for the children; if someone played the guitar and sang of Cananea or little doves or the names of girls, Liviana listened —she closed her eyes and cocked her head and swayed with the music, as if all songs were serenades and all serenades were sung for her. She was the mother of the house and the director; she planned the meals and made the purchases and said who would live in the block of houses and what would be planted in the garden. Sometimes she would spend a morning brushing and braiding a little girl's hair or supervising the grinding of corn. Sometimes she went early to the market to learn the prices or to buy newspapers that showed the fashions popular in the Capital.

She complained to Villa that it was a good life and destined not to last. The smoking star augured ill for them, she said. He would go away again, the rurales would come to the house and drive him away; she would be alone in a great empty block of houses, living like a widow, an old woman of fewer than twenty years. She said those things on the best of days, in the midst of holidays or birthdays or saints' days, while others were singing, after he brought gifts for her; she complained in the middle of laughter, bringing herself to tears.

He answered with comparisons, he told her of his own life in San Juan. He said there were times when the flavor of meat thrilled him, when it was as candy should have been, when he chewed a piece of meat soft and sucked the juice of it and chewed it again and again until there was no sweetness left in it. He told her the taste of weeds and the bitter flavor of an empty stomach complaining in one's mouth. And most often, he spoke of the work without end, the work without reward, the crop that one may not eat, the milk that one may not drink. He reminded her of the darkness of mines and the despair of dry fields and the life without firewood or oil for the lamps.

To soothe her, he listed the goods of their lives in the city of Chihuahua: chocolate and fresh meat, water from a tap, a bed with a mattress, tables, chairs, glass windows, a choice of clothes, the difference of the days. They were rich in matches, light, the number of rooms of their house; they owned a couch and two soft chairs. But most important, he said, they were not owned, they did not live halves.

Liviana would not be comforted. She cried until the tears were exhausted, and then she spoke of others, she recited the armies of the poor, she listed the names of the hungry, she described the nakedness of the children, she mourned the young dead. There is no hope, she said, no justice. She swore she could not bear to live even one more day in this world.

Then Villa agreed to speak of politics. "Francisco Madero is our deliverer," she said, her beginning always the same. And his answer always the same: a shrug and, "I know the ranch in Coahuila. They're rich Jews with friends in the government. Why should he care about the poor? Don't deceive yourself, Liviana; if the rich replace the rich, the poor will still be poor."

"He is our redeemer."

"Is that what Don Perfecto says? One day I'll come home and find Don Perfecto Lomelí in my house, then Mrs. Lomelí will become the widow Lomelí."

"You could talk to him."

"I would rather shoot him."

"You don't care about the poor; their misery means nothing to you. And you lie to me: you agree to talk about politics, about the antireelectionist groups, and then all I hear from you is jealousy."

He took her hands in his and led her to a chair and sat her down and walked up and back in front of her, telling her the same thing every time: "You are not a rich woman who lives in a great house filled with servants; you are the wife of Pancho Villa, a bandit, a man whose head is worth five thousand pesos to our esteemed Governor Creel. I sleep with a pistol under my pillow and a rifle beside my bed. I pay Claro Reza a thousand pesos every month to keep his rurales from finding me here in my own house. It is not possible for me to have a business or a job or a ranch or anything that your rich friends can have. I am a bandit and you are the wife of a bandit. When I first went into the hills, Nacho Parra told me what bandits do. 'We rob and kill,' he said, and that was the truth. I live by robbing and killing, and so do you. I steal cattle to buy you chocolate and I rob mines to put furniture in this house where you live. Liberals are rich men who tell other men how to die. The ones who die are the poor. I will not die for a rich man, because no rich man would die for me. If you brought your redeemer to this house, I would steal his watch and Tomás would pry the gold out of his teeth. And if he wasn't a dwarf, we would take his boots too."

"So you care nothing for the poor."

"I care nothing for the rich."

It was always the same, until the beginning of the summer of that year when the newspapers told of the arrest of Francisco Madero and his imprisonment in San Luis Potosí. "Now they will arrest them all," Liviana said. "Don Perfecto will be next." Villa told her to bring him to the house.

"Will you steal his watch?"

"Is it a gold watch?"

They prepared nine days for the visit of Don Perfecto and his wife. Liviana cooked mole sauce, she arranged for fresh fish to be brought to the house on the day of the dinner, she bought a young goat to roast, and every day she went to the markets to look for the best chiles, to find the perfect asparagus, the most delicate myrtle. She bought cinnamon chocolate and amaranth, wine from Delicias, brandy from Parras, and tiny, sweet mangos de manilla for desert.

The house was decorated with flowers from the market, a trio of violinists was hired to play during the meal, Liviana bought a blue satin dress, and Villa had the tailor make him a suit with a vest and a jacket that had a belt sewn to it. Beside Don Perfecto and his wife, the guests were to be Urbina, Soto, and Hipólito and Martina Villa. Twenty men with rifles were gathered in the yard behind the main house for the protection of Don Perfecto, twenty men with rifles were gathered for the protection of Pancho Villa; a stranger was coming to the house, one of the Liberals who sat in the Plaza de Armas with González and Mayo and Herrera, one of the men whose friends were now in the dungeons of San Juan de Ulúa.

Urbina and Soto arrived early. They were costumed as wealthy ranchers, their pants and jackets were embroidered, their shirts were ruffled, their boots creaked with newness, they wore perfumed grease in their hair. Villa greeted them with snorts and pointings, walking around them, touching the braid and embroidery that decorated them, taking their hats and pretending to stagger under the weight. "You must have robbed a silversmith," he said.

"We were going to buy serious suits, like yours," Soto said, "but the tailor said three old men died last week and he had to use the cloth for shrouds."

Villa put his arms around their shoulders and led them into the house, steering them to the parlor. "Farmer's jokes," he muttered.

As soon as they were inside the room, Soto closed the door behind them. "Lomelí was a colonel in the Federal Army," he said, rushing the words out in a whisper. "How can you allow him into your house? What guarantees did he give?"

"What guarantees do we give him?" Villa asked. "There are twenty armed men in the yard."

Soto nodded, "And twenty more in the streets."

"He's the one who takes the risk," Villa said. "He's the brave one."

Nothing Villa could say would satisfy them. They asked why a colonel was coming to his house, what need they had to talk to Liberals, how they would benefit by the end of the Porfiriato. Villa could not answer the questions. He said he wanted to look at the man, that Liviana trusted him; he reminded them that the leader of the antireelectionists was in prison. They responded with pacing and sour faces. Urbina toyed with his pistol, swinging the chamber out to the side, examining the cartridges, spinning the chamber, closing it into the frame again. Once, he reached over and patted the right side of Villa's coat at the hip, and, feeling the shape of the pistol underneath, he nodded, tightening his face to show the seriousness of the moment.

It was after nine o'clock when Don Perfecto and his wife arrived, and Liviana led them directly to the dining room, calling to Villa as they passed the parlor. The men shook hands when they came out of the parlor. Soto, Urbina, and Villa, each in turn, bowed to Don Perfecto's wife. They smiled, but there was no feeling of welcome in the portico on the way to the dining room. Liviana spoke like a flock of birds, so quickly did her words come out, so scattered were her apologies for the newness of the house, the brother and sister of Villa not yet arriving, the poor quality of the meal, the dishes, the silverware, the candleholders.

Liviana and Mrs. Lomelí walked ahead; Villa, Soto, and Urbina walked with Don Perfecto, surrounding him, studying his striped suit, his narrow, stiff body, the pinkness of his hands, the old paper of his face. They also looked at Don Perfecto's wife, her long black dress, the fit of the sleeves and the way they bloomed at the shoulders, the wooden bearing, the flat, flowered hat no wider than her head. These were people seen passing in carriages; these were the faces and the clothes that came out of coaches, timid and angry, to give their gold to bandits; these were the landlords living in the city; these were the eaters of the halves given up by the people. Neither Villa nor Urbina nor Soto spoke a word, while Don Perfecto said the required compliments about the house, the smell of the food coming from the kitchen, the size of the flowers, roses so early, so many buds on every branch, all seen through columns so neatly stuccoed, so newly whitewashed in this fine house, this well-built house, this handsome house.

They sat at the table, not waiting for the empty chairs to be filled. The wives of the men who lived in the block of houses served the salad of fish and tomatoes. "Bass," Villa said, holding up a piece of fish on his fork. "Caught yesterday night and put in the lemon juice right there at the lake."

Don Perfecto nodded, but did not taste his salad. Instead, he raised his glass of wine: "A toast!" He waited for the others to lift their glasses. "To the Puma of the Sierras, Pancho Villa." Everyone drank but Villa, who touched the glass to his lips and put it down on the table.

"You don't drink?" said Don Perfecto.

"Nor smoke. Smoking shortens one's breath and drinking is best left for old men; that is a rule I learned from the mountain people; it's the way our race was meant to live. Taste the bass; it's better than the wine. Fish is good food for the brain and wine makes the brain spongy."

Don Perfecto ate the fish. "Excellent," he said, nodding to Liviana, "my compliments to you, madame; you set an elegant table."

"In the house where I was born," Villa said, "we didn't have a table. We didn't have chairs and we didn't have beds. The first time I ate meat was when I was five years old, and the only milk I knew was from my mother's breast. Where did you grow up, Don Perfecto? Did you eat meat?"

"Some years yes and some years no. My father was a teacher, Mr. Villa. When the town wanted to pay the teacher, we had meat and milk; when the town didn't like what the teacher was telling the students, we ate gifts from our neighbors. In those days, all but a few schools were run by the clergy; my father had very little luck, so we had very little meat. I went to military school because of the food, and I became an officer and stayed in the army because of the food."

"In the Díaz army," Villa said.

"Yes. I was a colonel in the army of Porfirio Díaz, I was a believer in the idea of science, one of the scientists."

"And now you oppose Tata Porfirio?"

"Yes."

"I don't believe you."

There was quiet around the table. The women came and took the empty dishes. They brought bowls of rice and pots of chicken in mole. They brought hot tortillas to make into spoons for the sauce and chicken. They brought bowls of shredded lettuce in garlic sauce. They brought chía and roast goat and myrtle water and more wine. "I came to your house," Don Perfecto said, "and I came unarmed and unescorted."

Urbina, who was sitting next to Don Perfecto, leaned toward him and said quietly, "If you had come armed, sir, you would have been dead twenty times before you arrived at this house; I gave the instructions."

"But you see, I was not armed."

Urbina smiled broadly. "Of course; what looks smoother than quicksand?"

Don Perfecto defended himself: "It's well known that I oppose the dictatorship." He ate a forkful of the chicken. "Magnificent!" he said, "absolutely magnificent. Mr. Villa, the old saying is true, a woman should be judged by her mole, and you are a very lucky man."

"It is also true," Villa said, "that mole is eaten with a tortilla and not with a fork." He scooped up chicken and sauce in a piece of tortilla and put it in his mouth.

Don Perfecto took a tortilla from the basket and tried to imitate Villa, but the chicken fell off onto his plate and the sauce dripped onto his suit. Liviana quickly dipped her napkin in water and stood up, ready to clean the sauce from Don Perfecto's suit.

"Sit down," Villa said, "he has a napkin."

Liviana took her seat and the meal went on, long and quiet. Near the end, Don Perfecto, who was the first to finish, wiped his mouth, wetting his napkin to clean his mustache. He pushed his chair back from the table to speak: "We would like to have you with us, Mr. Villa. The stories about you that are told in the hills are known to us; the poor people speak of you as if you were a legend. Some say you have the powers of an ancient war god, others say you are a wizard, others say a god protects you and enables you to change into various forms. We do not, of course, subscribe to such theories; however, the leader of the movement against Porfirismo is a man who also believes that certain of the things that happen in this world are beyond our knowledge; he is a spiritist, one who has effected miraculous cures through the use of herbs. All of that aside, we believe that you could be a most important man in our movement, and we are certain that following the success of our movement we can be of help to you, if I make myself clear.

"Our primary interest is in men who are able to talk to people in the mountains and even in some of the smaller towns, and bring them into the movement. It is, of course, a political movement, and you will have to be trained in the philosophy. But your credibility, sir, your prestige among these people would be of inestimable value to us. I am empowered tonight to offer you membership in the Antireelectionist Club of Chihuahua, and I am speaking now on behalf of the president of the club, Don Abraham González." He leaned forward, awaiting Villa's reply.

"I have met Liberals before, sir; they are the people who come to your funeral after you do what they tell you." Villa put his hand to his face and made the gesture of grateful refusal.

Don Perfecto stood, rising slowly, lifting his years. His face was a lantern. "Mr. Villa," he said, "I can assure you that in the event of any armed conflict between the reelectionists and the antireelectionists Colonel Perfecto Lomelí will be in the front line, leading his troops."

He remained standing to greet Hipólito Villa, who entered the room wearing a silk top hat and a morning coat, with a red satin sash diagonally across the front of his starched white shirt. On his arm was a woman in a shiny red dress, a darkskinned woman whose hair had been made the color of carrots and whose cheeks had been painted with thick red grease. The round roll of her bosom showed at the top of her dress. Both Hipólito and the woman were drunk, swaying like sick birds. "Good evening," said Hipólito. "My sister did not wish to come this evening, so I had to find another lady, one who was more interested in the company of bandits and Liberal colonels. May I present the lady who knows the Mexican army best." He poked the woman in the ribs with his elbow: "Come on, cutie, tell them the true strength of a division, tell them what a division is worth to you."

Liviana nodded to the three violinists, who sat in a far corner of the room with their bows poised, and they began to play softly, slow music, with mixed rhythms and variations of melodies that seldom were repeated. Hipólito removed his high silk hat and bowed to the woman in the red dress. "Shall we dance?" he asked, and she answered by holding her dress and bending forward over one knee. Her bosom swelled; the men watched. The drunken couple danced around the table, turning and turning, to a song Hipólito seemed to be singing into the woman's ear. The musicians played,

Don Perfecto remained standing, Mrs. Lomelí sat very straight in her chair, as if there were no dancers in top hat and tight red dress, as if she were concentrating on the music of the violinists. Villa ate, Soto and Urbina watched the woman, turning their heads to follow her, and Liviana sat with her hands covering her face.

On the second turn around the table, Villa reached out and took his brother's arm; he dragged him to the table, he bent him backwards over the point of the narrow end of the table, he shamed him with the strength of his grip. "Sit yourself down," he said, "and eat your supper, little brother."

Hipólito went to the place beside Mrs. Lomelí. The woman sat between Soto and Urbina. "Remove your hat," Villa said to his brother.

"Why? It's a beautiful hat," Hipólito answered in the thick and cheerful words of a drunken man.

Villa reached under his coat, drew his pistol out of the holster, and shot the hat off Hipólito's head. The sound of the explosion thundered in the room. Mrs. Lomelí paled, looking for someone to hold her up, but the only one close enough was Hipólito, who extended his arms, letting her fall against his chest.

"Sir!" Don Perfecto shouted, taking his wife by the cloth of her dress and pulling her up out of Hipólito's arms. "Never, never in my life have I been in the company of such barbarians, such animals."

"For people like us," Villa said, "there is only one way: bread or the stick."

"I said no such thing. The Indian people of Mexico are the soul of the country."

"Please, Don Perfecto, let us be realistic, let us be scientific."

The words were the sign to everyone that it was permitted to laugh. The sounds came from the portico outside the room, from the kitchen, from everyone at the table but Liviana; and behind her hands, which still covered her face as if in shame, it was possible that even Liviana was laughing.

Army officers came to Chihuahua, the garrison was reinforced, cannon and automatic guns were unloaded from the trains. Claro Reza came to the house on Tenth Street to ask Villa to double the amount of money he paid each month for Reza to keep his rurales from Villa's house. Everyone was nervous, Reza said; Liberals, antireelectionists, Masons, and bandits were being arrested in every state, in every city. He and Villa negotiated; the amount of money was increased by half.

In the Capital, a great celebration was being prepared to mark the centennial of the Republic, a column was being prepared as a monument to the heroes of the Independence: Hidalgo, Allende, Aldama, Abasolo, Matamoros, Morelos, and the other dead, the other heroes. A man would dress as

Cortés, another as Motecuhzoma; the ancient clothes were being made again, musicians practiced the old rhythms on drums, flutes, and raspers; a woman was to walk the streets of Tenochtitlán in the costume of La Malinche, the whore of Cortés.

A message was brought to the house on Tenth Street from Abraham González, the nephew of Don Cruz González, who had been the governor of Chihuahua: the head of the antirelectionists in Chihuahua wished to speak with Francisco Villa. The meeting was to be in secret, for Don Abraham was no longer a rich and comfortable man; he waited to be arrested, and he feared he would be treated far worse than Madero, for he had no friends so close to Tata Porfirio, and his protests had begun long before those of Madero—he was the first man to have spoken of the horrors of the massacre at Temosachic.

Villa agreed to the meeting. He told Pedro Aprisco, the go-between, that it would be held in six days, at night, in a place to be named by Villa on the afternoon of the meeting. Villa said he would bring twenty armed men with him and two of them would stand beside him during the meeting. On that day he would also send a sign of identification, which Don Abraham was to show at the beginning of the meeting. To Pedro's questions about the need for such secrecy, he said, "For us to meet is a gift to the rurales; they can kill two birds with one stone." He swore Pedro to secrecy; no one else was to know of the meeting, not Soto, not Urbina, not even Liviana.

For all the six days Villa thought of the meeting. He wished to see the man's face; he could read faces, eyes, the shape of a man's mouth. He did not want to follow a man whose eyes had the narrowness and the hidden red light of his own eyes. He did not want to follow a man like Don Perfecto, a Spanish stalk. And there were so many questions about González: why should the nephew of a governor oppose the government? why should a rich man choose the poor for his allies? what would be changed if the antireelectionists came to power? After Hidalgo there was Temosachic, after Morelos there was San Andrés, after Juárez the grandfather of Liviana Aprisco Villa died of shame, after Allende Agustín Arango died in his half of a field, after Matamoros the son of Micaela Arango was unable to kiss her corpse, after Aldama the thighs of Martina Arango were forced open with the barrel of a rifle; after the antireelectionists what would change?

He thought of the history he had heard, the stories of his house and my house and his years in the hills; men died squealing, like pigs, or they died in anger. All men died; it was best to die in anger. He was afraid.

On the morning of the sixth day, he gave a key to Pedro and told him it would be the sign, then he called Soto and Urbina to the house and told them where Pedro was going and what he planned to do. He asked them to suggest a meeting place. Urbina said, "Go to his house, the place where he's hiding. Keep the house dark. No one can see a target in the dark."

Pedro was sent with those instructions, told to give the key to his go-between in the last hour of the afternoon. Urbina went to watch Don Abraham's house, Soto went to gather the rest of the twenty, Villa went to find Liviana. He took her into the bedroom and closed the door. "I'm going to see Don Abraham González," he said. "I don't know what he wants of me, I don't know what use he has for me. If anything goes wrong at the meeting, Pedro will be here with you. There is money in the house at San Andrés. Tell Pedro it's buried under the stall where I kept Star Two, but don't tell him unless I'm dead—Pedro has his own share."

She showed him the eyes of the girl, the beckoning shyness. He reached around her and loosened the buttons of her blouse. The shutters were closed, the room was dim and still; dresses and nightclothes hung from a wall, shoes were lined up in rows on a stand, a rifle leaned in a corner, the suit of a businessman and the work clothes of a cowboy hung from pegs; soft hats, straw hats and a gunbelt hung from pegs. "It's like the first night," she said.

He stayed the afternoon in the room, sleeping until dinner, awakening in the dark, dressing again, washing his face in the basin, putting on the soft hat and the gunbelt. She cooked a simple meal for him: eggs, chiles, and tortillas. He felt pains in his stomach, his head ached, he could not eat. She brewed green tea for him, and he drank it, thanking her, telling her the pains in his stomach were soothed. He told her about Nacho, how his stomach always hurt and his bowels bled, how he bent in half on his horse and had to be lifted in and out of the saddle.

Soto came for him. "We should have waited two more days," Soto said. "There's still a moon."

"Farmers worry too much about the moon."

"We bagged the hooves for the noise."

"And Star Two?"

"He didn't like it."

"Part of being a man is the noise," Villa said.

The others were already in the street. Carillo held Star Two. When Villa and Soto came out of the house, the men waved to them; then they began moving off toward Don Abraham's house, walking the horses, drifting away from Tenth Street in groups of two and three, the muffled hooves of the horses sounding like wood on the stones of the street. Villa and Soto rode together; Tacea, Atme and the Solís brothers followed.

Urbina was waiting for them. "There are three men in the house," he said. "Lomelí, González, and one I don't know."

They gave the horses to Carillo and went to the door of the house. Villa reached for the doorknob, but Soto pushed him aside and went ahead. Villa and Urbina slipped in behind him, quickly closing the door, shutting out the moonlight that framed them in the dark room.

"I have a sign to return to you." The speech had a northern slowness, but there was no drawl, no singing, only a raggedness, as if the speaker had not slept for a long time.

A match was struck, revealing a man sitting at a table and two other men behind him. The man at the table held the match above the palm of his hand, showing the key to Villa. The match went out and the man struck another. Villa saw that the man's eyes were tired, but without sadness; they were the eyes of a man who had laughed.

The match burned down and went out. Lomelí lit another, leaning forward, illuminating the faces. "What's the use in looking at faces?" Villa asked. "We have to look at facts."

The man who held the key turned to the match and blew it out. In the darkness he said, "My name is Abraham González of the Antireelectionist Party. I believe in democracy."

"And then what?"

The rising of the man made windsounds and rustlings in the dark, quiet room. He breathed in sighs. "There will be a revolution."

Villa opened his arms to Abraham González and embraced him.

BOOK TWO

¡Como una flor es la batalla:
Vais a tenerla en vuestros manos!

Cantares Mexicanos
Translated from the
Náhuatl by A.M. Garibay K.

1

We spoke of war as poets speak; we invoked gods, calling them by their loveliest names: Obsidian Butterfly, Blue Hummingbird, Cloud Serpent, Jeweled Bird, Young Prince, Heart of the Mountains, Lord of the House of Dawn; we did not speak of blood, not ever, not by that name, only by its battle name, Divine Water, the water within the fire.

The beautiful war, the War of Flowers, was the thought of Tlacaélel, the advisor to emperors, the man of the red ink and the black ink. In the *Chronicles* it is told how he said to Motecuhzoma Ilhuicamina that war is like a marketplace of victims; we must never completely destroy the others, for war must go on without end; we must always have war close by, like the market; we must find victims as easily as we find tortillas. It was he, Tlacaélel, who had been the greatest of warriors, speaking in the end of his days, who made the rules: only those whose legs were scarred in battle might wear the long robes, the ankle-length robes. And it was he who made the rule that a common man could also tie his hair in a knot, could also be a knight. It was he who brought flowers to war and gave the Divine Water, Movement, to the Sun of the Age of Movement. Not an emperor but a wise man saved the world.

After his time there have always been the clouds of dust, the trumpets, the drums, the phalanxes clashing, the eagles screaming, the jaguars screaming, the arrows, the spears, the obsidian-edged clubs, the thick shields, the cotton armor, the young men dragged by the hair, by the knotted hair. Since the time of Tlacaélel, there has always been the gore of prisoners in Anáhuac; the streets have been fouled, the water has been bitter, there has been a taste of salt in the earth for five hundred years. And every morning we have seen the sun.

I told him that, all of it, when he was a young man. I showed him the drawings, the knights with their robes knotted over one shoulder, the princes in their paper finery, the warriors in their jaguar suits. I showed him the speech scrolls and remembered for him what had been remembered for me. In my house he found the school of war and the school of wisdom, the telpuchcalli and the calmécac. I taught him the strategy of war as it had been, the plan of battle, the quickness, the manner of making one battle an entire war, arriving, forming the ranks, and then, as if a battle were a man, defeating the enemy with one terrific blow: once the trumpets, once the drums, once the dust, once the war.

He was a boy when he sat in my house and looked at the folded books and listened to what I remembered. It was in the room of flowers. I gave him chía and turkey-egg tamales shaped in the form of a hand. We refreshed ourselves with cool water and the flavor of myrtle. When I told him those things, his shoulders were narrow and the knuckles of his hands were hidden in soft flesh; he was only a boy, it was only history.

Abraham González sat in cool places to drink beer and tell history. His belly rolled, his eyes were the mourners of the four hundred years, his face was a rich and generous house. He told the history longly, serving it as a meal, in courses, with the spices of detail, the corn and vegetables of names and years, the meat of politics, and for sweets the heroes. He did not begin at the beginning, he did not know Aztlán, he spoke from newer books. He neglected the Monk of Tula, he did not know the journey of Xolótl. González had been to the College of Notre Dame; his world began in Europe, in Spain; his history had no age, he spoke it in foreign languages; it was not even half of the history of one sun.

He spoke of the forces of history, as if these were the gods. He talked slowly, ponderingly, stopping now and then to drink his beer, to light a cigar, to ask questions of himself, to seek the meaning of the chronicle; he was the student of his own teaching—he doubted himself, he doubted the doubts. When he most doubted what he said, he turned to the details, as if the truth could be found in the examination of grains of sand.

He confessed to Villa that he taught him this history for selfish reasons: to enlist him, to make him loyal. Villa was grateful; he took the words for gifts, studying them in the wakeful hours of his nights, cultivating them into seedlings, flowers, the begetters of flowers. In the darkness, while Liviana lay sleeping, in the ringing night, the words grew smells and weights, dust, a surface to hold dust, color, colors, heat, movement; the hills were solid, the faces moved, the words spoke words in the vineyards of Dolores not far from the church where the priest sat in shame and anger, listening to the chopping of vines, the cutting of the roots. The room was dark but for the glaring square of the high window. The priest sat on a bench, a thin man, very tall, crumpled over his knees. His cassock was worn and shrunken; when he stood up straight, his ankles could be seen, his frayed and mended sandals could be seen. He looked up at Christ, he heard the sound of the mulberry trees falling, he saw the dark face of Christ, the wide nose, the cheekbones so close to the dark eyes, he heard the silence of Christ at the edge of the vineyard, dressed in old white cotton, dressed in hopeful embroidery, silent Christ, watching while the axes chopped the stalks and the hoes murdered the roots of the vines.

The general from Oaxaca said: Effective suffrage and no reelection.

The dwarf of Parras said: Effective suffrage and no reelection.

The Protestants would have taught us to read instead of making us spend our money on candles for saints.

Night multiplied the words González told in the cool places of afternoons; night fleshed the words, made life of them. Villa saw not in dreams, but in the silent waking hours when he walked the perimeter of the moonlit garden, where the silver lay upon the roses. He saw most clearly when he lay in the narrow bed beside Liviana, listening to her sleep breath. The battles were played out upon the dark ceiling, the room took on the heat of the jungles of Guerrero, he suffered the hungers of Cuautla, he lost his breath in the heights of Zacatecas. The executions took place against the wall of the room. Lerdo's Law rebounded in the room, as it had in the world, confusing him. He gathered questions for Don Abraham; he needed details, explanations. Sleep was an ululation in his nights, he could not separate the dreams from the darkness, the phantasms of Don Abraham's words rode in and out on the waves. He heard the shots of the Emperor's execution, the rifles of Miramon's cavalry as they charged up the hills of Zacatecas. There was answering fire, the coarse bark of a Winchester. Liviana awakened, caught in the bedsheet, her nightdress rolled above her hips, the aspect of her face awry in the sudden change from repose to fear. Tacea cried out, "Rurales!"

Villa raised up on his side to protect Liviana from stray bullets coming through the shutters. "Do what I tell you now," he said. "Roll off the bed on your side. Don't stand up, roll off onto the floor, then crawl under the bed; I'll pass the pillows and the quilt to you. Surround yourself with them, make them into little walls around you. Don't be afraid, you'll be safe there; it's my head they want." The sound of the firing was increasing, bullets sank into the adobe of the house with dull thumps. Soto was at the door of the bedroom, knocking, whispering that the horses were being saddled.

"When will you come back?" Liviana asked, raising her head to look at Villa.

He pushed her head down with his hand. "First I have to get away."

"Animal!"

"Old woman!"

"Tell me when!"

"I'll send word with your brother, I'll give him a message. Now roll off the bed before you get shot for being an old woman." He smacked her buttocks for emphasis. She started to speak again, to continue the teasing, but he shoved her over the side of the bed, tossing the pillows and the quilt after her. The firing had steadied, coming evenly from inside and outside the house. A bullet came through the shutters, cracking the slat, hitting the far wall, and falling to the floor. Soto continued his loud whispers, begging Villa to hurry.

"Not without my pants," Villa said. He took the rifle and cartridge belt that were kept next to the bed, and, bending himself over to keep below the level of the windows, he crossed the room to where his clothes were hung on a peg.

"Where are you going?" Liviana called out from her place under the bed.

"To the Municipal Palace to complain to the President," he said, laughing. "Goodbye, beautiful Liviana."

Liviana told him. She came on horseback from San Andrés, riding like a man, dressed in a man's clothing, wearing spurs and carrying a cartridge belt across her breast. Pedro rode beside her, they rode inside a wide circle of old men, Beltrán's followers, the ragged old men who were delighted with having horses, who were grateful for having food. Villa met her at the foothills of the Nesting Mountains and rode up with her. They did not say but a few words while they climbed to the camp: he asked if she was well, he advised her when to lean forward or back to help the horse, to keep her seat firmly in the saddle; she told him how lonely it had been since he had gone, she said that Don Abraham was safe and well, Madero was still in prison, a man named Orozco was raising an army in the southern part of the state, Cástulo Herrera was talking about another army of the center.

They left the horses in the camp and walked a little way to find a place to speak privately. At the edge of a small mesa they sat with their backs against the side of a hill and ate fat tortillas and dried meat. She apologized for not bringing food with her. Villa laughed. "One meal in two months makes very little difference."

"Do you bring women up here?" she asked.

"Mares, does, cows, one of the men has a bitch for a pet."

"Not even streetwalkers?"

"A long time ago, Ignacio Parra told me: 'Women follow the army and the army follows the women.' Do you understand? If I allowed the men to bring women up here . . . Well, the kind of women who would come up here go with more than one man. They talk. One man is the same as another to them. They would betray anyone."

She reached over and touched his face with her fingers, stroking, promising. Villa took her hand and lowered it to the ground, holding it there between them. "No," he said, "I can't be the only one."

"I miss you."

[*300*]

"It would be unfair," he said. "Besides, we wouldn't be alone." He pointed to a peak above them and to the south where a man with a pair of binoculars sat under the shade of his hat, gazing out onto the slopes of the mountain, slowly raising and turning the binoculars, following the trails, inspecting the draws and the rounds of the hills. "Pedro will take you back to San Andrés."

She withdrew her hand abruptly. "As you say, chief."

"Liviana!"

Then she lay her head against his shoulder, a child in answer, soft against the scolding. "You left me there in the house, you didn't care what happened to me."

"A troop of rurales is no match for you," Villa said. He lifted her face to laugh with her, but he saw that there were tears in her eyes. "I didn't know you were afraid," he said. "I'm sorry. It was the safest thing for you. If they had followed us . . ."

She told him how they had broken open the doors and the shutters, the sound of the wood cracking, the fall of the remaining glass, the boots on the tiles of the house, the spurs jingling, the rifle butts against every door. From her place under the bed she had seen nothing; in the darkness she had dreamed the splintering of the wood, the spray of glass shattering. They had come into the bedroom with their rifles pointed, ready. She had not dared to move, she had not dared to speak. Then they went out of the room, running, circling the patio, banging open the doors. The kitchen was destroyed; she heard the plates breaking, the lower, hollow sound of the pots as they split open on the floor. It was quieter after that. She put one of the pillows under her head and lay back, waiting for them to leave. Suddenly the running began again. They came into the room, stopped. Then another came, running, jingling, carrying a lantern, lighting up the room. One asked if this was Villa's room. It was, said another. They walked up and back across the room. She saw their boots, their thick silver spurs, their gray trousers decorated with silver, buttoned with silver, tight against their legs, their boots. She heard them tear the clothes from the pegs in the walls. She saw the red and white dress falling, the blue skirt, the blouse her mother had embroidered, the pink blouse, the white blouse, the thick brown sweater, the silk blouse, the long skirt, the riding skirt, all torn, all ruined. She cried for her clothes, for the cotton ripped, the silk slashed, the pleated skirt ruined. She told herself she would buy new clothes, her mother would embroider another blouse, the woman from San Andrés would knit another sweater. She comforted herself. She thought of new clothes. She smiled. Then the mattress was lifted away and she saw Claro Reza standing over the bed.

She looked away from her husband while she spoke. Below the hills to the southeast lay the city of Chihuahua. It could not be seen from there in daylight; the dust interfered, the heat curled the light. At night, when all the lights were on, the gaslights and the kerosene lamps and the electric lights, the city appeared as a pale star, low and strange on the horizon, breaking the horizon. The Tarahumaras said it was an omen, the first star caught by the sun, the beginning of the end of the proper order of the world. Liviana looked from the hidden city to the face of her husband. She could not see his eyes; they had become hidden, as if he were looking into the sun.

"Francisco," she said. He looked directly at her. She saw the coruscations in his eyes. They were the color of cinnamon, the surface of mirrors.

"And then . . ." he said.

"Nothing. He laughed. He went away."

"He saw you in your nightdress."

"Yes."

"And he did nothing?"

"Nothing."

"He saw you."

"Yes, but he did nothing."

"He thought something."

"A lot of men think something."

"Go and stay in your father's house."

He saw her back to the camp, and he waited while she and Pedro and the circle of old men mounted their horses and started down the mountain toward the east. They leaned back in their saddles, holding on with the press of their knees while the horses picked their way down the slope. Villa stood on the crest of the mountain above the camp, waving to them until they were lost in the circling rock. He called the old man Chavarría up from the camp to stand with him. It was not an easy climb for the old man; he came panting and coughing, he came on all fours, like an animal. Villa reached down and took the old man by the arms to lift him up the last few feet. He put his arm around Chavarría's thin shoulders, steadying him against the sudden winds that blew across the crest of the mountain. "Liviana told me who betrayed us," Villa said.

"I'll shoot him for you."

Villa patted the old man's arm. "You would steal that pleasure from me?"

"I would do it for a gift to you, a gift for both of us. Pancho, I don't want to die like a farmer. I don't want to go to the place where we become nothing."

"Jenaro, I have something to ask you, something so dangerous that if you do this and later you die in your bed, you'll still go with the Sun."

The old man turned the face of gratitude to Villa. The eyes shone, the

[*302*]

hollows of the cheeks seemed to smooth, the eroded skin was momentarily rich. "Tell me, my chief." He closed his eyes, the more to savor the sound of his instruction.

"The man is called Claro Reza. He is a captain of the rurales. Find him for me, Jenaro. Put on your oldest clothes, put on your huaraches, let the dust cover your feet; cover your head with a hat as ragged as your beard, a hat of a country man, tied with a tassel in the back; ride a burro without even a blanket for a saddle, make your halter with rope and tie rags together for your reins; go like a beggar, sit in the street, let your wrinkled skin hide your machismo. Learn him, Jenaro, learn the pattern of his day, spy for me."

"Like the puchteca."

"When they were mice, the ones who went before the soldiers."

Chavarría coughed, he shuddered in the wind. Villa stood there with him, holding the old man as if he were a child. He saw how the wind lifted his long white hair and shook his beard. He saw how the wind flapped his sleeves and trousers like empty sacks. The old man turned his face into Villa's chest to hide from the wind that stole his breath.

The sun was still high and hot, the sky was only beginning to redden. There was quiet in the streets, the workday was not yet over. They waited in front of a store that sold sweets. Pánfilo said he wanted to buy chocolate for his brother and himself. "Not now," Villa said. Pánfilo pushed his hat back, appealing with his eyes, not rebellious, but sad for the lack of chocolate, longing for the taste of it. "Not now," Villa said again. Solís wiped his forehead with his sleeve and pulled his hat down. He waited.

Carillo came around the corner of the sweets store, walking quickly, talking as he arrived: "Reza is there, inside. The old man says that we have to wait for more beer and pissing."

"How long?" Villa asked.

Carillo shrugged.

"Where is Chavarría?"

"In front of The Select, sitting like a beggar. He complains about the customers. He said that he didn't make half a peso in six days of begging."

Villa pointed west. "We'll go around that way," he said. "We'll come up the street with the sun at our backs. If he's not outside, I'll go in." He turned Star Two, touching him lightly with his left heel.

His neck was tight, he saw the lights running in the fluid of his eyes. They came as flashes and were gone, leaving the ache. He narrowed his eyes, he focused, he fought the blind holes, the emptiness in his vision. They came to the end of the block and turned left, passing a white house, like the house on Tenth Street. He looked at the shutters, closed now to keep the house cool through the afternoon, closed now to keep the privacy of a bedroom, closed now to keep the honor of a woman who lay on the bed in her nightdress. He touched the horse again with his heels. The riders came to the next corner. The iron shoes rang on the cobblestones; Villa thought he saw them sparking. Sour air came up out of his stomach. He knocked on his chest with his fist; more air came up, burning in his nose and the back of his throat. He coughed.

There was Jenaro, leaning against the wall of The Select. His legs were thrust out across the walk; the dust had dulled the skin of his feet, the dust had paled the skin of his hands. He sat, covered in tatters, torn straw over his head, faded shreds of cotton cloth upon his reedy limbs. He sat very still, his right hand was held out, open, begging, and pointing to the man who stood beside him, leaning against the wall, in repose, smoking a small thin cigar. The man was dressed in gray, decorated in silver; there were silver buttons on the legs of his trousers, there were silver swirls on his hat. He looked through the springs and wires of the bed, seeing the woman, committing the violation with his eyes. He smiled, as fathers smile, as owners smile. His face was young and haggard, his mouth had no color. He saw the men on the walking horses, the big hats, nothing more in the sun. He looked at his cigar, he saw the ash. There were other men next to him, a row of men leaning, one with his foot up against the wall, another with his arms behind his head, another leaning. A boy sat on the ledge of a low window, tapping the heels of his bare feet against the pale green stucco of The Select.

Villa reined in his horse, stopping a few feet before he came to the man in gray, wanting him to look up into the sun. "Claro Reza," he said, "I have to pay you something." He had thought the words since they left camp; before, since the day of Liviana's visit; before, since the night of the betrayal: *pay, owe, debt,* all the ironic words, all the unpleasant words, all the words and ways of disrespect.

"Who is it?" Reza asked, looking into the sun, holding his hand under the brim of his hat, shading his eyes. He was annoyed. The ash fell from his cigar. He made a face of annoyance.

"There is a common house," Chavarría said, "a place where everyone goes."

"Francisco Villa, at your orders."

"You better get out of here," Reza said. "It's not safe for you here."

"Will someone betray me?"

"I tried to warn you."

The men who had been standing against the wall were moving away, walking sideways, like vinegaroons. The boy who sat on the window ledge leaned forward; his head was turned toward Villa, his eyes were almost closed against the sun.

[*304*]

"I can hear the rattlebells," Chavarría said. He was grinning, his legs trembled.

"Do you know what's going to happen?" Villa asked Reza.

"Yes, I know."

"Are you sweating, Claro?"

"Yes."

"Good. Very good. I wanted you to have time to think about what I'm going to pay you. I want to watch your face now."

"I didn't do anything to your wife, I didn't let anyone touch her."

"Are you trembling, my friend? Do you feel like you have to piss?"

"Yes, yes."

"Do you want to pray?"

"Please." Reza lowered his head and crossed himself. His eyes were hidden. Villa watched his shoulders and the position of his feet. Reza turned slowly, placing one foot behind the other. His hands were together, touching, but not clasped; he slowly raised his right shoulder. Villa shot him. Reza's eyes and mouth opened, like a man delighted, about to laugh. He was thrown against the wall. His hat fell forward over his face and tumbled onto the walk.

"Cuauhtli," the old man Chavarría said, patting Villa's arm. "That means eagle; you are an eagle."

Villa pushed the hand away from his arm; the weakness of the hand chilled him. He looked down at Reza's body. "I knew him when he was only a thief. He stole goats."

In the month of Quecholli, six men came to a house in the village of Millas. They had left Chihuahua in the early morning, hoping to arrive before the rain; but two of them were old men who tired easily on the mountain trail, and one was sick—they stopped often to rest and drink water and brandy, they stopped too often to arrive before the rain. Six drenched men arrived at the house: two were cursing, one was a Protestant priest, two made jokes about the rain, and the sixth gave orders to the sky for the rain to stop. Villa waited inside the house, watching from the window. When he saw them coming up the trail, he told Urbina to send men outside to meet them and take their horses to the shelter behind the house. There was mash in a wooden tub, there were cloths for rubbing the rain out of the lengthening winter coats. Inside the house, Bárbaro had built a fire to cook coffee.

Villa and the six men sat around a table made from two split logs. Carillo served the coffee to them, then he retired to sit against the wall with the other men who remained with Villa, the eleven who sat with their hats over their eyes and their Winchesters standing against the wall beside them. All were ragged, some in buckskin, torn and scuffed, some in thick wool sweaters for the lack of coats, Eustaquio Flores without boots, José Sánchez in his morning coat with the threadbare tails and the sleeve missing from one arm, Tomás Urbina shivering under his rabbitskin winter cape. Colonel Lomelí surveyed them from his place at the table. "This is not my idea of an army," he said.

"Yes," Villa answered, nodding. "Eleven men do not make an army."

"No no no no," Lomelí told him, "you don't understand. I'm talking about their discipline. Look at them, sitting on the floor, like a collection of old urchins. Look at their clothes; they're in rags!" He pointed to Flores: "That one doesn't even have any shoes; how can you have an army without shoes?" He looked to Don Abraham. "This will never do, never. I can not command an army without shoes."

Flores gathered his legs under him, squatting over them to hide his feet. He took the Winchester from its place against the wall and laid it across his arm. The room was quiet but for the sound of rain and the sap exploding in the fireplace. The men glared at each other, at the thin and prissy colonel, with his thin wet hair lying in streaks across his scalp, with his arms folded in certainty and his face crinkled by some hidden pain. González tried to ignore the unsaid dispute; he introduced Villa to the men around the table.

"You know Colonel Lomelí and you know me. But we don't know you. There are rumors that you were the one who shot Claro Reza in cold blood. We don't know you, and we are concerned because these are serious times. Things have changed since we last talked: the Plan of San Luis Potosí has been published. Madero has called for an armed uprising on Sunday, November 20, at six in the evening. On that day the army will desert to our side, Díaz will be forced to leave his office, Mexico will be ours. We must have an army led by men we can trust."

González let the question hang in the room. He took a cigar out of his pocket and spent a long time lighting it. The men at the table were still; they looked away from Villa, one adjusting his belt, another patting his damp hair, Moya scratching his beard. Lomelí asked, "Are there facilities in the house?"

"In the back," Villa answered. "Outside."

"Savages," the colonel muttered; then he said aloud, "I'll wait until the rain lets up."

"As you like," Villa said.

Again the question was in the room. No one spoke, not the men against the wall, nor the men around the table. Don Abraham smoked his cigar, some of the men who leaned against the wall smoked corn-husk cigarettes. There were shuffling sounds, Soto dug a hole in the dirt floor with one of his spurs, there was rain on the roof, there was rain against the windows.

There was the question, the insult implied, the difference told, estrangement in the need for it to be answered. Villa looked at the men around the table. He could not find their eyes. Each man sat in a curl of himself, nothing of them was open; their feet were close together, their hands were closed, their arms were held tightly in place. Suddenly, Villa laughed: "Do you think I'm going to steal your watches?"

The words came back from the Rev. J. Hernández, as if the sound had bounced: "Did you kill Claro Reza?"

"Yes."

There was a pause again, the questions in the room. They waited for Villa to explain. He said nothing.

Don Abraham let out a long sigh; his face deflated, his eyes turned down at the corners. "I want to be truthful with you, Francisco; we're troubled by such things. The killing of a man in cold blood is wrong. It could be excused if he were an enemy, perhaps. But what excuse can we make for you when Reza was one of the men we counted on to come over to our side? We talked to him. He showed sympathy. He could have brought three or four hundred men with him, and they would have been fully equipped.

"We can endure the loss. Perhaps he lied, perhaps we're fools to think the army and the rurales aren't loyal to the Porfiriato. But murder, Francisco, murder in cold blood, gunning a man down in the street, attacking an unsuspecting man, what can we make of that? I don't think any of us could have done it."

"Then you'll all be dead in December," Villa said. He pushed his chair back from the table, and stood up. Slowly, but without hesitating, he walked over to the wall where the ragged men sat and took his place among them. His legs were drawn up, like theirs; he let his hat fall forward over his eyes. He paraded for the men at the table, he sat for them, he posed for them.

"We need you," Luis Moya said.

Villa kept his head low. He said, "Fight the army with lawyers. Attack the rurales with words."

The Rev. J. Hernández left his chair and strode up and back, taking the length of the room in long quick steps. He stopped in front of Villa. "And you are a horse thief and a cattle thief as well."

"I am a bandit, sir."

Hernández bent forward, pointing his finger at Villa. "Then you admit to murder, you admit to stealing horses, you admit to rustling cattle."

"I have never denied those things."

"Well, then, it's settled," said Hernández. "We can't have you in our army." He turned to the men at the table: "If we have men like this in the antireelectionist forces, all we will have, even if we win, is another Porfiriato. We must have an army of moral men. To fight criminals with criminals is only to assure that the criminals will win. We are not fighting the Díaz regime simply to win, we are fighting in the name of Jesus Christ, we are fighting in the name of Christian decency.

"To sit in the same room with this man is a betrayal of everything I believe; to consider allying ourselves with his kind is a mockery of the teachings of Our Lord Jesus Christ. I'm ready to go back to the city now."

One of the men seated against the wall said very softly, "Go with God." The others giggled.

Colonel Lomelí shook his head, he appeared to be groaning. "Gentlemen," he said, "we are deluding ourselves, deluding, deluding, deluding. Have you all forgotten what Madero has asked for? Read the prologue to the Plan." With the help of his arms, leaning on the table, he pushed himself to a standing position. It pained him to stand erect. They read the pains in the twitches of his face. They saw him shrug, as if to answer the question of the pains, as if he were arguing within himself. He was thin, he trembled, he smelled of wet wool, his hair curled as it dried; yet he lifted his head, he remembered his dignity. In a voice they had not heard before, a voice gathered in the deeps of his shallow chest, he shouted, "War!"

He paused, perhaps for the drama, perhaps to collect his breath. The room was quiet, the loudness of his shout seemed to have silenced the rain. He clasped his hands behind his back, straightening his shoulders, pulling them back, using that device of old soldiers. "Soldiers are not saints," he said. "I have seen war, I have been a soldier; it is not a saintly profession. In Heaven, I would be willing to command an army of saints, but on earth I would rather have an army of bandits. We have the Apostle, we have Madero to lead us in our politics. But he cannot redeem Mexico with politics. He knows that, he has called for an armed uprising. He expects the Army to desert Díaz. That will not come to pass, my friends, that will not come to pass. There will be war, and if there is war, Madero must have his sword."

Lomelí staggered once at the end of his speech, caught himself, and hurried over to Villa, who stood up, opening his arms, preparing to embrace him. "Help me," Lomelí said. "Show me the facilities."

Villa held him up. He nodded to Soto and Urbina, who took the colonel and led him outside.

The men who sat around the table spoke to each other in whispers and gestures, all of them leaning in over the center of the split logs. Villa addressed them, emulating the loud, certain tones of the colonel: "I am not a saint. My colonel told the truth about me. But I will be a good sword for the Redeemer. I hate the Porfiriato and the landlords more than any of you; they killed my father, they shamed my sister, they kept me from the funeral when my mother died. I have been shamed and betrayed and made to live

[*308*]

like a roaming animal because of Tata Porfirio. I have reason to make war on him, on all of them; and I've been at war with them since I was sixteen years old."

"Our goal," said Hernández, "is not war."

Aureliano González stood up to speak. He was thinner than Don Abraham and he walked with a limp. He hooked his thumbs in the pockets of his vest and paced up and back while he made his oration: "Members of the Antireelectionist Club Benito Juárez, friends of my friend Francisco Villa, Reverend Hernández: For thirty years, since all of us were young, before some of us were born, this great country of ours, this beloved Mexico, has lived under the dictatorship of a barbarian. There has been no law in the land but martial law. The chambers of our legislature have become a mockery of the very idea of law and representative democracy. The towns, the districts, the cities, the states, all Mexico, is governed by political chiefs appointed by a usurper, a thief, a man who has stolen our rights. Year after year he has continued in office, year after year, term after term, and that in spite of the banner under which he himself fought—effective suffrage and no reelection. And what has he done for Mexico? He has given our nation away to foreigners and monopolies. We are the servants of foreigners, the vassals of the powerful capitalists brought here by the Jew, Limantour. We are slaves of Wall Street. We are starving. Our children are like skeletons, our parents die before their time, our friends are hanged or languish in prisons. There is no alternative for us now. After the last election, Madero was imprisoned, after the last election Dr. Vásquez Gómez fled. Where then is the hope for lawful change? There is no choice: if we want our liberty, we must fight for it, we must go to war, we must buy our freedom with our blood!" He sat down heavily in his chair, he held his head in his hands. "You know the facts," he said softly; "my argument is based on the facts."

Luis Moya spoke then, the words coming from inside the stillness of his thick white beard. The light he said was given to him by Madero was there in his eyes, shining. The vein in his temple was a counting of himself, a numbering of his anger. He stood in one place while he spoke, and he kept his arms open and partly extended, as an invitation, an invocation. He was not humble, he had no questions; the whole of him was fierce. "I know it is true; I saw it, I negotiated it, I was among the sinners and the thieves who must be held accountable for it; the land was stolen. The government made it possible, the government made it profitable, and we took the profits, we robbed the poor, we cheated the rightful inheritors. Now, what may be done? Divide the land among the poor! Divide the land! That is the first reform. And before that can be accomplished we must bring down the government of Porfirio Díaz. By war! Yes, by war, by killing in the name of Christ the Prince of Peace! How can we do that? How can we kill in the name of Christ? We will do it because this war is in the name of the blessed poor, in the defense of the poor, for their sake, may God love them. Christ died for the sins of man. We will also die for the sins of man, for the sins we have committed, for the sins we have allowed to be committed. He died on the cross; we will die on the battlefield." He turned to look at Villa: "Will you die for Christ?"

"Will you die for Christ?" Villa repeated, studying Moya, the longness of him, the narrowness of his nose, the roseate, European skin of his cheeks. "If we all die in the name of Christ," Villa said, putting the imagined string together slowly, "there will be . . . it will be a victory for the Porfiriato. We will all be dead, and who will be left to defend the poor?"

"Will you risk your life for Christ?" Moya asked.

"Every day is a risk for me, sir. If I promised you that, if Pancho Villa said he would put himself in danger in the name of Christ, it would be like the rabbit saying he would put himself in danger from the wolf, it would be a joke. What do you want of me? What do you want of us? We accept the presidency of Francisco Inocencio Madero, we believe in democracy, we are willing to fight. What more do you all want from us? My name is Francisco Villa, I can ride a hundred miles in a day, I can go a hundred hours without sleep, I can live a hundred days on the scraps of the desert. I offer you that. I offer you men who will follow me in whatever I do. Do you want us? Answer me now."

Don Abraham looked around the table, measuring the vote of each man, counting him according to the expression of his eyes. "We are all students of history here, including you, Francisco. We know the errors of Hidalgo, Morelos, Guerrero, Allende, Aldama, even Juárez; they were errors in war and they were always followed by errors in peace. We know the bravery of Cuauhtémoc and we also know that he was murdered by the Spaniards, because he could not defeat them. We will not make those errors, not in war and not in the peace that follows. Men like Francisco Villa will win this war for our cause, men like Francisco Madero and Dr. Vázquez Gómez will maintain our cause after the peace. This will be the last revolution, the last war in Mexico. Francisco Villa is appointed a captain of the volunteers to serve under Colonel Cástulo Herrera. Viva Madero! Viva Mexico!" He embraced Villa, he called him captain. The men who sat against the wall also shouted vivas, they also called Villa captain; they crowded around him, embracing him as they could, patting his back, punching his shoulders.

Villa cried. He wiped his eyes, he blew his nose, using the act of crying, the cover of the handkerchief to hide himself, to make his face. When he looked up, they stepped back, forming a circle around him, waiting for him to speak. He could not. He surprised them with a laugh, tears came again, he hid in the handkerchief. When he raised his head again, they were waiting. They asked him to speak.

Soto and Urbina brought the colonel into the house, carrying him by his arms, pulling his feet after him. They put him in a chair, but he could not sit up without help. Urbina held him in place while Soto went to whisper to Villa: "He's shitting blood. He can't help himself. He needs cola syrup or haws. Tomás is going to chop up some maguey leaves and boil them out for him, just to give him something to hold himself together inside. It's very bad, Pancho. He's an old man, or maybe he could use geranium; I know an old man who died from geranium—it's too strong."

Villa went to stand beside Lomelí's chair. Some of the others stood with him. "I didn't know you were so sick," Villa said.

"From Quintana Roo," the colonel said. "We were all sick in Quintana Roo." His head wobbled, he lost Villa's face, searched for a moment until he found him again. He smiled weakly. "War is for healthy men. Listen to me, I tell the truth: I have seen more men wounded by dysentery than by guns. I have seen diseases in the jungles that make you shiver as if you had seen a ghost. Ears and noses are rotted away, eyes turn black. Listen to me, young soldier: guard the health of your army, guard what they eat and what water they drink. There are strange poisons; look at me."

"I thought you were a foolish old man," Villa said. "I didn't know you were sick. I didn't know you were a great soldier."

"There is no excuse for ignorance," said the colonel.

The meeting was ended, the men walked around the room, they demanded that Carillo cook the evening meal, they talked with each other; the men who had sat against the wall were in their group, the men who had come from Chihuahua were in theirs. Villa stood in a corner with Cástulo Herrera, who told him that it was time to raise an army. There were thirty cases of Mauser rifles and a hundred thousand rounds of ammunition. Villa was to raise his army, attack the towns to the south: San Andrés, Palomas, Sabinas, and go on through Satevó and Tres Hermanos to take Parral. González was going north to Ojinaga to raise an army there. Pascual Orozco, Jr., a muleskinner, was going to raise an army and attack in the west at Guerrero. Then they were to come back, three powerful and experienced armies, the armies of the revolution, meeting at Chihuahua to lay siege to the city, to make war until the garrison surrendered and the armies of the revolution stood in the main plaza.

There were plans, there were hopes: victory in a month if the army defected, victory in three months if the uprising took place everywhere at the same time; victory, there would be victory, the good men would triumph, the illegal government would fall. It was certain, there had been signs: a comet, earthquakes, the eruption of volcanoes; there had been political signs: strikes, the failed elections, meetings, the little revolutions in a dozen towns; and there had been signs that only the Redeemer had seen, revelations, a board of letters on which strange forces moved a pointer telling him to be President of Mexico, simultaneous dreams in places hundreds of miles apart, cloud formations, voices that could have been the wind. As Nezahualpilli had shown Motecuhzoma in the game of fives that the end of Tenochtitlán was coming, so Francisco Inocencio had seen on the board of letters that the end of the Porfiriato was coming. Everyone knew, everyone believed. Why had he not been sent to San Juan de Ulúa like the Liberals? Why had he been allowed to escape from San Luis Potosí? Why did a rich man care so much for the poor?

> *Mucho trabajo,*
> *Poco dinero,*
> *No hay frijoles,*
> *Viva Madero!*
>
> *Sufragio efectivo y no reelección!*

You may call him the Dwarf of Parras, Tata Porfirio, but we call him the Bridegroom of Mexico.

He is a Spiritist. He studied in France. He studied in California. He cures the sick by the science of homeopathy. He writes books. He speaks French, English, and German. He feeds the children of the poor. He teaches them. He has no children; Christ had no children. He does not wish a revolution; he has called for war. There is no hope for the poor but Heaven and Francisco I. Madero.

The men from Chihuahua stayed until dawn, eating and drinking and saying aloud the words of the Plan of San Luis Potosí. Article Three promised the return of the land to the natives of the land, even to the second generation; it promised indemnity even to the third and fourth generations. The Plan gave the rules of the war: prisoners were not to be executed, hollow bullets were not to be used. It was a Plan devoted to law, said the men from Chihuahua, and the men from the Blue Mountains asked what the law said about the long workday, the low wages, the company store, the difference between the pay for Mexicans and the pay for foreigners. Law, law, the men from Chihuahua answered; first there must be a legal government, a government elected by the people, then there will be the questions of working hours, of company stores, of unfair pay. And the health of the people, and the right to form unions? First the rule of law; and then the first of laws under the rule of law is the alleviation of the suffering of the poor; a Plan is not a Constitution, a Plan is but a beginning.

Before morning, the rain stopped and the men from Chihuahua went outside. Snow lay on the edges of the western mountains, where there is neither grass nor game. Villa went outside with Don Abraham when the light was almost good enough for riding. He told the older man that he feared a long war ahead, a war of months, perhaps years; he feared for those who would die and those who would wish they had died. There would be horses to shoot, men to bury, limbs to be sawed off, dead eyes to cover. Don Abraham shrugged: "Be loyal," he said. "Obey the rules."

Don Abraham looked away. The blue light of morning increased the white shock of the snow that lay between the dark western sky and the brown mountains. "If you're born in these mountains, like we were, Pancho, you always have to come back to them. Beautiful, beautiful mountains. Such wasted land! What use are these beautiful mountains when we have so many hungry people? How will we ever feed them? It's not easy to love the poor. How will we disappoint them?"

"We won't disappoint them. We won't welsh on them," Villa said.

González put his hand on Villa's shoulder. "Of all of us," he said, "you're the only one who can imagine what this kind of war will be. Tell me."

"Have you ever been to a slaughterhouse? Do you know the fear that comes into the animals when they smell death? It's worse with men."

"Then why aren't you afraid?"

"Who said I was not afraid? I'm uneducated, sir, but I'm not an animal."

Villa and Soto watched the town by turns, looking through a long brass spyglass until the picture blurred, then passing the glass to the other. Chihuahua was as always: the train was in the station, late in leaving; the carts were gathered around the market, the farmers unloading the last of the fruits of autumn; there was a steady movement of people around the plaza; a small herd of cattle was being moved into the pens of the slaughterhouse; the garrison was quiet, the horses were in the stables, one platoon drilled on the hard clay field, marching up and back, left and right, marching and marching, going nowhere, students of discipline and not of war that morning, recruits, surely only recruits, with shaved heads and ill-fitting uniforms. The roads in and out of the city were no less usual, no less quiet. Navarro did not appear in the circle of the glass, Guzmán did not appear in the circle of the glass. Soto and Villa watched. A full regiment had been ordered to go north from the Capital; they had to be somewhere. The Twelfth Battalion was in Pedernales, the city below was protected by cooks, stable boys, and a platoon of recruits. Villa wished for his troops. "They'll be here late tonight," Soto said.

"We should have brought them by train." Villa gave the glass to Soto, swiveling it on the long brass steadying rod.

"Hey, brother, I can see your house." The warning of a joke was in Soto's voice. "I think I see . . . Well, I wonder what he would be doing there in your house."

"Maybe he's tired of your mother."

"What a way to treat a friend, a brother."

"I don't like waiting, man. Can you really see my house?"

"Let's see. Number five hundred. A white house. Roses in the patio. Holes in the shutters. Could those be bullet holes?"

"I should know better than to trust a farmer."

Soto bowed his legs, pretending to straddle cornrows. They laughed. Villa left him and went over to where the other men waited. Most of them sprawled on the ground, a few slept. There were no cooking fires so close to the city. Chavarría polished his rattlebells with a strip of thick cotton cloth. "I expect something," he told Villa.

Villa touched the old man's shoulder. "How's your cough?" Chavarría made a meaningless nod. Villa patted his shoulder lightly and moved on.

José Sánchez was standing with his horse, cutting its whiskers with a sewing scissors. "Why are you doing that now?" Villa asked.

"It's a new horse. I won it in a card game last night. You treat a horse well and it will treat you well."

"Like a woman."

"Who knows about women? It's easier to make friends with a horse."

Villa punched him on the arm. "Women or horses, the best ones are stolen."

He went on to Pedro, who sat by himself, his head bent, hidden under his hat. "I heard you were drunk last night," Villa said.

"Did you hear that I'm sick this morning?" Aprisco did not raise his head.

"Were you with Hipólito?"

"For the last time."

"That's a good cure for a hangover, you know—to give up drinking."

"You sound like Liviana."

"She loves you."

"God put tails on horses because the flies love them in the same way."

"Would you say that to her?"

Aprisco shuddered. "I would rather face Navarro and his whole regiment."

"Try to sleep," Villa told him. "We'll be here most of the day."

Villa got a canteen of water and a piece of dried meat and sat down with his back against a rock to eat breakfast. It was after nine o'clock. His mouth was dry, he felt tired, his left leg was aching, predicting colder weather, perhaps snow. He closed his eyes and lifted his face up to the sun while he chewed the meat. It would have been good to have a cup of hot coffee or chocolate. Liviana was less than two miles away. There was coffee and chocolate in the kitchen. There was a big can of cinnamon. She kept sugar in a sack on the shelf above the sink. He took his nose between his thumb and forefinger and squeezed it, rocking the soft bone from side to side. Nothing came out, nothing ever did; there was never a flow from the hill. He laughed at the answer to the old riddle, thinking of the child in Parral, the scar, the garden. He sucked mucus down into his mouth and spat it out. Navarro was out there somewhere, equipped with artillery and a battalion of infantrymen who wore boots and carried Model 93 Mausers with two-thousand-meter sighting.

The sun rested him. He leaned back to swallow the last of the meat. Perhaps he would sleep. His eyes were still closed, the sun caused flecks of light in the green darkness, he felt sleep coming forward from the back of his head. Soto was there, watching; the farm boy could be trusted; they were brothers, sworn. He waited for sleep, feeling the air shuddering in his throat, hearing it vaguely, as if the noise came from some other hilltop, floating. It had been a poor time for dreams; he had seen ice, flint, darkness, wind, he had heard dogs howling. He wished for dreams of women, he wished for sunlight in his dreams. The canteen lay at his side, his hands were folded across his belly, the tickled numbness floated in him, he shivered in the cold that seemed now to come with dreaming. The wind blew, mixing with the sound of dogs.

Soto awakened him. There had been shots. Had he heard them? The sound had come from the south, somewhere on Tecolote Flat, perhaps the Spearpoint Ranch. The shadow of Soto's head lay across Villa's face. Villa pushed him aside to let the sunlight fall on him again. "Shooting the dogs," he said. "Shooting the dogs in darkness."

Soto shook him: "Wake up, man!"

"I don't mind the cold," Villa said. He tried to focus his eyes, having difficulty lifting them up to see.

The shots came again, three, and two more. "Let's go," Villa said. The men were already running for their horses, pulling up the stakes, tying on their blanket rolls. Chavarría was dancing, coughing and shaking his rattlebells.

They went half a mile, turned the curve of the hill, leaning with the horses, and came out onto the flat, a mile of hard sand, table rock, patches of grass, strings of grass, low cactus, scrub oak creeping down from the surrounding hills. Villa motioned them into a wide line across the north end of the flat. He shouted at them to watch the flanks, to be careful. The horses moved forward, trotting; he slowed them to a walk. They approached the center, the hill receded behind them, the curve was out of reach. Soto was beside him, Pedro was beside him; the row of horses, the row of men on either side. The men were quiet, the horses made a hollow sound, reaching through the sand to the table rock beneath. They were so far from the hill, the flat was so quiet. On the western edge of the flat, beyond the hills, they could see the tops of the trees that surrounded the compound of Spearpoint. The leaves were gone. Villa raised his hand to halt the line of horsemen. He had lost the time: ten o'clock? eleven? The winter sun moved quickly. He felt the watch in his pocket. The sun was better. Time was no matter. The sun was bright and cold. He tasted shreds of meat in his teeth. The wind touched his back.

Jenaro Chavarría dismounted. The heel of his left boot caught in the stirrup. He hopped on one foot, pulling himself free. His hat fell off. Long hair, gray-streaked, matted, shining, fell to his shoulders. The man next to him reached over to take the reins of Chavarría's horse, but he was not quick enough; the animal shied, turned, half rearing, and ran back toward the hill. Chavarría walked forward, lifting the cartridge belts off, dropping them as he went. His clothes hung now, loose, white, and long. He took the flute from under his shirt and blew into the end of it. He made peeps, then longer notes, rhythms. He continued to walk forward into the center of the flat, lifting his feet in sharp movements, shaking the rattlebells, his rhythm the rhythm of the flute: cuts of sound, long, shivering unrollings of sound. His feet lifted easily; he was in the air, the dust rose under him, flying with the music; he danced, turning, rising on the toes of his thick boots. He did not cough.

The troops appeared, squads, platoons, companies, dark stalks, shining brass, blue, gunmetal, dark wood faces. They rose onto the flat, they rimmed the flat. The old man danced. His horse was gone, he had no weapons, his long shirt sailed, the clumps of his hair bounced and shook. He blew into the flute, he made the flute scream, he surrounded himself with rhythms and rising dust. The crack of the Mausers broke the rhythm of Chavarría's music, drowning the rattlebells. The old man danced while the shots fell around him, dust around him, dust rising around him, circles of dust flying around him. He blew into the flute, he made the rhythm of the rattlebells. The troops ran onto the flat, firing as they came. Chavarría rose on one foot; his arms were extended. He was whirling, flying, dead.

José Sánchez hung from the stirrups, bent back across the saddle. His mouth was open, his arms reached for the ground. His horse bolted forward, carrying him like a pennant streaming from its back. It ran forward into the center, past the center. Its forelegs crumpled and it rolled, flinging Sánchez upright, smashing him into the dust.

The shots came from all directions. The horses panicked. Villa's people could not hold the reins and work the bolts of the Mausers. "Forward," he shouted. "Let them run! Forward!" The rifles fired into the converging blue, the horses ran, gunpowder smoke and dust rose across the field. The blue stalks halted, fell back, ran forward again. Villa fired his rifle, ramming the bolt home, trembling, unable to aim, firing in the direction of the oncoming troops. Pedro's horse went down. Villa saw him fall free, roll over and come up to his knees. The rifle was still in his hands.

Horses were falling everywhere, screaming, pawing clouds of dust. There was no wind; the dust, the gunpowder smoke, hung darkening over the flat. The bugles blew. He heard a drum, something like a drum. Chavarría was off to his right; his body was in a dancer's pose but for one twisted leg. Villa clasped the rifle and the reins in one hand and fired his revolver with the other. His leg was punched, driven against the side of his horse. The animal bucked forward. Villa felt his leg stinging, cold; he looked for the wound. The hind legs of the horse collapsed. Villa felt it going down under him. He kicked the stirrups forward and threw himself clear. He landed on one shoulder and turned half a somersault. The rifle was gone, but he still held the revolver. The bugles sounded and the troops in blue came running again, shouting now, a roar, a sound like rifles moaning. He lay on one side, loading cartridges into the revolver. Horses fell, screaming through the roar. Villa drew saliva into his mouth to wet his breath.

Soto passed him, working the bolt of the Mauser, firing as he ran. He stopped a few yards beyond and knelt to push another clip into the breech of his rifle. His hat hung from the cord; it lay on his back. There was blood on his side. He worked the bolt of his rifle, shooting into the oncoming Federals. Villa fired over him, into the nearing charge. Beyond Soto, dim in the dust, men fell. They screamed like children wounded, they screamed like children alone. Soto jumped backward, the back of his head burst open. He staggered. Thick, bloody worms poured out of his head. He fell suddenly.

The Federals retired again; they were lost in the dust. Villa fired at them until the revolver was empty. He lay on his side to load again when he heard the bugles and the roar, the long shout rising to a shriek. The dust thickened, the firing came out of the dust; they were coming again. He looked for the horses. They lay all around him. Nothing stood, not one man stood. The army was coming, running, roaring. Villa pulled his legs up under him and ran, scurrying, crouching, stumbling, and hopping toward the north end of the flat. He saw Carillo dead. A horse was nearby, following him. He ran from it, turning in one direction, then another, like a rabbit running.

[*317*]

Pedro Aprisco sat in a little hollow, holding his rifle across his lap. The lower part of his face was gone. Villa shouted to him. Aprisco turned to the voice; blood bubbled out of the wound under his nose. The horse was closer, following Villa. He was too slow, his leg was failing. He stumbled over a stone and fell. The horse came, shaking the ground beneath Villa's knees. He raised his arm to protect himself. The rider reached down and took his wrist, dragging him up, pulling him onto the haunches of the horse. Villa put his arms around the rider's waist and held on.

Liviana kept the little girls of the compound close to her. She brushed their hair and braided it. She wiped the tears from their eyes and washed their sores and scratches. In return, they made her laugh in the games of girls. They gathered around her in the kitchen or the parlor, sometimes to sing for her, sometimes to lay their heads on her lap or against her bosom. She held their tiny hands, she kissed their fingers one by one, counting the endearing names she gave to them: love, sweetness, light, purity, and succor; grace, beauty, charity, saintliness, and mercy. She told them stories and riddles, she sang for them, and in the darkness, when they had gone home to their rooms beyond the courtyard to sleep, Liviana lay in her bed and wept. The stories had come back on the afternoon of the battle: eighty Federal soldiers killed and the army of the revolution destroyed. The bodies of the revolutionaries had been buried in the field; the names of the dead were not known. Liviana prayed for the dead and she prayed for the living; she could not hope because she mourned, she could not mourn because she hoped. She kept the little girls close to her; she reminded them that they would be women; they reminded her that she had been a child. She thought of her own dead child, the handful she had hidden in the blankets.

Villa came in the night and threw pebbles at her window, like a suitor. She turned up the lamp behind the shutters, the window glowed. She opened the shutters and the window and stood there, looking out, a woman in her nightbraided hair, in her long, sunstreaked, washed hair, in her thick and formless winter nightdress; she stood between him and the light, a shadow on the light, her troubled eyes hidden, her anguish safe in shadow. He laughed for her, he sang a lover's song. She stood there, between him and the light, a woman weeping, still unsure.

Inside the house, she inspected him, his wounded leg, the bandage thick with pieces of charcoal. She asked if it had been washed with alcohol. He said there had been nothing but pine resin and breast of maguey; that was enough. "And is my brother also wounded?" she asked.

"Dead."

"How?"

"To save the rest of us. Standing up, with pistols in his hands; he was

[*318*]

an army." He saw the sorrow in her eyes become diffused, complicated. "Without Pedro Aprisco, the revolution would be over, the people would be without hope. He was like a god, Liviana, I swear, like a god standing there with his pistols and the hope of all of the people in his hands. The soldiers charged and he threw them back with his pistols. It was like a miracle, the accuracy of his shooting. They were terrified by him, they could see that he was without fear. It was like a miracle: when his pistols were empty, he took the pistols from the dead who fell all around him, he shot them with their own bullets. There never was a man like him, standing there, so young, standing there, so straight. A miracle, it was a miracle that one man could hold off a battalion. One day, when Madero is our president, he'll tell people about Pedro Aprisco; the children will learn about him in the schools—Pedro Aprisco, the hero of the battle of Tecolote Flat, the man who saved the revolution."

"And he died quickly?"

"Without pain. When we saw him die, we ran; all of us who were alive ran away. Some boys from Spearpoint took us up on their horses and saved us from Navarro. I lost a lot of friends there: Soto, Sánchez, Chavarría, Carillo, my brother Pedro, others, all friends. They're all dead. Urbina is the only one left. All my friends are dead, all my brothers. All my friends, all my brothers."

"Pedro was not afraid?"

"He was like a warrior of ancient times. The dust was all around him, the horses were blowing, the rattlebells were sounding. It was beautiful, Liviana; you would have been proud of him."

"You're telling me the truth, Francisco? Do you swear you're telling me the truth? Pedro was never brave, I never thought that of him. He was afraid of so many things when he was a little boy, he was afraid of me."

"You can never know what a man is until you see him in battle."

She embraced him, giving herself to him, soft and heavy on his chest, as she had never been before, supported by him, seeking him. Her mouth was turned up to him; she offered her lips, the interior red, the blood-colored flesh. He kissed her neck, her cheek, the tip of her nose; he could not kiss her mouth.

Before they went to bed, she bathed his wound, washed it with alcohol, and dressed it with egg white and charcoal. They lay together under the quilts in the cold room, in the winter room. He kissed her neck, lifting her hair to find the most tender place, he touched her breast, but she would not accept him. She spoke of her tears, her dead brother. The night grew colder; they heard the wind, they whispered. He felt her breath; she would not have him. Instead, she reached into the pillow beneath his head and took out a white feather. She stroked it smooth, she made it perfect. There was no light in the room, they could see the feather when she held it up. They studied it, the symmetry, the soft line, the ease, the firm core. She put it in her mouth and swallowed it.

A soldier rose from the bed. He carried a rifle, a revolver, cartridge belts across his chest and around his waist. A saber hung at his side. His face was stern, his uniform of blue feathers was decorated with gold, pieces of polished jade and stripes of black rubber. He kissed Liviana, he held her hands in his, gently, as a son comforting his mother. She gave him paper decorations to put in his hair and on his back. He brought morning to the room, blessed it, and went out to make war on the night. He was the most terrible of soldiers, but they did not realize that until he had gone, leaving behind the bodies of his slain brothers and sisters.

The house was still quiet when Villa left, although he thought he heard the women of the compound grinding nixtamal for the day's tortillas. Luis Beltrán was waiting for him on Eighth Street. The others had gone ahead, driving a train of burros loaded with supplies for the men who waited in the Blue Mountains. Beltrán asked if he had told Liviana about her brother. Villa said, "I told her he was a hero."

Beltrán helped him onto the horse he had bought the night before. "We could go back and get the body. It's not too late."

"No, I don't want her to see the wounds."

"There was no priest."

"Send someone with a dog and some pieces of turquoise to bury near them. Bury some red cord and tree branches too. Give them everything."

"Not a priest?"

"The priests are for the Porfiristas."

"I heard in Chihuahua that Navarro had eight hundred men at Tecolote Flat."

"Does that make me any less a fool? It was my fault, I didn't plan, I was careless. I've been in the hills for sixteen years and I led us into a trap that a clerk would have seen."

"I heard that he had seven hundred and twenty men when he left the flat." Beltrán giggled. "We lost nine. He lost nine times nine." He stuck out his tongue and licked the white stubble around his mouth. "Nine is the most significant number after three. I think it's a good sign."

"I lost my wife's brother and my best friend; how much more do I have to lose?"

2

The Citizen President of Mexico stood behind his writing table. From the window at his back light entered, shimmering in the dark room. He stood in the center of the light. It washed over him. Villa fell to one knee and bowed his head. "My President," he whispered.

Madero took Villa's arm and raised him up. "We are all citizens," he said.

"You are the Saviour of Mexico."

"And you are Pancho Villa. I thought—I don't know why—perhaps because I've heard about you for so many years—that you would be much older. Pancho Villa. I don't know—why should I? I suppose—I expected a—well, there is no use in talking about what I expected—you're here, and that's what is important."

It was a woman's voice, it was the tone of a bargaining woman, and the words came at the speed of argument. He was small, smaller than they had said. His bones seemed like the bones of a young boy, small and very round, giving the expectation of pliancy. All the seriousness, all the possibility of severity in him was promised by the triangle of his beard. He stood very straight, he seemed proud, like a tiny soldier. His arm, wounded at Casas Grandes, was carried in a white sling. There were stains on the cloth, darkness on the white of the sling and of the bandage that covered his wrist and hand. His thick jacket bore the marks of wear, his riding breeches were dusty, there were deep scratches and bloodstains on his yellow riding boots. He had been to war; he was not a distant prince. Only in the way the light flowed around him was he separated from other men.

"They told me that you would not come alone, because—all of them said —you would be too cautious, having been a bandit. I knew, however, I knew by a kind of understanding that goes beyond the predictions of this waking life, if you know what I mean. About two hours ago, I had a sudden thought that you were on your way. Things like that come to me, as they do to many people—those who train themselves—who realize there is a spirit as well as a body. It's not uncommon. Haven't you known people like that?"

"Yes, sir."

"And I have had—yes, very distinctly—the understanding that you were different from the man I read about in the newspapers. And now, seeing you —and more than that, knowing you by your name—we are both Francisco, both called Pancho—I am confirmed in my spiritual understanding, which is that you are not a cruel man or an evil man or a murderer or even a thief in your heart. Something made you a bandit, something—I know, but I don't know what it is—I feel it—you didn't choose that life. Is that true? Tell me, tell me from the beginning. I know that I'm getting the right sense. It's only that I've been so busy—there's so much to do—or I wouldn't even have to ask, I could just concentrate. But you tell me, from the beginning."

"I was a bandit, that's true. I would not lie to you, sir." Villa looked away. He waited for the next question.

"Captain, a man is not born—he becomes, he makes a choice in his mind to become—a bandit. That is what interests me in your case. If a man was truly a bandit—evil, a bad man, a criminal—we certainly have such men in Mexico—there can be no excusing a common criminal, I assure you— Díaz is in a certain sense a criminal, but of another and more dangerous type—we would not expect to find him risking his life to bring true democracy to Mexico—a revolutionary. Therefore, I ask you to think, Pancho, of how you came into such a life." He waved his free hand as he spoke; the wounded arm rocked in the sling.

"It was not for the money, sir. We were the poorest of the poor. After my father died, there was a drought. We ate weeds, we ate carrion; I ate dirt to fill my belly. And in all those years of being poor I never robbed or stole. I never thought of it, sir, not even to feed my younger brothers and sisters and my sainted mother. But when I was sixteen years old and we were living as sharecroppers on the López Negrete ranch, the landlord came to our house when I was away in the fields, and he brought gunmen with him, and he had the ugliest desire. He shamed my sister. He did it in my own house in the presence of my mother. When I found out, I took a gun from my cousin's house and I waited in the hills for the landlord and I shot him. From that day since I have been a hunted man. I've lived like a nomad, I've been a wanderer, I've never had one day of peace.

"Sir, it's not what I wanted. It's not the life I dreamed of. I wanted to be a farmer, but the poor can't afford to buy land. I wanted to open a store, and I did in Chihuahua; but the rich would not permit me to have a store of my own. What else could I do? How else could I live?" Tears came into Villa's eyes. He blinked and squeezed his eyelids shut to force the tears out onto his cheeks.

"Pancho—may I call you Pancho?" Madero waited for the motion of Villa's head. "Thank you. Pancho, the revolution we are making is first of all to bring democracy—the ability of the people to choose their own leaders —to Mexico. After democracy, true democracy, justice follows. What you ask—of course, it is only because you have been misinformed—certain elements—I mean by those elements most especially the Magonistas—democracy must be understood—on first glance seems to be the best thing for Mexico. I cannot blame you, just as I cannot blame you for the life you were forced into by the savagery of your landlord. But there must be order. If we suddenly—and without careful, very careful, deliberation and planning—turn the country upside down, we will have anarchy instead of democracy. And what will anarchy bring us? Think of history—we must be scientific when we consider these things. Anarchy always leads to dictatorship; the Magonistas are as great a danger for the future as the Porfiristas are for the present.

"The Magonistas have lost faith in government and law, not just in the government of the Porfiriato, but in all government. Now, I ask you, consider this: if there is no government—men living without any law, like animals—what will happen? A strong man will emerge—good men and strong men are not necessarily the same, as we have seen in our own country. Díaz began as an ally of Juárez—and what will come—there must be some order, because men cannot live without order—is another dictator. Anarchy, dictatorship, and then another revolution. Can we spill our comrades' blood in vain? Economic collapse, the takeover by foreigners, Spaniards, Germans, Chinese, and more North Americans; the radicals endanger everything.

"At the moment, the Magonistas are with us, at the moment. We need them—the size of the army opposing the Porfiriato is of major importance —how I recall Casas Grandes—the dead, the prisoners—poor Eduardo Hay captured in that house—they say his eye was torn out and he couldn't see to fire his weapon or direct his men—if we are going to be successful in our attack on Chihuahua, the force of numbers must be on our side. I am, however, troubled by their presence among us—they constitute too great a part of our forces—one in ten, although my estimates are not accurate in that regard. What will become of the revolution if they remain among us? They could attempt to gain power—in our ranks divisiveness is an advantage to the enemy—victory could be lost—the kind of victory that results in further wars is a loss—illusion can be the outcome. So you see why I am worried about Orozco. He is not in their camp, they are in his camp; nevertheless, the situation must be watched. I ask your estimate of him."

He came around to the front of the table, still speaking in his sudden stops and rushes, never quite pausing long enough to give Villa the opportunity to begin an answer. "How young, how young! I expected—knowing the range—the sun some days can redden a man in an hour—heat, of course, dries out the skin, contributing to premature aging—we concern ourselves so much with appearances—the heat and the sun would have the same effect on you as on other men. But you look so young, you are so young. The tragedy of your life—how many of the people of this country of ours have suffered at the hands of the rich—and the way you've been forced to live —amends must be made—the way a man suffers always shows in his face. You are different, youthful; you have the face of a man who loves music. Well, we don't know—limited, limited, this physical world—how many things happen in the spiritual world; there are explanations for the mysteries, mysteries we have not yet discovered, powers beyond imagining. I trust you, Pancho. There are others that concern me."

"Orozco?"

The President nodded. "Orozco. And others."

"I don't know him. How can you know a man who doesn't speak? All I know is what happened at Cerro Prieto."

Madero smiled and leaned his head to one side, nodding in appreciation of Villa's loyalty to his fellow soldier. "Of course, of course, he saved you there. His cavalry was brilliant."

"Sir, when his cavalry arrived, two hundred and thirty-one of my men were dead or dying. A hundred more were wounded. The officer he gave me to teach us to sit on a hill and wait for the cannon to destroy us, that man was already dead. Mister President, his attack was almost four hours late."

"But he was brilliant."

"As you say, sir. For my part, I count the dead. It cost ten times as many men to lose Cerro Prieto as it did to win at La Piedra. At La Piedra my cavalry was not so brilliant, but they were not four hours late."

"Do you think it was in his mind to cost you so many men?"

"They were good men."

"And his politics?"

"I have yet to learn politics."

Madero put his hand on Villa's shoulder. "Colonel," he said in the intimate voice of a friend, "I want you to be a colonel in my army—Colonel Villa, before I go to sleep tonight I will write a decree absolving you of any crimes that you have been forced to commit to keep yourself alive in this difficult world. When you awaken tomorrow morning, Pancho, you will no longer be a criminal."

Liviana came by train to Hacienda de Bustillos to meet the President. He gave a small dinner for her, with dancing afterward. She wore a long dress of satin, colored like wine and marked with pale feathers at one shoulder. Mariachis played, a soldier's band softened for the occasion. Liviana's hair was blond, she was all laughter, so light beside the men who were gathered to plan battles. When she danced with the President, everyone watched. And some men came to congratulate Villa for the beauty of his wife.

"And she's a good cook and a good revolutionary too," he said.

After her dance with the President, Liviana helped him put his injured arm back into the sling. "I was so worried about you," she said. "Was it painful?"

"Oh, no, my dear Mrs. Villa. I have—or rather I should say I *take* to be more precise—certain medicines." He brought her to a small white table where Villa sat and pulled out a chair for her with his uninjured arm. "Sit, sit, please. May I join you and the colonel?" He went on talking as he sat. "Medicine, although I am not a doctor, is, one might say, my specialty. Homeopathy. Have you ever heard of homeopathy?"

"There's a healer like that in Torreón," Villa said. "People say he sometimes cures you. But they say he always makes you sick first."

"Exactly!" The President became excited. He waved his sling in emphasis. "You have understood—instinct—perhaps inherited, perhaps merely cultural—such studies are in their infancy—the very essence of homeopathic medicine: it is sickening, but only in a well person."

"What's the good of making a well person sick?" Liviana asked.

"Now, now we're asking—ah, you're an intelligent woman, I can see—questions of theory. Consider the logic. How else? What makes the well sick makes the sick well. Very Germanic, don't you agree?"

"Once in Parral a doctor wanted to cut off my leg," Villa said.

"Tell me your symptoms."

"My foot was black and swollen and stinking and I had a fever. I was so weak I could hardly walk."

"Surgery would have been an error. Peppers." The President sat back in his chair. He sucked his lips inward and nodded with satisfaction.

"Peppers?" Villa asked.

"You doubt my prescription."

"Peppers." Villa looked over at Liviana, hoping for advice. She offered none. He saw that she was on the verge of anger.

"Of course, peppers," the President said. "Do peppers make a well person hot, feverish? Does a well person perspire beneath his eyes when he eats peppers?"

"Yes," Villa said.

"Then what makes a well person feverish makes a feverish person well. Isn't that the theory of homeopathy?"

"Yes, sir. But what about the stinking?"

"The stomach lining of a pig."

"And the blackness?"

"Tar."

"And the swelling?"

"Bees to sting you."

"It's so simple," Liviana said.

The musicians played again. There were few dancers; the army had come to Bustillos without women. The men wore riding clothes, pieces of khaki assembled into something like uniforms. Their boots were heavy on the tiled floor. The young girls from nearby ranches who danced with the revolutionary officers kept their heads bent in shyness. Their long black braids swayed with the dancing. Some were barefoot. The music grew louder and the notes came more quickly. President Madero shouted to be heard. "Is the truth ever complicated? Light and dark, good and evil, well and sick, up and down, positive and negative, husband and wife. Is there anything complicated about the rising of the sun in the morning? To complain—although I don't accuse you of that, my dear—about the simplicity—unless you want me to be more accurate—the word I use is *clarity*—of an idea, is a French vice, distinctly French."

"How are you curing your arm?" Liviana asked, having to shout, like Madero, to be heard.

"A difficult case. There's neither fever nor swelling. I can't hurry nature's course. Poor luck." Madero shrugged. "We can't all be blessed with the kind of problems that have homeopathic solutions."

"Would it help to wound yourself in the other arm?"

"In jest—the charms of a young woman are often in her high spirits— think of young mares—one often finds truth. Wounds, however, are not diseases; there is nothing homeopathy can do for a wound until it becomes diseased."

"Should I hope your arm becomes diseased?"

"Hardly, madam."

The President excused himself, saying he was tired. Villa walked to the door with him. "My wife is always like that," he said. "She believes in you and in the revolution, sir, but she's always that way: she's like a summer fly the way she bites."

"The trouble," Madero said, "is the same for every man: he falls in love with a girl and finds himself married to a wife."

"I understand the wisdom of what you say, sir."

"Of course, we're both married men."

"When my leg was diseased I wish I had known a homeopathic healer like you, sir. I believe in it."

"Colonel Villa, at our family ranch at San Pedro I saved the lives of countless numbers of children through homeopathic medicine. I thank God that the opposites that arise through similarities are known to me. Not for my sake, I assure you, but for theirs."

[*326*]

"I'm at your feet," Villa said. He bent his knee and lowered his head. Madero touched his arm to lift him upright again. "Remember, my colonel, democracy."

Villa said goodnight to the President and went back to the table where he had left Liviana. He pulled her up out of her chair and led her across the room and out of the house. "There's an eastbound train in a while. I want you to get on it and go home."

"Why? What's wrong with you, Francisco?"

"You insulted my President."

"He talks nonsense."

"Is democracy nonsense? Is revolution nonsense? War? Dividing up the land? You made me ashamed that you're my wife. I want you to go home. I'm sending you."

"Even a President can be a fool."

He dragged her toward the railroad station. She could not keep his pace; she stumbled, she ran, she twisted her feet in the ruts of the road. "Francisco, please, don't do this to me; I'm your wife."

"He's the Redeemer."

They stood in the small wooden building that was the railroad station. He gave her his jacket to comfort her in the cold. "I was going to stay for a few days, we were going to be together; don't you want that?"

"The shame," he said.

"You're choosing him over me. I hope you know what you're doing. I hope so, because I don't think he'll return your loyalty. I hope so, because I know he doesn't love you; I can tell by the way he looks at you. He thinks you're an animal, a killer; he's using you."

"He absolved me from any crimes. He made me free. Is that enough? Do you trust him now?"

"I warned you."

The President arrived on the early morning train. He wore his yellow riding boots. Aides walked beside him, armed men, tall men; they dwarfed the President, they protected him; their eyes were wary, they suspected rooftops and shadows, they looked into all the darkened windows. The President went to the main plaza of San Andrés. He walked in a stately way, with his head held stiffly, with his back held straight. When he was alone, walking ahead of his aides, he appeared to be a tall man, he had the bearing of a tall man.

The President and his colonel embraced. Villa lifted the President while he held him; the yellow boots touched the ground only at the toes. "I thank you for the decree," Villa said. "I wish my mother was alive to hear it."

"It was only deserved," Madero answered.

"If only my mother had heard before she died. . . ."

"Perhaps she heard."

Villa let go his embrace. He looked at Madero, expecting a rich man's joke in his eyes, an arrogant wrinkle, a teasing curl at the corner of his mouth. The President's eyes were wide open, revealed sincere; the curves of his face were smooth, he left himself no place for hiding. The belief caused a tremor in Villa; he shivered in his arms and the calves of his legs, he thought of her listening, young again, as on the day she had given him the sugary skull, before she leaned so heavily on her hips, before the crime was done in her house, as if in death she had descended from the hill; and he wept aloud there in the street in front of the plaza where the nine old men played march music and the children walked past their mothers in parade.

"Colonel Villa," the President said, as if it were an order. There was no sound of reprimand in the words; he spoke expectations. "We must review the troops."

Villa gave a sign and the horsemen rode past them. They came in twos, as he had instructed them, six hundred horsemen managing as best they could the bearing of soldiers. While the President's aides whispered to Villa: "We will send a train for you and your men. We will take only one hundred horses. In two days. In the morning. There will be two trains. One is for you and one is for the others. We will send a train from Chihuahua. Two trains. Two trainloads of troops will attack Juárez. Villa and Orozco. In two days, in the morning."

"I need all the horses, Mr. President," Villa whispered, while the President smiled at the troops and waved to them and the aides allowed the children to stand in rows of circles near the Bridegroom of Mexico.

"There are only two trains, Pancho."

"I need my cavalry."

"Máximo Castillo is in charge of the arrangements—he understands these things—for the journey. Speak to him in Bustillos. Send your captain —the cross-eyed fellow I've heard about, the one from Durango or Camargo, I can't remember which—to see Castillo."

"Captain Urbina has gone to Indé with a hundred men."

"Very good. Then send another captain."

"My best captains are dead."

"God save us; what are we doing?" Madero put his left hand to his forehead. The aides touched his elbows, they hurried him; the train was waiting, there were meetings to be held, decrees to sign, letters to send, the revolution needed money, foreign governments were asking questions, Carranza had not yet made his move in Coahuila.

"Walk with me to the train," Madero said, asking. "The Liberals remain a problem. We have talked before—our first meeting, my friend—about them."

"Is there no time for the President to address the troops?"

"Our primary goal, you see, is the same: the removal of the dictator. However, the nation—we must consider the nation—is a more serious question. A new, democratic Mexico is the goal. Do you agree?"

The troops rode in circles. They had no orders. Some galloped their horses, shouting, "Long live Mexico! Long live Villa!" The band had turned to playing waltzes. The mothers put their children to dancing.

"If my mother could see us now, sir. If my mother could see her son with the President of Mexico. It would rest her soul, sir."

"You remain suspicious—political reasons would be better—of our Colonel Orozco, because of his lateness at Cerro Prieto?"

"She was a cultured woman. Priests came to our house; I remember them."

The train whistle blew. The aides hurried Madero. He lengthened his stride. The yellow boots slapped the dust. "Security," the aides said. "We must hurry. The Federals are everywhere, everywhere. Do not forget the letter to Limantour, do not forget the message from your brother, Gustavo. And your mother has not had a letter from you."

"You understand this danger, Pancho. Lawlessness, the lack of control by the new government—they don't obey orders, the Liberals—could lead to yet another revolution. Oh my God, I think of the dead!"

"I was unable to attend my mother's funeral, sir. The white candles were all around her; the priests betrayed me. Now she would understand."

A horse passed too close to them; Villa pulled Madero back, yet the rider brushed him. Villa reached for the man, catching his jacket. The horse dragged Villa for a few steps, then the man came loose, wheeling over the hindquarters, landing on his back in the street. The man lay at Villa's feet, senseless, with blank eyes. Madero knelt beside him and put his ear to the man's chest. "You are too violent with your troops," he said to Villa.

"My sister doesn't speak. My mother told me it was worse than the shame, that I caused the shame. She didn't know you would forgive me."

"He's not dead." Madero stood up, slapping the dust from his riding breeches. The band played a polka. The children shouted laughter while they danced. Down the street a man caught the riderless horse and looked through the saddlebags for whatever could be useful to him. The aides pressed the President forward, reminding him of the train, asking him to listen to the whistle.

"Be careful of the enchantments of the Liberals," Madero said. "We have some among us—in time, I will tell you their names—who oppose me. It is all, all because of their radical ideas. Unity—if we love our country and truly respect the rights of all of our people to govern themselves—is foremost, unity under the banner of effective suffrage and no reelection."

"On my mother's grave."

"Attend to the wounded, Pancho. Obey the rules of war. We must be— we are, after all, the upstarts, the revolutionaries—careful to obey the rules of war."

"In two days," the aides said to Villa, "in the early morning. Bring a hundred horses, bring all your men."

They were within sight of the railroad station. Villa pointed to the wood stacked beside the telegrapher's building. "We fought our first battle there, Mr. President. It was the first victory. We killed a lieutenant."

"Is a killing a victory, Colonel? Are we not all Mexicans?"

Villa went along dumbly. He looked to the aides for an answer. They edged closer to the President, showing wooden faces to Villa. One looked pityingly at him, as if he had always known.

The sound of the band in the plaza was faded soft; the notes were indistinguishable. They could no longer hear the voices of the children or the urgings of the mothers. The raging horsemen were on other streets. Now they passed empty houses. Dogs barked at them; they made disturbances among the chickens by their passing. They heard the boiling of the train engine, the smoke was in the air. "Mr. President," Villa said. He could not find the next words.

"Negotiation," the President said, "a war can be won by negotiation."

"They didn't negotiate with you at Casas Grandes, sir. Navarro didn't negotiate with me at Tecolote or Cerro Prieto. Look at your arm."

"One of the aims of our party is to avoid bloodshed."

They were at the train. There were more aides. They saluted the President, they nodded to Villa. Madero mounted the first step and turned back to Villa. They were nearly the same height; the thought made the President smile. "You're so young," he said, making the comment idly, as if the aides were not rushing aboard, as if the trainmen were not signaling the engineer and the whistle were not sounding. "So young." The President looked over Villa's head toward the town. "I depend on you, Pancho. Of all my colonels, you are the one most to be trusted. In two days, when you're in Bustillos again, I'll feel safe. My regards to your good wife."

The train began its quickening rhythm. There were cinders in the air. An aide took Madero's arm and helped him up onto the second step and the third. The train was moving. Villa walked beside it. He saluted. Madero returned the salute. Villa hurried to keep up with the train. He saw the sadness in the President's eyes; it was revealed in the last glance, the instant

[*330*]

of turning away, between the sight of Villa and the sight of the aides who waited on the platform, between one face and the next. "My President," Villa said to the ashes and the steel dust. He feared for him.

Villa lay on his mat on the floor of the adobe house outside San Andrés. He slept and he did not sleep; he heard the wind, he felt it run across the floor. A blanket covered him; it was between him and the wind. Two soldiers sat at the entrance to the house. Perhaps they slept. It was late, it was cold. They too were wrapped in blankets, they too felt the cold and the wind.

A woman entered the small house, passing through the place where the blanket covered the doorway. She was bent over, wrapped in a shawl and wrapped in a blanket too. She whispered, "Francisco Villa, Francisco Villa."

He heard the woman's voice. She said his name clearly; her accent was cultured, like Liviana's. "I am here," he answered.

"Help me," the woman whispered, "help my son."

Villa rolled himself in the blanket and stood up. He struck a match and lit the lantern on the table. The woman was partly revealed in the small light. Her shawl was dark red, loosely knit, like a net. She wore colored papers tied in her hair. In the brown-and-tan blanket that covered her, she held something. He thought it must be the child. "At your feet," he said. He had heard it said. Gentlemen spoke so; he was a colonel, a forgiven man.

She opened the blanket to show the child. It was naked, covered with black pitch. Turkey feathers were tied in its hair. An odor rose from inside the blanket, from the child itself. The odor was not only the dark green cleansing of pitch pine; it was mixed with something cooked. "Help my son," she said. "I have prepared him."

"No, I am not Him."

"Help my son. He doesn't move." She held up the child's thin legs and shook them. They dangled from the knees, they dangled from the hips.

"I am not Him."

"Bless my son." She cradled the child in one arm, and with her free hand she drew something out of the darkness inside the blanket. A bundle of thorns and a ball of straw. She put the ball on the table and offered the thorns to Villa.

"I am not Him."

"I know you."

He took one of the thorns and pierced each of the child's calves. There was no flesh; the loose skin lay next to the bone. Small spots of blood appeared in each of the wounds. The pitch shone in the light, it gleamed, the blood gleamed. The woman took the thorn from Villa's hand and thrust it into the ball of straw, then she took the ball from the table and put it inside her blanket. The child did not stir. The odor of the pitch was very strong, like fish cooked over a fire of green wood, like pale rotted fish. The woman covered the child with her blanket.

"I am not Him," Villa said again.

"There is an Enemy on Both Sides," the woman said.

Madero sent for Villa. He said there were traitors among them. He said their names: Alaniz, García, Salazar. Disarm them, he told Villa. You disarm them; Orozco has refused. We are on our way to the City of Juárez, and Orozco has refused.

"If they resist, Mr. President, some will be killed."

"We should avoid bloodshed."

"And if we can't?"

Madero wore a blue vest. It was silk, like a sky in summer. His breeches and his boots were tan and yellow, like ready fields. He had no quiet inside him, he could not sit, he could not lie on the camp bed that had been prepared for him. "I've known you for a long time—we've communicated before—since I was in prison—before. I dreamed you; first I dreamed you." His glance paled, he turned away; his head was tilted slightly, a man listening. He nodded, his mouth moved; his lips, amid the beard, moved, not forming words, trembling. The thin, perturbed hand passed over the President's eyes. "None will die," he said.

"You saw?"

Madero nodded. His eyes were closed. A secret smile rounded his cheeks. "Do you believe it's possible? Tell me, not lies—I'm so tired of lies—the truth, Pancho."

"You would know if I lied."

The President sighed. "There is—and you would know if I were lying— no other true answer. No other. The question. It's impossible. I can't explain—I explain to the others—one either knows or does not know. The spirit is there, it can't be taught. In us all—it's there—discovery. Democracy is the same, exactly—the scientists are wrong, Comte is wrong—like the spirit; we discover—any human being can do it—inside ourselves, the ability to think—Indian as well as Spaniard or North American—how the country should be governed. Good men—a man who loves the people and wants to do the best for them is a good man—can be recognized by anyone of any, any at all race."

"It's getting late, sir."

"Yes."

"It will take time to organize the boys. We'll have to make a plan."

"You're going tonight?" Madero looked puzzled. "They'll be asleep."

"There is an old saying, sir: the sleeping fish is swept downstream. Let me go now and do this for you."

"For Mexico."

"Long live Mexico!"

"Save us from the anarchists."

The Liberals had made a separate camp. There were few of them, and they were mostly men from cities who did not understand how to live in the hills. Schoolteachers and clerks led them to camp in open places far from water. Lawyers instructed them in shooting, and philosophers told them it was not necessary to carry heavy blankets and tents on their backs. The wind burned their skin, they were often hungry, they were cold every night, and all but a few of them were weak and feverish from dysentery. In the first days of the revolution they were the cleanest of all the soldiers; they changed their suits every morning, they washed their underwear every night, they shaved their faces and slept with their mustaches in little gauze slings, as generals do. Now they were the ragged men, the filthy speakers, the lecturers in their fouled clothes, protecting their typewriters and their tiny printing press, carrying their books and pens and ink and crumpled papers. They coughed, they limped in their city shoes, they drank too much water, they often had nothing to eat. A rich woman in California sent money to them, but it was never more than a few dollars, it was never enough. Their ammunition came across the mountains from Baja California: some lay lost in the snow, some was spread across the rock-hard floors of the canyons, much of what survived the journey did not fit their rifles. They had attacked town after town. Sometimes they had won for a day, sometimes they had won for two days or even three. After every victory, while the printing press was turning and the lecturers were in the fields and the taverns and the churches, the army came and drove them out. The dead in their dark suits and stiff collars were laid in long lines. Blood stained their vests, the grave diggers did not button their suitcoats or straighten their hair. No one stole their thin city shoes. They had no money. Their papers were thrown to the wind. They were buried in rows, piled in deep holes; in summer they were burned. Only Orozco tolerated them. He gave them food and horses and allowed them to lecture to his cowboys. They said he understood; in his silence he was like them, he was an anarchist.

Villa sent five hundred of his troops to encircle the separate camp. They went crouching; they used the night. For a long time they lay in their circle around the separate camp, patient, flat against the sand, five hundred men armed with pieces of thick wood and bars of iron and gun butts and heavy stones. Villa lay beside them, watching the fires and the shadows of the men passing. A man went to the latrine. He let out a little cry of discomfort. They heard the long sputter of his wind. Near the place where Villa lay, a thin figure poured water into a cooking pot and washed his underwear and socks. He washed them and squeezed out the water on the ground and washed them and squeezed them over and over. He lifted each article to his face, sniffed it, and hung it out on a mesquite bush to dry. The wind blew, red ashes were lifted from the fires. Above the town, in the mining camps, lights glowed. There was a smell of horses, wood smoke, dust, horses again. The camp was quiet, the fires were dying. From Orozco's camp they heard singing, "the Railroad Woman." The lights were bright yet in Madero's camp; the tents glowed. The North Americans who followed Garibaldi sang their harmonica songs and drank their whisky. The Villista camp was to the south; they could not see it. Men snored. A man had a loud fit of coughing. Someone shouted at him to be quiet, someone else called kindnesses to him, offering to bring him water, advising him to sit up and take deep breaths. The coughing slowed, became loud again, stopped.

"Now!" Villa whispered. He arose running. The circle arose with him. They entered the camp and fell on the sleeping men. They said Madero's name to identify themselves in the darkness. "Madero, Madero, Madero, Madero," they chanted to the startled men, and they beat them with the thick wood and the iron bars and the gun butts and the stones. The Liberals shouted warnings to each other, they called for help from Orozco and Villa; they thought the Federal Army had come.

A man struggled against Villa. His eyes shone white, lit by terror. "I arrest you in the name of the Revolution," Villa said.

The man tried to speak. Villa's hand was at his throat, strangling his words. The man tore at Villa's fingers, he kicked, the muscles of his neck were hard, the cords were pulled stiff. He wore a black suit, his arms and legs were thin, bubbles of mucus came out of his nostrils. Villa beat the man's head with the butt of his pistol. The cords in the neck went soft, the arms and legs were still. Villa went on to look for the next man, but there were no more; the Liberals had been subdued. They stood in shamed groups or lay senseless beside their fires. The Villistas threw brush and logs on the dying fires to light up the camp. They found Alaniz and brought him to their colonel; this is the leader, they said, this is Alaniz the Anarchist. And all they had was a paunchy man with a curled nose, a thick, unhappily curled nose.

"This is madness," Alaniz said. His lips were split and swollen; he wiped at his mouth with a bloody rag. "We're all in the same revolution."

"You betrayed Madero," Villa said.

"We wrote some letters." Alaniz had difficulty forming the words. His front teeth were broken; the rush of his breath made him shudder. "We disagreed with Madero. That's not a betrayal. How can you have elections, democracy, without disagreement? If that's what Madero tells you, he's another Díaz, nothing better."

"No!" Villa screamed, "no!" He smashed Alaniz's nose. The Liberal fell over backwards and sat on the ground near a fire. The red and yellow light showed the blood on his face. Alaniz wiped himself with the rag. He blinked his eyes rapidly, as if to clear them of some irritation. "I am not a soldier," Alaniz said. "Before this revolution I was a teacher in School Number . . . I can't remember the number now. I can't remember. I was a teacher, I read. . . ." He looked at the rag in his hand. It was wet with blood. "Oh, my God!" he said. "Oh, my God!"

The Liberals were herded into rows. They stood before the fires. Those who had been beaten were held up by the others. On the far side of the fire Villa walked up and down the length of the rows, looking over at them, preparing his words. They were anarchists, traitors, Liberals, followers of Flores Magón. They had written letters; Lazaro Alaniz had confessed to him. Madero had judged them. "For Mexico," he had said. They looked so pitiful; not one man among them wore a hat, some could not stand up without help, their shoes were tied together with rags, their shirts were filthy, their clothes were colorless. Alaniz toppled over. The men on either side picked him up. They held him up by his arms. The front of his shirt was bloodied; he no longer held the rag; his hands were dark with the blood that had dried on them; he worked his fingers absently, rubbing them clean. Villa stepped between the fires to stand close to him. Alaniz drew back, lifting his hands to protect his face. His lips were swollen thick as thumbs, the downward curl of his nose had been twisted. "I'm sorry," Villa said. Alaniz could not speak, he could not make his face into an answering expression. Villa turned away and walked back between the fires, through the line of his own followers and on toward his camp. He heard singing, he heard the filibusterers playing their Yanqui harmonica songs. The lanterns were bright in Madero's camp. He would tell the President in the morning; now he needed to lie down; his head ached, he wanted to sleep. He rolled himself in his blanket and tried to sleep. The lights born of his own eyes disturbed him. He thought of her in Chihuahua, of the smell of chocolate cooking, of the taste of chocolate from a clean cup. He lay on the hard ground. The train had come to the railroad station at Bustillos. She had not kissed him, she had touched his hand as lightly as unknown women do. The light was yellow in the train, the backs of the seats were green. She walked through the green-and-yellow car of the departing train.

The stories came back from Indé soon enough. Urbina had laid siege to the town; he had made war with snipers and dynamite thrown under cover of night. And when the town surrendered and all the rurales came forward with their hands raised and their faces wet with shame, he had done his horrors. He killed them in pieces, he used horses to tear them into halves, he sliced off the soles of their feet, he cut out their tongues, he blinded them, he buried them with ants, he opened their bowels on thick stakes, he hanged them slowly, nakedly, displaying all the weakness left in them. The people of Indé cheered him and called him the general of the town.

Madero named Pascual Orozco and Francisco Villa the generals of the Army of the Revolution. He embraced them and thanked them for all they had done for the people of Mexico. His wife was there, Sara Pérez de Madero. She had a witch's chin and a sharp nose. The sheen of her dark dress covered her arms to the wrist, her skirt brushed the floor. She nodded to her husband's generals, she did not speak to them, she did not give them her hand. The length of her chin puzzled them, the distance of her puzzled them; she was barren, her demeanor was barren; she was like the high mesas on which nothing grows.

The National Palace of the Revolution was across the river from the smelter. It was a gray house, adobe painted in the ash of boiled metal. On cold afternoons when the wind came out of the north the smoke of the great stacks settled over the gray house and seeped into it. The President's wife covered her nose and mouth with a small white handkerchief. Her eyes reddened; she looked more than ever like a witch.

Villa removed his hat when he was in the gray house. He listened to Madero tell how they would win the war by waiting, how they would force Díaz to resign, how they would not fight, they would not shed blood, they would not destroy the city.

"You tell me what we won't do," Villa said. "Tell me what we will do."

Madero lifted his hand, raising his forefinger in emphasis. "The ideals of liberty and justice will triumph."

"My people have nothing to eat, sir."

"We are laying siege to the city—not only the city, the dictatorship.

That's why we're waiting: we're laying siege to the most brutal dictator in the history of Mexico."

"We have no food and the water in the arroyo is making us sick; we're laying siege to ourselves. Sir, this is no army of young men. The men who came with me are the fathers; they understand time, they want the revolution now."

"We can hold out."

The aides pushed themselves into the space between Villa and Madero. They had papers to sign, letters to Washington, Paris, Mexico, San Antonio. Oscar Braniff said, Limantour said, Gustavo said, the reports from Mexico said, Carranza insisted, Dr. Vázquez Gómez demanded. Villa moved back toward the door. Over the shoulders of the aides he saw Madero signing papers, reading, listening; the President went back to the wooden table he used as a desk, he touched a white handkerchief to his forehead, he spoke and wrote and listened all at once. The voices blended; Villa could no longer hear what Madero was saying. The President's wife looked at Villa and smiled. Her mouth became a straight line stretched across the hanging square of her jaw. Villa put on his hat and went outside. Garibaldi was there, waiting under the canopy that had been put up to shade the entrance to the gray house. He and Villa did not speak.

Beyond the canopy, a North American waited to speak to Villa. He wore new boots and smelled of sweet tobacco. His face was pink and soft, like a fat flower. "Are you Pancho Villa?" he asked in Spanish.

"Yes."

"The bandit?"

"The general in the Army of the Revolution."

"Listen to me, General of the Revolution. You want to be famous? I can put you up there, write about you, you know. Not in some little Mexican newspaper—in the big ones, in the United States. Washington, New York, Chicago. You know what fame means? Money, women, respect. Now, what I'm looking for—all you have to do is give it to me on an exclusive basis. You talk and I'll put your name in headlines. Okay?"

Villa said nothing.

"How many men have you killed?"

"If I thought you were a man, I would make it one more."

The pink man backed away into the shade of the canopy. He looked at Garibaldi and shrugged. Garibaldi shrugged in return. They smiled at each other.

The generals stood on a hill west of the city. They waited for war. "What are they negotiating?" Orozco asked. "A city is not a horse. How can they haggle over a city?"

"He wants Díaz to resign," Villa said, looking out over the city, at the beginning of the day, the horses and the automobiles and the trolleys commencing, the people entering the streets in the morning cool, running before the sun. "He wants the city without a fight."

They looked at the city through a telescope, studying the rifle pits and barricades built in the streets, counting the mortars and the Hotchkiss guns. The revolutionaries had Charpentier's cannon and a little brass gun that had once stood in the San Jacinto Plaza on the other side of the border. There was no war, the city no longer expected war; it conducted its life in the most regular way: the Sunday bullfight was advertised, laborers in enormous hats extended the canal, the night lights shone like immortal children. Musicians, Orozco said of the men who surrounded Madero, a band of musicians; we are the only generals. They talk about anarchy, they talk and talk, and they never talk about war. Musicians. If we don't start the battle, there will be no battle.

Villa agreed. They made their plans, they gave their orders. It was the seventh of May. José Orozco and five hundred men crawled along the canal behind the drying piles of earth, and Francisco Villa and Pascual Orozco went to El Paso, Texas, to be shaved and barbered and anointed with rose water and pomade.

The little adobe house swirled in advisors and peacemakers and aides of all kinds. Heroes and attorneys filled the corners, orators stood on their toes and flexed their chests, waiting to be heard. The entrance of the generals slowed the room, quiet emanated from them. "The truce failed," Orozco said to Madero.

"Stop the shooting," the President said. His voice was thinner, from a knotted throat. He choked over the words, his face was burnt with anger. "Stop it now, right now, stop it immediately."

"It's too late," Villa said. "Herrera went over to the Federals. The truce didn't hold."

Carranza was there, the stately senator, the tall senator with his hand combing the hair of his white beard. "Withdraw the men," he said. "Order them to withdraw."

"Do you know José Orozco? He's my brother. He's there. I saw him."

"I order you to withdraw," Madero said. "We are retiring to Chihuahua. I gave the order. I gave the order." He tapped his breast with the end of his forefinger.

"There is no way, sir," Villa told him. "The men are trapped there. It's a very bad position. If we don't help them, the Federals will use grenades and mortars. It will be like Tecolote, like Cerro Prieto. They'll die, they'll all die; the shells will tear them to pieces."

[*338*]

"Nonsense," Carranza said. "Let them withdraw the same way they got there."

"Why don't you go and lead them out?" Orozco said. "Teach them what you learned in all the battles of Coahuila. Show them how a hero fights."

There was laughter from somewhere; Carranza withdrew. Madero walked in circles. He was made smaller by the moment, squeezed. "I can't —it would be immoral—abdication of my responsibility—to let them die." He hid his eyes in his hand. He stamped his foot; the yellow boot brought dust from the floor. "I didn't plan for this. It's Díaz, it's the waiting." He paced, he made circles, he was like a starched bird walking. He stopped in front of Villa and Orozco and looked up at them. "You never wear your hats in my house," he said.

"They're shooting at my brother," Orozco said.

"We must maintain order."

Orozco said, "I can hear the gunfire."

"They disobeyed my orders; we were to retire to Chihuahua." Madero paced, he circled; he stopped again before his generals. "Can we take this city?"

The generals smiled. "Yes, sir," Orozco said, and Villa added, "In four days."

Madero closed his eyes and turned his face up to heaven. "Please God," he said, "may it please God."

Orozco looked down at the President. He saw him through narrow eyes, he spoke to him with the flat voice of the battlefield: "Is that an order?"

Madero nodded. "In the morning, in the morning, my generals."

Villa spent the day in his camp along the river. He ordered the last of the rations to be distributed at noon and told his men to eat well and then to sleep; they would not go into battle that day. He stayed inside most of the day to think about how to attack the city from the south. His troops would face the machine guns and the mortars, Navarro would not be afraid to fire on him, the Americans would not intervene from the south. He lay on his low bed and hung one arm over the edge to draw in the dirt with the handle of his spoon. After he made a map of the southern end of the city, he pushed little piles of dirt into the street areas to indicate the barricades the mice had reported. Every street was blocked, every intersection was defended, impassable. It was a tactic learned from the French, someone had said, perhaps at Orozco's meeting; perhaps in his own camp, one of his men who had been an army officer had said it: across a narrow street a simple barricade becomes a fortress; three sides are protected and the fourth permits both supply and retreat.

He swept the floor flat with the side of his hand and began again, making only a single street, pushing rows of dirt into place to indicate the barricades and the walls of the houses. First he made only the outer walls that lined the street, then he made the inner walls and the windows and the doors. His people would be safe when they were in the houses, they could go in through the doors. But as they went from house to house, they would expose themselves to fire from behind the barricades; the riflemen and the machinegunners would destroy them; no one would survive the streets. He rolled over on the bed and felt the adobe wall next to him; no bullet could pass through it; behind the walls, inside the houses, his people would be safe. But they could not move.

He lay there, looking at his dusty hands, touching the walls of his model street; sometimes he was near sleep, sometimes he turned damp with the thought of men dying, with the thought of defeat, of rows of men, stacks of men, all bloody and curled or sprawled or neatly fallen, as if in different sleeps. At dusk, a man came into the room to recite a message from González Garza. He told of the situation in the city, the number of dead, the number of wounded, the positions of the troops, the problems of water, the problems of food. He told of how the wounded died on both sides and how the dead were buried in the streets.

Villa listened. He did not interrupt the messenger except to ask him once to repeat the locations of the troops. When the recitation was completed, he said: "Go back now and tell them to shut off the electricity. Tell them it's very important to me." The messenger saluted lazily and strolled out. He had been standing in Villa's model of the street and its houses; his footprints were there; he had flattened the walls. Villa ran out the door. He knew, he saw the walls falling, it had come to him, the city was his.

The first barricade was at the end of the long block of houses. The fronts of the houses faced the street in long lines. The side walls of the houses were close to each other, some of them almost touching. The walls that made a chute and a slaughterhouse could also be the walls of a barricade. Villa explained his plan to the assembled troops in the railroad yard. He asked the men who had worked in mines to come forward, he asked for the dynamiters to work their trade.

Yes, it could be done, they said. Railroad spikes would serve as drills and tamping bars, blankets could be used for wadding. They could use dynamite sticks or black powder. The dynamite sticks were quicker, the black powder could be better controlled. There was only one problem, they said: to blow open the side walls without destroying the front walls of the houses. They would have to work carefully. It would be slow, they said; a large explosion inside a house could level all four walls. That was the danger; every man warned him.

He went with the dynamiters to the first house. They chopped a small hole in the outside wall that faced the cross street. Black powder was poured into the hole, tamped solid, touched by a wick and secured with pieces of a blanket. The wick was lit and they stood back to watch the explosion. The center of the wall was blown away as sand. But the hole was too high. They set another charge near the ground to clear out the space and make it easy for a man to pass through.

On the other side of the street, also in the first wall of the first house, a stick of dynamite was wedged into the second brick above the ground. The explosion opened a perfect hole. It reached from the ground almost to the roof and it was wide enough for two men to walk through at the same time. The dynamiters on that side of the street cheered. They shouted for the revolution and for Pancho Villa.

After that, it was only work, it was like the mines, as dark as the mines. They went forward from house to house, the riflemen following the dynamiters, all of them safe from the Federals who waited behind the barricade, all of them moving behind a barricade of their own. When they were close to the end of the block, the Federals fired at them from their barricade in the street, but it was no use; the machine guns could not penetrate the thick adobe of the front walls of the houses. When the Federals saw that they were going to be outflanked, they retreated to the barricade at the end of the next block. The dynamiters followed, moving slowly, wall by wall, house by house toward the center of the city.

The pattern of the battle was made. The night advanced in screams and explosions, in accumulations of the shrunken dead, the not yet paled dead. The fat mortars painted the cold light with instants of red, and afterward the sand spraying upward and the smoke rolling. Prisoners curled in the lee of houses and looked up with white shining eyes at the revolutionaries passing, those who went to fight and those who came back soft with weariness and relief. Anaya's volunteers, dressed in their red crosses and bloodied aprons, drove their wagons in close behind the battle and lifted the wounded onto the wooden beds; they took them away from war, the revolutionaries in their blankets and great hats and the Federals in their blue and red. There was no food, there was little water; the faces of the men blackened in the smoke and sand; even those who rested could not wash—their eyes were circled in darkness, their hunger seemed permanent, a hunger of long standing.

From all sides the revolutionaries moved toward the center of the city. The battle reached into the houses where the people waited in fear of the night, not knowing where to run, seeing war on all sides. Women died in the cannon fire, the bodies of children lay in the streets. Villa ordered the prisoners up to the battle line to bury the dead. But they worked their shovels in fear, they made holes in the streets, they dug the shallowest graves; in the panic of the shellburst night a woman's hand was left protruding from a grave.

The Federal lines contracted, like a flower frightened of the night, closing up its vulnerability in soft shields. The revolutionaries converged on the center of the city, creeping along the sides of buildings, dragging cannon through the streets. They stopped at every store they passed to steal whatever they could carry. Men in three suits and stacks of hats carried rifles to war. A man with a sewing machine under his arm crept forward, stopping and stopping to change the heavy machine from one arm to the other. Some men carried dresses over their shoulders, some filled their blankets with pots and eating utensils, some hung shoes around their necks like scarves, some carried farm equipment, some carried furniture; a string of men ran through the streets carrying chairs, stopping whenever they were tired to sit on the chairs and rest while the others passed them as if on parade.

Villa ran from the doorway into the street, into the thieving stream of his army. He led them into the mute city, the wounded city. He was not afraid, he was not cold. With shouts and uncontrollable laughter, he took them to the next barricade and the next. They went together through the holes in the walls into the gore of the failed defenders. "Old men, my old men," he called to them. "Come on, old men; the revolution is a dream." He plunged into the city, the mute city; he saw them take everything. He laughed, he gleamed. The city was all around him, soft and bloody, stolen. He saw Félix Terrazas. They laughed for each other. "I'm burning," Villa said.

Madero called his generals to the little gray house. He gathered them in the room with all his aides, with all his advisors, with all his negotiators. The generals stood in the center of the room, four men dressed in glorious filth, stinking of war, sulphurous and bloody. Their eyes were too large, there was no strength in their cheeks; they smiled crookedly, their faces failed them. Orozco had the look of an old man; one shoulder drooped, his dark coat hung open. Garibaldi was stiff; his head nodded continually, running on the cogs of his neck. The elegance of Gonzáles was fouled in blood, he was crisp with blood; his mouth hung open, he scratched his beard, he scratched his head, circles of sweat rose up the crown of his campaign hat. Villa stood behind the others. He was the filthiest of them all: his shirt was torn open, his coat was burned and spattered with gore; his boots, his sleeves, all the parts of him, had been fouled by war and dusted over with sand. He could not keep his fingers still; even when he closed his hands the spasms rattled his fists.

Madero sat at the wooden table. Aides and advisors surrounded him in tiers. Papers covered the table: yellow cables, sheaves of folders filled with papers, long documents, handwritten papers, typewritten papers, books of papers. He cleared a place before him and placed his folded hands on the table. "We have asked for a cease-fire," he said. "In our desire—and I assure you, gentlemen, it is founded in the best intentions for us now, and more importantly, for the future of the nation—to save lives and property—you must remember that all property is not part of the Porfiriato—the homes and shops of ordinary people, the people for whom we are fighting, those good people—on their behalf we have asked for a cease-fire."

The men in all the tiers behind the President nodded while he spoke. Don Venustiano Carranza, the tallest of them, touched his fingers to his beard, he combed his beard, he looked across the room through the darkened lenses that hid his eyes. "I concur," he said. "The Secretary of War concurs."

"It's too late," Orozco said.

"I gave orders," Villa said.

Carranza stepped forward through the tiers to stand beside the President. He wore a long gray jacket, like a coat. It had the appearance of a uniform from some earlier war. He spoke softly, he let his words descend over the others. "Then give new orders."

"It's not so easy to stop an army," Villa said. "I gave orders, I pulled the trigger. Don't you think I was afraid? Now there is a war."

González Garza put himself forward. "To whom did you ask for a cease-fire?"

"Colonel Tamborel," the President said.

Villa shook his head. He made a snorting noise. "Tamborel is dead. We buried him this morning. I had his own men dig a hole for him."

"Tamborel was a fine officer," Carranza said, as if he were speaking over a grave. "He was a loyal officer and a brilliant defensive strategist. In an army with so many ambitious generals we needed men like him."

Villa stepped through the space between the generals and the advisors. He put his face up close to Carranza. "Tamborel lost the city, Mr. Carranza. He had cannon and mortars and machine guns, and we took the city from him with nothing but rifles." Carranza made a sour face. He showed his contempt for the smell of battle by stepping away from Villa; but Villa pushed forward, following him, keeping his words in Carranza's face. "Do I disgust you, sir? Come into the streets then, come and smell the dead, come and listen to the wounded." He turned back to the other generals. "Mr. Carranza wants a cease-fire. Mr. Carranza concurs. Mr. Carranza wants new orders. Mr. Carranza is all perfumed; the smell of battle disgusts him." When he saw them laughing, he turned back to Carranza. "I gave orders. I told my colonel to bring me the sword of a Federal general, and when I have the sword, I'll put it on my President's table. There will be a cease-fire, Mr. Carranza. There will be a cease-fire when Navarro surrenders. And if he doesn't surrender, there will also be a cease-fire—when the last Federal is dead."

"Our country has a history of uncontrollable generals," Carranza said. "We have one in the presidential palace now."

Orozco stepped up to Madero's desk and leaned forward over him. "We would like to speak to you privately."

"I have no secrets from these men," Madero said.

"Then we have nothing more to say."

"Very well," Madero said. He excused himself to the tiers of men who stood behind him, saying, "These are my loyal generals."

They went out together, the President followed by his generals. There was a crowd around the little building that was being made into a hospital. The carts that were not used to carry the wounded across the river had been collected there. Men were being unloaded from the wooden beds of the carts and laid out in a row. The area smelled of blood and horses; there were flies everywhere. Women in white aprons walked along the row of men, washing them, giving them water, swatting away the flies that fed in the open wounds.

"Carranza is a bad choice," Orozco said.

Madero looked up at his generals. He walked in a valley of generals. "Don Venustiano is the commander of the military forces of Coahuila, a respected—not only by me, but by men of all political variations—officer and gentleman. He has stature, he gives stature to his office. Everyone agrees. Vázquez Gómez, the doctor, agrees, as does his brother."

"He's a Porfirista," Orozco said.

Madero stopped. He shook his head at them. "No, no, no, you don't understand, not in this situation. Politics—not war—is our job—the most important task before the nation now is a political agreement that can heal —we're weak if we're divided—the wounds the Porfiriato has made: anarchists on the one hand, scientifics on the other, and between them— there is a center that can hold, I have seen it, I know—are those who love our country and every person in it, rich or poor, pale or swarthy, Catholic, Freemason, or Jew."

"Not the Chinese," Villa said.

The President took Villa's arm in his hand. He gave him a loving shake. "Even the Chinese, Pancho, even them." Villa pulled away, sulking. "Remember," Madero said, "our slogan: effective suffrage, that means everybody, even the Chinese."

"They destroy the race; they'll make us into a race of mules."

"We'll discuss that another time; we came out here to talk about Don Venustiano."

Orozco said, "He served under Díaz. He's a landlord."

"I am also a landlord," Madero said. "I have friends in the government. Limantour has been a friend of the Maderos since before I was born. Do you also want to remove me from office?"

"Every tree has different leaves," Orozco said.

"What does that mean?"

"We don't want him."

"Venustiano Carranza is my Minister of War."

"And will Juan Navarro be your general?"

Madero smiled; he took comfort in the question. "Of course not," he said, "under no circumstances."

"He'll be executed," Villa said.

Madero raised a cautionary finger, "He'll be tried. Such decisions are neither for generals nor for presidents. There are courts of law. He'll be tried in a court."

Villa was satisfied. "Good enough, he'll be tried and then executed."

"No, he'll be tried and then we'll do whatever the courts decide."

"And who will be the judge?" Orozco asked. "Carranza?"

"We're negotiating now for the resignation of General Díaz. I asked for a cease-fire to help in the negotiation. You tell me it's too late. If you say it's too late, then I believe you. But you must give me time—a government needs time to operate, to change, to make decisions, to set up a method for governing—the time to do these very important things. Let Navarro wait. There are other issues."

"Carranza tried to make an agreement with Vázquez Gómez to declare against you," Orozco said. "He's loyal to General Reyes, not to you."

Madero rolled his head from side to side. His lips were pursed. He made a schoolmaster's face. "There is a philosopher of war, a German—you must know him, Clausewitz—he said that war is a continuation of politics by other means. What happens in war? Men negotiate, as in politics—we know that much about politics, don't we? Now what has Mr. Carranza done but negotiate? If such a discussion took place—not that I question you, General Orozco—between the doctor and Carranza, what is it but a negotiation? Remembering our philosophy, the very reason for our going to war— effective suffrage and no reelection, democracy—how can we attack a man for following the ideals of our struggle?"

"He'll betray you," Villa said.

"If he opposes me in the election, it is not a betrayal; it is only democracy. Oh, my brave generals, we have so much to learn about democracy." He wiped his face with a white handkerchief. He had not taken a hat when he left the gray house. The sun bothered him, he shaded his eyes with his hand. "Now I must go back," he said, "because there is so much to do. The Liberals have taken Tijuana. We must be sure that the end of the Porfiriato is not the beginning of a civil war between us. When a government falls—this is what we're all working for, men are dying right now to bring down a government—there must be another government ready to take its place —a vacuum is the loss of everything, chaos, the opportunity for the worst forces to try to gain power—and that new government must keep order."

The generals followed him back to the gray house. They mounted their horses and rode back to the city, circling around the center, going their separate ways to their own lines. They came upon a silent city. The soldiers waited in their places, the buildings seemed empty, there was no wind, even the bloody carts did not move in the streets. General Navarro had surrendered.

There was to be a parade in the afternoon, the official entrance into the city by the army of the revolution. The parade was to follow the burial of the dead and the business of war that is left over after a battle. For the soldiers the business was the looting of stores and restaurants and houses; for Villa there was other work: from the second-floor windows of a building just off Juárez Avenue a sniper had wounded more than twenty men, and now it was time to find the sniper. Villa went to the building, a hardware store owned by Antonio Mestas, a small building with a wooden porch and apartments above the store, an innocent place, run-down, with peeling stucco and an unpainted ladder reaching up to the porch on the second floor. The hardware store was closed when he arrived, the shade was pulled down over the glass in the door, and the large window was boarded over behind the broken glass.

Three soldiers went ahead of him and pounded their fists and rifle butts on the door, demanding entrance. After a long time, a little man in a white shirt with thin maroon stripes opened the door. He bowed to the soldiers and welcomed them. He was apologetic, he squeezed his hands together and walked quickly from counter to counter inside the store, telling the prices of the merchandise. "Pancho Villa," he called out, "I am a poor merchant. Spare me, save me; you are the saviour and the defender of the poor. Don't let them rob me, please."

Villa entered the store, walking heavily, wearily, his boots thumping on the board floor. More soldiers followed. The little man in the striped shirt backed away from them. He was frightened, he held his hands out before him; they were clenched together, as if in desperate prayer.

"Where do you live?" Villa asked.

"At the eastern end of the avenue. I live at the eastern end in a modest house with a modest garden. I'm a poor man; my prices are low. Ask me, ask my customers."

"Who lives upstairs?"

"Strangers. Boarders. I'm a poor man, sir; I take in boarders to earn a little more. I need the money. Business is not good; there are too many hardware stores, and across the border they sell some things for less."

"I want to look at the rooms," Villa said.

"Oh, no, please. The rooms are not fit for a general."

Villa leaned over and whispered to Mestas: "But there's a certain woman who might be very comfortable here."

Mestas smiled, he leered; his hands were no longer clenched, his shoulders widened. He led Villa through the curtain to the back of his store and up the stairs to the sleeping rooms. "There are three rooms, General Villa. Who knows? Maybe you'll have need for all of them." He sang the words. He waggled his eyebrows.

Villa opened the door to the corner room. The window was open and there were water jars and cups on the dresser and on the floor. The bed was not unmade, but the bedcovers were wrinkled, as if someone had slept on top of them. "You don't turn down the covers?" Villa asked.

"Well, sometimes. You understand, comrade." Mestas spoke familiarly. He made generous motions with his hands. "It's a good bed. You can really use the sword in this bed." Mestas rubbed his crotch.

Villa went to the bed and touched it. There was a faint odor of gunpowder. He reached down and took the side of the bed frame in his hands, lifting it, standing the bed on its side against the wall. On the floor under the bed were hundreds of empty cartridges and a small-caliber target rifle. Villa scooped up a handful of cartridges and sniffed them. He looked at Mestas. The small man clenched his hands again. "It wasn't me," he said. "There was a Federal soldier up here, a sergeant."

"Yes, there was a Federal soldier up here," Villa said. He took the pistol from his holster and aimed it at the center of the small man. Mestas opened his hands and spread his arms as if to embrace Villa. His eyes were shining, his mouth was open. Villa shot him.

The small man was thrown back against the wall. He stood there, holding the wound in his belly and making short humming sounds, like the sounds of pleasure. Villa waved two soldiers into the room. "No doctor," he said to them, "no doctor for him." The soldiers nodded to the order. They pulled the bed over onto its four legs and sat down to watch Mestas die.

A few women came to the camp in the afternoon. They were old with hunger, they were accompanied by young children. The women sat at the edge of the camp, folded in the Indian way, covered with widow's shawls, dark objects, black and brown, still as stones, waiting, encircled with children in pale dresses, in nakedness and filth. Then the old couples came, the slow-moving women with their hands on the elbows of bent men, and they stood in the sun, pairs and pairs, behind the widows. They accumulated. A line of them came slowly walking, appearing out of the last of the rows of houses, a line as long as a town.

Soldiers went among them. "Who are you waiting for?" they asked.

"Pancho Villa," the waiting people said, the standing people and the sitting people. "We are hungry."

"There is no food," the soldiers said.

"We will wait."

The soldiers walked among the waiting people. They did not know what to do. The sun was hot, there was no wind, the earth was paled, the people were drying up. When Pancho Villa came back from the city, riding on his heavy horse, ready for parade, the people did not speak to him; they only looked, they only watched. They did not beg, their hands were not held out. They were there. They were like ashes on the sand.

"They came to see you," a sergeant said to Villa. "They know your name."

"Is it because they are hungry?"

"There is no food."

"Then get food. If there is corn, go to the mill and grind it. If there are cattle, slaughter them and give the first pieces to the widows."

"And if there is nothing, sir?"

"There is something, the rich always have something. Give it to the people, give something to everyone who is waiting."

"An order came from the President: we are to shoot looters."

Villa stood up in the saddle, balancing in the stirrups. He looked out over the waiting people. He saw their patience, he smelled the dryness of them; they were vulnerable to winds. "Feed them," he said, "feed the people before you feed the troops."

The soldiers brought fresh water, they brought ground corn in great white sacks. They slaughtered steers and butchered them there on the sand where the people could see the cutting of the meat. All that could be found was given, first to the widows who sat waiting and then to the old who stood behind. The people took the water and the corn and the meat and hid the food in the secrets of their blankets. As quietly as they had come, they went away, a long line of them, a line as long as a city; the widows and their children, the old women and the old men. They returned to the city. They said nothing, their hands were not quick; they walked slowly, the feet of the women could not be seen.

Villa remained outside the city. He stayed in his camp with all his troops, talking to them, speaking of their courage and of the decorum of victors. Visitors came to the camp. They brought cameras. They made pictures of the troops, they asked Villa to pose for them, to preen himself. He did whatever they asked: he smiled, he looked into the sun, he made his horse rear up on its hind legs to please those who asked if he was truly half man and half horse, a beast like the one told to Motecuhzoma.

A messenger came from Orozco in the early evening, asking Villa to meet the general in the Café Central. Villa put on his dark suit and his shiny boots that covered his knees, and he rode into the city. He sat at a small table with Orozco and a tall thin boy with staring eyes and one hand trembling, waiting to reach for his pistol, a defender of generals, a boy with mountain manners and no appetites. The boy sat with them but he did not speak. He drank only water. He was like a folded grasshopper. When the people with cameras came to the table, the boy looked at them with curiosity. He watched the bellows of the cameras open, he listened to the winding and clicking sounds. After a while Orozco signaled to the boy that enough pictures had been taken. The boy snapped into his full height. His hand held a pistol. The people with the cameras ran away, all but one, and the boy beat that one with the barrel of his pistol, bloodying the photographer's face and smashing his camera and flash powder stand.

Orozco looked around at the other tables, at the staring people. They saw his eyes and turned away. He said nothing, he looked out the front doorway to the street. "I saw Madero today," he said. His voice had no light, he had no light in his face.

"When do we get Navarro?"

"I had a visit from Dr. Vázquez Gómez."

"What about Navarro?"

Orozco said nothing. He put money on the table. The money was uncounted; he did not look at the bills, he did not read the amounts, he let the paper float down onto the marble top of the table. "Let's go outside," he said.

They walked north to the river and turned west, moving away from the center of the city, out of the yellow light. They saw the fires of the chimneys across the river, the burning smoke of the smelter floated over them. The wind changed; they smelled the water and the dusty earthworks of the canal. "Here," Orozco said, pointing to a low place in the earthworks. "Navarro walked across here. He wrapped up his clothes and tied them on his back and swam over to the other side."

"It's impossible," Villa said. "He was a prisoner in his house. There were guards. I sent some of my own people to watch the house."

"The President gave orders. Your President, Villa; your Bridegroom of

Mexico, your Apostle, your Redeemer, your fucking dwarf Jew bastard from Parras. He moved him to the German consulate and the old son of a bitch walked out of there and swam the river."

"It's true?"

"General Villa, you are as stupid as a side of beef. And don't reach for your fucking gun because I'm insulting you. The next beef on the next hook is General Orozco. What a pair we are! Didn't we know when he put that Reyista bastard in his cabinet? Didn't we know when he took the city and he made Carranza his Minister of War?" He lifted his hands and drew his fingers into trembling fists. "We're stupid, two stupid country boys screwed by the Jew and his rich friends. He stole Navarro from us. He stole Navarro! God damn him! May he die without a priest!"

"He was good to me," Villa said. He watched Orozco, he saw the cramped lines of his neck, the chew and grit of his jaws.

"He used you! He used your gratitude. He betrayed you, he betrayed me. He had a choice between us and Navarro and he chose Navarro! He chose a man who murders women and children over us!

"Villa, they tell me that after the battle the poor went out to your camp because they knew you would give them food and water. That's true, isn't it? You fed them until there was nothing left for your own troops. You didn't eat that night, did you? I know you, Pancho Villa. I know what matters to you. Is Madero your man? Did Madero miss a meal? Did he go one day without shining his yellow boots? Villa, when the ambulance drivers were taking the wounded to the other side, they passed Madero and his father and his brothers in their fine clothing going to a fancy dinner. Is Madero your man? Inocencio, he calls himself; he even insults us with his name.

"He's a landlord, man, and all landlords are the same. Carranza is a rich man, Limantour is a rich man, Reyes is a rich man; they're all rich men, they all sleep on feathers, all their wives wear silk. Do you think Madero is going to do anything for the poor? He makes games with them. He feeds them herbs to make them well so they can pick more of his rubber plants. He uses the poor like he used us. You know how you can tell? Look at his skin, look at the color of his skin. He's not one of us, he's not one of our race.

"Villa, I swear to you, if that man is President, you'll stand before a firing squad. I swear to you on my mother's soul."

Orozco loosened himself from Villa; he withdrew to make turns on the sandy ground, to mark a faint circle with the toe of his boot. He settled, he became again the muttering man, the slowly graceful man; his face was again appropriate to the celebration of the Day of the Dead, a northern mountain face. "Where is your anger?" he asked. His voice fell away, his words were taken into the vagueness of the city, the mistaken silence. "I expected you to have more anger."

"Don Abraham rescued me," Villa said. "He's a good man." The flatness of his words left no doubt; it was a test.

"Yes, he's a good man; I believe that. But what power does he have in a nest of Jews and secret Porfiristas?" Orozco shook his head. "No, nothing, no power. The plan is to push him out, to make him the governor of the state, Vázquez Gómez told me. And you, do you know what they call you? The animal, Madero's puma. They laugh about your clothes. Madero amuses them with imitations of your accent. He shows them how Pancho Villa can swallow an *s* without even chewing it up first."

"He says that?"

"Worse."

"You heard him?"

"Yes. We argued over it. I could have been the Secretary of War, but I argued for a brave man."

"What did he say? What more?"

"There are some things I can't say."

"Tell me what he said."

"No. I promised not to say the words. I swore to myself. I owe that to you, as one general to another, as a comrade, as a member of the race. God hears, Pancho; I can't say the words before God."

Villa threw his hands up to hide his face. He sobbed. He covered his eyes with the thickness of his arms. He sought a place to rest, to lean himself. He swayed, his feet turned and scraped in the sandy place.

"It should be a government of generals," Orozco said.

"Yes."

"The revolution should benefit the poor."

"Yes."

"Madero is a rich Jew who should be arrested."

"Yes."

"He betrayed us."

"Yes."

"Tomorrow at ten we'll each bring fifty men."

"Yes."

"Swear!"

Villa took his arms from the protecting of his face. He leaned over and touched one hand to the earth. He ground the sandy earth between his fingers, he felt the grit and dryness of it.

"Swear!" Orozco insisted. "Swear!"

Villa ate the earth. He kissed the earth from his fingers.

＊　＊　＊

He lay on the bed in the fine clothes and shining boots he had worn in the evening. His mother watched him. She was the summer mother, she had given him sugar candy. She was surrounded by white candles. He saw her through the mirroring darkness. He asked forgiveness from her, a promise. She remained the summer mother among white candles; a dust of bones cannot come down the hill. He called to her, he called to his sisters. He went out into the camp and called the name of his brother who had come with him to the City of Juárez. Men awakened, complaining, but when they saw it was he, they were quiet, afterward laughing, showing a second face.

Félix Terrazas walked back into the adobe house with him. "They know about Hipólito," Terrazas said; "they saw him in the city."

Villa sat on the edge of the bed. The room was dark but for the reflected light of the unseen moon. Terrazas lifted the globe of the lamp to light it, but Villa told him to leave the room in darkness. "I was dreaming," he said. "The light gets rid of the dreams."

"I saw my dead mother."

"Forgive me."

Villa washed his face with the dry palm of his hand. He rubbed his eyes clear. "Do you see how they change when they know it's me? I never wanted to be a general. How can a general trust anyone? They know I have power over them. Why do they do what they do? I don't know them anymore; I don't know anyone."

"You lead them, sir. Of course they trust you."

"Félix, you're already a colonel; what do you want of me?"

"To serve you, sir."

"The Judas goat has power. Did you ever think of that? He goes first and he goes alone. The other animals follow him."

"I don't understand."

"Madero. Madero betrayed us! He let Navarro cross the river! After everything, after so many dead, he let Navarro cross the river! Now, Madero is the enemy; there's nothing else left to do. We'll arrest him in the morning."

"Hail Mary!"

"I can't sleep, man. I don't know anything, I'm not a wise man; but I'm a general, and who can a general ask? I didn't want to be a general. I had a meat market; it was my store. Now there's a revolution, and who knows what will come after this? I can't sleep, man; the sweat keeps me awake. You would lie to me, you would show me the face I want to see. How can I ask you?

"Before I was married, I trusted my wife; I had no power over her. Now

I'm her general too. I had a friend, Eleuterio Soto, who never lied to me. He died at Tecolote Flat; Navarro killed him. I need him now. My brother, Hipólito, what is he? I can't ask him. The sweat is so thick, a stinking syrup comes out of me, a general's sweat. I can't sleep. My mother doesn't answer, my father died so long ago, my sister doesn't speak. Should we arrest Madero? Tell me what you think, Terrazas. Don't lie to me."

"Do you want me to light the lamp so you can see my face?"

"I'll know by what you say."

"You won't be pleased."

"Tell me."

"I don't know what you should do. I thank God I'm not a general."

"That's all?"

"Yes."

"Félix, if you lit the lamp, it would still be dark in this room."

"No one ever proposed that I should be a general. When Navarro surrendered to me, I remember, he asked for a general in my place. He said he only wanted to surrender to a general. I asked him what difference it would make, and he told me I couldn't understand. Now I know what he meant. Now I know that I should have killed him there in the barracks. For Mexico. For what's going to happen."

"You take Madero's side, don't you?"

"I'm tired, sir. Forgive me."

"Did you ever hear of Ignacio Parra?"

"No, sir."

"I'll need fifty men in the morning. Tell them to be ready to leave here at nine o'clock on the dot. Now I'll try again to sleep."

Villa lay back on the bed as Terrazas made his way to the door. The colonel stood in the lighted space for a moment, looking back. "I'm sorry," he said. "This business . . . we're all alone, even colonels."

Villa lay with the night. He spoke to the figures that wandered the walls.

The President was in the main room of his house in the city. His brother Gustavo and Roque González Garza were with him. Sánchez Azcona, the President's secretary, led Villa and Orozco into the room. "The generals," he said, presenting them as if they were strangers in the white stuccoed house. Madero looked up from a sheaf of papers and smiled. He walked about the room, reading the papers, putting one after another at the back of the sheaf. He had a hummingbird's pace.

"Mr. President," Villa said, "I came to talk about the problem of General Navarro."

"He's next door—I put him there—in the German consulate."

"No," said the President's brother, "not anymore. He escaped across the border. The old man swam the river, imagine that!" Gustavo chuckled. He was fat, his face was soft, uncooked, clerk's dough. Villa was beside him. They faced the President.

"Well, well," Madero said. He could not keep from glancing at the papers as he spoke. "Maybe—and I'm not certain—it's all for the best. A war—this battle, at least—seems to be—the dictator could change everything—how he lies! all the time, all the time—over. Why, considering that, should we—revolutions must end sometime—continue the killing after the peace is made?" He looked at the papers for a moment, then returned to the men in the room. "Swam the river in the night!" Madero giggled. "Ignominious!"

"I wanted him," Villa shouted. "I earned him!"

Madero put the sheaf of papers on his writing table. He showed his weary eyes to Villa. "What good are executions?" he asked. "We didn't go to war to take prisoners and have executions."

"You're under arrest," Villa said. Something poked him in the side. He reached for his revolver.

"I'll kill you," Gustavo said. He pushed the barrel of his revolver hard against Villa's side.

Halfway across the room González Garza stood behind Orozco, holding a pistol to his back. "And I'll do the same for you, general."

"Me?" Orozco showed the innocence of open hands. "Why me?"

"My boys are outside," Villa said to the President. He looked over at Gustavo. "Do you understand me? Can you understand my country accent?"

"We were raised in the country," Madero said, imitating Villa's speech. "Don't insult me."

"You were the one I never feared," Madero said. He stayed in his place, unmoving, the hummingbird poised. The perfume of him was in the room, its own flower. He had old eyes; his face could not bear the weight of them. "You were the one I knew beyond flesh. In what cannot be understood I understood you—one spirit and another touching—Francisco and Francisco—Pancho and Pancho—they are always surprised that we are so young. And you betrayed me."

"There are troops outside," Gustavo said.

Madero's head turned, sudden and distinct, as if on a bird's neck. He ran out into the street.

They heard him, his voice reached into the house; he stood on the back seat of an automobile and his voice carried over the heads of the gathered soldiers; the thin, urgent sound came over the walls and into the rooms. He spoke in the straightest way, without digressions; the words did not come at the same time from all the separate doors of his mind. "Brave soldiers," he began, "men of the revolution, victors in the battle of the City of Juárez, Mexico is ours! We await the resignation of the dictator Porfirio Díaz!" They cheered, a hundred voices and more arriving. "Together we have won the freedom of Mexico, we have returned the nation to the people. There will be free elections, there will be effective suffrage, that is where I have led you, that is where I believed you wanted to go.

"I opposed the Porfiriato not for myself, but for what I saw in our country. I see people without food when food is plentiful. I see houses without corn when the silos are full. I see children who have not tasted milk since the day they left the mother's breast. I see people, women, children, people like us, Mexicans, who do not taste eggs or meat or fish year after year. And I see landlords who have gobbled up everything. I see that the rewards have gone to those who stole the land and not to those who work the land, and I say that is the injustice suffered by a people who do not have free elections. I say that is the injustice suffered by a people who do not have democracy! And I say the beginning of the end of that injustice came on the day I led you to this city! The yoke is lifted from our necks!" Again they cheered. Some crossed themselves. They said he was the Redeemer, they said he was the Bridegroom of Mexico. Women came with their children, they held up their children to show them the Apostle, the Innocent.

"And now that the country is ours, now that there will be a government which has a base in the will of the people, what have we won? Will the Plan of San Luis Potosí keep its promise? Will power be taken from the hands of the few and given over to the people, the free people? I fear that is not the will of some men who fought here. I fear that some brave men, some good soldiers, have lost sight of the goals of the revolution. They do not seek justice and freedom, they do not seek the return of the uncultivated lands, they do not seek the removal of corrupt judges, cowardly legislators, and a dictator who forced us all to live in shame. There are some, some good soldiers, some good men, who have lost sight of the goals of the revolution. They seek power for themselves, they believe they are wiser than the people, they believe their will is greater than the will of the people, they put pride above compassion, vengeance above honor. The Plan of San Luis Potosí said we would not loot the cities that fell to our revolutionary army, we would not kill defenseless prisoners. That is what is said in Article Eleven, Section B. Looting and the shooting of defenseless prisoners are crimes; the most severe punishment is to be applied to those who perpetrate these crimes. That is what it said in our Plan. And that is the Plan to which I swore my allegiance. That is the Plan from which I will not deviate. That is the Plan to make Mexico free!"

Villa turned his face to the President's brother. He showed him the eyes of a child frightened by darkness, he showed him the open, incapable mouth of a penitent. Then he turned away, looking in the direction of Madero's voice. Tears seeped out from the corners of his eyes. "Go to him," Gustavo said.

"Judas," Orozco called, rumbling and hissing the word.

Villa looked around at him, wanting to be certain it was Orozco who had said the accusation. The general gave him part of a smile, but nothing from his eyes. Madero was still speaking. Villa could no longer hear the words through the murmur of the crowd coming. He followed the sounds into the entry room and out into the garden. He could see Madero through the open gate. He was above the people, taller than the people, his voice was heard over them, the sun was on him; he shone, his skin shone, the lines of his beard were like ink on the shining paper of his face.

The crowd made a place for Villa, they let him pass. Mothers gathered their children up from his path, soldiers stepped aside. They saw him take the pistol from its holster.

He tried to walk with a soldier's grace. The inward turn of his left foot tripped him, failed him; he made a trail of dust. His hand was outstretched, the pistol was raised. He saw the face of the President, the sweat beading at the temple, the nostrils, the darkness that erupted breath and words. Other faces appeared along the way: teeth, eyes, chins, unrecognizable collaborations. Villa ran. The President saw him. He no longer spoke. Like the crowd, he made way for Villa, he gave him room by his silence. Madero's face gleamed in the sun, he was painted onto the day, the most certain form.

Villa reached the car. With one hand he took hold of the yellow painted metal of the door. He knelt there on the dark, rubber-covered running board. With his free hand he held up the pistol to Madero, offering the handle to him. "Shoot me," he said. "I betrayed you. Shoot me, please shoot me."

A woman fell to her knees and crossed herself. She walked forward on her knees; on the rough street on her bleeding knees she prayed, the beads were in her hand, running between her fingers, she prayed, she came forward praying, as she did on Easter Sunday when she climbed on her knees to kiss the crucifix at the summit of the Mountain of Christ the King. She was the first woman, and then there was another.

Villa removed his hat and lay his head on the yellow painted metal. He wished for a dog to be beside him, he tried to think of the west. Tears streamed from his eyes. He heard the women now. Hail Mary, full of grace! The Lord is with thee. . . . Glory be to the Father . . . as it was in the beginning, is now, and ever shall be, world without end. The Agony of Our Lord in the Garden. Two. The Scourging at the Pillar. Three. Holy Mary, Mother of God, pray for us sinners . . . He heard them, the quick words mixing, the song of his Autumn Mother heavy on her hips, given to the black-skirted men, the brown-skirted men, the women framed without hair, the stern women. The gun was heavy in his hand. He asked Madero, he begged him, "Shoot me, shoot me now." The voices of the women went on; they made a mourner's song.

A hand took Villa's arm and lifted him up. He saw Madero's face framed by the sun. It blinded him. "I would not shoot you," Madero said. "You could do no harm to me, I knew it, I never feared you. Remember that, Pancho: I never feared you, and you need never fear me." He looked out at the crowd, the kneeling women, the waiting soldiers, the hundreds now. "I would not shoot a brave man, a general of the revolution. He is one of you, my soldiers, a hero. Like you, he suffered hunger and heat and the horrors of battle to bring about the end of the Porfiriato.

"No, I will not shoot him, I will not punish him, I will not shame him. I know this man and I believe he is a good man. I am grateful to him. He is my fellow citizen, my comrade-in-arms and my friend. May God protect him."

Madero stepped down from the seat and embraced Villa. Then the people were upon them, full of blessings and congratulations to the leaders of the revolution. Their hands were on the President and his General. They touched them with crosses, rosaries, and paper pictures of the saints of their lives. The saints were thrust everywhere, they surrounded Villa; the Virgin of Guadalupe in her encirclement of roses, St. Maurice of the infantrymen, St. Barbara of the gunners, and St. Dorothea of the gardeners, she of his name, his mother's dream of him, St. Dorothea laden with flowers, the child laden with flowers, the child arrived too late. He felt himself moving through the saints, the people, wool and straw, leather, hands upon him, the blood burning in his neck, his eyes stinging. The pistol was in the holster again and he was mounting his horse, the reins put in his hand. He was riding west. The sun was overhead, almost noon. He felt the sun on his sweat-curled hair. He had lost his soft hat. It was back there somewhere near Madero's house, it was in an earlier time.

He left his horse in front of the little house. Someone tried to follow him inside—Félix Terrazas or Hipólito or the sergeant who had shared his tea early that morning; he could not understand the signs of the face that followed him. He shut the door before the man could enter the dark room. He permitted no one to enter the room. He lay on the low cot and slept and saw the darkness and slept again. He went to the latrine trench blinded by the sun, stumbling dangerously near the edge. There was fresh water and food, beans and tortillas, when he returned. He drank the water. He scooped up beans in a tortilla, tasted them and dropped the tortilla back into the plate of beans. He slept again until dark. He awakened and saw the darkness and lay still and silent on his cot until he slept again. Without dreams, he craved night, he suffered the cold of the darkness, he suffered the cold of the light.

The President's brother Raúl came to the small house on the third day. He entered the house without announcing himself, and he left the door open behind him, he let the sunlight into the room where Villa lay in continuing sleep. Raúl wore a dimpled campaign hat and riding breeches. His upper lip was arched to show the length of his teeth; this defect of his face could not be hidden by his mustache. He had a foreman's loud voice, pinched in his nose. "Good morning, General Villa," he said. It was late afternoon.

Villa was drunk with sleep.

"The President has ordered me to deliver ten thousand pesos to you for your services to the revolution. I have the money here. Will you sign for it or make your mark?"

"And my boys?"

"Your work is completed. You are to retire from the army with the permanent rank of colonel. I will assume command of your troops."

"Madero said that?"

"President Madero said that."

Villa rolled from side to side on the bed. He was wrapped in his arms, like a man shivering. He could not raise himself up. "Leave the money."

"Sign for it, please."

"Make the mark for me."

Raúl Madero made a languorous nod; his head rocked slowly to stillness. "I am to assume command at dawn tomorrow." He threw the leather bag of money onto the bed beside Villa. "At your orders," he said, saluting.

"Well, good enough," Villa said, "good enough. When it comes to grazing, the sheep is better than the wolf, the sheep is better, yes, better the sheep than the wolf when it comes to living off the grass."

"You're drunk."

"I'm retired, so you can say whatever strikes your fancy."

The President's brother left the room. He did not close the door behind him. The light streamed in, drowning the room. Villa lay back on the low bed; he hoped to sleep again. Spines of beard grew on his face, his eyes and cheeks were swollen, he felt diseased, his bones clicked when he moved. The sun persisted.

A face appeared in the doorway, peering around the corner, watching. Félix slipped around the edge of the door into the room. He walked with a hunch of deference. "I brought coffee, sir."

"Chocolate for the general."

"There is no chocolate, sir."

Villa signaled Terrazas to come close to the bed. "Then the general will have to drink coffee." He laughed. His breath was fouled and his eyes were hidden from the sun; but he laughed, and that caused Terrazas to laugh in return, to thank God. Villa clapped his hands around the colonel's back, he embraced him, drawing him forward. "Félix," he said. "Comrade Terrazas. You have the worst name and the best heart in Chihuahua. You couldn't tell me the truth and you couldn't lie to me. Félix. Félix, I'm going away. You saw who was here, the President's brother. He has the devil's own face, but he's a good man, a true revolutionary. He brought me news, orders; the President does not trust important matters to writing."

"What orders?"

"I can't tell you now. I swore I wouldn't tell anyone, not even you. There is something very special I have to do for him."

"A secret mission?"

"No one else is to know. Félix, I swore. The boys are to be commanded by Raúl until I complete my work. You tell them. There's a lot for me to do, because I have to leave tonight. Now get me some hot water so I can shave. And find me some atole or some eggs, something; I can't keep eating those cold beans for every meal. And get my brother, get Hipólito. Tell him we leave at sundown; I don't want to be followed out of camp by some Porfirista with a knife in his teeth."

It was late in the day, nearly four. Colonel Terrazas brought a barber and a bucket of hot water. At six thirty, two soldiers brought Hipólito into camp. They herded him in, driving his horse with slaps of rope. Hipólito sat in the saddle, stupefied, drunk, lolling with the movements of the horse. He wore a filthy white suit and a bullfighter's hat. A woman's silk scarf was tied around his neck. The two men dismounted and tied up the horses in front of the little house. They pulled Hipólito down from his saddle. He hung for a moment, upside down, the scarf over his face, his left foot caught in the stirrup. The men urged him to be sensible, to cooperate. Hipólito collapsed and fell through their arms.

Villa came out and stood in the doorway. He looked at his brother lying in the dirt, his legs sprawled with the carelessness of the dead. "Get up," he said, "get up and wash yourself. We're going home."

He led Liviana into their bedroom and closed the door. "The old man Orozco sent a messenger to me this afternoon; he wants a meeting. You know what it means: it's the right time for Orozco. If I were Orozco, I would declare now. He has money from the old scientifics, he has Vázquez Gómez to talk for him. He'll declare now. He sent his father to get me out of his way, to set a trap for me."

"Ask Madero's protection."

"I protect Madero," he said. He put his arms around her and gave the rough and friendly embrace he would have given a man. He was laughing. "You're still a girl, a sweet little girl." He kissed her forehead. "How old are you now? Nineteen? Twenty? You're getting soft, Liviana. You used to have a tongue like a lizard skin, but you're getting soft now. I think it must be this easy life. A soft bed's not good for a man or a woman." He laughed again, continuing the embrace, kissing her cheeks and her nose and her eyes. He called her darling, he said she was his life and his love.

"When are you leaving?" she asked. Her voice was flat and as bitter as old coffee.

"I'm not leaving, I'm only preparing. You know, I have this business and we have a good house and we've been to the President's palace, but I'm still a farmer at heart. And you know how we are, you remember: a farmer is always afraid that he won't get his seed in before the rains start or that he won't get his crop in before the frost; a farmer prepares."

She sucked her cheeks in. She made a bitter and disbelieving face. "Save that kind of nonsense for your troops."

"Sometimes a wife should believe her husband's nonsense. She should have faith in him. A man's troops love him; a man's wife should love him."

"I'm a wife without children."

"If Orozco has his way, you'll be a widow without children."

She sat on the side of the bed. There was a basket of sewing there. She put the basket in her lap and touched the cloth and the spools of thread. "I don't like to sew. This basket is always full."

"When I was a boy in Canatlán, I was a salesman for a good man who owned a store there. He sent me into the hills to take orders for thread and needles and buttons and dyes, all the things women need to make a home. I always remembered the orders: one spool of blue thread, two spools of white, a needle and a little piece of shiny red cloth in a square shape; and for the next house three spools of thread, two black and one white, a widow's house. I knew all the houses, I knew all the people. I was the salesman, and the salesman knows what people want. And he remembers. Sometimes I took fifty orders before I went back to the store; I could have taken a hundred. It was good work, the people liked me. I shot game and gave it to the poor."

"You were a saint."

"Josefina Liviana . . ." He stopped. He did not want to leave in anger.

"What? Speak up. Do I annoy you? Would it be better if I was glad when you were going away? Speak to me, Colonel Villa; deliver an address to your troops."

"It will be tomorrow or the next day, not much longer." He sat down beside her on the bed. "I don't want to leave you," he said. "Don't argue now; it's not the right time."

She awakened shivering. It surprised her to find him also awake, leaning on one hand, looking at the dark and quiet room. He got out of bed and put several pieces of wood in the round metal stove. "The room is too big," he said. "The roof is too high. This is only a good room in summer."

"Did you wake up because you were cold?"

"Sometimes my leg bothers me, but not enough to wake me up. No, I was thinking of a man I knew. He killed his horse with a machete. It was a good horse, about five or six years old. It was a little mule-faced, but it had good stamina, it was a good climber. He needed the horse, but he cut it to pieces with a machete. I was just thinking about him and about Orozco. His name was Refugio, and Orozco's man here is Refugio Mendoza. I was just thinking how we all kill our own horses. You know, when we were fighting up north I had to tell my boys not to take the uniforms from the Federals, because I couldn't tell us from them except for the uniforms. And now it's coming again, I know it.

"If we opened up the shutters now, we could see the moon. We would remember why she has no body. When Our Lady was pregnant with the Sun, the Moon came leading all her brothers and sisters to kill Our Lady. They came to do that because they were afraid of what she carried in her belly. They were afraid of a child born of a ball of down. Then the Sun was born. The Sun was born before the rebellious sisters and brothers could kill the mother. The Sun defeated them with a ray of light, as he does now every day. He chased them away with light. He did worse to the Moon. She was his closest sister and she was also the leader of the rebellious brothers and sisters. He cut off her head. And that's all we see of the Moon. The Moon has no arms or legs or breasts. The Moon is not a whole woman now.

"My mother said it was only a story. She said that Tonantzin could not have a child without a man, only Christ's mother could get pregnant without a man. Perhaps. When I was a boy, I believed her, I believed everything she said, I was afraid of the priests. But I'm not thinking about that now, I'm thinking about Refugio's horse and the Sun cutting off his sister's head and the battles that are coming, all the betrayals, all the traitors, all the dead of our race. I don't want to go to war again; I'm a merchant now, my life is the most comfortable life I ever dreamed. I want to stay home."

"I yearned for you to be home, to stay home. I'll do it again."

"Thank you."

The fire in the stove had become too hot. While they talked, the air of the room had been cooked dry. His breath came rasping, he uncovered himself. "Should I open the window? Will it make you too cold?" he asked.

"The Moon will look in," she said.

Refugio Mendoza attacked the State Penitentiary in the morning. Aurelio Gómez, the interim governor, exchanged cables with Pascual Orozco and the commander of the guards at the penitentiary. Orozco advised that the white flag be raised over the penitentiary.

All that day men came to the house on Tenth Street to report the progress of the uprising to Villa. The interim governor sent word that Orozco had cabled Madero to ask for ammunition and weapons to mount a campaign against the rebelling Vazquistas. "And what did the President say?" Villa asked. "Do you know?"

The messenger lowered his eyes.

In the back corner of the house Liviana worked with the other women, packing food for her husband and the men who would go with him. They sacked beans, bacon, dried chiles, dried beef, and balls of salt. They made kits of bandages. They ground coffee and packed it in tins. Beyond the house, in the open yard of the compound, the men unpacked the heavy Winchesters and loaded ammunition belts. They brought the pieces of a Hotchkiss gun from the storerooms, digging them out from under the summer's corn and beans.

A message from Orozco arrived in the late afternoon of the day after the siege of the penitentiary. He asked that Villa lead a troop of militia in search of the rebels. "Tell him I'll do it," Villa said to the messenger. "And tell him this too, tell him that Pancho Villa is loyal to the Madero government. Until death, tell him that."

He instructed the men to saddle the horses and load the mules while he waited for a reply. When the answer came, it was dark. They were all sitting in the dining room, eating a supper of grilled beef and beans. Orozco had asked Villa to take command of a contingent of militiamen who would be waiting for him at the railroad station in the morning. The interim governor had granted permission for him to raise an army and supply it as best he could. The State of Chihuahua could promise neither money nor supplies. Villa fed the messenger and sent him back with the promise that he would be at the railroad station at dawn.

They finished the meal with cups of chocolate, toasting the Madero government, and some of them remarking that it would be a long time before they drank chocolate again. "There is no chocolate in the desert," Villa said. He lifted his cup for a toast to the desert, to chocolate; he did not know. He looked at the others holding up their cups, waiting for him to speak. He drank off the last of the chocolate and left the table.

In his bedroom he changed into his riding clothes. Liviana came in while he was pulling on his boots. "Well, I'm going again," he said. "And I'll be back again."

"Again." Her eyes were swollen. One of the braids of her hair had come partly undone.

"I hope you're not going to cry."

"There are six widows in this compound. They cry all the time." She made herself stiff. She put on arrogance. "They set me off. All their weeping; they're always weeping."

He sat on the side of the bed and stamped his feet down into the boots. "I was thinking. . . . When we were eating, I was thinking that two years ago all the faces were different. Eleuterio, and your brother, and that crazy old man Jenaro, and Tacea. And the old man Beltrán is gone. Carillo, the brothers. Urbina is down around Camargo, I think, or maybe he went back up to Canutillo; I'll find him."

"You'll come back?"

"Of course. And you know, I was thinking too that I won't make the same mistake this time; I should have killed Orozco after Cerro Prieto."

"A general signs his name."

"I'm grateful to you for that."

"You write it like a painter, you draw a picture of your name."

He draped the heavy cartridge belts across his shoulders, shifting them until he was comfortable. "Thirty-thirties, the best."

"I'll be alone again."

"Maybe I left you with something in your belly." He laughed. "It would be company for you."

[*363*]

"Mother of God," she said. She kissed him. The spice in her breath was going stale.

The old soldiers went with Villa. They wrapped their feet in rags and tied scarves over their faces to keep the cold from entering their throats. They wore blankets and rags, they clothed themselves in hides and woven cactus fibers. They sang. The wind stole their voices. They sang louder. At night they slept between fires or they lay in rows in the barns and hallways of ranch houses. Villa spoke to them of the alliance between Orozco and the Terrazas and Creel family, he told them of the lies behind Vázques Gómez's complaints against the President. He was their teacher and their general. He shot a man who carried newspaper drawings critical of the President.

With a hundred and fifty men he went high into the mountains west of Parral to Saint John of the True Cross. He had known the owner of a ranch there since he had first traveled with Ignacio Parra. He trusted the man to give them food and to let them sleep in the houses of his compound until the weather changed and they could sleep out in the open again. Pascual Orozco, Sr., came to see him there. A man drove him up the narrow road to the compound in an automobile without a top. It was the middle of the day and the sun was warm. The old man Orozco came smiling.

Villa greeted him and took him into the house. The old man brought a bottle of brandy with him. He showed Villa the swelling in his hands. He said the brandy was for the pain and the swellings.

"And what do you drink for the pain of having a traitor for a son?"

Orozco smiled. His face was less like that of his son than it had been when Villa first saw him in his house before the battle at Cerro Prieto. In two years the flesh of his cheeks had fallen lower. The hollows were gone, his lip hung out over his teeth; his mouth fell at the corners. There was a permanent sorrow in his face. He sat at a table in the main room of the house to drink his brandy. For a long time he did not speak. His hands occupied him. He pressed on the swollen parts and watched the flesh turn pale, he flexed his fingers, he watched for the bones of his knuckles hidden under the swelling. When finally he spoke, it was to complain. "Typhus in the south, rheumatism in the north; what a country!"

"I like it."

Orozco poured himself another glass of brandy. "My son has been offered the position of Governor of Chihuahua," he said. "It's true. Don Abraham offered him the appointment. The state needs a strong man and González wants to stay in Madero's cabinet. I advised him to accept the appointment, but a son doesn't always listen to his father. He said they had only paid him a third of the hundred and fifty thousand Madero promised him for his service to the revolution."

"That's not the reason."

"Why should I lie to you?" The old man's voice was slow. He lit a cigar. The match quavered in his bent fingers. "He has no faith in Madero. The Plan of San Luis Potosí has been a failure. That's what Pascualito says. I don't know. I ask myself, what has he done? There is now a Department of Labor, but who earns a decent wage? He has Reyes in jail, but what can he do about Zapata? I ask myself, Pancho, what has he done? He said he would right the wrongs that were done under the old wastelands law, but who has land now who didn't have it before? You know what they're saying? That the only good thing about Madero is that he might not be reelected. But there aren't many who say that, because it's hard to find anyone who thinks he'll last out the term. It's a bad time, kid; the country is very divided."

"He deserves loyalty."

"What he deserves and what he gets are two different things."

They argued away the afternoon. The old man sipped his brandy, but he did not become drunk. Villa sat across the table from him, watching his eyes, expecting the brandy to open him up and reveal secrets. The old man gave away nothing. He massaged his hands and pressed his knuckles and talked from a grand distance of the failures of the antireelectionists and the scientifics and the Reyistas. They talked and talked; they had a game of patience, an old man's game.

"Who sent you here?" Villa asked.

"My son."

"For what purpose?"

"To talk, nothing more."

"Then we've talked," Villa said. He stood up.

"I'm prepared to offer you three hundred thousand pesos," Orozco said. "Take it and retire. Here or across the border."

"No."

The old man shrugged. "Then I can go."

Villa went outside to the automobile with Orozco. It was dark and snowing. The old man called for his driver. Snow touched their hair and their clothes. It stayed a long time before melting. The wind drove the snow into their eyes and fed the flakes to their lips. Snow collected on the brim of Orozco's hat. He shivered, he turned up the collar of his suitcoat, he stamped the snow from his feet. The driver lit the lamps in the front of the automobile. The lighting took a long time in the wind. The old man waited. His arms were crossed and his hands were tucked into his armpits. "Three hundred thousand pesos," he said. "I came to offer you three hundred thousand."

A boy came out of the house carrying a blanket for Villa. The old man watched while Villa covered himself. He stamped the snow from his feet, his breath blew white in the wind, he groaned softly. "Why don't you put on your overcoat?" Villa asked.

The old man did not answer. He was watching the driver, who stood bent over the front of the car, turning and turning the metal crank. Villa took off his blanket and put it over the old man's shoulders. Orozco gave a nod of acceptance. Snow caught in his mustache; it gave the appearance of his age, it was comfortable with the fall of his flesh.

"I thought of shooting you," Villa said.

"I know."

"It made me sad to think of what you did for your son. He put you in danger here. He's a traitor to his country and to his own father." Villa shook his head. "My father died when I was a boy. I tried to save him, I would have saved him, I would never have sent him to do a thing like this."

The motor of the automobile began to run. It roared and banged; a white cloud poured out of a pipe at the tail. The driver opened the doors and swept the snow from the seats with the brim of his hat. The light of the headlamps yellowed the snow. The wind made yellow rosettes of snow in the air in front of the headlamps.

"The cold hurts me," the old man said. He went to the car. The snow was collecting again on the seat.

"It's a long way to Parral," Villa said.

"I think we'll have to stay in Balleza tonight." Orozco reached one arm out from under the blanket. He banged the metal door shut. "I'm an old man," he said, "but I have sons."

"Then I'll be sorry for you when the time comes."

The old man did not answer. The car made a wide circle in the snow and went down the road toward Balleza. The chickens complained at the noise. The snow made a close horizon.

The Villistas moved into Parral at night, going on foot to the army barracks at the edge of town. There was no fighting. The commander of the troops welcomed them and asked to join up with Pancho Villa. He sat in a corner of his room, hidden from the circle of light made by the kerosene lamp, a thin man, very tall, with the hardened hands of a miner and the skin across his face like a glove over the bones. When Villa entered the room, he leaped up, stopped to make certain of the face, and rushed to embrace him. They danced and laughed. "Maclovio, I thought all the old Liberals were with Orozco. Where's your red flag?"

"I thought you were still robbing banks."

"Who taught me to steal from the collection plate?"

"How's your foot?"

"If you had musicians here to greet an old friend, if you didn't have the manners of a mole, I would dance for you."

"And I'd have to rub you with mint again so you could walk tomorrow morning."

They talked through the night, and in the morning, they took the town. Orozco's colonel offered no resistance; a few of his troops even deserted to Villa and Maclovio Herrera. Volunteers also came from the town and the mines to join them. The army of sixty increased to six hundred. The sergeants drilled the new soldiers in the streets, teaching them military commands and formations. They wrote down their names and formed them into military units. They sat them on the dry grass of the plazas and taught them to use Mausers and grenades. Children and dogs followed them everywhere. The old women of the town sat in their black wrappings and watched. When the troops moved, the old women also moved, and when the troops halted, the old women found new places to sit. The children were like swallows, the soldiers said, and the old women were like crows.

To raise money for the new army Villa called a meeting of the rich men of the city. He prepared himself by putting on a white shirt and a blue silk tie. He oiled his hair and combed it flat and perfumed himself. The meeting was to be held in the lobby of the Miner's Bank. Villa sent armed guards to escort each of the rich men from his store or office.

The rich came querulously. They asked for chairs to be brought to the lobby for them, they said Villa was a bandit, they said his troops were thieves, murderers, rapists, drunkards, marijuana smokers, and gluttons. Villa stood on a table to speak to them. "I do not want to keep you away from your business," he said, "and I know you don't want to spend a long time listening to my country accent. The interim governor has given the authorization to me for the purpose of raising money for the purpose of the defense of our presidential government from the rebel barbarians and Vazquistas who are commanded by the antagonist, Pascual Orozco the younger."

He cleared his throat, he sought words. Manuel Andana held up a glass of water for him. Villa rinsed his mouth, gargled and spat. "Gentlemen, therefore I ask of your assistance," he said, wiping his mouth with a handkerchief. "My troops are masticated from hunger and elemental exposure. They have not had a single consideration since the second day of February in the year of Our Lord nineteen hundred and twelve. A depreciated army cannot serve the President. I ask your help, chiefs, for democracy and preservation."

The men in the lobby whispered to each other. They showed insulting eyes and the meanness of half-laughter. They wore gray gloves and hard round little hats with small curled brims. Their mustaches were curled upward at the corners; they slept with cloth bands under their noses. A man in a striped coat raised the ivory knob of his cane to attract Villa's attention. "Colonel Villa. Or is it General Villa? One never knows." There was light, scornful laughter. "If I may speak for my fellow citizens, I should like to inform you that no funds will be subscribed by the business community of Hidalgo del Parral for your adventure. The subscription you propose is merely a variation upon the banditry for which you are widely known. Perhaps you think it more efficient to rob so many of us at once, but I can assure you it will not be effective. I consider your request not as a patriotism but as extortion, and I am determined to resist. And sir, if you persist in this, I shall have to telephone President Madero to insist that you be removed from command." There were nods, the rich men purred.

Villa looked over at Maclovio Herrera for advice. The miner showed him a clenched fist. Villa rinsed his mouth and spat again. "Landlords and merchants of Hidalgo del Parral, if a little animal has big ears and a strong back and it kicks and brays and shows its teeth when you give it a command, the little animal must be a burro, true? If a man has money and the man refuses to give any of his money to help the President's loyal troops, the man must be a Vazquista, true? And Vazquistas are traitors, true? And the law of war is that traitors must be shot. Do you understand me? If there is anyone here who does not understand me, my secretary, Lieutenant Andana, will explain to you in his city accent what I have just said. He will write it for you on a piece of white paper."

The rich men were quiet. "Good," Villa said, "I'm glad there are no traitors in Parral. When my secretary passes among you, gentlemen, please tell him your contribution. Remember, the Vazquistas have rich friends even though they are anarchists. We will need money to defeat them, two hundred and fifty thousand pesos from you." The merchants and landlords groaned and shook their heads, but no complaints were spoken. While Andana walked among them, writing down their names and the money they were willing to give, Villa sent three old women with trays of sweetcakes into the room to show his hospitality. The women were barefoot and dusty. They took the trays down from atop their heads to offer the sweetcakes to the men in dark suits and hard round little hats. The rich men ate nothing. The women went to the edges of the room and gave the cakes to the soldiers.

Only one hundred and fifty thousand pesos were pledged. "It is not enough," Villa said, "but we are not bandits. The defenders of your elected government accept whatever you are willing to give in defense of Mexico. But we do not thank you, gentlemen: all you gave is money; we will go to war."

Emilio Campa came with fifteen hundred men to take back the city. They carried red flags and wore red ribbons. They attacked at night and again in the morning; and in the afternoon they left off fighting and the city was quiet. Then Emilio Campa came back with four trainloads of men and equipment and thousands more marching south from the meeting of the rivers in the Zaragoza Valley. Villa and Maclovio Herrera abandoned Parral and marched south to Durango. Tomás Urbina joined them in Las Nieves with four hundred men. They moved on to Mapimí, where Raúl Madero had recruited a contingent of railroad men.

The battles went badly for the government troops. González Salas, general of the army, defeated at Rellano, wounded in both legs and one arm, retreating, sat in his personal railroad car and watched his chief of staff die. He was quite calm. He said to his generals that his only thought in retreat was to save his artillery. Then he went into the private room of the car, his personal place, and killed himself. The artillery was lost to the men with the red flags. The Northern Division was without a leader, and the Northern Division was being defeated everywhere.

Villa listened to the reports of the losses, making a list in his mind of the traitors: Orozco, Campa, Inés Salazár, Braulio Hernández, Vázques Gómez, de la Luz Soto, de la Luz Blanco. They were the men who reproached Madero. They criticized him, saying that effective suffrage and no reelection was not a good slogan; land and liberty was what Mexico needed; liberty, land, justice, and law was what Mexico needed. Villa listened, he learned the words of the letters they sent to him, the offers they made. In his camp beside the railroad tracks leading into Bermejillo, he told Manuel Andana to write a letter for him. "Send this to Pascual Orozco the younger," he said. "Tell him we should gather our troops in a field, the traitors on one side and the loyal troops on the other; and in the center of the field Orozco and Villa will meet in hand-to-hand combat. Whoever lives will be the winner in this war, and it will not matter very much who wins, because the war will be over."

"He won't do that," Andana said. "No one's done that for a thousand years."

Villa laid his cheek against his shoulder and smiled as if he were dreaming. "No," he said, "not now. He's winning; why should he accept such an offer? No, that's not the purpose, Manito. I want him to know what I think of him. I want him to know that he didn't accept the offer, that's all. It's not a big thing, it's for his dreams. One day we'll be sitting on one side of a field and his boys will be on the other side, and then I want him to remember who made the offer and who didn't accept it. That's part of fighting. A man has to be known; I think sometimes that we live or die by how we're known."

Villa waited there in Bermejillo for an answer, but he did not wait happily. A new commander had been appointed for the Northern Division,

General Victoriano Huerta. He had been a Porfirista, everyone knew; he had defeated the Maya rebellion in Yucatán and destroyed every sign of the rebellious spirit by executions and enslavement, everyone knew. He was a drunkard and a marijuana smoker, a man who spent his nights in dark places among people who were not known. He was all of those things; but he was a good soldier, a general who had never lost a battle; and because he was a good soldier he could have been forgiven his flaws, had he not been a Huichol.

"A peyote-eater," Herrera said. "I don't like them."

"I don't want to fight for the son of a bitch," Urbina said. "I know those fuckers, and they're all made from the same clay. They'll cut your throat in the night, and they'll steal your children. I remember, my mother used to tell me that the Huicholes come in the night to steal bad children."

Villa laughed. "All mothers say that. When my wife has a baby, she'll say that too. But it's just something to say to them, like telling them they won't grow if they don't put water on their faces every day."

"Oh, wait a minute," Urbina said. "I have a midget in my house in Las Nieves. He's only this big." Urbina put his hand out at a little more than three feet. "His name is Rafael, but naturally I call him Rafaelito. He's a good midget too; he has a hunchback and everything, a cock like a stallion; it's as long as his arm." His eyes crossed with wonderment. "But you know how he came to be a midget? I asked him. I stood him up there in front of all the children, my children and my officers' children, all the children, and I said to him, 'Rafaelito, when you were a boy, did you put water on your face every day? Tell the truth now, because I'm going to cut off your cock if you lie to me.' Well, man, he confessed right away.

"And now, Colonel Villa, I want to tell you something about the Huicholes that maybe you never heard. Their women show off their cunts. It's the truth. You know when they do it? At night, only at night. They have to put their cunts up so close to the fire that the hairs burn. I know men who were in their camps. The whole camp smells of burning cunt hair. And what kind of son do you think comes out of a woman like that? A Huichol! A treacherous, crazy Huichol! And that's what we have for a general."

"He's Madero's choice."

Huerta passed the days in conference with his officers or he went to a small tavern two blocks from the main plaza and sat all day in silence, drinking brandy and smoking black cigarettes. He had no women. He rubbed his eyes and cleaned his small, thick eyeglasses. His hair was white and cut short, like a conscript's hair on his first day in the army. He wore his officer's cap squarely on his head and he buckled the strap under his chin. When the people of the town came to visit him, he was polite to the men and he kissed the women's hands, and said, "At your feet, Madame." A woman was brought from Jalisco to cook chicken wings for him in an old brown pot. He ate alone.

Villa went to see the general in the house he had made into his headquarters. It was a small house, stuccoed, whitewashed, decorated with two tall but meager palm trees. An aide met Villa at the front door and led him into the room Huerta used for an office. The General of the Division sat on the edge of a desk, drinking brandy and talking with his officers. Trucy Aubert was there, a fat man with loose jowls and a great belly that was not contained by his officer's coat—only the top button was closed, the coat hung open, spreading as it reached his waist, showing a pyramid of belly. His hair and mustache were light brown. No sign of his defeats could be seen on his face; the fat crowded his eyes, masking them. He greeted Villa and embraced him. Villa heard Aubert's breath, short and hurried, like the breath of a man running.

Antonio Rábago was there, the young general, dark and slim, the adventurer general. He wore his hat slightly tilted, he laughed easily, showing the whiteness of his teeth. He was as pretty as a poet. And Rubio Navarrete was there, the dry colonel of artillery, a pale winter stick of a man, educated in France, pressed and polished, a counting man. He removed one glove and gave his hand to Villa in greeting. "We look forward to the assistance of your irregulars in the destruction of the enemy," he said. He bowed slightly.

"God willing," Villa said.

Rábago punched Villa's shoulder. "If you speak to God, tell him to keep the Hotchkiss guns from jamming. Oh, God," he prayed, "keep the devil out of the ejection mechanism." He laughed.

"We have a worse problem," Villa said. "I have six hundred men with Model 93 Mausers and three hundred men with Winchesters, Colts, Mannlichers, Remingtons, and Enfields. I need Mausers, seven millimeter, regular or cavalry models. If I could get three hundred, my men could all use the same ammunition."

Huerta looked up from his brandy glass. He pointed one finger at the aide who had escorted Villa into the room. "Give Colonel Villa what he needs." Huerta's voice was loud. He had the voice of a much larger man.

"Ammunition too?" the aide asked.

"What good are rifles without ammunition? You damned fool, I'll send you into battle someday and you'll learn what it's about." He turned to Villa. "You see what we graduate from our military college? He speaks French like a native, but he doesn't know you need ammunition for rifles. Now we have Felipe Angeles, an artilleryman, running the school; the next thing I know, they'll issue howitzers to the cavalry."

"I need uniforms and hats and shoes for every man."

"Why? Are you going on parade? Is someone coming to review your troops? I'll send Aubert to review them. He looks like a pig; your men will feel better."

"And provisions?"

"We're short ourselves."

Villa nodded. "Well, if you give us the rifles, I'll take care of the rest."

"No looting," Huerta said. "Looters will be shot."

"I have money."

"Where did you get the money? Thieves and looters are the same to me, I warn you."

"The merchants and landlords in Parral wanted to help President Madero."

"Irregulars," Huerta said. He looked down into the brandy glass. He drank a mouthful, showed his teeth, and looked down into the glass again. Trucy Aubert left the room, the other officers followed. An aide took Villa's arm and led him out. Huerta remained sitting on the edge of his desk looking into the glass of brandy. He lit a cigarette. The tight skin over his skull contracted when he drew in the smoke.

When Urbina and Herrera asked Villa what kind of man commanded the Northern Division, he made a fist and lifted it to his mouth as if it were a glass. "But they'll bring the rifles out from the city in the morning," he said. "And that's what I wanted."

Every few days Huerta's officers came to Villa's camp. They always came in a group, elegant in their uniforms, riding combed horses, smoking white-paper cigarettes and wearing soft gloves. They asked questions of the men who had come with Villa, and whatever the men answered made the officers laugh. They gave written messages to Villa, saying they were orders from General Huerta; and when Villa went to Manuel Andana to ask him to read the orders, they turned out to be fairy tales and love stories and recipes and lists of children born in the city that month. After a while, Villa learned to hide when the young officers came to his camp. Sometimes he sat on the side of one of the little hills to the west of Gómez Palacio and watched the officers riding on their shining horses, and he thought about going home. Liviana would give birth to a child in summer; she had asked if he could be home then. He had not answered her letter; it seemed wrong to him to have to tell intimate things to another man and never to know if the words on the paper were the words he said.

Only one officer came to Villa's camp without arrogance: General Rábago. He came with orders for Villa to send scouts north to Bermejillo or out on the flanks of the city, into the mountains, and he came back to hear what the scouts had found. When they captured Orozquista scouts, they carried them on litters to be questioned by Rábago. Not until one of the prisoners complained did Rábago realize that Villa's men sliced off the soles of their prisoners' feet to keep them from running away. "It's barbarous," he told Villa. He lifted up a blanket to show Villa the black scabs that covered the bottoms of a prisoner's feet. "There are rules of war," he said. "Civilized men don't do such things."

Villa took him aside. "Walk up here with me," he said, pointing to a hill above the camp. "We'll sit down, and you can smoke one of your cigarettes, and we can talk about war and rules and what civilized men do."

They climbed the hill slowly. At first, Rábago slid on the loose rock and scrambled to keep up with Villa, who walked easily without sliding. "You're like a goat," Rábago said.

"No man can climb like a goat, sir; at best, a man has only two good legs. But look—" he took Rábago's arm and pulled him over behind him— "there's no sense walking over there; walk here on the ridge, where the stones don't slide. Take little steps and you won't tire yourself. You see, it's not so difficult now. And I'm not a good climber because I have this bad foot that hurts me when I step a certain way."

They sat on a smooth rock that was like a bench, and looked over the camp, watching the men cooking, caring for the horses, often just sitting curled over their folded legs, quiet in the sun. It was the first of several visits they had together. Rábago brought gifts for Villa: an officer's sword, a leather waterbag made in Spain, a leather gunbelt with a shoulder strap, the kind officers wore. Villa gave him a gold toothpick and a goat-hair saddlepad and a monocle with a black ribbon.

On the first day, Villa explained why they mutilated the scouts: "Imagine, if you are a scout, what is the best thing you can do? Be captured and escape, isn't that true? An escaped prisoner has seen everything; he can tell the place, the number of troops, the condition of the horses, how the men are feeling, how many are sick, and how many are too afraid. That's on the right hand. On the left hand, if you capture a man and he thinks he can escape, he won't tell anything to you. He could even tell you lies to set a trap. But cut off the soles of his feet and he knows he isn't going to escape, he has no hope, he depends on you for everything, even to hold him up while he empties his bowels. He depends on you, he becomes your son, and a son tells the father whatever he wants to know. All of Orozco's troops know that we do this. It's not easy for him to find scouts who will go very close to my camp."

"But he must do the same thing to your scouts."

"No. Orozco has a different kind of army. They all want to behave like rich men. You understand? Orozco gets his money from Terrazas and Creel; that's why he threw out Vázquez Gómez, because the Vazquistas were too close to the poor people, because they were too much like Madero. No, his red flaggers don't do those things, they're too Frenchified. When they take prisoners, they shoot them. That's what they did to that American who was with us in Parral. But what good does that do? If a prisoner knows you're going to shoot him, he might as well be a brave man and tell you some lies. Isn't that true?"

"After you do that to a man's feet, is he ever able to walk again?"

"How could it be otherwise? If there's no infection, the skin will grow back in a year, more or less. The bottom of the foot is just soft, a cushion. It's not like cutting the tendon behind the knee or in the back of the ankle."

"I should tell you," Rábago said, "that there have been stories in the newspapers about this business. It doesn't make you look good."

Villa shrugged. "Well, I don't read the newspapers."

"Maybe it's an advantage."

They laughed. When Rábago told Villa of the advantages of artillery support for an infantry attack and of the need to protect the artillery with infantry, Villa told him of the advantages of cold. "Always attack at dawn," he said, "when it's still almost dark, at the coldest time of day. Men are afraid when they're cold, their blood is slow, they have very little move-ment. Dawn is the worst time to be waiting and the best time to attack. The attackers are warm, right? Because they're running or riding hard. Their blood is hot, they're full of movement. The ones who have to sit and wait are the only ones who suffer cold."

"According to your theory, it would be even better to attack at night."

Villa put his hand over Rábago's eyes. "Are you sure?"

If Rábago told Villa of modern methods of troop movement, methods of massing troops at a railhead, distribution of units in a division, numbers of batteries of cannon and machine guns to numbers of troops, Villa would answer by explaining how it was best to send runners as scouts. "A man doesn't leave trails, like a horse," he said. "You can't touch a man's manure and tell if he went by recently or days before. Men were here long before horses. Our race came up out of the ground in this country, but horses were brought here by the catzopines in Motecuhzoma's time. And that's true, because the word *catzopin* isn't a word for a man who was born in Spain; it means a man who wears spurs, a cruel man. So that's how everyone knows that horses aren't good for scouting. Maybe you can't see a horse from far away in Spain, but if we stand up here and look over that desert out there, if we close our eyes until only a thin line is left open, we can see the horses from very far away. If you do that with your eyes, and there are horses, it will look like the ground is shaking; it's like looking for birds in the forest —one leaf moves. But a man is different: he fits the land, he's the right size and the right color; if one man stands out there in the desert and moves carefully without kicking up dust, no one can see him, not even a person with binoculars. Yaquis are good scouts, but the Tarahumaras are better, because they're the best runners. That's the way I think about it; if I have a man who can run like a deer, why should I send a man who can only ride on a horse?"

They traded secrets, they became friends, they made a contest of friendship. Rábago told Villa about total war. "I'm telling you the theories of the most brilliant man who ever wrote on the subject—Clausewitz." He said the name with pride, he rolled the strange word in his throat. "He's made a science of war. He's studied every one of the great battles. He knows Napoleon's strategies. You have to understand that; there are classic strategies in war: flanking movements, sudden charges, the splitting of the middle of a line of defense. War is a business of softening and probing, trying here, trying there, moving all along a line and then suddenly cracking through."

"I don't know about any battles except the ones I've been in, but I've seen some good fighters. I learned at Cerro Prieto not to sit and wait to be destroyed. If I can't win, I know now that I have to run away. But I don't wait. I only attack, and I don't attack by trying here and trying there. One terrific blow, that's how to make war. Maybe that's not what your brilliant man said, but I remember once when I was a boy I saw a puma kill a deer. He did it with one blow of his paw. He made one move, he delivered one terrific blow. The puma is the best killer."

"Villa, be careful. A battle isn't like a puma killing a deer. If you commit everything and the defenses are too strong, you'll lose everything, you'll be destroyed."

Huerta stood on the rear platform of his private railroad car to watch the victorious troops returning from Tlahualilo. He called Villa up to him and embraced him there in sight of all the troops. In front of all the elegant officers he congratulated his dusty irregular colonel, he pressed the battle-fouled jacket still worn by his colonel to his own perfect uniform, he took the dust and sweat unto himself. Urbina stood below. He wore a white rag for a headband, his clothes were torn and bloodied; he had lost a horse in the first charge, he had been in the close fighting, the war of pistols and machetes; when Huerta and Villa embraced, he looked away.

The trains were loaded in the morning, and the division moved north to Peronal. José Inés Salazar and Cheché Campos were camped on the plain near Conejos. They were waiting, the artillery and machine guns captured from González Salas were waiting. On the night before the battle, Huerta assembled the division. They stood with their regimental flags, with the flag of Mexico above them all. The band played. General Huerta stood on a platform. He was surrounded by his officers. They wore their swords. He called Villa to the platform, and he said in his loud voice, in his voice that carried over the assembled regiments, "In the name of Francisco I. Madero, the elected President of the United States of Mexico, I commission you Honorary General of the Irregular Forces of the Northern Division." He embraced Villa, the band played dianas, there were cheers. Tlahualilo had been the first victory, they were moving north, few of them had seen war. They were a cheering army; the women who followed them also cheered; they stood at the edges of the regiments, wrapped in their shawls against the night, mountain women with corn flour under their fingernails and babies in their arms.

After the ceremony, Huerta invited Villa and the other officers to his private rail car to celebrate. He served French wine and ground goose liver. The room was full of loud laughter and cigar smoke. They toasted the end of Orozco, the end of Vázquez Gómez, the end of Zapata. Villa and Rábago stayed at the far end of the car near the door; they spoke to each other of Tlahualilo, of the plains of Conejo, of artillery support and the quick removal of the wounded.

Huerta's voice stopped the room. "A toast to Honorary General Villa," he said. "A toast to the overlooking of certain individuals by the inflexible laws of social evolution, a toast to Pancho Villa the General." The room trembled with the sound of laughter, the sound was in the walls and in the floor; it was as if the rail car were traveling on laughter.

Villa kept his back to the wall. "I have letters from President Madero," he said. "I have a telegram from him. It came yesterday. He congratulated me, he sent his affection."

He heard the light laughter, he heard someone whisper, "How does he know what it said?" It was meant for him to hear. He heard the laughter again. Huerta stared at him. The General of the Division held his wine glass in a toast. It was still full. "Will you drink with me?" he asked Villa. "I'm waiting. We're all waiting. Surely, you would not deprive us of this honor, this surpassing honor."

"I've tried to be a friend to all of you," Villa said. "When you were hungry, I sent my boys out to bring beef cattle back to this camp. When it was time to send men into the desert to scout, I sent my boys. When it was time to go to Tlahualilo, my boys went. When you needed the first victory of this campaign, my boys gave it to you. They're in the desert now, counting the troops at Conejos. When you go into battle there, you'll know the location of every battery of artillery, every regiment of cavalry. I do that for you, I do it gladly, gentlemen, because of my loyalty to the President.

"You drink wine and eat whatever comes from France. You were all born rich, you were all born to sleep in soft beds. You wear elegant uniforms. Your women babble, they waste food, they throw away good clothes because the styles change. Your women decorate themselves; you decorate yourselves. Your mustaches curl up, you have time to teach them to curl up.

"If I look at myself through your eyes, I see an animal, a wordless thing. Only one of you, General Rábago, consents to speak to me. The rest of you belong to that kind of people who ruined my life, who hunted me and wanted to kill me. I know. All the people of my kind know. We are your regiments. We cook your food and raise your children. And you want to kill us, we know.

"You laugh at my loyalty. You laugh at my speech. You laugh at my clothes. I hear you; I know. But fates change, my friends. Whatever saved me from you before will save me from you again. You are the wellborn boys of some other place; I am at home in Mexico."

The officers applauded. They tapped the fingers of one hand on the palm of the other. "Pericles," one said. "They should have made you a senator instead of a general," said another. Laughter mixed with the continuing applause. Villa spat on the floor and went out onto the platform. The door slammed behind him, opened again, and Rábago came out. He put his hand on Villa's shoulder to comfort him. "They're cruel boys, children; don't let them upset you." He pushed on Villa's shoulder to turn him around, to look into his face and show him compassion. The face that turned to him was not what he expected; there were no tears, no trembling lips. Villa was red. His eyes were translucent, like animal eyes. In the mixture of moonlight and kerosene fires, his eyes were like red glass. Rábago let go; he stepped back against the door to the car. Villa walked down the iron steps into the rail yard. He walked carelessly, crunching the gravel. His steps were not even.

A woman came out of the dark. She was barefoot, quiet on the stones. "I'm abandoned," she said. "I have no man, nothing to eat. Help me, Juan."

Villa took her shoulder in his hand. He held her. He took her shawl and unwound it. He uncovered her neck and her hair, he lifted the shadow from her face. The woman was young, but she was not pretty to look at: her face was closed, as if some unseen hand had grasped it when the clay was still soft and forced all the flesh into a mound. He unbuttoned her blouse and reached his hand inside to hold her breast. He squeezed her breast.

She cried out, "General Villa!"

"Did I hurt you?"

"A little, sir. I'm embarrassed, can't you see?"

"My wife, too. I was thinking of my wife."

"My sweetheart is a cavalryman. I haven't seen him since he went to Tlahualilo. Is he dead, sir? What will I do if he's dead? We came together from Veracruz. I knew him there. He sang to me, he went to sea and brought back red snapper and bonito. I went with him and General Huerta

[*377*]

to Yucatán. We had a child there, but it died of rot. Our second was born in the Capital and I nursed it and nursed it, but it never grew. We buried our second there, a girl, in the Capital. Everything is taken from me, sir. I cooked for him before he left for Tlahualilo. We eat meat now; there's no fish in this country. And we have no tomatoes. It isn't easy to cook without tomatoes. I cooked for him, I made fat tortillas for him to put in his breadbag before he went to Tlahualilo."

"We took the wounded to the hotel in Tlahualilo. Did you go there?"

"Yes, sir. I asked for him by name, I looked in all the beds, I asked the others if they had seen him. And when I came back, I asked the sergeant if he was on the list of the dead. I asked him to look for Santiago de Olmos, a swarthy man with a big lower lip, a mouth like a trumpet. He's not among the living, General, and he's not among the dead. I'm abandoned. I have no man, and I'm embarrassed, can't you see?"

"Go home," Villa said. "Do you know how to get to Veracruz from here?"

"It's behind me on the left."

"It's very far."

"Yes," she said, "it's too far to walk."

Villa took money from his pocket and counted a hundred pesos into her hand. "Can you walk to Bermejillo? It's only twelve miles. The trains are running there. If not, it's only twenty miles more to Torreón. You can buy a ticket there to Veracruz. Ask the price from three people in three different places to be sure you aren't cheated."

"Do you want me to stay with you tonight? You could imagine I am your wife."

"Can a general take a woman away from a cavalryman? Go home. Give birth. If you have a son, teach him to be a fisherman, like his father. Teach him all the songs his father sang to you. If you have a daughter . . . Well, it's not important; I can tell from the way you carry it so high that it's going to be a son."

She kissed him on the mouth. She held his mouth a long time before she said goodbye and walked down the tracks. He saw that she walked slowly and that her shoulders were thrown back very far. The child was heavy in her.

Everyone knew about the woman. She said he had taken her there on the railroad tracks and that being with him was like lying under a locomotive gone mad. He had left her in a faint, the woman said, and when she awakened her belly was swollen and she felt his child inside her, kicking to be born. She showed the hundred pesos for proof.

Rábago sent his colonel, Rubio Navarrete, to ask if the story of the rape was true. Villa had been sick for two days when the artillery colonel came to his camp. He listened to the story from his bed of blankets and hot stones. He listened while he lay sweating away the fever. "No," he told Rubio Navarrete, "it's not true. When I rape a woman, she always gives birth the next day."

"It is true," Urbina said. "I remember one time in Casas Grandes, we were lying side by side, raping virgins, the daughters of priests, nothing less, man, and Villa pulled out his cock and a kid came out right after. It was full grown, like a five-year-old boy. The kid was mad, too; he said someone came into his house and spat at him."

Rubio Navarrete said, "Rábago told me to look for the woman. He wanted to be able to confront her with the tale, but she appears to have disappeared. We've telegraphed down the line as far as Torreón, but we have very little hope of finding her. He's worried about your reputation, General Villa; the men may not want to serve under you."

Villa only laughed. Urbina only laughed.

The fever grew worse. During the battle for Conejos Villa fainted. He lay like a dead man on the field. The Orozquistas had been routed and the dead were being collected for burning when Urbina found him and brought him back to camp. For nine days Villa lay in a bed of sweat. He ate only atole and drank only medicine.

The fever passed and came back and passed again. Villa no longer lay in his bed when the fever came. He drank the thirteen teas and began to drink the wormwood tea. He led his troops at Escalón, and he led them down the steppes to Rellano, where the battle lasted twenty-two hours. Orozco was broken. Huerta had come north with five thousand men to meet Orozco's twelve thousand, and Orozco was running, past Jiménez to Santa Rosalía. Taft, the American President, had said that no more weapons could be sent across the border to Orozco. The weapons and ammunition factories Orozco had built in barns and garages in Chihuahua could not supply his army. He abandoned Parral, and Villa and Rábago were sent to secure the town. They were met with flowers and gifts. Their troops came as the guests of the town, the brothers-in-law of the people.

Rábago warned Villa to keep his troops quartered outside the town. "People are speaking against you," he said. "Not here, but in the Capital. You saw the problem with your friend Urbina. I don't know why Huerta had him arrested, but everyone in the Capital knows that you said you would desert and take your boys with you if he wasn't released. They accuse you of a lot of things. I'll count them for you: rape, disloyalty, murder, robbery, looting, and torture. The businessmen here say that you stole one hundred and fifty thousand pesos from them. There are rumors, Pancho, stories in the newspapers against you. Lane Wilson, the American ambassador, is complaining to Madero about you. Huerta embraces you after every battle, but I don't know what he's telling Madero. They have you in a classically bad position, a pincer movement, with Lane Wilson and the newspapers on one side and Huerta on the other. It's awkward for Madero, and that's not good for you. Be careful."

"Did you see how they greeted us?" Villa asked. "Did you see?" He put his arm over Rábago's shoulder and led him to the window of the hotel room. Bands played in the streets, march time and polkas and music for singing. The buildings were hung with banners, there was dancing in the plazas; even the old women danced, even the old men danced; the streets smelled of flowers, the streets were rows of movement, the intersections were a froth of firecrackers and flowers. "The people know Orozco is beaten. They know who beat him, they don't have to read the newspapers to hear lies about me. Those people in the street are all I know about politics, brother. Those people in the street are the only people I trust. I know them, man. You see that group on the corner? Over there, near the church, where the little girls are standing. The little girls are my nieces, the man with the big horn is married to the brother-in-law of my aunt's cousin, the woman selling tacos helped me when I worked in the mine here, the men standing against the wall worked with me in the mines—we were sick together on the floor of the dormitory; I pulled one of them out from under a piece of timber after an accident. You see the man standing behind the union table in the plaza? Maclovio Herrera and I rubbed his legs with mint leaves so he could walk again after his first day in the mine. And the boy standing next to him is my cousin by marriage. At the pulque stand are men I worked with here building the walls of houses. I could take you through the streets and tell you the name of almost everyone we meet. I know the muleskinners and the carpenters and the gunsmiths and the butchers and the women who sell sweetcakes; I know the whores and the drunks and the marijuanos and the cowboys and all the men with shoulders like mules who work in the mines. We're the same race, the same blood; they're my house, Rábago. I'm not afraid of a gringo ambassador or a Huichol general; I live here."

"I warned you," Rábago said.

"Good, I'm warned, but what difference does it make? Advise the jaguar, but don't expect him to change his spots."

"Pancho, no one is as deaf as a man who doesn't want to hear."

"I like to hear you talk like a Mexican," Villa said, giving Rábago a friendly shake.

They went out into the street, where the irregulars of Villa's battalion had gathered to present him with a gift. There were cheers, and a band came to play dianas, and women moved forward through the crowd to throw flowers. A sorrel mare, perfect, with four white socks and a student's face, was brought through the crowd and presented to Villa. A wounded man, his head and chest and one arm wrapped in fresh bandages, led the mare. He put the lead rope in Villa's hand.

"We defeated Orozco," Villa said. "At Santa Rosalía we will defeat him again. And at Bachimba, where he says our cannon will be useless, we will destroy him!"

Villa returned to Jiménez the next day and took a room in Charley Chi's Hotel. He did not like Chinese, but there was a sweat bath in Chi's Hotel. Villa sat all day in the damp gray room, wrapped in blankets, feeling the fever in his joints, hearing it, hearing the sound of insect wings from some great distance inside his bones. He drank wormwood tea and sat by himself in a corner of the room. He crushed eucalyptus leaves in his fingers and rubbed them on his chest. In the afternoon, he went to his room and slept; in the evening, he returned to the sweat bath. He was full of sickness. He thought he saw pus in his urine. Two Chinese men came in and out of the sweat bath. They carried the hot stones and poured water over them to make steam. They wore no shirts. The color of their skin sickened Villa; he had to look away. When they spoke, he covered his ears. He could not eat or drink anything they had touched.

An old Chinese man came into the sweat bath and sat down next to Villa. He unwrapped himself and sat naked on the wooden bench. Villa stared at him, making an inspection of his parts. The old man's skin was smooth; only his face was wrinkled, the skin of his body hung smooth and loose, like a soft sack. His pubic hair was sparse and white, it hung down in thin clumps, like the hair on his head. "How are you? What's your name, cowboy?" the Chinese said in Spanish. Villa went to his room.

He slept. He heard noises in the street, rumblings, caissons; he slept again. There was a sound at his door, rapping. "General Villa, General Villa!"

"Let me alone," he said. "I'm sick, I have a fever."

"General Huerta wants you to come to his headquarters."

"I'm sick. I have a fever."

"What should I tell General Huerta? He wants you."

"Tell him what I told you."

"General Villa."

"Let me alone."

"Yes, sir."

There was quiet, Villa slept again. The sound of caissons awakened him. The wheels were loud, like pigs dying. Hushed voices sounded between the squeals of the axles. It was quiet again. He wondered at the time. The shutters were closed, he could not remember the direction of the window.

Had there been wind? From what direction? The Chinese opened the door. He stood there inside the room, in his shining red robe, in his round black skullcap; he took the key from the door and let it fall into the side pocket of his robe. "Visitors, General Villa," he said cheerfully. His long teeth showed in a smile. He laughed, as if to apologize for being unable to pronounce the general's name. Two officers followed the Chinese into the room. They wore fresh uniforms and pith helmets. "General Villa, by order of the Commander-in-Chief of the Northern Division, General Victoriano Huerta, you are under arrest." The officers knocked the heels of their boots together, they stood stiffly, they pointed their revolvers at Villa.

He looked at them, the flats and corners of officers in fresh clothing, the boots so high and shining. "Colonels, to arrest a general? No."

One of the colonels stepped forward. His face was red, with no brown, no earth in the color. "Get up, Villa. Get up or I'll carry out the order here. I'll shoot you in your bed or against the wall; it makes no difference to me."

"I don't know if you're my fever speaking."

"Let him put on his uniform," the other colonel said. "You can't execute a man who doesn't have his pants on."

"What time is it?" Villa asked. "I don't know the time."

"Get up, Villa. Get yourself dressed."

"Is it morning? Are the shutters closed?"

The Chinese went to the window and opened the shutters. The room flashed in sunlight. Villa rolled over, hiding his eyes. He was colder in the light, his knees ached, he felt the fevered humming in his wrist bones and the column of his neck. The colonel touched the muzzle of the gun to the back of Villa's head, he worked the muzzle through the sweated curls of hair until it was solid against flesh. The cold of the metal was unbearable for Villa. "Please," he said; "I have a fever."

The colonels dressed him.

"Do you have any money, any valuables?" the red-faced colonel asked. "Something to tip the men who do the job?"

Villa showed him a confused face. "I have a few pesos there on the dresser. They don't matter."

"Anything of value?"

"A sword. Rábago gave me a sword."

"No. Anything you want to have with you? A rosary, a medal, a blessed medal, a watch, anything you'd like to have in your pockets, anything you'd like to hold in your hand?" The colonels were pushing Villa toward the door. "We'll collect your effects and send them to your wife, unless you'd like them to go somewhere else."

"Micaela Arámbula Widow of Arango."

"Who's that?"

"My mother is dead."

They pushed him through the door. The Chinese stood aside for them. He bowed as they passed, he laughed. "Pay for the room, please."

Soldiers waited in the hall. Villa looked in their faces to find someone he knew. They turned away, they looked again after he had passed. The hall smelled of cooking lard; it had a burned smell. A dark woman in a dress for evening, her hair loose and thick, ragged at the ends, uneven, looked out a door at Villa. She bent her head as he passed; her neck was thin.

Rubio Navarrete waited at the bottom of the stairs. Villa stopped when he was close to him. The colonels pushed him forward, but Villa would not move. Rubio Navarrete made a sign to the colonels to stand back. He looked at Villa for a moment, he said nothing.

"I don't understand," Villa said.

"Huerta gave the order."

"Is he going to put me up against the wall?"

"Yes. He gave the order."

"For what? If I'm a criminal, man, what is my crime?"

"Insubordination, attempted rebellion, looting."

"Do you believe that?"

"He gave the order," Rubio Navarrete said.

"He has no reason. You know me, what have I done? Is it the horse? Is it because the political chief of Parral says my boys stole his horse and gave it to me for a gift? Would Huerta shoot me for the price of a horse?"

"He gave the order."

"Does Madero know?"

Rubio Navarrete did not answer.

"At Conejos you told me the shells would go past us. I trusted you and your rolling barrage. I sent my boys ahead on your word. I went at the front of them on your word. And now you won't even answer my question. Does Madero know?"

Rubio Navarrete looked over at the red-faced colonel. "O'Horan, find one of the brothers, Raúl or Emilio. Ask them to be present at the execution." He turned back to Villa. He put his hand on Villa's shoulder. His arm was stiff. He stood at the full distance of his arm. "Do you want to see Huerta? That's all I can do."

"Let's go."

A battalion lined the street; all the men were there in battle dress, the rows facing the center, the officers in their places, the sergeants in their places, the machine guns behind the bags of sand, the gunners on their metal seats, the first clips inserted in the guns, holding there like tiny wings, and after all the soldiers, the cannoneers, with their thick guns facing outward, their shells stacked in squares, the gun layers ready, the breeches open, the trios standing by the shells, ready to fuse them, ready, ready, and without war, with only the shadowed street to see, with no movement to study but the growing of the morning light. They were quiet. Somewhere the horses made their shudderings, their stampings; the men were quiet, the light moved down the sides of the buildings.

Villa walked in the center, between the lines. Rubio Navarrete followed, taking longer steps, his slow measure. He wore a sword with a gold handle. The colonel and the soldiers from the hotel marched behind. A sergeant whispered the pace. The Chinese in his red robe came after all the rest. He wore tiny black shoes, he carried the hotel bill in his hand.

"What time is it?" Villa asked.

"Dawn," a soldier said.

"Shut up," a sergeant said. "Keep in line."

They arrived at the rail yards and went to Huerta's private car. The General of the Division was in the outer room. He wore his dress uniform. Rubio Navarrete saluted; the general responded with a nod. Villa advanced toward the general with open arms; Huerta turned away. He sipped coffee from a white cup decorated with one pale rose.

"I never disobeyed your orders," Villa said. "I was sick. I have a fever. It's the same fever I had at Conejos; it comes and goes. I'm better for a few days and then my urine starts to stink again and I can't shit. It's bad, a bad fever. I had it when you sent for me. I was in the saddle seventeen and a half hours, to Bachimba and back to look at Orozco's lines. I was too sick, I couldn't answer your order."

"I'm not a physician," Huerta said.

"Why are you doing this to me? Was any soldier more loyal than Pancho Villa?"

"It's a question of honor."

"Please, will you let me sit down?"

Huerta raised his hand and pointed to Rubio Navarrete. "I gave you orders. In time of war insubordination is a capital offense. Do you know the rules, Colonel? They apply to all soldiers of all ranks, even to those whose mustaches turn up at the corners."

Rubio Navarrete took Villa's arm.

"No," Villa said, pulling away, shaking loose from the colonel's grip. "I have one more question for General Huerta: does Madero know?"

"We all serve at the pleasure of the President." Huerta put the coffee cup down and went to his inner room.

Rubio Navarrete whispered to Villa: "You've got to go now, friend."

[384]

He led Villa to the door. "I can't do any more. There's nothing more."

"And Rábago?"

"You know he's still in Parral."

"What time is it?"

The colonel took a gold watch from his pocket. He clicked it open, looked, and showed the face to Villa. "Six nineteen. Correct?"

"I left my watch in the room."

"You can have this one."

"No, thank you," Villa said.

Below them, in a circle around the platform at the rear of Huerta's car, the colonel and the soldiers from the hotel were waiting. The Chinese was with them. "He wants two pesos for the room," the colonel said.

"Give him one," Rubio Navarrete answered.

"I left the money in the room," Villa said.

The colonel pointed to a soldier carrying a gray sack. "We have the prisoner's personal effects," he said, looking at the Chinese, taking a peso from his pocket to pay him. Then the two soldiers took the Chinese and ran him beyond the farthest track and pushed him forward into the street between the lines of soldiers. The Chinese fell. The soldiers laughed. The sergeants ordered quiet. The colonel looked up at Rubio Navarrete: "I'll assemble a firing squad.

"Let him speak to a priest. Have a clerk take down any message he wants to send to his wife or mother. Treat him with respect." He looked at Villa. "You're a general officer. You will be dignified."

Villa wiped his forehead with the sleeve of his jacket. It came away drenched. "I have a fever," he said. Rubio Navarrete was gone. The colonel had his arm, he pulled him toward the high metal steps. "I'm sick," Villa said.

"Dr. Alemán Pérez will be there. He attends all executions; it's the rule."

"I can't think," Villa said. "I'm dizzy. I have a fever."

They walked down the tracks, the soldiers were alongside, the sergeant calling out the step. A drummer joined them. He skipped twice to find the step. He touched the drum with his sticks, he made a whispered sound. They walked on the stones, their boots rattled the stones. The drummer struck his drum harder, he made a counting sound, dull, dull, and hum hum hum. The boots counted on the stones, the stones were a rattle lying along the track.

"What time is it?"

"Six twenty."

"Only six twenty."

"Only six twenty, sir."

They turned into a street. Their boots were quieter, the drum sounded alone. Villa stumbled. The colonel caught his arm. "Don't be afraid," he said.

"My left foot is turned."

A dog came out from behind a house. It came barking. It came with flattened ears. A soldier swung his rifle butt. The dog rolled in the street. It lay in the street. Villa asked the time.

They came to the wall. The colonel spoke in whispers to the sergeant, the sergeant called out four names. Four soldiers trotted out into the center of the yard. They made a line and faced the wall. They wore battle dress, they leaned forward to balance the weight of their packs, they rested on their rifles. "There's the doctor," the colonel said, pointing to a man with a camera. "I think it's better now to see a priest."

"No priest."

"Do you want to send a message to your mother or your wife?"

"My mother is dead."

"And your wife, sir?"

"Liviana."

"I'll call the clerk." The colonel went to stand with the doctor. Other officers were arriving. They talked softly, they shaded their eyes from the sun. A clerk went to stand beside Villa. He held his paper and his pencil in his hands. "What is the name and address, sir?"

"What's your name, boy?"

The clerk looked up at Villa. He closed his eyes because of the sun. He moved to one side. He was awkward, he shuffled his feet. Dust rose. "If it's a long message, we should hurry, sir. They don't always let me finish."

"I'm not afraid."

"No, sir."

"What time is it?"

"I don't have a watch, sir."

"You can have mine, write down that you can have mine."

"They won't believe me, sir."

"Well, write to my wife: Josefina Liviana Aprisco de Villa, Tenth Street, Number Five Hundred, in Chihuahua." He leaned forward to look at the clerk's notebook. "Listen to me, kid," he said very softly, "no one's going to shoot me; Madero won't permit it. Huerta wouldn't dare. I need time. It takes time. Now you just write down anything you want. You know any songs? Write down a song. You know that song about the strike at Cananea; that's a good song, write it down. You know: 'In the jail at Cananea, situated on a mesa. . . .' Write the whole song, all the verses. Then 'The Swallow,' that's a good song too. And 'The Bicycles' and 'The Horseman,'

[386]

all the songs. How about Veracruz songs, you know any good songs from Veracruz? Oh, I'm so sick. What a fever! It's more than the grippe, I know that. Look at my clothes, how much weight I've lost! Fever burns up your flesh, like a piece of wood. When the fire is over, what's left? Fever is a fire in a man, if it burns too long, only ashes are left. You don't know what time it is?"

"Would you like a cigarette, sir?"

The clerk wrote, Villa talked. He said the words of songs, he drank from the clerk's canteen, he looked at the railroad tracks, the telegraph wires, he looked at the wall, the line of soldiers, the sergeant waiting beside them. "It's time," the colonel said. The sergeant came and led Villa out into the center of the yard. He left him there, before the squad of four soldiers. "Wait here." The sergeant went to the wall and marked an X with his machete. "Here," he called to Villa. "Stand here."

Villa could not see the soldiers. The sun was behind them, their shadows reached all the way to the wall. He held down the brim of his campaign hat, he bent it to block out the sun. The soldiers were only shadows.

"Here," the sergeant said. "Stand here, where I made the mark."

"There's time," Villa said.

"There's no time," the sergeant said.

The shapes of the soldiers darkened, the sun flashed on the barrels of the rifles. The rifles were real, the time was gone, the sergeant was shouting. "Why are you going to do this?" Villa asked. "What crime am I charged with? What trial have I had? No, boys, don't do this thing. Think of what you're doing, think of the service I've given."

The sergeant came to stand beside the four soldiers. The colonels and the doctor stood behind them. Raúl Madero came and stood with them. And Rubio Navarrete. Villa called out to them, he asked them to consider his loyalty, to remember his victories. No one spoke in answer. The sergeant came forward. "Stand against the wall," he said, "at the mark." He held Villa's arm and pushed against his chest, forcing him back to the wall.

The tears burst from Villa's eyes. "There was no insubordination," he screamed. He lost control of his knees, the sergeant could not hold him, he fell and fell again, he lay at the sergeant's feet. "I need time, I need time to speak to Madero. He knows me, he wrote to me with affection. Just wait a while, just give me time, give me a little time. Don't shoot me, for God's sake don't shoot me."

The sergeant took the collar of Villa's coat in his fists. He turned him around, he dragged him back. Villa's hat slid away, the dust of the sergeant's heels covered his face, he scrambled on his knees, he lifted himself up by his arms, he walked on his hands. The sergeant threw him forward into the wall. "Now stand up," he said, "like a man."

Villa wiped his mouth with his wrist. He watered his mouth to wash the dust away. The sergeant picked up the hat and put it lightly on Villa's head. "Like a man," he said, "like a man. We'll be quick; my boys are good shots. You won't feel anything."

Villa stood up. He tried to think of dying. He talked; he didn't know what words he said. The sun was hot; he noticed that there was no shade. The sergeant went back to his place. Another man came forward. Villa could not see him in the sun. He raised his hand to shade his eyes, to protect himself. "It's Rubio Navarrete," the man said. "Wait here. I'll see Huerta again. I'll try again, my friend. It's all I can do."

"What did Madero say?"

"Raúl is over there. He'll go with me to see Huerta."

"No, the President."

"It's not even seven o'clock in the morning; the President is asleep."

"Wake him up!"

"I'll see Huerta again."

Villa brushed the sand from his clothes. A soldier brought him a cloth to wipe his face. He stood alone in the sun in the center of the yard. He asked for the bag of his personal effects. The sergeant permitted it. Villa gave ten pesos to the soldier who brought the gray bag. He gave his watch to the clerk and he divided the rest of the money among the sergeant and his four soldiers. "Aim well," he said to them, "be marksmen." He walked to the wall and stood in front of the mark the sergeant had made. The sun was not so low now; it was easier to see. He thought of himself dead; he saw nothing, nothing came into his mind. His bones ached, the fever would not go away. He leaned against the wall. He wanted to sleep, to lie with Liviana beside him, smelling of soap and not of perfume, talking to him, talking, the salt of her in talking, whispering, the wife Liviana, the woman Liviana, of his house, tasting of chocolate. He recited the names of his brothers and sisters and all his relatives, beginning with his mother, reaching from the dead to the living. His mouth was dry. His left foot hurt. He looked around him for a stick to hold, some tiny piece of the beginning of a tree to make the rich tree. He listened for the sound of the drummer.

When Rubio Navarrete and Raúl Madero came to tell him that he would not be shot, he thanked them and he embraced them, but he was not happy. He felt the dust in his clothes and he thought for the first time of the shame; he thought that for the first time he had not been a man.

There were no penitentiaries in Tenochtitlán. The judges were the five captains. Some criminals died by stoning, some died by the stocks, some were strangled. Those who were not killed were made into slaves. They were forced to untie their hair, they were forced to hide their scars. They were lower than the common people. They had no land, no voice, they lived in other people's houses. That was the law.

Villa was entered into the Lecumberrí Prison. He walked slowly. The guards pushed him. The gates closed. The prison was made of iron, of clangs and locks and stone floors and metal bowls and thin spoons. The prison was made of debts and bribes and long rows and buckets stinking in corners. They wrote his name in a ledger and took his belt and his hat and coat. They took the laces from his shoes. When he spoke, they did not look up from their ledgers, they did not pause in the thumping of their stamps. Men pushed him from room to room. His hands were chained. They unlocked the chains and locked them again. They pushed him to a next room and a next. There were no windows, the floor was made of thick stone, the walls were made of thick stone, iron bars separated the rooms, the corridors, the cells. The guards touched him. They felt in his hair and under his arms. They removed his clothes, they threw his clothes back to him. He waited for the unlocking of the chains, and when he was dressed, he waited again for the locking of the chains.

"You begged," a guard said. "We heard that you fell on your knees and wept." The guard laughed. His cheek was rotted. The stink came from his mouth.

The doors of bars clanged, the locks clanked. The guards carried keys in metal rings attached to their belts. They wore thick clubs attached to their belts. Villa asked the guard, "What time is it?"

"Do you have an appointment, Mr. General?"

"I'm waiting for the President."

"Has he been arrested? Only criminals come to Lecumberrí. This is not Chapultepec, Mr. General; they don't shit in buckets in Chapultepec."

The stone walls were plastered and painted; the paint fell away in flakes, in pale dust, in ragged patches. They entered the corridors of prisoners. Men lay on their beds in the cells, men sat on their beds; there were no chairs, no tables, only beds, only buckets, only the men on their thin and narrow beds.

The air was cool and thick, the light had no warmth. It was winter light, rain light. The stench of the buckets lay in the air; one thick stench, like a camp latrine, and a hundred stenches, layers of stenches, the separate bowels of each man, the separate bladders of each man, the waste lying in the buckets, the buckets themselves, the waste putrefying, the slow making of wind in all the stages of the days of the years of the buckets. And somewhere food was cooking; the odors lay on the air: beans, fish, innards, lard. The fish was old, the innards had not been cleaned.

The guards removed Villa's chains and pushed him into a cell. The door clanged. The keys and the lock were like broken bells sounding, tuneless rattlebells. "Use the bucket," a guard said. "Keep yourself clean. Keep yourself quiet."

"I'm expecting the President," Villa said.

The guard said, "The President of Mexico will come to Lecumberrí, sure he will. When nuns fuck. When pulque squirts from my wife's tits and birds shit chocolate. Go to sleep, man; if you dream when you're sleeping, no one will think you're crazy." The guard walked down the row of cells, looking in at the prisoners, calling to them as he passed, "Let go of your chile, you son of a bitch, you'll wear it out. How come you're so sad, Blondie? You must be wondering who's fucking your mother tonight. Little Cat has a peso; he must have raised the price of his asshole. Hey, Fatso, if you're still hungry, you can eat my crabs." One man threw his cup at the bars in answer, another asked if the guard wanted a drink from his bucket. All the rest lay quietly; they did not seem to hear.

Villa sat on his bed. He raised the round welting at the edge of the mattress and looked in the dark crease; the bedbugs lay in a thick black line. They huddled in the darkness of the seam, pressed together, waiting. Villa squatted next to the bed and began pulling the bugs out of the seam. He cracked each of the hard shells with his thumbnail and dropped the broken insects on the floor. There was still blood in some of them. He saw the color of it on his fingers, under his fingernail; the cell had not been empty for more than a day.

A prisoner called from across the corridor: "Surrender, brother; you'll never live long enough to kill all those suckers." Villa persisted. His legs grew tired, he rested on his knees, he squatted again, he sat on the floor. The killing went slowly. He hurried, he was not careful; some of the bugs fell unbroken onto the floor. He saw them moving among the dead ones. The light from the electric bulb was not strong enough to find the live ones. He fished for them with his fingers, feeling among the still ones for the tiny legs that moved. The prisoner across the corridor called to him again, "It's impossible, man; they're laying eggs while you're cracking them. Ask the guard for kerosene. Give him a peso and he'll pour kerosene in the seams for you."

"They took my money a long time ago, in Jiménez."

"Shit, man, you're really in trouble."

"I'm not worried," Villa said. "I'm waiting for a visit from the President."

"Not down here. We're the worst down here, the ones who gave the world a good fucking and got caught doing it. When you're down here, you're a real criminal. You don't get sent down here for pinching wallets or not paying your rent. This is what they do with you if you're not lucky enough to get hanged. You see Little Cat over there? He buggers schoolboys and robs them. That's pretty good, huh? And Fatso, he's something: he battered people for a living, he loaned them a peso and collected the loan every week for years. We're the worst; after the ones who get hanged, we're the worst. Take me, I used to make fifty pesos a day collecting from the beggars. If one of those pricks wouldn't cough up the wool, I fixed him so he was a real cripple or a real blind man. They caught me for cutting out a man's tongue. It was a lousy job; he still could tell the police my name. Shit luck. Shit luck. We're all here for that reason. We don't have luck, but one thing is for sure, nobody throws any shit at us down here. They know what kind we are."

"Yes, good people," Villa said, "people with class."

"Hey, don't get smart with me, tittysucker. That bastard who was in there before you woke up hanging from the bars. A country boy, like you. Didn't know his ass from a hole in the ground. I told him, 'Stick your thumb in, and if you can walk away from it, it's a hole in the ground.' He was like that, eh? Like you. You just keep up that smart talk and we'll have an empty cell again."

"How do you get out of your cell?"

"Goof! We pay the guard. A little bite here and there for the guard and you can do what you want. You're really a dumb cunt, aren't you? What's your name?"

"Pancho Villa."

"The bandit?"

"The general."

"Son of a bitch!" He shouted to the others: "Hey, you bastards, you know who's here? Pancho Villa! Pancho Villa, the biggest fucker of them all! And he's here, right here in our row. Oh, son of a refucked mother! Pancho Villa!"

"Now leave me in peace."

"Whatever you like, Pancho. Pancho Villa, oh, shit! Man, I always dreamed of being as big as Pancho Villa. Listen, you're the big daddy for me. Anything you want, the Pug will do it. I'm your man."

Villa went back to pulling the bedbugs out of the seam. In an hour he had cleared most of one side. He estimated the time, thinking he could be lying on the bed before midnight. Then he realized that the lower-welt seams were equally thick with insects. "Pug," he called to the man in the cell facing him, "it's no use this way."

"Leave it to me! Don't you worry about it, Pancho."

The guard came and Pug talked with him. He went out and came back with a clean mattress and a can of kerosene. He passed the mattress through the bars to Villa and asked him to pass the old mattress out. After the exchange was made, he asked Villa to stand back while he splashed kerosene around the cell. "Don't smoke for a few hours," he said, "not until the smell goes away."

Villa lay on the mattress, breathing the fumes; he was sickened by them. He lay still, his legs ticked, he covered his eyes with his forearm and tried to sleep. The guard turned out the electric lights in the corridor. In the darkness the cell doors opened, the men shuffled into other cells. They whispered, they made the sounds of prisoners at their pleasure. Villa heard his name, he heard the delight they took in his name. The darkness was a mirror; they showed him a face in the darkness. He recognized himself, he saw himself as he was known there. It was as if he lay in the flood of an ugly river. He did not want to touch himself; he parted his legs, he spread his fingers, he suspended his tongue in the center of his open mouth, he drew the lids back from the lubricious fluids of his eyes. He lay mute and blind in the darkness, in the whispers and secret laughters.

New guards came in the morning. They took him upstairs into the light to wash himself. A barber came into the room to shave him and put oil on his hair. They led him to a new corridor, where the ceilings were high and the cell doors were open in the day and locked only at night. A captain of the guards came to apologize for keeping him all night in the cells with the incorrigibles.

"I wouldn't keep an animal in a place like that," Villa said.

The captain leaned his head to one side, nodding, "I wouldn't keep an animal there, either, but it's a good place for vermin."

"Yes, I saw that. You raise fine vermin, Captain, one of the largest herds in Mexico." The captain laughed. Villa put his arm around the captain's shoulder. "I want you to do something for me; it's very important. I want you to send a message to the President."

"You can send only two messages. That's the rule. Tell me what you want to say."

"Say that his loyal general, Francisco Villa, has been unjustly accused and that he solemnly requests the assistance of his elected friend and comrade of the spirit to come to his aid in this time of a bad jam. No, not a jam, don't say a jam. Say in this time of his suffering of deception and retreat to bad fortune. Will you remember that?"

"I'll give you a pen and paper and you can write it yourself."

"No, go ahead, you send it."

The judge came that afternoon to read the charges to Villa. They stood outside the corridor together, watched by a guard. "I was a colonel in the army," the judge said. "As you can imagine, I'm understanding of the problems of a soldier, but I'm also aware of the need for discipline."

Villa looked down at the judge's feet. They were far beyond the size of most feet, half again the size of the feet of the largest man. The judge's feet flopped when he walked, they rose at the ends in long curls of black leather. He shifted his feet while he read the charges to Villa from the typewritten pages. He was uncomfortable with his feet or with the words he read; Villa did not know which. He studied the judge's feet, he listened to the words; the judge seemed to dance with discomfort.

"Well," Villa said at the end of the reading of the charges, "if that's all, Mr. Judge Armendáriz, you can let me out of this place now. The Governor of Chihauhua gave me the authorization to raise money for my troops; you can ask him or you can look at the paper he gave me; my secretary, Manuel Andana, keeps the papers. As for not going to General Huerta's headquarters, I was too sick, everyone knows I had a fever. Ask the doctor, Alemán Pérez; he treated me. The horse, the horse, I don't know what to tell you about the horse, Mr. Judge. My boys gave it to me in Parral. There was a ceremony, a band, there were speeches. In such moments what is a general to say? Does anyone of good manners ask the cost of a gift? And rebellion! I was there to put down a rebellion! And I fought well to do it; they didn't make a general of Pancho Villa because he ate goose liver or slept in a private car on the Northern. My boys were always the advance, we were always the first to reach the enemy lines. I lost so many dead, so many wounded. Urbina was the bravest officer in the division, Urbina was a hero, sir. Without Urbina, the usefulness of my troops would have been half. We needed him, Madero needed him. It goes without saying that I would make noises to get such a man out of jail. Sir, you must understand that Orozco's troops outnumbered us by twelve thousand to five thousand. He had artillery, machine guns, railroad trains. My only thought was to defeat him, to defend President Madero. And for that loyalty I am here in the Federal penitentiary! Why do you punish the ox for pulling the plow?"

"The charges are serious, General Villa. They can't be dismissed. There will be a trial, you'll have an attorney, the right to defend yourself, that's the law. But a trial doesn't happen overnight. It will take time to prepare. That's for your benefit; the army's case is clear."

"I sent a message to the President."

The feet shifted, the far ends curled and tapped and curled again. "The President has already forgiven you once. How often do you expect him to forgive you? Rebellion is not a child's prank and this is not a private business. There are public pressures: the newspapers, Lane Wilson and the American colony, the military. If you're truly loyal to Madero, you won't expect him to do anything for you in this; you'll stand trial, like a man, like a soldier."

"I would give my life for Madero."

"General Villa, every soldier who goes into battle is willing to give his life for the President of his country."

"Madero needs me."

"*Au contraire,* my General, you need him."

Villa waited. For a week he spoke to no one but the captain. He sat in his cell during the open period. In the exercise yard, he ran around the perimeter, tiring himself, hoping it would enable him to sleep at night. He dreamed of an answer from Madero. He spent hours thinking of his loyalty, concentrating his mind on loyalty; Madero could hear such thoughts, he read a man's spirit from a thousand miles away.

There were two Zapatistas in corridor nine: Abrahám Martínez, Zapata's chief of staff, and Gildardo Magaña, a burly young man, hardly more than a student. Martínez said he did not want to speak to Villa: "I don't trust anyone who supports Madero. Fuck Madero! And fuck all the Maderistas! Anyone who supports Madero is a traitor—Article Nine of the Plan of Ayala. A Maderista is a man who would kill his brother for a fistful of coins. Stay away from me; I don't have the money or the stomach to buy you."

"He didn't make me rich, that isn't why I supported him."

"Well then, Villa, you're not only a traitor, you're a stupid traitor. He has an unlimited supply of money. He sold out to the gringo oil company, Standard Oil. That's how Huerta is destroying Orozco. Standard Oil put an embargo on arms shipments across the border. Orozco's making shells in garages. How the hell can he fight Huerta and Standard Oil too? And you never got any of that money? You're a fool."

"And you're a liar," Villa said. "If Zapata and Orozco and Reyes and

[*394*]

Vázquez Gómez would stop trying to become dictators and leave the elected President some peace to carry out his programs, we wouldn't be shooting our brothers, and all the money that's being spent on war would go to feed the poor. Do you know how much one Mauser rifle costs?"

Martínez looked pleased. "Yes, I know how much one costs: one Federal soldier. A machine gun costs two, and one piece of artillery costs six."

"You can't fight a war that way."

"Zapata's in the mountains and Villa's in Lecumberrí. How long have you been here? How long have you been waiting for a trial, a letter from Madero? How long?"

It had been almost a month. "Oh, I don't know," Villa said. "Time flies. I don't worry about it, because I'll be out soon."

"You poor bastard."

They had no more conversations. Martínez stayed away from Villa, but he did not interfere when Villa and the other Zapatista in corridor nine became friends. The young man from Zamora initiated the friendship on the day after he and Martínez were brought to corridor nine. "General Villa," he said, extending his hand in the most formal way, with his feet together and his head bent slightly to avoid the embarrassment of eyes suddenly meeting, "Gildardo Magaña of General Zapata's staff. I'm pleased to meet you, sir. Your name is well known in Morelos."

"Yes, like the smallpox."

"A man is known by his enemies."

"Then I must be very well known in Morelos."

"Orozco's people speak of you very often, it's true." Magaña laughed, his whole person shook with the laughter. "They speak of you so often and with such passion, sir, that we think you must be a very good soldier. But I would not have recognized you from their descriptions; I expected a man at least nine feet tall, with horse's hooves and fire coming out of his eyes. You don't have the little horns either, the ones that come from having a pact with the devil." The laughter came again. He was fat, like a child; the laughter trembled in his soft flesh. "But we hear other stories too." The laughter fled him, he became solid, a promise of darkness appeared beneath his eyes. "They say you're a man who cares about the poor. After you took the City of Juárez, they say, you gave all your provisions to the poor. And before the revolution, they say, Pancho Villa gave cattle and money to the poor. So we know in Morelos that half the stories must be lies: the devil doesn't help the poor or they wouldn't be poor."

"Maybe the devil had a falling out with the rich."

"If I believed that, I would have been a priest instead of a revolutionary."

"You don't think God is on the side of the poor?"

"General Villa, I think the poor will have to take up arms in Heaven."

Villa embraced him. They were friends. They walked together in the exercise yard, and when the time in the corridor came that afternoon, they sat together at the corner of one of the wooden tables. "Are you really close to Madero?" Magaña asked.

"He's the President and I'm in prison."

"There could be reasons; politics aren't simple. He needs Huerta, he needs the army. The man has trouble on both hands: the circle of scientifics is still strong and the Liberals are getting stronger. Look at his problems: he can't defeat Zapata. You can put down a military revolt by military force —Porfirio's nephew is already in another corridor here—but he can't defeat Zapata, he can only make concessions, compromises, he can only take him in. If he doesn't make the concessions, his government will fall. Sooner or later it will fall."

"I could defeat Zapata."

"In your home country, not in his."

"That's possible."

"And Zapata would be helpless in the north."

"It goes without saying."

"Then what's the answer?" Magaña leaned back from the table. He waited.

"Hey, kid, how old are you? I keep looking at your face and seeing a baby."

"Twenty-three."

"That's a good age for a woman."

"You know what Cervantes says about that: 'Don't mention rope in the household of a man who's been hanged.' "

"I don't know Cervantes. If that's what your Zapatista says, it's all right with me, but in Chihuahua we say, 'The only food you can be sure to enjoy is what you've already eaten.' "

"Cervantes says, 'Don't go around looking for a cat with three hind legs.' "

"Villa says, 'Talk is cheap.' "

"That's true enough, but what else is there to do in prison but read and write and talk?"

"The only thing to do when they put you in prison is to get yourself out."

They made jokes, they exchanged proverbs, they talked about war, the suffering of the poor in time of war. "Whether the pitcher strikes the stone or the stone strikes the pitcher, it's hard luck for the pitcher," they concluded. Magaña talked often about Zapata and his Plan of Ayala. Villa listened when he spoke about the man, but when Magaña spoke of a revolution against Madero, Villa touched his finger to his lips. "Say what you will about me, but don't insult my mother or my friends."

[*396*]

An attorney came to see Villa. He stood outside the corridor with him and spoke of the difficulty of the case: Villa had no evidence, Villa had no proof, only the charge of extortion could be dismissed; in the others he was certain to be judged guilty. Plead, the lawyer told him, beg, ask the judge to be merciful. Sometimes Villa listened to the lawyer, Bonales Sandoval, and sometimes he watched him without hearing. He saw the care that turned the lawyer's mustache up and around in two circles coming from the center of his nose. He saw the stiffness of Bonales Sandoval's collar, the discomfort and the comfort of it. He saw the certainty of the attorney's eyes, and he knew who was the pitcher and who was the stone.

He sent the attorney away and he waited for him to return. What the attorney said did not change from time to time. Villa waited for him, but he was not eager; he expected nothing. He listened to Magaña. He thought of his child and why it was not yet born. Huerta defeated Orozco at Bachimba and Chihuahua. The Federals moved north, they made Orozco's corner smaller and smaller. The Zapatistas blew up a train in Morelos. Money for Villa's defense came from the governors of Chihuahua and Sonora. There was no answer from Madero.

Magaña said, "There's a great difference between you and Zapata: he had advantages, a family, a little money, a share of the communal land. He reads, and reading makes him a more subtle man. You know, General, if you tell something to him, he can write it down, he doesn't have to fill up his head with useless remembering, he doesn't have to lie awake at night remembering to remember what he has to remember. You should learn to read; I could teach you."

"You can't teach Peter to be a goatherd," Villa said.

"Can you sign your name?"

"Yes. My wife taught me."

"And when you sign your name to a paper, what does the paper say?"

"Whatever is written on the paper."

"What? How do you know what's written on the paper?"

They sat in the corridor at the corner of the wooden table. The thieves were around them. They listened, they stole into the room of the words. Villa stood up and waved his arms at them. He shouted, as if he were chasing birds from a cornfield. The thieves ran to another table, they pretended not to listen.

"Well," Magaña said, "tell me. How do you know what's written on the paper?"

Villa went to his cell and lay down on the bed. He turned his face to the wall and tried to sleep. It rained. He smelled the rain on the air. It had always rained in summer, since the city was called Tenochtitlán, since there were two schools: one for war and one for books.

[*397*]

Magaña was there again in the morning. He walked with Villa to the exercise yard, he said to him: " 'There is no book so bad that it doesn't have some good in it.' Cervantes said that, Miguel de Cervantes Saavedra."

"Spaniards turn my stomach."

In the afternoon, Magaña sat next to Villa at one of the wooden tables in the corridor. He had a newspaper with him. He showed the front of it to Villa. "Look here," he said, "look what Orozco said about you."

"What did he say?"

Magaña passed the newspaper over to Villa. "Read it yourself. I'm not your secretary."

Villa reached across the corner of the table and took the throat of Magaña's shirt in his fists. He reached slowly, in a killing way, as executioners move. He stood up, dragging Magaña with him. The skin of the young man's face yellowed. "Don't put any more banderillas in me," Villa said. He turned his knuckles into Magaña's softness, he forced his bones into the hollows of his neck, he closed his veins, he paled him.

"I did it for your own good."

"Children learn to read. Let me alone!" He discarded Magaña, sending him tumbling backward over the bench.

The guards came with their clubs raised. Magaña lay on the floor. His limbs were in confusion. He found his arm and held it up to Villa, extending his hand. "What an oaf I am! Help me up, please. My mother always said I grew too fast to keep all the size of me together. Aaahhh, my feet are even more tangled than my politics. Give me a hand, will you?"

Villa pulled him upright. The guards watched; they kept their clubs raised. "No fighting," one of the guards said. "If you want to fight, you can go to San Juan de Ulúa. You can go there and fight the tides."

"The injustices of the judicial system are endless," Magaña said. "First you put us in prison on absolutely ridiculous charges, you violate agreements, confidences. Not you personally, but the system you represent, the federal government, which is no less corrupt now than it was during the Porfiriato. And now that you have us here at your mercy, you make further accusations, you turn a fall into a fight—anything to condemn us, anything to find a way to continue to keep the men who truly care about the welfare of Mexico and your own welfare from having the opportunity to do what must be done." He poured the words onto them until the weight forced them back, until they shook their heads and put their hands over their ears, until they put down their clubs and backed away.

Then he turned to Villa: "You see? Only a man who can read can talk enough to defeat two guards without raising a finger."

"You don't have to read to do that. I know some old women who could defeat whole regiments that way; they could turn back cavalry charges with their prattle."

They had a moment for laughter and another for thanks. Then they sat down again around the corner of the table, and Magaña said, "Anyone can learn to read, and everyone should learn. In Morelos, up in the mountains, we're teaching old men to read and write. That's what a revolution is about, man. You see, those bastards, those filthy bastards who sat around Díaz were partly right: people who can't read aren't really ready to govern themselves. Madero knows that. He's not doing anything about it, he's not building enough schools, he's not teaching the adults, but he knows as well as Díaz did that you can't have true democracy without educated people. If the people can't read, they will never have power; the power will always go to the rich because they're educated. How could a man who can't read be the mayor of a town or the governor of a state? How can we have senators who can't read the laws they write? Judges? Presidents?

"Villa, our slogan is Liberty, Justice, and Law. Without law, you can't have justice or liberty, true? But what good is the law if the people can't read it? The power of the law belongs to those who can read."

"There were laws before people could read."

"But there was no justice, there was no democracy before people could read."

"Mexico was a great country before the catzopines came; the race was pure."

"This is 1912. We can't go back four hundred years. In 1912, people have to know how to read or they'll continue to be slaves."

"You can't teach Peter to be a goatherd," Villa said. "I tried to learn to read, a telegrapher tried to teach me. It's impossible. And I don't want to hear about it anymore. It's too late. You have to learn when you're a child."

"I'll teach you in three months. Will you try for three months? What else do you have to do in jail?"

"I have to get out."

Bonales Sandoval came often to talk with Villa about the progress of the case. He said he needed evidence, witnesses, papers. Villa had nothing to give him; he could only swear his loyalty, he could only ask when Madero would answer his message. And always the attorney answered that the President had other problems. He told Villa that the people were not satisfied with Madero, he told him that Madero's promises had not been kept. On some visits he brought newspapers and read the stories to Villa. He showed him the stories and the murderous drawings. He did not defend the President, he only told about him, speaking in a cool way, as if he were telling gossip from another town.

"Then help me," Villa asked, "you help me. Get me out, convince the judge." But Bonales Sandoval could only ask again for evidence, papers, witnesses. He reminded Villa that the truth was in question, that a regular general spoke against an honorary general. He said that there were rules. He read the rules of the army to Villa, he explained them.

"Then get me a cleaner cell, then make them allow me to have visitors. I haven't heard about my wife. Find out about my wife, you find out."

The rule was three months without visitors, the lawyer told Villa; after three months they could complain, they could make demands. He knew nothing about Liviana; he said that was not a lawyer's work.

Time in the prison was not time; it did not pass quickly, it did not pass slowly. The days were days because the days were counted. The sun rose in the morning, rain came in the afternoon, the sun set, the rain stopped, it was night. The time was summer, the days had names; they had numbers, they followed.

"Read," the young Zapatista said to Villa, "learn to read and the days will be different. There are seventy-four adventures in the book about Don Quijote de la Mancha. Read one adventure every day for seventy-four days and you will remember the days by the events and not only by the names of the days. Cervantes calls him an imaginative landlord; I call him a meddler, a good fool, a troublemaker with the best intentions, the most impractical man—he's a knight who rides on a nag and attacks windmills, he's innocent about women. Some days you'll laugh at him, some days you'll be angry with him, some days you'll cry for him. Cervantes knew the world: he was a soldier, he fought duels, he had women, he went to prison three times and he never committed a crime. Learn to read by reading this book, General Villa. Do that, and prison will not be a punishment; do that, and the days will be more than numbers. Read the book and laugh and the laughter will help you to see the world more clearly. You'll know more about Madero by reading this book than you would know if you were his brother."

"What kind of man owns land in a place called The Stain?"

"Read the book."

"Yes. All right."

"Do you know the letters? How they sound?"

"Some."

Magaña opened the book. With his pen he pointed to the letter *A.* He said the sound, he asked Villa to say it. They went on to *B* and *C.* After the letters, they read the first words; they began. Villa made the sound of each of the letters. He made the sounds very quickly. It was a word, and he knew the word. "I'm reading," he said.

"You're beginning."

"No, man, I can read. Didn't I look at the letters and say the word? Didn't you hear me?"

"Read more."

Villa said another word. He stumbled. Magaña helped him, he whispered the sounds to him. He asked him to go back, to read the row of words, to read until the dot said to stop and take a breath. Villa said the words, from the big letter to the dot. He read.

"I'm not too old."

Magaña replied by a half-hidden smile.

"But it takes a long time to read," Villa said. "It's very slow."

"It becomes quick; one day you'll think talking is too slow."

Villa took the book with him to his cell. He examined it there: the bundles of the pages, the yellowing pages, the odor of age hidden in the back, the coarse cloth pasted across its back, like shirt-sleeves. A book. He held it up, he laid the flat side of it against his cheek. A book of words; it had a voice, it was a container of voices. He could draw out the voices, he could hear them; the voices were there at his will. He opened the pages. They spread. There was a fan of pages. He let them fall. Seventy-four days passed, all the voices passed. He did not know them; he expected them, he listened for them; the surprises were in the letters that marked the pages, the life was in the marks on the pages—color came from those black lines and curls as flowers came from black earth. He turned to the first page again, and he read, "At a certain Village in La Mancha, which I shall not name, there lived not long ago one of those old-fashioned Gentlemen. . . ."

Who spoke? He spoke. Whose words? The words of the life of the book. His voice spoke them; the book had entered him, he held the book and said it out of his mouth; he was the book and the book was him. He closed the covers and put the book beside his pillow, then he lay down and watched the book and wondered what words it held and what might become of him.

"Say the sounds quickly," Magaña advised, "to understand the words. Say the words slowly to understand the book."

Villa could not read without Magaña's whispers. He waited for the exercise hour and again for the hour in the corridor. They read together. Villa listened to the voice and he saw what it made. "You won't always have to speak the words to hear them," Magaña said. "One day, they'll speak without any sound. You'll see the sound."

"That would be magic."

"Yes, magic."

[*401*]

* * *

He learned about the child, a boy, born in summer, in the month Tlaxo-
chimaco, which is the birth of flowers, the celebration of flowers in dancing,
the month when men and women dance together and touch each other.
There is no happier month.

Liviana went home to San Andrés for the child to be born. Her mother
sent for a woman from the mountains to count the days and to wash the
child and to put ashes on its joints and the vulnerable place in its head. It
was a good time: they made cakes of corn and honey, they invited neighbors
to sit beside the wife of the general, they prayed for a daughter to be born
in that month, knowing that she would be beautiful.

The old woman came down from her house in a steep place in the Blue
Mountains. She brought her bags of medicines and charms. She brought a
jade knife to put under the bed to cut the pain. "We must be careful," the
woman said. "The child is almost due and it could be born on a bad day:
the water sign is tomorrow. The baby should be born today or on the day
after tomorrow." There were discussions in the kitchen, in the yard behind
the house, in places where they could not be overheard by Liviana. The
mother and her sisters in the long black dresses talked with the woman from
the Blue Mountains. "It's too dangerous to hurry the birth," the woman
said; "the child can lose its breath. If she's too close, we can slow down the
birth with cold water, balms, and jimsonweed leaves."

"It's better to get the baby out sooner," the sisters said. "We can massage
her and give her wormwood tea; the tea always brings the baby."

"I won't endanger the child," the midwife said. "Even if it's born under
the water sign and it's a male, we can name it on another day. Then it won't
be weak and sickly all its life; the days mix, the signs change each other;
we can choose the best of the second signs. Maybe it will only be a grumbler.
Maybe the month will be stronger than the day. We'll paint its head with
pitch until the second sign. I'll stay with her until the naming, but the
wormwood is too dangerous, too dangerous for the breath of the child."

They brought the problem to Liviana. She sat in the patio in the afternoon
shade, fanning herself and sipping cool myrtle water from a thick cup. Her
belly was large and still pointed, even after it dropped; she was sure the child
was a boy. The midwife and the sisters spoke to her; they told her the day
sign and all the things that could be done to spare the child the bad luck
of the water. Liviana laughed at them. "The child will be born when God
said it should be born, and if there's any trouble, we'll call Dr. von Schoech." She shooed the women away. She sat alone in the garden. It was hot
even in the shade. Beads of perspiration ran between her breasts. She picked
a dark rose and pulled off the petals and pressed them to her breast. By the
scent of the rose and the flavor of myrtle she cooled herself. The child

moved inside her. The muscles in her back were tense. She could not be comfortable in the chair.

The pains came the next afternoon. They were not severe, and they came far apart, without rhythm. "It will be a long labor," the midwife said. "The baby will come in a day, and that will be the wrong day; the sign will be One Atl, the water sign. She should be slowed, for the sake of the child."

"We can hurry it," the sisters said. "If she starts the wormwood tea now and eats the meat of nopal leaves."

Liviana lay in the center of them. She was surrounded by dried women, all thin, all in black, all with hard hands, smooth only over the knuckles, smooth only where the knuckles swelled. The hands pressed her belly. The midwife reached her fingers inside Liviana to measure the progress of the birth. "A long time," the midwife said. She washed her hands in a bowl and rubbed them with scented alcohol.

"In its own good time," Liviana said. "Let the child come when it's ready."

The sisters and the midwife met outside the room. Their faces were sharp. Liviana's mother stood with them, but she did not speak; she tried to remember the birth of her own child, but she could not recall the time, she could not recall the pain, only the child itself was clear, only the pleasure of it.

They did nothing. Liviana permitted nothing, only the warm oils and the gentle massage to soften the muscles and take away the pain of stretching; she drank no medicine, she ate no herbs. The midwife examined her. There was something wrong, she said; the position of the afterbirth was wrong, it was loosened and the baby was not yet born. Liviana said she wanted the doctor. The women agreed, even the midwife.

Liviana's father rode into San Andrés to Dr. von Schoech's house. He had gone to the Terrazas Ranch. A daughter of the landlord was sick with fever and coughing. They had sent an automobile for the doctor. Aprisco asked the doctor's housekeeper to telegraph the ranch. At the other end of the line someone told her the doctor was busy and could not be disturbed. She told them of the difficult birth, she demanded to speak to the doctor, but there was no one at the other end of the wire. "Go there," the telegraph operator told Aprisco. "Maybe the line is down. They won't answer."

Aprisco rode north all that afternoon and into the night. His horse was lathered, winded. He dismounted and picked up a stick to beat the animal. At the entrance to the main house two cowboys met him. He told them his name, he told them he had to see the doctor. They beat him with pistol butts until he was like a dead man. They tied him across the saddle of his horse and led him out into the desert. When they were far from the house and miles from any road, they untied him and threw him down on the road.

They beat the horse across the fetlock joints to make it lame. They took Aprisco's boots off and made deep cuts into the soles of his feet with their machetes. They hacked open his feet so that he could not walk. He screamed for his pain, he screamed that the life of a child would be on their souls. They beat him again and spat on his face before they left him.

The afterbirth was born in the early morning. The sisters screamed when they saw it. "Be quiet," the midwife told them. "Push on her belly, massage the child down, push down." She told Liviana to push hard, to force the child out. "There's time," the midwife said. "If we hurry, there's still time." She took hold of the bloody cord with both hands and pulled. Liviana wept. She said the afterbirth was her child, she said a monster had been born. The sisters and the midwife shouted at her and tried to comfort her. Liviana wept. She screamed with every pain.

An hour later, the child was born. It was well formed, a long, thin boy. The midwife held a mirror to his lips. She felt for movement in his neck. She rubbed his chest, she kneaded the soft bones above his heart. There was no movement. She touched sneezeweed to his nostrils, she immersed him in the coldest water, she held him upside down, she slapped him and shook him. The flesh was gray, the boy was dead.

Liviana lay back on the bed. Her eyes were dulled; she appeared to be blinded. Her breathing slowed, she was quiet. The sisters prepared to change the sheets under her. They brought clean sheets and basins of water. But the midwife said it was not yet time. She put on a glove of soft deerskin and reached inside Liviana. "Be still," she told her. "Be still while I find out if you're clean inside. Be still; don't try to push my hand out." The midwife turned her hand inside Liviana. Her eyes were closed while she worked, as if to increase the sensing of her fingertips inside the glove. She withdrew her hand slowly, talking softly to Liviana, comforting her, but she showed the sisters by her face that she had found some trouble.

"Push hard now," the midwife told Liviana. "Push out the rest, clean yourself."

Liviana lay still. She made no movement in her belly or her bowels. The sisters and the midwife watched for ripples in Liviana's belly, they looked for the arching of her back. There was nothing. "Please," the midwife said, "push, clean yourself, empty yourself." Liviana did not answer, she did not move. The tears and the sweat dried on her face and on her bosom, the red flush of her breast paled, her feet fell open, she breathed at a slow and even pace. Suddenly, the midwife pulled the pillow from under Liviana's head and held it over her face. Liviana lay quietly until her breath was gone. Then she raised her hands to lift the pillow away. The midwife leaned over onto the pillow. She was small and old and age had dried the weight out of her, but she made herself heavy, she pressed the pillow hard over Liviana's nose and mouth. Liviana tore at the pillow, she beat at the old woman's arms, she kicked and arched and twisted. The blood poured from between her legs. The old woman bore down on the pillow; she held the breath away until Liviana lay still.

The sisters bent over Liviana's bed, cleaning away the clotted blood, wiping her with white rags, washing her with copal and clear water. The midwife leaned against the wall, holding her hand over her heart, counting, counting herself and the time of Liviana's sleep. When her own breast was calm, the midwife took a pinch of sneezeweed from a sack and held it under Liviana's nose. The sneeze did not bring anything more from Liviana's birth canal. The sisters wiped her with a clean cloth to be sure. When they held up the unmarked cloth, the old woman smiled. She slapped Liviana's cheeks to awaken her to understanding. "You're clean inside," the midwife said. "You won't have fever, not even a little. Sleep now. The next child will be a girl; it's always that way. And she'll be born under some good sign, she'll have good fortune. Think of the next child."

In the late afternoon of the next day, they buried the dead child. Because no priest would come to the burial, the midwife presided. She put a piece of turquoise in the baby's hand and she laid a small dried branch of pine against its shoulder. They wrapped the body in red cloth and buried it sitting up, facing the Morning Star. The prayers were brief: the sisters knelt and crossed themselves and spoke rapidly in Latin; Liviana and her mother stood together, stiff, still, in black cloth, in black veiling; the midwife marked her face with ashes and sang softly a Nahuátl song.

The next morning, the old woman went back to her house in the Blue Mountains. She took the afterbirth with her, carrying it in a blue jar.

It was all told to Villa by Bonales Sandoval. He stood in the corridor, touching his forehead with a perfumed handkerchief and toying with the curl of his mustache while he spoke. Villa held on to the bars. His face was pressed against the bars, forced between them, constricted, protruding. His fingers were white and trembling, the blood was squeezed out of his fingers. "And two days later," Bonales Sandoval said, "some Indian brought Aprisco in on the back of a mule. His feet were swollen up like watermelons, but he'll be all right, everyone is going to all right. In the end, after all, it was not so bad."

The lights appeared in Villa's eyes, the blank, dead holes came into his vision. He could not see the lawyer; the lights were like stars bursting in water, they were like fluids of light, like the moon molten and shimmering. He pushed himself away from the bars and stumbled back into his cell, blinded, turning. His knee touched the metal frame of the bed. He reached down and took the metal in his hands. He lifted the bed up on its hinges, he threw it against the wall. He threw it again and again. He strained to tear the bed loose from the wall, to smash it.

A flat, trilling scream came from his chest. He mourned. He roared with mourning. Again, he lifted the bed frame, twisting it, tearing at the hinges. The springs came loose, the steel wires fell out of the center of the frame. He threw it against the wall, he caught the frame returning, he took it in his blind hands and threw it again. And then he wept. He stood in the center of the cell, blinded and trembling, and he wept.

The guards allowed Magaña into Villa's cell to sit with him. "I heard," Magaña said. "I want to say something to comfort you. It's difficult to know what to say. We have to mourn. It's human to mourn."

"The doctor."

"I heard that too." He put his arm around Villa, he held him as if he were an injured child, he comforted him by that closeness. "I can tell you this: we'll take the land away, we'll take the power away. That's what a revolution is about, Villa: power. To take away power you have to take back the land. Can you understand me? Can you hear me? That's where Madero is mistaken. Elections are not enough. We have to go beyond elections. We have to take away their power, and to do that we'll have to take away their land and their money, everything; we'll have to begin again. Villa, we'll have to take land from every rich man—even Madero, even him. Do you understand? That's the only revenge, that's the only thing that matters. If you ever get out of here, remember that."

"I'll be out soon," Villa said. "Madero knows; he heard me, he heard what they did to my son. He knows those things, he hears from a great distance; the words come to him like dreams. Now he'll let me out."

"Who told him?"

"He doesn't have to be told; he hears, he listens to thoughts; he told me, and I believe him. He knew I was a revolutionary before we ever met. He pardoned me because he knew about my life before I told him. He hears; thoughts come to him. We have the same name, Francisco, Pancho; even that is a help to him in hearing me."

"Nonsense."

"We'll see." He patted Magaña's knee. "Thank you; you're my friend. But I want to be quiet now, I want to think about Terrazas."

"Not only Terrazas, all of them."

"First Terrazas."

Every day Villa read, and every day he was disappointed: the words did not come easily, nor was he able to see the sounds. He learned to recognize words; he did not have to make the sounds of the letters of each word, but he could not read the words without saying them softly to himself. Nor could he write anything but his own name, which he still drew as a face or a figure is drawn. At Magaña's suggestion he asked his new attorney, Aguirre Benavides, to bring him a typewriter. Then he made words as they were made in books; he did not have to learn another language of writing. He wrote a letter to Liviana:

> Dear Liviana, How are
> you? I do not like the
> jail. You are far from me.
> Do not be sad. Your
> husband, Francisco Villa.

Magaña helped him to spell the words; he showed him the keys to hit with his fingertips. Villa was not satisfied with the letter. He told Magaña it did not say enough.

"It's better than nothing."

"It's not my voice."

Villa did not send the letter. He put the typewriter aside.

Luis Aguirre Benavides promised a woman, a young woman, a beautiful and innocent woman. He said her name was Rosa Palacios; he made the shape of her in the air, he described her with his hands. She lay in dreams in Villa's narrow iron bed.

On the day after Colonel Mayol assumed command of the federal penitentiary the woman was brought to corridor nine. She walked with her hand in the bend of Aguirre Benavides's arm. She was like a rouge-touched spring mango beside the stiff, unhappy attorney; so sweetly turned, so promisingly colored was she. The prisoners in the cells closest to the gate followed her with glances, with staring, but they did not call out promises or endearments to her; it was as if she had been washed, as if Aguirre Benavides were merchant and priest. The lawyer and the woman walked in a formal way, with their chins lifted and their steps slow and regular; they were a procession—he in black cloth, a trunk and sticks, and she in green and rose, swaying, rustling, perfume and the illusion of music.

The lawyer made the presentations: the lady to the general, the general to the lady. "At your feet," said Villa the general. "I've heard so much about you," said Rosa the lady, with a laugh, with a quick, girl's laugh in her voice.

They spoke through the bars, they saw each other striped by the bars. She put her hand through the bars to touch him. From another part of the corridor came an enormous, uncontrollable sigh. She laughed; the sound made her bosom tremble.

The guard unlocked the door to the cell, and Rosa went inside. She walked about the square of it, she read the walls, she looked into the bowl

[*407*]

of the toilet, she stood on her toes to peer out through the small, high window. "It's not a bad little shack," she said.

"I won't be here long."

"It's funny to think of a general in jail. Why don't you call your army to get you out?"

"Is Luisito paying you?"

"Yes."

"Is he paying you well?"

"Yes." She turned her face away; she lowered her head to make herself modest.

"How much?"

"General Villa . . ." She implored him by the tone. She clasped her hands in front of her, in the lap of her thighs, as if in prayer.

"How much?" He sat on the bed, against the wall. He spread himself, he made himself thick.

"A little now—clothes, a few pesos, gifts. When it's over, he promised to give me a little house in Coyoacan."

Villa sat up. "And when will it be over?"

"When you go."

"On what day? When? Did he say when?"

She cried very softly, with shrugs and little steps to keep her from toppling over onto the floor of the cell. She said she was afraid.

Villa hung blankets over the bars to make a room of the cell. He made her stand in the center of the room and remove her clothes. "I've already undressed once," she said. "A woman looked in all my clothes. She felt me naked. I'm not shameless."

He insisted. He took her clothes as she removed them, feeling everywhere, in the seams, in the folds of her skirt, inside her shoes. He stood behind her and felt in her hair.

"For what?" she asked. "Why are you looking in my hair?"

"A small knife, a razor, a poisoned needle."

She held her hands over her eyes, as if to hide from his estimation of her. She stood lightly on the cold stone floor, shifting from one foot to the other, shivering at each step, like a girl putting her toes in cold water. "Why?" she asked again, "why?"

"I have enemies: Huerta, Orozco, Terrazas, others—so many others that I don't even know all their names or their faces. Ten thousand others. More."

"But I came to make love."

"How do I know that someone didn't send you to kill me? I don't trust anyone, Rosita; I watch them spoon out the food every morning, every afternoon, every night, I always watch, and I never eat until all the others have eaten; I'm always the last one to eat. No one will poison me; I'm too careful."

He took her to the metal bed. She held the chain with one hand. She gave him neither cries nor illusions. She was still. Her face was damp with sorrow.

She washed and dressed herself, she rolled her hair and laced her shoes and made herself rose and green again; rustling, swaying, she made the illusion of music.

"Will you return?"

"Yes."

"Do you want to?"

"Yes."

"I'll always look inside your clothes."

"I understand."

They began to speak on the next visit. She asked childish questions, she made him laugh. Could he really change into the shape of an animal? Did he cut off the soles of men's feet? Had he tied men to horses and pulled them apart? How many women had he raped? How many men had he killed? He answered her with riddles and promises: if he could escape from prison by making himself into a cockroach, he would have six legs. Would she love him more if he became a horse on her next visit? Are men's feet immortal? Is half a man a boy? Can a man find a needle in a haystack? He said he had killed men, but not enough; he made a list for her.

She wore rose because it was her name, because it was the color of the blush in her cheeks, the color of her years. She went to his cell three times every week, and she lay beside him on the narrow bed and spoke to him more with every visit. She told him she was the child of women, the daughter and the granddaughter and the great-granddaughter of a great-granddaughter. She was scum, she said, descended from scum, from the léperos who were crucified in the streets of Mexico and at all the crossroads for miles around the city. It was her history. She recited it: the slums are not the hills; we are the hills, the rich walk on us. There are no beasts in the slums; we are the beasts, the rich devour us. We are the children of women; the rich rape us, we do not know our names. There are no men in the slums; there cannot be, the rich have murdered them. I was first fucked with a knife at my throat; I have been fucked strangling, bleeding, beaten, bound, and in my precious dead sleep; I have never screamed, I weep only for my dead sister, the burst heart of my sainted grandmother, and the suffering of Our Lord Jesus Christ. I am the direct descendant of the rape of La Malinche; and when I saw her in the parade, I was only fifteen years old, but I spat because I knew that the sight of her in the streets of Mexico would bring the beginning of the end of this world; and it was true, I was

[409]

the only one who was not surprised by the comet or the earthquake; it was true, I saw her in the street, in her long dress, in her braided hair; she spoke Spanish, but we knew her Nahuátl name, we all knew, but I was the only one who spat, I was the only one who called her grandmother, and spat.

Because of her I joined the revolution, I became Juana the wife of Zapatistas, Magonistas, Villistas, Vazquistas, and even Orozquistas. I am the wife of the revolution; I want to know a man, I want to give light to the child of a man, a daughter or a son named with a father's name, a child made for after the revolution, a farm child, a mountain child, a child that eats meat and reads books and knows all of its names; and I will be happy if it is the child of a revolutionary, because I have seen birth and I know that all children are born bloody; I am ready, I will wash my child and put ashes on its knees and keep a fire burning in my house for days and days, I will make a famous child by the duration of the fire.

The reading went on. It came to the place about the island and Sancho Pança's work as a governor. "The main point in this point of governing," Sancho said, "is to make a good beginning." Magaña asked if Madero had made a good beginning, if sending a vicious general against Zapata was a good beginning, if failing to act on the land question was a good beginning. Villa defended the President, saying that everything could not be done at once, accusing Zapata of failing to give the President time to carry out his programs, blaming Zapata and Orozco for the poor beginning.

They talked about land. They agreed that the land should belong to the people who work the land, they agreed that the Law of the Wastelands had been turned against the poor, they agreed that the land should be returned to those who had worked it and owned it before the rich had taken everything in Mexico, they agreed that the communal lands belonged to the village people; but Villa would not agree that Madero had made a bad beginning or that he would not soon return the land to the poor. Magaña laughed, he said that Villa was sentimental, he said that Little Madero's government would not last another year. "He has no support among the rich and no support among the poor, the gringos want him out, the big European countries have no interest in anything but a rape, and the army would put its mother in the streets for a silver peso."

"Then we should be loyal to him," Villa said. "He needs his friends."

The Zapatista gave Villa a friendly whack across the shoulders. "Comrade, a man who puts me in jail is not my friend, and if he takes my mother for a hostage the way he did to Zapata, I will consider him even more unfriendly."

"Madero wouldn't order that."

"He's the President."

Their arguments ended in shrugs and embraces, they wept together at the death of Don Quijote, at the finish of his madness. They turned from reading to the study of numbers by tens. Villa wrote additions and subtractions, he learned the rules of multiplication, he studied the lists of answers Magaña made for him, he agreed that tens were more useful than twenties and hundreds more manageable than four hundreds; he did not count by fingers and flags, he made numbers on the page.

And they also talked of revolution. "Perhaps a revolutionary is nothing but a meddler," Villa said, "milking his cows into a sieve."

"You read the book wrongly," Magaña said, and he opened it to one of the places he had marked and read a part of a poem:

> No slave, to lazy ease resigned
> Ever triumphed over noble foes.
> The monarch Fortune most is kind
> To him who bravely dares oppose.

They began another book, *The Three Musketeers,* but Villa found it less to his liking. He told Magaña that the new book had no face, he put it down, he turned the pages without care; the book passed by him without entering. He asked Magaña if there were not other books more like *Don Quijote,* books with voices and faces, books that were written by people who were old and suffered and wise enough to laugh. Magaña said that there was another book, a book of plays written by an Englishman who lived at the same time as Cervantes. He promised to get the book; but before it was brought to Lecumberrí, Villa was moved to the military prison in the old convent of Santiago Tlaltelolco.

On the day before the guards came to transfer Villa, he gave Magaña all the useful things he had collected in his cell: the warm blankets, the plates and forks and spoons, the jars of hair oil, the rubber shoes, a razor, a shaving brush, two mugs of shaving soap, towels, and a goose-down pillow. Villa embraced Magaña and thanked him, he said they would always be friends; and Magaña answered: " 'There's no friend; all friendship's gone: Now men embrace, then fight anon.' "

Villa shook his head; he was full of laughter, he felt the heat of tears behind his eyes. "Rozinante and Dapple," he said.

"One day, we'll all be shepherds," Magaña said.

Santiago Tlaltelolco was for the comfort of generals. They lived at their ease in the great halls, they walked in the gardens, they received visitors in the manner of generals. The finest whores came to the prison, the best food was served, the generals wore soft leather shoes and perfume and slept with their mustaches in gauze nets. In Santiago Tlaltelolco there were no cells;

[*411*]

the generals lived in rooms with doors, they had privacy, they were more comfortable than the nuns of the convent had ever been. Beyond the halls where the generals lived were the courtrooms and the rooms of records. Those rooms had been the chapels and sacristies of the convent. On the upper floor of the building, in the rooms where nuns had once slept and lived in prayer and poverty, in rooms smaller than prison cells, in rooms that only the worshipers of martyrdom could tolerate, lived the ordinary prisoners. The generals did not see these ordinary prisoners, the generals were the princes of the prison, for the jailers knew that governments fall and imprisoned generals, who survive the anger of one government, are often the generals of the next. The jailers were practical men; they saluted the generals, they accepted gifts from the generals, they were the aides and the orderlies the generals had left behind.

Villa was imprisoned on the lower floor in a corridor that bordered on the Third Court of Military Investigations. Only a row of thin bars separated the corridor from the offices of the Third Court. There was no wall. He looked into the offices and saw the clerks at their desks. At the other end of the corridor was the door that led to the dining room and the barber's room and the garden where the generals often met to talk about their luck and the certain failure of the government that had imprisoned them. It was a garden of generals; there was a smell of roses and Havana tobacco. At first, Villa stayed in the corridor. He left his room only for meals. Then he was lonely, and he went into the garden to listen to the generals, to learn the style of generals.

General Reyes spoke to him every day. He was polite, he called Villa "sir" and "the General of the North," he said Villa was truly "the Lion of the Sierras," a hero to the poor, a man of accomplishment, a man for whom promises were not enough.

Villa was not at ease with him; he apologized for his accent, he was sorry he did not drink wine, he asked the general for advice about Liviana, he asked him for the names of books, but always he reminded the general that he was loyal to Madero.

"Your loyalty is admirable," General Reyes said, "but I would admire you more, sir, if your first loyalty was to Mexico. A nation is dying under Madero, a tragedy is being enacted here in Mexico that will affect the lives of unborn generations, the whole world is feasting on the weakness of a man of good intentions."

"Give him time."

"Time passes and it cannot be recovered." Reyes paused to appreciate himself, the resting of his limbs, the languor of smoke in the enclosed garden, the pale, freckled, blued skin of his hands. "I consider time often here—this garden is a contemplative place, crowded though it may be. It

[*412*]

appears, sir, that my time is being wasted here, that I am undergoing a hiatus in my life, as prison is meant to be. Let me assure you that it is not so. I sit here like a farmer waiting for the proper combination of moisture and sunlight to sprout his corn or a herdsman taking his ease while his flock crops grass, preparing itself for market. Life is made of successful plantings, fermentations; there are some occasions when biding one's time is the best use one can make of his time. Everything is completed, plowed and seeded; Madero is finished."

"Are you going to declare?"

General Reyes leaned back in his chair. He raised his face to the pale sun of the hour before the rain. There were casts of yellow in his beard: age, cigar smoke, some ancestor wearing spurs in the heated plains of Andaluz. "We've talked enough, I'm resting now. A busy time is coming, General Villa; if you would accept an old man's advice, be part of it, for the sake of Mexico. History will vindicate you, if you act when you are needed; otherwise, history will forget the number of your cell and the letters of your name."

"You are going to declare against Madero."

"From the garden of Santiago Tlaltelolco?" He laughed. "I'm a soldier, not a philosopher."

"I'll defend him."

"You have." General Reyes closed his eyes. He dismissed Villa by closing his eyes. The smoke of the cigar rose in a stream, whiter than the general's beard. A liquid sound came from the general's belly; he smacked his lips.

Villa lived in the small room, the cell. The walls were painted white, they were clean. He slept on a thick mattress, he closed the door to use the toilet, he put aside the book about the musketeers and read again about Don Quijote, he used the typewriter to make words, he copied the words from *Don Quijote,* he waited. There was no message from Madero, the lawyers came less often now that the case had been decided and he was declared guilty. He waited. The guards brought letters to him; they contained nothing more than a name, his name and a few bills, a hundred pesos, three hundred, never more. The letters came from Don Abraham, from Maytorena in Sonora, Urbina in Durango, and from Antonio and Hipólito in Chihuahua. There were no letters from Liviana.

The rains stopped, the air cooled and became lighter; his mouth parched and his lips cracked, Rosita brought him an oil of Canaigre Root to soothe and heal the fissures in his lower lip. He passed afternoons with Rosita; sometimes she stayed the night, sleeping tightly beside him on the narrow bed, responded to the shape of him. She ironed his clothes and spoke to him of revolution, she urged him, she told the value of land to him, the meaning of land, she lay beside him and whispered that war and poverty were brothers, the wounds of one no less than the wounds of the other. He said she was a soldier, she said she would be a soldier, but only until the revolution was completed; after that, she said, armies only make wars, after the revolution a soldier is nothing more than a maggot.

"I'm a soldier," he said.

"You're a general."

"I wanted to be a farmer; I was named for St. Dorothy. I wanted to have a store. I had a meat market in Chihuahua."

"You stole cattle."

"I charged the lowest prices."

"Revolutionaries don't steal."

"Do you know what Cervantes says about women?" He found the book and read to her. He did not read easily, the words came panting:

> *The Wife that expects to have a good Name,*
> *Is always at home as if she were lame:*
> *And the Maid that is honest, her chiefest Delight,*
> *Is still to be doing from Morning to Night.*

He said the rhymed words over again, laughing. Rosa began a disagreement, but he touched his fingers to her mouth, he told her she had said enough.

The neat young man who sat in the clerk's office beyond the bars at the end of the corridor wore garters on the sleeves of his shirt and protected his white cotton cuffs with stiff false cuffs made of Celluloid. He bowed to generals and judges. His mustache was not offensive. He was neither a lawyer nor a clerk, he was a young man in passage, a young man who wished to become. He spoke through the bars to the generals imprisoned on the other side, he offered favors to them, he saw them expectantly. The government was falling: the Standard Oil scandal was in the newspapers every day, the railroad workers were threatening to strike for an eight-hour day, the textile workers had been on strike, the Zapatistas were not defeated by the gentlemanly maneuvers of Felipe Angeles, as they had not been defeated by the cruelty of his predecessor, and the generals were in constant contact with each other: Reyes, Huerta, Mondragón, Rubio Navarrete, all of them, waiting now, in dispute only over who would be the next President, held back only by the change that was coming in Washington, uncertain only there. He wanted to be with them, he saw an opportunity; he was a neat young man, he was not offensive.

Of all the generals who stood on the other side of the bars to speak to the young man, General Villa was there most often. He gave the young man gifts of ten pesos or fifty, he sent him on errands, he asked him about books, the law, the news. The neat young man always did as General Villa asked, he always told him the truth about the news, he did not make things better, he did not make them worse, he was a good lieutenant, accurate and dependable. He told Villa he would help him to escape from Santiago Tlaltelolco. He urged him to escape.

"It's not worth the trouble," Villa said. "Madero will pardon me, I'm waiting for a pardon."

"I looked at your records," the neat young man said. "You've been in prison since the beginning of summer." He looked away, he said softly, "If he intended to pardon you, he would not have promoted Huerta."

Villa did not answer. He went to his room. He sat in the dark and ministered to his cracked lower lip. He knew the young man, Carlos Juáregui, was a good lieutenant, accurate and dependable.

For more than a week Villa spoke to no one but Rosita Palacios. He asked her to get two thousand pesos from Aguirre Benavides. She brought the money in two days. It was not the first errand she had done for the revolution; she hurried, she asked no questions. But she no longer spoke to Villa in the same way: she was quieter, like a man waiting for the first shot to be fired; she lectured Villa on the revolution, she spoke in whispers about the land, she argued for a new law about the division of the land, as Magaña had, in the words of the Plan of Ayala; and she made intimate jokes, ugly soldier's jokes followed by stifled laughter, by the hoarseness that comes of too many cigarettes and too much shouting. The flush of her cheeks deepened. She wore thick wool sweaters and heavy walking shoes. She was ready for something; she did not say what it was, and he did not ask. She continued to visit him regularly. The days were short. It was very cold.

A man came to see Villa. "My name is Antonio Tamayo," he said. "General Reyes sent me."

"He could have come himself."

The man closed the door to the cell. Villa was standing behind him. He pushed the man up against the wall and held him there, pressing the palms of his hands against Tamayo's shoulder blades.

"Talk to me," Villa said.

"I can only talk to the wall."

"The wall is my friend; it tells me whatever is said in this cell. Talk to the wall."

"I was sent to help you."

"Or to kill me."

"Don't be a clown. If General Reyes had wanted someone to kill you,

[415]

he would have done it weeks ago, and I can assure you, sir, he would have sent an assassin instead of a lawyer."

"Sit down there on the bed. Keep your hands flat on your knees."

Villa stepped back and Tamayo went to the bed. He sat very straight and he did not take his hands from his knees. "They're going to declare," he said.

"When?"

Tamayo let his shoulders fall. He smiled; the corners of his mustache were raised. "Soon, very soon. There are still details to be worked out. The country mustn't be thrown into chaos, Madero must be allowed to resign, everything must be honorable, reasonable, in the best interests of the country."

"What about Zapata?"

"A hundred barefoot Indians. We're talking about fifteen million people, a whole nation."

"Gonzáles in Chihuahua?"

"Weak; he can't control the state; he gave it away to Orozco. You know how he let Orozco take it from him. We need a strong man in the north. There have been discussions about you; even Huerta says you're a good soldier, even Huerta admits that the people would be satisfied if you were our man in the north."

"Do I have a better friend than Huerta?"

"Why should I lie to you? Huerta doesn't like you, but that's not important; we're not talking about friendship here, we're talking politics, power. The generals are talking about the future of a whole country; what does it matter who's invited to a party or a dinner?"

"Why should I trust you?"

Tamayo shook his head. He sucked his lip, thinking what to say. He shook his head again. "I'm revealing a plan that could put the generals up against a wall, and you ask why you should trust me. How can I answer? They're offering you the north, the whole north."

"It could be a trick."

"We've arranged for you to leave the prison; you'll think more clearly when you're out of here. Everything is arranged for the twenty-eighth: clothes, a car, a place to hide until the declaration is made."

Villa sat down on the bowl of the toilet to think. Tamayo asked if he could smoke, and Villa answered with a wave of his hand. The lawyer lit a cigar and dropped the match onto the floor. "Pick it up," Villa said. "This is not the street."

The lawyer picked up the match. He smoked. He studied the ash of the cigar. Villa stood up and went to the window. He saw the street: stores, two carriages passing, a woman carrying a bundle of wash, children playing with a red-and-yellow ball; a prison guard going home, his shirt collar unbuttoned and his hat tilted and pushed to the back of his head. "Does Juáregui, the clerk, work for General Reyes?"

"The little faggot? He works for anyone. But why should you care? You have the Palacios woman; isn't she enough for you?"

Villa continued to look out the window. A brown dog had come to watch the children. He knew the dog, he knew the children. Every day, the children played with the same red-and-yellow ball in the same place outside the military prison; every day, the brown dog came and lay down and watched the children. In summer, the dog lay in the shade; now it lay in the sun, with its belly shown to the sun. "I could betray the generals."

"Which general? Did a general ever come to your cell? Did you ever go to visit a general in his cell? Did General Reyes ever say anything to you while you were out in the garden together? Did anyone ever hear him? Sir, the courts operate on evidence, not on rumors."

"You're here."

"A lawyer interested in your case."

One of the children fell. A girl. There was blood on her knee. She cried out, but the other children went on with the game. While she cried, they did not throw the red-and-yellow ball to her. "Arrange everything for the twenty-eighth; if I'm ready, I'll go with you. But I'll tell you now: I don't like what you said about Don Abraham and I'm worried about Madero. If you could give me some proof . . ."

Tamayo went to the door. "Nothing will happen to Madero. He'll resign, there will be new elections, everything will be better, you'll see." The ash fell from Tamayo's cigar and shattered on the floor. Villa looked at the pieces of burnt tobacco; an unnoticeable breeze carried the pieces of ash across the room, spreading the grayness.

The arrangements with Juáregui were made quickly; the young man answered Villa's questions innocently, his eyes were soft, by the softness of his eyes he submitted. "And if we're caught," Villa said, "if they find us out, they'll shoot me and you'll say you gave the alarm."

"No, sir, if they shoot one, they'll have to shoot two."

Villa reached through the bars to take the young man's hand. Juáregui's fingers were soft, his palms were damp; there was no force in his hand, no weight. "I'll bring a file for the bars," he said.

"No. These are nothing more than wires. They were meant to keep old men from wandering. When the time comes, we can pull them apart and walk through the space. Worry about the pistols; bring two, not little ones —Colts or Smith and Wessons; bring one box of shells for each pistol. If we're caught, we'll defend ourselves. But do it fast, Carlitos; I'll be a dead man on the twenty-eighth, if I'm not out of here."

"How do you know?"

"Because that's when they said they would save me."

The young man brought the pistols on the next day and the boxes of cartridges on the day following. On the third day, he brought a Spanish cape, a round black hat, and a pair of dark, striped trousers. "A car is outside," he said. "Put on these clothes and we'll go. Pretend you're a lawyer when we go out. Walk slowly and let your feet drag, the way lawyers do." He laughed; Villa did not return the laughter.

"Do you know how to use a pistol?"

"Not very well."

"A little?"

"I was born in the city. We had no reason."

"It's all right, Carlitos; you be the scout and I'll be the artillery. You walk ahead."

"It's better if we walk together. I'll tell you about a case in the court here. Sometimes the lawyers ask me to do that. The guards have heard me, they know it's the way things are done."

"When should we go?"

"Now, sir. The car is waiting."

"I have some things in my cell. I'll need a little while; you surprised me."

"Yes," the young man said. He smiled; for the first time he seemed confident. "If I surprised you, I'll surprise them too. We should go now, right now, sir."

Villa put on the lawyer's clothes. He gave the prison trousers to Juáregui, who hid them in a drawer of his desk. The thin bars spread easily; one came loose at the bottom and hung from its place in the ceiling. Villa stepped through the space to the other side. He stood in the clerk's office, gathering the cape around him, raising the collar to cover his face, while Juáregui pushed the bent bar back into place. They walked through the clerk's office, into an empty courtroom, out into the corridor. Juáregui talked, describing the case of a captain who had found his wife with a lover and shot them both. He defended the captain, he spoke of the rights of the home, the sanctity of the home, the justice of what the captain had done. Villa listened. They walked slowly. Villa dragged his feet, as lawyers do.

The car was waiting, a black thing, shining, spokes and lanterns, leathery, oiled, long sides of painted metal with silvery fittings; it had a medicinal smell. They drove west toward Toluca. Juáregui was very calm; he smiled into the glass, he did not curse at chickens or horses. When old women stopped in the middle of the street to look up at the threatening monster, Carlos tipped his hat to them and called them Little Mother.

"Are we safe?" Villa asked.

"Please wear your hat straight. When you wear it pushed back like that, you look like Pancho Villa."

"That bandit!" Villa pulled the hat forward, he forced it down low over his eyes. "How is this, Mr. Driver?" He turned his half-hidden face to Juáregui. The young man laughed. They were free.

He told Don Abraham. He sat in a small room that stank of age and heat and told Carlos to write down everything the governor needed to know. "I am safe and sound in El Paso, Texas," he began. He told the plans of the generals, how they had offered him freedom if he would betray Madero, and he told his loyalty to the President and Don Abraham. He was ready to cross the border, he was ready to fight again for freedom, for land, for Madero; he waited only for orders from Don Abraham or the President.

The letter was written and read and written again. He did not know how much to say, how best to say his fears, how best to tell his loyalty. For three days he said the letter and read what the young man wrote and said the letter again. He spoke of the snow in Nogales, his lack of money, the misery of his room in El Paso, and when he read that part, he drew a line through it and asked Juáregui to write the letter again.

The room was cold or the heat roasted him. He looked out on the worst of streets, the most dismal of people; he saw children shivering, he saw thieves and unclean men and women, he saw the people who bent themselves to avoid the wind, who wrapped themselves in rags and blankets and did not know how to warm their hurrying feet. It snowed. The room was not dark at night, it was not light in the day. He sat with the pistols beside him, he parted the dry, dusty curtains to look out at the street, he listened for the cluttered sound of too many boots on the hall stairs. He sent Carlos into the street to buy tacos and beans, and he made him taste the food before he ate it himself. He was often sick; his head ached, and sometimes he lay in bed all day, feeling the blood moving in waves against his skull. He counted his breaths, he counted the sounds of his heart, he read the letter and told Carlos to write it again. The days were lost. Carlos told him that the letter would do no good if it arrived after Madero was dead or in exile. Villa listened to the letter again. He said, "Put this in: 'Time covers up as much as it uncovers,' and then send it." He lay back on the bed. The fire was drying him out, burning up the air, his lips were roasted to crackling. He told Carlos it would be a good time for a dish of ice cream. There was no money.

Don Abraham sent his brother, Aureliano, to visit Villa. The brother said only to wait. He offered to pay Villa at the rank of colonel, but Villa asked instead for a loan of fifteen hundred pesos. The money would be sent, the brother promised; it would help Villa to wait. If he was needed to reassemble the irregulars, Don Abraham would send word. Until then, he was to wait, and he was to be careful not to be arrested by the gringos and turned over to the Federals. The money arrived in a week. A thousand pesos more came from Maytorena, mailed from Tucson. Villa waited. With Juáregui's help, he read the newspapers. He sat in the dry room and ate ice cream and kept his pistols by his side and waited and watched in dreams and the dulled light of the room while the government turned to dust. He saw everything; the ten tragic days were in his room, he smelled them, he heard the guns in the streets of the Capital, the walls of the room trembled, the smoke of the bodies burning in Balbuena came into the room, his head ached, he saw Reyes murdered, he whispered to Madero, he warned him.

The train had started toward the capital and then turned back. It had not even reached Torreón when the order came to turn back. Don Abraham complained to Colonel Camarena: "Your damned fool generals can't seem to make up their minds. Where are we going now? Chihuahua? The City of Juárez? Do you know? Are you lost? It's the middle of the night; if you can't tell your direction by the stars, I'll help you." Camarena gave a mild shrug in answer, he showed an innocent face, he was only a lieutenant colonel. Don Abraham held out his wrists for Camarena to see the raw spots. The colonel shrugged again. "Orders," he said.

The train stopped at Mapula. A trainman opened the door of the compartment and handed a lantern to Camarena. He and the other officers stood up together. They helped Don Abraham to his feet and led him through the narrow corridor to the open platform at the rear of the car. The junior officers walked down the stairs and stood on the gravel beside the tracks. Camarena pushed Don Abraham to the edge of the stairs. The chain between his ankles was not long enough for him to walk down the steps; he jumped. He was a big man, heavy and grown old in the revolution; the officers steadied him.

It was very cold, the wind was from the northwest; it smelled of snow and pine trees and dust. The officers led Don Abraham to the end of the train. They were small men, slim, dressed in hard cloth, dressed in shining leather; Don Abraham was very wide, he had a belly, his mustache was thick and gray, his hair fell over his forehead, he was a rumpled man, his neck was fat, his cheeks were fat, his eyes shone, he had a soft voice, his collar was loose, his necktie was pushed to one side; he was an old man and he was a boy, he knew sadness.

The junior officers pushed him backward, they tumbled him onto the gravel. Colonel Camarena waved the lantern, the rhythm of the locomotive began, the wheels made the first slipping rotation. Don Abraham struggled to sit up, to turn himself over, to crawl; he was grown old in the revolution, his hair was gray, his neck was thick, he had a belly. He let out a great sigh when the wheels reached him.

A newspaperman entered the room. He raised his hands to show that he had no weapons. Miguel Saavedra, Manuel Ochoa, Juan Dozal, and Carlos stood against the walls of the room. They wore shirts without collars, their suit coats did not fit them. They stood quietly, they leaned, their faces were dark, they were beyond the light of the oil lamp. The newspaperman removed his soft hat. His hair was thin; he had arranged it over the bare spots of his scalp.

"Pancho Villa?"

The man who sat up against the headboard of the bed shook his head. "José Jesús Martínez." A pistol lay on the bed beside him; he touched it, his hand hovered over it. "Pancho Villa is in the hills somewhere. He's in Mexico; why don't you go to Mexico and look for him?"

"Are you empowered to speak for him?" The newspaperman spoke Spanish comfortably, he drawled in the northern way; but the hardness of his words betrayed him, his nose was too involved; the thickness of his tongue betrayed him, his mouth was too wet.

"No."

"Do you think he knows that Madero and Gonzáles are dead? Do you think he knows that his worst enemies, Huerta and Orozco, are now in power?" The newspaperman saw what he thought was a response, a change in the eye light; he went on: "Orozco joined Huerta right after the coup. He went to the Capital. There are photographs of them standing together. Do you think Pancho Villa knows about that?"

"Why did you come here to bother me? I'm only a lawyer going about his business. These men are ranchers from Coahuila; they want to buy a bull for breeding. You know we have a lot of cattle in my country, but they don't pick up weight quickly, the meat is too lean, too tough, it needs a nice sprinkling of fat, that nice yellow fat, corn fat, you know."

"What about Pancho Villa?"

[*421*]

"I don't think he'll steal any cattle from these gentlemen."

The newspaperman put his hat on, he pushed it down on his head. "Look, man, I'm going to print a story in tomorrow's *El Paso Times* saying that Pancho Villa is living here in a hotel in the Little Chihuahua district. So if you're afraid to talk, that's something else."

Villa's hand settled over the pistol. "Did you come here alone, sir? It's not safe for a Yanqui to be in this section alone."

"No, I left a couple of friends outside."

Ochoa went to the window and looked out at the street. "I don't see any Yanquis. Where are your friends, Mister?"

"In the tavern."

"There's no tavern on this street."

"I think you must be a spy," Dozal said.

"Maybe you're a red flagger," Saavedra said.

"Maybe you work for Huerta," Carlos said.

The men moved away from the wall. Villa threw his legs over the side of the bed, he stood up, the pistol was held loosely in his hand. The newspaperman moved back toward the door. "Tim Turner," he said, *"El Paso Times,* unarmed, search me." The men advanced on him, they forced him back toward the door. Suddenly, Dozal pulled the door open. Mr. Turner fled.

"We wasted him," Carlos said. "Newspapers are an instrument of politics; newspapermen have no imagination; even their lies are someone else's lies. You can tell a newspaperman a lie and he'll print it in his paper the next morning; and even if he says it's a lie, everyone who reads the newspaper will believe it because it's written in the newspaper. It's like the Bible; people don't believe the priests but they believe what's written in the Bible, and the newspaper is the Bible of the day.

"We have to learn to use the newspapers. Let me give you a case to study. President Wilson is already giving Huerta trouble; he says he wants to see an elected government in Mexico, he says he won't recognize a Huerta government. How can you get President Wilson to support you? If you tell the newspapers that you were loyal to Madero and that you want to reestablish democracy in Mexico, the newspapers will tell Wilson; and he's no different from anyone else who reads the newspapers, he'll believe what you tell him there."

"What a lawyer!" Villa said. "You know, Carlitos, if a lawyer like you turned against the Virgin, he could have her hanged for stealing flowers."

"I was serious," Carlos said. "I've heard important men talk about the same thing: Reyes, Blanquet, Mondragón, others." He stepped back out of the light. The strength was gone from his voice, he was a young man with fine manners; his eyes did not presume, his posture did not offend.

"Don't be afraid, kid. I listened to you, I believed you. But you don't have to be a Porfirista to be realistic. There are five of us here in this room. What should I tell a newspaperman? That five men are going to defeat the Mexican army? They'd say I was a marijuano. This isn't the time, kid; it's too soon.

"It costs blood to make people listen. Who listened to Madero until we took the City of Juárez? You have to buy the right to speak. Like Cervantes. Do you know why people listen to Cervantes? Because he wrote that book in prison. He paid. We'll pay, then we'll speak."

"Yes, sir." Carlos withdrew into deeper shadows, he curled himself down into submission. "I talked too much," he said. "I haven't earned the right."

"All revolutionaries talk too much. It's to be expected. A canary chatters at a cat."

They crossed the river on rented horses, nine men armed with pistols, two Winchester rifles, and a Mauser with a broken stock that had to be fired from the hip. The water was cold, colder in the night wind. They wanted to stop and build a fire, but Villa forced them on; he said it was because of the horses, he said the fire would be seen, he reminded them that they rode on stolen horses.

They rode until morning, going south, keeping the railroad to the west of them. When there was enough light to hide a fire, they stopped and cooked coffee and beans. All that day they rode south, sometimes sleeping in the saddle, walking the rented horses, urging the nameless horses. They were careful not to hurry; the horses lathered easily, they were old and used to comforts, they were standing horses, deafened in the city—too old to buck, they sat down in anger, like mules.

After seven days they arrived in San Andrés. They approached the Aprisco house from the northeast, circling, closing slowly, waiting for the dogs to announce them, waiting for someone to come out of the house. They saw Liviana's father. He walked on the sides of his feet, his legs were spread at the knees. The dogs were close around him, like a herd. He carried a short Mauser; a cartridge belt hung from his shoulder. "Who's there? Who's there?" he shouted. His voice was dull, the wind turned it. He wiped his forehead with the back of his hand, the barrel of the rifle sank. "Who's there? Who's there?" A dog squeezed between his legs. It upset him; he was turned around, stumbling for his balance. He swung the barrel of the rifle at the dogs.

"Your son-in-law." Villa remained around the side of the house, beside the windowless wall.

"We're alone. Come on!"

Villa greeted Aprisco with an embrace. "I heard about your feet."

[*423*]

"They always hurt me now. I was very sick. Look how thin I am! The color of my eyes changed, my eyes turned yellow. They ruined me, Pancho: ants crawled inside my feet, there is always blood in my stool—it comes out black, it pains me; I wake up in the night to piss and I see blood in my piss too. I'm bleeding to death inside; I eat nothing but livers just to stay alive."

"Liviana? Is she here?"

"She's stronger than ever. She takes care of us all now, like a daughter and a son. Don't take her away, you'll kill us all if you take her away." Aprisco handed his rifle to Villa, he lifted one arm for Villa to slip under it and become his crutch. "Help me to the house; you know what they did to my feet."

Liviana had cooled. Her hands were strong, her breasts lay heavily on her breath, she walked without swaying, her hair was tied up, it was pulled tight. She kissed Villa on the cheek. "I heard about the baby," he said. "I cried for you."

"The order was wrong."

"I heard. I heard about Terrazas too. We'll have our revenge."

"The child is dead, my father is an old man, I have no husband." The corners of her mouth trembled, the beginning of her afternoon. "How long will you be here this time? We have seed corn and no one to plant it. There is nothing to feed cattle; we raise goats. The dogs live on what they can find. My mother stays in her room, my aunts are thinner, Christ's spinsters; my cousin and his wife went to Tampico, he works on the boats and she waits for him. The house is empty, Francisco. I can't remember the taste of chocolate, I can't remember the last time I was warm."

"There's going to be a revolution," he said.

She laid her head against her own shoulder. She sighed. "There's always a revolution. I'll be alone again, like a widow. Why? Why don't you stay home?"

"They would come after me. Dear Liviana, I would like to stay home here or in Chihuahua. Isn't that what we always said I would do? But not now, not anymore. I'm like something caught by the wind or the water of a fast stream. They'll come for me here. They'll bring a whole army to this town.

"Liviana, I don't decide anymore. The revolution is the revolution; it goes on, it doesn't get completed, the circle goes around and around, and I'm in the circle, I'm one of the dancers. In a few days I'll go out to find an army again, because Madero is dead and Don Abraham is dead, and something has to be done. Can I stay home? Even if it was possible, would you want me to stay home?"

"Our baby died."

"I was more afraid for you."

"Stay home."

[424]

"They would come with an army, with cannon and machine guns. They would destroy this house and everyone in it. The war is started, the war will have to be finished."

"That's your choice."

"I have no choice."

He stayed three days in the Aprisco house. In the corners of the house and the stables and in the earthen floors, in the fields and the hills beyond the house, Villa had buried rifles and ammunition, no more than three rifles or one case of ammunition in any one place, no more than one sack of grenades in a single hole. Now he remembered them, he dug them up, he took off the oiled rags and cleaned the barrels with turpentine and oiled them with neat's-foot oil. There were forty-one rifles, all cavalry Mausers. He lined them up against the wall of Liviana's bedroom, but he did not put the grenades or the ammunition in the room. He told her it was dangerous to sleep near explosives. She gave him scorn for his concern, she recounted the deaths of her grandfather and her brother, she told him the stench of her father's feet when they dumped him in front of the house.

"You insulted Madero, you thought he was a fool," Villa said. "I remember very well. If you thought differently about him, maybe you could understand my loyalty."

"If you had been loyal to him at Juárez, you could stay home with me now."

"I didn't come home to fight with you. I wept when I heard about our child. I came home to comfort you."

"You came to San Andrés because there are rifles and ammunition here. A wife knows her husband. Lie to your troops, but not to me."

"Do you think I want to go to war?"

"Yes."

In the following silence he thought of having to go away; he didn't know what to say; he didn't want to leave her at such a great distance. "I learned to read in prison."

"Do you remember that I showed you how to sign your name?"

"Yes."

"Well, Francisco, now you're a rich man."

"It's true: a man who can read and write is rich. But I haven't forgotten the poor. I told you I was going to raise an army because I have no choice, because they're going to send an army to kill me. That's true, but there are also the poor; I haven't forgotten the poor. A revolution is for them, so they can live like human beings."

"Charity begins at home." She made a rubber sneer.

"There was a time," he said, decorating the sadness in his voice by the fall of his eyes and the opening turn of his hands, "there was a time . . .

I remember when you were a different woman. I cared for the poor then, but you cared more, you loved them, you urged me into the revolution, you brought the revolution to our house."

"I'm older now."

"And what does that mean? Old, old, I had an army of old men. Who do you think I took to Juárez? Old men! Older than you. Old men are the best revolutionaries. Because you're older now? Is that what chilled you? I don't believe it, Liviana, not in my head and not in my heart. Because you're older! I look among old men for my army; only the old ones know."

"I had dreams."

"Why should dreamers go to war?"

"The order was wrong when I gave birth. I saw my dead child. He was gray and yellow, like pork fat. A dead child came out of me. I want to be in peace now, I know enough about the world: the first thing is to be alive."

He looked for signs of sadness in her, he expected weeping; but her face was as flat as brick. "Do you still dream?" he asked.

"I don't know. There's so little time; I'm the woman and the man in this house. How can I think of other houses, dream houses? Dreams are another house, Francisco, and I can't go there anymore. My son is buried in another house. Do you know now what I mean?"

"No," he said. "It's not possible; my father died when I was seven years old."

They slept in the same bed. She was his wife, but when they slept she did not touch him, she lay at the edge of the bed, curled away from him. He said they should have another child. She permitted him; there had been a church marriage and a civil marriage, she was his wife; she permitted him, she lay with him like a pot, she said she was thinking of their child born out of order.

He found five kernels of seed corn in the bed. They were placed at the points of a star; hard and dark yellow, the kernels cast shadows on the white sheet. He gathered the kernels in his hand and threw them into the fire. He asked her if she could smell the corn roasting.

"I'm left to live with women," she said.

"I'll leave three men here to make a farm. They'll do the plowing and put in seed."

"And where will my husband be?"

"I'll raise an army. It won't be long this time."

"Here comes Pancho Villa," she said. "I've heard them say it. I can hear them again. Pancho Villa, the Saviour of the Poor! I would like to tell them that your chin is too thick and the hair in your beard grows like cactus spines. I would like them to see the scars on your leg and let them know

[426]

how you make faces some days when you take your boots off because one leg isn't right anymore. I would like them all to know how you flatter cooks and servants when they come to your meat market. My general, do you think they should know how you smelled when you came into this house? Do you think they should know the noises your belly makes? Do you think they should know how you whine like an old woman about your headaches? The Lion of the Sierras! What if they knew how you worry, Mr. Lion? Why don't you wash your teeth? Mother of God, why don't you wash your teeth?"

"Is that what you have to say to your husband?"

She turned to the wall.

"Are you ashamed?"

She said nothing. The five kernels of corn burned in the fireplace. The room was warm. The smell of the burned corn and the wood smoke mixed with the odors of her that seeped upward out of the blankets. He listened to her breathing and waited to feel the sweated stillness of her night. He left her sleeping.

Come with me! If you do not have a rifle, the revolution will give you a rifle, if you do not have a horse, the revolution will give you a horse, if you have nothing, the revolution will give you land, the revolution will give you something, no one fights without reason, no one is a gift to the revolution, ask for what you need, ask for what you want, the revolution will provide. I need you now, good soldier, brave man, revolutionary; come with me, fight beside me, this is the last revolution, this will be the death of Huerta, the end of war, your children will bless you, come with me and be as rich as any man, the revolution will provide. Do not ask the name of our president or the color of our flag, the revolution is for you, I remember you, I remember your name; kiss your wife, bless your children, and come with me, come now, in the name of the martyred Bridegroom of Mexico, the martyred Redeemer, the saint who loved the poor, Francisco Inocencio, come with me in his name, in the name of your children, in the name of Mexico, come with me, kiss your wife and bless your children, and come with me. Bring your machete and your best weapon, ride a good horse, carry salt in your saddlebag, wear your warmest blanket, come with me, come on, let's go, these men are waiting, this long line of men, this army is waiting, the revolution is waiting for you, can't you hear the music, the men singing, the hope, the bells, the bells of war, the bells of revolution, are you deaf, are you a woman, come on, come on, man, this is the revolution!

The others cheered, they waved their hats, they sang; every man was a victory.

Sánchez Azcona had seen the results of the battle at Casas Grandes, the houses destroyed, the town without windows, with nothing left but women, children and old men; he had heard of the men lined up in rows to be shot three at once, three with a single bullet, and the hundred dead dumped in the well. He came north to Ascención, following Villa, arriving at the end of the battle for the town, entering to the sound of the last gunshots, the beginning of music, the first wails of the women who found their men in the long row of dead, the neat row of shoeless, pillaged dead on the town street. He found Villa in the tavern, sitting at a round table, listening to his colonels and his captains.

Villa greeted him with an embrace. He said it had been a long time since Lecumberrí, he asked about the last days of Madero, he took the secretary to a quiet table and sat there with him and ate ice cream and wept and listened to the details of the death of the Apostle. "Take a little ice cream," he told the secretary. "After a battle, your insides are heated up, the taste of your gut comes into your mouth. Ice cream cools you. Take some ice cream." He wiped the tears from his eyes and blew his nose. He ate ice cream. The sleeves of his jacket were bloody.

"There was close combat," Sánchez Azcona said, looking at the bloody sleeves.

"Yes."

"You used a knife?"

Villa lifted up his arms to examine the blood on his sleeves. "I eat with a knife," he said. "The wounded did this to me. We don't have a doctor with us, so I'm the general and the doctor too; I help to pick up the wounded. Now they're gone; I can eat my ice cream. Juan Dozal and his brother are taking them to Agua Prieta. Calles has doctors there. He's a good man, Calles; Dozal is bringing him forty-three wounded and he'll come back with thirty-five thousand cartridges." He watched the secretary's face. He saw that his mouth was watering, that he was swallowing quickly. "If it disgusts you, look the other way."

Villa continued eating ice cream. "Raw meat for courage before, ice cream for calm after."

"I've come from the First Chief," Sánchez Azcona said.

"Who is that?"

"Venustiano Carranza."

"Carranza isn't even the First Chief of Coahuila. He doesn't understand war. I hear what's going on there; don't you think I hear? He's lost control of the state, he can't mount an army, he can't do anything but make proclamations. The man wants to be the First Chief, good! let him fight for it."

[*428*]

Sánchez Azcona nodded. "Okay. Then who should be the First Chief? Who's ready to take Madero's place? Francisco Villa? Is that what you want?"

"I never said I wanted to be President. I'm not an educated man, you know that; I don't even consider such things. But I know about war, Mr. Secretary, and I know what I'm going to do to Huerta and Orozco. I know what kind of men they are. When I was in San Andrés, I sent a telegram to my old comrade, Rábago, the new Governor of Chihuahua. I told him I was back in Mexico; they didn't have to worry about extraditing me anymore. And you know how he answered? He offered me a hundred thousand pesos and the rank of general of a division. Imagine! A hundred thousand pesos to betray the memory of a saint! I told him to give the money to Huerta so he could swill it down in aguardiente.

"I can't be bought and I won't be sold. That's all."

"If not Carranza, who?" The secretary put his hands on the table, he folded his fingers together and pushed his hands out to Villa. "If Obregón takes Sonora and you take Chihuahua and Carranza takes Coahuila and Zapata takes Morelos and Calles takes Tabasco, what will we have? Not a government, not democracy; we'll have anarchy, Mexico will be destroyed, someone will come from outside to take over the country: Yanquis or Spaniards or Japanese or Chinese. Then we'll begin again in a hundred years with a war of independence and a revolution and a dictator and another revolution and another and another and another. Madero knew the dangers of anarchy; how many times did he tell you? How often did he say he feared anarchy more than the Porfiriato? If you loved Madero, if you believed in him, you know that anarchy is the worst thing that can happen to Mexico."

Villa finished the ice cream. He licked the spoon clean and wiped it with a white handkerchief and put it in his breast pocket along with the knife and fork. He moved slowly, he looked over the spoon and the cloth to watch the secretary's face. The man had been close to Madero, no one had been closer, no one had been more trusted. Villa nodded. "Carranza."

"And Obregón will be in charge of the armies of the northwest, including Chihuahua."

"No."

"Obregón or anarchy."

"What does Obregón know about Chihuahua? Do I go to Sonora to tell him how to plant his beans? Shoemaker to your shoes, that's the rule. No meddling, nothing good ever comes of meddling; haven't you read Cervantes? Obregón in Sonora, Villa in Chihuahua. And don't argue with me, because I won't change my mind."

"Then it's anarchy."

"Yes," Villa said, "anarchy." He stood up and bowed in the manner of

[*429*]

generals, in the style he had seen in the garden of Santiago Tlaltelolco.

Villa remained in Ascención, organizing his army, waiting for Dozal to come back from Agua Prieta with ammunition. Juan Medina joined him there. He came alone, a small man with a wide, thick mustache and watery eyes. He had been a soldier since he was sixteen years old. "I have no wife, no family," he said. "I belonged to the army; it was my house. But Huerta is the army now, my general is an assassin. I came to the revolution because I do not want to serve an assassin, I came to you because I believe you are the general who will defeat Huerta."

Villa welcomed him and made him a colonel in the revolution. "An army is like a man," Medina said. "It has arms and legs and fingers and toes. It needs a head to make all the parts move correctly, it needs to be in order. That's the kind of soldier I am: I help to put an army in order. I can't lead a cavalry charge or direct artillery fire, but I can make the hands and feet of your army do what you ask of them." Villa made Medina his chief of staff.

Medina sat beside his general at the second meeting with Sánchez Azcona; he did not speak himself except to greet the secretary, but all through the meeting he spoke to Villa in coughs and glances, and at the end it was Medina who defended the execution of prisoners. "The law was made in 1861. It was the law of Juárez and the law of Maximilian. It was under the same law that Maximilian made in 1865 that Juárez had him put against the wall. Whether it was written or spoken, the law always has been the same in Mexico, since the Spaniards, since before the Spaniards; whoever revolts against the government is killed. I think the law is just; it gives men pride, it makes war honorable. To do anything else is to prolong war; to fill the prisons with captured enemies only creates the cadre of the next revolution."

The secretary did not agree and he did not disagree; silence was his answer. There was no use in saying more, nothing more could be done in that town; the agreements had been made: Villa had sworn himself to the Plan of Guadalupe, to the leadership and certain presidency of Carranza, and the First Chief's emissary had finally promised that no man would give orders in the state who was from outside; he had promised artillery, ammunition, coal, and supplies. It was agreed, it was over, the war could proceed.

The sound of pistols carried to the Aprisco house on the hill above the town. Liviana and her father went outside and climbed a little knoll near the arroyo to look down at San Andrés. He used a cane and leaned on her with his free arm. They walked very slowly; the bowing of his legs had begun to tear open the joints of his knees, fluids swelled his knees. They stood on the high place and watched the Federal advance troops circle the plaza and enter the tavern. They saw the troop trains arriving, the soldiers inside and the women riding the roofs of the cars, hiding under umbrellas and tents and shelters of boxes and leaves, avoiding the sun and the smoke that sometimes poured down over them. The trains came in close to the town. They carried 75-mm. cannon on flatcars. The troops came out of the cars and formed into companies, the women took down their umbrellas and their tents and their shelters made of boxes and leaves and set them up again alongside the railroad tracks, the horses were led out of the boxcars, the cannon were dragged off onto the loading platforms.

Liviana led her father back down to the house. She helped him to his bed and gave him a glass of myrtle water to cool him, then she and her mother and her aunts gathered up their clothes and their food and whatever was valuable in the house, the silver things, the metal pots, the rifles, even the crucifixes that had been nailed to the walls before Liviana was born. They put what they could into suitcases and tied the rest into bundles made of sheets and blankets. Liviana saddled the horses and put the halters on the burros, then she and her mother dragged the suitcases and the blankets out to the stable and loaded them onto the horses and the burros. The aunts lit candles to the Virgin on the altar in the little room where they had slept since they were born. They left the candles burning and took the statue of the Virgin and the crucifixes with them.

Aprisco said he could not mount a horse himself, the stirrups hurt his feet, he could not grip the flanks with his swollen knees; he asked to be left behind in his bed. "Just give me a large pitcher of myrtle water and a few tortillas," he said. "I can last a long time, I don't require much to keep alive, not at my age and in my condition. Go on without me, save yourselves." The women lifted him out of his bed and half carried him to the stable. They pushed and pulled him up onto the seat of the wagon, and from there they lifted him over onto his horse. He complained of the pain in his knees, he said it made him sick to his stomach; but the women pretended not to hear, they did not even bother to be gentle with him. There were a thousand troops in the town, Liviana said, and they were Orozquistas. Everyone knew that Villa was lining up prisoners in threes and shooting them, everyone knew what he was doing to the red flaggers; they would not be kind to the family.

The troops were building barricades, the artillery nags were dragging the cannon into position, and the camp women were gathering firewood and starting the cooking fires when the Apriscos left the house. Liviana walked ahead, leading the horse that carried her father; her mother led the other horses. The aunts, in their black shawls and black dresses, paling in the dust, walked beside the burros, punishing them with sticks, calling upon St. Nicholas, St. Christopher, St. Rafael, and St. Anthony of Padua to exorcise the stubbornness of the devil from the beasts, to make them tractable, quiet, and not so unpleasant to smell. The aunts said to their sister, "We are like Agape, Chionia, and Irene fleeing to the mountains because we will not renounce the good ways of Our Lord Jesus Christ."

"Irene, Irene," the father shouted back at them. "I knew it all along. You wear those pious faces, but you'd really like to be stripped of your clothes and put in a brothel. I knew it, I knew it all along."

"Filthy, filthy, filthy," the aunts said. "You see how you're punished! Look at your feet! Look at your knees! The mercy of God is tested by your filthy mouth and your sinful thoughts. Heaven help us, our sister is married to a Jonah."

Liviana led the horse. She wore a cartridge belt and carried the rifle slung over her shoulder. There was a place in the Blue Mountains. It was not so far. They would live in a cave, they would eat tuna and mesquite beans and chiles and wait for Villa to take Chihuahua.

The generals came to Villa's railroad car to sit at the round table, drinking coffee or eating ice cream; they were a conference of generals, sitting together, reading maps, discussing women, vilifying the cowardice of Juan Dozal's resignation from the revolutionary army, telling the names of their heroic dead; and each general also came alone to sit in the railroad car with the curtains drawn and the daylight in the room as centerless as old smoke. They spoke softly then, as if Medina's pen could not hear their whispers.

VILLA

Have you been in the Guerrero or Juárez districts? Have your men come from there? My wife was in San Andrés when the Orozquistas took the town. She must have gone to the mountains. Ask your people about her. No, they weren't killed, there were no graves. We asked the prisoners before we shot them. The house was empty, the windows were broken, the doors were taken for firewood, we found chickens walking in the house, but there were no graves. Ask your people about her.

Maybe I'll find her after Torreón.

CHAO

When the First Chief visited with me on his way to Sonora, we discussed the military situation at some length, his assumption being that I would direct the attack because of my long and most thorough familiarity with the use of artillery.

We have no other hope in this engagement but for me to direct the attack

[*432*]

asshole anymore, so I gave him sixty pesos and an old saddle. Not a bad joke, huh? You know, brother, we took so much gold from Durango—over a hundred thousand pesos from one church. They had everything gold: cups, plates, everything. I wasn't going to do it, but I have this man with me now who really is a killer, Rodolfo Fierro. I was afraid to loot a church, but that son of a bitch, nothing scares him.

This Fierro's all man. I made him a major right away. He's a railroad man, you know; he understands everything about trains, everything. He could handle the transportation of a whole division. He's smart, but crazy, a real fucker.

The old man Orozco went down to try to buy off Zapata, and they put him up against the wall.

A woven cane chair was brought from the tiled lobby of the Hotel Salvador; it was brought for General Villa so that he might be a center for the celebration of the fall of Torreón. The chair was placed in the light of the hotel, kerosene lamps were hung on the wall behind it; in the midnight darkness Villa appeared to the passing troops as a man sitting in the sun. The light stunned their eyes; they cheered him, they said his name.

His face was red with laughter, he was in a fever of sleeplessness; he ate ice cream. The days of the battle were in the creases of his body, a thick and stinging sweat. He was not comfortable in his chair; his skin burned, he recognized the tiny white blisters that grew in hideouts and trenches. The ice cream did not sweeten the juices that came into his mouth from tiny vomitings. He wanted to sleep, he could not sleep, he could not remember when he had slept.

Women came to see him, to stand beyond the passing soldiers, to crowd themselves onto the sidewalk in the spaces between the squadrons, to dance and to throw laughter to him, to reflect the light. He ordered music: dianas for the troops passing, polkas for the women, waltzes for the women. The musicians played with the slowness of frightened men; their uniforms were muddied, the brass of their instruments did not shine. He ordered marches, he demanded glorious music: "Jesusita in Chihuahua," again and again, until the passing soldiers broke from their narrow ranks and took the women dancing in the street and on the crossing paths of the plaza.

Generals stood beside the cane chair, leaning, whispering: in a walled yard in Avilés, with two pistols and a terrified lieutenant to load them, with nothing more than moonlight to guide his aim, Rodolfo Fierro had killed two hundred and thirty-seven unarmed men; Maclovio Herrera had run his troops beside the flooded river, following the flight of the Federals, search-ing for a place to cross over, any place to swim the horses, to float the guns,

[435]

to destroy the defeated army, and he had instead been defeated by the river, left to run his brigade into exhaustion; Navarro had burned the Federal dead on the battlefield, he had sickened battalions with the stench of the hair and the innards roasting, with the sight of the corpses in the shape of charred grasshoppers, lacking hands and feet, the ash-covered limbs bent in hard angles.

The band played dianas for the passing soldiers. Villa saw them, their muddied boots, their sweat-ringed hats. They pushed their feet along the hard walk; their horses were irritated, stiff with dried lather. Sleepless children came through the ranks of men, they carried gifts for the general: piglets, hens, wooden charms, yarns woven into charms, cotton cloth made from the puffs of the fields that surrounded the fallen city. He saw the poor women lingering in the background, squatting on the grass beyond the dancing soldiers. A soldier stopped to look at his general; his eye had been cut open, the wound had not been cleaned. The wind blew, it was the middle of the night, the lights of the town burned; above the flat buildings of the city the palms of the plaza shook in the wind, like the palms of Manzanillo, like palm trees near the sea suddenly growing in this defeated town beside the desert.

The band played, the soldiers were fewer, the dancing went on, the women turning and turning, kicking their skirts to the rhythm of the drum, to the rhythm of the guitarrón. The faces of the women were shining, the city smelled of horses, beer, and unwashed men. After the fearful hilarity of battle the night was quieter, slow, slowing. He thought to make a formal celebration in the morning, he told Medina to arrange a great review of all the heroes of the battle of Torreón, he told Medina to put food in the hands of the waiting poor, to put medicine in the hospitals where the wounded lay, where Dr. Navarro stood in his bloodstained smock, telling a face he did not recognize that bandages were needed and alcohol and morphine, telling anyone to tell General Villa.

The Morning Star appeared for the first time. The dancers stopped to look, to cross themselves and ask the indulgence of Our Lady of Sorrows. A soothsayer passed among them, a man or a woman dressed in black cloth and strings of red mescal beans, a soothsayer with clotted hair and white eyes gleaming. He said, "They dressed the knight like a God and served him. They bent the knight over the temalacatl. The people saw his steaming heart." He did not speak to Villa, but the words were carried to him, they were repeated for him.

Villa ordered the band to play a last diana, he ordered the people to go to their houses, he ordered the soldiers to go to their camps, he said it was time to sleep. A room had been prepared for him in the Hotel Salvador. He went inside, through the blurring brightness of the lights, waving to the people who called his name, reminding them of Madero, of the revolution. In the room that had been prepared for him he lay on the bed and thought of bathing and of sleeping and he saw the Morning Star in its second appearance and its third appearance. His clothes were stiff, he lay inside the odor of himself, he felt the greasy sweat in the creases of his groin. There had been no word of Liviana, there had been no congratulations from Carranza. He lay on the bed, wrapped in his sweats. When the sun came up, he went to the window and closed the shutters.

A girl came with a garland of flowers for the General of the Division. "You are sweeter than the flowers," he said. Her throat was dressed in white lace. He saw the pulse beneath the delicate bone of her chin. She raised the garland, he touched her hand. "Your skin is soft," he said.

"A blanket and a woman should be soft."

"Tell me your name."

"Juana Torres."

"Juana Torres of Torreón. The city is yours."

She lowered her eyes, as children do. "In Torreón everything belongs to General Villa, everything."

"And who does Juana Torres belong to?"

"She lives in Torreón." Her lower lip trembled, she brushed his face with the flowers, she leaned forward to include him in the aura of perfume at her throat.

"May I call on you, Miss?"

"We're poor people. My mother and I help in a tailor's shop; we don't live in a house fit to receive a general."

"It's me!" he said, touching his fist to his chest. "Pancho Villa, not some perfumed Spaniard! You think you're poor! When I was a boy, we had nothing to eat but weeds and carrion. From the time I was weaned I never drank milk. You think you're poor! No one could be poorer than I was and still live. Anyway, it's no shame to be poor, every revolutionary knows that. Believe me, it makes you a better person, because one who has suffered much can be consoled with little."

She dropped the garland over his shoulders and ran away. He watched her buttocks in the cup of her skirt. Urbina also watched. "Follow a woman who's followed by a suitcase," he said.

"Be careful how you speak of my fiancée."

Urbina punched Villa's shoulder. "You don't even know her. How can you buy a horse before you try it out? You have to be careful, brother; some of these women are so beautiful they set your balls on fire, and when you get close to them you find a bad smell. Listen to me: look before you leap. Every cunt is its own world."

[*437*]

"Are you Liviana's messenger?"

Urbina drew back in mock horror. "Me? Did you forget who I am? I don't speak for women."

"You forget, brother; I don't have a wife. If I have a wife, where is she? You see? I'm free to marry."

"Aren't you going to look for her? Look, it's not my business, Pancho, but you know no one ever found a body."

"And no one ever found a wife. She's gone, man. What can I do? I see women. This one excites me. Should I just take her? Is that an example to my troops? I need a wife; it's the only way under democracy."

"I'll dance at your wedding, I'll be your marriage broker."

"Find out where she lives and bring her a present from me, something nice, something important."

There were no more garlands in the morning; the distribution of food began: Villa led the wagons through the poor sections of the city, he went from house to house, leaving bundles of food in the doorways of houses built of brush and tin, giving sacks of wheat flour and sides of bacon to women whose children had never tasted meat or milled flour, carrying cheeses and chunks of beef to the shacks where cripples and widows lived. He stood beside the wagons in the streets and called the beggars to come and be fed. When they said his name, when they praised him, he accepted their thanks in the name of Madero, in the name of the revolution. The old women fell at his feet, saying that he was the Saviour of the Poor. He lifted them up: "No, mama," he told them, "the revolution is the Saviour of the Poor, the revolution."

Urbina conducted the marriage negotiations with Mrs. Torres. He did his work in the old-fashioned way, going every day to her raw house on the outskirts of the town, bringing gifts of sweets and shawls and a golden surprise. Every day he perfumed himself and brushed his blue uniform and wetted down his hair and reminded himself to speak without curses or obscenities. But Mrs. Torres was difficult: she demanded to see General Villa, to make her negotiations with him, to be direct.

"Be careful," Urbina warned her. "The man has a terrible temper. You're a very forthright woman and he's a very forthright man. Perhaps this meeting is not such a good idea. He has a lot on his mind, Mrs. Torres: war, the government, the problems of food and hospital supplies, other battles coming. He has so many papers, so many messages, so many people to see. Take my advice, madam; don't be another problem in his life."

Mrs. Torres insisted that Urbina arrange a meeting in the general's rooms prior to any further negotiation. "I want to see him there," she said, "to know how he lives, how he keeps himself. All these things are important. By the house we know the health, isn't that so?"

[438]

Urbina arranged the meeting. Mrs. Torres traveled across the city by trolley to the Hotel Salvador. She came with her hair in the tightest braids and with her dress hanging from the outcropping of her bosom like a shining drapery. Urbina warned Villa: "If you believe 'like mother, like daughter,' the wedding will never take place. The old woman has tits like two sows and the disposition of a wasp in a smokehouse. I'd rather negotiate with starving Jews."

"If you were my friend, you'd give her a little stab to soften her up."

"You know me, man; I'd fuck a snake if it wiggled, but Mrs. Torres? I'd die in a monastery first."

"My friend."

Urbina shook his head, sitting down to await the arrival of Mrs. Torres.

She came late, a heavy bird carrying a potful of sweet biscuits baked by her daughter. Villa kissed her hand and offered to kiss her feet. "Never mind," Mrs. Torres said. "I came to ask questions of great seriousness. No sayings, none of that. I'll ask straight questions and I expect honest answers."

"As you like," Villa said. "But won't you sit down and let me give you a cup of chocolate?"

Mrs. Torres let herself down into a cane chair. The outline of the pillars of her legs was clear under her skirt. She breathed heavily, fanning herself with a folded newspaper. Villa paced back and forth before her, on parade, dressed in a new uniform with a tight collar. He leaned forward to show her the buttons. "Real gold," he said.

"Very nice, sir, but what will you do for my daughter? Will you dress her in real gold?"

"Gold is heavy, Mrs. Torres. Perhaps it would be better to dress her in silk."

"I heard you were a shrewd man."

"Would you want your daughter to marry a fool?"

"How many wives does a fool have?" Mrs. Torres sat back in her chair to bask in the sharpness of her question.

Villa paced, stroking his mustache. Only when he had an answer did he stop and face her. "Mrs. Torres, one wife can make a fool of a man; why would he need two?"

"Do you deny that you already have a wife?"

"Tragedy takes away a man's spirit. I don't know why you would choose to sadden me now when I'm thinking of the joy of marriage and the pleasure of raising a family. Mrs. Torres, you're a fierce woman, you give no quarter. Here I have surrendered my heart to your daughter, I come to you under a white flag, helpless in love, and yet you attack me, you twist the blade in the sadness of my life."

[439]

"What will you provide for her?"

"Ten times her dowry, madam; a hundred times her dowry, if you like."

"You know I'm a poor widow."

"Tomorrow you'll be the mother-in-law of a general."

The marriage was set for the afternoon. Villa said he would make the celebration. "You'll be kind to her," Mrs. Torres said. "You'll give her things, nice things, won't you? A woman should have a little treasure of her own, something to protect her. I speak as a widow; I know the sorrows of being alone, without a man to provide for me."

Villa led her to the door. "Out of kindness, please, don't bury me on the day before my wedding. Your daughter will have such a lonely wedding night."

The wedding was held in the lobby of the Hotel Salvador. The generals and the colonels and their women stood on the tile floor or sat in the woven chairs. They wore uniforms and carried swords, they brought their women with them. The priest stood with his back against the clerk's counter. Villa and Juana Torres stood before him, the bride in her white silk gown and long white veil, the bride with the green leaves and pale yellow flowers of roses held in one arm, the general in his blue uniform with gold buttons, with a red sash and a long sword in a silver scabbard. The mother of the bride stood behind them; she held a gold chalice, the gift brought by Urbina, the important gift.

After the wedding there was a banquet and dancing in the Casino de la Laguna. The band played polkas and marches, mountain rhythms and waltzes. The generals and the colonels and the captains drank and danced until they fell down dancing, until they saw morning light in the windows of the casino. Villa went back to the hotel with his wife and her mother. Mrs. Torres followed them up the stairs. She still carried the gold chalice, she pressed it to the great baskets of her bosom.

Mrs. Torres kissed her daughter goodnight; she said she would pray for her. She did not cry; she was a stern woman, standing inside a corset, wearing a net to cover her braided hair. She embraced Juana and Villa and herded them together toward their room.

Juana put out the lights and drew the curtains and went to the farthest corner of the room to undress. She did not speak much, except to say that it had been a good banquet and that she had enjoyed the dancing. The sound of her clothing embarrassed her; she tried to hide the sound by softly singing. Villa was not patient. It was morning, the light was growing stronger, beginning to penetrate the curtains, the trains were being loaded for the attack on Chihuahua. He whispered to her, asking her to hurry.

He was gentle. Even so, she cried out once. And her mother answered from the next room, "Don't be frightened, I'm right here."

The bride went north with Villa in his railroad car. She cooked for him and sewed buttons on his suit coats and uniforms, she promised to sew new curtains for the windows of the railroad car. All day she sewed and looked out the windows at the desert passing. Late at night, when the generals and the colonels and the secretaries had gone to their own quarters, Villa pushed the table to one side of the car and pulled the wooden bed down from its daytime resting place against the wall.

He whispered trusts to her: the secrets of money and war, the fears of betrayal; he told her how Juan Dozal had never come back from Agua Prieta, he lamented the execution of Benjamín Yuriar, who had revolted at Torreón, he asked her to watch the counting of the money in the other room of the car. "You have a working woman's shrewdness about money—your mother told me so. In money matters a man can trust his wife more than his brothers, especially when his brother is always drunk and chasing whores."

Her voice was thin and filled with little peaks. She seldom laughed, but she seemed always to be in good spirits. "You're such a big man," she said, "and heavy, like a general."

She clawed him. The blood oozed and hardened in thin lines on his back and on his shoulders. He said that she was like a certain desert in Durango not far from the place where he was born.

She asked for silks and golden things. Nothing pleased her more than the sound of tiny silver bells. He gave her what he could. "I am only a soldier," he said for his apology.

She pouted. "You're a general," she said. It was always her argument.

She pleased him only at night. During the day he avoided her, eating with his officers, planning the attack on Chihuahua. He said it was for her own safety, but he did not believe what he said when he sent her home to Torreón to be safe.

The Apriscos came down from the hills after the first freezing night. The women complained that it swelled their joints with burrs. Liviana told them to sit close to the fire and to wear their warmest clothing, but she could not answer her father when he said the cold made the pain of his torture echo again in his body, shooting up from the soles of his feet directly into his mind. She loaded the animals with whatever was left of their belongings and led the little pack train down the slopes of the hills toward San Andrés.

Her father complained of returning to a country house. He said that a sick man would be better off in a city like Chihuahua, he said that he needed the good doctors and the modern medicine that was available in the city. "They give injections in the city," he said. "Perhaps injections could cure my feet so that I could walk like a man again instead of a monkey without a tail."

Liviana reminded him that she had crossed the summit of the Blue Mountains to watch the battle of Chihuahua. She had seen it from the middle of the second day through the retreat of the revolutionaries. From her place in the mountains the battle had looked like a map, the brigades had appeared as squares or pieces of circles. She had seen the forming of the encirclement that destroyed so many of Maclovio Herrera's troops, and for a moment she had thought of warning him, of saving the revolutionaries from the slaughter, but she was no closer than dreaming distance: it would have taken two days or more to descend to the city. She had prayed, she had seen Aguirre Benavides break through, and she had seen the diminished square of Herrera's troops running out of the circle. She had not known that it was her husband who was defeated in the field below, for they had not spoken to anyone since leaving the house at San Andrés, they had avoided even the woodcutters and the hunters for fear of betrayal.

"Liviana, Liviana," her father said, rocking with despair. "Are you a general, Liviana? Do you know which side won the battle, do you know who is in command of the city now? Ay, Liviana, you're exactly like your grandfather."

"I know," she said. "I saw it."

"From the top of a mountain! I'm the father of an eagle."

She left her family on the east side of the arroyo and crossed over to the house. It was silent, a dead house, after a season of ruin. Liviana walked through the rooms. All the windows had been broken, all the furniture had been stolen or burned for firewood, all the walls had been stained, all the floors had been torn. An owl had made a nest in the room where she and her husband had slept, where her children had been stillborn. She pointed her rifle out the window and fired two shots, then she went to the other side of the arroyo and brought her family home.

They put the animals in the stables and tied them there, because all the gates and all the doors had been torn off and burned for firewood. Their beds in the house were the same as their beds in the hills; they unrolled their blankets and slept on the ground. In the morning, the sisters in black dresses unpacked their crucifixes and their paintings of the Virgin. They decorated the walls and made an altar, they blessed the house, they exorcised the spirits of the Evils who had destroyed their home. "It can be repaired," they said. "God will give us strength. The house is only a little worse now than it was when Francisco first came here."

"It's fit for animals," Liviana said.

"I'm tired of living like this," her father said. "I'm a sick man, I need comforts."

The sisters knelt together. "Our Lord Jesus Christ was born in a place that was only fit for animals."

"Damn you," Liviana said. "Damn you, get up off your knees and help us look for something to eat."

They searched the fields and found nothing but a patch of onions. Liviana and the sisters dug up the onions, cut away the rotten parts and made a soup as thick as stew. The next day they found a turkey and some ears of parched corn that could be scraped and put in jars of water to become nixtamal. They ate. They blocked the doorways and covered over the holes where the windows had been. They collected firewood and built thorny brush pens for the animals. They bought beans, they made goat cheese, they repaired the roof, they pruned the dry and broken rose bushes in the garden. "You see," the sisters said, "the house is again a place to live; the meek *shall* inherit the earth. Blessed are the meek."

"Worms," Liviana said.

Felipe Angeles, former director of the military college at Chapultepec, former General in Chief of the humane campaign against the Zapatistas, graduate of the École Militaire, the one friend of Madero who was too beloved of the army to be executed by the usurper, the secretary of war of the Constitutionalist Provisional Government, wrote to General Francisco Villa: "The taking of the City of Juárez was a classical tactic, a feat that will be compared with the fall of Troy. It is surpassed, however, by your brilliant strategy at Tierra Blanca. Rarely in military history has a subtle advantage of terrain been put to more effective use. Nor have I often heard of men more daring or more courageous than your Colonel Fierro. His action in boarding the fleeing Federal train in the heat of battle and stopping it by pulling the emergency braking device is absolutely extraordinary. I congratulate him, I congratulate you. Sir, I stand in awe."

General Hugh Scott of the United States Army met with General Villa at the Juárez Hippodrome to watch the horses run. He brought a guest, the famous horseman, Colonel Matt Winn of the Kentucky Derby. They bet on the horses, they talked of war. It was a cold day; General Scott wore a thick jacket with a sheepskin collar, General Villa wore his finest suit and vest.

"Aren't you cold?" Scott asked. "I could have one of these jackets brought over for you."

"I'm a Mexican. When I'm cold, I wear a blanket."

They spoke in Spanish. The Yanqui general said he had learned the language when he fought Indians. "It was a long time ago," he said, "when I was a young man."

"Mexicans are Indians," Villa said. "The Spaniards destroyed our great

[*443*]

Indian nation. The Porfiristas celebrate the destruction of the Indian nation; I do not."

"I fought Apaches, sir. That was quite different."

"Yes, different," Villa said. He turned away to watch the horses.

Colonel Winn spoke of a great Mexican Derby, a race between the best horses in the Americas; but after the revolution, of course, when there was peace in Mexico. There was agreement. All the aides nodded, everyone said there would soon be peace. Colonel Fierro removed his hat and said he prayed for peace, democracy, and the repair of the railroads.

"It won't be easy," Villa said. "Huerta buys from the Germans. They sell him very fine rifles, precision-made cartridges and artillery shells, and they give him credit."

"And they've made the same offer to you?" General Scott asked.

"Yes, of course. A weed grows wherever it can."

"You're aware of President Wilson's feelings in this matter," Scott said. "He favors peace and democracy, very much as you do. It's important to him to protect American citizens and American property, but he's deeply concerned that it be done in an atmosphere of peace. He loves peace, General Villa, he loves law and democracy. Wilson is a very deep thinker, a man of great honor. He knows about you, he trusts you. He's very impressed by your loyalty to Madero, but even more important, he feels the fact that you don't smoke or drink and that your language is clean means something very good about your character. Nothing could be more important to him than a man's good character, and nothing could be more odious to President Wilson than a man who murdered the democratically elected president of his country."

"When will we be able to buy arms from President Wilson's government? We do it now in secret. Everyone knows. You don't stop the arms shipments; there are hundreds of vendors in El Paso now, Medina's office is filled with them. But we have to buy in secret, we have to pay four, eight times the real price. When will President Wilson open the border?"

"Soon, very soon. It takes time. There are political considerations."

Villa looked out at the racetrack. The animals were moving into a line behind the thin wire. The day was sunless; it had no color. The riders' shirts flapped in the wind; they did not shine. "We all bet on the horse that gets to the finish line first," Villa said.

General Scott laughed. He hunched forward in his seat and slapped Villa's knee. "Then don't bet on the Germans; they have too far to go."

7

General Francisco Villa, First Chief of the Constitutionalist Army in the State of Chihuahua, and in accord with the Plan of Guadalupe, Provisional Governor of said State, by virtue of the powers invested in him, decreed:

Confiscation of the great ranches owned by Terrazas, Creel, Cuilty, Falomir, Lujan, Molinar and Sánchez.

Equitable distribution of all confiscated lands and other property. First, to the widows and orphans of the men who fought in defense of the cause of justice since 1910. Second, to those who fought in defense of our cause. Third, to those who worked the lands and were not fairly compensated. Fourth, to the original owners of the lands, who were victims of usurpation by the capitalists.

The goods and properties confiscated are to become the property of the State Bank, where detailed records will be kept of all goods and properties confiscated and distributed.

Alcoholic beverages are prohibited in the City of Chihuahua.

All Spaniards must leave the State within twenty-four hours; any remaining after that time will be shot.

Chinese may not engage in business in the State.

Crimes of rape and robbery are punishable by death.

Money printed by the State Bank and signed by the Provisional Governor will be the official legal tender in the State.

Marriage between Chinese and members of our race is prohibited.

Legally owned property of foreign nationals, excluding Spaniards and Chinese, is guaranteed.

Children will attend school at the expense of the State through completion of the sixth grade. All schools of the Catholic Church of Rome are closed.

Matrimony is a civil function, and henceforth only those marriages performed by civil authorities will be legally binding.

He lived in the house on Tenth Street, where the women brought him tortillas and meats enriched with sauces; and he lived in the Governor's

[*445*]

Palace, where the old man in black livery carried ice cream up to him from the basement storehouse. He went to the cockfights and the bullfights, and he was the leader and the reviewer of every parade. He was not alone, he had no privacy, except in the nights when he lay with war and loneliness in a bed of memories, in the room of memories, in the house where the revolution had come to him at his dinner table in the pompous shell of an old soldier.

There were days of merchants and days of politics, all the days came in unhappy streams to the office of the Provisional Governor of Family Disputes and Sour Milk. He gave out justice from an old man's chair, he sent the problems of pesos and boundaries to the colonels and majors who walked between the banks and the courtrooms of the city. All day he heard explanations, all night he was alone without explanations. He heard Martina weeping in the streets, in dreams, between parades, under the sound of bands playing, gray amid the blue and the brass, lonely in the crowded streets, smoke weeping, gray, slipping between the touching shoulders of the joyous crowds, heard in the empty instants of the breaths between their laughing cheers. He went to Antonio's house to see her.

She sat in the winter's garden wrapped in two blankets. A fat yellow dog lay at her feet. The cactus grew green in the garden, the rose bushes were all in thorns and gray wood. She did not look up when Villa entered the garden. The fat dog rolled out a long growl.

"I brought you a shawl," Villa said. "Look at the colors."

Martina's head was bent, her hair was parted in the center; he saw her scalp like the weakness in an infant's skull.

A steady wind climbed over the garden wall and chilled them and died against the house.

He folded himself down in front of her and looked up into her face. The sleepless dark around her eyes glistened. Her arms and legs were sharp forms in the blankets, bones only, dying limbs. She smelled of onions.

"Forgive me, I beg you."

Silence. Her lips were dry and narrow, mute.

"Forgive me. It has been long enough." He began as always. He put his hand on her knee. The bone was clear to his touch. He took his hand away. He began as always.

"Martina."

The bones had died, the eyes had died, she sat in her blankets, mute. She accused.

"Liviana lives in the house in San Andrés again. Tell me how to go there to her now."

The fat dog lay sleeping.

"Have I shamed her? Have I shamed myself? The other woman is no pleasure now. She never was. I married her because it would have been a crime. Generals can't take women, Martina; the rules of landlords are for them the rules of war. I'm a good soldier.

"Everyone lies to a general; he has as many enemies as a rich man. And what do I own? They come to me with papers. There are more papers than I can read, more than I can ever hear; I am in a boat of papers on a river of papers.

"Do you remember San Juan del Río? We had a farm, the best land was near the hills; we planted the gentle slope of the hills even though the rain washed away the young corn. If our father had not died, I would not have been the one, it would not have happened. Do you ever think of that when you sit here in the garden?

"Your face is pale. Are your hands also pale? Will you let me see your hands? Your face is pale even though you sat here all summer in the sun. You need to eat, sister. You need to walk. Keep your silence. You can keep your silence even though you eat, even though you walk.

"I have no choice but talking now; they ask me questions all my life. I have no quiet now: they come to me with arguments, they haunt me, they try to deceive me with questions and arguments, they meddle in everything I do. Ask me: who are they? Do you wonder? They are the aides, the general's hands and feet, the general's mouth, the general's tongue, the general's eyes; so they tell me, they insist. I know their names and the names of their friends and the names of their wants and dreams; I am familiar with all the ambitions of all the men who have become the parts of the general. I don't trust them, my parts have escaped me and taken other names. I tighten my fists, I bite my tongue, I no longer believe my eyes.

"There is nothing they are afraid to ask of me, and I know they are all afraid of me, afraid that I'll put them up against the wall in straight rows of threes, in rows of threes to spare the cost of them to the revolution.

"The bread is not good, have you noticed? Is that why you don't eat anymore? What should I tell the bakers? The soldiers are now baking bread and the bread is sour, the soldiers are now running the power plant and we live in darkness, the soldiers are now brewing the beer and no one will drink it, the soldiers are now printing the money and no one will accept it. I am a farmer; do you remember? What can a farmer do? They make sure my bird wins at the cockfights; no one dares to outrun my horses; if I cape a bull, the bull dies to win my favor. Tell me how the world works. You've been watching. Tell me how the world works before Carranza asks.

"I'm not afraid of him, that old man, those whiskers. He wears dark glasses; I'm not afraid to take off my hat.

"Have you looked at his fingers, how long and thin they are? He has a rich man's hands, he says things I believe because I don't know. I don't know. Who asked him to be the First Chief? There was no election, he didn't ask me, he didn't ask the people in Coahuila; did he ask you, Martina?

"I'm afraid of him; he knows how to talk, he carries books in a trunk wherever he goes. If he hasn't read them, what can I say? If he's read them, what can I say?

"I'm a soldier. What's my wife's name? That one in Torreón, she'll never have children. Have you seen Liviana? Does she come in secret to Chihuahua to visit you? Would you speak to her if she came to Chihuahua? I am so tired, and nothing is going right, and I've won all these battles, and I don't know who could be the next President, if not Carranza.

"Tell me the name of a man I can trust. Reading makes liars of men; I know that now. But how can a mountain man live in the city? You see how their feet can't survive.

"Advise me, I'm ashamed."

She sat wrapped in two blankets with the fat dog at her feet. She was more silent than the wind that climbed over the wall and died against the house.

He put the shawl over her shoulders and asked her again to look at the colors. She did not move. He went into the house and brought out a bowl of soup to feed to her. He put a spoon of soup into her mouth; and when he took the spoon from between her lips, the soup flowed out over her thin lip, down her chin, and onto the blanket, and was nothing more than a little darkness there.

"Help me. I have two wives, I'm wrapped in lies, the war is not over, Carranza has no right to order me; tell me what tomorrow will bring, tell me what the gringos want, tell me what is wanted by the farmers and the ranchers and the bakers and the soldiers who fail at everything I put them to. Tell me the value of a peso and tell me why my house is so empty and why it is so far to San Andrés; there is no one I trust but you; tell me."

She sat in winter's garden and was mute. He left the bowl of soup on the ground and went inside to give Antonio money to care for her. The fat dog ate the soup.

General Villa looked at his army and he asked himself, what was the use of an army when it was not at war? He saw the soldiers in the streets of the city, he saw them marching in the flat fields that preceded the mountains, he saw that they were eaters of meat, corn, beans, bread, everything that came from the land; and they only marched in the fields and walked with aimless patience in the streets, and folded themselves up before their cooking fires to devour what the farmers made in their agreement with the land. The army seemed to him like a flock of ravens, and what do ravens do? What is the good of ravens?

The good of an army is to be an army, the generals said. The work of an army is to be the army. How like the old man Chavarría they were, dreaming of dust rising and the sound of rattlebells! War is beautiful for the sake of war.

If an army has no work but war, then there will always be war, Villa said to the generals. Send your soldiers to the bakeries and the meat packing plant, let them run the telephones and the electricity and the water system, put them to building schools. I have made a list of all the schools that must be built in this city; I have forty places marked on a map. Let the army build schools, send them now. Make bricks, plane the wood for doors, build chairs and desks. If her children can't read, what will Mexico be?

Feed the army, Villa said, and feed the people too. Put the prices of bread and meat back to the prices of 1910. If anyone charges more, call him an enemy, and do with him what you would do with any other enemy.

The world is not like that, the generals said; you'll ruin the army and the city. Reconsider, please.

Tell the bakers and the meat packers to wash their hands, Villa answered; keep everything clean. Let the world see that we're not savages, let the world see that after the revolution Mexico will be a good place to live.

Villa sent Panfilo Natera to Ojinaga to destroy the Federals who had escaped from Tierra Blanca, to finish the war in the State of Chihuahua. Natera laid siege to the town. He shelled it from a distance, he attacked it with cavalry, he attacked it with infantry; he concentrated his forces and attacked in one place and he spread his forces and attacked everywhere at once. The Federals defeated him, they stood behind their low walls of defense and shot down his troops on the cactus-flecked plain. The losses were terrible. There was no hospital within a hundred miles. The wounded lay under the stars, the wind blew over them as they died.

It was the beginning of the year, the first battle of their year 1914, and they took the defeat for an omen. "The soul of the revolution is in danger," Villa told his generals. He hurried them. In two days they left Chihuahua to relieve Natera. When they arrived in Ojinaga, the weather turned against them: the wind came down from the north, so terrible that it blew down tents and overturned light wagons. They did not know what to do. The plain before Ojinaga was open, dry and cold. They hid from the wind, they wrapped themselves in blankets and tied kerchiefs over their faces and lay in the protecting shadows of their horses. And then it snowed. They despaired. Some said the north had abandoned them, the cold had turned against them, the flint was on the side of the enemy. The snow and the Federals, the mountain people said, Yaótl, The Enemy on Both Sides.

The snow fell all night; it was apportioned by the wind into soft banks and deceptive blankets over the rocks and hollows of the cold plain. Villa went alone among the troops. He wore a hat tied under his chin. The snow collected in the brim of his hat and was emptied by the wind. His blanket was piled with snow; it held to the wool by the ice of a man walking in the snow, by the heat of a man overcome by wind. The ice was thick and white on the back of Villa's blanket. When he squatted beside a fire to take a tortilla or share a cup of tea, the ice cracked and the pieces were like white glass shattered, yet clinging, rows and rows of jagged white-glass beads clinging.

He said to the troops not to be afraid, he pointed to the smoke going east. They saw only the snow. He ordered food to be distributed, he gave them coal to burn. They showed him their fingers bloodied in the cold, they said they were afraid to sleep; men who slept in the open in the snow drifted, like the snow, the wind took them to other places, they never returned. He promised the sun, the sure coming of morning, he told them the number of hours until morning.

At the western edge of the camp a group of mountain men sat together around a fire built in a pit. They had found a mouse frozen in the snow. It was a bad sign, they said; the mouse had not found its home. Why had the mouse gone out into the snow? they asked. It was a fat mouse; there was time for such a mouse, a season, unless the season was not to change, unless the earth itself was cold.

Villa stood nearby. He listened to them, he was not seen. The men were turned to the fire, averting their faces from the wind. They spoke to each other, they looked down into the heat. The odor of coffee and wet wool was in the center of the group, as if it came from the fire. "Bad luck," they said. "Too cold. I have not seen a bird. Where are the owls tonight? Could it be that the owls are busy with something else? Did the mouse know?"

They were men from the same village, a high place in the mountains near the Rough River. The oldest of them was a singer. His eyes were very narrow; he shielded the secrets the singers know. He removed his hat and tore a strip of red cloth from his headband. It was for the mouse. He sang while he wrapped the frozen mouse in the red cloth:

> *The tomato stands in flowers,*
> *The tomato stands in flowers,*
> *Getting ripe, getting ripe;*
> *The tomato stands up.*

The singer put the mouse wrapped in red cloth into the fire. The cloth blackened, the odor of burning fur came from the fire. The singing continued, the singer drew three crosses in the snow. A gust of wind covered over the crosses. The singer drew them deeper, forcing his hand into the snow up to his wrist. A coyote stepped between the men into the small circle around the fire pit. There was no snow in its fur, and its eyes were red, a reflection of the color of the fire; its eyes were black mirrors reflecting the fire. The coyote dipped its muzzle into the fire and pulled out the mouse. The wrappings were all blackened, pieces of the wrappings fell like ashes. The coyote laid the mouse in the snow. There was nothing but a black bundle in the snow. Then the wrappings fell away and the mouse was revealed lying on its side. The tail moved, the mouse breathed. Suddenly, it jumped to its feet and ran away.

Before morning, the appearance of the coyote and the miracle it had worked were known by everyone in the camp. Those who knew also said they saw the smoke going west. Many remembered that they had seen the sun setting red the night before; it had been difficult, looking into the driving snow, seeing beyond the heavy clouds, but they had seen the red sun. They said they were not surprised when the snow stopped and the wind came warming; they had expected the morning.

Villa ordered extra food to be distributed. He told the generals to give the men warm clothing, he told them to take their cold, wet clothing and find a way to make it warm and dry again. When the troops were fed and clothed, he called the brigades to order. The day was cold and very clear, the air had a sound, like the wind crackling; but there was no wind, and the sky was cloudless, a whitened blue. Villa called for the troops to march in review. He told the band to play in march time, he told the men to sing, to march to their singing and the glory of the band playing in the bright day, to be an army in the sun.

"We'll fall on the town," he told them, shouting the words for hundreds to hear. "We'll give them one terrific blow. And the town will fall to us. An hour and a half, an hour and a half from the first shot until we take the plaza. In the name of God, boys; in the name of the Redeemer, Francisco Inocencio; in the name of the revolution, put it to them!"

The soldiers cheered, they rode their horses on parade. They were no longer cold; the sun was above them, there was light and warmth, the world was not dark anymore. They sang, they went to war laughing; no man believed he would die that day.

On a hill east of Ojinaga, Villa stood with his secretary. He watched through binoculars, waiting for the attack to begin. "You promised a lot," Luisito said.

"They have no ammunition."

"How do you know?"

"My stomach asks the same question."

"Are you sick?"

Villa put the binoculars down and looked at Luisito. The dark bird face of the man was kind, the concern was in his eyes. "Are you worried about me or the battle?"

"Both."

"Ojinaga is ours."

"And you?"

"My eyes are clear."

"You could take something for your stomach."

"Victory cures my stomach," Villa said. He laughed and looked through the binoculars again. "Until I see the wounded."

On the east, the Federals collapsed in fifteen minutes. In five minutes more, the cavalry broke their center. They fought on the west; they endured Martiniano Servín's artillery, they stood up to the cavalry charging and the infantry advancing from line to line, they returned the fire, they obeyed their officers, and in forty-five minutes there was nothing left of them. One hour and five minutes after the first shot was fired the revolutionaries entered the plaza of Ojinaga; the Federals had crossed the river into Texas. Nothing was left of them but their wounded, nothing was left of them but their dead.

General Scott served pot roast and baked beans to his guests. "It's our native food," he said. He laughed, showing his teeth under the mustache; his eyes were nearly closed in laughter. The Mexicans had come to his house straight from reviewing the troops at Fort Bliss, and they were still quiet with awe. Villa had said, "It's the best army in the world. I never saw such an army. Even under Huerta the troops were not so well disciplined, even under Felipe Angeles the cadets were not so perfectly dressed. And in my division—well, you've seen my troops, General Scott—I still don't have shoes for every man. And I have one brigade dressed in purple shirts and one with pink socks. I have a whole company dressed in red pants. Our underwear is blue. Why blue? We buy whatever is cheap, we take whatever we can get. But those boys are good soldiers; if they had the training and the equipment, they would put up a good argument against any army."

General Scott leaned across the corner of his table, he put his face close to Villa. "It's not the troops, General; it's the man; the man who leads makes the army. By God, I thought I'd seen it all when I fought the Apaches out here, but you're something unto yourself, Villa, *sui generis.* I've seen wolves that didn't have your instinct for terrain. And at Ojinaga, you knew they were weak, didn't you? We've got men in the jail here who say they didn't have fifteen cartridges a man when you hit them. You knew, of course you knew; that's the instinct of a general. Let me tell you, I think that's what made Napoleon great; I'd never say it in front of my junior officers, but I think the man operated on instinct, pure instinct, like a wolf.

"That's you. But your First Chief is another matter. He's nothing but

[452]

politics. He threw away Coahuila. He's ambitious, he's sly; he has an instinct for that, all right; but for war, for war he's worse than an old woman."

Villa leaned closer to Scott. He breathed the Yanqui general's breath. "Then give us the prisoners, just the Orozquistas."

"And you'll put them up against a wall."

"Yes."

Scott leaned back in his chair, he made himself formal, he used the distance: "The killing of prisoners is an abomination, the conventions of war forbid it."

"I have never killed prisoners," Villa said. "Orozquistas are traitors. Do you think I would shoot those poor skinheads who were forced into the army? Never. Do you think I would shoot an officer who serves in the army because it's his life to serve the President of Mexico? Never. But an Orozquista is different; they're traitors and the Law of Juárez says they should be shot."

"Then the law is wrong."

"Sooner or later, they'll cross the border; you can't keep them in jail because they lost a battle at Ojinaga. You'll let them out and they'll cross over the river, and then I'll kill them. Before I'm finished, there won't be an Orozquista left alive on either side of the border."

"You disappoint me," Scott said.

"Should I have lied? A liar's credit soon runs out."

"Blessed are the merciful . . ."

"Is the wolf merciful? Is an Apache merciful? When the Apaches hate a man, they hang him upside down over a small fire and cook his head until it bursts. My boys do that too; I've seen them."

The officers at the table ate without looking up. General Scott sawed at his meat; the sound of his knife on the plate dominated the room, like an order. Villa gave a shrug, he picked up a piece of meat in his hands and chewed around the fat. He made a scoop of a slice of bread and picked up his beans with it; the beans softened the bread, they fell out onto the tablecloth. Villa scraped up the beans with a knife and licked the knife clean. "It's not like a tortilla," he said. "The bread is too soft." He laughed. No one laughed with him. He put his hands palm down on the table and stared at his plate. The meal had been ruined, there was no more conversation.

They went into the parlor to sit in soft chairs and drink coffee and brandy. An orderly brought cigars. The afternoon light was growing red. General Scott called for the photographs made that morning during the review of the troops. He showed Villa a picture of his face.

"My face is only my face," Villa said. "What's the use of making a picture of my face? A face doesn't tell you anything; I can make it whatever I want.

[453]

Anyone can do that. Go into the mountains and talk to the people; they won't look at your face, because they don't want to be deceived by a stranger's mask." He handed the picture back to Scott. "Why do Yanquis love pictures so? A man, not much more than a boy, paid us five hundred dollars a day in gold to make moving pictures of a battle. He came with us to a small town near the Conchos, where the Federals had left a garrison of twenty men. We were seven hundred when we came to the town. Seven hundred! The Federals fired a few rounds for the sake of honor before they surrendered. No one was killed, no one was wounded. All twenty men, even the lieutenant, joined the revolution; they asked to fight with us against Huerta. The Yanqui boy came to me with tears in his eyes. He begged me to make a battle for him, for his pictures; he paid us two thousand dollars in gold to run across a field and shoot a few cartridges. I gave the orders." He interrupted himself with laughter. "I told the boys it was for training. What a sight it was! They all ran standing up straight, like a row of corn. Some women ran with them. It was like a game. No one was afraid, no one crawled. Some men fell into a ditch and lay there laughing. One had a broken leg and he was still laughing. The Yanqui came to me later and thanked me. He said the pictures would be history, they would show people how a war was fought, they would be the first true pictures of war. Why do you Yanquis love pictures so? Do you think it's good to make a mask of war? A lie? One day, your credit will run out, like a priest's threats or a poor doctor's promises."

"Those pictures are only for entertainment," Scott said, "for amusement."

"Is that true?"

"Yes, people will enjoy themselves by looking at those pictures."

"I prefer dancing," Villa said. "And something else." Then all the officers laughed, and for a moment they were like friends. Villa called them to order, "Listen, listen to me! You know what I bought with the money the moving picture boy paid us?" He opened a button in the center of his uniform and pulled the pieces of cloth apart. "Look! The great bargain: the Jew's blue underwear!"

Medina had brought the letters to him: secret correspondence between Juana and her mother. Villa had become feverish when he first listened to the words, his eyes had gone blind with lights. They had talked, Medina had spoken of forgiveness, of the need to show mercy to women; he had said it was for the sake of the revolution, a general who executed his wife could lose the respect of his troops; execution was too harsh, prison was too harsh. They had talked away an afternoon, an evening, they had talked until the sudden fever passed. Afterward, they had gone walking in the streets,

[454]

passing by the open doors and windows of the first warm evening since the beginning of the year, seeing the families inside, in the lamplight, the husbands at their leisure, the children sleeping, rows of children in their wide beds, the same blanket for them all, the women washing the dishes and kettles of the evening meal, the women beside their men in the promising breezes of the first warm evening. There had been singing in some of the houses, a party in one, a lullaby in another, the accompaniment of the tiny laughter of children, girls sighing, lovers imperfectly singing. Villa had said, "When Liviana and I were married, there were mariachis outside the window all that night. We had to be quiet so they wouldn't hear us. It was a long time ago, but I was already a man; sweethearts in Chihuahua now are only children. Maybe the revolution makes them hurry."

He remembered the warm evening while he waited for her to come to the sitting room, he used it against the fever that threatened to overtake him again.

Juana was not changed from the first day he had seen her in Torreón: the innocence had not left her face, there were no corners, she was as gentle as a pebble. He kissed her in a husbandly way, he held her hands lightly while she sat down on the couch. She was perfumed, she wore silk, her hair was combed up into rolls, her hair was soft, it shone, it moved, swaying with her movements. He said to her, "Tell me, Juana, do you still sew? I've been away so much that I don't know: is that a dress you made?"

She raised her eyes. They were dark and seemed imperfectly defined, soft rounds within softer. They were the eyes of a child awake in the night. "A girl gets used to her husband, and then he sends her home, and then he goes away."

"That's such a pretty dress; did you sew it yourself? Silk is expensive."

"I longed for you."

"There is a revolution."

"Some men are getting rich," she said.

"God willing, that's the purpose of the revolution. Give a poor man twenty-five hectares and he's rich. But there are also some men who are stealing from the revolution, which is the worst crime, even worse than being a traitor. A traitor could be confused, he could think he's doing the right thing, he could believe in the wrong side; but a man who steals from the revolution knows he's a thief, he knows he's stealing cartridges from the troops, food from the poor; a man who steals from the revolution has to be shot. When we catch one, we always shoot him, always; we can never let one live, we can never forgive that crime. If my brother stole from the revolution, I would kill him. It's right to do that, isn't it?"

"It goes without saying." She was calm, her eyes did not change.

Villa let the room go quiet. He waited for her to speak, to move, to make some betrayal of herself. He wished for her to be afraid, to begin repentance, to enable him to take the child of her into his forgiveness.

"The servants in this house are surly," she said. "Would you speak to them? They don't understand that I'm the mistress of this house."

"If a man's wife stole some money that belonged to the revolution, like twenty or thirty thousand pesos, she would have to be put up against the wall. Even if he loved her, he would have to do it, don't you agree?"

"Yes." Her eyes wandered, she appeared to be bored, she found a loose thread on the arm of the couch and twisted it back down against the fabric.

"Tell me, how would you do it? We don't shoot women. It would be the first time."

"I don't know about those things. Ask your generals. Ask Medina, your bookkeeper."

"Yes, I'll ask him. Meanwhile, would you read this letter for me? You know I'm not a very educated man. It takes me so long to read a letter. Help your stupid husband, Juanita. Please, do that for me." He took a letter from his pocket and held it out to her. His hand was open, the writing on the envelope was plain to her.

"The letter is meant only for my mother to read."

"Tell me what it says, Juanita; read it to me."

"It's not intended for you to read."

He let the letter float out of his hand onto her lap. "Read it!"

She took the paper from the envelope and read aloud. She did not weep, her voice did not tremble, but the sound was thin and hollow; it came from a distance not in the room.

" 'Dear Mama, I will be coming home soon. I have enough money to take care of us. I have thirty thousand pesos. He doesn't know. He is so stupid, like an animal, a fat bull, a fat, curly-haired bull.

" 'I will be glad to be home. I will be glad to be away from him. He makes me sick to my stomach. You should see how he eats, like a pig. When he's on the train in his car he even smells like a pig from being all day with horses and sweating. He never talks about me or things I like. He only cares about war. He always has bristles on his face, like a pig.

" 'I have thirty thousand in real money, not in those bilimbiques with his name on them. Thanks to God, I'll be able to get away from him soon. Please have everything ready to leave for when I can escape from the animal.' "

He told her to read it again. Her voice did not change, there was no sign of fear in her face. She read more quickly the second time. "No tears?" he asked. "Aren't you afraid to go up against the wall?"

She did not answer.

Villa stood over her, expecting his anger. He felt only a mourner's loss;

[*456*]

her death had been done to him. He touched her cheek, stroking her to soothe himself. His tears surprised him, he coughed to hide himself. "Give the money back to Medina. He'll give you a paper, something, a receipt from the Provisional Government. And that will be the business of it, the business will be done. I won't ask how you stole the money; you would only lie to me. From my pockets, from this house, from the railroad car. I'm not a careful man, I think too little of money, of papers of all kinds; country people are like that.

"You're a city woman; Torreón is a paper city; it feeds on cotton, like a pest in the flower. You were made in the city, you were made with paper. I should have known, I should have known; I should have known by the smell of you. I should have seen the color of your face, your shaded city face.

"I never loved you, Juana Torres.

"That's not true."

"I never loved you in the way I loved Liviana. How much can a man love a girl? In time, maybe, I don't know, if girls become women—do girls know? I should have known: a virgin is not shameless. I should have known.

"Go away now. Don't go to Torreón, go to some other city; there's going to be fighting in Torreón. We'll be taking Baby and The Kid to Torreón; the shelling from those guns will be terrible, whole blocks will be destroyed. Go somewhere else; there is paper everywhere, in every city."

He took her arm in his hand and lifted her to standing. With his other hand, he felt her belly. "It's empty," he said. "Corn grows from the earth. When the weeds grow, we pull them out. Corn needs a clear place. Go away now, Juana Torres. Leave me in peace."

Liviana came home to him. He fell to his knees before her and laid his cheek against her skirts and wept. His house was whole again, he said he had been blessed. He celebrated her, he filled the house with dancing, with flowers and laughter. She went with him to the bank to see the interrogation of the son of Don Luis Terrazas. The landlord's pain was a gift to her. And when they broke open the column in the bank and found the Terrazas fortune hidden there, he gave her the first gold piece for a sign to put in her father's hand.

"Is it true you married a woman named Juana Torres?" Liviana asked.
"Yes."
"Did you love her?"
"For a moment."
"How can I forgive you?"

[457]

"What have you lost?"

"There is a summer sun and a winter sun; I have lost the summer."

He came back from the City of Juárez sick with fever. He could not eat for the nausea, his legs pained him when he walked, the headaches came all day and all night, the watery flashing lights of the next headache began before the pain of the last headache had passed. Liviana took him from the aides as if he were a package delivered to her. She led him to their bedroom and undressed him and gave him apple tea to quiet his stomach.

"It will take more than tea," he said. "I'm sick for what I've seen. This is no revolution, Liviana; the Zapatistas are right about Carranza, they understand him. Oh, Liviana, my heart is broken.

"You know how I was when I went there; I went to thank him, I was grateful; truly, I was grateful. The trouble over the way Rudi killed the Englishman was so bad, and Carranza stood with me, he defended me. When the Yanquis asked him about Benton, he answered like a revolutionary, like a Mexican.

"He's perfumed, Liviana, the First Chief of the revolution has the soul of a landlord. He told me, with insults, with arrogance. He told me again and again that he was an educated man—he speaks French. He insulted me, he lectured me, he spoke to me as I would speak to a child or an animal, yes, an animal.

"Carranza wants to be the President of Mexico. Nothing else interests him. The poor disgust him; he says that farmers have a bad smell. He has a saddle made of jaguar fur. The dark glasses he wears are to hide his eyes; he lifts them up to read. I saw his eyes, that's when I knew him; his eyes are small and empty, and he can't keep them still. In all my life I never saw a good man with such eyes."

"Drink the tea," she said. "Then close your eyes. I'll bring a cold cloth to put over your eyes."

"I don't like to close my eyes now. I see a desert. It's after everything has died and rotted, even the ants have died. Without the ants, no new life can be brought into the world. But the sun is shining on the desert; there should be flowers. I don't know what it means, it frightens me, it makes me afraid to sleep."

"My grandfather lived in dreams," she said. "Be careful that you don't become like him. Only what you see with your eyes is true."

"I know better. Think of this: your heart was beating before your mother gave you light. You dreamed before you were born, you came into this world from dreams."

"And now I live with my eyes open," she said.

"Yes, dreams were different then; we didn't know the world."

[458]

General Angeles stepped down from the train to the sound of shouting, to the music lost in the practiced unison of the cheers, and into the embrace of Francisco Villa, who said to him, "I am at your orders, sir."

Angeles lifted his head from the embrace, he spoke over Villa's shoulder to the crowd, his voice was a soldier's trumpet. "I place myself at the orders of General Francisco Villa, First Chief of the Army of Chihuahua, hero of the revolution, Saviour of the Poor. Viva Villa!"

The brigades replied, the words came pumping, "Viva Villa!"

Villa turned out of the embrace, he raised his hands to quiet the brigades. "I stand beside the soldier of soldiers, the man even Huerta was afraid to kill, Madero's friend, the greatest general since Cuauhtémoc of Tenochtitlán. Felipe Angeles!"

The brigades cheered, and Villa led them, making music of the cheers, composing the sounds with his hands. Angeles whispered through the noise to Villa: "Between Cuauhtémoc and me there was that Corsican runt."

"Who is that?"

"It's not important, but let's hope our luck is better than his or Cuauhtémoc's."

"Cuauhtémoc was a great fighter."

"Yes," Angeles said, "and the Lord loved him, so he took him to his bosom at a very early age."

From the railroad station they went to the governor's palace and then to the theater. They went to banquets and evenings of speeches and songs, to parties, dances, and the presentations of medals made for the moment. Everywhere General Angeles sat beside General Villa, and everywhere he was Villa's teacher, interpreting to him the formal world, the military world, the political world. He gave advice:

Don't be ashamed because you can't speak French; the inevitable end of speaking French is indigestion.

If you put your napkin under your chin, your clothes will stay clean, the women will have nothing to wash, and the devil will take them in their idleness. The moral character of the Western world is dependent upon spilled soup.

The difference between a dictator and a democrat is that the dictator has the job and the democrat wants it.

It's perfectly reasonable to carry your own eating utensils in your breast pocket; you can be sure you'll never put a dirty fork into a poisoned pie.

If you must choose between brave men and machine guns, choose machine guns; the guns have to be imported at great expense, the fools who are willing to stand in front of them are born at an alarming rate.

Never trust a rich man; he knows what can be gained.

Women who want to marry soldiers like to be left alone; by not marrying, one pleases them all.

If Huerta fought like a Huichol instead of a Frenchman, we'd both have been in our graves a long time ago.

Think of this that Clausewitz said: "The most distinguished generals have never risen from the very learned or really erudite class of officers."

He also said that moderation in war is absurd, adding that one must be immoderate in the most temperate way.

I am an artilleryman by profession, but I will be the first to admit that the force of artillery is moral and not always predictable: a troop that survives a terrible bombardment may emerge the moral victor; like a woman who outlives a miserable husband, the troop will consider itself invincible.

Neither of us should be President of Mexico: when the state serves the military instead of the other way around, the grass grows khaki in the springtime and the milk tastes of gunpowder all through the year.

Is everyone who is not an anarchist a capitalist? And is everyone who is not a capitalist an anarchist? Think of them as two horses, and you're the driver of the wagon. Each horse is pulling in a different direction. If you want to get where you're going, you have to keep the horses in balance. Where are we going? I would say the goal is justice, but I can't steal a definition of justice from the man who first thought of the example of the horses—he couldn't define justice himself. Democracy seems a good place to begin; we may as well lay the blame at the doorstep of the people.

You ask me why I left Carranza and came here to the Division of the North. This is my answer: if we get to the Capital first, it will be first come, first served; if Carranza is the first to arrive, the rule will be first come, first served.

Dr. Raschbaum came to the house on Tenth Street to examine Villa. He stayed in the bedroom with him for almost an hour, thumping Villa's back and his chest, listening to his heart and the sounds of his innards working. After the examination, he told Villa to get dressed and come out into the parlor to discuss his case.

"Am I sick?"

Raschbaum pursed his lips. He said nothing.

"Don't do that with your mouth, Herr Doktor. The way your nose sticks out it makes your face look like a trombone."

"To make a man your personal physician and then to insult him I can't understand," the doctor said. He spoke with a German accent. He was always serious. Angeles said it was because he believed the world was dying.

Dr. Raschbaum was sitting in the parlor, chatting with Liviana, when Villa came into the room. "Sit yourself down," the doctor said to Villa, "and don't worry yourself. There's no disease, nothing to worry about."

"But the headaches," Liviana said, "and the trouble with his eyes; it must be something."

Dr. Raschbaum sipped from the cup of chocolate Liviana had brought for him. He looked up at the ceiling to let time pass, perhaps to think, perhaps to force Villa to a weaker position. "A doctor hears everything in confidence," he said. "You understand that. So I ask you a secret question, a confidential question. You will answer me?"

Villa nodded.

"He will," Liviana said.

"I consider the rages, the headaches, the ophthalmological—eye—problem all of a piece. This is not like a man who is shot in the foot and also has a toothache; this is one thing, all connected. Yes? Now, I ask you a confidential question: do you like this work, being a general, a governor? Tell me the truth now; it's a question of your health."

Villa looked to Liviana for advice. The confusion was a paleness in his face. She nodded, she asked, "What good is a sickly general?"

"Well, Herr Doktor, I'll tell you the truth. But it's a secret. No one is to hear but you and Liviana; and if you tell my secret to anyone else, I'll have you executed. I won't put you up against the wall, like an honorable criminal, I'll have you killed in the Apache style. Do you know what that is?"

"Enough," Liviana said. "The man is here to help you."

"Let him answer me first."

"Yes, yes," the doctor said. "I have done an autopsy of a man killed in this fashion. The head does not burst; this is a myth. The effect is similar to death from fever. Possibly there is no pain of an extraordinary nature, only delirium. One cannot say without observation. But yes, I am familiar with the method. Now, if you wish me to solve this problem of your rages and your headaches and so on, you must answer my question."

"It's not easy to frighten a doctor," Villa said. "I remember when Dr. Navarro was killed here when we tried to take Chihuahua the first time. A piece of shrapnel opened up his whole belly, it put him inside out. He talked all the time, until he died. Even the stink that was making everyone sick around him didn't bother him."

"Yes, yes," the doctor said.

"Why aren't doctors afraid?"

"I am not sick, that is not the question."

Villa combed the ends of his mustache with two fingers. He looked out into the garden; it had not yet begun to grow again. That afternoon he had knelt among the wooden branches of the roses to search for the first buds. "The answer is no," he said. "I don't like the work of a general or a governor. I'm an ignorant man; I draw my name, I read as slowly as a child; how am I prepared to be governor, how am I prepared to be a general?"

"How does your blood feel?" the doctor asked.

"When I'm wounded or when it's inside me?"

"Inside."

"After we took such a blow at Chihuahua, my blood was all in my head. We were going up the tracks, north, when I saw the coal train, and we took it and emptied out the coal and put our troops inside. All the way to the City of Juárez, every mile, every telegraph station, I felt the blood in my stomach. I kept thinking they would find out, they would be waiting for us, the trick wouldn't work. And when we pulled into the railroad station and I saw that the city was asleep, that I had come in on their own train, right into the middle of them and found them all asleep, then the blood spread out in me again and I was not sick anymore.

"But in a few days after that we fought them at Tierra Blanca and I was sick again: the blood was like a veil over my eyes. When we broke their middle and we were running across the sand dunes to their trains, I saw a man hiding, a soldier who was afraid to fight, and I killed him. A general doesn't kill his own soldiers, I can't be that way, I can't have rages. Do you understand me, what's wrong with me?"

"Perhaps."

"What medicine should I take?"

"Do you eat meat?"

"Every day. Before a battle we eat raw meat. It gives a man courage."

"Well, clearly, this is the problem. No more meat. None. For a man with thin blood meat is good, but for a man like you meat causes the problem: the blood gets too thick, you have too much blood. You see, if you eat some potatoes and a little milk or cream before a battle, this will make the difference. But no meat. Tortillas, beans, chicken, fish, milk, eggs, potatoes, tomatoes, squash, anything but meat. You will begin now not to eat meat and you will have no headaches, no rages, no ophthalmological problems in the next battle. This goes the same for a general or a soldier in the line."

"Herr Doktor, I'm going to take you with me to Torreón. If one of the rages happens there, you'll be nearby."

"For what purpose? This diet does not work overnight. Time is required."

"To clear my eyes," Villa said. He laughed until the doctor understood.

The doctor turned to Liviana: "You'll help him with this. A woman is most important for the man's health in such a malfunction of the mechanism that regulates the volume of blood. I don't criticize your cooking, Mrs. Villa; I say this only for his health."

"He's eaten his last good meal," Liviana said.

"When was my first good meal in this house?" Villa made an unhappy face. He said with longing in his voice, "When I was a boy, that was when I ate well. My mother was a great cook. How I remember the meals she fixed for us: weeds, carrion, corncobs, all the good things."

"This is true, that you ate weeds and carrion?"

"One day, when I'm cured, Herr Doktor, I'll take you to a real Mexican fiesta."

Villa and Angeles gathered the brigades, they trained the men in war. There were ten thousand, a division, sixty doctors, four thousand horses, six thousand women following, children beyond counting. They moved south, the slow-moving trains stopped in all the towns, taking on food, refilling the water tanks, exercising the horses. In Villa's private car the walls were hung with maps and drawings of beautiful women; day and night men sat in the car, meeting around the table, planning the battle. Villa lay in the wooden bed that folded down from the wall. He listened, he agreed, he shook his head, he was quiet. The generals watched him; his eyes were open, but he seemed to sleep—his face was the color of angers. At Camargo, in the early evening, the generals realized that Villa was no longer with the division: he had disappeared. They said nothing outside the privacy of the car. The Division of the North continued toward Torreón; General Angeles maintained the schedule.

In Tula, where Quetzalcóatl lived as a monk, this earth was perfect. There were cacao trees, the land was green, the city was beautiful. It was a city of flowers, a city of song; the craftsmen lived there. In Tula, Quetzalcóatl lived alone in a room of four colors; he thought of the gods, of the Close and the Near. But the wizards envied him. A wizard came into his room and showed him his face in a mirror. How sad it made the monk to see his puffy face, his aged face! He put on a mask of jade.

A second wizard came and gave him wine to taste; he made Quetzalcóatl drunk, he set him to singing. The third wizard brought the monk's sister, and she too drank wine and became intoxicated. The monk and his sister drank wine all night, they wore masks and disported themselves, they were not real, they were in dreams. In the morning, the monk thought of what he had done; he knew his shame. Quetzalcóatl fled from Tula, he went east to the sea, he rose there in flames, he went to the place of red and black. And Tula belonged to the wizards, it was their city; they looked on it, but they were not pleased: the cacao trees had turned to cactus, the green land had turned to desert, there was no more beauty in Tula.

All of this was known before the catzopines came; the truth is as I tell you. The world is as it has been described. Men are always in revolt, usurpation has always produced deserts, no man who knew himself was ever satisfied. Think of this: a wise man is one who knows something. Ask yourself: How are we different from the ever-withering flowers? Ask yourself: Do we live here on earth?

Villa answered that he was sick.

Is your body sick? Is your heart sick? There are as many ways to be sick as there are men on earth. More. There are sicknesses yet to be born. How are you sick? Have you lost your face?

He said only that he was sick.

I saw that it was true. There were swellings around his eyes and his skin had lost the rubbery quality of health; he had become the ember of himself. I asked him to tell me how the sickness showed in him.

Blindness, nausea, and pain.

I put butterflies into the fire, I burned a snake. I made him spin himself around until he was guided to stop. He stood facing north, as always. It was clear that his náhual was still with him, and in the form of the coyote. I told him so.

He said there was no magic, that the náhual was an illusion. War is real, he said, the machine gun is magic; he had seen it, he was going to see it again. He told me of the wounded he had seen, how men wept when they lost their limbs, how the blind foundered and the stink came out of men's intestines. He spoke of cities after the artillery had done its work, of women dead in the rubble, of their houses and children lying in the streets, the living more horrible than the dead. He said that the old songs did not tell the truth, that the place of the fleshless was here, that he was Death, he made it so.

Why now, Doroteo? Ask yourself.

He washed himself, he washed his clothes; he put on white cotton and sat among the roses. He pierced his leg with a thorn and threw the blood into the fire.

I'm sick, he said. When I close my eyes, I see deserts. It is long after everything is dead, even the ants are dead; but the sun is bright and I know now there is running water nearby, just out of sight, beyond a hill, in the plain below, in secret arroyos, canyons I cannot see. There should be flowers.

Do you see dust? Is there an echo of rattlebells?

He laughed aloud.

We sat on opposite sides of the room where the roses grow. The fire burned all night and all the next day, with no more wood than what had been between the three stones when he laughed. It was magic, but he could no longer see magic. I told him his wife was carrying a child, a girl who would be born healthy and beautiful, but he gave no sign that he had heard. I put thorns through my tongue and sang for him with the blood bubbling in my mouth. It was Xipe's month: I offered him cocolli, I gave him a garland of the twisted tortillas to wear around his neck, I striped amate paper with black rubber and threw it into the fire. He shuddered, as if he knew of the skinning, as if he remembered. It made no difference to him that I did these things to cause flowers to grow in the deserts of his dreams; he believed now that the only truth was here on earth.

At the end of the day in my house he said that he was no longer sick. The swelling around his eyes had left him, and when he moved I could see that his skin again had the healthy rubbery quality of his youth. He told me how he had once eaten the Root of Gold and entered himself through the top of his head. In the time he had stared at me across the fire, he said, something similar had happened: he knew now that life here on earth was the most important life, the certain life, the one that must be considered first; he understood that the next world was in the children of this world, which was reason enough to go to war.

He put on his clothes that were washed and cleansed in the sun, and prepared to go back. Before he left, he held out five gold coins to me as a payment.

The shame! I put on all my mirrors. When I went out into the hills, I dressed myself in mirrors to conceal the shame.

On his way back to the army he ate nothing but tzoalli. If he came to a place and the people there lacked either amaranth or yellow corn or dark honey for the making of tzoalli, he ate nothing. Thus he purified himself, thus he made himself well. My shame was lessened. Xochiquetzal danced; the stolen bride is lovely, her hips are swaying.

Crocodile

Dust everywhere, then the night so cold. No grazing for the animals, the mules in their strings, each man's horse found in the dust, in the confusion of the railroad cars, pulled and pushed down the ramp, tied in the night to a mesquite bush, with nothing to graze on and no place but the cutting rock and cactus floor of the desert to sleep.

All night the scouts came and went, the riders whispering to their muffled horses, the runners like a faint wind, no more than breath and shadow. Laughter came from the generals' cars. There was singing from the men spread across the flat desert. Women crooned to their babies. Quiet came. It was so cold, so clear. The click of the telegraph carried in the pauses of the wind. The challenges of the sentries were heard in all the distances of the camp.

Wind

The brigades came by train, on horseback, and walking. They gathered in Bermejillo, they flowed into the town, like rivers into a lake. In the watered fields, where the grass of spring lay in its beginning, in the timid fields they squabbled over places. The women hunted for hearth stones and firewood. The women patted tortillas and cooked them in ashes. Cattle were slaughtered, and the meat was prepared for cooking; none was hung in the sun to dry; Peronal, Tlahualilo, Bermejillo, had fallen in a day; everyone knew, Torreón would fall before the end of the week.

Villa walked in the fields, among the people, taking a piece of a tortilla from one campfire, a chunk of meat from another. A woman handed a cup of coffee up to him. He squatted beside her to drink. "Pancho Villa, your suit needs to be ironed," she said. "It's all wrinkled, like you stole it a week ago." She lacked teeth. When she laughed she pursed her lips and shook her head from side to side. Children were all around her. The small ones wore only shirts; their hair hung straight and ragged; they were powdered with pale dust; their noses ran in watery hangings.

"Listen, cutie; you should be drying some of that meat; sometimes it takes a while to get a tick out of your skin."

The smallest boy opened her dress and put his mouth to her breast. "I'm raising up another Villista," she said. She wiped the boy's nose with her fingers, pinching it clean. She smiled down at him. "Right, snotnose?"

Villa put the coffee cup down and gave her a light tap on the cheek, standing up, going on. "Get yourself a clean suit," she said after him. "A good pair belongs in clean pants."

He made his way through the camp to the railroad car. The round table in the center of the car was set with silver utensils on a white cloth. "We shall celebrate," Angeles said, "we shall honor the victories of the dancing general."

"It was a wedding; northerners dance at weddings. I would have arrived in Torreón before you if the girls hadn't been such good dancers."

"There is dancing and there is dancing, sir; just as there are battles and sieges."

"Nothing from Urbina?"

Angeles shook his head. "No word."

"Why is he taking so long? We can't move until he takes Mapimí. I can't have Velasco between us and the border."

Villa paced, he quickened, he took the shape of crouching. "I see those people in the camp. They eat everything, like black vultures. They tear the meat with their teeth and swallow it without chewing. What will they do next week? This is not cattle country, cattle don't eat cotton. I tell them to start drying the meat while the sun is still up. And they laugh, they all laugh. They think Torreón will fall by magic. Have they seen La Pila? Have they seen that hill? Before this is over they'll think the devil made it. They'll die hungry on that hill. They'll have shit in their pants, they won't have the strength to run another step. They'll see, they'll see. And so will you. This won't be what they taught you at the French school, I promise. Magic, everyone wants magic. Pancho Villa is the devil, and the devil will take the city by magic."

House

The day began with all the bands playing. It was the birthday of Benito Juárez. The music reached the length of the ten trains. The army spread out on both sides of the main track, like a city without houses. Cattle were slaughtered and more corn was used up. It was another day for victory to be celebrated: Mapimí had fallen to Urbina, and he was coming in with the Morelos brigade. The division was growing: with Urbina and Robles joining them and Calixto Contreras and his two thousand guerrillas moving down the Nazas toward Huarache Canyon, they were more than fifteen thousand. General Aguirre Benavides set out for Sacramento with three brigades; they went singing, with cheers following them and the bands furiously playing. The artillerymen still worked on the mountain guns, trying to assemble them. General Angeles had been with them all night; his brown sweater was stained with grease, he complained of the cold. During the night, Rodolfo Fierro killed a drunken soldier in the town.

[*467*]

Villa and Fierro took a thousand men south. At Noé, the last station on the main line before Gómez Palacio, the Federals had destroyed a bridge. After Noé, the track had been destroyed all the way to Torreón. Fierro put his crews to work rebuilding the bridge and laying new tracks. Villa met with his officers. They set back the time of the attack from six o'clock to seven; the artillery wanted one more hour. "You'd keep the devil waiting," he told Angeles.

"Forever, sir, and the day after for good measure."

Herrera asked for news from Sacramento.

"We've moved them out of the Municipal Building," Luisito reported. "General Aguirre Benavides says the resistance is now confined to the area around the church. He expects the church to fall by morning."

Angeles gave Luisito a slap on the back. "Speak up, man! You should be proud of your brother: the Church has lasted nineteen hundred years and your brother is going to bring about its fall overnight."

The generals said their troops were ready, excited. José Rodríguez said he worried about the mood of his brigade. He had never seen the men so agitated. "It worries me, too," Fierro said; "it's like being too long without a woman: you get a gunfighter trigger and you have to be careful you don't shoot off your foot."

They laughed, they looked at the sky; the form of the sun was gone, only the last of the light remained. Faces cooled, the light made mirrors of their eyes. The artillery was behind them. The brigades were spread over a six-mile front that curled around Gómez Palacio and Torreón and on the right reached almost to Lerdo. The attack was to come in the center, with Herrera holding the right wing and Rodríguez holding on the left. As the center moved forward both wings were to follow to keep the center from the danger of being cut off and surrounded; Villa did not want to make the same error that had hurt him in the attack on Chihuahua.

The center moved forward. They were to seem like cavalry, walking their horses forward in line in order, awaiting the bugler. When they dismounted and went forward as infantry, the Federals would be confused: the elevations and the timings of their artillery would be wrong, they would not be prepared for Villa's rolling barrage. The evening wind blew low across the unplowed fields, carrying the dust eastward. The horses crushed the dry plants, making an enormous whisper.

The first of the Federal shells landed among a group of officers. Saúl Navarro, the brother of the doctor who had been killed at Chihuahua, was the first to die at Gómez Palacio. The firing was uneven, the Federal gunners were hunting, waiting for the attack to reveal its shape, looking for the first sign of Villa's artillery.

Villa stood on a low hill between the advancing troops and his artillery. His staff stood around him, talking softly, pointing to the location of the Federal guns, which seemed up too close. Or were they mistaken about the elevations? Villa watched the brigades advancing. He spoke to them softly. Calmly, boys, calmly, do what I tell you. Calmly, now, get ready to dismount. Easy, easy, Angeles is ready. Do what I tell you. Surprise! Surprise! Surprise them and we'll have the town.

He saw the officers rein in their horses, preparing to dismount. And then the troops passed them, trotting, giving the spur to their horses, speeding the charge, running, at a gallop, their rifles ready, into the sudden cannonade, the shrapnel bursting pale green light and smoke above them, the timed shells sending their pieces of metal to tear through the cavalrymen and their galloping horses. The line wavered, the horses stampeded toward the town, the waiting riflemen and machinegunners opened fire, knowing the range. The line scattered, covered the plain before the town, came leaping over the fallen horses, into the machine gun's rasp and the Mauser's crackling. Men and horses fell. There were no patterns. The closest ran on, the far ones fell, the closest fell, the shrapnel burst over the center, the earth erupted at one side. The unhorsed men ran back. One stopped to shoot his wounded horse, another carried a saddle over his shoulder. The wounded were dragged back. Men crawled in the field, in the dead and trampled cotton of the season past. Men hid in the shadow of dead horses, they curled up in shell holes.

On the right, the guns of La Pila had found Herrera's brigade. Villa could see the shells landing in the midst of Herrera's positions, at the place where his staff should have been. He looked behind him to Angeles. In the last of the light he saw the general in his brown sweater, standing on a hill, his head bowed, unable to fire even one shell for fear of killing the revolutionaries who had passed beyond the first houses and into the town.

The firing stopped after dark. Villa ordered the men to be given food and water. He rode down to the edge of the battlefield and waited there with the doctors and the stretcher bearers while the wounded came crawling back in the darkness. Luisito stood beside him, keeping count of the numbers. Villa asked for the numbers again and again. At midnight, there were no more men alive on the field. "We lost four hundred and fifty," Luisito said.

"How many dead?"

"A hundred and twenty-five, maybe a hundred and fifty."

"Wounded?"

"Dr. Villarreal has three hundred and fifteen in his hospital car."

"My God!"

"Four and a half percent isn't so bad, sir."

"The battle hasn't started."

Snake

Aguirre Benavides brought his troops in. Sacramento had fallen, he had chased the Federals all the way back to Gómez Palacio.

The armies faced each other, too far apart for the cannon to be effective. There was the sound of rifle fire somewhere along the line all day, but no battles developed, no one moved. The revolutionaries lay in shallow trenches, irrigation ditches, or on the flat ground of the cotton fields. They played cards or threw plum stones to pass the time. Some prayed, some slept, a few ran away. The track repair crews worked in twelve-hour shifts, the big railway guns moved forward, not yet in range, but closer.

Death

General Angeles addressed the generals of the Division of the North. He pointed with a riding crop to a map of Gómez Palacio as he spoke. "This is La Pila, which is the center of their defense. It controls the town and the approaches to it, as Maclovio knows. The slope of the hill is steady at thirty degrees, which makes a cavalry charge impossible; we'll have to go on foot.

"Our plan is to surround the hill with artillery, aiming and getting the fuse times before dark. We can use the cover of darkness to minimize the effectiveness of Velasco's guns in the city.

"We estimate five hundred Federal troops on the hill. The conventional theory is that between four- and six-to-one superiority in numbers will be needed to achieve the objective. Thank you. General Villa has assigned the brigades to their positions."

Angeles stepped back and Villa took his place in front of the map. He drew a circle around the base of the hill with his finger. "The artillery here." He looked at the generals; they waited uneasily, shifting and sighing; their spurs were like gentle bells, a whisper of bells. "Maclovio here. José Rodríguez and my brigade here. And my cross-eyed buddy, Tomasito, here."

"Son of a refucked mother," Urbina said.

Villa looked at him. "Are you speaking to me?"

"No, man, to him." Urbina raised his eyes to Heaven. "He gives me rheumatism and lays my brigade on the grinding stone for good measure. Shit!"

[*470*]

"It's the only thing to do," Rodríguez said.

"Yes," Villa said. "When you're the anvil, bear; when you're the hammer, strike."

Deer

The day was hot and drying, the fields crackled, the troops lay in shaded places, erecting tents of rifles and blankets, hiding beneath packing cases and umbrellas. Crews moved up and back from the water tank car, driving mule carts loaded with barrels of water. Fierro went through the trains, seeking out the men who had gone back to spend the night in the company of women, shaming them, driving them back to the front as if they were cattle.

Villa rode up and down the line, talking to the troops, sitting with his officers to talk the strategy of the battle. He heard a man playing a concertina and sat with him and a dozen other men of the Zaragoza Brigade to sing and mourn the lack of women at the front. On the far right, near Lerdo, he saw a man sitting in a tree, looking into the town through a telescopic sight. "Are you a sharpshooter?" he asked the man.

"Who's asking?" The soldier kept his eye to the sight.

"Pancho Villa."

"Yes, sir, I'm a sharpshooter."

"Do you see any beauties there among the troops?"

"There's one who comes in and out of the bakery. Oh, she makes my balls itch."

"Be careful you don't pull the trigger."

"I would die first."

Villa reached up and tapped the man's foot to get his attention. "If you touch that woman after we take Lerdo, I'll give you to Fierro for target practice."

The man took the sight away from his eye. He looked down, revealing the face of a boy. "If I met such a beautiful woman, I would fall on my knees and worship her like the Virgin herself. Oh, God, let me live long enough to meet a woman like her."

General Angeles lay under a sun shade made of canvas caisson covers. He ate an orange. Villa sat with him. He was red and dusty, he smelled of sweat and the lather of his horse. Angeles took another orange from his breadbag. He made four cuts in the skin, sliced off the top and bottom, and removed the peel in four pieces. "The French way," he said, offering half of the orange to Villa, "very efficient."

They ate oranges and looked across the fields to La Pila. The hill was brown, stony, rough-skinned, without even the relieving green of cactus. "Do you know what lives on that kind of hill?" Villa asked. "The worst things in the desert: Gila monsters, blind snakes, scorpions, vinegar ants. If a wounded man fell on that hill, the creatures would come out after him."

"Have you changed your mind?"

"We'll make a lot of widows tonight," Villa said. His eyes were unclear, his voice was very soft.

"There's a story about Napoleon that you should know. He was waiting for a battle to start—they began in the morning instead of at night—and he was thinking about the widows too. But he said, 'The wine is poured, it must be drunk.' That's how generals have to think."

"Maybe Velasco's dog will open its mouth and tell him we're going to destroy the town."

"And if he kills his dog, maybe his turkey will speak."

Villa fixed his eyes on Angeles. He looked at him with suspicion.

"What's the matter? Did you forget that I'm Mexican?" asked Angeles.

"You're not like us, you don't even look like us. Your face is different, you use different words."

"Ignorance and ugliness are individual blessings, not racial characteristics."

Villa laughed.

"I'm not joking, not this time. The Porfiristas didn't stay in power because of the rurales or the old man's fat-bellied generals; they did it by making people believe they were ugly and stupid. It was perfect: as long as the people believed they were stupid animals, they kept themselves in chains; the old son of a bitch didn't have to do a thing.

"Madero understood. I think he understood better than the Liberals. They were worried about economics; he knew that effective suffrage alone would destroy the dictatorship. The slogan was all he needed. Even if the people didn't vote, the idea that they were human enough to have the right to vote changed the country forever.

"When Carranza takes office, there won't be any confusion over who should vote and who shouldn't. He doesn't believe in democracy, he has no interest in it. Think of how he speaks to you. He lectures you, he tells you about his own class. What Carranza did was to try to make you chain yourself; he tried to make you surrender your soul to him. Exactly like the Porfiristas. He learned from them, he was one of them, a political chief, a senator. He knows you're vulnerable, and he also knows you're dangerous; I've heard him say as much.

"A lot is being decided in this war. If the symbol of the war is Villa or Zapata, it will be a revolution; if the symbol is Carranza, it will be another barracks revolt. He knows that; Carranza isn't a fool. You're his enemy on two counts. Defend yourself."

Angeles took another orange out of his breadbag and peeled it. He held the orange to his nose and took a deep breath. "My God, Villa, nothing I've said makes you smell any better."

They shared the orange, chewing slowly, watching the hill. By squeezing their eyes until they were almost closed, they could see the shimmerings that were the movements of men.

Villa sucked the pieces of orange out of his teeth. "If not Carranza, who? Do you want to be President?"

"I've thought about it."

"Do you want it?"

"History is against a soldier being a good President. If we have another general for President, we'll have another dictator. Generals are dictators; aren't you? Don't you shoot men who disobey your orders? You don't really even have a choice; if you don't shoot them, the army will disintegrate. Presidents can't think that way; a democracy has to permit dissent."

"Then who should we make President?"

"It's not for us to decide, Don Porfirio. The people will decide, all those ugly, ignorant Indians. It's a terrifying thought, I admit, but those are the risks of democracy. My guess is that this war won't produce a democratic government, and even if it does, the people will elect the wrong man. Is that too terribly pessimistic? Blame it on the French. I spent too much time with the French. Never go to Paris, Francisco; it teaches you what we could have been and how badly we failed. Well, why go to Paris? You can go to San Juan Teotihuacan and feel just as hopeless."

The light does not die. It passes. It returns.

All day there was rifle fire, like trees breaking, like sticks breaking, like twigs breaking. Quiet came at dusk, as if the battle paused to resupply itself with food, like a man. The brigades stood in their rows. All the men were laden. The mountain guns were loaded on the backs of the mules. The horses were strapped to the field guns, the riders sitting on the right horses of the pairs. The last three horses of the nine waited beside, mounted, pulling-horses under saddle. It was the parade. There were no drummers, there were no bells, no horns; there was no dust.

Villa passed them on his horse, going slow, seeing them from his walking horse. He saw the hats of his army: straw hats with tassels hanging, hardened hats turned up at the front, straw hats with tall cones, soft straw hats wider than the man, Texas hats, English jungle hats, caps, headbands, fedoras, peaked caps, a round derby hat, brown campaign hats bought from the merchants in El Paso and San Antonio.

Herrera rode beside him; his beard was growing, sorrowful, black. Urbina rode beside him; he wore the winter pain in his face, he wrapped himself in a blue cape, he still had a boy's ungovernable hair. Rodríguez rode beside him; his cheeks were smooth, he had not grown a mustache to a man's fullness, he seemed to have been washed and put back into his wrinkled clothes. Angeles stood with his gunners; his brown sweater was torn at the shoulder, the grease of the guns marked his hands and face, he was pale straw.

Villa looked at the field after the troops had passed. Cotton had grown there in summer, the water had run between the rows. There was nothing now, no sign; the field was flat, dust, the straw of the dead season's plants had disappeared. He rode back to his camp at El Vergel and ate potatoes and milk. For an hour he slept. When he awakened, the sky was dark, the lights had gone out in the town of Gómez Palacio. The taste of blood was in his mouth. He could not remember if he had dreamed.

Luisito waited while Villa washed. "What time is it?" Villa asked.

"Eight twenty-five."

"It's quiet."

"They're waiting for Angeles to begin."

"What's the sign?"

"Soldiers. And the countersign is Chihuahua."

"What time is it?"

"Eight twenty-five."

"Slow enough, slow enough." He looked for a towel. There was none. He pulled out the front of his shirt and dried his face with it.

"What time is it?"

"Eight twenty-six."

At the places where the troops waited there was a strong odor of urine. The lieutenants were still walking among the troops, awakening the sleepers, when Villa arrived. Men passed him in the dark, going off to urinate, returning half asleep, lost in the dark, asking for their units, saying the names of their lieutenants in loud whispers. The men used their water to wash the sleep from their eyes, the lieutenants warned them to save it. Villa felt his own face cool. He thought of washing his hair.

Angeles began the bombardment at nine o'clock. The first target was the roundhouse. The shells exploded around the building: red, yellow, purple, smoke rising in the light of the next shell burst. The noise was close, sharp. For ten minutes the shelling of the roundhouse went on. The pattern was rapid, regular; the light blinked. The roundhouse was destroyed, it did not burn.

[*474*]

The shelling stopped. The silence gossiped, waiting. The guns fired a single volley, and in the fading of the explosions the troops roared, rising up, running across the railroad tracks, crouching, bent, upright, angles cranking, men leaning, firing as they ran. Slow, in the incessant blinking light they were slow, running at the speed of escaping dreams.

Amid the runners some men sank, settling, their limbs all made of leaves, floating downward through the thickness of air, settling, downward, dead.

The holes in the roundhouse lit up with gunpowder light, the mask had many eyes. The cannon began again, aiming higher, at the hill itself. The longer fall of the shells was a black whistle sounding through the boom and cracking of the night and the roaring throats of the men urging themselves forward.

General Villa watched. He sat his horse heavily, holding it still by the weight of himself. He had seen death in his mother's house, watching from the field, away: death lit small fires.

The dynamiters reached the roundhouse. The explosions were inside the metal of the building. The windows the cannon had not reached burst outward in sudden light. There was a cheer, the roundhouse was silent. Rifle fire came infrequently, echoing; the men were putting their rifles into the gun ports, shooting the survivors of the dynamite bombs.

In the gathering moment the stretcher bearers went forward, dressed in white, marked with blue crosses, running in pairs. The wounded did not wait. They came back in strands. A man carried another on his back; they were a hunched beast in the darkness. Calls for God were softly said somewhere in the night. "I'm here," a voice said, "over here," as if the voice of the wounded man was the answer of God. They went past Villa, the long strands of wounded, following each other toward the lights of the camp at El Vergel and the ambulance trains waiting there. A blinded soldier came toward Villa. He walked cautiously, holding on to the shoulder of a comrade who walked before him; his arm was stretched to its full length, keeping the distance between them. The soldier who led the blind man did not appear to be wounded. Villa thought to lean down and send the unhurt man back to the hill. As they came near him he heard the unhurt man talking: "Still far, still far. No, there are no colors, there is very little light. The light is dim, the moon is new, almost no moon at all." And the wounded man speaking at the same time: "There were white roses that my cousin Silvestre brought from Durango and the prickly pear blooming red with yellow centers and the fields greening around the fresh water and the sky like the color of a handful of water and my horse is black and my pet dog is yellow and brown and the color of my wife's skin is like copper before it goes to the smelter—she is bronze not copper and her hair is black, her eyes are black but not always, depending on the light, her mood, the time

[475]

of day, the time of year, the color changes, her eyes reflect colors that are all around. . . ." He let them pass. He was quiet, waiting for the assault on the dark hill. He washed his mouth with water and spat.

"Luisito, what time is it?"

"Nine seventeen."

"Were you ever wounded, Luisito?"

"I broke my arm when I was eight years old."

"Do you consider your crossed eye a wound?"

"No, sir. I see quite well with eyeglasses."

"What time is it now, Luisito?"

"Nine eighteen."

"When we take the city, see that the liquor is destroyed. Looters will be shot."

The buglers gave the order; they were a chorus of separate brass. The brigades advanced up the hill, firing as they went. In the night they were a circle of teeth, the little fires of them devouring the hill. The shelling came from the guns on La Pila and from the guns aimed at La Pila. The noise was enormous, battering; it muted the men who fought there. Explosions were everywhere, making a continuous wavering light, a piece of afternoon on the hill.

The revolutionaries moved up the hill and stopped; they fell back. The revolutionaries moved upward again, and stopped, and fell back. The shelling did not cease, the dynamite bombs did not cease; the circle of men, shadows colored in the false afternoon, moved up and down the hill in a rocking motion, like the wind-driven water of a pond. With each rocking motion the revolutionaries moved closer to the top of the hill and the stone reservoir where the machine guns worked.

Angeles aimed his guns only at the reservoir. The cannon beside it were quiet; only the reservoir remained unbroken by the exploding shells and the dynamite bombs. When it fell, the revolution would possess a piece of the hill, half of the fortifications, a safe place for the night. The bugles sent them forward again, the teeth of the light moving up, close to the top, within reach of the reservoir. They were too close for Angeles to trust his guns, the shelling stopped, the light dimmed, the small fires faced each other in the closing circle.

For a long time the revolutionaries lay in their places below the reservoir. They hid in shell holes and behind tiny piles of rocks. The machine guns crossed over them in brief arcs. They waited.

The sound of them was like the shells screaming. They hurled themselves forward, bombs, propelled by the constant order of the bugles. The first of them to reach the reservoir threw dynamite bombs into the gun ports. Stones crumbled, the reservoir was a flashing lantern, half of the hill of La

Pila belonged to the revolution. It was a safe place in which to pause for the night. The men rested, the stretcher bearers rushed forward, the wounded came back.

"How did it go?" Villa asked a man who carried his bloody fist in his hand.

"They slaughtered us, sir. And we slaughtered them."

Rabbit

The cold night had slowed the fouling of the dead; the men on La Pila hoped the day would be cool.

Dark yellow dogs came up the hill from the town. Their tails were down and curled in under them.

The creatures of the hill had come during the night; they had entered the clothing of the dead.

A counterattack had been expected, a rush of men coming across the face of the hill. Instead, Velasco used his artillery, firing steadily, round after round; the shells burst as they hit the ground, lifting brown fountains in the fire. The shells burst above the trenches, the green fire threw its killing storm in the air, cutting pieces of the earth, cutting pieces of the men who lay on the earth.

Angeles located the Federal guns. He aimed his batteries, he timed his fuses, and the shells failed him: the crimping machines in the sheds in Chihuahua had no consistency. He could not predict where the shells would fall, he could not be certain the guns would fire, and when the shells reached the Federal guns, he could not be sure they would explode. He moved his batteries closer, he endangered them, because he saw the hill and the men dying there.

Velasco sent his troops forward. They endured to the limit of their courage and fell back. The artillery fired again. Velasco sent his troops across the hill. They moved closer to the revolutionaries. And then the barrage and the troops running forward and the barrage again. In daylight the guns were accurate; hundreds of Velasco's troops fell, and yet he sent them again, climbing the hill; like water rocking and rocking, climbing the bank of a river, soaked into the sand, dying there, yet climbing, reaching with the next wave for a higher place.

"Give them the hill," Villa said to his generals. "Dynamite the reservoir and the trench walls, leave nothing; but give them the hill. We can't hold on in daylight, the cannon will kill us all. In the dark we'll take it again; his artillery can't find us in the dark. Sound retreat. Bring the wounded down. Don't leave the wounded on that hill."

Villa spent the day among the troops who had come down from the hill.

[*477*]

They knew they would go back again after dark. They could not sleep. The Ballad of La Pila was composed in the afternoon; the singer walked through the resting soldiers telling of the courage and the glory of the men who would dare to attack the hill a second time. He was not cheered.

The doctors reported the number of wounded. More than four hundred had been treated and sent on to hospitals in Parral and Chihuahua. They estimated the number of the dead; it would have been foolish, the generals agreed, to count deserters as dead. Herrera, who had been on the hill in the morning, said there were no deserters. "Our dead lay in five rows," he told Villa. "They all faced forward. I didn't see any who were shot in the back."

"Did you keep a count of the dead?" Luisito asked. "We need it for the report."

"Fuck the report! Fuck all your papers!" Herrera shouted. His face was filthy, he had the look of a miner at the end of his day. "You want to count the dead? Come with us tonight. I invite you."

A nurse came to ask Villa if he would visit a bugler who had been wounded on the hill. The boy lay on a blanket beside a ditch. The doctors had seen him and stuffed his wound with a great wad of cotton and gauze. His chest was torn open, the cotton and gauze grew like a white maguey plant out of the wound, the blood crawled upward, softening the cotton, collapsing the gauze. He was dying. The doctors had left him there.

Villa squatted beside the bugler. "What's your name? What's your regiment, kid?"

The boy did not answer. He burped loudly and a gout of blood came out of his mouth, spilling across his face. The nurse wiped the blood away with a swab of cotton. "They told me he asked to see you," the nurse said to Villa. "I don't think he can talk now."

"You were very brave," Villa said. "We're going to give you the Cadet's Medal. General Angeles, who was the chief of the cadets, is going to give you the medal. You get well now so you can thank him when he gives you the medal."

The boy's eyes were unmoving. His breath came through fluids, bubbling. Villa patted the boy's bare arm. It was cooling.

At dark the troops moved into position to attack the hill again. The roundhouse was empty; the metal walls hung loose, splintered clangings in the wind. The troops moved up close to the railroad track, lying in the dust and gravel. They did not know where the Federals had taken their positions on the hill, how far they had come down from the top.

Scouts were brought to Villa for instructions before they went up the hill. They were slim men, shining in the moonlight, barefoot hunters dressed in knives and arrows. They rolled in the dust before they went. Villa watched through field glasses, looking for the burnished stripes he had sent up the face of La Pila. He saw nothing; the hill loomed colorless and still, the broken walls of the trenches were like jagged teeth. The moon was increased. The three stars of the fire drill were seen in the eastern sky.

The scouts came down the hill in leaps and turns, with their arms outstretched, running in the air. They laughed and screeched, imitating birds. Only the dead waited on La Pila. Velasco had abandoned the hill and the town. Gómez Palacio had fallen to the revolution.

Water

Villa walked to the top of La Pila, followed by his clerks and generals. In the dim yellow light of the lantern the shadow of a rat crossed the floor and ran up the wall of the reservoir. It startled the men inside; they aimed their guns, too late for the shadow. "The water," Urbina said. "It came up here to look for the water. The men say the Federals poisoned the water in the ditches. Some of them are all twisted up with cramps, puking and shitting all night. The rats know; they can smell the water."

Down below the men slept, all but the doctors, all but the track repairmen clanging and steaming in the cold night, laying the rails for the big guns to move closer to the town.

All day the bodies were gathered, stripped, dragged or carried on carts to a single pyre at the top of the hill. The burning began in the late afternoon; the fat of the dead men burned black; the ashes floated over the city, falling as tiny black feathers.

Villa and Angeles met in Gómez Palacio to have dinner. It was not a celebration; they grasped for joy, but the odor of the burned dead was in the air. Angeles wore the most elegant of his uniforms and Villa wore his filthy brown suit and Texas hat. They tried to make each other laugh: they exchanged hats, they turned their backs to each other to show the face of Velasco in battle, they sang of the three little whores sitting on a saddle, shouting, "Viva Pancho Villa."

"We will compose a letter to General Velasco," Angeles said. "We will compliment him on his courage and the brilliance of his tactics, and in the end, we will ask him to give Torreón to us." He read the letter aloud to Villa as he wrote, speaking of the men who came every day to join the revolutionary forces, speaking of public opinion that favored the revolution, excluding only the privileged classes, who favored a dictator to protect their interests at any cost. In the beginning he appealed to Velasco's patriotism, and in the end he threatened him with the judgment of history.

[479]

Dog

The Federal guns started firing at dawn. They continued all day. Angeles moved his guns, keeping them concealed. At dusk he answered. A fire started in the city; the flames grew brighter with the night and died out before morning. The Federal guns kept up the shelling during the night. Villa rode up and down the lines, urging the men to sleep; he told them the safest place to be during an artillery attack was lying close to the earth, like a man sleeping.

Monkey

Villa rode into Gómez Palacio, running his horse, anxious for sleep. Luisito and his staff of clerks and runners followed. It was two hours before dawn, the shelling had declined to a slow, booming pulse on the eastern flank, and the troops in the town lay sleeping, wrapped in their blankets, curled against the walls of houses, avoiding the wind. The sound of the horses drumming on the hard streets frightened them awake; they greeted Villa with passwords and curses and aimed rifles. He laughed at them: "It's all right, boys, you can go back to sleep; Pancho Villa's awake and watching over you." The derision was soothing; the soldiers lay back in their positions, pulling the blankets around their shoulders.

Four soldiers sat against the walls of the room where Villa lay on the bed that had belonged to a cotton merchant and his wife. There was no linen on the bed. Villa lay on his back with his spurs cut into the mattress. The room was dark and cold; the soldiers had been told not to turn on the lights or build a fire. Villa talked to the soldiers, calling them by name, asking if they missed having women with them, asking how many of the golden ones had been killed, how many had been wounded, asking, "What were the names?"

The soldier began his list, starting with the dead.

It was after four. "Wake me up at five thirty," Villa said, interrupting the list. The soldier continued his recitation. Villa slept.

The firing started at five, echoing out of Huarache Canyon. Villa awakened with the sound of the first shells, sitting up suddenly, leaning on his elbows. Angeles came into the room. He wore a maroon silk dressing gown that reached to his ankles. "Eighty-millimeter shrapnel," he said. "I hope that poor bastard Contreras has dug himself in."

Angeles paced from the bed to the door. "I think this is Velasco's day," he said. "Damn him, damn him! We'll take a beating before he wears himself out. I know the man, I've listened to him lecture: he's not what you'd expect, he has the mind of a kitchen fighter, a brawler; he wants to hit and hit and hit and suddenly knock the legs out from under you."

From his position on the bed Villa could see out the small, high window on the west side of the room. The shrapnel exploded low and green over Huarache Canyon. The small arms fire was a yellow glow under it, sickening the green. He remembered Cerro Prieto, the dead men lying in the arroyo, the breast of the red-haired officer torn by an artillery shell.

Angeles went on packing and talking. "He'll continue for a day, two days, perhaps three. The man understands Clausewitz, he knows war; I've heard him lecture on Napoleon's errors. He's a student of the moral aspects, he knows when troops turn into a mob and fail. He'll surprise us, he'll frighten the men with surprises. And he'll keep attacking; he knows the moral force of continuous attack." He stopped and faced Villa, standing over him. "That's my analysis. We'll suffer Hell for two or three days. If our moral force fails, he'll turn this battle into a rout."

The shelling began on the east wing. Villa rolled himself out of the bed, tearing the mattress with his spurs, pulling up little tufts of feathers. He went to the window on the south side of the room and looked out. They were using shrapnel on the east too. There was no small arms fire below it; the color was cooler, water green.

A soldier came from the center of the house, carrying coffee and milk-sweet tortillas. Villa ate without interest. "A good piece of roast meat would give a man more strength," he said. The words had no more meaning than the food. He remained standing at the window, watching the shells bursting while he ate. When he had finished the tortilla, he turned back to Angeles: "I like it when you make jokes. I trust you when you make jokes."

"Do you think this is the proper time for levity?"

Villa looked out the window again, drawn to the lighted sky. "When a bull isn't a bull anymore, it's meat."

"If that's a line from Cervantes, it's new to me."

"No, it's not from *Don Quijote;* I was just thinking about how things change. It's always for the better, you know. Like a tree. When a tree isn't a tree anymore, what is it? Firewood."

"A worm becomes a butterfly."

"Yes, that's true," Villa said, speaking lazily, looking out the window, thinking elsewhere. "But the worm becomes a butterfly in its own good time. You changed in a hurry, more like the bull or the tree. I like you better when you make jokes." He was drawn again to the shell bursts. He counted them. "So much ammunition. If we had that much ammunition . . ."

"It won't last forever," Angeles said. "Sooner or later, we'll wear him down."

Villa walked across the room to Angeles and put his arm around the

[*481*]

artillery commander's shoulders. "Felipe, you're a good general, a professor of war. And what am I? A man who has read one book, a poor orphan, a victim of this life, an ill-tempered peón, but a Mexican, like them. They won't wait for two or three days while Velasco tires himself out, they'll go home. You understand what I'm saying? In a military way, in the way they taught you in France, you're right, we should wait. But I know these men. The hammer will die for you, but why should the anvil take any risks? We'll attack Velasco this morning. Wake up Luisito and tell him to send out the orders."

"As God is my blacksmith," Angeles said.

"That's better, trustworthy."

On the right, Contreras drove a force of two thousand Federals back through Huarache Canyon to the outskirts of the city. The fighting spread all along the line. Robles, Herrera, and Aguirre Benavides attacked on the left, driving into the city, destroying two fortified buildings, and arriving at the tree-lined Alameda on the eastern edge of the city. Robles was shot in the thigh, and he could not stop the bleeding. Villa ordered him to the hospital, and Robles sent back a request for a doctor to treat him there on the Alameda. "Send him here," Robles wrote, "the Alameda is lovely under fire."

Urbina and José Rodríguez attacked the center at noon. Calabazas Heights fell at three o'clock to Contreras. Angeles bombarded the Federal fortifications in the city. The main attack came at dusk, driving the center of the Federal lines back toward the river. They had never known war so terrible, even the taking of La Pila had not been so intense. Men could not speak. They shouted; the sounds of artillery, rifles, bombs, and machine guns took away their shouting. There was no speech, there was only fear and noise. The troops entered the dusts and smokes of the evening battle; they ran through the cloud, firing at what they saw dimly in the gray ahead. Night came earlier in the touchable air of war. The men lay down in their ditches, they built stone shields before them on the flat ground, they moved the protecting mounds of sandy earth from the north sides of the trenches to the south. The firing stopped at the completion of darkness. The little winds of chill came along the ground. The water bearers filled the canteens. The dead were discovered in their places.

Dead Grass

Velasco would not surrender the city; he asked for a forty-eight-hour truce to attend to his wounded and bury his dead. He asked for food for his troops and for the civilians who suffered in the besieged city. Villa refused; his dead were burned or buried, his wounded were cared for in the white-enameled railroad cars, the civilians would be eating again soon; he needed nothing, not time, certainly not time.

Reed

The courthouse of Gómez Palacio had been arranged in a formal way. General Urbina sat as president of the court martial. The room was closed in by the wooden shutters, cooled and darkened; no more than sticks of light entered, no more than whispers of war could be heard through the thick wood and the adobe walls. General José Carrillo stood in the center of the room. His uniform was buttoned to the chin. He had asked permission on the way to the trial to wash his face and wet down his hair. His eyes were clear. A gold watch dangled from a chain that ran through the sixth buttonhole of his uniform coat.

The room was severe, the faces of the generals were serious; Carrillo had refused an order, he had not moved his troops forward at the command of the Chief General of the Division of the North.

"They were shelling us," Carrillo said. "We were facing machine guns across an open space. I needed artillery support. I would have lost the brigade, the entire brigade. I couldn't send all those men to die. They're from my town, gentlemen; some are my cousins, some are my relatives by marriage. I couldn't send them to die, surely to die. It's true, they would all have died, every one."

"You knew it was an order from General Villa," Urbina said. He leaned forward, his skin was the darkest of any man in the room, his hair fell over one eye, the boyish hair, the Mexican hair.

"Yes." Carrillo's legs were thin. The wrist bones showed at the ends of his sleeves. His fingers hung like wisks.

Urbina slapped the flat of his hand on the table. He sat back, satisfied. "Up against the wall," he said. There was no pleasure in his face; he had not laughed for a long time. His eyes were yellowing; cat's curves were coming into the shape of his eyes.

Villa entered the courtroom. Everyone stood. "Go on," he said, "go on with the trial."

The members of the court martial sat down, except for the prisoner and General Aguirre Benavides. The general leaned on the table in a lawyer's stance. He was a small man, his thick round spectacles did not hide the bold crossing of his eyes. "If it please the court," he said, "the question is whether this man did not obey an order because he was a coward or a traitor—even that is possible, although I doubt it—or because he was a true patriot who risked this court martial because he did what he thought was best for the revolution. I submit that this court, composed of men who are now actively

[*483*]

engaged in fighting the enemy, is not fit to judge fairly and without prejudice the case of General Carrillo. The very idea of justice that we are fighting for is sullied by our trial of this man in these circumstances. I urge the court to suspend this trial until a later date or to send this man to Chihuahua where he can have a fair trial now."

Urbina agreed to send Carrillo to Chihuahua. "Let him be shot there. We can't afford to waste ammunition here."

As the prisoner was being led out, Villa reached into the aisle and put a hand on his shoulder to stop him. "You owe your life to Dr. Raschbaum."

Carrillo looked puzzled. He was unable to speak, his eyes were tearful, so relieved was he.

"I'm a calmer man because of him. Before I started his treatments I would have shot you myself. Now, who knows? Maybe in Chihuahua they give medals to cowards."

"It wasn't cowardice, sir."

"The men who died on La Pila weren't cowards," Villa said. He looked over Carrillo, eyeing him all the way up from his boots. Villa's eyes reddened, sweat came out on his forehead. He spat in Carrillo's face.

Ocelot

There was no food in the city. The refugees came out; the women were draped in shawls, carrying their children, leading their children; they walked through the lines of fire as if they did not know, as if they did not care. Whatever was valuable to them they carried in blankets slung across their backs or piled on their heads. They made burros of themselves, they carried their lives in panniers. The soldiers in the line would not share their food or water, they sent the refugees back, north, across the river to the trains.

Villa was in the center of the line. The refugees went around him. He could not see their faces; their heads were bent, their backs were curled; they went forward, yet they had no forwardness; they passed and passed; all the colors of them were without light; they moved with the speed of grief.

"They're eating the dogs in the city," Angeles said. "It's the last stage."

"The men in the line say they hear children crying all day," Urbina said. "We have to be quick now."

"I never saw so many wounded," Dr. Villarreal said. "My hospital is a charnel house. My heart is sick."

Eight hundred fresh troops arrived from Chihuahua, sent by Governor Chao. Villa ordered them into battle at eight o'clock. There were no open spaces now, no great charges to make, no terrific blows to give. At Coyote Dam four hundred men were wounded in two hours. In the city the fighting went from house to house. Every wall was a trench, every house had to be destroyed with dynamite or artillery. The Orozquistas were old soldiers now, fighting from all the advantages, lying on rooftops, always seeming to come from behind the little knots of young men who had just come glorious and innocent to the revolution. There were wounded men to carry out for every house that fell. Yet the brigades moved deeper into the city. At ten o'clock, the lights of the city went out. A terrible fire rose in the center of the city. The revolutionaries did not know what it was. The fire was like a torch, without smoke.

In the dining room of the house Urbina had taken for himself in Gómez Palacio, three generals sat in the light of candles and counted the wounded, counted the dead. The numbers were given to them by Luisito. "Twenty percent," he said. "One out of five. Too many. An army can win a battle and still be defeated. It's worse for Velasco, much worse; I estimate 40 percent, maybe more. Overall, for both sides about 30 percent, one in three. One in three! Oh, my God!"

Urbina had destroyed the room: the dour Spanish paintings framed in gilt and darkenings were cast in a broken pile, replaced by revolutionary flags and paintings of women greater than the corsets that defined their middles; dirty dishes were piled on the sideboard, glued with yesterday's sauces; the pale oak dining table was pocked at all its edges by the cuts of spurs; and the floor was thick with the wastes of soldiers' meals.

General Angeles cleared a place around his chair before he sat down, pushing the debris away with the tip of his sword, sweeping it with the sides of his boots. He sat stiffly, dressed in his blue uniform, a formal officer in the broken light of a disarray of candles.

"You take a town and you need candles," Urbina said, "take them from a church; those bastards always have boxes of candles. Wine and candles, that's all they're good for."

"I told Fierro to start the electricity," Villa said. "He says a shell hit the power plant. I don't know what's wrong." His voice was weary. The sentences were interrupted by long yawns, the sound of mucus trilling. There were swellings under his eyes, outlined by dark rings. "The city is a slaughterhouse," he said.

"We're losing too many," Urbina said.

"Total war," Angeles said.

Villa answered with a slow nodding. "There are dead children in the streets."

"The responsibility makes danger weigh tenfold on the mind of the chief," Angeles said. "Clausewitz tells us that."

[485]

"Fuck Clausewitz! My boys are dying in the streets. I'm sick of it," Urbina said.

"Velasco won't surrender," Villa said. "His heart is broken, he can't surrender now, but he would give us the town—if we gave him a way, he would abandon the town."

"And what would we have won?" Angeles asked.

"Torreón."

"No! We would have won nothing; all we would have done is to have put the battle off until another time. All the lives would have been wasted here, all the blood would have been spilled for nothing. Finish him here."

"Not here," Villa said. "The cost is too high. We'll do it in another place. I won't ask so many more to die. We'll give him the road to Saltillo."

"Listen to what Clausewitz said: 'There is hardly any celebrated exercise in war which was not achieved by endless exertion, pains and privations; and as here the weakness of the physical and moral man is ever disposed to yield, only an immense force of will, which manifests itself in perseverance admired by present and future generations, can conduct us to our goal.' "

"Clausewitz is an animal," Villa said. "All Europeans are animals in war, rich men sending the poor to die for them. We're not animals, we don't just whip our troops and watch them die, we speak to them, we know their names; we're human beings." He called for Luisito. The secretary came the third time his name was called. He was not wearing his eyeglasses, he had been weeping. "Calm yourself, man; and do this for me right away: get word to Robles to open the road to Saltillo. If Velasco wants to run, we'll give him the path."

Eagle

The night axe came to Villa in his sleep and awakened him with a wailing that shook his eyes. He lay in his bed until the sweat cooled on him, and then he dressed himself and went out into the camp. Sentries challenged him, and he answered as any soldier would; he did not say his name, he did not wear the slouch hat the soldiers recognized, he did not wear the blue general's uniform with the gold buttons sewn tight by Juana Torres.

He felt a discomfort in his ears, as if a storm were coming.

A mountain woman, sitting beside a small fire, holding a coughing child to her breast, asked him, "Do you know the time?"

"I saw the Morning Star."

She put a piece of green pine on the fire and held the child over the aromatic smoke. "My son was born on Two Water; he has a weakness in his chest. A storm is coming. I'm afraid it will take his breath away."

"Build a tent over him."

"It won't be enough; the spiders are hiding."

"Where is your man?"

"Over there on La Pila. He was with Maclovio Herrera."

"How are you living?"

She shrugged. The fumes of the burning pine had cleared the boy's throat and nose for the moment. She held him to her breast again. "When this battle is over, I'll go home. We had a cow and four sheep. I left them with my mother."

"The revolution gives land to widows of soldiers."

"Yes, I've heard. But no one gives the widows plows or horses to pull the plows or seed to put in the ground."

He found money in his pocket, a thickness of paper money—he did not know how much. He gave the money to her.

"I knew you were Pancho Villa. Your eyes are exactly as they say."

"How is that?"

"Take back the money. I'm afraid of you." She held the folded paper up to him.

He turned away sharply and walked a few hurried steps. As he continued through the camp, he saw that the women were awake, restless, as if they all knew the spiders were hiding. Some lay on their backs, looking up at the sky, most lay curled in their blankets; the only sign of wakefulness was the reflection of their eyes. Villa crouched beside them to ask why they were awake. Some said they feared a storm, others feared fire, more said they were awakened by their dreams.

Villa watched the day from a distance, he circled over the day, he kept his gaze on Velasco, studying him by the patterns of his troops, comparing him to the battle for La Pila, measuring him against what Angeles knew. Temptations entered him: if he waited for Velasco on the road to Saltillo . . . if he laid back and let starvation do its work . . . if he poisoned the water. He saw the children dead.

The storm came from the west, a brown cloud advancing, as if the mountains themselves were moving on Torreón. The people took down their umbrellas and tents of blankets, they abandoned the tops of the railroad cars, they gathered in the lees of houses, hills, railroad cars, ammunition crates, whatever was solid and could endure the wind. The horses cried out in fear, standing against the halter ropes, piteously comprehending; the cowboys led them in close against hillsides and secured them. People crowded into the houses of Gómez Palacio, they filed into the great iron roundhouse, they loaded themselves into boxcars.

Quiet lay on Torreón; there were neither birds nor insects in the air, the spiders and ants hid themselves in the earth; the fear of the horses and the shouts of cowboys flashed in the stillness. Luisito brought Villa a pair of goggles with a rubber strap. They stood together quietly, looking at the brown west, listening to the rash voice of the storm.

Wind. The surface of the earth was hurled on the air, blinding, spikes, cuts, all points and edges. The wind was a roar of tiny woundings; it took everything, it attacked everything, it stole the breath of every living thing. The first shells were unheard in the storm. In the waverings of the wind the pounding became known. Velasco was bombarding the revolutionaries everywhere along the line, seeking them in their huddlings. The roundhouse was hit, houses burst, giving themselves to the wind, trench walls were turned to fleeing dust. On the left Velasco's cavalry charged, became disorganized in the storm, and turned back into the city, leaving horses and men behind, lost, wandering until they found their own lines or the revolutionary rifles picked them out of the brown cloud.

Villa called Luisito. "It's the same as La Pila," he said. "Tell your brother, tell Herrera and Robles. Give them room, give them the Saltillo road."

"And if you're wrong?" Angeles asked.

"Use the railroad guns. Drive him out."

"Heavy artillery doesn't last long. It has the failings of swarthy women: you get an enormous charge, but not for very long," Angeles said, making the joke he had made to his students of Chapultepec, the teacher speaking rote. "The size of the charge wears out the metal on the inside of the barrel. The guns lose their range and accuracy very quickly. After a while, they're nothing but big tubes with no firepower."

"Drive them out."

"We may need those guns later."

"Use them now."

The railroad guns set fires in the city, and the wind lifted the flames from building to building. The fires shone through the dust, red soft circles, dusky summer suns. Velasco's artillery ceased firing with the darkening of evening. The wind slowed. Through the paling dust the fires took ragged shapes; the smoke leaned upward. An hour later the rifle fire stopped. On the east wing Herrera, Robles, and Aguirre Benavides moved their brigades into the city, going cautiously, each house a step.

Villa walked down to the edge of the Nazas with Angeles, Urbina, Luisito, and José Rodríguez. The wind had become a breeze, the river ran smoothly, lowering; summer neared. A sergeant came out of the darkness bringing cups of cinnamon chocolate. "We could have destroyed him," Angeles said.

"To know your limitations is not to give up," Villa answered.

"A bird in hand . . ."

[*488*]

"A tiger by the tail."

"You can't catch fish without getting your breeches wet."

"I am also an admirer of Cervantes," Villa said, "so I know that God suffers the wicked, but not forever." He walked upriver to stand by himself and watch the moonlight on the water. He thought of nothing, he looked for fish in the water; there were sometimes trout, even that far downriver. When the people began to come out from between the houses near the river bank, he knew that Velasco had abandoned Torreón. He went back down to where the others stood. "There will be no looting and no drunkenness. We'll be fathers to virtue and fathers-in-law to vice."

He told Luisito to send a telegram to Carranza. "Tell him we have won the city. Say we lost fifteen hundred wounded and five hundred dead. Say the Federals lost twice as many."

"There were more," Luisito said.

"I have no pride in that."

Vulture

Music was not permitted. They rode to the slow rhythm of the drums. The revolutionary dead lay on the sidewalks in rows. Music was not permitted. None.

The dead were buried, the starving were fed, the light was put into the wires, the city of Torreón rested, nothing was left of war but destruction.

Motion

"They slaughtered the Maderistas in San Pedro. They did it because it was Madero's home, because he had the school there. But there is justice in the end, Tomasito. Follow Velasco to San Pedro, hold him there, and when our boys are rested and ready, we'll destroy Velasco in Panchito's town. Tell Raúl. Take him with you. Put the knife in his hand."

Flint Knife

Fierro had collected the catzopines on the day they entered the town. Some had been killed, all that survived were herded into the vault of the Laguna Bank. They remained there in that confined place, without room to lie down, without food, given water once a day, crowded, fouling themselves, like animals in the last pen of a slaughterhouse. Fierro told them the order of the General in Chief: they had forty-eight hours to leave Mexico.

The catzopines replied with tears and slithering, they asked everyone to defend them, they used their old friendships, their old powers, the color of their eyes, the narrowness of their noses, the raw pink of their skin. The Americans had pleaded for them, the English had pleaded for them. Neither Villa nor Carranza would change the order. "But Spain is the Mother Country," the American, Carothers, had said to Villa.

And Villa had replied: "No, sir, you are mistaken. Mexico is the mother; we are the children of a raped mother. Haven't you heard us saying that? It's the name of our race."

"This thing you're doing is barbarous," Carothers said.

"The Spaniards came here and killed us and it was not barbarous, the French came here and killed us and it was not barbarous, your people took away half of our country and it was not barbarous; it is only barbarous when our race defends itself. If you want to let them cross the border, I'll send them tomorrow; otherwise, I'll kill them all, even the women and children."

"I don't believe you'd do that."

"There are seven hundred locked up in the bank, Mr. Carothers. Are you a gambler?"

Rain

Villa brought the catzopines out of the vault to be fed before they were loaded into ammunition wagons and driven north to the border. They were weak and dazed, they stank of their own excrement, but none had died.

The young children went first through the food line, they stood with their spoons and bowls of food, they did not eat. The American said to Villa: "Do you expect my government to support a revolution that does this to children?"

"Does what?"

"Those children are too weak to eat."

Villa pointed to the men and women coming through the food line. "Now, you'll see, Carothers. They'll feed the children. You know why? Because there has always been someone to feed these wellborn babes. They are three and four and even five years old and they don't know how to feed themselves. There has always been a maid to put the food in their mouths. One of our women fed them so the wellborn wouldn't have to trouble themselves lifting the spoon. When she was finished, she got to eat the scraps that were left in the bowl. And if there was too much, they beat her for not coaxing the child to eat more. That's what my sisters did: they were servants to babies, they took orders from children." He watched the children sitting with their mothers, eating now that the spoons were put into their mouths. "I should have put them up against the wall," he said. "All of them, even the children."

Other men had taken her, officers in his army: generals, colonels, majors, whoever would give her money, whoever would endure her laughter, her aftermath of derision. They whispered to him: not Otilia Meraz, not a whore like her for the General in Chief.

She painted her face, she showed the fleshy beginnings of her bosom. Her perfume caused Villa to lose his breath. Everywhere she moved her hips in promises. Men watched her, she invited them, her glance was always intimate. When he was with her, she bit and tore his skin with her teeth and fingernails. She licked the blood that came from the small wounds.

He beat her, he cursed her for what she could have been, for the warmth of her body squandered and the beauty of her face wasted. She laughed, saying the names of other men, speaking lists to him.

In the streets of the fallen city the general swaggered for the sake of his used woman, because of her, in spite of all those who had climbed her. He walked with her past tumbled houses. They saw widows and the still-expectant eyes of newly orphaned children. They saw children staring into the next moment. She touched the children and set the men to leering. The women did not complain; they thought of food and how to shelter their children from the night.

When Otilia lay beside him in his bed, he often pulled the sheets away and looked at her brown skin, the earthen shadows in lamplight, rich and dark as the gifts of rivers. He wondered that her breasts were dry and her hips were empty. She was an oiled woman, not sweet, but promising access. She eluded him.

He deserted her there in Torreón. She sucked the end of her finger, withdrawing it from her mouth slowly, wetting her lips. She laughed. "You weren't the first, and you surely won't be the last," she said; but he was beyond hearing.

BOOK THREE

I am feared. I am dreaded.
My captive is covered with feathers.

Song of Uitznauac Iáotl
Florentine Codex Book II

1

The Zapatistas are gone to Aguascalientes to the Convention, Luisito said. How softly they go! All but Soto y Gama; well fed on bitterness, he shrieks: socialism, anarchy. I trust him.

I do not.

How long since Torreón! From this mountain it seems so far behind us.

Eight months.

What is the history of this town?

In 1546 it was discovered by one Juan de Tolosa that La Bufa was a veritable mountain of silver. But it was not until 1557 that a method was discovered for separating the silver in a productive manner. From that moment on, New Spain began to supply great amounts of silver, though of relatively low grade, to the Mother Country.

Angeles showed his genius here.

You sent your men in waves, General, you assaulted the Federals.

And for that Carranza crippled my army: he refused to send me coal for my trains, he refused to send me the ammunition he imported at Tampico. He cares nothing for the revolution, he cares nothing for Mexico, he wanted only to be the first to enter the Capital. I do not understand; what can be done?

It is done, sir.

His General Obregón marched into the Capital while I was left in the north with my crippled army, while I was left to sell cotton and cattle and whatever could be gathered from the mines; all of that for a few carloads of coal and some crates of ammunition. Obregón marched into the capital with his Yaquis playing their little drums, terrifying the people. They killed men in the streets and imprisoned every man who believed in giving the land back to the people. I should have killed Obregón in Chihuahua. I should have killed him when we went to see Maytorena in Sonora. You opposed that, Luisito; explain yourself to me again.

Nothing motivates me but my love for Mexico, sir.

Why did we have a revolution and make those mountains of bodies in the streets of Torreón and Zacatecas? Why did we kill so many that morn-

[495]

ing at Paredón? I thought it was for the land, Luisito, that's what I thought. Let me tell you my dreams, even though you've already written them down: a school for every two hundred and fifty children, elections in every town, land to the widows and orphans, land to everyone who wants it, no more land for any man than what he can work. It was seemly to have broken Huerta's army here at Zacatecas, a pleasure of history to have sent him into exile from this place. And now what? They are starving in the streets of the Capital and the land has not been divided in any of the states. Nothing has been given back but the few small parcels I returned in Chihuahua and the hectares returned by Blanco and Zapata.

He was so generous to me in Parral. What friends we were! It did not seem serious then. If Carranza was allied with the unions and I was more concerned for the farmers, what difference did it make? How could that have destroyed my best division?

When Maclovio told me he would desert if I split with Carranza, I lay awake a whole night, I wept, I could not eat. My friend, a true revolutionary, and he spoke of me in that way, he accused me of reaction and cowardice, he dared me to come back to Parral. You heard him, everyone knew; if it had not been known, if only it had not been known, I would have left him there, I would have tried to heal him, as once he had healed me. But there was no choice, comrade, none; I had to send the troops.

Maclovio defeated, routed; oh, man! the tears that ran from my eyes; and yet I wanted him defeated, I sent Raúl to destroy him.

What does he want, that old man, combing his goat's beard with his fingers and drinking chocolate, that perfumed old man?

He made you a General of the Division, the highest rank.

First he promoted Obregón and Pablo González; and for what? How had they earned such rewards? Obregón took the easy route down the West Coast; and Pablo, poor Pablo has never won a battle. He made them Generals of the Division and he ignored me; after Torreón and Paredón and Saltillo and San Pedro de las Colonias and Zacatecas he would not promote me. Is that just? Can such a man be trusted to lead a nation? My promotion was arranged by Obregón, and he did it out of fear. Pablo González! I'm waiting for him. Pablito, the general who has never won a battle, is Carranza's balance weight. How long would it take us to defeat him? A day? What part of a day? We are the greatest soldiers since the Aztecs. There has never been a division like ours. Send a message to González, tell him I'll meet him anywhere: invite him here to Guadalupe, tell him about the silver just behind us in La Bufa, or see if he wants to invite us south. Anywhere he wants to meet us, anywhere; I would consider it a gift.

It would be civil war.

Where can I go, Luisito? What does he want of me? If he would resign,

I would resign; I told the Convention, I swore, I stood there in the theater and wept and swore that I would abide by their decisions. I wrote my name on the flag. What more?

Do you remember in Torreón when I resigned? He was so helpful then, he asked my generals to elect a man in my place. He was so democratic, he would not appoint a chief for my division. How his face must have trembled when they refused; it should have shattered him. And then Maclovio called him a son of a bitch on the telegraph. Maclovio. I cannot keep up with the times. Should I trust anyone? I watch you, even you, even now I'm watching you.

Send the message to General González, Luisito.

It will be the beginning of a civil war.

Is there any choice?

Generals don't die in war.

You're becoming a brave man, Mr. Aguirre Benavides. Don't think I haven't noticed the change. It's good, it's very good. A general should surround himself with brave men, he should hear everything, all the arguments, before he decides.

When the convention is over and I am no longer a general and there is no more war, what will there be left for me to decide? I'll tell my wife to cook fish instead of meat for dinner. I'll give her an order to cook fish. "Make fresh fish," I'll say. "Let the fish pass in review after they've been cleaned."

You have a wife, a daughter, family, friends; you'll be very busy, sir.

Can you see the hills of Zacatecas, the way they make an aisle for the sun? What an advantage it is in war to hold hills like that! Huerta gave the advantage to one of his best. Carranza knew that; yet he sent me to Saltillo and he gave Zacatecas to Panfilo Natera. Poor Natera, the Federals sent him home bloody. Then Carranza asked me to send him another five thousand men to die on the slopes of those hills. We were right to go ourselves, Luisito; I have never doubted that, never. Angeles went like a good soldier, even after Carranza had taken away his post as Under Secretary of War. I saw him after the shell exploded in the gunner's hands and his own men lost their nerve. I saw him picking up the shells himself and carrying them to the breeches. And Carranza said he was disloyal. How can I see Carranza in the Eagle Chair?

When I went to the Morelos Theater and I spoke to the Convention, I told them I was a man without culture, I excused myself. They understood. You will also have to understand: I'm worried about the land; I don't want to see another Lerdo's Law used to take the land away from the people, and I don't want to see them lose the land for lack of money to buy seed and a few animals, either. When the Convention is over, we should try to start another bank for the poor. Carranza stopped us in Chihuahua, but he won't be able to do that after the Convention. If we can't print a few million pesos, we'll ask the Convention to do it. There won't be a Carranza to tell us not to print a few million when he prints over a hundred million himself.

That man in Parral, Pedro Alvarado, maybe he would help you to start a bank for the poor. They say he throws his money out the window to them now.

It's true, I've seen him.

Start a bank with him.

He's afraid to make any more money. He doesn't want it.

Then don't charge interest.

Is that possible?

Anything is possible, sir.

I'm not so hopeful anymore. They made me a dreamer with their dreams back in Chihuahua. Madero was a magician in Bustillos. And when I was in prison with Gildardo, I came to think that anything was possible—I learned to read. But now there has been war and war and all I see is another war, and after that. . . . My hope is dimmed. When Wilson sent his troops to Veracruz, he swore to me it was to keep the Germans from delivering arms to Huerta. Why should I have doubted him? He opened the border to us, he refused to recognize the Huerta government. But Carranza saw his advantage in it; he made himself a hero. Was I wrong? Luisito, was I wrong?

Foreign troops landed on Mexican soil.

Luisito, the German ship was just outside the harbor.

Maybe you were too quick to be convinced, sir?

So I'm a reactionary. Do you believe him when he says that Villa and Zapata are reactionaries? Then why did he refuse to come to the Convention? Why does he refuse to subscribe to Zapata's Plan of Ayala? Why does he say that he'll be the one to decide the reforms? And if Wilson is so against the revolution, why is he trying to make peace between me and Carranza? Why should I consider myself at war with the Americans when they're selling us arms? I'm not a traitor, everyone knows that. He should not have said that about me, not if he wanted peace in Mexico, not if he wanted the best for the poor people.

I made all my mistakes early. I should have destroyed him before he became strong, I should never have let him take the Capital. Now he sits there while the rest of us hold a Convention in Aguascalientes. We say that Eulalio Gutiérrez is the interim President, and he disowns the Convention. Then what do we have? War again, war again. There has never been so little corn planted in Mexico in a thousand years. There have never been so few cattle in two hundred years. We starve to make war. I keep selling gold to

Silberberg and buying uniforms on credit from Carusoe. And one day, the Jews in El Paso will lose faith in the revolution and there will be no more uniforms. Then we'll be hungry and naked too, and that's how it will all end: the Spaniards will come back, or the French, or the Americans will truly invade Mexico. They can do it; the Americans are the greatest danger. When I was in El Paso with Obregón and we visited with their General Pershing, I was frightened by the troops he paraded before us: they were so many, and they marched so well, and they had everything an army could ever need. They will invade us if the war goes on; I saw it in Pershing's face.

The world would not permit it.

They know how to deal with the world.

I know now what has to be done, I've known for days. Send a telegraph message to the Convention. Tell them there is only one answer in this world, and that is to put Villa and Carranza up against a wall and shoot them. Villa is ready.

No, sir.

Send it.

General Villa, it's not a reasonable solution.

Why not? Everyone dies, mostly for nothing. I can do more.

Not dead.

I'll dream, I'll be in dreams. Bury me with twigs and jewels and a dog that doesn't bark too much. Put good omens in my pockets.

2

In Tacuba, the generals disagreed: Angeles could find no pleasure in the presence of a delighted army. He refused to listen to the singing, he would not laugh, he turned his back to dancing and the preparations for Villa's entrance into Mexico. "Do it now," he urged Villa. "Cut his supply lines, hunt Carranza down and destroy him there in Veracruz."

"If I could," Villa answered.

"You can, if you do it now. *Now.* Act now before he can bring supplies in at Veracruz, before he can make a machine out of the pieces he has left."

"My lines are too long, it's too far to the border; they could cut me off. You say it's not important, but I know better. I didn't go to school in

France, but I know what a gunfight is: the man who has his back to the wall never dies with a look of surprise on his face. Do you understand me? He cut off our coal after Zacatecas, and we just sat there while he took the Capital. They have a division in Jalisco, they could cut us off at Celaya or even Torreón. Then we'd be left like crippled cows: they'd eat little pieces out of us, they'd pick our bones."

"He has oil at Tampico, the oil gives him money; and he has the port of Veracruz to bring in ammunition and supplies. It won't take him long to build up the divisions again: he can pay them and the Germans will supply them. Why let him get strong? Think strategically, Villa, for God's sake think strategically. There is a rule in war about demoralization and the time it takes to recover from it. You're giving Carranza the time."

"I don't want a knife at my back."

"You'd rather have a cannon at your throat."

"I'm going to see Zapata tomorrow in Xochimilco. I'll ask him to march on Veracruz while I go to Guadalajara and back up north to protect my lines."

"He's a good revolutionary," Angeles said, "but he's not a general. I fought for Madero against him, I know him. Zapata doesn't have an army. You'll see, when the planting season starts, his troops will go home."

"There's time."

"Time is on Carranza's side."

"I need allies."

"Carranza has oil fields and seaports for allies. And all you'll have is a little dandy in a big hat. Be realistic, Villa. Zapata thinks his best general is his brother, and no one has ever seen that idiot sober. He has an army of farmers who take their orders from the seasons and the weather. The man has no munitions and no access to munitions. He has never fought a major battle, and you're expecting him to defeat Obregón."

"What battles has Obregón won? The battle to kiss Carranza's ass!"

"Don't underestimate him."

"I know the grapes on my vine, brother; Zapata has an army of farmers, he leads the meek, and those are the best and most trustworthy soldiers: The revolution is for them and they're for the revolution; there's reason to trust them."

"You're changed," Angeles said. "I don't know what changed you, but I see a different man here. Carranza insulted you, he rebelled against the Convention, he made a horror of Mexico, and yet you don't seem to be angry. Maybe Herr Doktor did too good a job."

"I sat for a long time at Zacatecas."

"And did you go to sleep there?"

"I thought a lot. One day I tried to remember all the names of all the men who died in this revolution. I tried to remember in the same way that I used to remember all the orders for threads and needles and pots and pans. I remembered and remembered, I said names for a whole day, and when I woke up the next morning I was thinking about Liviana and my daughter and I knew I had forgotten my own brother-in-law's name. That makes me a poor general, wouldn't you say? Didn't you tell me not to get too close to my troops so that it won't hurt me when I have to send them into battle? Felipe, I'm getting tired of being a general. I don't want to make any mistakes."

"What happened to your anger?"

"I'm getting older now. I'm thinking about being forty years old. Now I think about why we made a revolution. We didn't do anything good yet, Felipe, not one thing, and the revolution has been going on for almost four years. I want to finish it now, I don't want to make any mistakes."

"That's a rule, you know: when you're afraid to make mistakes, you make the worst mistakes. It always happens that way; you're doing it now."

"So we have a choice, a decision to make: whether it should be my mistake or yours. Well, I think of you like a brother, Felipe; my rich, educated brother from France, my brother whose hair is getting thin from worrying so much. Let it be my mistake."

"Yes, sir." Angeles struck the pose of a cadet. But he saw no light of laughter in Villa's face. He laughed at himself alone. "Whenever we disagree," he said, "I think of my three horses: Ney is obedient, Madero has great heart, and I've yet to be able to ride the one I call Pancho Villa."

It was an army beyond the dreams of Ahuitzotl or Axayacatl or Motecuhzoma Ilhuicamina or Cuauhtémoc the hero. For eight hours the army marched in the streets of Mexico. In the beginning were General Villa and General Zapata and all their generals around them and Villa's Golden Ones following on their pale horses, the young ones, the fine young ones who carried two rifles and wore great hats the color of gold. How the streets were filled! All soldiers in the center and the people of the city lining the way along the street now called Francisco I. Madero and down the great Paseo de la Reforma all the way to the Presidential Palace, where Eulalio Gutiérrez stood on a balcony waving to the citizens. It was a glorious day, an invincible army. Francisco Villa was dressed in his blue-and-gold uniform of a General of the Division, and beside him, riding on a horse decorated to parade in rosettes and tassels, was Emiliano Zapata, the sober man in bejeweled trousers and a deerskin jacket colored with scrolls and braid. The crowds cheered and the bands played: there were the marches written for Tierra Blanca and Zacatecas, the National Anthem, and because it pleased the Chief of the Army of the National Revolutionary Convention, the

[*501*]

horses pranced and the children in the streets applauded to the gaiety of "Jesusita in Chihuahua." The war was over, the parade said, there would be no more murder in the capital, no more artillery fire in the streets; there would be coal for the stoves, the parade said; there would be corn and milk and bread and one kind of money and one kind alone, the sun-colored face of Francisco Villa said. The people in the streets cheered when they saw him; they said to their children that they had seen the Saviour of the Poor.

They celebrated in the Presidential Palace at the end of the parade, all the generals in their harsh finery walking in the long marmoreal halls, all the generals, loudly, penetrating the draperies, a din and a crowd, blue cloth and deerskin, gold, gold braid and silver buttons, swords from Spain, hats, caps, and cloth helmets, touching everything with their hardened hands. The photographers followed them, carrying their tripods and cameras and black sheets, ready to set up their flash-powder hods: General, general! Over here! Sit here! Stand up! General, general, remember me? Just one picture. And Luisito between the generals and the photographers, saying the importance of it, scurrying and pleading, complaining that the afternoon was getting out of order.

The photographers persuaded the generals to sit and stand in rows beside and behind the Eagle Chair. Villa offered the chair to Zapata, who offered it to him. They were allies now, sworn in Xochimilco; they had agreed to executions, even to the deaths of some of the men who had sat beside them in the schoolhouse, dining on country food and listening to speeches while the band played outside in the hall. They bowed to each other, making comedy of the chair; they served up the chair to each other, like waiters in a French restaurant. Even Zapata laughed.

Finally, Villa sat in the chair. While the photographers made their preparations, Eufemio Zapata stood beside him, a little drunk and with his clothes in disarray. His brother motioned to him with a glance to move away—he did not want him in the photograph. Eufemio spoke to Villa, ignoring his brother. "You know I was the first Conventionist to be in this fucking Frenchified palace after Obregón the beanfarter pulled out. And the one thing I wanted was to destroy the presidential seat. Comrade, I thought we'd had enough trouble from sons of bitches who thought they could have power over us because they sat in some special seat. So I started looking. I went to every room and then I went to every room over again, looking for the presidential seat. Well, I couldn't find the fucking thing. I looked all day for it, a whole day, a whole fucking, drunken day. And you know what, Pancho? I saw that chair you're sitting in fifty times. I would have made it into firewood and gold buttons, but I didn't know that was the seat. You see, I didn't know that the seat of power was a chair; I'm a horseman, a general of the cavalry; I thought about it, and to me the seat of power had to be a saddle."

Villa sprawled with laughter. The hods exploded light. General Zapata looked beyond the cameras, disapproving of his brother. The others attempted to remain serious. Zapata's son, standing beside him, laughed, and Fierro could not hold back a smile. Eufemio rocked in staggers, like a pile of heavy timbers about to fall. "Hey, Villa," he said, "if I had known, you wouldn't be resting your ass on the seat of power now, your ass would be hanging out in the fresh air, like laundry." Eufemio pulled up an imaginary chair and sat down on it, descending slowly, until he suddenly fell over on his back and sprawled on the floor. Villa laughed, the hods exploded, the laughter was forever.

Without Madero, there was no certainty, there was no center. Gutiérrez was a temporary man, he had no power. The Convention met now in the Capital, making argument, but not law. Zapata had no artillery, Obregón's army had disintegrated, the Division of the North was the army of Mexico, and Villa was its general. He was in Mexico, he wandered there: to see Juan Silveti kill a bull, to eat in restaurants, to seek a house to make his own, to place flowers at the martyr's tomb; he emptied the prisons; he sent an army to Jalisco and another army to the border, he urged the Zapatistas toward Veracruz; he rode in parades of motorcars to dine at long tables in somber halls, and afterward he put on his Texas hat and thick brown sweater and went with his sure friends to walk in the streets of the Capital.

Villa saw her on his way up to Angeles's room in the Hotel Auberge. It was no more than a glimpse, without detail. She had red hair. Or was it blond? She was pale, her skin was fair, the light in the hotel had no sun; he could not be certain. She was behind the wooden counter near the entrance, she was the keeper of the heavy room-keys with the brass bells for handles. It was the sound of the bells that attracted him. He smiled at her as he turned up the stairs; she returned a nod, like a bow, answering a guest.

"There's a good-looking girl at the counter downstairs," he told Angeles. "Very fine hair. Is that why you stay in this little place?"

"She's related to the concierge, a niece or a distant cousin or something. The French petite bourgeoisie, wonderful people; they'll steal the gold out of your teeth while you're eating a pastry."

"Did you see the color of her eyes? I wasn't close enough. I'll bet you they're blue. Around San Juan, where I was born, there were a lot of French; the women had blue eyes and very fine hair."

[503]

Angeles pinched Villa's cheek. "Oh, brave knight, you've found your Dulcinea here in Mexico. But I warn you, sir, this is not a good-hearted tavern wench, but a mean-spirited concierge's cousin with a pen that's sharper than her nose."

"It doesn't matter. She has fine hair. Do you know her name?"

"Dulcinea?"

"I'm not in a mood for teasing."

"Rozinante?" Angeles giggled.

"Why are you always making jokes?"

"What do you want me to do? A revolution is dying. You're making the classic mistake of applying moderation to war. We could drive Carranza and Obregón into the ocean, and instead we're giving them time to consolidate an army. Villa, two German ships docked at Veracruz yesterday. They unloaded munitions, and they'll be going up the coast to Tampico to take on oil in payment. Or maybe Carranza will pay them in gold or Yanqui dollars. God knows, he's collecting enough from the wells."

Villa listened and argued, but he was not interested; he was thinking about the girl. "Felipe," he said, musing, interrupting a sentence he had not heard, "a man in my position, a General in Chief, goes to banquets and ceremonies; he should have a woman of refinement to go with him."

"You have a wife; bring Liviana to Mexico."

"It's not the same; she has a baby."

"Listen to me: I'll call the woman up to the room; you can throw her down on the couch or the floor or the bed, whatever you like, put the sword to her, and have done with it. Enjoy yourself; rape is an old military tradition, like keeping your boots shined. I'll call her up now, you can get it over with, and we'll go to Veracruz."

"I tell my boys that rape is just like looting. Isn't that so? Instead of looting a house or a store, you loot a woman."

"You know I oppose rape."

"Then why did you say that?"

"This ridiculous romance you're imagining."

"What's her name?"

"Marie."

"Marie what?"

"I don't ask clerks their family names."

"Well, I'll have to find out, because I might marry her."

"Don't make a fool of yourself."

"If I love her, it won't be foolish," Villa said. He answered Angeles's stare with a slow, serious nodding. "Maybe you've already tried with her. Maybe you're jealous of me, Felipe. It's possible."

"Mother of God! The revolution is in danger and we're arguing over the affections of a desk clerk."

Villa went back down to the lobby. The woman was still there behind the counter, now sitting at a small desk, writing numbers in a heavy leather-bound ledger. Her hair was red and blond and very fine; the wisps that escaped the knot at the back of her neck could not be seen except in certain glancing lights. She looked up at him, and he saw that her eyes were blue and her skin was fair—it had not been the light. Her nose was sharp, as Angeles had said, but it was not cruel, it was only another showing of the fineness of her.

"What's your name?"

"Marie Ledoux." She made the French sounds, as if her throat were wetted with sweets.

He pushed his hat back and leaned on the counter, crossing his legs, balancing on the flat of one foot and the toe of the other. Her voice heated his face, he could not speak without wetting his lips. "Your hair is like an angel's glory, a halo; and your voice is softer than a flower. I never saw such beautiful skin until I looked at you. Maria Ledoux, you are the most beautiful woman in Mexico."

"Thank you, sir," she said, as if he had just paid his bill or left a small tip for a favor.

"Maria . . ."

"Marie," she answered, instructing him on where the r was to be made in one's throat.

"Marrie."

"Come now, is it so difficult for the Mexican tongue?"

"Marrie." His mouth was too wet. A drop of spit fell onto the counter. He wiped it off with his sleeve.

She sneered.

"I'll come back, I'll visit you again. This evening."

But he could not go back that evening: Fierro had assassinated a Zapatista journalist, and there was an uproar in the city. Newspapermen came to Villa's hotel, the interim President sent a note of protest, Zapata made a public condemnation of the murder. He sat in his room with Fierro and Luisito and listened to the protests and avoided the newspapermen. Zapata's statement made him laugh. "You see how politics are done," he told Luisito. "When we were in Xochimilco I made agreements with Zapata. I wanted a general who was an Orozquista and I wanted the journalist because of those things he wrote about Madero. He wouldn't give me the general, but the journalist, who was sitting right there in the room, he agreed to. Now he condemns the execution. Politics."

He sat on a small couch, with his back against one arm and his boots resting on the other, he reclined, drinking strawberry-flavored soda water. "What do you think of your friend Zapata now?" he asked Fierro.

"Zapata's full of shit."

"But he's going to Veracruz instead of you; aren't you grateful for that?"

"He'll be lucky to come back alive. Zapata's not a soldier; he's a politician, a dandy. That coat he wears looks like he stole it off a whore. Shit, he's got more silver on his pants than the Bank of Mexico. Don't waste your time on him. If you want to put it to Carranza, let me do it or do it yourself."

"You talk like Angeles."

Fierro drank brandy from a blue glass. "Angeles is right. Zapata's nothing. He sets fire to outhouses and he shoots down cornstalks. He won't get halfway to Veracruz."

Villa sat for a long time with his strawberry soda, sipping again and again from the long bottle. "You can't change my mind," he said. "I made a bargain with Zapata. It's decided."

There was no more argument, the room was quiet; disagreement was there unheard, in the air, like the air. After a long time Villa spoke again to tell Fierro and Luisito to go home. "I want to think about it," he said. "Maybe I'll change my mind." But after they were gone he thought about the woman at the Hotel Auberge, nothing else. He planned to see her again in the morning. He lay awake all night, thinking about her, preparing his words, practicing the sound of her name. The men from the newspapers waited in the lobby of the hotel, but he did not see them. Whenever the telephone rang to say that a new one had arrived, he hung up the receiver without answering.

He dressed in his best blue general's uniform and put French perfume on his face and in his hair and under his arms and across his chest and between his legs before he went to the Hotel Auberge in the morning. Six of his Golden Ones went with him to keep the newspapermen away. He walked through the streets singing and saying her name in the wet, French way. It was a cool day, but he wore his cloth jungle helmet, he wore his only hat that was made in Europe.

She was behind the counter, sitting at the desk, bent over the same ledger and the same pile of bills, writing with the same pen. In the morning light her hair glowed. He stood at the desk to look at her before he spoke. She wore a different dress, more closely fitted to the form of her bosom, revealing the delicacy of her. It was like the dresses he saw at the theater and on the Reforma. "Good morning, miss. How lovely the weather is, how lovely the sun shines on you, how lovely you are."

"Good morning, sir." She did not look up.

[506]

He wondered if she smelled his perfume; he wanted her to see his helmet.
"Do you have a room for me?"

"They're all occupied."

"Marrie."

"I'm very busy now. Please."

"Yes. I only came to ask if you would like a gift from me. Tell me
something you want, anything."

"To be left in peace to do my work."

"Very well, I really came here to see General Angeles."

He went upstairs and found Angeles reading the morning newspapers.
"You smell like a whore," Angeles said for a greeting.

"I think she liked it."

"Who?"

"Marrie Ledoux."

"I thought that was yesterday's infatuation."

Villa went to the window and looked out. He could see all the way to
Popocatepetl. "Mexico is beautiful, Marrie is beautiful. Felipe, you should
see how she dresses! So fashionable! I'm in love with her, in love, in love."

"You're not in love with her; you have a wife and a child; you're married.
She's not beautiful; she has a pinched nose and crooked teeth and she walks
like a plow horse. And don't be impressed with her clothes. Every shop girl
in France is well dressed; that's all French women care about, fashion—that
and money. Mostly money. Yes, money first, always money. Someday, after
this is all over, we'll go to France and you'll see what they're like: stingy,
bitter people, selfish people, ingrown, arrogant; they perfume their garbage
and never wash anything that can't be seen."

"I love her."

Angeles put down his newspaper. "Don't make a fool of yourself. We
have enough trouble: the papers are full of stories about the works of your
friend, Fierro the Butcher. Gutiérrez, our brilliant interim President, is
complaining. Gonzalez Garza is having trouble in the Convention because
of the assassinations. There's enough trouble, Villa: the people are hungry,
Carranza is making promises, insulting you, threatening you, God only
knows what Zapata is doing. Don't make any more trouble, not for the
Convention and not for yourself. We got a note of protest today from the
Yanquis; Wilson is upset by the executions."

"Speak to her for me, speak in French."

"No."

"It's an order."

"Shoot me."

Villa came away from the window. He approached the small table, where

Angeles sat with his newspapers. "You wouldn't be the first man I shot."

"And I wouldn't be the first man who died for giving good advice."

"Don't force me."

"Let Luisito be your broker."

"Felipe, what's wrong with me? I saw Zapata in Xochimilco. He had two women with him, two women, laughing and laughing, all the time they were laughing. Why does he have two women and Marrie won't even speak to me? She only insults me, she only makes fun of the way I talk."

"Well, you're not Demosthenes."

"Who is he?"

"A man who put pebbles in his mouth when he practiced speaking."

"Should I try that?"

"Worry about Carranza. The problem is Carranza. Do it now or you may live to regret it."

"You hate Carranza more than I do."

"The man is preparing to destroy you. Do what you have to do now, do it while you can."

"I'm going to send Fierro to Guadalajara. I'll clear out the west and the north before I go to Veracruz. Maybe I'll send you to the north, maybe I'll go to the border to see why we aren't getting enough arms and coal. I'll marry Marrie, and then I'll go."

"Do what you like. Leave me out of it."

He sent Luisito to speak to Marie Ledoux, and Luisito came back willing to say only that he had failed. Villa pressed him: "What did you say? How did you ask her?"

"The usual," the little secretary said.

"And what did she say?"

"Not much."

"You're not telling the truth."

"General Villa, there are so many problems: the Convention is torn apart; Gonzalez Garza fights all day and all night with the reactionaries. The trouble with Gutiérrez is getting worse and worse; I don't know what we'll do with him, he even talks about resigning if he can't have control of his army. And there's trouble in Coahuila and in Guadalajara, and Carranza is taking money out of Tampico and buying arms in Veracruz. How much can we think about this woman? She's not even a Mexican."

"Tell her I invite her to the French opera as the guest of the General in Chief of the Army of the Confederation."

Marie Ledoux refused the invitation. Villa did not know what to do next. He walked in the streets with Fierro and Luisito. They were conquerors and prowlers, uncertain of their direction, sometimes recognized, then surrounded by newspaper reporters and women asking favors on behalf of the revolutionary dead, taking a host of beggars and children with them like a curly tail. They carried pistols and innocence into the old quickness of the Capital.

A child said to General Villa: "You want a woman, sir? I can get you a twelve-year-old, beautiful, perfumes her cunt like a French countess. But you have to pay in silver or gold, none of those Villista bilimbiques, and we don't need any bedsheets, either; this woman's already fixed up and waiting for you, sir."

Villa peered down at the child and saw a shadow. He grabbed the child's arm and lifted him into the light. The bone was small in his hand, the flesh around it was no more than a soft string. He held the child in the air with one hand, and with the other he lifted off a torn cap and pushed back the long dirty hair that fell in the child's eyes. "Are you a boy or a girl?" Villa asked, seeing the softness in the child's eyes, the promise of wounding he associated with women.

"Man."

"Pimps are not men."

"Are you the police?"

"No."

"Then put me down or I'll call the police."

"Where is your mother?" The boy struggled, but he had no weight; Villa held him easily.

"Moved away."

"And your father?"

"Who knows?"

"And the girl is your sister?"

The boy did not answer. Villa lifted him high over his head to inspect his feet. They were bare and they had been filthy for a long time. The boy kicked to hide his feet. Villa caught one ankle in his hand. The filth had thickness, pieces of it came off in his fingers, the outer layer of skin crumbled. The boy's body slackened, he began to weep, a soft sound, failing in his throat, as if he were sadly going to sleep. Villa lowered the boy and held him against his chest in a cradling way.

"How old are you?"

"Nine."

"Only nine."

"Can you read?"

The boy shook his head.

"Have you ever been to school?"

There was no answer. "Poor thing," Villa said, "poor thing. I'm going to send you to school, I'm going to see to it that you learn to read and write. Maybe you'll be an engineer or a lawyer; you won't be ignorant like some of us. But I can't do it here, kid; I'll have to send you up north. In Chihuahua we have schools for all the children, and we give them milk and meat every day, we give them eggs. I'll send you there. And your sister, if she wants to go."

The boy led them through dark streets. The houses were rooms, they shared walls. There were no gardens in these streets. The ground was dry, but giving, as if there had once been burials in the streets. The children's house was a room. The boy led them to where his sister lay on a bed. She was dressed in a white bedsheet sewn into the pleats of a gown. Her face was tiny, a triangle painted with red greases at the mouth, spotted with red grease on each cheek. Oils and curling irons had made her hair thick. She sprawled, she held herself lewdly. She lifted a cigarette to her mouth. The thumb was missing from her right hand.

"Come in, boys, disport yourselves." She flung her legs open, she made her voice low, like a growl.

The walls of the room were hung with red paper. Incense burned in a shallow bowl beside the bed. "Will you give me a drink of whisky?" she asked. "I like whisky, it loosens me. I'm so small for you big fellows, I've got to be loosened up first. Come on, boys, let me see your money and your cocks."

"How old are you?" Villa asked.

"She had some hairs on her cunt," the boy said, "but she pulled them out."

"Get them out of here," Villa said to Luisito. And to Fierro, "Make up a train, get twenty cars, get thirty cars, find all the orphans and put them on this train to Chihuahua. We'll find a place for them there. I'll build schools for them. Get the train ready now, tonight." He turned to Luisito again. "Clean them up and give them children's clothes. Find shoes for them. And before they leave for the north, sprinkle water on all their faces."

Fierro lifted the girl in one arm and he took the boy's hand. "I have a daughter," he said. "She's almost as old as you are. My daughter sews and she can sing rhymes. Do you know any rhymes? Say them for me. Do you have a doll to play with? You should have a doll. And you must not smoke, little girl; good girls don't smoke and they don't drink whisky." He carried her away, walking through the streets, saying his admonishments, wiping at her lips and cheeks with his handkerchief. Luisito followed him. The boy was not strong and could not walk far. Villa carried him.

Fierro killed the young colonel, David Berlanga. The newspapers said that Berlanga had not been afraid, that his hand had been so steady he had not lost the ash on his cigar even when he was up against the wall, waiting for the executioners to fire. They said the ash was the entire length of the cigar. Fierro said it was not true, but he asked Villa to send him to another part of the country, out of the Capital, to a place where he could be a soldier again. Villa sent him to Guadalajara.

Villa went again to see Marie Ledoux, and again she would not speak to him. "I'm an important man," he told her. "I'm moving into a house now, a house on Liverpool Street, one of the best."

"You're stealing a house, and you'll steal all the furniture to go with it."

"Not me. I oppose looting, rape, all the bad things. I don't steal, Marrie. I don't."

She laughed, two sounds made in her nose.

"You don't believe what you say about me. You'd be afraid to insult me if you believed what you say."

"The French are not frightened of Indians."

"I'll show you the hill where your emperor died. Come out from behind that counter and I'll take you there in a motorcar."

"Go away. I don't want to go anywhere with you."

Dear Francisco,

Our daughter is a big girl now. She lifts her head and looks around. She is very healthy and she weighs more every day. You would be very happy in your heart when you see her. Her head is round now after the giving of light. Her cheeks are round too. She is a beautiful baby girl. She will be a beautiful woman with eyes like yours. We miss you. She would like you to hold her. I would like you to hold me too. When I read what General Obregón is saying about you to the newspapers I think how ungrateful he is for the hospitality of our house we showed him when he was here in Chihuahua. Perhaps you were right when you wanted to shoot him for his Carrancista doings. I was like the rest and said you shouldn't but I was not right I think now and I should have listened to you as we all should have listened to you. My father is not well because of his feet that keep him from moving around and give him pains in his knees and his hips. His legs are getting so thin. My mother is good to him. She helps him. My aunts help him. But God knows a person is not healthy who does not walk around and live like people should in their lives. I see them getting old. It can be seen in their faces but more in their hands and their skin and the knuckles and joints of their hands. Gray hair may deceive you but wrinkles never lie. And knuckles and joints the same. You brother Antonio is running the business which is going well and making money to feed us all and all the families in the compound.

[*511*]

He helped me fix up the windows where the wind was blowing in so much cold air this early part of winter. I miss you my husband who could do the same work better because you have experience as a stonemason. In the cold weather I dress up our daughter in blankets and take her out to the patio to be in the sun. With all the blankets wrapped around her she looks like a flower that didn't open yet. Your sister is still too quiet and I always wonder what can be done for her to make her a happy woman. I think sometimes in a dream that she will meet a knight or a prince who will kiss her and she will suddenly change and become happy and marry him. She is a pretty woman and it is always sad to think of her not marrying and living happily. She is good too I can see in her eyes as everyone else can but no one knows what to do for her. When will you be coming home again? I would like to hear about the capital and what the women are now wearing. The trains of children to go to our schools arrived here and everyone went to greet the poor orphans and give them food and make them welcome. It is such a good thing you have done by paying attention to the aims of the revolution regarding education and land distribution too but everyone is still wondering when you will be able to start up the bank for the poor who need your help even after they get land. Well I miss you and I love you and I and your daughter would like to see you again as soon as possible even if we have to come on the long train trip to the capital which I have not seen since we went to visit the late President.

> I send you a thousand ardent kisses,
> *Yours,*
> *Josefina Liviana*

The birth of a child blunts a woman and makes her soft; she falls from girlhood, a milky heaviness weighs her down. Little drops of sweat would come from under her breasts in summer, she would sway, she would have fallen upon herself.

She was shared, the letter said.

When she lay back, the breasts would spread, they would lie sleeping upon the bed of her ribs. He thought of the press of her against him.

She gave sugar candy to the child. The child shouted for the glee the sweetness made, and it hid in the soft folds of its mother's skirt. The sun was bright on the whitewashed houses and the light gray stones that rose in high steps from the street. There was dust. She cradled the child. Her bosom accepted the form.

At night, she listened for the sound of the child's breathing from the cradle—awakening, awakening, always to listen, to heed with her stroking hands and the milk of her breasts. The child cried, she did not know why. She sat in a deep chair to nurse the child. She was careful not to let the engulfing possibility of her breast steal the breath of the suckling child, she sat up very straight; her back ached, her shoulders were weary and sore. She tied a shawl across her back and shoulders and knotted a kerchief around her neck.

She ate to make milk, fattening and slowing herself; the milk was held in a sponge of flesh. Her hair was tied behind in a roll she could not remember; strands fell long over her forehead, over her cheeks; she blew the strands back, aiming with the shape of her lower lip. She needed sleep, she lived and could not live by the child's hungers, she lost her true form, she became mother only.

War terrified her. She watched the days and the grass and the colors of the evening sky, thinking always of rain, corn, and the child sleeping, the child lying in her lap, the child at its suckling. Nevermore was she disagreeable in the things of the world. She ate, she softened herself; there was no taking of her, she was given. She worried, she sought warmth; her eyes were deepening and dark. He saw the downward curl of her fingers and toes, the thickening of the toenails that would grasp the earth; he knew that after the softness came the bone. He loved her, he did not want her.

There was another woman, one dressed in blue and flowers, one whose hair fell over her forehead in bangs, one who wore a hat of red leather. He invited her to dance with him, to visit him in his new house on Liverpool Street; he sent her gifts of flowers, he sent her gifts of gold; he offered her an army, a capital, a nation. "Come with me and walk on the Reforma, see what it is to walk with General Francisco Villa: people will bow, everyone will know you, everyone, you will be known." And she attended to her leather-bound ledger and her bills and her keys with their reminders of bells.

Arrest her, lock her in a room in that French hotel; she has insulted the revolution, the Convention, the nation. If there are no empty rooms, make one empty. Leave her in the room with guards posted on the door, tear out the telephone wires and board up the windows. Give her food and water, but nothing more. Do not speak to her, let her wait for me, let her become hungry to talk to me.

Luisito put her in the room next to Felipe Angeles and posted four of the Golden Ones at her door. She was not to come out, no one was to be permitted to enter but General Villa. Marie Ledoux was a prisoner, an enemy of the revolution. They were to be firm with her, but not cruel; no one was to touch her—orders from General Villa.

While Fierro was defeated in Guadalajara and Gutiérrez said he would resign if order was not restored to the Capital and the Minister of Education fled to Washington and Angeles prepared to go north to begin his campaign in Coahuila and Zapata prepared his army to attack Puebla on the road to Veracruz.

The concierge made a contest of the arrest: she went to the newspapers and consulates, she complained to the Convention, to anyone who would listen, even to passersby on the street in front of the Hotel Auberge. She said it was rape, she implied that Villa had brought slavery back to Mexico. He is a Negro, she said, out to turn the tables on the whites. The main protest came from the French, who said that the kidnapping of a French citizen could lead to action by the French military forces. The English said it was another incident like the killing of William Benton; Argentina, Brazil, and Chile began an informal investigation with promises to revive the ABC Commission; the Americans sent Carothers to make inquiries.

Give me time, Villa told Luisito; all I want is to talk to her. She needs a few days of loneliness, she needs to understand that a man doesn't permit insults, she needs to learn respect for our race.

You're starting an international incident. Carranza will use it.

Tell the protesters that this is Mexico.

Please, General Villa, I beg you; we're making a mistake.

Villa said he would go to see Marie Ledoux that day and release her before morning.

You won't touch her, Luisito said.

Oh, man, stop biting me. I want to marry the woman. Would I rape a woman I want to marry? Would I rape any woman? You're talking to Pancho Villa. After all this time, don't you know me?

She could tell lies.

Then it makes no difference what I do.

Luisito clapped his hands to the sides of his head and nodded with woe. When he took his hands away, the earpieces of his spectacles were bent.

He walked through the lines of his Golden Ones who stood guard over the Hotel Auberge. They saluted him, all the fine young men in the brilliant hats and the tight trousers some said had been taken from dead rurales. He went by the counter in the lobby, passing the concierge and her curses, laughing at her, telling the Golden Ones by his laughter that she was not to be punished. Now, now, he told himself, running up the stairs to the room where she waited, now she is ready, softened, like a bride.

The room where Angeles had lived was now the headquarters for the men who guarded Marie Ledoux. They sat on the couches, smoking or resting in half-sleep. At the table Angeles had used to read his newspapers and eat his meals of coffee and French pastry rolls five young soldiers played a game of cards. Villa dismissed them all, even the two who stood beside the door to her room.

"Has there been a trial?" one of the Golden Ones asked.

"I think she's going to join the revolution," Villa answered.

The soldier made the sign of intercourse and gave a little cheer.

The room was filled with flowers. Marie Ledoux wore her blue plumage, her flowery blue plumage, and her red leather hat. She posed for him; her arms were open, like a woman dancing.

"Have you been happy here?"

She whirled, speaking in French.

"The flowers become you," he said.

She lifted a marigold from a basket and tore off the petals, scattering them on the floor.

"Marry me."

"I would hire you for my gardener."

"Marrie, don't make me angry. I could keep you here forever. I could do anything I want with you."

"Don't you think I expect that? I know you and your kind. We have our criminals in France too. And we have our pigs. But in France we use pigs to hunt truffles and in Mexico you make them generals."

He removed a basket of flowers from the seat of a chair and sat down to think about her. She posed before him. Her mouth was painted red. What was the perfume of her and what was the perfume of the flowers? The room was soaked in sweet odors. He would have opened the windows, but they were nailed shut and covered with boards. He would have opened them for air, for light; the yellow electric light marred the pink of her skin, it turned her hair to thick strands leaning toward orange.

"Why did you come to Mexico?"

"To make money. I am like an explorer who goes among the savages to hunt for gold."

"Were you poor in France?"

"I wanted more."

"I could give you money. If you were my wife, I would give you a gold mine and you could keep everything that came out of it. Is that why you came to Mexico?"

"I didn't come to marry an Indian."

"In the town where I was born there were many French people, the district was settled by them. Look at my hair, you can see by the color of it, by the way it curls; my hair is red and not straight." He bent his head to show her his hair.

"I bet your mother's hair was straight and black." She let out a long laugh through the narrowness of her nose.

Villa reached for his revolver, aborting the gesture in the act, turning it into a slap on his thigh. She saw the movement, the work of will in the changing, and it quieted her. Marie backed away, looking behind her for a place to sit. She pushed aside a basket of flowers and sat in a narrow space against the arm of a couch. Her knees were together, she was suddenly prim —her chin was lifted.

"I would like to instruct you in Mexico, Marrie. If you took off your shoes, I would take you to green fields, I would show you grasslands and fig trees, gardens of oranges, mountains where there are beds of pine needles that go on for miles and miles, all so soft, all the way up from the desert to the snow. I would do that."

"You really aren't an ugly man. I understand that now. I was unfair to you. That was my fault. But you were at fault too, my dear general: you hurried me, you invaded me as if I were a town on your way to the Capital. That's not what women want. Whisper to women, don't order them to love you. Give a woman time. I didn't know you, how could I have known you? Did you expect me to marry your army or your uniform or what I read in the newspapers?"

"But I wanted to marry you from the first time I saw you."

"You were impatient. Have you never heard of courting?"

"Will you marry me now?"

"You didn't hear a word I said, did you?"

"Don't make fun of me. I have a bad temper, I have rages, everyone knows I have rages."

"You see! You're threatening me again, besieging me. That's what turns me away from you. Perhaps in time I could learn to live with your bad manners, your country speech, the cheap perfume you put on your hair. Perhaps. I don't know; we're from different worlds—not France and Mexico, the city and the country. Perhaps. But the threats, the war you make on me, I could never live with that, never. Compared to you I'm weak, but I don't want to be afraid."

"I'm not threatening you. You're free to go now. I only had you arrested so I could talk to you, so you would listen to me. Last night, I thought of standing outside your door and singing to you the way we used to do in the country."

"I wish you had."

"I will. Tonight."

"It's too late now."

"I love you, Marrie. What can I do?"

"In time, perhaps in time . . ."

"I have no time. I have trouble. Zapata took Puebla, but he won't go on. Gutiérrez is making proclamations against me; he threatens to abandon the city; I have to keep the interim President here under guard. My brother is not sending the arms we asked for. Fierro is defeated in Jalisco, Carranza is getting stronger. I have no time, Marrie, I have only troubles."

"And a wife."

"From a long time ago."

"When your troubles are over, when you have time, when you no longer have a wife, when I know you, then perhaps—only perhaps." She took a flower from the basket and carried it across the room to him. "Keep this," she said. "When you have time, bring it back to me."

She opened the door and walked out of the room. He said nothing. He sat on the hard chair in the soaked air in the flowery room, he sat for a long time with the flower in his hand. Then he threw it on the floor and went out among his troubles.

González Garza came to the house on Liverpool Street in the late morning. He sat with Villa at one end of the long dining table. They ate boiled potatoes and milk. "It's good for you here," Villa said, patting the lower part of his belly. "In a man this is the weakest part, just above where his cock begins. When you're having troubles, you get little flutterings there, you know what I mean?"

"When I have troubles, it's always higher up, in the area of the stomach. But who knows? Every belly is a world."

The table was polished, a long brown mirror. The chairs were delicate, the seats were covered with red silk. The two men were small and their voices were soft in the space of the room.

"You're thinner," Villa said. It had been a long time since they had gone to take Juárez for Madero.

"Age."

"These four years . . . I miss him."

"He would have been forty-one."

"Still young."

Villa sighed. "Instead of him, we have Eulalio Gutiérrez in the Eagle Chair. It's a mistake."

"There'll be elections."

"I trust a man who has a beard."

"You flatter me, I think, but I must tell you in response that the stability of the government is now more important than the man who heads it. We can't afford to lose the support of Wilson. Carothers says Wilson will turn to Carranza if we begin fighting among ourselves; he wants a stable government above all."

Villa cut a brown spot out of a piece of potato and put it on the table beside his plate. "You see that? It's rotten, you have to get rid of it."

"You could have eaten it. That piece wouldn't have bothered you."

"We should be thinking more alike," Villa said, "like brothers, like old soldiers together." He put his spoon on the rejected piece of potato and smashed it.

González Garza touched his napkin to his beard, he dabbed away the intimacy of eating. The president of the Convention spoke: "What I fear most at this moment is the dissolution of the Convention. We are suffering now from factionalism within the Convention, which is Carranza's only ally and his only hope. If you make a move against Gutiérrez, the Convention will come apart: Blanco will desert us and I think we could have problems with Robles and Aguirre Benavides. Zapata would side with you in a move against Gutiérrez, but it would only be temporary; you and he would split apart almost immediately afterward. The end result would be chaos; Carranza could destroy us by chopping away at the pieces."

"Gutiérrez called me a traitor; did you know that? He plans to leave the Capital and set up his government somewhere else; did you know that?"

"We can't afford to let him go."

"That's right," Villa said. He leaned across the corner of the table, smiling. "And I won't let him go, comrade. If you look at the Reforma now, you'll see cavalry in a long line, a line the length of the whole street. The interim President isn't going anywhere and he isn't going to call me a traitor anymore. Fierro is moving two thousand troops into the city now; they'll be going with me to visit our interim President. I have some things to tell him. He doesn't have to listen to me, because I'm only an uncultured man, my voice is soft; but two thousand troops and a regiment of cavalry have a very loud voice."

"You're trying to hold the Convention together."

"If I have to nail Gutiérrez to the front door of the Presidential Palace."

"If you go to see him with such an army, he'll just agree with you and do what he pleases later, after you and the army are gone."

"I know, but what else can I do? Nothing is going right for me. There's trouble everywhere."

"The French woman."

"Her too. I told Luisito to buy the hotel. Then she'll work for me, she'll be like one of my sergeants."

"What difference will that make?"

"Do you have better advice?"

"Enjoy yourself. See the city, go to the theater, eat in good restaurants." He leaned closer and whispered. "Visit the girls, man. Some of the girls here in Mexico are absolutely extraordinary."

"How would you know?"

"Would I send you to a restaurant if I'd never eaten there?"

Villa's face glowed with delight. He slapped the president of the Convention on the back. "Hey, you're all right. You know, brother, I always thought you were a stuffed shirt, one of the wellborn boys, but you're a real Mexican."

"We're revolutionaries together, man, and that's more Mexican than the chile."

"Maybe you should be the interim President."

"Give my regards to the girls."

The night had begun in a theater with laughter and song. He had been applauded, he had stood in swirls of perfume and the sound of silk in graceful movement, the orchestra had played "Adelita" to honor him, the audience had sung the words. After the theater there had been parties of gentle dancing, bowing, white gloves, the lies of politeness. He had said little, knowing that the women laughed at his accent. He had not danced, knowing that the women laughed at his clumsiness, the failings of his left leg. Urbina had stood beside him, describing the dancing women, comparing them to mountain birds. He had nodded toward the wife of the British consul: "Look at her, brother, a vulture that shit her pants." Villa had laughed at the match of the pictures, he had not been able to stop laughing. The room had stopped, he had been made alone in his laughter.

They had left the parties to go in a closed car, in secret, to the Bandit's House, where the music was loud and the women waited in a row of organdy, silk, and tulle, showing the shape of their breasts. He had chosen the woman for the quality of her laughter, for its sound of trills played softly on a piano. He was not gladdened by her. Lying under a canopy, shielded by curtains, beside her in the velvet room, he did not think of her. There was typhoid in the city. Zapata had taken Puebla and freed the Huertistas from the prison there, and all of Villa's complaints to the Zapatistas at the Convention had produced no explanation. And what did Zapata care? He had not been able to take the city without artillery from the Division of the North, and no sooner had he taken Puebla than he had gone home. There was no move toward Veracruz; Angeles had been right. Worse, the Carrancistas were preparing to attack Puebla, and Zapata had left nothing but a small garrison to defend it. U.S. citizens were being killed in the border towns, and Carothers was warning that the complaints of his government would soon turn into threats of intervention. Veracruz again, Veracruz again.

"I saw you in the parade," the woman said.

Something was wrong in Jalisco, perhaps with Fierro, with his staff, with his troops. Holding Guadalajara was not certain. The Division was being spread: Fierro in Jalisco, Angeles in the north, Urbina would have to be sent to Tampico. Fierro was back in the Capital now with two thousand troops who should have been in Jalisco. He needed Fierro here, he needed Fierro

[*519*]

in Jalisco. There was Angeles, chasing Maclovio. How had that come about?

The woman showed herself, she touched him. "Have you ever killed a woman?" she asked.

Gutiérrez was the problem now. How had they ever agreed on him for President? He complained and complained. Now he had published a circular attacking the executions of Huertistas and Carrancistas, he had attacked the chief of his own army. It could not be permitted.

The woman laughed and tossed her head. The thickness of her hair was perfumed.

Order was failing in the Capital: there was not enough food, there was not enough coal, cars crashed in the streets, people were run down, there were drunkards everywhere, prices in the currency exchanges no longer made sense. Why was this city so different from Chihuahua? Why was it even more difficult to manage than the City of Juárez?

"Other men want me," the woman said. "Of all the women here I am the one who is most desired; I choose my men."

What had brought the Japanese to the house on Liverpool Street? Surely the admiral had not come all the way from Japan to flatter a general in Mexico. He spoke of Texas, California, and the ambitions of the United States in the Pacific Ocean. Had he answered the Japanese correctly? Could they provide arms through West Coast seaports? Why had the Japanese officer sailed his ship all the way to Mexico? There were echoes of the race in his eyes and the shape of his face; he looked like an Otomi, an Otomi in disguise. Otomis did not carry swords and wear uniforms. Who had sent him?

The woman's legs were fleshy, rich. She drew them up and spread them, she slapped the inside of her thigh.

Marie Ledoux was most beautiful when she spoke r's. Then her voice was a purring, the promise of a woman in her satisfactions. She was no longer locked in the room, perhaps she would now change her mind. Luisito was arranging to buy the hotel; he had two hundred thousand pesos. When the purchase was completed and the hotel belonged to the revolution, perhaps then. How the French consul had complained! A citizen of the Republic of France was being held against her will: barbaric, illegal, the beginning of an international incident. Had he forgotten the Hill of the Bells? The woman was so beautiful. Her hair was blond, red, fine. Each of her fingers was a reed, whispering to whatever it touched. Her eyes were the endless blue that appears only over wheat fields in autumn; they were a color never seen over mountains or grasslands or fields of corn, a color of Europe, the father's color in a woman's eyes.

"I am a dancer, my laughter is a song, my sighs are the petals of dark red flowers." The woman rolled in the bed; her skin was smoother than the sheets.

In Canatlán they said the French had been the first to farm the land. They had left light brown hair and pale eyes for their history. How else was an Indian woman pleasing to see?

"Are you the quiet one? I thought it was the other one."

Insults from Obregón, Carranza, Herrera, Huerta, and now Gutiérrez. War was coming again, the buglers, the bloody fields, the horses charging, and afterward the wounded; and in the end, the stench of pork and hair fried in kerosene. The French machine guns were so delicate! The slides were always jammed, the springs were always broken; men died hunched over their delicate French guns. The barrels of the Mexican cannon wore wide in a single battle, the shells from Chihuahua were, as Angeles said, as lovely and as varied as snowflakes, unpredictable, impossible to aim; and it seemed not to matter what he said to the factories, how he threatened them, how he rewarded them.

Zapata the quiet one! His women giggled for him. He took what he could and went home. Zapata, Zapata, the lover of the land, did he think he could make an island of land reform? Did he think Anáhuac was Morelos? that the world began there? He came in the door with a peso in his pocket to bargain for the whole store!

"Speak to me. I'm here beside you. Look at me!" She wet her fingertips on her tongue and touched them to her nipples, raising them to shining.

"There's too much in my mind," he said.

She touched a finger to his lips. "Don't say that. When there's too much in your mind, it brings a fever. It can kill you."

Villa laughed. "My little healer. You're right, you're right. My mind is full of dancing. What's your name? My mind is filled with you." He embraced her, he rolled with her in the canopied bed.

Josefina Liviana Aprisco de Villa.

The French woman with the endless blue eyes.

Trophies.

Toys.

He had asked Marrie to permit him to see her feet, if not all of her feet, only her toes, only her toenails. He had asked her to come with him to a field and stand barefoot on plain earth.

Death, dogs, and wind.

Flint.

Black.

[*521*]

3

The train passed through Chihuahua. He thought of her.

There was no time, there were only troubles. He could not think of his daughter's name; all the way to the City of Juárez he tried to think of his daughter's name.

Hipólito took the General to the Club Tivoli. They sat in the reddened light. Waiters carried roast meat to their table; they also brought wine and chocolate. In other rooms women sang and orchestras came and went, playing violins and marimbas; the managers of the gambling tables sang like herbalists in crowded markets; the rooms smelled of cigar smoke and American whisky; everyone spoke English, even the Mexican women who let themselves be half seen in candlelight.

"I don't eat meat," the General said.

"Then we'll eat fish, bass, or huachinango. There is one dish my chef prepares: a bass stuffed with little fish and seafood from the Gulf of California and tiny spices from France, the whole thing baked in wine, surrounded by saffron rice and tomatoes browned with cheese. Would you like that? Would you prefer squab, an omelet, cheeses, an omelet of cheeses, eggs, and herbs?"

"I would like a boiled potato and a bowl of warm milk."

"For the Chief of the Army of the Convention? Doro, we can do better than that. Mexico is not an uncivilized country; the north has changed, we're sophisticated now."

"I have a sick stomach; the change in altitude, the different waters bother me."

Hipólito drank colorless wine. He ate bits of salted fish mixed with egg and onion. "I'll cure you. Tonight, I'll send two women to your bedroom. Did you ever have two women at once? They'll put on little shows for you, they'll teach you pleasures you never imagined."

"You have soft eyes, brother; do men take advantage of you?"

"Isn't the revolution getting its money's worth?" Hipólito took a cigarette from a thin silver case. He tapped both ends of the cigarette on the flat side of the case. A waiter held a lighted match out to him. "What brings us more money than these gambling clubs? What brings us more guns and ammunition than these women? In my way I'm as important to the revolution as any of your generals." He blew out a stream of smoke in the form of a long trumpet. It was like red milk in the colored room.

"I'm bothered by whores," Villa said. "A whore is somebody's sister."

"You always went to whores, Doro. You took me to whores when I was a baby; they had to show me what to do."

The waiter brought a bowl of potatoes in warm milk. He asked the General if he would like a raw egg in the milk. "To give the soup a little body," the waiter said.

"No, no, this is fine, a soldier's meal." Villa took a spoon from his breast pocket, wiped it with a napkin and began to eat. "I'm hungry," he said, "but I have to keep my blood thin. It keeps my anger in control."

Hipólito nodded. He smoked and drank wine. "The whores," he said.

"A whore is a sharecropper: a rich man owns the house she lives in, he takes most of the money she earns by her work, and when she's old and tired and can't work anymore, he kicks her out and puts someone else in her place. She has nothing, a rich man steals her work. We talk about such things in the revolution. Magaña talks about them, others too, mostly Zapatistas. Giving back the land is just the beginning."

"But you take the money from the whores."

The General threw the spoon down into his plate. Milk splashed onto the table. Hipólito touched a napkin to the drops that spilled on his suit. The General made a fist, he squeezed his hand, he made himself tremble with squeezing. "I take money from anyone, even from whores. You know what it's like to be in battle with no ammunition? You know what it's like when their artillery can reach you and your artillery can't reach to the end of your arm? The casings we're filling in Chihuahua aren't any good, they have no range, they're never the same, we can't aim them. To get good artillery you have to buy it, to get good ammunition you have to pay the salesmen, and without it a battle turns into an execution: the boys lay in their holes until the shells drive them out; and the machine guns and the shrapnel, the grenades and the Mausers, they tear them to pieces. Don't tell me about money."

"And don't tell me about whores."

"I saw the railroad yards when I came into the city," the General said. He opened his hand and took up the spoon again. "There's confusion: some cars full of ammunition have been there for weeks, some cars are in the wrong order, the switch engines run around in circles."

A woman came to the table. Her hips swayed, she was made of exaggerations. She posed in the red light. "A gift for you," Hipólito whispered.

[*523*]

"Tell her to go away."

Hipólito signaled to the woman with a turn of his head. She made a pouting face. Her lips were thick, oiled, and swollen, like secret flesh. A feather of blue cloth fell from her shoulder and touched the table. She went to another room.

"You were rude to her," Hipólito said.

"Talk about the trains."

"Do you think it's easy to manage a city? Do you think the war is any help in doing my job? I have to raise money for you. Where do you think the money comes from? Munitions salesmen don't accept the money that comes off your printing presses. They want American currency or gold. Everything falls on my head: the gambling, the railroad yards, and the racetrack, how could I forget the racetrack? The stalls are too small, the track is too hard, the feed is dry, the odds are too low, why don't we have ice for the drinks? Everything falls to me and everything costs money, and we just don't have enough money. I'm doing my best, I'm not having a good time. You get the glory, brother, and I get the bills."

"You wear nice clothes. The French ambassador has a shirt like that, I saw him."

"Well, if it's a crime against the revolution, why don't you have me shot? I'm sure Fierro would . . ."

"Don't fail me, Hipólito. If you fail me, we'll die out there."

There were meetings every day: Scott came across the bridge to meet Villa, Villa went across the bridge to meet Scott. The newspapermen were always there, waiting at the bridge, watching them, following. The generals met in secret, in forts and in the guarded rooms of white wood houses. Carothers was with them, advising, the cautious, heavy arm of Washington. "What are they talking about?" the newspapermen asked Carothers.

He made shrugs, he reminded them that he had been a grocer, he wore the bland face of a man who sold sacks of flour, he questioned the reporters about the tensions in Europe.

Scott said nothing, he pushed the newspapermen aside. He was the biggest man, as big as Villa, bigger in his sheepskin winter coat. There was no humor in the Yanqui general, the yellow-white mustache did not curl in laughter, the pale eyes seemed always to be on guard against some damaging light; he coughed and took medicine from a small brown bottle. He threatened intervention. "Against my wish, against my fondness for the Mexican people, against my hope and Wilson's hope for the success of your government, but we won't permit American citizens to be killed."

"Calles and his reactionaries are finished at Naco," Villa said. "Just give my friend Maytorena a little more time; the border will be calm."

[524]

"Either Maytorena agrees to the cease-fire and signs it or we'll cross the border," Scott said.

"Don't lose Wilson's support." It was always the advice from Carothers.

Villa made himself stone. The telegrams came regularly from Maytorena: another day, another week, a month at most; it's all I ask. He sent messengers to show their eyes in pleading, to describe his patriotism as he could not, to remind Villa of his good support in the days of Villa's weakness; he sent men to beg, to collect his debts.

"I have a book that was given to me by a man in Chihuahua," Villa said. "It shows Mexico and the rest of the world. The maps are all in different colors, the maps are smooth, flat; they don't show the mountains or the rivers or the canyons, they're flatter than the cold desert plains. Then why should the maps be in different colors? What was in the mapmaker's mind when he painted them? I think it's a book of accidents. If a child breaks a pot, he doesn't say that he broke it, he says that it broke itself. Things seem to happen by themselves, and that's how countries are, that's how cities are. It's not necessary for Naco to be on the border, it's an accident, the states broke themselves in that place. Would we go to war because a pot fell from a table? Why should this accident be more important? Let Calles come out of the town and fight us there, let him come into the fields and make the dust fly."

"Calles is hiding in our skirts," Scott said. "I know it and he knows it, but there isn't anything I can do to change the situation: the protection of American citizens comes first."

"The Americans always come first."

"Not to you."

"If I could make war without weapons or ammunition."

"Cheer up," Scott said, slapping at Villa's shoulder. "While Maytorena moves back from Naco, Angeles will be destroying a whole brigade at Saltillo."

"There won't be a battle at Saltillo; they'll meet in another place. But it won't make me happy wherever it is: Maclovio Herrera was my friend, I knew him when we were both very young men. He was a unionist then, he didn't worry about land problems, he didn't care about the land. When Carranza started his negotiations with the House of World Workers, I knew I would lose Herrera to him. There were other problems, but I knew the House would be the difference for Maclovio. Now Angeles is going to finish him. Poor Maclovio, in battle his beard grew and the suffering made his face thin; he looked like Christ. But he got bad advice from his father and his brother, he was ruined, he forgot the names of his friends. At Tierra Blanca, he was my best general; Fierro was the best man, but Maclovio was my best general."

[*525*]

"Don't think of Fierro as a friend," Scott said.

"He's hurting your cause," Carothers said. "The man executes prisoners, he's a savage. You lose a lot of friends, even in high places, the highest places, because of Rodolfo Fierro."

"I trust him."

"I was only advising you," Carothers said.

"Give me a little less advice and a little more ammunition, Mr. Carothers."

The child wept when he touched her. He picked her up in his hands and put her cheek to his and sang to her and told her she was a dove and very beautiful. She screamed. In the reddening of her face he saw the first rage again, the rage against the light. He made a cradle of his arms, he rocked her in his arms. She exhausted herself with screaming.

Liviana took the child from him. She was careless in her intimacy, she sang absently, she rocked the child in unthought rhythms. When she looked up at Villa, she said by the darkness in her eyes that he had been away too long.

"The war," he said.

"Always the war."

"There was a time, Liviana, when your grandfather said you were more like a man, more like a revolutionary than most men. I remember."

"I have a child."

He caressed her face, pushing back a fallen wisp of hair. Her face was so round now. She bent her head to the child when she carried it. "The war is for children; I sent children here to study in our schools. Dear Liviana, the war is not for men."

"I'm a mother."

"You have enough to eat; you have chocolate, you have coffee. Every day you eat eggs and meat and drink milk. In the Capital I saw women whose breasts were dry, I saw the children of women whose milk was like water."

"A mother sees her own child first."

"You lied to me in your letter."

"You expect me to be a saint."

"I expect you to be a good wife."

"And I expect you to be a good father."

The child screamed again. Liviana rocked her. "Look what you've done," she said, "look what you've done. She's a good baby. She never cries, not even when she's wet; I have to feel her to know. Now, with you home, her own father, she screams. Look what you've done! Are you happy? Your daughter screams when she sees you, there is no distribution of land, there is no bank for the poor, there's nothing but war and war and more war. What use is the war?"

"The apple of discord," he said.

He went to visit the schools and the banks and the governor's office and the water purification plant and the slaughterhouse and the military barracks. In the evenings men came to the house on Tenth Street; they ate and sat in the parlor to smoke cigars and plan for the distribution of land and the bank for the poor; they talked about racehorses and bullfighters and airplanes and oil fields in Tampico; they remembered certain battles and certain women; they remembered the dead, speaking their names softly.

Liviana sent other women into the parlor to serve coffee and fruit and cheese. She did not greet the guests, she did not eat with them, she stayed in her bedroom beside her child. After the men left, Villa went into the room and found her sleeping. He awakened her on the second night, and she said, "I need sleep; if I don't sleep, my milk will sour."

He walked under the porticos around the garden. It was cold, the sky was colored by clouds that had lost their rain. He saw the moon, he listened to the conk of his heels on the tiled floor. He thought of Angeles, the defeat of Herrera at Ramos Arizpe. He turned himself in circles, dancing, singing the words. From a window near the kitchen a voice hushed him. He walked again, his left foot ached. Maclovio would die soon. The sisters had died, the garden of herbs was gone. His foot was swollen, he limped, he walked round and round the square of the garden, looking for the place where it ended, where it began.

The message came in the afternoon. Angeles had captured letters from Gutiérrez; the interim President was making arrangements with Carranza, a meeting was planned with Obregón. The letters were put on a train to Torreón for Villa to read them there.

He said goodbye to Liviana, he kissed the sleeping child. "I'm sorry," Liviana said. "Is it because of me that you're leaving?"

"The war, the revolution; it goes on and on. There is always another weed in the garden."

"Gutiérrez?"

"I thought I knew him. After the Convention he asked me to be his general. I thought this was going to be the end of it, but nothing ends so easily, the garden is never free of weeds; I always have to be there or nothing good will grow."

"There's so much killing to grow a garden," Liviana said.

"Yes, that's what has to be done. First you cut down whatever was there, and then you burn it to make the soil rich; and when the garden begins to grow, everything that isn't good has to be killed at its roots."

[*527*]

"And when is the end of it?"

"I don't know."

"Mothers are against wars."

"Our daughter is fat; you can afford to think that way."

Liviana's father came into the room, rolling himself on his chair with wheels. "The train is waiting," he said. "Your lieutenant is outside in the motorcar."

"Your daughter is against the revolution, sir."

Tears came into Liviana's eyes. She turned away. Her father wheeled himself next to her. "Don't you care about getting revenge for what they did to me?"

"I have no other dreams," she said. Her back was bent, her shoulders curled in; she had the thick weight of an old woman.

She walked with Villa to the front door of the house. In the foyer before the door she took his arm and pulled him back to her. "I read in the newspapers about the French woman in Mexico. I forgive you for her. I don't want you to go away thinking I don't forgive you."

"There was nothing to forgive."

"What you thought."

"Liviana, if I thought I was the king of Spain, would you forgive me for the rape of Mexico?"

He said nothing more to her. After the revolution there would be time. In the evenings, after the store was closed, after the work of the farm was done, there would be time to make her laugh, to win her back from the women, to win back her youth. They would plant gardens, grow fruit trees; on summer nights the blossoms of lime trees would make a perfume as thick as rain.

He thought of her on the way to Torreón. He watched the desert passing. The rivers were still low, some were dry. The snow would melt, the rains would come. He thought of gardens.

The letters revealed everything: Gutiérrez had made agreements with three of Villa's generals: Lucio Blanco, Eugenio Aguirre Benavides, and José

Robles. Along with the letters came descriptions of the Villista victory at Ramos Arizpe. The northeast was secure, Angeles was marching on Monterrey; the only problem now was Gutiérrez. There was a chance that Robles, Blanco, Aguirre Benavides, and the others were not really with him, that he was only using their names to seduce Herrera and Villarreal. Villa called in his secretary and told him to write a letter in code to Robles. "Tell him we've captured the letters. Tell him to put Gutiérrez up against the wall."

"They'll say you're another Huerta."

"No. I want you to show the letters to the newspapers. Let everyone know who betrayed the Convention."

The generals met in April in Torreón. The cotton had begun to bloom, the farmers worked as if there had been an end to war. Children swam in the Nazas, the irrigation canals were full. There were fish in the rivers, flowers grew on La Pila, the Division of the North moved through the city in train after train, gathering in the outskirts of Irapuato and Salamanca. Bands of musicians played along the railroad tracks, women climbed aboard the trains; there was a festival in the railroad city of Torreón— Mexico belonged to the Villistas.

Angeles came on crutches, a soured man; the draw of pain had changed his face, it had taken the pad of optimism from his cheeks, it had painted his eyes in shadows. He used the crutches to move from place to place, dragging his smashed leg and the heavy plaster cast. There was always dampness on his forehead now. Streaks of gray had come into his hair. "I'm not much good to you anymore," he said for a greeting.

"It's your head I need, not your leg. I have a thousand cowboys who can ride better than you, and the Tarahumara isn't born who couldn't run faster than you by the time he was five years old. So just sit down there in a comfortable chair and use your head. I'll get you a cigar and a little of your famous French cognac and we'll talk."

"Will you listen to me?"

"It goes without saying."

"You never listened before."

"A horse never fell on your leg before. You see, there's a first time for everything in this life."

Two lieutenants helped Angeles into a soft chair. They lifted his injured leg and put a stool under his foot to make him comfortable. When they changed the position of his leg, his face was marked with white lines in the creases and he squeezed his eyes shut. The lieutenants poured a glass of cognac for him. After the cognac he breathed deeply, keeping his eyes closed. He spoke slowly, without hiding his weariness. "Don't go to Celaya, make Obregón come to you. Stretch his supply lines, harass him, let Zapata cut him off from the east, isolate him. Meanwhile, let Fierro finish up in Jalisco, and Urbina and Chao in Tampico, bring everyone in, the whole army: when he's weak and you're strong, destroy him."

"You came all this way, and in such pain, just to give me bad advice?"

Angeles jerked himself forward. "Damn it, Villa, if you attack Obregón now at Celaya you'll lose the division and the war and the whole damn revolution! He's counting on you to make mistakes. He's counting on the length of your supply lines, he's counting on the stupidity of your brother, he's counting on Urbina and Fierro and Chao and everybody else being a thousand miles away when you need them. Don't go to Celaya; you'll lose everything there."

"Do you remember what Cervantes said about the stone and the pitcher? Well, brother, I'm the stone and he's the pitcher, so it doesn't matter whether I strike him at Celaya or he strikes me in Chihuahua, it's hard luck for Obregón."

"Then you've made up your mind."

"The trains are going through to Irapuato now."

Angeles called for his lieutenants to take him to a place where he could lie down.

"We'll have dinner together," Villa said, "later, when you're rested."

"I'll have soup in my room."

"Is it so bad?"

"Villa, let me try once more. If you lose at Celaya, you lose everything. Everything! Think about it. Obregón won't engage you unless he's sure to win. He's got the unions with him now, he's got German ammunition and German officers. We let him pull his army together, we trusted Zapata, and Zapata went home to raise corn. Villa, if he defeats you at Celaya, the moral force of the victory will be much greater than the actual victory: you've won battle after battle, you're the Centaur of the North, the Lion of the Sierras, the Napoleon of Mexico; even if he outnumbers you the moral effect will be the same. You understand what I mean, we've talked about it before, the moral effect, the moral force, you can replace lost troops and lost weapons, but once the moral force is lost you may never be able to recover it. Think of Borodino; we've talked about it so many times. Napoleon wasn't defeated there. It was actually the Russians who retreated from the field, who abandoned Moscow to him, but the very fact that he left them an army to retreat, that he didn't destroy them there was enough; he lost the moral force at Borodino, his army rotted in Moscow, it was the end for him. Keep that in mind. You're in Napoleon's situation: if you attack Celaya, you have to destroy Obregón; anything less will destroy you. Why take that risk?

Why give him the advantage? Why depend on Zapata, who failed you once, to cut off his supplies? Why go without Fierro and Urbina?"

"He's getting stronger."

"Weaken him. Would you try to kill a bull before the picadors lowered its head?"

"I can't wait."

"Why not? Tell me why you can't wait? Give me a reason."

"A violent storm is soon over."

"Don't hide from me in proverbs; tell me the real reason."

"I'm tired of war and I'm more tired of politics. The longer the war goes on the more I'm betrayed, the more I'm wounded by my friends. If I don't finish soon, I'll be all alone. So I'm going to Celaya to finish it now. I'm going to give them one terrific blow, and then it will all be over and I can go home."

Angeles shook his head in despair. The lieutenants helped him to his feet, gently lowering his leg to the floor. They put the crutches under his arms and walked beside him. As he was leaving, he stopped and swung himself around to look at Villa one last time. "For god's sake," he said.

"Rest yourself," Villa said. "Get well." He sat back in his chair and drank orange-flavored soda from a bottle. There was no kindness to say to Angeles, there was nothing but to wish him well again, to wish for him to be the general of Torreón and Zacatecas again, the general of certainty and laughter. It was the accident that hurt his thinking, the bad luck of it, the pain, the weakening of the spirit that came from walking with crutches and needing two young men to help him in and out of a chair. Bad luck, bad luck for Angeles, but there were other good artillerymen now; Angeles had taught them the tricks of war, even how to use the poor shells that were made in Chihuahua.

It would be sad to go to Celaya without Felipe Angeles, to cheat him of the last great battle of the revolution—he had been so brave at Zacatecas; but it was not good to go into battle with a man who had lost his faith. War is not for a man who doesn't trust his luck. Poor Felipe, missing Celaya, the end of Obregón, the last of the great charges, the last of the glory. After Celaya there would be only skirmishes and surrenders. What generals did Carranza have after Obregón? Fools and drunkards. Traitors. He had German colonels to promote, he had battalions of factory workers, poor pale things.

Celaya, Celaya, he said the word aloud, making the middle of it liquid on his sweet orange tongue. There would never again be a battle like Celaya: the wings of cavalry, the rows of infantry, the artillery deafening the day. After Celaya no one would remember Zacatecas or Torreón or Paredón or

Tierra Blanca, after Celaya there would be no more great battles. There would be bands playing and the bells ringing in the painted churches and officers walking with their women under the porticos. They would pass Irapuato, assemble at Salamanca, and from there move in for the great blow, for the ending at Celaya. He sat with his sweet soda in the empty room and he thought of the glory. It was getting late, the house was quiet, he no longer heard the whistles of the trains moving through the city toward Celaya. He lay down on a cot in the corner of the room and waited for sleep. His boots were too hard at the ankles; he sat up on the side of the bed and kicked and pulled himself out of the boots. He lay down again to wait for sleep. In the darkness the bands were playing, the war was over, all the bells were ringing, the war-stained men were marching in the street, all the soldierly stiffness was gone, they marched in a mob, with their hats gone, thrown away in some earlier cheer, and their packs left behind and their rifles held at every angle; he ordered them to be paid one last time and sent home to vote in the elections and remember the war while they walked the rows of their fields and herded their animals. His mouth was dry. He drank the last of the orange soda and lay back again to wait for sleep. Maria, Marrie, Marria, Marrie Ledoux; Juana, Socorro, Rosita Palacios Meraz. He wrote the orders for the morning in his mind, he made revisions, interrupting himself with old intimacies; he walked in the garden of the house on Tenth Street and he slept in his own bed beside his wife, who smelled of chocolate and onions and barely breathed for listening to the breath of her child.

A band was there in Salamanca to play a greeting to his train. They were all in blue and playing brass and drums. The soldiers shouted and the women cheered; they were so certain. This was the last battle, the end of war. Getting ready was a celebration. In the flat fields the women had already begun to dance.

He looked at them for a while from the window of his car. They wanted him. He was a thing to them, like the paper saints they wore into battle. After the war, would they know him? Would they remember this clamoring in Salamanca? He put on his hat and pushed it back from his forehead, he put on the coat of the suit he had slept in that afternoon, he put the knife and fork and spoon in his pocket, he put on the gunbelt, he put on all the things that had been painted on the paper that was him, and he prepared himself to go outside to them. Should he smile? How should the general's face be on the day before the beginning of the last battle? Would Angeles have been stern or laughing? What had the most moral force? Luisito would have had some advice to disagree with, but he was in Mexico, still negotiating for the Hotel Auberge; and the professor who had become Luisito's replacement was too dry and too thin for laughter.

With the whiskers of Carranza
I'll make a little hatband
To put on the sombrero
Of his daddy, Pancho Villa.

Sing, he told them, still unseen, still secretly watching them through the curtains Juana Torres had sewn. The army of the revolution—did they know they were eight thousand going to meet twelve thousand? Angeles was wrong. If he could see them now, eight thousand singing, he would be dancing on his broken leg.

He went out to them. He sang with them, he danced through the band to the delighted women, he took them in his arms and skimmed the flat ground, dancing them, raising storms of celebration with the winds of their whirling skirts. They kissed him, he kissed them, he embraced them, they perfumed him with the sweat of their gladness. The last one, Pancho! Put it to them! Goodbye to the war! God bless you, Pancho! Oh, what a man! Yes, we'll do it this time, cutie, yes, we will, my dear, this is the last war and the last battle and you are so beautiful I wish I could stay here with you and let the battle take care of itself, but if I don't go, who will harvest Obregón the bean planter's beans? Let's get on with it! I'll dance with you in the plaza of Celaya. Save me that next dance! He whirled them and whirled them, he sang to them until the colonels and the captains came and took him off to where the brigades waited, getting ready for war.

The battle plans were made in the evening, all the details were drawn on maps and written into orders by the secretary-professor. In the morning, Obregón made them the gift of his forward brigade; and the trains that came to rescue that brigade were almost lost to them as well. By evening the Villistas had advanced to the edge of the town; less than a mile of open field separated them from the first houses of Celaya.

The secretary-professor found a little hill and made it into a command post. He took Villa to inspect the position just before dark. They could see the town and beyond it to the groves of mesquite trees, yellow-green, paled by the dust that floated over the dry fields. "We have them," Villa said.

"I envision a great victory," the secretary-professor answered.

"The end of war."

"Culminating in the realization of the aims of the revolution and the implementation of the reforms spelled out in the Plan of Ayala."

"Yes, that too."

"I should say that the rout at El Guaje this morning adumbrated the victory we may expect tomorrow."

"Speak plainly, man; don't teach me now."

"Are you worried at all?"

"No, but I want to get a good night's sleep. Have everything ready in the morning. Find out where the train is that was coming from the border." He started to leave, then he turned around and walked back up the few steps to where the secretary-professor stood with his notebook, making drawings of the places for the telegraph and telephone wires and the latrines and the low barricades that would not be needed. "Tell me, maestro, have they heard the Yaquis yet?"

"Not yet, but tonight we'll be close enough for our boys to hear the drumming."

"That's too bad," Villa said. "I wish they'd heard them before." The secretary-professor answered with a shrug, and Villa shrugged in return; what did it matter? On the way back to his railroad car he did not even think about Celaya; the problems were not here but in Tampico, where Urbina had been stopped again and again, unable to break through to the city or to the oil wells. Urbina had asked for money to buy supplies and ammunition, gold, and he had sent it, but it seemed strange that it should cost so much and take so long to win one small city when Carranza's main army was six hundred miles away. Urbina complained of the dampness. He said his midget suffered too.

Villa moved through the crowd of aides and journalists to his railroad car. He was not comfortable, he missed Luisito, although he felt certain now that Luisito would not be coming back: his brother had deserted, how could Luisito not go with his brother? Luisito, Maclovio, and before them so many others. What was Urbina doing in Tampico? Why did he want so much money? And Triana, a good general, had a relative who was with Obregón in Celaya. Could Triana be trusted? So many. It made his head ache to think of so many traitors. Fierro was safe. And Angeles. Hipólito could be bought; the ammunition had not arrived. Had Hipólito already been bought? He washed his hand over his eyes to clear his mind. What kind of war was this?

The supplicants reached out to him near the steps of the railroad car. "A piece of land, my general, please. I have not eaten for a week, my general, please. Help a widow, sir. Do something for my children; we are Duranguenos, like you, sir. God bless you, I need a hundred pesos to bury my mother, sir." And the journalists asking questions that were the province of colonels: "What's the plan of attack? How many troops do you have? Has the ammunition arrived? What's the news from Tampico? This is your first major battle without Angeles, isn't it? Where's Fierro? Why isn't Zapata with you?"

He pushed his way through them, holding onto the rail, pulling himself up the stairs to the platform of the car. One of his Golden Ones stood beside him on the platform. He used his rifle to bar the journalists and supplicants from mounting the platform. "Well done," Villa said to the soldier, and to the crowd below: "I have work to do. Get yourselves some sleep now, my friends; tomorrow will be a long day."

The inside of the car was dark, lit by only one small kerosene lamp. It smelled of cigar smoke. Someone had been there. A soldier? The cook? The cook did not smoke cigars. A bowl of boiled potatoes and a pitcher of milk had been left on the table. He put his nose into the pitcher and smelled the milk. Had it been sitting too long? There was no freshness in the smell, there was something old, a metallic smell. Soap? The scrubbing brush? He went to his bed and lay down to think about the morning. The orders had been written: the cavalry would be the wings, Triana would be in the center, the artillery would be up close. They would be in the plaza by evening, the war would be over. He heard the bells and the bands. When he closed his eyes he could see the flat-topped trees and the painted churches of Celaya shining in the lights of celebration. He was hungry. There was no more flavored soda, there was no ice cream, there was nothing to soothe him; he feared the milk in the pitcher.

The French woman was lost to him now; the flowery room, the blue tunic, the red hat, the dancer's pose, were beyond his reach, in another city, perhaps in another country. He wanted to go home. This was no battle, this was the dying breath of the war; it could have been left to a colonel. One day, one great blow, and then the celebration; it was the rhythm of war. With Luisito gone and Angeles crippled, there was no one for talking. Not the secretary-professor, the spindly lecturer. He removed his gunbelt and put the gun under his pillow. No light came in through the windows, the camp was quieter now, he heard the night wind touching the wooden sides of the car. Liviana was now a mother, no longer a wife. Juana had been the prettiest, but not so fine as Marrie, and no woman was as mysterious as Socorro, no woman had so many darknesses.

He could not sleep. Perhaps it was the hunger. He got up and took two of the boiled potatoes from the bowl and lay down again to eat them. They were cold in his hand and they had a mealy taste. He could not clear his mouth of the mealiness. The smell of the milk was strong in the room of the car; he did not dare to drink it. He lay with his face to the wall, reading the orders he had written in his mind. He heard soft sounds, scratchings. He went out on the rear platform and looked up at the roof of the car. There was nothing. He went back inside and put his ear to the floor, hoping not to hear the ominous sound of mice. There was nothing. He lay down on the bed again. He heard the sounds, whisperings.

I had never deceived him. A man is privileged to know his own calculations. I had told him why he was not named when he was born, I had told him everything, even the name of the one who set the path of his life, Tlaloc, the Prince of Sad Omens.

The attack proceeded according to his orders, the day went as he had imagined it: the artillery found Obregón's batteries, the cavalry routed Obregón's forward positions, a company of Triana's infantry found a corridor between Obregón's Eighth and Ninth Battalions and ran forward into the center of the city—they rang the bells in the plaza of Celaya. All day Villa watched through his field glasses, waiting for the counterattack by Obregón's cavalry, but no counterattack came; he saw only the flat fields, the houses of the city, the yellow-green groves of mesquite beyond the city; he saw only the dust of his own troops moving forward, displacing the Carrancistas from their shallow trenches. He thought mostly about the taking of the city, how to do it honorably, how to give dignity to the end of this last battle. He called Francisco Escudero up to the hill and told him to write orders for the dignified taking of the plaza of Celaya. "But not too solemn," he told Escudero. "Make a celebration for soldiers, not for lawyers." Escudero smiled and went off to write the orders; he never laughed, he had no laughter.

At the end of the day the Villistas held strong positions all across the face of the city. There was one more field to cross before they entered the dirt lanes between the houses. The generals met in Villa's railroad car. There was no planning to be done; the final thrust into the city was to begin early so that it could be completed before dark. Triana talked about his troops, who still held the plaza, ringing and ringing the bells of the painted churches. Jurado, who fought in the place of Angeles, spoke of the accuracy and regularity of his artillery. The cavalry generals were the loudest; they pounded the table and stomped heavily on the wooden floor when they spoke.

"I looked all day for their cavalry," Villa said. "I made these rings around my eyes from looking through the glasses."

There is no cavalry, the generals said. We destroyed them at El Guaje. There has been no cavalry since yesterday. You passed through the fields of dead horses on your way to the front, you saw them, the carcasses of Maycotte's cavalry, the carcasses of Cesáro Castro's cavalry.

"I saw them," Villa said, "but that could not have been all of them, not all of them. Some of them must have got away."

Some, the generals answered, yes, some: enough to drag the bean planter's hearse through the streets.

Calixto Contreras got up from the table and paced the length of the car. He pulled at his thin mustache, he hung his head. When they asked him why he behaved so strangely on the night before a victory, he began to weep. "The whole damned thing is over now. We're all washed up. We'll take Celaya tomorrow and that will be the end of Obregón and the end of Carranza and the end of us too. Who will think about us when the war is over? The Frenchified generals will take over, the irregulars will go home. I'll be herding cows and selling firewood again. Women won't even look at me anymore; I'll be as good as dead. Worse. What a pity! Because we'll win tomorrow, we'll lose everything."

"Maybe you'll be lucky and you'll be killed tomorrow," Villa said.

"Generals never get killed. When you're a general, your náhual gets angry at you and he only lets you get wounded. Look at these scars I got from Torreón! This one next to my ear looks like an old cunt, it's so deep and red."

"Well, if you can't get women," someone whispered, "maybe you can get some queer to fuck you in the head."

Everyone laughed. Contreras said, "Only a queer would think of that. Who said it? Stand up, whoever said it, you queer. Stand up and I'll shoot your fucking queer heart out." He drew his pistol and waved it in the air, pointing at the roof of the car. He tried to look menacing, but laughter finally overtook him.

"I know what you mean," Villa said, "but I look forward to going home and living a quiet life. I'm older than you, Calixto. I think it's because I'm older."

"Oh, man, don't talk to me that way. When I go home, I'll be a cowboy again. When you go home, you'll be Pancho Villa. They'll be singing songs about you when you're a hundred years old. Who will know Calixto Contreras? Shit, even my mother will be dead by then."

The other generals agreed: it's different for you, Pancho; everyone knows you, everyone knows your name, everyone knows your face.

"And when the assassin comes for me, he'll know my face, but I won't recognize him."

Jurado got up from his place and went around the table to where Villa was sitting. He slapped his hand on Villa's shoulder. "Stop it," he said, "stop talking like a crazy Mexican."

After the generals had gone back to their troops, Villa lay in his bed and tried to sleep. It was over. They were all washed up now, even him. Maybe

[537]

the next President would give them something, as Madero had after they had thrown Díaz out. Maybe. He could not sleep, he lay awake and listened to the rustlings somewhere around the wooden car and sang to himself the words of the songs about Pancho Villa. Adelita. Who had imagined her? Who had imagined her abandoned? The woman soldier, Adelita. He closed his eyes and made himself dream of other women.

The runners came up to the hill early in the morning, asking for ammunition. "It's no matter now," Villa told them, "we'll have the city in a few hours." He sent them back with orders to begin a general attack at nine o'clock.

The artillery fired for ten minutes before the attack. At the end of the barrage, the commanders blew their whistles and the troops went forward, running in the fearful crouch. Then they slowed, they walked, they stopped in the middle of the shining green field of wheat. The machine guns opened fire, the standing men fell, they drowned in the wheat, their arms waved, they called for help, they sank. The officers shouted and blew their whistles. The men turned, but they could not run. The Spaniards who owned the fields around Celaya had opened the floodgates of the irrigation system, the fields were lakes growing wheat, the men stood sinking. Villa ordered them to retreat. But still the men could not run; they died facing their own lines, hundreds died, a thousand died, the mud was soiled beneath them, their blood lay like rust on the wheat. The lucky ones crawled back toward their own trenches. And Villa sent them forward again, and again they died in the mired fields, the green watery fields, the bloody fields.

We were in the center of the plaza, sir, waiting for the ammunition bearers. Celaya was ours, we rang the bells. Did you hear us ringing the bells? We could hardly see the sun; there was a chill in the air under the trees. Oh, my general, we thought the battle was won. Then their bugler played dianas, he played and played, and they came at us from everywhere, from the houses and the streets. They fired through the windows and from the rooftops. It was Hell there in the plaza. We didn't know where to run. We all ran, every man who could use his two feet ran on them. Not many came out alive. I came out. But look at my arm, sir, look what they did to my arm. My fingers are dead, my hand is dead, my right hand. I'm all washed up; I'm alive, but I'm all washed up.

This is my General Estrada's sword, sir, and this is my General Estrada's hat. This case was lying beside him, this money was in his pockets, these papers were in his pockets. I don't know what the papers say; I can't read, sir. The money is wet. I'm sorry, sir. The field was like a swamp; I lost one boot in the mud. He fell in the water, sir; I saw him fall. He was face down in the water. He no sooner fell than I was there to lift him up. I rolled him over and sat him up to get his face out of the water, but I could see in his eyes that he was dead. I'm sorry. He was a good general; everyone who served Agustín Estrada said he was a good general; we were all paid.

Villa, where is the fucking ammunition? Damn your brother, damn your fucking fancy brother!

Villa went down to the trenches to give the troops the strength of the sight of him. The hat was pushed back on his head, he walked upright; the anger showed in his eyes. "We'll go back, kid. Hey, brother, we'll have supper in Celaya tonight. Cross yourself, why not? God's on the side of the Convention. Hold your ground, hold your ground." He touched the men, he took their hands; they called him Slouch Hat and Pancho. Their hands were cold.

It hurts me here, sir. I was shot here in the side and it hurts me here in the chest over my heart. I don't understand why it hurts me here, sir. My lieutenant fell in the water. He was hurt too; I saw him. He lay in the water and then he got up to his hands and knees. He coughed and coughed. I couldn't see where he was hurt; there was mud all over him. His head was down, he was looking at the water and coughing. The bullet went in the top of his head and it exploded him like a grenade. A piece of his head hit me, a piece of my lieutenant's head hit me right here on my shoulder. Mother of God!

The Carrancistas came on the right hand and on the left, galloping out of the mesquite trees, firing as they rode, charging to the bugler's call. The Carrancistas came, thunder and splashing. The horsemen staggered at the Villista lines, they lost their order, the horses milled in dust, in mud. The horses fell, the men fell, the Villistas gutted the horses with machetes and bayonets, the standing horses ran over the fallen men, the wounded horses spilled gray entrails from the baskets of their bellies.

Villa stood between the two wedges of the attack. On the right, Contreras weakened; Maycotte circled around behind him, and Castro's squadrons rode into his trenches in the frontal attack. His fire was divided, his men did not know where to turn; they stumbled, they died; the wall of fire broke and fell, mixing into the cavalry, losing its space on the field; it was no longer a wall, there was no line.

Men retreated in the center too, walking back, then running. Villa sent Miguel Trillo and a squadron of the Golden Ones to hold the center; he sent the rest of his escort to help Contreras on the right.

[539]

There was no one left on the hill with Villa but the secretary-professor and the boy who stood below them on the other side of the slope with the reins of three horses wrapped around his fist. On the field that lay between the city and the hill the Villista lines gave way. First the wings fell back before the cavalry charges; then the center retreated, trying to form another line. The flanks could not hold, the center was afraid; they retreated again; they made a line in the last trench before the artillery and waited there for the Carrancistas to rise toward them again.

The dust and the burnt powder darkened the air, rising and swelling, reaching the hill where Villa stood. He did not need the field glasses now; the battle had reached him, he could smell the errors, he could see the fear. The Carrancistas came like driven rain. His men fell before them like seedlings. The mistake was lodged in his belly, twisting inside him, like a piece of shrapnel or a hollow-nose bullet expanding. He felt the front of his uniform and looked at his hand to see if it was bloody. There was only the thick flesh, the hardened skin. He watched the curling of his hand.

He looked at the secretary-professor, who had been pushed into a crouch by his fear. "Find the bugler. Tell him to sound retreat."

"The line is holding now."

"Find the bugler. Tell him to sound retreat."

The troops ran wildly for the trains. The officers fought and swore and beat them to keep order. Men climbed over each other to board the trains. Those who could not fit into the cars climbed onto the roofs or stuffed themselves into the undercarriages. The trains left with men hanging from the sides, gathered on the ladders like aphids on a leaf, piled onto the roofs. They had come in fifteen trains, they retreated in six. The cavalry followed the trains. They passed the artillery on the way to Irapuato.

Villa called the generals to his railroad car. They crowded into the unkempt room. Only Bracamontes had washed and put on fresh clothes, the others stank of battle. Three were wounded, freshly bandaged. The blood was still wet on the white gauze band that was wrapped around Miguel Trillo's head; one side of his face was swollen and pale under the bandage.

When all the generals were gathered in the car, Villa went to them one by one and embraced them and held them back at arm's length to look into their eyes. He had not washed himself, he had slept only a few hours in three days: a dark red beard had begun to emerge from his face, his eyes were swollen and dark. He stood before the map of Celaya, rubbing his eyes with his fists.

"It's not a defeat," he said. "Battles have stages. Can you remember La Pila? How we suffered there! Here we don't have to climb a hill of rocks,

[*540*]

we don't have to look up at the enemy guns. We'll go back in a week. I'll call the brigades in, I'll get more cartridges and artillery shells, better shells. In a week, we'll go back and destroy Obregón. Then we'll march straight to Veracruz and put Carranza up against a wall.

"I sent a message to Obregón this morning. I told him I would be back in a week with sixty pieces of artillery and twenty thousand men, thirty thousand men to put him between the grinding stones."

"How many did we lose?" Contreras asked.

"Three thousand dead."

"Does Angeles favor going back to Celaya?"

"I offered him command of this army, I did that a long time ago in Chihuahua. He refused."

Carothers came to Irapuato bringing admonitions from his Secretary Bryan: the gold mines and the silver mines belong to foreigners; you can't force them to work, you can only demand that they pay taxes. He argued that Villa's decree that the mines must be worked was illegal. He told of the complaints in Washington.

"I'm fighting a revolutionary war," Villa said. "I need money, my troops have to be paid. We borrow from foreigners, we sign papers; everything we do is legal, my lawyers assure me. About the Chinese I will do nothing. Let them starve, let them die. I don't want Chink blood to infect our race. And the Spaniards! It was the Spaniards who opened the irrigation gates and flooded the fields at Celaya. Mr. Carothers, when I take Celaya, I'm going to kill every Spaniard left alive in the town."

"Even the children?"

Villa did not answer.

"Be reasonable. The Wilson government supports you."

"How? Do you send me ammunition? Only what I can pay for and only when it pleases you. Did you close the port at Veracruz? Did you stop buying oil from the fields at Tampico? No. You threaten me with intervention, you tell me to do this and that, you allow Huerta to live on your Long Island. You were a storekeeper, Mr. Carothers; did you give your goods to people without taking anything in return?"

Carothers shook his head.

"Then why should your government make such demands when it gives so little? And your complaints that people are being killed in the revolution! How could it be otherwise?"

"Don't force Wilson to close the border." Carothers spoke in a whisper, he made himself a conspirator.

"Germans have come to me, Japanese have come to me; they make offers, they don't ask for everything without giving anything."

"Are you threatening us?"

"If an animal has four legs and a tail and it howls like a wolf, is it a wolf?"

The mice brought strange stories back from Celaya: Obregón spent most of his time reading about the war in Europe; he sat at a desk covered with photographs of that war. Sometimes he sat for hours reading and staring at the photographs, refusing to see anyone. The defense of the city seemed to have been left to his German artillery officer, Kloss. The defenses Kloss built were also strange: instead of barricades that could stop a cavalry charge, he ordered the men to dig ditches; and instead of piling stones in front of the ditches to shield the riflemen, he strung barbed wire in a great circle around the outside of the town, as if he could make a wall of wire.

Villa listened to all the reports. He heard madness in them, the tale of a man who mistook the high plains of Mexico for the old fields of Europe. "One cowboy with a rope and a good pony can bring down a mile of wire fence," he said. "And a ditch is good protection against infantry, so we'll use cavalry; but first we'll use artillery to destroy them in their beds."

Villa did not sleep well, his stomach was sour, the doctors told him to drink more milk, and he was tired of milk: "It makes me shit little stones," he said. The doctors conferred and ended with shrugs; it was the only cure. He sent them away.

A mad dog appeared in the camp. It frightened the women, who armed themselves with stones and pieces of wood. The dog was shot six times before it died. Everyone said the dog was a demon sent by Yaqui witches. Villa told his officers to say that it was true, they also believed the dog had been a demon, and then to say how good it was that the demon, which was an ally of the Yaquis, had been killed.

There were only thirty-one pieces of artillery, there were not sixty. The shells Hipólito promised did not arrive. Everything was slow coming from the border, even the trainloads of provisions; the animals could be fed only once a day.

More messages arrived from Secretary Bryan. "It's important that you succeed this time," Carothers said. "There are pressures in Washington, Carranza has the support of the American labor unions."

The House of World Workers sent two more Red Battalions to Celaya.

> *Battle is like a flower;*
> *Take it in your hand.*

On Tuesday morning they marched on Celaya. The attack went on that day and that night and the next day and the next night, without rest, without end. Men hung on the barbed wire, they could not be rescued, the Yaquis would not finish them; the men died in agony, in the way of the new war; they screamed for help from God or man. They lost their courage, they lost their hope; they hung on the barbed wire and were the inglorious flags of the battle.

In the trenches the Yaquis raised up and killed the leaping horses; they opened their bellies with bayonets and machetes; they slaughtered the horses, they cut into their hearts. The dead horses lay like hills behind the trenches. The riders lay beside them, beneath them, mixed with the dead horses. Rats came on the second night of the battle. The silent things of the high plain came to eat the dead. Owls carried pieces of flesh to their secret roostings. The vultures floated above the battlefield, waiting, more patient than timid.

In the sun of the second day since they had died, the corpses swelled with wind and the soured-nut stench of death floated across the fields. The Yaquis lay in their trenches, the wire fences stood, the machine guns looked out from the city across the nakedness of the fields. The Villistas laid siege to Celaya.

The battle went on slowly. Now and then a machine gun rasped, like a yawn. Obregón's artillery fired a few shells, the Villistas answered. The rifles were silent. The day heated, the flies came.

A woman in a red skirt and a white blouse walked past the Villista lines and into the middle of the field. She searched among the bodies there, she went forward in the direction of the Constitutionalist lines. There was no wind. Her skirt lay heavily on her hips. The flies rose at her passing, the flies buzzed and swarmed at the shadow of the woman passing. Her hair was black and thick. She wore huaraches with high leather backs that came over the tops of her ankles. The troops watched the woman, they raised up in their trenches to watch her. She went to the barbed wire fence and walked along the row of poles, looking at the men who hung there. The Yaqui drums sang to her. She came to a place where several men lay together, wrapped in the strands of barbed wire. She separated one man from the group and threw the others down. They made the dust rise. She took one dead man by the arm and dragged him across the field, away from the barbed wire fences, across the slaughtered green wheat. The body made a trail of rising dust. She pulled the dead man as if she were an ox. The body slid over the dead wheat and the smooth dusty field. When she was halfway across the field, she stopped and wiped her face with her forearm. There was one shot, a bark, a Winchester. The woman fell. A man with a blue cross armband ran out into the field to attend the woman. The Winchester fired again. After the crude sound, the man with the blue cross fell. The man and the woman lay still, the flies settled again. There was no wind. The stench grew like a flood.

There was a disturbance south of the city. It was in a thick growth of mesquite trees, obscured by the mesquite trees. The Villistas saw the sun rising from the direction of the trees. The disturbance was reported to General Bracamontes, General Ruíz, and General Contreras. They sent messages to General Villa: scouts had been dispatched to the area, they would keep the General in Chief informed. "Tell me the shape of the dust clouds," Villa demanded of the messengers.

"They're faint clouds, sir. Wide and very faint. Wind. Maybe it's only wind."

Villa shouted for his aides, he screamed for them, giving orders as they arrived: "Tell Jurado and Durón to split the artillery, ten, ten, and ten; protect the flanks, load shrapnel, fuse it short. Tell them it's the cavalry again. Tell the brigades to withdraw to a line west of the city. Abandon the encirclement, pull back, form a line. Get the cavalry behind the line at both flanks. Tell the men to use their bayonets, shoot the horses, bring the horses down first. Send messengers, go yourselves, run, for the sake of the revolution, run!"

The cloud split. Two thick clouds emerged from the mesquite trees. They came racing toward the city. It was too late for the troops to pull back, too late for the artillery to move, too late to form a line. Two brigades were cut off. The Carrancista cavalry grasped them, as in two terrible hands. The machine guns and artillery cut into them. They did not know where to turn; the Carrancistas were everywhere, on all sides. The brigades fired the last of their ammunition, they threw down their weapons, they surrendered, they ran, they died where they stood.

From the distance of the hill, Villa saw the defeat as if it were drawn on a map. The attacks came in thick, dark arrows; the brigades crumbled as if they had been painted away. A Yaqui infantryman broke through the lines and came running toward the hill. He wore nothing but a pair of black-and-white-striped bib overalls cut off above the knee. He ran up the hill in leaps, like a dancer; he floated over the rocks and stubs of cactus. The little drum hung at his side, the Mauser was in his hand. Villa held his pistol at arm's length, aiming. He breathed and let his breath slide out, he breathed again, he saw nothing but the leaping man, he waited, his breath slid out, he breathed again, he saw the man's chest above the squared cloth, the meeting of the bones, the hilly countryside of muscle, he let his breath out slowly, squeezing the trigger. The bullet met the man in the middle of a leap. It was a wall in midair. He stopped, he reached for something, he crumpled there; his empty hands were the last of him to fall.

The fleeing men passed the hill. Their mouths were gaping, their faces were twisted; their eyes were too open, they did not defend their eyes against the dust.

Villa called the secretary-professor over to him. "Listen to me now, Mr. Professor. I want to turn this battle into a trap for them. At El Guaje." He opened a map and spread it on the table of stone at the front of the headquarters area. "We'll move the artillery to here and we'll put the brigades in front of it in two long lines. You see? Like a path, a wide path. They we'll lead them into the artillery, we'll drive them in from behind. The brigades will be the hammer and the artillery will be the anvil. You see?"

"My general, sir, the artillery is lost and the men have no ammunition. I'm sorry, sir."

"All the artillery?"

"Look for yourself, sir."

Villa stood up and looked out over the field. The swarming shape of the defeat was changing: the surrendered men stood in great soft circles, the Carrancista cavalry was forming again to begin the next stage of the attack. Miguel Trillo took his arm and pulled him back from the low wall. Villa looked down at the smaller man. He wore a suit and a vest, he did not look like a soldier. Trillo pulled him across the top of the hill to the far side. A squadron of his Golden Ones waited there, mounted and waiting. Their short Mausers were pointed upward, the butts rested on their thighs.

"Let's go," Trillo said.

Villa and the secretary-professor ran down the hill with him, and the Golden Ones cheered: "Here comes Pancho Villa!"

General Alvaro Obregón dressed himself in cowboy clothes to proclaim the celebration in Celaya. The bands played in the plaza under the flat-topped trees, the city was lighted yellow. The bells rang all night in the Church of Our Lady of Carmen. The women danced and the soldiers could not stop singing. In the fields around the city, the dead were burned. The ashes floated down upon the dancers and the singers and the musicians incessantly playing.

The hero of the battle was Colonel Kloss, who said, "You see, you see, war has changed since Clausewitz wrote his book: The frictions, the impediments, have been overcome by modern weaponry; absolute war is now possible."

In the early morning, the captured Villista officers were marched into a goat pen on the edge of the city. The insult of the goat pen made them surly: they were now the goats, the cuckolds, the bastards. They kicked the goats out of the way, into the sheds at the far corner of the pen. The filth of the pen was terrible; the wounded were afraid to lie down. They waited without food or water in the hot sun, in the filth. The wounded cried for help. No doctors came. A man died screaming. His mouth continued to move after his breath was gone.

Two machine gun crews came in the early afternoon and set up their guns with the barrels poking through the spaces in the fence. Colonel Kloss arrived in an open car. He sat in the rear seat with a major beside him. They stood up in the car to look at the officers in the pen. The major got out of the car and spoke to each of the machine gun crews. There were more than two hundred men inside the goat pen. They demanded water, they demanded doctors for the wounded. Colonel Kloss made a sour face. He nodded to the major, who nodded to the machine gun crews.

They killed all the officers in the goat pen. They left the dead in heaps, one fallen upon the other. The goats came out of the sheds in the late afternoon, they walked over the piles of men, they chewed at shreds of uniforms, they ate the tender parts.

Maclovio Herrera was killed by his own troops. It was an accident of war, the telegraph said.

Eugenio Aguirre Benavides was executed by order of Venustiano Carranza. His brother Luisito hid himself, perhaps in some narrow street in the Capital, perhaps in the United States.

Urbina was defeated at El Ebano. He retired without ever reaching Tampico. His midget, Rafaelito, died of a jungle fever and was buried in a child's coffin.

Villa retreated north to León and took an old house with thick walls and a rich garden for himself there. He gathered his brigades again to make a division, he replaced the artillery that had been lost at Celaya, he executed Dionisio Triana, who had been the first to run away at Celaya, he mourned for the twelve thousand dead, he bought an airplane and hired a pilot, and he sent for Felipe Angeles and for Liviana.

Angeles came to León, a thin and sickly man, walking with a cane, a soured man, speaking of his weakness. Liviana replied by telegraph; she said her daughter was too young and her father was too old, she could not go to León.

The airplane frightened people wherever it passed. They said it was a great dragon in the sky, they said it was the devil himself, surely the shadow was the shadow of the devil passing across the land. And the noise, they said, was the sound that would accompany the quaking, crumbling end of the fifth and final sun.

"It's not a weapon," Angeles said. "It's a bird, use it as a bird, send it over Obregón's camp to give you a bird's-eye view. Use the airplane and you'll never again be surprised by his cavalry. If you had been able to use an airplane at Celaya . . ."

The pilot wore a white silk scarf and a leather hat that covered his head like an Olmec helmet. He protected his eyes with large goggles. When he was not in the airplane, he staked it out in a field, like a horse. The men who passed by the field where the airplane waited looked at the ropes and the stakes and concluded that it was a great bird and very wild. Those who had seen the airplane tied down to its stakes argued that it was not a devil at all; they said it was a gringo bird. A deputation went to the house in which Villa stayed to report the presence of the gringo bird. We do not know, the spokesman said, but we think this may be intervention. Perhaps the gringos have trained these birds.

An automobile is a machine like a horse, an airplane is a machine like a bird.

The pilot said the air was thin over León; he did not think he could fly much higher. No one doubted him; he spoke with authority, he said he had been trained in New Jersey. Everyone knew the pilot was being paid in gold. He made no secret of it.

On clear days the pilot flew his airplane over León. He made it turn and roll over in the air, like a puppy. After a week of exuberance, Villa sent him over Obregón's camp with orders to count the troops and be ready to show the location of them on a map. The pilot saluted and clicked his heels loudly. He was a brisk and serious man. He wore his goggles and his Olmec helmet and his white scarf. His assistant helped him into the airplane, then he turned the twisted blade of the propeller and the airplane engine started.

The airplane ran down the center of a wheat field and rose into the air. Villa and Angeles watched it through field glasses. They saw the airplane go east toward Trinidad and fly in circles over the town. During the third circle, the Constitutionalist riflemen shot at the airplane. It caught fire during the fourth circle and fell out of the sky onto a low hill. The airplane burned very brightly, and at the end it sent up a thin line of black smoke.

"It's too much like shooting quail," Angeles said, and Villa agreed. All the modern young men who had volunteered to learn to fly in airplanes returned to their brigades.

The battle of León lasted forty days. The green flies of June stung the men in the trenches, the heat weakened the horses and the men and dried up the rivers, the lice grew like a plague. In the beginning of the battle the fields smelled of leaf dust and ashes, but the dead soon rotted and the men fought with kerchiefs over their faces to blunt the stench. Villa and Angeles argued over this new kind of war, this war of death and waiting, this filthy war. "It is the kind of war that ends wars," Angeles said. "In this kind of war the patient one wins." Villa said it was a coward's war. They argued. Angeles left León.

An artillery shell destroyed Obregón's right arm. He tried to kill himself, but his pistol was empty and he could not load it with one hand. His shattered arm was amputated and put into a glass jar filled with undertaker's fluid. The hand was preserved in the shape of a fist.

Villa sat in the cool house in León and listened to tales of the rivers drying and the men eaten by rats and green flies. He crawled through the trenches to cheer his troops and afterward he burned his clothes and washed himself in pine smoke and yellow soap. Liviana complained that she had no money, and he answered that there was none to send. Fierro came north from Jalisco with the last of his cavalry, men too weary and too defeated to be of use in war. Lawyers and financiers came to León to make it a city of banquets and music. Trains carried the wounded back to Chihuahua; every day the hospital train left for Chihuahua. Villa sat in his cool house and listened to munitions salesmen and German officers and Mr. Carothers. The revolution twisted itself around him, it wrapped itself in papers; the revolution was like strings of paper, knots of paper; there was no time to know all the words. Only at night, while the salesmen and the lawyers and the foreign officers pleased themselves in the restaurants and the dance halls and the dining rooms, was Villa able to sit quietly, drinking cool myrtle water and studying his maps.

After thirty-seven days in the trenches, Villa could wait no longer. He assembled his cavalry, twelve thousand men, and he told them to be ready to attack in the morning. He led them in a great circle around the Carrancista lines, and while they were dying in the hills of the Otate Mountains, the Carrancistas leaped out of their trenches and overran his lines. Villa retreated to Aguascalientes.

Fierro and Canuto Reyes went to Villa with a plan to suddenly win the war. They found him in the hotel room where he spent much of the day now, studying his maps, falling asleep over them, awakening sour and cramped, going back to the maps, passing the days in the dream-filled edge of sleep, waiting.

"Have you tried the baths?" Fierro asked.

"They'll get your pecker up," Reyes said. "You come out of those baths like a bull from Tepehuanes."

"It saps your strength," Villa said. "I'm always tired now; it must be my stomach. I'm eating meat again to get my strength. The Jew doctor weakened me, he made my blood thin with all those potatoes."

"It's true," Reyes said, "the Jews are worse than the Chinks."

Villa looked up at his cavalry officer; he saw him through the darkening of heavy eyelids. "They say Madero the Incorruptible was a Jew."

"And Our Lord Jesus Christ," Reyes said.

Villa nodded. He rubbed his hand over his eyes. "But Raschbaum was a bad doctor. Our race is different from his, we have different stomachs. It causes a different smell. Did you ever notice when a Chink or a gringo lets gas how different it smells?"

The three men sat around the heavy hewn table in the corner of Villa's room. They leaned their elbows on the maps that were spread across the table. "It's our time now," Fierro said. "Canuto and I are going to make a raid down through the center. We're going to take the towns and destroy the railroad tracks and telegraph wires behind us. We have four thousand good men and every one has a well-fed horse. We'll go right down the center and join up with González Garza in the Capital."

"Four thousand," Villa said. "In this kind of war you need forty thousand. This is a German war."

"Hey, man, you're talking to Rudy Fierro, not to Felipe Angeles. I know how to move, I'm a railroader. Did you forget? All aboard! Highballing! Full steam ahead! I don't walk—I ride. I roll! We'll go through those towns at full steam. Silao, Irapuato, Celaya, Toluca, they'll just be whistle stops for my boys on the way to the Capital."

"No parleys, no prisoners," Reyes said. "Behind us, they won't find anything. We'll go like fire."

"What do you want of me?"

"Ammunition," Fierro said.

"Do you know what I lost at Celaya? Do you know what I lost at León? I won't tell you the numbers, I don't want anyone to know. My friends, I invite you to go to the trains and take whatever you find. I'm waiting for a shipment now from my brother. Waiting. My friends, if Obregón attacked Aguascalientes tomorrow, we would have to throw stones at him. Do you know what my boys are doing out there now around the Calvillo Canyon? They're burying dynamite in the fields so that if Obregón attacks before the trains arrive, we'll have time to run away in good order. That's why I study the maps. If we can't hold Aguascalientes, where will we go? Zacatecas? Torreón? Chihuahua? Should we put our backs to the Bravo and hope the gringos threaten intervention? I'm doing what Felipe said, I'm taking his advice. This time I'll stay in my trenches, this time I'll be the patient one. I'll fight the flies, I'll fight the rats, I'll stay in these trenches until the lice pick us up and carry us out of them. Hipólito will send me the ammunition. It'll be here soon. Meanwhile, take what you can find. Give me some time, let my boys rest."

Fierro embraced Villa before he left. "Watch what you eat," he said. "Remember, a little wine is good for the digestion."

Villa followed the cavalry maneuver on the maps. Fierro and Reyes moved down the center like a sword cut. The towns fell to them: Silao, Irapuato, Celaya. Fierro, the railroader, destroyed the track behind him, he cut off Obregón from his supply centers on the east coast. González Garza was coming out of the Capital with another brigade. Villa drew their positions on the maps. They were so isolated, nothing was near to help them, they had no reserves, the towns behind them fell back to the Carrancistas. He leaned over the maps, he could not stop the tears that blurred his vision. They were not making war; it was a raid, a gesture; Fierro did it for him, to weaken Obregón, to make it possible for him to be defeated in the mountains before Aguascalientes. Somewhere in the high plain Fierro and Reyes would come upon a defended city, somewhere they would suddenly hear the sounds of artillery and machine guns. The horses would turn and plunge crazily in the box canyon of steel-jacketed walls, the dust would rise, floating, swirling, a dust of birds; and the men and the horses screaming, dazed in the sudden canyon, would wet down the dust with blood. The canyon would disappear, the dust would fall down again, the scavengers would come creeping through the pockets of the dead. And then the fire; before the coyotes and the vultures came the fire; before the ants and the flies had eaten, there would be the fire. He wept. He thought of Fierro in the Presidential Palace, he thought of him in his white cowboy hat, he thought of all the liquor Fierro had drunk without ever losing himself, he saw him gallant with women, dancing in his stately way, he saw him at war —the hero and the executioner, the butcher laughing. Every day he studied the maps, knowing that somewhere in one of the black circles that lay beside the blue veins Fierro was dying.

His army of defense burst like a rotten gourd. Obregón had not stayed in his trenches; Aguascalientes was lost in a day.

Villa left a garrison at Zacatecas and moved north to Torreón. The Army of the Convention stayed for six days in Torreón. They paraded through the streets of the city. The bands played in the plaza. Villa met with Carothers, he showed Carothers his army. The news came to Torreón that the Convention had been driven out of the Capital. Carranza announced his victories, he said he controlled seven eighths of Mexico, the war was over and the Lion of the Sierras was once again what he had always been, a bandit, nothing more.

As Villa moved north again to Chihuahua, the news came that Fierro had driven the Carrancistas out of the Capital. He had joined with González Garza and they waited only for Zapata to begin moving east to destroy Carranza in his own bed. But Zapata stayed in Morelos; he said he had no ammunition, he complained against Villa's Agrarian Law, he said politics came before war. Fierro went to Pachuca with six thousand men to meet Pablo González, General Backwards, the general who had never won a battle. He lost everything there. When he turned north toward Chihuahua, Fierro had fewer than a thousand men.

"I saw them throwing flowers at you," Liviana said. "I saw the way the photographers looked at you and the little boys tried to touch you. You're home now, Francisco."

Villa walked in the patio with her. He picked roses from the garden, wrapped a handkerchief around the gathered stems, and gave the flowers to her to hold.

"You weren't here," she said. "I took care of the garden."

He looked down at the garden. The summer was cooling early, the flowers were hurrying to seed. "We have to begin again," he said.

Liviana did not answer. She put her arm in his, she leaned her head against his shoulder. The patio smelled of roses, of fish and onions, of cinnamon and pepper.

"Is your father well?"

"He sleeps."

"And your mother and your aunts?"

"It's the end of summer; they worry about winter now."

"Are you angry?"

"You were away a long time, you had other women. It takes time to become a wife again. I live in a house of women. Valeriana doesn't know her father, my husband isn't familiar to me. I forgot the sound of your step, I never remember how much red is in your hair. Pancho Villa is in the newspapers, a stranger. A general is in my house."

They ate alone in the dining room. "The food is good," he told her. "It's been a long time since I ate well." She said she was pleased, she said she had been waiting for him to come home.

"They're building a tomb for me," he said. "I ordered it."

She laughed.

After dinner, they walked around the garden again. He asked if she knew about the battles, the terrible losses. "I saw them throw flowers at you," she answered. "I laughed when the man with the movie camera stumbled and almost fell down the steps of the palace. I heard the bands playing for you and I heard the people shout your name."

"You're a generous woman, Liviana."

"I'm your wife."

"And what do the other people say?"

"I hear only the cheering."

In their room, in the darkness, with the top shutters open and the breeze blowing comfort over them, he held her hand in his. The skin of her fingers was not soft, she worked; the wife of the Chief of Operations had not weakened. He said to her: "At León the bodies were like garbage in the fields. The dead smell like meat waiting to be made into tallow. The fat rots first. The bellies swell up as if the dead went to banquets. But when they're moved the swelling comes out of them in farts.

"We had trenches in León, we made war like Germans. It was so hot. Those big green flies came. Once when I was in the trenches, I heard a shell coming and I fell down next to a dead man. The flies were all over his face. I couldn't see his skin; it was all green lumps; his face was buzzing—it had little wings everywhere, thin little wings and shiny green bumps. I couldn't move because of the shells coming. I was so close to him, I could see the flies eating, pushing their black mouths into his dead flesh. They rubbed their back legs while they ate. Their bodies were shining like fat green mirrors. The shells kept coming and coming. The flies saw me, they came over and tried to eat my face.

"I was all alone there. Felipe was gone. He argued with me there: he said I should have brought the battle here to Chihuahua, he said I should have waited here for Obregón to come with his artillery to fight in Chihuahua; and he was right, Liviana. I knew he was right, but I couldn't do it. I remembered Torreón after the fight. The old people picked the oats out of the horse droppings and ground them up and cooked them in pans. They couldn't wash the oats before they cooked them; there was no water. I couldn't bring the battle here.

"I couldn't wait there, I didn't have the patience. I was all alone. I asked you to come. It was safe in the city. I asked you to come to León to give me patience.

"Didn't you see the hospital trains arriving here? Didn't you read the newspapers? I had no patience, I made the mistake, worse than the mistakes I made at Celaya. I had no patience.

[552]

"Did your father need you so much? Would Valeriana have been so lonely in this house of women? Thousands died at León."

"You're home now," she said. "Rest yourself, sleep." She kissed his temple, she caressed him, she held on tightly to his hand.

They had washed and perfumed themselves, the roses were sweet in the room, the creases in the bedsheets were still fresh, the cotton was not yet shamed with sweat.

"When you fought in the towns, did you spare the children?"

"We had artillery."

He felt the opening of her hand.

Villa and Fierro sat together on the train to Parral. Fierro talked about the sound of the locomotive, the lack of sand that was causing the wheels to slip. He said the roadbed was not in good condition; it needed work if the trains were to move at full speed. Villa drank orange-flavored soda and watched the dry land passing. There had been almost two months of negotiations with Washington, Huerta was dying in El Paso, Pascual Orozco had been killed by Texas Rangers, the Carrancistas were moving north, town after town was abandoned to them. It had not been easy to raise money; he had become a tax collector, a cattle merchant, a haggler. The munitions salesmen gave him gifts of jeweled pistols and gold rings and failed to deliver the weapons and ammunition he bought from them. He sold the gifts in El Paso and used the money to pay for more munitions that were not delivered. The army was increasing again; there were sixteen thousand, but they demanded payment now, they deserted when the money was late. Gutiérrez was finished, José Robles had gone over to Carranza, Urbina had robbed the revolution, Angeles was in Washington arguing for the Convention.

Near Parral the land was better; it was familiar. He told Fierro where the water was sweet and where the canyons cut through the rising mountains, he pointed to the faint scars that had been the mule drivers' trails.

They saw a young woman riding in a buggy. She sat in the shaded seat.

Two cowboys rode in the front. One carried a rifle; the one who drove the buggy wore two pistols. "I also have a daughter," Fierro said.

Villa looked surprised. He put the soda bottle on the floor between his feet. It tipped over immediately and lay on its round, rocking with the motion of the train. He captured the bottle with his feet and held it still. "What do we talk about?" he asked. Fierro did not answer; he knew he was not expected to answer.

Villa looked out the window. He recognized the ranches, he had been in some of the houses. "Tell me about your daughter," he said. "Where is she?"

"She lives with my wife in Guaymas. I have a new photograph of her carrying a parasol. She's so dark and my wife makes her carry a parasol; that's funny."

"Is she pretty?"

"Was the Mother of Our Lord a virgin?"

They took the horses off the train at Parral and rode over the high divide to Las Nieves. There were sixty of them, the Golden Ones, all that was left of the Golden Ones.

Villa rode beside Fierro. He made jokes about the way the railroader sat a horse, he pointed to the thickness of Fierro's waist, he said he must be getting old.

"It's not fat," Fierro said. "I keep some money in a belt for my daughter. It's heavy. When I feel the weight of it here, it makes me think of her. I don't have anything but my house in Guaymas and the money I carry in this belt. Not like Urbina."

"Once a thief, always a thief."

"Do you think he buried it?"

"Maybe he bought himself from Carranza?"

They approached Urbina's house in the early morning. There were no sentries. They saw the smoke of cooking fires. Half a mile from the house they dismounted and made a picket rope and left the horses there. No one saw them until they entered the courtyard of Urbina's house. Two men who were eating beans out of brown plates drew their pistols, fired once and surrendered. Urbina rushed out of the house. He had a pistol in each hand. There was no direction in him: he fired crazily, shooting into the dirt and over the heads of the oncoming men. He wore a woolen undershirt and blue military trousers. His suspenders hung from his hips. He ran turning from side to side on his stiff legs. A bullet hit him in the arm and knocked him down. "No more," he shouted. "I'm wounded. No more."

The courtyard became quiet. Villa walked through the line of soldiers to the place where Urbina had fallen.

"Panchito, thank God it's you. These fuckers shot me. Look at the way my arm is bleeding. These pricks, these sons of bitches, I'll have them all shot."

"You stole money from the revolution," Villa said. "You betrayed us to Carranza."

"Who says that about me?" Urbina lay on his back; the wound bled in spurts, pumping; his arm was useless; he could not get to his feet. "What son of a bitch says that about Tomás Urbina?"

"I do."

"Help me tie up my arm and I'll explain everything, brother. Jesus God, help me tie up my arm: all the blood is running out."

"I needed your brigade."

"What brigade? Every man had fever, every man had the shits. I lost it all, man: my troops, my health, everything, even my little friend, Rafael. It was bad there, Panchito; the worms were eating up Rafaelito before he died. It was so bad, it ruined me. My fucking hair is turning white, like an old man's. In the name of God, Villa, tie up my arm."

"You still have a face like a boy. How is that possible after what you've done?"

"I wash with the juice from young cunts. How do I know? I don't make my face. Hurry up, please. I'm dying. The blood is pumping out of me." Urbina could not keep his legs still; he climbed the soft dust of the court-yard. "Okay, God save me, I took a few pieces of gold and put them away for my old age. Would you let a comrade, a friend from before the revolution die for a few pieces of gold? Shit! You knew I was a thief. I was always a thief, but I'd never betray you. And, hey, Doro, you're a thief too. Did you forget that?"

"We'll take you to Chihuahua," Villa said. "We'll have a trial."

Villa called a man from the medical unit to bandage Urbina's arm. He squatted in a shaded place in the courtyard, leaning against the adobe wall, to watch the wound being cleaned and pressed with white cotton to stop the bleeding. Urbina moaned and cursed the man who attended him. The bone was broken, splints could not be made until the bleeding was stopped. Urbina called for a real doctor. He asked for a bottle of sotol to help the pain. "Do it right," Urbina demanded. "Be careful, you faggot bastard, you're bandaging the right arm of a general. You fuck me up and I'll have your balls cut off."

Fierro came out of the house and squatted next to Villa in the shaded place. "I didn't find anything," he said, "no papers, no money, nothing but filth. The whole house is filthy, like pigs lived there."

"His mother didn't keep a clean house," Villa said. He looked above the walls at the sky, the autumn blue, the paper white clouds. "The sky is darker at this time of year, the daytime sky is more blue than in the summer. Clear autumn, windy winter."

"What's the use of bandaging him?"

"We'll have a trial in Chihuahua."

"Urbina's a thief and a traitor. We know what we have to do. You said the revolution is like a garden, you said the evil things that grow in the garden have to be killed at the roots. We came here for an execution."

"The rheumatism is bad now; did you see how he walks?"

"If Urbina can betray you, anyone can betray you. We can't have an army without discipline, you said so yourself. An undisciplined army runs away. Didn't that happen to us? Wasn't the true difference between us and the Carrancistas the discipline? How many lives will you give up to save a filthy-mouthed traitor? We should do what we came to do and get out of here."

"Who's safe, Rudy? You're a butcher, an animal. The name they use for you is your true name. Butcher. When will you come to kill me? Butcher, butcher."

"Revolutionary."

"He made a cape for himself out of rabbit skins and deerskins, whatever he could find that was warm. How he hated winter! I never knew a man who was more afraid of the cold. But he didn't run away then; he wrapped himself up in that cape, like a bear, like a bear with a little boy's face. If he didn't run away from the cold . . . I don't understand. Why did he go to Carranza? If he wasn't afraid at La Pila . . . He was always a thief, I know he was always a thief."

"Villa, would you die for the revolution?"

"Yes."

"Urbina will die for the revolution."

"Don't do it for the pleasure."

Fierro stood up. He was out of the shadow, but the brim of his white hat shaded his face. Straight black hair fell from under his hat and lay across his forehead. His eyes were hidden in narrowness; the lids were swollen. "For the revolution," he said.

Villa nodded.

Fierro went to the place where Urbina lay. He motioned to the man who was wrapping gauze around Urbina's wounded arm. "Enough." The man dropped the roll of gauze, stood up slowly and walked to a shaded place. There was dust on his knees. He brushed them clean. Fierro pulled Urbina to his feet. The gauze unrolled, hanging like a faint strip of rag.

Urbina's wounded arm hung like the gauze. The front of his underwear shirt was dark with drying blood and the back was brown with dust; there was dust in his hair. Dark, crumbling clots of blood and dust fell from his

[556]

shirt. His suspenders hung halfway to his knees, his trousers had fallen to his hips; he walked with his thighs pressed together to keep his trousers from falling. Fierro led him out of the courtyard.

Urbina's wife came to the open door of the house. She knelt there, divided in the hard line of the sun and shade, and crossed herself, and called to her husband, and heard no answer. "Mother of God," she said, "Oh, Mother of God." She saw her husband in Fierro's grasp, she knew Fierro, she called to her husband not to go with him. But Urbina did not look around. He stepped on the bottoms of his trouser legs, he tripped; his trousers slid down, a space opened between the bottom of his shirt and his trousers. The skin was dark and smooth, touched with dust. He walked on dry bones, like an old man. Fierro held him upright.

Villa remained in the shaded place, looking up beyond the wall of the courtyard to the sky, the passing clouds, the promises for winter. Urbina's wife called to him, saying his name.

Fierro was gone a long time. He came back leading two horses; one was Villa's.

"Was it quick?" Villa asked.

"He said ugly things."

The reporters stood in the hall of the Juárez Customs House. There were few of them, but they made a crowd of pushing and cigar smoke, of languages and speculations in the loudest voices. They sought the place where Villa would stand, asking his officers, making their demands, complaining all the while of the earliness of the hour and the lack of coffee, the lack of consideration for the press. All of them knew that Angeles and González Garza were in Washington, arguing against recognition of Carranza. All of them knew that Samuel Gompers and his unionists and now all the oil companies and mining companies and the representatives of Argentina, Brasil, and Chile favored Carranza. General Scott and Mr. Carothers favored Villa; Wilson and Bryan favored Villa. Or had they changed? And what did Wall Street say? They pushed and whined and demanded sweetcakes and coffee; there had always been coffee, there had always been sweetcakes; had Villa now forgotten them and what they had done for him?

Villa sat in a hard chair, where he had been all night. Odors of night sweat arose from him; he asked for perfume. Was his jacket English? Was his hat clean? He drank orange soda and sat in the chair. He looked at his watch, he asked the time, he saw his shadow coming back to him. The room was cold, made of tile and narrow lines of sun; he sat in the sunlight, it warmed his back. His secretary came to tell him the newspapermen were waiting; he asked what the telegraph said.

"Nothing," the secretary-professor answered.

"Nothing?"

The news had come from Angeles; desperation, he had said, the recognition of the Carranza government, the closing of the border, the end of money from the United States, the death of the revolution; and there was nothing more he could do, there was nothing more he could demand of the men who controlled the unions or pumped the oil from the fields at Tampico; they knew of Celaya, León, Aguascalientes, Zacatecas, Torreón, Saltillo, Durango, Guadalajara, Pachuca, and the Capital; there is nothing left now but you, there is no hope now but you; speak to them, you are the revolution.

I am an uncultured man, he had answered, without English. They know me as a lion. What can I say to them now? Write something for me.

Speak from the heart, it will go better for us if you speak from the heart.

Yes, he said, now that I've come to this cold room in the Customs House, at eight o'clock on the morning of the eighth, in my English coat and my best hat, with words I've read and the best sayings.

With words you know.

Angeles could not convince them; what can an uneducated man do here in this room of cigar smoke and questions? The faces are rude, the Spanish words elude them, as if they cannot hear; they whisper, asking questions, always asking. But the photographers are not with them. Because there are no horses, there are no dead, there are no bands playing for the picturesque men and unbelieving boys about to die.

The faces are rude, little veins are painted broken on their cheeks, they are unhappy in the morning listening to a man begin with the history of dictators and the lives of those who begin their days before dawn and have never tasted sweetcakes.

A man yawns.

They write on folded paper, but they do not write much and there are so many words: Wilson will recognize his enemy, the one who refused to make peace, the one who has always spoken ill of him, damned his people living in Mexico, starved the citizens of the Capital, favored the execution of prisoners, listened to the Germans, took ammunition from the Germans in return for who knows what promises against Wilson's country. Is it possible that Wilson will make recognition his reward?

Their eyes are dull; it's getting warm in the rooms of the Customs House, they rub their eyes, they are hungry, their bellies rumble.

In the end, they draw back, hearing anger, hearing promises that Wilson's recognition will not end the war, that his heartfelt sympathy is only politics, that he takes his ease in the matter of the hungry, that the cause of liberty will die by his hand. And they are not pleased in the end to know that the Chief of Operations of the Convention does not believe Wilson will recognize Carranza. They are not pleased, they do not understand, they protest contradictions, yet they have few questions, they leave the room hurriedly, talking to each other, but not exchanging the words on their folded papers. The secretary-professor tells them to wait, he will give them all of Villa's words in English, in proper English, he studied in Philadelphia. They will have coffee and sweetcakes and then they will return, they say. Someone will be sent to collect the English words. Soon. Yes. It is most important. Wilson should know, all America should know. Yes. Yes. Good morning, General Villa. Tell the General it was a fine speech. You're right to put your faith in Wilson, General Villa. Can the General document those charges? Will the General go to war against the United States if Wilson recognizes Carranza? Laughter.

A journalist from St. Louis stayed behind, asking for a private interview with the General. "I speak Spanish," he said in English to the secretary-professor. "I believe in the Conventionist cause. And I can promise you that a private interview with General Villa will get more coverage than anything he says in a speech."

"It's possible," the secretary-professor said in English. "I'll ask him." He turned to Villa and translated the request.

Villa walked up close to the journalist and looked in his face to see what kind of man he was. He saw milk and potatoes, but for the eyes, which were small and tight, dark, blemishes in the blandness. "Are you serious?" he asked in Spanish.

"I studying of politician," the journalist answered in Spanish.

"Good, good. Like John Reed."

"I have many to asks for to talk."

"You speak Spanish very well. Where did you learn?"

"I studying in the school. College. Princeton."

"What do you want to know? Ask me questions."

"Why do you have so many husbands?"

"Wives?"

"Yes, wives. Pardon me."

"To avoid sin."

"How this, sir?"

"To make love to a woman who is not your wife is a sin, adultery. True?"

"I want to say so. But, sir, to have much husband is condemned."

"I prefer wives."

"Yes, wives. Pardon me."

"What do you want to know about Wilson and me?"

"If he gives recognition to Carranza on eggs, what goes?"

"We'll have breakfast."

"To breakfast is all?"

"Well, a nice lunch and a little supper too."

"To eat?"

"Exactly."

"No war?"

"On what?"

"On eggs."

"Not at the moment."

"Then you love Wilson. Is it true? Tell him?"

"Tell who? The professor. He knows what I think of Wilson, everyone knows. Didn't I just say so for all the world to hear?"

"And for the women?"

"Chocolate and pretty dresses. Sons and daughters, beans to cook and corn to grind."

"And Carranza?"

"No chocolate, no dresses, nothing. Up against the wall for Carranza."

"I am writing you to say, Mr. General."

"Goodbye, Mr. Journalist. I must go back to the war."

"Pleased to meet you, Mr. General. Thank you very much."

"At your service."

The secretary-professor guided the journalist to the main door of the Customs House. "An impressive man," the journalist said in English.

"We are most appreciative of your interest and understanding, sir. The cause of justice is in your hands."

"Rest assured."

The next day Wilson recognized the Constitutionalist Government of General Venustiano Carranza.

Villa went home to his house in Chihuahua to sit with his anger. He stayed alone under the portico, wrapped in a blanket, while rain fell on the garden, while winter came. For the first day Liviana did not speak to him, nor did she allow their child to play where her voice might disturb him. The house was quiet, the rain fell, the garden browned, the new branches lost their strength, the seasoned wood remained. He looked for meaning in the seasons and the garden's life, but he found nothing. Politics, he thought, is not the natural way of things; he turned his mind to war.

He held the child in his arms on the second day, he spoke to her of rain, he told her how to look at clouds and what to expect of the seasons. The sound of his voice made her sleep. He held her wrapped in a blanket to keep the cold and the dampness away, but he often reached inside to touch her fingers, to hold the soft miniature of her hand. Liviana came to sit beside him, to take the baby for suckling. "Is it over?" she asked.

"I was thinking of a quilt, the way it becomes larger by sewing one square onto the next."

"Do you like the rain? My brother loved the rain. Valeriana sleeps best in the rain. I suppose it's in the blood. She doesn't like summer, she pees so much in summer."

"Chihuahua is next to Sonora and Sonora is next to Durango and Durango is next to Sinaloa. That's the mistake we made, the mistake I made. Angeles told me, he tried to draw a quilt for me. Now there's no other way; I have to begin again."

"For what? Mexico wants a strong man, another Tata Porfirio. No one wants a revolution that ends up in democracy and land reform; it's too much trouble.

"When I was a girl, I believed in democracy. I listened to the Freemasons and the Liberals, I thought Don Abraham was a great man. Oh, Francisco, I was so sure. I married a revolutionary, I saw my grandfather and my brother die, I saw my father lose the use of his feet. For what? We had the Porfiriato, now we'll have the Carranzazo; the people get what they want, which is what they deserve. No one cares for them, because they don't care for themselves. Wilson knows; he recognized oil instead of democracy, you said so yourself—I read it in the newspapers.

"Be as smart as Wilson, make an agreement with Carranza. What's the use of this? You're alone."

"I had thirty thousand troops," he said. "I had hospital trains and artillery that rode on the flatbeds of armored cars. When we came to cities, I built schools and wrote laws, and I appointed mayors who trusted me, knowing that I would not permit my soldiers to be drunk, knowing that I would not permit rape or looting in the towns taken back for the people. They came from all over the world to see my army of thirty thousand. I was not alone. I am not alone now.

"It was not a lie, Liviana: I hate the oppression of the poor, I believe in land reform and democracy. It was not a lie: Madero taught me, he made a revolutionary of me."

"Madero left you in jail," she said. "He wouldn't even answer your letters."

"I had allies, friends."

"They betrayed you."

"Not all of them."

"Not yet."

"Women and blankets should be soft."

He described the quilting plan to Fierro and Fierro agreed. They spoke of Fierro's raid through the center of Mexico, how he had gone too far.

Angeles had been right about the supply lines, Angeles had always been right. "He should be President," Villa said. Fierro was full of noddings and smiles. "First we'll take Sonora," he said. They laughed.

"And you'll see your daughter."

"I miss her, man. When I see you with Valeriana, I think of her and I want to be home."

"And stay there."

"No, not me. I'm a railroader, I move, keep rolling, highballing, moving on. That's how we are. My wife knows; she could have married a farmer or a fisherman or a shopkeeper; I wasn't the only man in town. She liked the smell of smoke. Some women are like that."

Fierro informed the brigade commanders: everything was to be done quickly, in secret, even the officers were not to be told where they were going until they had left the city. If there were any questions, the answer was to be: The puma growls after he eats.

Fierro went ahead with the light cavalry, moving quickly. Villa followed with the main body of troops and the artillery. He marched slowly, saving the animals for the crossing of the Sierra Madre to the west. When he arrived at Casas Grandes, he was almost a full day behind Fierro.

A young officer told Villa what had happened: "The local people said to go around the flooded area, sir. You see, they dig pits here in the summer to find the underground springs. Then the rains come and this whole area turns into a swamp. You can see by the reeds, the way they grow. The point came back and told General Fierro about the waterholes, but the general wouldn't listen. He spat on the man, sir; I saw him. He spat on the man and rode out into the swamp. He called us cowards and he made other insults too, but no one followed him.

"General Fierro spurred his horse," the officer said. "Oh, he tore the skin off a horse! That mare went splashing through the water like it was running on hard sand. We heard him laughing, we started to laugh with him; he made us embarrassed, small; he showed us that we were afraid. Suddenly his horse was in water up to its belly. He kicked it with his spurs again, harder; we saw him kicking the horse. Then his feet were in the water and he was shouting filthy words to the wind, he was shouting at the wind, cursing it. His hands were up in the air when he disappeared into the water; he went like a ghost, so fast. Big, thick bubbles came up from the water, muddy bubbles, dark brown."

Villa went to the line of pack animals and pulled out one of the long ramrods. He took off his shoes and his gunbelt, and he went back to the officer to ask him where Fierro had gone into the water. The officer pointed to a hill across the lake. "In line with the hill," he said. "He rode in a straight line toward the hill. And it didn't happen until he was halfway across, maybe a little more."

"Eighteen is wind," Villa said, "one wind." He walked out into the water. The sand was soft under his feet, it sucked at his feet. His stockings were gone. "Eighteen. He carried the dead woman's arm. One wind. Eighteen." The ramrod was heavy on his shoulder. He did not let it sink down into the mud until he was near the center of the swamp. Then he stood among the green reeds, raising and lowering the ramrod, feeling in the deep sand for a man and a horse. The sand sucked at his feet, his legs; he walked from place to place, moving slowly, lifting his feet high out of the muddy water. He stood in water up to his knees, his waist; the reeds touched his face, the ramrod sank into the sand. "One wind. Eighteen. He carried the dead woman's arm." At dark, Miguel Trillo waded out into the swamp and took Villa's arm and led him back onto a low ridge where a fire had been built and fresh clothes had been laid out for him. "Eighteen," Villa said.

"Today is the thirteenth," Trillo said. "Tuesday the thirteenth."

"Eighteen was his birthday, he told me so. I always forgave him; he was the best he could be, and he was not a witch."

There was no burial at Casas Grandes. It rained all night and into the next day, a cold, continuous dark rain. The men had no dry clothes, fires only smouldered in the wet sand, the animals shivered, the water leaked through the canvas covers of the mountain guns. They rode northwest toward Janos in the early afternoon. The road was mud, the fields beside the road were mud. The animals tired, the men could not dry themselves, they rode northwest in the darkness and the cold rain. They moved through Janos like a river, six thousand, five hundred men, sweeping along what could be eaten—for themselves, for the horses and the struggling mules.

From Janos they could see through the rain to the brown peaks of the Sierra Madre. The storms were gray slantings in the canyons, the water came down from the mountains in overflowed streams, in new arroyos; it made rivers. The wind was cold, the men trembled in the rain, but there was no ice, there was no snow, the mountains were brown. Villa led them up the long slope to the foothills of the Sierras, he kept them moving. Six miles out of Janos a horse stopped walking. It stood for a moment in the rain, shivering like the others. The rider kicked it. The forelegs buckled, the animal's breath was cold. It was dead.

The rain stopped early in the evening. The wind was colder; ice formed on the pools of water. Greasewood burned, the men dried their clothes, but they could not get warm: their shoes would not dry, there was not enough heat to dry their blankets, there was no shelter. A few men slept, the rest passed the night cleaning their rifles and caring for the animals. They split prickly pear leaves for the horses, they held the sweet pulp out in their hands.

Villa walked among his troops all night. He advised them, he told them there was no danger unless it snowed, and it was too early for snow, even in the high passes, even on the peaks. "But we have to keep moving," he told them; "you mustn't stay still for a long time in the cold or your blood will thicken."

The snow fell suddenly, before them and behind them, the snow fell all around them. They stood like summer trees while the piling snow climbed them, while their legs drowned in the cold. The first man died before morning; an old man sitting with his burro in a small hollow away from the wind lay down in the warm bed of snow and slept while the blue-white color of the dawn snow entered him.

The column spread out into a long line, a string of mules. The mountains were like a wall before them. They climbed the slope, the growing steepness, leading the horses, pulling and driving the mules. Ahead in the distance, dimmed by snow and the mist of morning, beyond the green and brown and sickly white faces of the mountains, was the flat face of The Pulpit, and below it the deep pass across the Nacori Range, the first of the three rows of the Sierra Madre. They climbed toward the pass. The animals slipped and faltered on the frozen ground. The column moved slowly, the string was longer.

Now the soldiers found strawberry trees and curls of oak. They made low shelters with their blankets and built fires and collected the heat on themselves. They ate jerked meat and chiles and fed the corn to the animals. Villa called a meeting of his officers to tell them what to expect in the next days. He described the three ranges of the Sierra Madre: the steep Nacori, the deep valley before the Huehuerachi, and the gentler slopes of the Bacadehuachi leading down to the Bavispe River and the high plain of Sonora. He said the cordon of the Nacori would be the worst of the crossing, the wind would come through Pulpit Pass like the breath of Hell.

"I'm an old muleskinner," he told them. "I've been through these mountains before, I know them, in the sunshine and in the snow. The trail is narrow in some places on the way, the mulepacks will hit the walls and get off balance; there won't be time to get them on straight before the animals roll over the side—it can't be helped. But you tell the boys not to abandon a mule just because it falls and rolls down a few hundred feet. Go down after them, get them up, tie the packs on again, and drive them back up to the trail. Don't let them abandon those animals. We'll lose some to our bellies and we'll lose some to the rocks, but I don't want to lose an animal because some muleskinner was born without a midwife."

[564]

We should go back, the officers said. We should go back and wait for the weather to clear.

"We should go back and wait for Calles to get reinforcements at Agua Prieta," Villa said, "is that what you're telling me? My answer is no. I don't want another Celaya. When we reach the Bavispe, we'll be on the plains again, and we'll run to Agua Prieta, we'll run all day and all night for that last seventy miles."

The officers were not satisfied. We have no food, they said. The men are sick, the animals are dying. We were not prepared for snow.

Nicolás Fernández, a captain who had served with Fierro, disagreed. He said his argument in spurts, stopping often to think of the correct Spanish word. "I saw a bear," he said. "The bear is good. I am born in these Sierra Madres. Do not be afraid of these mountains. I tell you." The other officers nodded; they were not interested. Fernández stood up and walked out of the shelter of blankets into the snow. He removed his clothes and threw them away into the night. He stood before them in his white loin wrapping. He was dark brown, red in the firelight, made of ropes and bones; his legs were scarred. "Look! Nicolás Fernández is not afraid. The snow is white, the good water is white."

The officers, who had seen Tarahumaras in winter before, turned back to Villa.

"We'll go across," Villa said. "We'll go with our ally against our enemy. We'll keep the mountains between us and the wind and we'll let movement keep us warm. We'll go across."

The old ones died first; they lay down to sleep in the snow and the fires went out and in the morning they were dead. The blankets began to come apart on the third night. The hand-spun wool tore first; the strands unraveled and the soggy threads parted and the weight of the wet wool tore itself apart. The snow blew all night, the air was white. They ate the first of the horses.

There were no resting places. In the wind of Pulpit Pass the animals lay down and turned their heads into their bellies. Villa stood at the entrance to the pass. He was snow-crusted and steaming. He tore at the ears of the mules, he jerked their tails until they got up biting and kicking, bucking to throw off the packs. He had no gloves, his hands were puckered from drinking cold snow. His knuckles bled. He wore his underwear shirt over his head and ears and wrapped around his throat, and he protected his eyes from the snow with rubber-rimmed desert goggles. The column moved through.

In the flat places where the snow blew blinding, he told them to hold on to the tail of the animal that walked before them, to lead their own animals by their halters or their ears. But in the flat places the men wandered away into the whiteness, they faded away from the line as if there were some purpose in their going, as if they had seen some warmth in the distance, some sheltered place where a fire would last, where the wind failed.

In the valley between the Nacori and Huehuerachi there had been a Mormon colony. The land had been good for their corn and the slopes of the hills had provided grazing for their cattle. Villa had been there. He had seen the deer come down from the stands of pine to drink at the stream that ran through the center of the valley. Now there was snow and the broken walls of long-abandoned houses and the piled stones of Apache monuments. There were no deer. The stream had flooded and frozen in the fields. The string of mules walked through the places where the Mormon houses had stood.

In the deep snow of the valley the animals foundered, sinking. Villa watched them dying into the snow, as Fierro had died in the swamps near Casas Grandes, as the brigades had died in the flooded fields of Celaya— the drowning soldiers, going west where the milk trees bloomed, the drowning gift, the dying soldiers, drowning.

His hands were bloody, ice grew in his mustache, his horse had been eaten; he walked. Movement! he shouted to the foundering men, keep your blood moving! The snow was up to his knees, the snow was up to his waist. He reached into caves and wells of snow to take the hands of fallen men. He dragged them forward, running with them until their legs began to move again. "It's Panco Villa, comrade! I'm the North and I'm with you. Don't be afraid, comrade; Pancho Villa is with you. I've got hold of your hand."

Leather hardened and cracked; the soldiers wrapped their feet in rags, they washed their frozen limbs in snow, they put on the skins of dead animals, they put on the clothes of dead men. The snow fell, the snow fell upon the snow. There was nothing more to burn, the snow covered everything. They fell more in the descent than in the climbing, the animals could not hold the packs, their bones broke, the soldiers ate the raw meat of them —there was nothing left to burn.

They came down out of the mountains eleven days after they had crossed the Río Carretas on the eastern slope. Four artillery pieces and almost a thousand mules and horses had been lost. Of the six thousand four hundred men who left Casas Grandes, only five thousand seven hundred entered the town of Batepito on the Bavispe River. They bought corn in the town and feed for the animals and a herd of goats to slaughter for themselves. Villa called his officers together and told them: "We won a victory over the Sierra Madre. We made an impossible crossing and by that we defeated an enemy greater than any army we'll ever face in battle. Go back to your boys and tell them to celebrate, tell them to sing. They're the first heroes of the new stage of the revolution."

The officers stood staring at their general. His feet were still wrapped in rags, the brim of his hat was puckered and stiff, his hands were crusted with scabs, a beard grew like filth on his face, the skin below his eyes hung in slack quarter-moons. The officers walked away without speaking.

There was no singing. The men slept on dry ground; they wanted nothing more that night. In the morning the whispering began: How many had died? How many were still lost back there, freezing in the snow? Villa's luck was bad; it never snowed so early in the Sierra Madre, it never snowed so much. They were all going to die at Agua Prieta.

Candelario Cervantes, who had been with the old Cuauhtémoc Brigade, brought one of the whisperers to Villa. The man coughed, he said he had a fever; his boots were gone and one of his toes was black. "What more can you do to me?" the man asked. "You can make me die a few days sooner, you can end my suffering a little sooner; that's all."

Soldiers were gathering; they came to see an execution. Cervantes let the wretched man sit down on a bench to remove the weight from his dying foot.

"Up against the wall?" Cervantes asked.

The soldiers were coming from their camping places along the river, all quiet men, all haggard men, all walking slowly, carrying the goat meat in hard mounds in their bellies. Villa watched the massing of them, like cattle, with the unspoken politeness of cattle, shuffling into all the spaces, taking on the heaviness of one, growing tense by the weight of them on the small space. The wretched man sat before him on the bench, lumps and sticks, covered with what had been a red sweater, bent, curled at the shoulders, with his head thrust forward as if for a noose; a man about to be dead, no more a soldier, no more a man, to be a cripple, to be a beggar, a load to carry, a weight upon an army, festering, dying sour; nothing would be wasted in the example.

"Up against the wall?" Cervantes asked again.

The thickness of men waited in a circle; they made a heavy collar around Villa, Cervantes, and the wretched man. They pressed forward, like the crowd at a cockfight. They were quiet, the whisperers were poised.

Villa knelt before the wretched man and took the stinking foot in his hands to examine it. The flesh was black and very soft, the toenail floated in the fluids that were collecting in the dead flesh. "I'm sorry," Villa said, looking up at the man. "We don't have a doctor with us. There was no way to bring the medical train across the Sierras. But Maytorena has doctors in Naco. You go to Naco instead of Agua Prieta. Tell Maytorena that I sent

[*567*]

you. He'll see that you have the best doctor." He knelt close to the man's foot, sniffing it to determine whether there was gangrene yet. "If you go now, comrade, there's still a chance to save your foot. But hurry."

The man crossed himself. In the crowd of watching soldiers several men knelt and crossed themselves. Villa stood up and put his hand on the wretched man's shoulder while he spoke to his troops: "This is a revolution, comrades. Some of us have to die, because a revolution is also a war. But we're comrades. When one of us is wounded, we care for him; when one of us is sick, we heal him. They say you know when a war is lost, because the man next to you runs away. This man is my comrade; I'll never run away from him. Let the Carrancistas run away from each other; they only came to this war to fight over the spoils. We're true revolutionaries, comrades, we're the defenders of the poor."

The column marched as far as Fronteras and made its base there. The artillerymen set up the mountain guns, the machine gunners oiled and cleared their weapons, the cavalry rode in its formations, and the telegraphers spoke to Maytorena from the small office in the railroad station. The news was reported to Villa: Wilson had closed the border to him. Wilson had permitted Carranza to move troops from Piedras Negras to Agua Prieta on American trains. Calles now had seven or eight thousand troops at Agua Prieta; the reinforcements had passed through El Paso on the thirtieth of November in the early morning.

Villa left the telegraph office and walked back to the little house that had been given to him for his headquarters in Fronteras. Townspeople stopped him along the way to wish him luck, to swear their allegiance to him and to Maytorena, to ask him how soon he planned to move north with his troops. He nodded to them and walked on; they had revalued Villista money in Fronteras: it had been worth thirty cents in U.S. money, now it was worth two cents, and people preferred gold or silver. He contained his anger toward them, but he tried to remember their faces, the twitchings that showed through their lips when they told him the new prices.

The headquarters house was dark and small. It seemed to have been empty for a long time, as if the people who lived there had died or gone away. He could not find an oil lamp or a candle. He lay down on the corn-shuck mattress, but he could not sleep. He went outside to urinate. The sky was clear and very dark, the stars were very bright. He looked at the formations: the Fire Drill and the S-shaped stars and the Scorpion with its curled and deadly brilliant tail. What did the stars tell? The wind blew from the north, a bad luck wind. He went back into the house and lay down on the mattress. Through the open door he saw the moon's bright half. He thought of her, round and beautiful, the moon of betrayal, decapitated by the sun. The shadows of two men passed before the moon and entered the house: one wore a cowboy hat, the other was tall, with a thin neck wrapped in a high round collar.

THE COWBOY

I was weighted down. That's what a man gets for having children; he thinks about them when his mind should be on other things.

THE THIN MAN

I have the greatest sympathy for him and all others like him. My deeply compassionate view of the suffering poor is widely known.

THE COWBOY

When a rich man gets aboard a train, the first thing he wants is to take the throttle.

THE THIN MAN

I want peace more than power, more than anything. My melancholia is a direct result of the frustrations I have suffered in attempting to bring about peace among the peoples of the less sophisticated nations of the world.

THE COWBOY

Is that why I died?

THE THIN MAN

Death is a de facto situation. God knows, I gave you every opportunity. It was your own impetuousness that killed you.

THE COWBOY

You permitted the death of democracy.

THE THIN MAN

The charge is absurd; no man favors democracy more than I do. What you fail to realize is that democracy can only survive by its own strength. We must be neutral in action as well as in name.

THE COWBOY

And for that you let me die.

THE THIN MAN

Sometimes people call me an idealist.

The Cowboy lifted the pistol from his holster. The shadow of the weapon was unclear until it fired and the flash illuminated the weapon and the wounding of the Thin Man. The wound was not fatal: the Thin Man lay sickly and weakened on the dirt floor. He complained, but his words were not clear.

The attack on Agua Prieta began in darkness. The Villistas went riding across the plain that led to the city, they charged across the wide plain, all the thousands of them went riding to deliver the terrific blow, to break through one place in the defenses, to flood the city with horses running and rifles firing. Their cannon fired over them, their machine gunners came running behind. It was night when they went riding, the men and horses running and all the whistles and all the bugles blowing, sending them north into the blind night.

The suns appeared in the north, rows of searchlights shining, blinding the riders, marking them in the light like forms painted on an executioner's wooden wall. The machine guns fired and the horsemen and the horses died. Hundreds died, a thousand died in the first moments of the charge. Villa abandoned the attack on Agua Prieta.

He led the last of his army in doublings and circles. They were the rabbits, they rode their horses until the backs of the animals bled and the blankets grew into the bloody galls. There was no retreat but the Sierra Madre again, there was no other place where the Carrancistas would not follow, no other place where the Yanquis could not help Obregón with railroads and munitions. Villa led his troops to the foothills of the Bacadehuachi Range. They made a camp there beside a white water stream and they slaughtered two good steers and a pig and they ate and sang and all the soldiers whispered, wondering where next the Carrancistas were waiting for them, what battle Villa planned.

After the food was eaten, Villa climbed up on a rock above the camp and shouted to the soldiers to come and listen to him. "This is the end of the Division of the North," he said. "Many have died. Enough now!" He cupped his hands around his mouth to make the words reach the men who stood at the back of the crowd. "I am going across to Chihuahua. Come with me; I will take you home! Come with me! Not as soldiers, as my comrades, as my true comrades! It is not an order! Listen to me: it is not an order! The Division of the North is finished, washed up, the war is over!" He paused to breathe less violently, to rest his throat. "From Chihuahua I will go to the mountains again. As a guerrilla. As I began. I will not surrender! I will wait in the mountains. Carranza will know I am in the mountains. He will know I am the defender of the poor!

"Whoever loves democracy can come with me! Whoever gives his heart to the poor can come with me! Whoever loves Mexico more than himself can come with me!

"Decide now! Choose tonight! Whoever is here in the morning goes with me! Whoever leaves in the night leaves without shame!

"You are all heroes! You are all revolutionaries! I am grateful to you all.

"Comrades, we are all Mexicans, we are all of the same race. Long live the Race!"

The soldiers held up their hands to him and lifted him down from the rock. They held out their arms to him, they embraced him. He felt their rough faces, he smelled their weariness, their defeat. He kissed them, he wept with them; he knew they would be gone in the morning.

The officers passed the order that there would be no campfires that night; the men who left would go in darkness, without farewells, without shame. The camp was quiet in the early hours of the night, as if the men were sleeping. Villa sat high up on the side of the mountain, in a place where the moonlight could not reveal the faces of the men who chose to leave. He watched over the quiet camp. There was a washed wind, the smell of promised snow was in the air. He covered himself with his blanket and leaned back against a rock. The camp was quiet; he heard the horses stamping their hooves in the cold. He watched the quiet camp. He sighed and saw his breath white in the air.

He heard them first: the whisper of the stirring, the metallic sounds of the gathering of things, the brush of pebbles disturbed. They stood up, lifting their saddles, walking down to the place where the horses were picketed. The slope of the hill rose up in shadows and fled to the place where the horses were picketed. The soldiers whispered, they spoke aloud, they laughed. There were so many.

Villa did not sleep. He sat against the rock, looking down over the hill, waiting for first light. Color came to the hill while the stars could still be seen and the moon was bright. Almost five thousand men had come with him to the beginning of the Sierra Madre. He counted those who were left, whispering the numbers aloud. As the light grew and the forms of the sleeping men were more certain, he counted again: there were four hundred. He closed his eyes and considered sleep, but he had seen the heavy gray snowclouds coming down from the northwest; it would be best to go as far as they could before the snow fell.

BOOK FOUR

Solamente yo busco,
recuerdo a nuestros amigos.
¿Acaso vendrán una vez más,
acaso volverán a vivir?
Sólo una vez perecemos,
sólo una vez aquí en la tierra.

Nezahualcóyotl
Translated from the Náhuatl
by Miguel León-Portilla

1

A thick film, yellow and hard as a fingernail, grew across my right eye. The joints of my fingers and my knees swelled, and rough shapes seemed to have grown inside in the places where the bones meet. The pain was most severe in winter, even willow-bark tea did not dim the pain in winter. I slept closer to the fire.

Fewer people came to see me. My former visitors said the garden room of my house was no longer well tended; they asked how a healer could be unable to heal himself. I explained: my ills are the ills of age, which have no cure. At the end of every day the day dies and cannot be made to live again. Time is not a circle. If you want to hear lies about time, go to the Chichimeca or the Huicholes or the Tarahumaras. Lies are not a cure. Look at me! I am old, I reek of an old man's sweats. Shall I tell myself that I can chase rabbits with a stick? Shall I tell myself that women desire me? What comfort will those lies be when I am hungry and lonely in my bed? How will I eat fresh meat if I have no teeth?

I said to them: Do not abandon me because I am old and full of memories; listen to me, I am rich now, I am a storehouse, I am a book.

Some said I was too old to have a life. They brought me the charity of their visits on days when I preferred to be alone, they brought me gifts of things I did not want and would not use, and they spoke to me as if I lived in Motecuhzoma's time. My few visitors spoke to me of thundersticks, iron birds, and magic torches, when they meant to speak of the new Colt machine guns and Wright biplanes and incandescent light bulbs. I told them to speak plainly to me; I could hear in both ears and I could see with one eye and half of the other. I told them how much one learns through observing war. I told them how war has changed everything that men use, but it has not changed men.

No one was happy with me. Many acted as if oldness were madness. Children said I was a witch. More and more I lived alone, watching, comparing this time to time past; and nothing I saw, nothing I divined showed that men had changed. I thought often about the nature of change; I used my great age, I used what had been told to me, I used what I saw, and I could only conclude that men are a circle within the dying days.

Those who came to the saddle of the mountain to sit with me in my house did so out of kindness or to have a spell removed. They did not stay long, they did not want to talk. The war had changed people's speed, I thought. Automobiles, airplanes, machines, had hurried their hearts. There was no time for philosophy, no time for remembering. Perhaps it was the numbers of the dead, more than a million, as many as two million, that rushed them. Perhaps it is impossible to think of philosophy when so many have been killed.

The towns were crowded even though so many had been killed. The people came back from the cities, where there was nothing to eat and no one knew the value of money or the price of anything. They came back from the cities because Carranza had betrayed their unions the moment he no longer needed them: strikes were outlawed, the House of World Workers was closed. They came back from the cities because of the executions and the murdering and the thievery and the executions that followed the murdering and the thievery. Everyone was afraid; peace was more capricious than war.

Twelve thousand Villistas surrendered in Chihuahua, the Zapatistas continued their small war in Morelos, Villa took his four hundred men and two hundred more who joined him in Chihuahua and went to the hills. I wanted Villa to come to my house, I wanted to talk to him, but the calculations said it would not happen. I watched. I drew in red ink and black ink. It was a cold winter; my joints swelled and ached; I slept close to the fire.

At the end of the year 1915, Villa gathered his six hundred comrades in a small box canyon in the Blue Mountains. He served them roast pork and fried stomachs and tripe soup and beans and flavorings of amaranth seed and mountain chiles. There was even goat cheese to melt over the refried beans. It was a bright day and there was no wind in the canyon; the smell of the meat roasting gave the meeting the air of a country festival. Men played guitars and sang and told stories of battles and whores and horses. They had not been so comfortable since Aguascalientes, they had not felt so safe since then.

The men spoke to each other of a golden army, an army of heroes, as lean as a snake. There was talk of attacking towns, small towns at first, then perhaps Chihuahua or Agua Prieta. Six hundred heroes, an army as lean as a snake; they would be invincible. Villa told them it could not be so. An army of six hundred is too large to live in the hills, he said; it is too fat, too slow, too heavy on the land. Where would they find food for themselves? he asked. Where would they find grazing for their horses? Six hundred men

"My faded friend, I have the pleasure to inform you that this is Mexico and that you are speaking to a Mexican citizen."

"Let's be realistic."

"Okay. Angeles tells me that Secretary Lansing has offered me asylum in the United States. There are restrictions, but they're not unreasonable. The problem is that by accepting his offer I would be another rotten fruit who abandoned his country. What Yanquis and renegades like you don't believe is that I am a revolutionary. I have no money, I never took anything from the revolution. I believe in liberty and democracy and an end to the oppression of the poor. Of all the bosses who fought in this revolution, only three ever tried to distribute the land: Blanco, Zapata, and Villa. Blanco is dead, Zapata is a good man who was never able to leave his own garden; only Villa distributed the land, only Villa put thirty thousand men behind the words of his Agrarian Reform Law. If that is true, why do you think I would abandon the people now? If that is not true, why do you waste your time talking to me?"

The man drank his beer. He looked over the bottle at Villa, who sat unmoving in his chair, looking down at the paper spread on the table. "I didn't come to talk about asylum," the man said. "Mr. Stone is arranging an interview, a meeting between President Wilson and General Villa. We can bring you across the border at Columbus. Obregón has no troops at Palomas, and we have only a small garrison at Columbus. Secretary Lansing guarantees safe passage once you're across the border."

"What's your name?"

"Juan."

"Don't you have a father?"

"For my father's sake, Juan."

"Make the arrangements. Maybe I'll go. I have advisors. We have to discuss the offer. We have very little reason now to trust Mr. Wilson."

Liviana moved the whole of her family back to the house in San Andrés. They went quietly, traveling together on the regular train. Only her neighbors noticed, and they said nothing: it was a family going home from the city, in defeat, surrendering, the family of a hero become an ordinary bandit again. The neighbors did not offer to help with the loading of baskets and boxes into the hired wagon; the widows of the compound on Tenth Street did the work. Only the old man Aprisco was a problem; he refused to permit the driver of the hired wagon to lift him out of his wheelchair, he demanded to be rolled on boards up onto the bed of the wagon. "Like a mule being put into a boxcar," Liviana said, and the old man smiled and waited for the wide boards to be lined up against the back of the wagon.

The old house was slow to be repaired. The windows had been broken again, the wood had been stripped from the doors and shutters again. Liviana hired a carpenter to make new doors and shutters. He was an old man who had lost two sons in the revolution. He wrapped himself in sweaters and blankets and never worked more than a few hours in the middle of the morning. Liviana and her mother and her aunts swept and washed and arranged the few pieces of furniture they had brought with them from Chihuahua.

They had no animals and no one to plow or seed the fields that had given way to sage and cactus and the beginnings of live oak. The women hoed patches to make a garden. They worked every day, turning and chopping the soil, killing the roots of all the useless plants in their garden. The old man insisted on always being with them. He sat in his wheelchair, a bloated curl, piled with blankets, telling the women where to chop, how deep to dig, never pleased, saying always that women were not fit to work the land, that their menstrual blood poisoned the earth.

Villa saw them from the road, the wheels and blankets that were the old man, the mother and her sisters black-draped even in the fields, bent, chopping, pausing again and again to throw the shawls across their chests, and Liviana, big again, broad as a man, bent over her belly, chopping and sweating, carrying the burden of them all, thickening under the weight of it. He took the hoe from her and embraced her and kissed her sweated face. He offered to do the work for her, but she said they were finished for the day, it was time to go inside. She asked him to push the wheelchair.

"Go slow," the old man said. "Don't jiggle my feet."

The women went ahead. When they were out of earshot, the old man put a hand out of the blankets and motioned to Villa to bend his head close to him. "I suffer this way because of you, my son. Not only pain, but humiliation. How do you think I shit? It's no trouble to piss; they wheel me outside and turn me away from the wind and I piss a good stream. But shitting! Imagine! Go ahead, imagine. Tell me how you think I shit."

"It doesn't matter. You're an old man and too much trouble. In war one learns not to worry about the hopeless cases. What do do you think of that?"

The old man had no answer. He slumped in his chair, groaning at the pain of his jiggled feet. Villa wheeled him into his bedroom and left him there. "I have to piss," the old man called through the closed door. Villa went to find Liviana.

"Your father is like a baby," he told her.

"He was always that way, even when I was a baby."

She took Villa to the room where Valeriana slept. They whispered; he kissed the child without touching his lips to her. His mustache grazed her cheek. She gave a twitch at the irritation. He lifted his hand to stroke her back into sleep, but Liviana pulled him away. "Let her sleep now," she said when they were outside the room. "If you awaken her, she'll be frightened."

They went outside the house to be away from the listening women and the complaints of the old man. The wind was cold and bearing dust. They walked together. Liviana bent her head to avoid the dust. Her shoulders were heavy; she walked with her feet set widely, as farm women walk. She said, "I'm due to give birth in April, but I'm always early. Will you be here when this one is born?"

"I'm going to Washington."

"When?"

"I don't know. I haven't made up my mind about going."

"Do you want my advice?"

"Cervantes says that a woman's advice isn't worth much, but the man who doesn't take it is a fool."

"I don't want to be a widow," she said.

"That's a riddle."

"And this is a riddle: how can a virtuous widow bear children?"

They came to the edge of the broken ground. The wind was picking up the topsoil. The women had chopped it too finely; the soil had dried to dust. The rains had stopped, there was only wind. The ditches that had been cut from the arroyo to the house had long ago filled up with sand; sage grew on them, mesquite trees rose from the places where the water had run. There would be no garden. The wind would uncover the seeds, the roots of the useless thorny things would grow again. Villa stood looking at the hoed ground. He knew the taste of weeds.

"My mother thought I would be a farmer," he said. "She gave me a farmer's name. But we never had a farm; we had a field of stones. So I'm not a farmer who stays in his fields and waits for rain. My wife is a widow because I am a soldier. And I am a soldier because our farm was a field of stones. I'll go to see Wilson because I'm a soldier. I don't know what else to do. I want to rest and I have no place to lie down."

He unfolded his blanket and arranged it over her shoulders. Her hair was knotted into a bun above the blanket; her hair was light brown, more yellow than the dust. "I'll leave a few of the boys here to take care of you."

"Is that what a widow needs?"

"They'll plow the fields and put in corn and beans. They can start a little herd of cattle. I'll see that one of them is a good carpenter to help you with the house. Liviana, it will be better than five husbands."

She pulled the blanket closed over her bosom and walked back to the house.

[*581*]

* * *

Every night Villa packed his blue metal suitcase and dressed himself in
a white shirt and a silk tie and a brown suit with a vest and a gold watch
chain. Every night he waited in his camp in the hills south of Palomas while
the water froze in the canteens and the troops complained that they could
not stay any longer without fires to see them through the night. There was
no food left in the camp. The men were worn, the horses ate the buds from
the little trees that grew along a stream, the horses cropped the young grass
like sheep, and it made them sick. Every night Villa waited for Miguel Trillo
to come back up from the town to say he had seen the man from the
Associated Press. Every night Trillo stayed in the plaza, waiting until he
saw the morning star the second time before he went back up into the hills
to say to Villa that Juan had not come. And every morning Villa took off
his American suit and folded it into the blue metal case and went alone to
sit in the sun and think about the Americans.

Four hundred men had come with him to the border, his escort, his
guarantee that the man from the Associated Press would not present him
for a gift to Carranza. But there had been no troops waiting, there had been
nothing. A week had passed. He waited now out of stubborness, he waited
now out of shame. He was going to Washington, he had told them all, and
his first stop would be in Sam Ravel's store to collect forty thousand pesos
for weapons not delivered. He would go to Ravel's store with the man from
the Associated Press and an escort of Yanqui soldiers, and they would all
listen to him, for he was going to Washington under the protection of
President Wilson.

There was nothing, only the wind, the dust coming every afternoon like
a brown mist from the mountains, the freezing night, the bent trees, the
horses lying down, nothing, humiliation. At night he sat in the hills and
watched the lights coming on, circles in the circles of the towns, the towns
a divided abdomen separated by the waist of the border crossing. The dust
was in his hair; there was always grit in his teeth, an alkaline odor always
in his nostrils. He did not want to shave anymore with cold water, he did
not want to perfume himself to wait out any more nights; he sat in his place
in the hills and looked down at his troops and looked down at the towns
and did not know where to turn.

Fernández came up to the place where Villa sat alone in the midday sun.
He ran, he always ran uphill, slipping on loose rocks and laughing. "Good,"
he said, patting his thighs. He was always dusty, coated with tan or gray,
never shining; Villa was always surprised to see him move.

"I'm not going to Washington," Villa said.

"Sons of bitches."

"White Chinks."

Where was the field telephone, where were the runners? He had advice to give, orders to say.

No Wilson, no Washington, no peace now. The Japanese, the Germans; it had been so long, they spoke only to Carranza now. He saw the Morning Star, he saw the making of the eastern horizon. It was cold. He squatted there on the hilltop and put himself inside his blanket. The time sailed on the wind. He did not sleep; he was with the time, he put himself beside the sailing time.

Trillo found him in the early light. "Very bad," Trillo said. "A hundred dead, a hundred and twenty-five."

"Tell the boys we'll head for the Big Mouth Mountains. Save the wounded."

Trillo ran down the hill toward the hole in the fence where the men were coming back across the border. Villa stood up slowly. His knees were stiff and the long muscles of his thighs ached. He could not remember when his knees had been stiff before. It made him think of Urbina, Fierro, the old man Chavarría. He heard the rattlebells, he thought of the old man's glorious moment.

Villa listened to everything that could be found out about the Yanqui general, who was either forty-six or fifty-six or sixty-three years old, who was either a murderer and a coward or a schoolteacher and a drunkard. The news often made him laugh. He told Trillo and Cervantes: "If Pershing survives the summer in the desert, he'll die in the winter in the mountains. Don't worry about Pershing; let him try to feed his six thousand men in Chihuahua, let him try to find a Mexican who will betray us to a Yanqui army. Let him try to find us; to him we're the color of the desert; if he stepped on us, he would think we were stones.

"If you want to worry, worry about Murguía; he's a good soldier and he can find people who still trust Carranza. Pershing has six thousand, ten thousand troops, and they're all deaf, dumb and blind; but in time Murguía will be able to put thirty thousand troops in Chihuahua.

"No, my friends, don't worry about Pershing; he'll destroy Carranza, not Villa. The old goat is the one who has to carry the gringos on his back now. It's the way your father says, Cervantes: 'God suffers the wicked, but not forever.' There's still time for us to put Carranza up against a wall."

The Yanquis wandered in the deserts and climbed aimlessly over the mountains. They ate their saddles and abandoned their airplanes and automobiles. Their Apache scouts could not tell them which tracks belonged to Villistas and which belonged to Carrancistas. In the towns the people told them Villa was just ahead and just behind and only a little to the west and if the Yanquis would look over their shoulders they would see Villa riding off to the east.

General Pershing rode in a Dodge automobile while his troops walked on their ruined shoes over the cutting rock. The general forced his troops to stand up while they rested. By accident his soldiers found Candelario Cervantes and killed him. They fought all of their other battles against Carrancistas. When the Yanquis passed through a place, the people laughed and gave them gifts of carrion and spoiled food. They directed them to alkali springs and box canyons. If the Yanquis came with someone who spoke Spanish, the people spoke Tarahumara; if the Yanquis came with someone who understood Tarahumara, the people lied.

You will always know Villa, the people said, because there is the sign of the cross on his back; but it is not a Christian cross. Look for the cross you see on the belly of a tortoise. It is the sign of a man who has a pact with the devil.

The mistake you are making, mister, is that you keep looking for a man. Sometimes Villa is a man—you can ask the women—and sometimes he is a coyote or an eagle. Well, you can laugh, mister, but if you see a small dog following you, watch out!

If you want to find Pancho Villa, you must eat a special root and lie down beside a river, and then you will see where he is. Ask the Yaquis, ask the Tarahumaras; they can always find him.

The root is the one you call Loco Weed. Feed it to your horses first.

It's true, mister, that if you find Pancho Villa's wife, you'll find Pancho Villa. Yes, I know Pancho Villa's wife; I know two of his wives. But go north, he has more in the north. In the City of Juárez he has ten. And in the City of Chihuahua, he is the father of all the children under the age of twelve; ask them.

To find Pancho Villa, mister, all you have to do is wait by the place where he buried the gold he took from the Cusi Mining Company. Look for a mountain where pine trees grow; it's buried there, I swear it.

You'll know Pancho Villa by his horse, Mister. He changes all the time, but you can always recognize the horse. Sure, I've seen it. And I can tell you what it looks like. This horse has four legs, each with a hoof, and it has a tail and a head, with two ears, two eyes, a nose. . . .

[586]

Villa moved like a rabbit, which leaves a trail that runs in both directions and then disappears. If he rode southwest all day, in the late afternoon he divided his troops into four squadrons and sent each of them in wide circles that ended in a northeasterly direction. After riding a few miles in the wrong direction, the squadrons dragged mesquite or pine boughs behind them for a mile or two before circling around to the southwest again. Sometimes he rode up and back over his tracks, sending men off in all directions to meet later in some difficult, rocky place. The Apache and Yaqui scouts who tracked him knew exactly how a rabbit moves; they explained to the Yanquis and the Carrancistas that the best way to catch a rabbit is to sit down somewhere and wait for it to pass by. The most difficult thing, they said, was that Villa often rode in the tracks of the Yanquis or the Carrancistas, following them for miles, until he came to a river or an area of hard rock, where he went his own way.

Think this way, Villa told his troops: Do the stars chase the sun or does the sun chase the stars?

The men who rode with Villa now were Tarahumaras and Yaquis. They were comfortable in the high plain and in the mountains, they knew by the colors of the sky when a storm was coming, they knew by the smell of water and the plants that grew near it whether the water was sweet. They hunted armadillos and woodpeckers, rabbits and deer; they argued like wolves over the sweet innards of the animals they killed. When they came to a house or a village of Tarahumaras, they did not rush in; they sat outside in the proper way, they waited for the man of the house or the head of the village to come out to them; they waited an hour or three hours, they said nothing, they did nothing, they were welcomed.

Wherever he went, Villa was a surprise. He traveled north one day, south the next, southwest the next, going from town to town, never staying more than a few hours, meeting the small garrisons of Carrancista troops, defeating them quickly, taking their horses, weapons, ammunition, and shoes, going on. He executed no one, he told the men who surrendered that they were nothing but skinheads, that true revolutionaries did not execute men of the race; he left them to be his newspaper and his telegraph.

Villa attacked Guerrero before dawn. The Carrancista garrison there was small and armed with old weapons; the mice had said they did not even have a machine gun. The main attack was led by Francisco Beltrán, the Yaqui, and Nicolás Fernández; Villa rode in behind them, thinking more of who lived in the old Orozco house and the trenches at Cerro Prieto than of the skirmish against José Cavazas, the general without a machine gun. The fight went quickly: Cavazas had no plan but withdrawal; he moved back through the town, across the railroad tracks, seeking only to give his troops time to save their horses and equipment. As soon as he could, Cavazas gave the

[587]

order to run away. The Villistas followed, shooting and calling insults. It was not war, it was a horserace, and some of the men were laughing. Villa rode with them, running his horse for the exercise, for the feel of the wind.

The bullet pulled his leg out of the stirrup. He fell over on his side, as if something had clutched onto his leg and would not let go. The horse was running out from under him. He took the saddle horn with his left hand. The horse was coming over on top of him. He pulled his left leg over the saddle and let himself fall. The horse went over in front of him, screaming, rolling on the saddle. Villa rounded himself and rolled over and over. He spread his arms and legs to stop the rolling and came to rest on his back. Stones had cut him; he felt stones under his back. He had lost his hat. The horse was struggling, up on its forelegs. The dust was in his eyes. He lay back and closed his eyes to rest while the dust cleared.

His leg was bleeding from below the knee on both sides; the bullet had gone through. The pain was in his thigh. He sat up and looked at his thigh; there was no wound where he felt the pain. The chase had passed him. He heard the shooting in the distance, perhaps over a hill or in a little valley. The dust was settling. He felt sick, perhaps from the fall, from losing his breath. There was some sage near him, and he took it up in a handful and crushed it between his fingers; he thought the odor of the sage would clear the sick feeling from him, but it did not. He threw the sage away and sat leaning back on his elbows, waiting for someone to come and help him up.

A stretcher was brought out from Guerrero. Villa said he did not need to be carried; all he wanted was someone to lean on. Beltrán and Fernández took Villa's arms under the shoulders and set him upright. He shivered, his mouth was open, chewing; he could not speak. They laid him on the stretcher and carried him to the German doctor who lived in the town. "Don't let him cut off my leg," was all he said.

The doctor's house was hung with bones and drawings of human bodies without skin. He worked in a room lined with shelves and cabinets with glass doors. Everything in the room had been painted white, even the coat rack was white, even the floor was white. The room shone with whiteness, the room frightened with whiteness. It smelled of paint and alcohol. Villa was lifted from the stretcher to the white metal table. The lights above were hung from mirrors. He saw himself, a darkness in the white room; the blood had dried black on his wounded leg.

The doctor dressed himself in a white coat and covered his hair with a brimless white cap. He was a pale man, he quivered. "Well, who have we here?" he asked, preparing himself, taking his instruments from a drawer. He had a foreign accent. He spoke cheerfully, the way rich women speak to poor men's children.

"General Francisco Villa," Beltrán said.

[588]

"Very good, very good," the doctor said. He cut away Villa's trouser leg and threw it into a white basket. The quivering was magnified in his hands, but he was quick. "Well, well, I see you've had some trouble. How do you feel?"

"Sick."

"Dizzy? Nauseated? Tell me exactly; the doctor must know."

"Sick."

The doctor examined the wound without touching it. He called Beltrán and Fernández over to a corner of the room. "Are you in charge here?" They nodded. "One of the bones, the tibia, is broken, very badly broken. The wound is filthy. The old-fashioned soft-nose bullets do that. The lead itself is poisonous. He won't be able to walk on the leg again, even if he doesn't get blood poisoning. The best thing is to amputate. The man's life is in danger."

"You cut off his leg," Fernández said, "I cut your throat."

The doctor looked to Beltrán, who nodded. "Very well, he's your friend. Leave him here and I'll do what I can, but I can't work miracles. I'll do my best, but I can't work miracles. The wound is filthy, that's the danger now."

"I'll clean it out," Beltrán said. "Then you take care of him." He went back to the table where Villa lay, quiet now, his shirt collar unbuttoned and his belt loosened. "We always clean out a wound," Beltrán said. "You know?"

"It's the best way."

Beltrán took off his hat and threw it to Fernández. He patted Villa's belly once; his hand was gentle. "Comrade," he said. Villa smiled. Beltrán bent his head to Villa's leg and put his mouth over the wound. He sucked hard, turned his head away, and spat blood on the floor. He sucked and spat until the blood ran freely from the place where the bullet had entered. There was blood on his mustache and on his chin. He went around to the other side of the table, washing his mouth with saliva and spitting as he walked.

"The other side, too," Beltrán said. Villa did not answer. His face was wet, his neck was knotted tight. His hands lay at his sides in failing fists.

Beltrán bent to the wound again. The place where the bullet had come out was wider, too large for Beltrán to cover with his mouth. He squeezed half the wound closed and sucked the open place, spitting out the dark blood and slivers of bone as his mouth filled. When half the wound was bleeding freely, he closed it with his hand and sucked the other part clean. His face was washed in blood. There was blood on his forehead and in his eyes. He held out his hands for someone to give him a cloth to wipe his face. He spat and spat, wandering in the room, looking for water to wash his mouth.

[589]

The doctor brought him a white cloth and a bowl of water to clean himself. Beltrán used the bowl for a cup, washing his mouth and spitting the pale red water on the floor. He used what water remained to clean his face, washing his eyes first and wiping the lids clean with the white cloth. "I felt pieces of bone," he said to the doctor. "And I tasted lead. The bullet came out, but not all of it. I tasted lead."

Villa saw the bleeding wound in the mirrors above him. He saw the shape of himself and the spattered table and floor. The blood was in great splotches and in sprays of drops; it was black and darkening red, drying. He looked for the pieces of bone. The light hurt his eyes. "I need something to wipe my face," he said. "And a drop of water for my lips." Someone touched a cold cloth to his lips and someone wiped his face. "It's worse than I thought," he said.

The doctor washed the wound with a red liquid. He talked all the time, speaking to a child, asking questions, not waiting for answers. "Brave soldier," he said while he lifted Villa's leg again and again to pass a long piece of gauze under it. "You're a good soldier. Now, that didn't hurt so much, did it? You're feeling better, aren't you?" After he had taped the bandage in place, he asked the two men to lift Villa onto the stretcher again and follow him to a small room on the other side of the house.

A woman came to the room with a bowl of soup, but Villa did not eat. He said he was tired, he wanted to sleep. The woman closed the shutters. She said she would come back later. Villa felt the pulse in his leg; he counted, he slept.

Beltrán awakened him. The room was dark, the shutters opened on a pale window. "We have to move," the Yaqui said; "Pershing is at Namiquipa."

"Don't cut off my leg."

"I would cut off my own leg first."

Villa was placed in a dark carriage. He lay across the seat, his shoulders were pressed against the sidewall. Two men sat opposite him, their hands were held out, showing their palms. The carriage leaned back; he felt the pressure against his leg. The driver cursed, the road rolled and fell; he was jolted. The wound bled, the wound stopped bleeding. There was the pulse in his leg and the pulse of the carriage; he could not separate them. He was rolled over on his side, urinating into a bowl. The men were laughing. He was cold, covered with thick blankets, he slept.

Two men lifted him out of the carriage and placed him on a litter of pine sticks and blankets. He saw the carriage rolling backwards, crashing and turning over the rocks. They went uphill. It was colder. A man lifted him up, carrying him in his arms; he heard the man's breathing; he sank between the man's arms, his legs dangled. The blue powder turned red in the water;

they washed his wound with the red water, they bandaged his leg again.

He was carried higher, he did not know where. He heard the altitude, he felt the cold. His leg was hot; but the warmth did not come into his face or hands, he shivered. There were fewer people around him. He called for Beltrán, he told him about the heat in his leg. The man who sat beside Villa said his name was Cifuentes, cousin Bernabé. They were sitting in a cave, at the entrance, watching the snow fall. There was a thick and rotted stench in the cave; something was dead inside—a pig: the gut had burst. The man with Villa wore a mask over his nose and mouth, he carried prickly-pear leaves in a sack.

A goat walked past the entrance to the cave. The bell that hung from a collar around the goat's neck made a loud noise, it clanged. Villa took the goat's horn in his hand and forced the head against his chest. He cut the throat deeply, thoroughly. The goat's head hung loosely, the blood rushed over the clanging bell. He buried the goat in soft ground at the base of a long hill and marked the place with a flat piece of wood. He cut his name into the wood.

The man with the mask over his face cooked rice and dried beef and chiles in a tin pot. He cooked water in the pot. Villa did not smell coffee, there was no coffee. The doctor was a Frenchman, his voice was rough and wet. He wore a mask over his nose and mouth while he peeled the prickly-pear leaves from the wound. Villa asked the doctor to wash the blackness away from his leg. The doctor put knives and spoons in the tin pot. He spoke, but his words did not come through the mask.

Yellow blood came from the wound. The doctor put his forks into the hole and brought out small stones. Socorro showed Villa her scar; he had not seen her since he lived in Parral. The old sisters did not know her. The garden of herbs was destroyed. The house burned in his leg, the monster had taken hold of his foot. He knew fire.

It's a long, long way to Tipperary.

He heard them passing, making camp near the spring. He pulled himself to the mouth of the cave, but they were downhill and he could not see them. They were close by; he heard them walking through the brush, gathering firewood. They talked, and when they were not talking, they whistled: hunters who warned the hunted. He was not afraid, he knew they would not find him. To be certain, he pulled himself deeper into the cave, dragging his wounded leg and the heavy splints. The Yanquis passed near the cave all night, sometimes singing, sometimes whistling, sometimes silent, walking heavily, sleepily walking.

[*591*]

He walked again in the middle of May, when the air was warm in the mountains and the flowers bloomed over the dry ground and the birds talked all day. He was thin and his face was as white as his belly. He walked slowly, using one leg and a heavy cane, touching the splints to the ground only to balance himself. There was very little water in May; the snow had run off and there was no rain; the men who took their turns caring for him were often gone all day to find food and water. Villa was not lost any longer in stories of Tierra Blanca and Zacatecas; he no longer was obliged to tell them what had happened at Celaya and León. He sat with himself in the mountains and looked down through the clear air at the plain, seeing the shapes of fields plowed, the spread of cattle grazing, the houses of the ranch compounds like boxes fallen on the land.

For six years he had not been alone for even a day, and now he sat with pines and maples and the grass that grew where it could and the cactus that grew where the grass could not, he sat with breezes and infrequent clouds, he sat with the prospecting ants, the birds that tapped, the birds that hunted, the birds that drank the flowers. He listened. He saw the lizards walking widespread and the rabbits reading the wind. He lay back in the sun and let himself become red and brown again. He shaved off the beard that had grown in the cave; it was the winter's end.

There were no messages. He thought about Wilson, he thought about Liviana, the color of her hair, the thickness of her now, the second child, perhaps a boy. He thought of Martina, Antonio, Marianita, Hipólito. The mute sister had come in dreams, floating; her weeping could not be heard, the quiet of the dreams frightened him.

On the plain, men worked in the fields, making puffs of dust, long lines of dust.

Windmills.

What lesson did Cervantes give to revolutionaries? The unwanted old gentleman. In time it is clear that Sancho did not govern well. Which did Cervantes love more, the dreams or the solid earth? A revolutionary can be a fool. Flores Magón.

Felipe Angeles and Pancho Villa.

Angeles is without dreams.

Battles are lost when others make the rules.

Villa took heavy stones in his hands and stood on one foot, raising and lowering the stones, tiring himself to bring back his strength. He rode half a mile on the back of a burro, a mile, and then down to the white water spring. He wanted to hunt for his food, but he could not chance the noise of a rifle shot, and when he tried to kill rabbits with stones, he lost his balance, sometimes falling, always missing the rabbits.

In June, he began the two-hundred-mile trip south to San Juan Bautista. The rumors of his death came to him along the way: the Yanquis had seen his grave, Nicolás Fernández said he had seen Villa die in the snow in the Coscomate Mountains, Dr. Riquetti said his examination of Villa in Guerrero showed the necessity for immediate amputation to avoid blood poisoning and a painful death. The news about Candelario Cervantes was not a rumor: the Yanquis had found him at a ranch near Namiquipa and they had killed him there. It was not a rumor either that the Yanquis had killed seventy men near Carrizal.

He went south, riding twenty miles one day, too weak to ride more than ten miles the next day, forced to rest for all of another day. He was greeted as a ghost, he was greeted as a saint. An old woman came walking on her knees to see him. "Bring back my grandson," she said. "He went with Urbina when he was fourteen years old. They left him at El Ebano in the rubber country."

"We pass this way only once," Villa said.

"You returned," she said. She wavered on the pain of her knees, she held out her hands in prayer.

Villa took her clasped hands and covered them with his palms. "Leave him in the west; the next life is for soldiers, Granny; we're all happy in the next life."

The miners told him what the Yanquis owned, the railroad workers told him what the Yanquis owned, the sharecroppers said the prices in the company stores were higher than ever. The unions were broken, the landlords were taking back the little pieces of land, the widows were hungry, Carranza was going to make himself President. Nothing had changed since the Porfiriato. Villa went south. They would be waiting for him in San Juan Bautista, they would all be coming to Durango on the sixth of July.

The old man came down from the hill. He and Villa spoke in Tarahumara and in Spanish; they used the words that were common to them. The old man squatted, resting his elbows on his knees. He looked at the splints on Villa's leg. "Bad luck," the old man said. "You have enemies."

Villa said he was hungry and very tired.

"Do you eat mice? Many mixed-breeds are afraid to eat mice. The political chief of this district is a mixed-breed and he is afraid to eat mice."

"I'm not afraid."

"We have no salt."

Villa took a ball of salt from his breadbag and gave it to the old man.

The old man nodded and put the salt inside his shirt. "I'm in my summer house," he said, pointing to the top of the hill.

"Will you help me?"

"You have a burro over there in the thicket, but maybe it's worn out. I can carry you on my back, but I will have to stop to rest halfway up the hill, because you are as big as a bear."

"No, no," Villa said, "just let me lean on your shoulder." But the old man had turned himself around to offer his back.

Villa put his arms around the old man's neck and climbed on his back. The old man stood up slowly, wobbling. He leaned forward, holding Villa's legs in his arms. He stopped twice on the way to his summer house. Both times he asked Villa if he was well and still able to hold on.

At the top of the hill the old man let Villa slide down his back until his feet touched the ground. "Can you stand up now? It's not far."

They walked across the tabletop of the hill; Villa leaned on his cane, following the old man. The other Tarahumaras did not look up as they passed. Only women and old men were on the hilltop. They ground corn, they boiled water in kettles, they worked at their looms; no one looked at Villa, who followed the old man past the crosses of the Sun, the Moon, and the Morning Star into the leaning boards of his summer house.

No sun came through the boards, but there was a light breeze in the house, as if a fan were slowly turning. The old man sat cross-legged on the west side of the house, looking beyond Villa through the entrance. He waited patiently while Villa lowered himself to the ground. "I will give you corn and meat and teshuina. The teshuina has the power to cure wounds, if you will share it with Him."

The old man's hair was streaked with white. He was thin and powdered with dust. His house was perfumed with pine. "First, tell me why you took our sons away."

"Me?"

"You're Pancho Pistols, I know you."

"Did your sons fight in the revolution?"

"Died. Killed."

"Good men died in the revolution."

"Why?"

"We are fighting for democracy and justice. Democracy is when the people decide who the President will be, when the people vote, and no one can do anything to them that they don't want. In democracy all the people are a council. Justice is when everyone has a piece of land and the political chiefs and the landlords don't have any more than the common people."

"We have always lived that way," the old man said. "It's the mixed-breeds who don't know how to live. Why should our sons die to teach the mixed-breeds what we already know?"

"Why did your sons fight in the revolution?"

"The blackbirds made them go."

The old man sat quietly for a long time. He looked around the walls of his house. There was a long and ancient rasping stick on one wall. The old man stood up, touched the rasping stick, and went out of the house. He came back carrying tamales and gourds of teshuina. "I gave Him some; this is for you." He put the food and the beer down in front of Villa. He took his place again opposite the entrance to the house. "I have never seen a bear," he said. "I'm an old man and I have never seen a bear. When I pray, I hear the voices of my sons. One was a good runner, the other one was cross-eyed. All my daughters are cross-eyed and none of them have husbands. My sons are killed. I hear them. They are in the night, they float. Now I spend my days making arrows, perfect arrows to hunt blackbirds. I'm not afraid. I kill blackbirds and take out their hearts and cut them in four pieces and bury each piece in a different place. My sons know. They told me to do this."

"Do your sons speak of the revolution?"

The old man leaned his head to one side, as if he were listening. "What is a revolution? The blackbirds made them go."

They celebrated in San Juan Bautista. The celebration lasted for five days. There were so few of them, they did not know what more to do.

2

The old man Aprisco said he was pleased when his second grandchild was born. But it was not true. Liviana seldom went to his room to see the old man anymore. She was careful not to nurse her son in his presence; she said there was something ugly in the old man's eyes, something too similar to what she saw in Valeriana. The men Villa left behind took care of the old man. At first they were gentle with him, but they soon tired of his unhappy humor. They handled him roughly, they neglected him, they said he was a pig who made shit in his own bed, they shamed him.

The old man complained to his daughter, he complained to his wife and to his sisters-in-law. He wrote a letter listing his grievances to General Villa. He showed it to the men who cared for him with so little affection. There were no pleasures left to him. He put his scarred and useless feet outside the covers of his bed for everyone to see, and no one looked. He surprised his wife by pissing on her when she came to pray with him before sleep.

The room where the old man lay stank of his filth. No one bathed him. The men who cared for him forgot to bring his food. When Liviana came to visit him, he spat on her and her child. He insulted his sisters-in-law, he said they fucked themselves with candles before they lighted them to God. No one came to his room. He ate only rosary beads. He died.

The carpenter who worked on the Aprisco farm was the first to lie down with the fever of the winter of 1919. He was a small, careful man, who went about with the tools of his trade attached to his overalls by a system of loops and pockets. The hammer did not swing when he sawed and the saw did not cut when he hammered. When he became sick, he hung all his tools on their proper pegs in the little room where he lived and did his most careful work. As the fever progressed, the odor of wood shavings in his room was replaced by the sourness of his sweats. When the sisters in their black dresses and shawls came to care for him, he cried out for them not to take him, he asked God to give him his health again. The sisters quieted him, they washed his face with cool cloths and gave him dogwood bark tea to drink. He coughed, he could not breathe enough. The priest came from San Andrés to hear the carpenter's confession. The priest was quick. There were so many.

The carpenter's body lay in his room for three days before a coffin could be made for him. So many died in San Andrés.

The sisters became ill on the day the carpenter was buried. They lay down on their narrow beds, side by side, as they had always been. Liviana and her mother came to care for them, but the sisters said they did not want food or medicine. They asked only for water, they asked only that incense be burned in their room so that there was no unpleasant odor when the priest came to hear their confession. The sisters were not unhappy. They prayed together, speaking in unison, speaking to the rhythm of their beads clacking. Sometimes they reached out for each other and held hands while they looked at the bleeding Christ hung on his cross of pain on the far wall of the room. The sisters spoke of the next life, saying they would wear white in Heaven. They did not suffer, there was no pain. The priest came and heard their confession and anointed them. The sisters blessed him. They lay in their beds and waited to die. They were impatient. On the second day after the priest had come, the sisters sat up in their beds and prayed to God to take them to His bosom. The heaviness in their chests gladdened them; they smiled and their eyes shone like candles. They died.

The fever was called the Carranzazo. It spread everywhere; in some towns there were not enough of the living to give proper burial to the dead;

in some towns the priests died and left the sick without hope of Heaven. The people wept, the people prayed. O my God, they said, after the revolution, the plague.

The battles of guerrillas are the most ancient way of war; they are separate from the world, each one; they are a world, each one. Guerrillas are alone; they are uncounted; on the days of their celebrations and the days of their deaths they are a group alone in the world. Like the Chichimecas who came south to the Valley of Mexico, guerrillas do not have the rules of nations; they are not Toltecs, they make war to become Toltecs. It is better to be a craftsman in a quiet place, living among craftsmen by their rules, than to fight a war of envy. Death without rules is not more glorious than a death of sickness. The uncounted remain uncounted, they are alone, they do not know of other beginnings, they do not know of other ends; the touches of the world surprise them.

Villa had lost the world when he fought in Parral. He brought his guerrillas out of the darkness, charging up the rising land; they came all the way from Moctezuma, almost from the border, to attack Parral. They came south in circles, hunters running like rabbits, not touching the towns. When they took the Hill of Santa Cruz they did not know what had happened in Chinameca.

And in the angriest moment, when Villa rode his horse through the streets of Parral, hurrying José de la Luz Herrera to the cemetery, it was still not known. He killed the old man there, Maclovio's father, the one who had won Maclovio for Carranza. He did the work himself, refusing the old man Herrera the dignity of a military death. He shot him in anger, after the old man had walked through the town with his hands raised and his eyes turning from side to side in search of some other way, after the old man had been shamed.

Nor did Villa know the next day. He married Alma Rótulos in the afternoon, in a moment of laughter; he made a dance of the marriage, the celebration of Parral. "You dance too well for a woman with innocent eyes," he told her. "You're as soft as a blanket should be. How I love you!"

He sang to her. She liked to stand next to him, with his arm over her shoulders, making her small beside him, lost beside him. Her skin was milky; she carried a parasol whenever she went out in the sun. Her eyes were large and very dark; she had a timid and secret aspect. When Villa was with her, he spoke loudly, he laughed from his belly, and there was nothing he feared to say. "Yes, I have another woman," he told her, "but she's stuck up and sour. And fat. Don't let it worry you; a priest will marry us. A good priest, a revolutionary priest will marry us; you don't have to be ashamed if you're married by a priest."

Martín López told him after the wedding. He took him away from the dancing, he shouted the news in the room of mariachis and dancing soldiers. "Zapata is dead. Assassinated. There was an exchange of letters. A Colonel Guajardo did it. He tricked him. He made promises, he gave evidence, he was going to bring Zapata a whole brigade, surrender a whole brigade to him. This Guajardo told Zapata he supported the Plan of Ayala. They had a meeting in Chinameca. He gave Zapata a horse. He greeted him with bugles and a guard of honor. The buglers played honors to Zapata three times, then the guard of honor turned their rifles on him. Some people say Zapata went out after he was shot and got on his horse and rode away with his arms straight out, like Christ. The truth is that they took his body to Cuautla and put it on exhibition. The face was swollen and discolored. Zapata looked fat and stupid; they left him with his mouth open."

"Well, he drank too much," Villa said. "He had too many women, and his brother was a fool; he trusted his brother too much. And I never saw a revolutionary with such fancy clothes, with so much silver sewed onto his clothes; he dressed himself up like a landlord and not like a soldier. He wasn't a good soldier, brother; he couldn't control his generals, he couldn't take the revolution out of his own cornfields. What did Guajardo promise him?"

"Rifles and troops."

Tears ran down Villa's face, streaking his anger. "Don't think I'm weeping over him, a fool like him. He welshed on me at Celaya. He was a better man than I am, more cultured, more political; he was the soul of this revolution. What are we going to do now? I agreed to the Plan of Ayala, I embraced him at Xochimilco. He was a fool, all that silver. What are we going to do now? We're all alone, López. The man was such a rotten soldier! He should have stayed on his farm, he shouldn't have put on shoes."

Villa left the wedding room, walking through the congratulating hands, between the smiles and the wishing words. He went to the river where it came down into the city, still cold in April, snow melted, running slower now and very clear. He washed his face in the clear water, kneeling on the soft bank to dip his cupped hands out where the current could be seen. The knees of his wedding suit were stained, the mud dried gray and pale on his boots. He climbed the hill toward the house where the sisters had lived, where the herb gardens no longer grew in neat patches. He saw flowers he did not know, he remembered the secrets of the healing room, the pouches and the jars, the color of marigolds, the scent of copal burning.

There were no other houses on the hill. He was alone, an old man. He lay down on a bed of leaves and folded his ancient hands over his chest. She was there in the garden, holding Zapata in the claws of her feet. Her faces spoke to Villa, but he could not understand the different words of the same

[598]

time. He rolled away from her, frightened by the snakes. She followed, a heavy-footed woman, graceless, thick. Whose head? Whose heart? He spoke demands, but the voice that emerged was thin, a leaf of grass brayed between a child's lips. Men served her. Zapata's face was blackened in several places, fattened with lumps. His mouth hung open; he could have been a servant sleeping after a brawl. Her faces were made of children crowned with feathers; their eyes were newly opened, they could not speak. He listened to them, unable to understand their wailing. Were they pleased to be? The feathers would fall, they knew, the feathers would be underfoot, the writhing grass, and falling. Villa was no longer afraid of the snakes; he saw how the wind blew them. Once he had wanted to kill the snakes; now he was at home with them; he was an old man, afraid only that the snakes would be cold to touch. Villa shouted to her; he was the only voice and he was old. He ordered her to retreat, he pushed her back with the reedy sound of his old man's voice. He was very tired, wishing for sleep, but he roused himself and went back down the reversing slope of the hill. His hands became strong again; he walked quickly in Parral.

Alma was gone, no one knew where. Villa sat in the rooms he had planned for them. He went to the bed and lay down for a while. The pillows were cool, like heavy clouds; he pushed them aside and lay with his head resting on his folded hands, like a young man at his ease on a grassy field. The canopy over the bed was dusty; a spider had begun to make a web in one corner. Would she have cleaned it? He did not know her, he did not know where she had gone. She had seemed so timid. He had mistaken her eyes.

A crowd was filling the plaza. The murmur of the crowd covered the voices of the vendors, blunting their cries. The speeches would begin soon. After a battle there were always speeches. "You are the cruel man, not me," Fierro had said. "I only execute men, you make them listen to speeches." Fierro never made speeches, Urbina never made speeches. Zapata said only aphorisms: It is better to die on your feet than to live on your knees. Or someone had told him to say that. Magaña? Soto y Gama? Zapata had died on his feet. It doesn't matter whether you die on your feet or on your knees, they bury you on your back. Zapata dead, Zapata dead. Maytorena in California making war with letters. Villa was very tired. Later, in the afternoon, he would make a speech, after he slept in the bed he had planned for Alma. Later he would stand on the top step of the bandstand and say, "I am not a cultured man, but I speak to you from my heart. Emiliano Zapata, the Chief General of the Army of the South, is dead."

He would not speak of deaths or burials; he needed them. What could be said? Battles end in words. He was tired, the sun is hot in April in the afternoon. There was a humming of heat beneath the sound of the crowd

[*599*]

spreading into the room. The bottles of soda were empty: orange-rimmed, red-rimmed at the bottoms. He undid the buttons of his wedding shirt. The sharp stems of his beard scraped his neck. He looked at the tile floor, the dust of the canopy, the squares of sun on the smooth walls, the unopened gifts: gold, perfume, lace, a comb cut from a seashell, the little boxes glued in squares, printed, painted; he could send the gifts to Liviana now.

Which of the laughing women who had sat beside him in Xochimilco was the widow of Zapata?

General Felipe Angeles was forty-eight years old when he became a socialist. He wrote to his wife, who had remained in Boston, that it was not poverty that made him a socialist, not his poverty. "The love of justice," he wrote, "compels me to accept this form of economic organization. Perhaps I would have embraced socialism earlier if it were the habit of socialists to bathe more frequently.

"Among other problems common to my fellow socialists is a lack of money or connection to money; i.e., I have not yet found suitable employment. I have not accepted the offer to dig coal in Pennsylvania, which astonished my patron, a gentleman who has twice invited me to attend his parties in native dress.

"The Liberal Alliance continues to pay for my meals and lodging here in New York. They are generous, but not in the extreme. My room is in the area known as the Lower East Side. No one in this building speaks Spanish and few speak any more English than I do. My only regular contact with my neighbors is an exchange of smiles outside the toilet. Which is not to imply that these people are either unfriendly or ungenerous; I have been invited to several meals of dumpling soup, chopped fishballs, and roast chicken. The meals are most peculiar in that they are constantly interrupted for the saying of Hebrew prayers. You will be interested to know that it is the custom here for married women to wear wigs.

"I wrote to Maytorena in Los Angeles to ask if he would have us as his guests over the Christmas holiday season. He was negative, of course. If I did not know how well he lived, I would not have lowered myself to write to him. Am I too harsh with him? Is it unfair to dislike a man because his chins rumble when he belches? What a good Christmas it would have been! What a good Christmas in spite of the belches and rumblings! Los Angeles is warm now. You are used to snow, but the winter here is very difficult for me. I suffered in Paris in the winter when I was a student, but Paris provided warmths for a young man that are not available to a poor and creaking former general in New York.

"The prospects for 1918 are better, however; shortly after the New Year I will have an interview with the owner of a restaurant on Fourteenth Street.

He is partial to former general officers, I am told. Very well then, I shall cleave sausages with my sword and lead charges of scullions."

A year later, General Angeles crossed the Bravo into Mexico to meet Villa and form the National Army of Reconstruction. He explained socialism to Villa, he taught him to discipline his troops with exercise and hard work; even Villa ran and jumped and squatted and twisted, leading his troops in exercises. At first, Angeles followed Villa in his doublings and turnings, in his guerrilla tactics, in his imitation of rabbits; but it was not a comfortable way for Angeles, he said it was not a soldier's way, it was not fitting for the National Army of Reconstruction to drag branches behind it in the sand. They argued too over the execution of prisoners. "Murguía hangs my troops," Villa said; "shooting is more merciful." Angeles argued that the National Army of Reconstruction was a moral army, that it had moral force on its side. He compared conscripted soldiers to exploited workers; he convinced Villa, the captured Carrancistas survived.

They made speeches, they carried a printing press with them on a wagon, they loaded burros with paper and ink, they met with the generals every night to talk about socialism. The government must own the railroads, Angeles said, and the workers must own the mines and the factories; all foreign ownership of property and business will be terminated; Mexico belongs to the Mexicans; the means of production, including the land, is the true property of the people who work. The Plan of Río Florido was published, the army took the town of Parral, the army prepared to move north to take the City of Juárez. They marched in rows in the desert, they exercised; Angeles taught them maneuvers, he taught them all that had been learned in the war in Europe. "We are a modern army," he said, "guerrillas with discipline, hard men, workers and soldiers. A conscript is a man sacrificed to the machine of war; that is the key to modern warfare. We are soldiers in the cause of socialism and democracy; that is why we cannot be defeated." Angeles was to be the interim President; the law was that no general could ever become President of the socialist republic to come.

They needed the City of Juárez, there had to be a place to bring arms into the country; they needed money, the gambling halls in the city could provide them with money. They fought for two days and two nights to take the city, and when it was theirs, the Yanqui troops came across the border, regiments of black men, fresh and armed with the best horses and the best weapons, armed with an unending supply of machine guns and grenades and new Springfield rifles, with airplanes and artillery and mortars and trucks and cars crossing over the bridges behind them. The soldiers of the Army of National Reconstruction were too weary after the days and nights of fighting; they withdrew, they sent a letter of protest to the Yanquis. The city was lost, Murguía was coming north with brigades of his own; the Army of National Reconstruction fled to the mountains.

Carrancista troops were everywhere in Chihuahua: militia in the towns, regular troops pursuing the Villistas in the mountains. Villa explained to Angeles that the army could not stay together, that they would have to split apart into small groups to survive. In a few months they could gather again, perhaps in Sonora, perhaps in Coahuila, perhaps in Durango. "Guerrillas attack small garrisons," Villa said: "We can't meet an army in the field." Angeles agreed. He said he was tired, he had fevers, his gut was weak, he needed to rest. A doctor gave him paregoric for the pains in his belly, he slept away the fevers and the pains and the fevers came again. He lost weight, the flesh darkened beneath his skin. He said he had a Yanqui stomach, he apologized.

"I am fifty years old today," Angeles wrote to his wife, "and I am vacationing here in the mountains with a staff of four in help. The weather is pleasant: sunny, warm days and cool nights. One of my staff plays the guitar and sings in curious and varied keys, so talented is he that he is able to sing the same song innumerable times without ever repeating the melody. I call him Orfeo, because he is a thief and a murderer and will surely descend into Hell. His real name is Félix Salas, an attentive fellow really and quite pleasant. My only fear is that he will discover that today is my birthday and serenade me as my reward for having lived fifty years.

"The paregoric prescribed by Doctor Villarreal is quite effective for my mild case of dysentery. The weight loss has not persisted and I am not reduced to bones and hair, as you feared. How fortunate! For I have so little hair. Soon I shall have to wear a wig, like those ladies in New York. Or a skullcap, like their husbands. In that event, I will appear to be either a Hebrew or a Prince of the Church, neither of which would be dear to my General Villa's heart.

"Speaking of Villa, he continues to astonish me with his knowledge of the terrain and the people. I do honestly believe he is acquainted with every man, woman, child, rock, arroyo, and stream in the state. Your fears that I will be captured are really quite groundless. In these guerrilla games of hide and seek, Villa is a master. I have a great deal to learn from him in a military way. Perhaps I should begin by drinking orange soda. Can a graduate of the École Militaire lose his taste for wine? This homegrown bitterness that passes for wine in Chihuahua may be helpful."

The fevers persisted, becoming more frequent, worsening; sometimes he did not know his name, sometimes he spoke in French or German. He led his escort in circles, he became lost in the Nonoava Mountains, shivering and weak, unable even to sit his horse. The four men who traveled with him hid Angeles in a cave. They made a bed of corn husks and grass to comfort him and built a fire deep in the cave to protect him from the chill of the autumn night. Félix Salas went into Parral to find a doctor. He came back instead with the town militia. "Take him quickly," Salas advised the militiamen, "because he keeps poison in a little pocket in his belt. Take him quickly; we won't get the money if he commits suicide."

Angeles could not sit his horse. The militiamen tied him face down across the saddle and led him down out of the mountains to Parral. The movement of the horse sickened him. He asked to be allowed to rest, to try again to sit his horse. The militiamen laughed. He is a pig, they said, he even disgusts the horse. When they came to a stream, they used cooking pans to throw water on the side of the horse.

Visitors came to see Angeles in his cell in Parral. He was ill and the light was poor; he could not make out who they were, he did not know what they wanted of him. To everyone who stood at the bars of his cell to look in at him, to his jailers and to those who came with promises to rescue him, he said, "My death will do more good for the cause of democracy than all the acts of my life. The blood of martyrs enriches good causes."

A voice said to him in the darkness, "My General, my dear General Angeles, we will not let you die. Tomorrow, before the sun comes up, we're going to attack this prison and take you with us to the mountains."

"Too many will die," Angeles answered.

"But, sir . . ."

"You have my orders."

"And the Judas?"

"I forgive him this betrayal, but I cannot forgive him his singing."

"What do you mean, sir?"

"Let General Villa deal with Salas."

There was a sigh, a lover's anticipation.

General Angeles was moved by train to Chihuahua for his trial. President Carranza sent a letter of praise to the commander of the militia in Parral. There was no mention of Félix Salas.

The people waited for the arrival of the train in Chihuahua. There were thousands, all of them silent. They saw Felipe Angeles step down from the train. How thin he was! He carried a book in the curl of his left hand. He leaned. Yes, he had been ill, something had attacked him in the mountains. He lifted his head for them, he was a soldier. The people wept, they followed the automobile through the streets of Chihuahua. The old women were kneeling in the streets, crossing themselves, praying for him, raising their eyes only to look into the windows of the automobile as it passed.

The telegrams were sent to Carranza. The students in the Military Academy asked that the life of General Felipe Angeles be spared. The Liberal Alliance asked that his life be spared in the name of Francisco Madero, that mercy be shown in the name of the mother of Venustiano Carranza. General Alvaro Obregón asked that the life of Felipe Angeles be spared; he sent telegrams to Carranza and to General Diéguez, who would preside over the trial.

During the trial, which was quick and certain, General Angeles spoke for only a few moments. He sat in the great room of the Theater of Heroes, leaning his head to one side, weary and thin; he seemed to be thinking of other times, other places. He said to his judges what Seneca had said, "A sufferer is a sacred thing."

Soldiers in white uniforms sat behind him, holding their rifles, wearing their white kepis and shining boots. The judges sat before him at a long table. He saw their boots under the table, he saw the comfort of them in their chairs. His head fell onto his chest; they gave him no medicine for the fever. He told his attorney that it was cold in the room. The judges watched him fallen in his high-backed chair. The walls of the room were white, the wood of the walls was carved, painted gold.

He lifted his head once to say, "While the poor work, the rich eat."

When it came time for him to rise in his own defense, he spoke of the brotherhood of socialism. "I have loved all Mexicans of all beliefs," he said. "That has been my flaw: to love all Mexicans, to love all humanity, to love even the animals of this earth, for there are times when we are less good than the animals.

"I admire the United States, because they are a great people, the equal of Rome; but I do not want those people, like Rome, to absorb all other nations. I want the people who are now in power, the Constitutionalists, to consolidate this nation, to open their arms to all their brothers, to be an example among governments, to exploit the riches of the nation, to bring Mexico to flower."

He said he expected to die, he asked only that he not be thought of afterward as an evil man. And when they said the sentence, he was quiet, he made no answer, not even with his eyes or the place of his body on the high-backed chair. The attorney touched his arm. "My General," he said.

Angeles looked up at him. He glanced around at the room, as if he had only just entered. He smiled. "I will want to write to my wife tonight. They will permit me that."

"And we've petitioned the courts in the Capital. It will be important for you also to write petitions. This court has no authority over cases of this kind. There is a body of law in our favor. The petitions will be granted, you'll see."

"I'll want to read tonight," Angeles said. "Will you see that there is a good light."

He wrote to his wife, then he said goodbye to his friends, and he lay down

on the narrow bed to read *The Life of Jesus* until the priest came to wait
with him during the last hour before the light.

Villa was camped in the hills southwest of Bustillos. It was a comfortable
time: the horses had been turned out to graze; the troop was divided into
small groups of cobblers and saddlers and tailors; long strips of beef were
drying in the sun; a few men knelt by a stream to pound their clothes on
the flat rocks; the camp had no urgency, they rested. Villa thought now of
the winter and where to wait; perhaps in the valleys of the Sierra Madre
where the Tarahumaras lived, to eat corn and play kickball games and think
of the spring campaign of the Army of National Reconstruction. There were
fewer than two hundred men with him, a squadron of officers and sergeants,
the bones of the army that would be fleshed out, muscled in the spring. A
sergeant—Mules they called him—came back from Bustillos with bags of
salt to use in curing meat. Villa went to meet him, for he had also asked
Mules to bring back a few bottles of orange soda.

"They assassinated General Angeles in Chihuahua," Mules said.

Villa's face died, his arms and legs failed; he fell, like a killed man. He
lay a long time on the torn grass at the beginning of the valley, he did not
move. His hat was overturned, crushed beneath his shoulder. The troops
gathered around. He looked to them as if he were dead. The weeping burst
from him in screams. He tore the earth with his hands and the heels of his
boots. No one touched him. He did not become quiet until after dark. They
brought him a wet cloth then to wash his face and a bowl of atole to calm
him inside. He did not speak to them. He walked to the end of the valley,
passing through the herd of grazing horses, wading across the cold stream
that ran through the center of the valley. He climbed the first hill, leaning
into the steepness, sometimes touching the rough ground with his hands.

He sat on the little peak of the hill and looked up at the sky. He could
name a man killed for every star he saw.

Mules came up onto the hill in the middle of the night. He came crawling
in the darkness, prepared to turn and run away if he met anger. "We should
have taken Tampico," Villa said to him. "The Yanquis wanted the oil, they
would have given the revolution to us if we had taken Tampico. I didn't
know then, I didn't understand. How could I have known? I'm a man
without culture, I was never fit to be more than a colonel."

"General Angeles said something before he died, sir. He said that his
death would do more for the cause of democracy than all the actions of his
life. He said that the blood of martyrs was fertilizer for the good cause."

"Felipe was talking like a man who knew he was going to die. It's better
to die suddenly, then you don't have to tell yourself so many lies.

"War is not good for anyone, and soldiers have no use, and the blood of

[*605*]

martyrs doesn't fertilize anything but the grass. The gringos, the white Chinks own everything. That's who we fought, not Carranza or Huerta or Obregón. We fought the gringos for the oil, and we lost. Angeles knew that, he knew the war was with Wall Street. But what can we do? You can't shoot Wall Street.

"We stopped the executions after he told me about Wall Street. Why should one person of our race kill another to serve Wall Street? The enemy is American Smelting and Refining and Standard Oil, he told me so, and I believed him, I still believe him. So what can we do? What's the use of killing more Mexicans?"

"What are you going to do?"

"Continue."

In half a year Carranza was also dead, betrayed by Obregón and Calles and his general who was always defeated, Pablo González. Miguel Trillo read the accounts of Carranza's death to Villa. He sat in a camp chair in a grove of oak trees on the slope of the Sierra Madre. The squared flesh of his face was red with pleasure. He turned the pages of the newspaper with great care, mindful of the sudden winds of the Sierra. "Son of a bitch," he said, "there are no more sinners; what's left for the priests?"

Trillo folded the newspaper and put it under his arm. He adjusted his tie, he rearranged himself inside the shoulders of his bureaucrat's suit.

"I'm tired," Villa said. "Maybe now I can go home."

"Where?"

Villa shrugged. He could not speak. The death of Carranza was bringing tears from him. He shrugged again. The tears were coming.

BOOK FIVE

Quenamican

1

I thought he would come to see me then, after the revolution was over, after
he took the offer from de la Huerta and settled himself in the ranch at
Canutillo. Perhaps he thought I was dead; it had been a long time and I
was very old. My cheeks were as thin as paper and my hands were bony
and curled, like chicken feet. The hard film covered over my eye; there was
nothing left for me on that side of the world but a yellow glow. I thought
often of death, of what the poets had said of the Place of Mystery, the Land
of the Fleshless, the Lower Worlds and the Upper Worlds. It was only
poetry; they did not know. I had already withered, like the flowers; I had
already been broken, like the emeralds; I had already been torn, like the
feathers; and yet I had a face, my heart was whole. I cared for myself, I kept
warm.

No one came to see me in my house in the saddle of the mountain, no
one smelled the flowers or saw the smoke roiling in my dark mirror. Mexico
had changed: garlands of flowers were hung on locomotives, people sang
in the mines, children read forgotten books, painters made gods of factory
workers and peasants; it was a hopeful time, a new age. In Canatlán they
planted peach trees and opened stores, a new bridge was built across the
river into San Juan del Río, automobiles became as common as horses,
factories steamed and men and women worked all day and all night, roads
were made of cement and buildings in the form of artless stelae were raised
to the heavens.

But the poet is right, there is no truth on earth. There was hunger in the
cities and in the villages, children were born blind, children died, there were
schools only for the few, there were shoes only for the few. Land was
distributed to people who had no money for seed and no cattle or sheep or
even chickens to raise; they starved, they sold their gifts back to the landlords, they went back to the company stores, and when their children were
grown, they sent them to the mines and the railroads and the factories. I
can answer the poet's questions: nothing is stable and lasting, nothing
reaches its aim. There was no need to tell these things to Villa; he knew.

He brought Liviana to the compound at Canutillo. A different woman arrived; he knew her only by the color of her hair and the shape of her mouth. She had grown fat and soft; her breasts weighed against her blouse, they were two soft melons. She wore sweaters and sat with her knees spread. "You're a rich man," she said to him; "I want a cook and a housekeeper and a nurse for the children and a seamstress to make my clothes. President de la Huerta made you comfortable; make me comfortable. Tell your fifty Golden Ones to call me Mrs. Villa, tell them to marry their women and to attend church. I suffered for you, my father and my grandfather and my brother died for you, and you are no longer a revolutionary, you are another landlord; let me live in the style of a landlord's wife. Buy lace dresses for your daughter, buy a pony for your son. I want a Victrola; Urbina had a Victrola and he was nothing but a swine and a traitor; his widow is not permitted in this house. I am the wife, the house is mine, the fields belong to you."

Villa listened to her. He said nothing; he was afraid of what he might say. A Victrola with a great speaking horn was brought from Torreón, Valeriana was dressed in pale lace and patent leather shoes, Agustín rode on his own pony, a seamstress with a soft neck and gently waved black hair was brought from Parral, and all of Liviana's cousins came to live at Canutillo.

A nest of women now lived in the house at Canutillo. They cooked and gossiped and were always seen with white aprons hanging from their waists. The women who lived with the escort permitted to Villa under his agreement with de la Huerta were separate from those who stayed in the main house; Liviana called them streetwalkers who were too lazy to walk the streets, she would not speak to them, she would not permit them in her house. When Liviana and the women of the main house went to hear the mass in the church of the compound, they sat in the front rows, they avoided looking at the women who lived in the rows of rooms behind the main house.

Men came to Canutillo to make photographs and to write down what Villa said. He spoke to them about hunger and poverty, he told them that every soldier should be a soldier for two days of his week and a farmer or a factory worker for three days. "What is the use of an army?" he asked. "The revolution is over, now is the time to make the revolution." He showed the place where he planned to build a school, he told them he made loans to the poor at no interest. "No one should make money just for having money to loan," he said. "That should be the first rule of a socialist revolution."

"Ah, but you own the hotel there on Gabino Barreda Street, and you charge rent for the rooms, sir."

"You all know about the hotel," Villa said. "Well enough; it's a journalist's work to know such things. But let me tell you something about a hotel:

it's pure luxury; any man who wants to save his money can sleep under the stars. Ask me. Ask me how many nights I slept that way.

"It's always different when there are choices. For example: the government has the choice to pay the soldiers or to pay the teachers. I say that the teachers should be paid first, but the government is more interested in soldiers. To me that is like giving free rooms to the men who can pay to sleep in my hotel and charging the farmers who have to borrow to live. Imagine! Cervantes says there is no book so bad that something can't be learned from it, and I say there is no soldier who can't earn his keep by doing an honest day's work. Work and education, gentlemen! Work and education, those are the answers to the great problems of the nation."

And before the conversations were completed, the journalists always looked at the revolver Villa carried on his hip, and they always had some question about it. "Yes," Villa told them all, "you see clearly. I carry a pistol, and it is loaded."

He was more comfortable with the salesmen who came from El Paso and San Antonio to show him pictures of new plows and machines to do the work of his wheat fields. He talked with them about crops and the weather and the good that machines could do. They slept in his house, he put a bed for them in his own small room. There was no doubt between Villa and the men who sold machines for the farm. "You sell good things to make money," he told Mr. Beers. "I trust you. When your company makes a machine for picking corn, I'll buy one of those. But corn is a problem; it tires the land. Why is corn so heavy on the land? I prefer corn to wheat."

The fifty men of his escort went with Villa into the fields. He walked behind a plow to show them how a straight line was made, he advised them on the use of the thresher and the tractor. He showed them how to fit horseshoes and he worked with them to brand horses and cattle; he taught his soldiers to be farmers, but he always left some at the far corners of the field with nothing in their hands but rifles, with nothing to do but watch the fields that spread beyond the fields of Canutillo.

He walked behind his guests, he carried a pistol with him wherever he went. "I have enemies," he explained, "reactionaries. The bankers tried to have me killed in my own fields, because I do not charge interest to the poor. There are also Carrancistas left in this country, men who blame me for the dead of the revolution, men who blame me for their land lost to the poor. There are assassins, men who kill from ambush, poisoners, men who want to kill me in my sleep. I'm careful. Obregón sent me two machine guns for my protection. I keep them hidden, but there are always two men with each gun, and they don't sleep when they're with the guns."

Cervantes said to Villa: "Journey over all the universe in a map, without the expense and fatigue of traveling, without suffering the inconveniences of heat, cold, hunger, and thirst." And Villa agreed; he sat in his small room into the night, with books of maps lying on the small table, with books stacked among the gifts, the unopened perfumes that had been sent to him. He read the rivers and the mountains, the blue and the dark brown; he sailed the pale blue seas, crossing the intersections of thin black lines, parting them with his mind; he rode the green plains of Illinois; he stood among the wheat fields of Kansas and Nebraska; in Paris, he walked the narrow streets Felipe Angeles had described; he stood on fields where Caesar had fought; he walked along the route of Napoleon's mistaken retreat from Moscow; he took himself to the trenches of Gettysburg and Verdun; he remembered the irrigation canals of Celaya, the green flies buzzing at León, the hills of Zacatecas, the hills of Gómez Palacio. He sat with the maps until the lamplight in the room had paled away, until he heard crowing and the women stirring in another part of the house.

A journalist advised him to read Dante; and word by word, through the long nights, he made the descent with the poet into Hell. The book of punishments, the book of sins, the book without hope; he thought of the heavy walk of his mother in her last days, he thought of Liviana, sleeping in some other room, so wide, with her breasts nursed into fat melons, with her hair darkening and her eyes falling into the thickness of her face. He sat the nights with that hopeless death, the death without forgiveness, the death that did not know glory, not even in birth, not even in war, the death that damned children. He put the book of Dante on the shelf among the perfume bottles and the unopened wines and cognacs, he preferred to sit with his maps, he preferred to read Cervantes again—it went so quickly now that he knew the words, it made him laugh, he wept each time he read of the knight of sad airs sickened and dying dreamless.

The ball court was made of hard clay. There was a smooth wall at one end. Villa played there, hitting a small hard rubber ball against the wall. He did not use a stick or a paddle, he hit the ball only with his hand. He often played with Miguel Trillo. The ball players covered themselves with sweat, their skins darkened in the sun.

It was not like the ball courts of the old, old time; the players wore no hip pads, no protection against the weight of a heavy ball, the players did not contest the outcome of the game, nothing was wagered, there was no danger. Villa played only for exercise. He was uncomfortable with the fat that collected on his chest and around his waist; he said it weakened him, he said it endangered him; he grasped the fat around his waist in his hand as if it were an enemy.

After the ball games he sat with Trillo in a shaded place and drank orange soda water and talked or listened while Trillo read the letters to him. The

[*612*]

ball game tired him, he felt like sleeping after the games; but he did not permit himself to sleep, he overcame the cool softness around his eyes. "Now I am the age of generals," he said to Trillo, "and I have an army of fifty men."

"If a man is a general when he is young, he can retire and be a statesman."

"Or a farmer."

"People write letters to you, they come to see you; that's the way a statesman lives, not a farmer."

"Miguelito, you're a good friend and a flatterer. The truth is that I'm asleep now; memories are dreams, it's a sleep without rest."

"I've ordered stationery for you from England, the kind befitting a statesman. It has your name and the name of the ranch printed on it at the top. The paper is made partly of linen; they say it will last a thousand years."

The garden was planted on the south side of the house on a piece of low ground, beyond the stables, beside the river. Oranges and lemons grew in the garden. It was a thickly green place; in every season but winter it smelled of flowers. On some warm nights in summer when there was no wind the perfume of the garden was smothering, the pollens were a mist.

Liviana sent women from the house to pick fruit and flowers from the garden, but she did not walk there herself. Villa walked in the garden with other women. The laughter of the women was as sweet as the pollen. The women ate oranges and mangos that grew in the garden. Villa saw their teeth in the moonlight. He tasted the sweet juices that overflowed the lips of the laughing women.

On their first day at Canutillo, Villa stood the children in a row and asked them to say their names. He spoke very firmly to them, he made their upraised eyes round with fear of him. "I am your father," he said. The children nodded. "And you are the children. Do you know the difference between the father and the children?"

"We're small and you're big," Valeriana said.

Villa paced up and back before them, stalking, head lowered in thought, considering her answer. After a long time he stopped in front of Valeriana and stared down at her. His eyebrows were curled down and his lips were thrust out under his mustache. "Yes," he said.

He stood in front of each of the children in turn, asking them if they agreed. The boy, Antonio, said, "Yes, my General." The others laughed.

"Very good," Villa said, "but there is more to the difference than our sizes. When the father speaks, the children listen. When the father gives orders, the children obey. The children wash. The children kiss their father on the cheek. Children do not tell lies. All children go to school, girls as well as boys. All children study hard and learn to read and write. Children work on the farm; they ride horses and help in the fields and in the corrals, girls as well as boys." He looked at Valeriana. "In the revolution women were soldiers, women carried guns and rode horses and fought in the trenches. Can you shoot a gun?"

She was the prettiest of little girls. Her eyes were as innocent as the darkness that came before the first sun. Her legs were straight and slim; she wore short white stockings and black shoes with little straps. Her face was always prepared; tears and laughter were waiting in her cheeks. "Papa," she said, promising a question, "I don't like guns."

"Then how will you fight? Will you smoke marijuana before you go into battle? Will you get yourself drunk? What will you do? How can you fight without a gun?"

"I'll sing songs."

"Will you kill people with your singing? Is your singing so painful to hear?"

She squeezed her face and tears came flowing. The tears spread down the row of children. Villa caught the children in his arms and lifted them up. He held all four children close to him. He kissed them and gave them sugar candies. When they misbehaved, he left the spankings and the shoutings for Liviana. He kissed them and told them stories and gave them sweets and gifts. They sat on his knees and curled their arms around his neck, they followed him like a row of ducklings. He brought them ponies and boots and pretty dresses, he told them riddles, he kissed away their tears and blushed with pleasure at their laughter; the feel of them in his arms was the morning of his life.

Liviana found him in the stables. She asked him to walk with her in the garden. "I have something to tell you," she said.

Villa nodded to her. "In a while. Tomorrow."

She did not move, she was a heaviness in the stable, a demand. The men saw her, they went around her, they looked away, they did their work according to Villa's directions. Liviana waited, she maintained the width of herself in the aisle of the stable.

"Tomorrow," Villa said.

"It's important."

He saw the men watching, he saw how much they knew. "All right, Josefina Liviana, the garden is pretty now, we'll go walking there."

They walked together without touching. He did not take her arm as they descended the wooden steps to the garden. They went deep into the garden, they went into the confining silence of the trees before she spoke. "I know," she said.

[*614*]

He wiped his forehead with a red kerchief. He knew what the gossips told. He took a peach from a tree and offered it to her. "Take it. It's sweet."

"I know," she said, declining the offered fruit with her hand, waving it away. "I know, but I do not know why."

"Love does not age gracefully."

"Nature asks more of women."

"Men go to war."

He had expected anger, he had expected her to weep with anger; but there was only a sadness in her, weighing in her, adding to the heaviness of her. "I was your wife before you went to war," she said.

"You came here to live like a rich woman. You put on airs, you made yourself a landlord's wife, you surrounded yourself with cousins and servants, you made a world of women around yourself; your husband and your children aren't near you anymore."

"I gave you children."

"And I gave you children," he said.

"Yes. That's why I can't understand. Why, Francisco, why in my own house? In this garden? In the war I was your wife, you came home to me, we had children; why now?"

"You made a wall of women around yourself, you busied yourself, you became the keeper of this ranch here at Canutillo, you forgot that you were also my wife, you forgot that you were also the mother of your children."

"I am their mother."

"I am their father, and I have had to look after them the way a mother should too."

He leaned against a tree, eating the peach, leaning his head forward to keep the juices from dripping on his shirt. "I planted this garden; how could I not offer you a peach? You brought her into this house, you asked for her; like a rich woman, you asked for her."

"I nursed your children. I ate for them, my breasts were filled with milk. A woman changes; is that reason to humiliate her? I ask you, Francisco. Tell me what I should have done, tell me what mistake I made. Is it my age? I could be thin again. Do the children bother you? Does the food displease you? Tell me what I should have done."

"One love drives out another."

"How can you humiliate your wife for a seamstress?"

"A man can choose to begin love, but not to end it."

"And a fool at forty is a fool indeed!"

Villa held the peach between two fingers, gnawing close to the pit.

"You think you make yourself more virile by taking another woman in my house, you think that shows your virility. I had a grandfather and a father and a brother, I know men. I know how you think, how you want everyone to know. Forgive me, my General, but you can take a thousand women into this house and Obregón will still be Obregón and Villa will still be Villa. How wrong you are, Francisco, how you err about life! What you do to make a fool of me in front of your escort makes a fool of you in the eyes of God."

He dropped the peach pit at her feet. It rolled toward her, collecting dirt; strands of fruit hung from the gnawed pit.

She looked a long time at the pit, understanding what he had said with it. "There is still the house in Chihuahua," she said.

"Leave the children."

"And the seamstress?"

"Yes. I like the way she laughs. I remember when you laughed, I remember when I called you Blondie. It was a long time ago, before the revolution. You were a girl then, you were hard, but you were not bitter. There was a lightness in you, like your name, you were the girl of your name. That's gone now. Time took away your lightness. I was away too much, I saw it. I saw the women gathering around you, I saw the girl Liviana become a hen. The door was closed to me."

"You keep that scarred horse, Seven Leagues, in the stable."

"I remember you."

"Now I'll eat a peach," she said. "Would you pick one for me? A ripe one, red, with a sweet flavor in the juice."

He took her arm and led her through the garden to the steps. She ate the peach he picked for her. The juice fell on the soft hanging of her bosom. "I thought we would be buried together in the park in Chihuahua."

"We'll be old," he said. "Perhaps we'll know each other again when we're old. Who knows? There will be time."

Liviana went to her husband's room. It was night, the book of maps was open on the shelf of the dresser, the lamps burned dimly, the light did not reach the edges of the room. Villa stood before the dresser shelf, hunched over the book, as if in prayer. She stood beside him, she looked with him at the map of Africa bending into the meeting of the pages. He spoke to her in a whisper: "I can imagine elephants, striped tigers, lions with great heads, endless herds of deer and striped horses, cobras and pythons and giraffes and gorillas. The mountains are higher than our Sierra Madre, there are grasslands bigger than Mexico, and rivers, the greatest rivers in the world. I've seen pictures. I can close my eyes or look in the darkness of this room and the pictures move, the skin of the elephants has its roughness."

"I can't leave the children," Liviana said.

"Women don't dream. I've always looked for a woman who dreamed like a man. I've always wanted a woman who could sit with me in this room and be in Africa."

"I'll live in another part of the house. Give me one of the rooms in the compound."

"Two women in one house, two dogs and one bone."

Liviana sat on the bed. She bent forward over her knees. She was a solid round, the legs hung from her. "They need me," she said.

"You leave them with maids, you raise them like a landlord's children. They don't know you. My children are alone. You cook for me, you smile for guests, you have no time for children. You live for gossip, you're the mother and the daughter of your cousins. The children won't know when you're gone."

"The Carrancistas knew more about you than I did."

"I don't know what changed in you," he said. "In the worst of times you were the best of women."

"You always betrayed me."

"I always came back to you." He closed the book of maps. The lamps fluttered, the light became steady again. "Go to Chihuahua now. In the morning. Go."

"I'll need money to live."

"To have chocolate in the kitchen, to have cotton that can be pressed into edges. I remember that too, along with your laughter. I'll send you money. Go to Chihuahua and I'll send you money. Go and drink chocolate in Chihuahua."

"God punishes adulterers."

He answered with mulish laughter.

He married Austreberta the week after Liviana went to Chihuahua. For her wedding Austreberta wore a satin dress that reached only to her ankles. She made faces at Villa's children during the ceremony, and when the mayor of Las Nieves halted the reading of the marriage vows to chastise the children for laughing, the giggles burst forth from Berta's mouth in a stream of wet bubbles. The children laughed all the more. The mayor stamped his foot at the indignity of it all; he threatened to terminate the ceremony. Villa turned to the children and asked them to be quiet, and the ceremony went on. At the party afterward, Berta danced with her husband until morning, and then she said it was hunger and not weariness that made her want to stop.

Berta could ride a horse like a man. She was slow in aiming, but she could shoot as well as Villa. Her hatred of Carrancistas was greater than anyone else's. When Gildardo Magaña came up from Morelos to visit Villa, he told her that forgiveness was divine, and she answered that retribution was also divine. She attacked Magaña for his religious view of the world, saying that he was no longer the man who had inspired her husband when they were in prison together. He said she was a shrew, she said he had become a churchmouse. During the last days of Magaña's visit, they did not speak.

Berta taught the girls to sew, she lifted the boys onto ponies. She ran footraces with the children and led them in hiding games, she read stories to them and sang with them and held them up over the gate of a stall to watch the birth of a horse. They would not eat unless she ate at the table with them, they would not sleep until she kissed them and wrapped them in their bedclothes; she was their mother and their sister, she led them to laughter.

"I'll be your wife," she told Villa, "if you'll let me be your friend." She looked at the maps with him, she dreamed with him, she said she heard the roar of lions on the African plain. There was an air of sureness in her: she expected the corn to grow well, she was not afraid of de la Huerta's mood, the anger of bankers made her laugh, she knew the hearthstones would not explode and the tamales would not stick to the bottom of the pot. When she walked in the garden with her husband, she talked to him about the problems of the farm, the speed of the fattening of the cattle, and the efficiency of the thresher. She knew which men plowed best and which men walked in crooked lines or pushed the plow too deep. The diseases of corn angered her and the worms that lived in cotton gnawed at her. When they walked in the garden in the evening, she stopped to pull out the roots of weeds and she stretched upward to prune the sickly branches from the fruit trees. Villa took comfort from her, she calmed him. He took her for long rides in the Dodge touring car; she was the only escort he wanted. He leaned on her, he put his arm around her shoulders as if she were a man. They talked of going to Africa.

I had not gone down from my place in the saddle of the mountain for twenty years. I had watched and listened, living in this place in the style of a monk, following the old ways, sacrificing snakes and butterflies, maintaining the count of the days, thinking of the folded books, the red ink and the black ink. But it was the fifty-second year again, the end of the old fire, the anxious year, the year of the consideration of endings. I saddled my horse and went down to the world of others.

The journey to Parral was very difficult. I am old, the movement of a horse jars my bones. The cushions of my body are worn away, the bones touch, an ache comes into all my bones. It was deep summer when I began my journey. I wore a wide paper hat and a mantle to protect myself from the sun. People laughed at the style of my clothing, they whistled to me, thorns have fallen off. I live in the same house, in the room you built for me. I've been waiting for you there."

Villa went to her house in the evening. He brought gifts of honey, gold, and perfume. She dressed in red, she wore white paper cones in her hair. A yellow dog, festooned with ribbons, sat at her feet. Quail walked through the rooms, eating the bones that lay on the floors. Socorro flattered Villa, she obliged him. They ate together, they spoke of the past. He wept for the dead child, the riddles, the first planting of the garden, the chocolate served in the uncounted evenings after the child was asleep.

A rose thorn cut Villa's finger.

Socorro held a picture of the dead child in her hand.

A conch shell.

Flurries of quail feathers startled them.

They looked out the window at the perfect darkness of the clouded night. The festooned dog walked under them.

He arose without waking her. The car was waiting. Miguel Trillo sat beside him, half-asleep, already dressed in his bureaucrat's suit and uneven necktie. The others sat on the rear seat. They were six. It was quiet in the city, in the cool sun. Villa drove the car down the hills into the center of Parral. It was very early, the air was not cooked, the dust was heavy.

In the main plaza a man stood beside an empty cart. "Seeds," he wailed, "seeds." He was alone, the plaza was empty, there were no seeds in his cart. The man waved his white handkerchief to the men in the passing car. The plaza was empty, summer grass and the settled dust of morning. Villa turned the car onto Gabino Barreda Street. The white house was on his left, the shutters were open; rifles pointed through the dark squares of the windows. He heard the rifles. He was dead.

The bodies were laid out in a row in the largest room of the Hotel Hidalgo; his was the first. A sheet was wrapped around his groin. His body had been arranged on the iron bed, his eyes had been closed, his arms and legs had been straightened. The undertakers had not yet done their work: the flesh was not drained, the wounds were like patches torn from stucco, the blood dried darkly in the wounds, darker than adobe.

Men with cameras were invited to the long room to record his mortality, to show him naked and broken in his final form. Fluids leaked from his nose, the slow stiffening of his body forced blood from the wounds. The bedsheet was stained.

In the street, the people spoke of the assassins, of the number of dead men in the hotel. I walked among the people, I stopped to listen to what they said. They were not afraid of him, they were not able to ask anything more of him. The first questions, the first calumniations, were whispered in the street. I paused in my long journey to the east to reply:

He brought the brigades together, all the brigades from all the towns and all the states, the cowboys and the farmers, the professors and the wanderers, the storekeepers and the soldiers who sought a different army. The trains of his army overflowed the railroad yards, his horses filled the spaces between cities. He was the general of artillery and infantry and cavalry, he was the general of generals; thirty thousand men passed in review before him in a single day. He learned reading and socialism, he loved the poor. He built schools for the children of the revolution, he began the division of the land.

Smoke